MORE TOMORROW
& OTHER STORIES

Other books by Michael Marshall Smith

MORE TOMORROW
& OTHER STORIES

Michael Marshall Smith

EARTHLING PUBLICATIONS 2003

FIRST EDITION, FIRST PRINTING.
October 2003

Numbered hardcover edition ISBN: 0-9744203-0-1
Traycased lettered hardcover edition ISBN: 0-9744203-1-X

EARTHLING PUBLICATIONS
12 Pheasant Hill Drive
Shrewsbury, MA 01545 USA
Email: earthlingpub@yahoo.com

WEBSITES OF INTEREST
Earthling Publications: http://www.earthlingpub.com
Michael Marshall Smith: http://www.michaelmarshallsmith.com
John Picacio: http://www.johnpicacio.com
Stephen Jones: http://www.herebedragons.co.uk/jones

Dedicated to the memory of my mother,

Margaret Ruth Smith
November 1937 – November 2002

What we all were to each other, that we are still.

Acknowledgments

Thanks to Nicholas Royle, without whose initial and continued friendship and encouragement this book wouldn't exist; and to Stephen Jones, without whose encouragement and friendship it would be a very slim pamphlet indeed. Thanks also to Peter Crowther, Ellen Datlow, Al Sarrantonio, Bill Shafer, Richard Chizmar, Andy Cox, Stefan Dziemianowicz, David Sutton and others for providing inviting homes for some of my stories, often before they existed; and especially to Paul Miller, for building this luxury, all-modern-conveniences condo for them to share—and for doing so with such enthusiasm, creativity and, frankly, patience.

Love and thanks to friends and family, and in particular to my father David, sister Tracey and wife Paula (who reads everything first, and is always kind); and finally to everyone out there who keeps the faith and reads short stories, and who likes tales in which things sometimes are not quite right.

Without you...

Contents

Introduction:
Alias Smith & Jones

The job of an anthology editor is often a lonely occupation.

Most of us sit in an office all day, working our way through piles of submissions that, invariably, range from the unsuitable to the incompetent. We are always looking out for the 'next Stephen King' or the 'new Peter Straub', usually without much success. It can be a depressing and thankless task, sorting the wheat from the chaff, so that when you chance upon a genuinely impressive story or discover an exciting new talent, then those are events to be dearly treasured and celebrated.

Which is why, back in the early 1990s, when I read a short story submission from an unknown author which combined the lyricism of a young Ray Bradbury with the confident prose of a new Stephen King, I immediately snapped up the story for the anthology I was working on.

The story was, of course, 'The Man Who Drew Cats', and the author (as if you haven't already guessed), was Michael Marshall Smith.

We were first introduced, if memory serves, by our mutual friend, author and editor Nicholas Royle. Despite our age difference, Mike and I hit it off immediately.

With a background as a scriptwriter and performer in theatrical and radio revue comedy, he was an unlikely candidate to become a full-time horror author. However, Mike's discovery of the works of Stephen King changed all that.

My co-editor Dave Sutton and I bought 'The Man Who Drew Cats' for our paperback anthology *Dark Voices 2: The Pan Book of Horror* (1990). It wasn't the first story Mike sold—Nick Royle had already bought 'The Dark Land' for his award-winning anthology *Darklands* (1992)—but it was the first story of his to be published. Our editorial acumen was

11

justified when the story went on to win The British Fantasy Award for 1991, and Mike was presented with the award for Best Newcomer that same year. He was definitely on his way as a writer, and a consecutive British Fantasy Award for 'The Dark Land' only confirmed his reputation as a talent to watch out for.

Over the next several years he turned out a stream of superior short stories that were published in a wide range of anthologies edited by myself and others. These included such now-classic tales as 'More Bitter Than Death', 'Later', 'The Fracture', 'The Owner', 'To See the Sea', 'Rain Falls', 'To Receive is Better' (which eventually formed the basis of his second novel), The British Fantasy Award-winning 'More Tomorrow', 'Not Waving', 'Dear Alison', 'Everybody Goes', 'Welcome' and 'The Handover', to name but a few.

Many of his tales were regularly selected for 'Year's Best' anthologies on both sides of the Atlantic. It was almost as if he could effortlessly write a notable short story to order, although several of these tales were actually fledgling efforts dating back to before his first publication. This merely served to illustrate that he always had the talent to become a first-rate writer.

I am also lucky enough to count Mike and his lovely wife Paula (not forgetting their two attention-seeking felines, Spangle and Lintilla) as amongst my closest friends. They kindly asked me to read something at their wedding ceremony in London in 1998, and Paula and I (who share the same birth-date) have jointly celebrated/commiserated the passing of yet another year at numerous fantasy conventions. I have slept off countless hangovers on their floors, while Mike has sampled my homemade chilli, gumbo and barbecue, and occasionally enjoyed a close-up encounter with the bushes in my garden after a long Summer's afternoon of partying. We have been on vacation together in such exotic locales as New Orleans and Baja, California, and we continue to swap advice and put-the-world-to-rights over a beer or two on a regular basis. In short, I couldn't ask for better or more supportive companions and confidants.

However, nailing my colours firmly to the mast here, I have to admit that I was not a huge fan of Mike's first three novels, the British Fantasy Award-winning *Only Forward* (1994), *Spares* (1996) and *One of Us* (1998), nor the separately-published novella *The Vaccinator* (1999). All these books were a departure from the tone and subject matter of the stories I so admired, and in terms of ideas and execution, they were more akin to the 'speculative fiction' of such cross-genre writers as Michael Moorcock and M. John Harrison. As a reader, I preferred the edgier, darker tone of his shorter tales.

Of course, I was in a very small minority. These books were both critical and commercial successes around the world, published in numerous countries and translated into more than fourteen languages.

It is therefore perhaps all the more ironic that the first of his novels I actually finished and enjoyed immensely was published under the obviously transparent pseudonym of 'Michael Marshall' (I don't intended to go into detail here about the stupidity of publishers' marketing departments!). *The Straw Men* (2002) is a phenomenally intense psycho-thriller, involving a frantic search for a secret society of serial killers. For me, it was a return to everything I had admired in the short stories, but plotted and written by an author who had refined his craft after more than a decade of professional publication.

I think that *The Straw Men* would make a marvellous movie or television mini-series, but Mike's own brushes with the entertainment industry have, to date, been less auspicious than his talent has deserved.

Spares was repeatedly optioned by Steven Spielberg's DreamWorks SKG (the director eventually decided to make the disappointing *Minority Report* instead), while *One of Us* has been optioned by DiNovi Pictures and Heyday Films for Warner Bros. and currently seems to be consigned to Script Development Hell.

As a screenwriter himself, Mike has been attached to various high-concept projects such as adaptations of Clive Barker's *Weaveworld*, Robert E. Howard's *Solomon Kane* and Peter O'Donnell's *Modesty Blaise*, all of which apparently continue to languish on the desks of talent-blind production executives.

In the late 1990s, Mike and I teamed up to create a media development partnership under the somewhat obvious nomenclature of Smith & Jones. The brainstorming meetings in Soho pubs were certainly fun, and we also enjoyed the pitch sessions in Hollywood with such studios as Miramax, Warner Bros. and Universal. However, in the end, we apparently had more faith in our ideas than the men-in-suits did. Which is still of great regret to both of us, as we came up with some really remarkable and original genre concepts during a frenetic five-year period of intense creativity. Not least of these was a *Hellraiser* sequel that actually retained the integrity and imagination of the original and which disappeared into a black hole somewhere on Harvey Weinstein's desk.

However, Mike and I have continued to work together on smaller creative projects, mostly involving publishing and graphic design, and our innate ability to communicate with each other on an almost instinctive level has resulted in some worthwhile collaborations, usually followed by a few beers in the pub afterwards.

Previous selections of Mike's short stories have been collected in Britain in the promotional bookstore give-away *When God Lived in Kentish Town* (1998), which is now a fabulously rare edition amongst collectors of the author's work, and *What You Make It* (1999), a representative compilation of Mike's first decade as a writer.

Although Earthling Publications previously put out Mike's attractive three-story sampler *Cat Stories* in a printing of just 350 copies in 2001, *More Tomorrow & Other Stories* marks yet another milestone for this stylish young imprint. The substantial volume you now hold in your hands is a superb gathering of the author's very best stories (several of which may be unfamiliar to American readers), along with four brand-new tales that are appearing here for the very first time. If you only know Mike's work from his novels, then prepare to be dazzled by a writer whose deceptively lucid storytelling coupled with a distinctive narrative tone have put him at the forefront of young authors working in the genre of imaginative fiction today.

Throughout the 1990s, Michael Marshall Smith was one of the most accomplished and distinctive new voices in British horror. Today he has matured into one of our finest novelists and a best-selling author whose work commands the attention of publishers and filmmakers all over the world.

This is how it should be. The ever-upward trajectory of his career is not only richly deserved, but is a fitting testimony to his hard work and commitment to a field of literature he both knows and loves.

And I hope that, in some small measure, I have contributed to that success. I'm still sitting in that same office, still pouring through those piles of submissions. However, there is just one difference these days—now I'm looking for the 'new Michael Marshall Smith'.

And believe me, that's one hell of a label for any writer to live up to, as you'll discover for yourself in the exceptional stories of fantasy and horror that follow...

Stephen Jones
London, May 2003

MORE TOMORROW

& OTHER STORIES

More Tomorrow

I got a new job a couple of weeks ago. It's pretty much the same as my old job, but at a nicer company. What I do is troubleshoot computers and their software—and yes, I know that sounds dull. People tell me so all the time. Not in words, exactly, but in their glassy smiles and their awkward 'let's be nice to the geek' demeanor.

It's a strange phenomenon, the whole 'computer people are losers' mentality. All round the world, at desks in every office and every building, people are using computers. Day in, day out. Every now and then, these machines go wrong. They're bound to: they're complex systems, like a human body, or society. When someone gets hurt, you call in a doctor. When a riot breaks out, it's the police that—for once—you want to see on your doorstep. It's their job to sort it out. Similarly, if your word processor starts dumping files or your hard disk goes non-linear, it's someone like me you need. Someone who actually *understands* the magic box which sits on your desk, and can make it all lovely again.

But do we get any thanks, any kudos for being the emergency services of the late twentieth century?

Do we fuck.

I can understand this to a degree. There are enough hard-line nerds and social zero geeks around to make it seem like a losing way of life. But there are plenty of pretty basic earthlings doing all the other jobs too, and no-one expects them to turn up for work in a pinwheel hat and a T-shirt saying 'Programmers do it recursively'. For the record, I play reasonable blues guitar, I've been out with a girl and have worked undercover for the CIA. The last bit isn't true, of course, but you get the general idea.

Up until recently I worked for a computer company, which I'll admit *was* full of very perfunctory human beings. When people started passing around jokes that were written in C++, I decided it was time to move on. One of the advantages of knowing about computers is that

17

unemployment isn't going to be a problem until the damn things start fixing themselves, and so I called a few contacts, posted a new CV up on my web site and within twenty-four hours had four opportunities to choose from. Most of them were other computer businesses, which I was kind of keen to avoid, and in the end I decided to have a crack at a company called the VCA. I put on my pin-wheel hat, rubbed pizza on my shirt, and strolled along for an interview.

The VCA, it transpired, was a non-profit organization dedicated to promoting effective business communication. The suave but shifty chief executive who interviewed me seemed a little vague as to what this actually entailed, and in the end I let it go. The company was situated in tidy new offices right in the centre of town, and seemed to be doing good trade at whatever it was they did. The reason they needed someone like me was they wanted to upgrade their system—computers, software and all. It was a months' contract work, at a very decent rate, and I said yes without a second thought.

Morehead, the guy in charge, took me for a gloating tour round the office. It looked the same as they always do, only emptier, because everyone was out at lunch. Then I settled down with their spreadsheet-basher to go find out what kind of system they could afford. His name was Cremmer, and he wasn't out at lunch because he was clearly one of those people who see working nine-hour days as worthy of some form of admiration. Personally I view it as worthy of pity, at most. He seemed amiable enough, in a curly-haired, irritating sort of way, and within half an hour we'd thrashed out the necessary. I made some calls, arranged to come back in a few days, and spent the rest of the afternoon helping build a hospital in Rwanda. Well actually I spent it listening to loud music and catching up on my Internet newsgroups, but I could have done the other had I been so inclined.

The Internet is one of those things that everyone's heard of without necessarily having any real idea of what it means—or how it works. It's actually pretty simple. A while back a group of universities and government organisations experimented with linking up their computers so they could share resources, send little messages and play *Star Trek* games with each other. There was also a military connection, and so the servers were linked in such a way that the system could take a hit somewhere and reroute information accordingly. After a time this network started to take on a momentum of its own, with everyone from Pentagon heavies to pin-wheeling wireheads taking it upon themselves to find new ways of connecting things up and making more information available. Just about every computer on the planet is now connected, and

18

if you've got a modem and a phone line, you can get on there too. What you find almost qualifies as a parallel universe. There are thousands of pieces of software, probably billions of text files by now. You can check the records of the New York Public Library, book a plane flight or a hotel room, download a picture of the far side of Jupiter, and monitor how many cans of Dr Pepper there are in soda machines in the computer science labs of American universities. Chances are you already have. It all used to be fairly chaotically organised, but now there are systems that span the net as a whole. One of these is the web, of course, which everyone's heard of, the dotcoms and wwws and 'enter your credit card details here'. Another is the newsgroups.

The newsgroups are kind of a hangover from the early days, from before everything became point-and-click. There are tens of thousands of these groups, covering anything from computers to fine art, science fiction to tastelessness, the books of Stephen King to quirky sexual preferences. If it's not outright illegal, out there on the Infobahn people will be yakking about it 24 hours a day, every day of the year. Either that or posting images of it: there are paintings and animals, NASA archives and abstract art, and in the alt.binaries.pictures.tasteless group you can find anything from close-up shots of roadkills to people with acid burns on their faces. Not very nice, but trust me, it's a minority interest. Now that I think of it, there is some illegal stuff (drugs, mainly)—there's a system by which you can send untraceable and anonymous messages, though I've never bothered to check it out.

Basically the newsgroups are the Internet for traditionalists—people who want the news as it breaks and who take an obscure pride in doing it the hard way. They're like super-charged mailing lists, discussion forums that stick to the raw data rather than wasting time with layout and glossy graphics and java applets that play tunes and flip pop-ups at you until you go insane. People read each other's messages and reply, or forward their own pronouncements or questions. Some groups are repositories of computer files, like software or pictures, others just have text messages. No-one, however sad, could hope to keep abreast of all of them, and nor would you want to. I don't give a toss about recent developments in Multilevel Marketing Businesses or the Chinchilla Farming in America Today, and have no interest in reading megabytes of losing burblings about them. So I stick to a tiny subset of the groups that carry stuff I'm interested in—Mac computers, guitar music, cats and the like.

So now you know.

*

Michael Marshall Smith

The following Tuesday I got up bright and early and made my way to the VCA for my first morning's work. England was doing its best to be Summery, which as always meant that it was humid without being hot, bright without being sunny, and every third commuter on the hellish tube journey was intermittently pebble-dashing nearby passengers with hayfever sneezes. I emerged moist and irritable from the station, more determined than ever to find a way of working that meant never having to leave my apartment. The walk from the station to VCA was better, passing through an attractive square and a selection of interesting side streets with restaurants featuring unusual cuisines, and I was feeling chipper again by the time I got there.

My suppliers had done their work, and the main area of VCA's open-plan office was piled high with exciting boxes. When I walked in just about all the staff were standing around the pile, coffee mugs in hand, regarding it with the wary enthusiasm of simple country folk confronted with a recently-landed UFO. There was a slightly toe-curling five minutes of introductions, embarrassing merely because I don't enjoy that kind of thing. Only one person, John, seemed to view me with the sniffy disdain of someone greeting an underling whose services are, unfortunately, in the ascendant. Everybody else seemed nice, some very much so.

Morehead eventually oiled out of his office and dispensed a few weak jokes that had the—possibly intentional—effect of scattering everyone back to their desks to get on with their work. I took off my jacket, rolled up my sleeves and got on with it.

I spent the morning cabling like a wild thing, placing the hardware of the network itself. As this involved a certain amount of disrupting everyone in turn by drilling, pulling up carpet and moving their desks, I was soon on apologetic grinning terms with most of them. I guess I could have done the wire-up over the weekend when nobody was there, but I like my weekends as they are. John gave me the invisibility routine that people once used on servants, but everyone else was fairly cool about it. One of the girls, Jeanette, actually engaged me in conversation while I worked nearby, and seemed genuinely interested in understanding what I was doing. When I broke it to her that it was actually pretty dull, she smiled.

The wiring took a little longer than I was expecting, and I stayed on after everybody else had gone. Everyone but Cremmer, that was, who stayed, probably to make sure that I didn't run off with their plants, or database, or spoons. Either that or to get some brownie points with whoever it is he thought cared about people putting in long hours. The invoicing supremo was in expansive mood, and chuntered endlessly about his adventures in computing, which were, to be honest, of slender interest to me. In the end he got bored of my monosyllabic grunts from beneath desks, and left me with some keys instead.

The next day was pretty much the same, except I was setting up the computers themselves. This involved taking things out of boxes and installing interminable pieces of software on the server. This isn't quite such a sociable activity as disturbing people, and I spent most of the day in the affable but distant company of Sarah, their PR person. At the end of the day everyone gathered in the main room and then left together, apparently for a meal to celebrate someone's birthday. I thought I caught Jeanette casting a glance in my direction at one point, maybe embarrassed at the division between me and them. It didn't bother me much, so I just put my head down and got on with swapping floppy disks in and out of the machines.

Well, it did bother me a little, to be honest. It wasn't their fault—there was no reason why they should make the effort to include someone they didn't know, who wasn't really a part of their group. People seldom do. You have to be a little thick-skinned about that kind of thing if you work freelance. There are tribes, you know, everywhere you go. They owe their allegiance to shared time (if they're friends), or to an organisation (if they're colleagues): but they're still tribes, just as much as if they'd tilled the same patch of desert for centuries. As a freelancer, especially in the cyber-areas, you tend to spend a lot of time wandering between them; occasionally being granted access to their watering hole, but never being one of the real people. Sometimes it can get on your nerves. That's all.

I finished up, locked the building carefully—I'm a complete anal-retentive about such things—and went home. I used my mobile to call for a pizza while I was on route, and it arrived two minutes after I got out of the shower. A perfect piece of timing, which sadly no-one was on hand to appreciate. My last experiment with living with someone did not end well, mainly because she was a touchy and irritable woman who needed her own space twenty-three and a half hours a day. Well it was more complicated than that, of course, but that was the main impression I took away with me. I mulled over those times as I sat and munched my 'Everything on it, and then a few more things as well' pizza, vague-eyed in front of white noise television, and ended up feeling rather grim.

Food event over, I made a jug of coffee and settled down in front of the Mac. I tweaked my invoicing database for a while, exciting young man that I am, and then wrote a letter to my sister in Australia. She doesn't have access to Internet email, unfortunately, otherwise she'd hear from me a lot more often. Write letter, print letter, put it in envelope, get stamps, get it to a post office. A chain of admin of that magnitude usually takes me about two weeks to get through, and it's a bit primitive, really, compared to 'Write letter, press button, there in five minutes'.

I called my friend Nick, who's a freelance sub-editor on a trendy magazine, but he was chasing a deadline and not disposed to chat. I tried the television, but it was still outputting someone else's idea of entertainment. By nine o'clock I was very bored, and so I logged on to the net.

Probably because I was bored, and feeling a bit isolated, after I'd done my usual groups I found myself checking out alt.binaries.pictures.erotica. 'alt' means the group is an unofficial one; 'binaries' means it holds computer files rather than just messages; 'pictures' means those files are images. As for the last word, I'm prepared to be educational about this but you're going to have to work that one out for yourself.

The media has the impression that the minute you're in cyberspace countless pictures of this type come flooding at you down the phone, pouring like ravening hordes onto your hard disk and leaping out of the screen to take over your mind. This is not the case, and all of you worried about your little Timmy's soul can afford to relax a little. Even if you're only talking about the web, you need a computer, a modem, access to a phone line, and a credit card to pay for your Internet feed. With Usenet you need to find the right newsgroup, and download about three segments for each picture. You require several bits of software to piece them together, convert the result, and display it.

The naughty pictures don't come and get you, and if you see one, it ain't an accident. If your little Timmy has the kit, finance and inclination to go looking, then maybe it's you who needs the talking to. In fact, maybe you should be grounded.

The flipside of that, of course, is the implication that *I* have the inclination to go looking, which I guess I occasionally do. Not very often—honest—but I do. I don't know how defensive to feel about that fact. Men of all shapes and sizes, ages and creeds, and states of marital or relationship bliss enjoy, every now and then, the sight of a woman with no clothes on. It's just as well we do, you know, otherwise there'd be no new little earthlings, would there? If you want to call that oppression or sexism or the commodification of the female body then go right ahead, but don't expect me to talk to you at dinner parties. I prefer to call it sexual attraction, but then I'm a sad fuck who spends half his life in front of computer, so what the hell do I know?

Still, it's not something that people feel great about, and I'm not going to defend it too hard. Especially not to women, because that would be a waste of everyone's time. Women have a little bit of their brain missing that means they cannot understand the attraction of pornography. I'm not saying that's a *bad* thing, just that it's true. On the other hand they understand the attraction of babies, shoe shops and the detail of other people's lives, so I guess it's swings and roundabouts.

I've talked about it for too long now, and you're going to think I'm some Neanderthal with his tongue hanging to the ground who goes round looking up people's skirts. I'm not. Yes, there are rude pictures to be found on the net, and yes I sometimes find them. What can I say? I'm a bloke.

Anyway, I scouted round for a while, but in the end didn't even download anything. From the descriptions of the files they seemed to be the same endless permutations of badly-lit mad people, which is ultimately a bit tedious. Also, bullish talk notwithstanding, I don't feel great about looking at that kind of thing. I don't think it reflects very well upon one, and you only have to read a few other people's slaverings to make you decide it is too sad to be a part of.

So in the end I played the guitar for a while and went to bed.

The next few days at VCA passed pretty easily. I installed and configured, configured and installed. The birthday meal went pretty well, I gathered, and featured amongst other highlights the secretary Tanya literally sliding under the table through drunkenness. That was her story, at least. By the Monday of the following week everyone was calling me by name, and I was being included in the coffee-making rounds. England had called off its doomed attempt at summer, or at least imposed a time out, and had settled for a much more bearable cross between Spring and Autumn instead. All in all, things were going fairly well.

And as the week progressed, slightly better even than that. The reason for this was a person. Jeanette, to be precise.

I began, without even noticing at first, to find myself veering towards the computer nearest her when I needed to do some testing. I also found that I was slightly more likely to offer to go and make a round of coffees in the kitchen when she was already standing there, smoking one of her hourly cigarettes. Initially it was just because she was the politest and most approachable of the staff, and it was a couple of days before I realised that I was looking out for her return from lunch, trying to be less dull when she was around, and noticing what she wore.

It was almost as if I was beginning to fancy her, for heaven's sake.

Michael Marshall Smith

By the beginning of the next week I passed a kind of watershed, and went from undirected, subconscious behaviour to actually facing the fact that I was attracted to her. I did this with a faint feeling of dread, coupled with occasional, mournful tinges of melancholy. It was like being back at school. It's awful, when you're grown-up, to be reminded of what it was like when a word from someone, a glance, even just their presence, can be like the sun coming out from behind cloud. While it's nice, in a lyric, romantic novel sort of way, it also complicates things. Suddenly it matters if other people come into the kitchen when you're talking to her, and the way they interact with other people becomes more important. You start trying to engineer things, try to be near them, and it all just gets a bit weird.

Especially if the other person hasn't a clue what's going on in your head—and you've no intention of telling them. I'm no good at that, the telling part. Ten years ago I carried a letter round with me for two weeks, trying to pluck up the courage to give it to someone. It was a girl who was part of the same crowd at college, who I knew well as a friend, and who had just split up from someone else. The letter was a very carefully worded and tentative description of how I felt about her, ending with an invitation for a drink. Several times I was on the brink, I swear, but somehow I didn't give it to her. I just didn't have what it took.

The computer stuff was going okay, if you're interested. By the middle of the week the system was pretty much in place, and people were happily sending pop-up messages to each other. Cremmer, in particular, thought it was just fab that he could boss people around from the comfort of his own den. Even John was bucked up by seeing how the new system was going to ease the progress of whatever dull task it was he performed, and all in all my stock at the VCA was rising high.

It was time, finally, to get down to the nitty-gritty of developing their new databases. I tend to enjoy that part more than the wireheading, because it's more of a challenge, gives scope for design and creativity, and I don't have to keep getting up from my chair. When I settled down to it on Thursday morning, I realised that it was going to have an additional benefit. Jeanette was the VCA's Events Organiser, and most of the databases they needed concerned various aspects of her job. In other words, it was her I genuinely had to talk to about them, and at some length.

We sat side by side at her desk, me keeping a respectful distance, and I asked her the kind of questions I had to ask. She answered them concisely and quickly, didn't pipe up with a lot of damn fool questions, and came up with some reasonable requests. It was rather a nice day outside, and sunlight that was for once not hazy and obstructive angled through the window to pick out the lighter hues amongst her chestnut hair, which was long, and wavy, and as far as I could see entirely beautiful. Her hands played carelessly with a biro as we talked, the fingers long and purposeful, the forearms a pleasing shade of skin colour. I hate people who go sprinting out into parks at the first sign of Summer, to spend their lunchtimes staked out with insectile brainlessness in the desperate quest for a tan. As far as I was concerned the fact that Jeanette clearly hadn't done so—in contrast to Tanya, for example, who already looked like a hazelnut (and probably thought with the same fluency as one)—was just another thing to like her for.

It was a nice morning. Relaxed, and pleasant. Over the last week we'd started to speak more and more, and were ready for a period of actually having to converse with each other at length. I enjoyed it, but didn't get over-excited. Despite my losing status as a technodrone, I am wise in the ways of relationships. Just being able to get on with her, and have her look as if she didn't mind being with me—that was more than enough for the time being. I wasn't going to try for anything more. Or so I thought.

Then, at 12.30, I did something entirely unexpected. We were in the middle of an in-depth and speculative wrangle on the projected nature of their hotel-booking database, when I realised that we were approaching the time at which Jeanette generally took her lunch. Smoothly, and with a nonchalance that I found frankly impressive, I lofted the idea that we go grab a sandwich somewhere and continue the discussion outside. As the sentences slipped from my mouth I experienced an out-of-body sensation, as if I was watching myself from about three feet away, cowering behind a chair. 'Not bad,' I found myself thinking, incredulously. 'Clearly she'll say no, but that was a good, businesslike way of putting it.'

Bizarrely, instead of shrieking with horror or poking my eye out with a ruler, she said yes. We rose together, I grabbed my jacket, and we left the office, me trying not to smirk like a businessman recently ennobled for doing a lot of work for charity. We took the lift down to the lobby and stepped outside, and I chattered inanely to avoid coming to terms with the fact that I was now standing with her *outside* work, beyond our usual frame of reference.

She knew a snack bar round the corner, and within ten minutes we found ourselves at a table outside, ploughing through sandwiches. She even ate attractively, holding the food fluently and wolfing it down, as if she was a genuine human taking on sustenance rather than someone appearing in amateur dramatics. I audibly mulled over the database for a while, to give myself time to settle down, and before long we'd pretty much done the subject.

Luckily, as we each smoked a cigarette she pointed out with distaste a couple of blokes walking down the street, both of whom had taken their shirts off, and whose paunches were hanging over their jeans.

'Summer,' she said, with a sigh, and I was away. There are few people with a larger internal stock of complaints to make about Summer than me, and I let myself rip.

Why, I asked her, did everyone think it was so nice? What were supposed to be the benefits? One of the worst things about Summer, I maintained hotly, as she smiled and ordered a coffee, was the constant pressure to enjoy oneself in ways which are considerably less fun than death.

Barbecues, for example. Now I don't mind barbies, especially, except that *my* friends never have them. It's just not their kind of thing. If I end up at a barbecue it's because I've been dragged there by my partner, to stand round in someone else's scraggy back garden as the sky threatens rain, watching drunken blokes teasing a nasty barking dog and girls I don't know standing in hunched clumps gossiping about people I've never heard of, while I try to eat badly cooked food that I could have bought for £2.50 in McDonalds *and* had somewhere to sit as well. That terrible weariness, a feeling of being washed out, exhausted and depressed, that comes from getting not quite drunk enough in the afternoon sun while standing up and either trying to make conversation with people I'll never see again, or putting up with them doing the same to me.

And going and sitting in parks. I hate it, as you may have gathered. Why? Because it's fucking *horrible*, that's why. Sitting on grass which is both papery and damp, surrounded by middle-class men with beards teaching their kids to unicycle, the air rent by the sound of some arsehole torturing a guitar to the delight of his 14-year-old hippy girlfriend. Drinking lukewarm soft drinks out of over-priced cans, and all the time being repetitively told how nice it all is, as if by some process of brain-washing you'll actually start to enjoy it.

Worst of all, the constant pressure to *go outside*. 'What are you doing inside on a day like this? You want to go outside, you do, get some fresh air. You want to go outside.' No. Wrong. I don't want to go outside. For a start, I like it inside. It's nice there. There are sofas, drinks, cigarettes, books. There is shade. Outside there's nothing but the sun, the mindless drudgery of suntan cultivation, and the perpetual sound of droning voices, yapping dogs and convention shouting at you to enjoy yourself. And always the constant refrain from everyone you meet, drumming on your mind like torrential rain on a tin roof: 'Isn't it a beautiful day?', 'Isn't it a beautiful day?', 'Isn't it a beautiful day?', 'Isn't it a beautiful day?'

No, say I. No, it fucking *isn't*.

There was all that, and some more, but I'm sure you get the drift. By halfway through Jeanette was laughing, partly at what I was saying, and partly—I'm sure—at the fact that I was getting quite so worked up about it. But she was fundamentally on my side, and chipped in some valuable observations about the horrors of sitting outside dull country pubs surrounded by red-faced career girls and loud-mouthed estate agents in shorts, deafened by the sound of open-topped cars being revved by people who clearly had no right to live. We banged on happily for quite a while, had another cup of coffee, and then were both surprised to realise that we'd gone into overtime on lunch. I paid, telling her she could get the next one, and although that sounds like a terrible line, it came out pretty much perfect and she didn't stab me or anything. We strode quickly back to the office, still chatting, and the rest of the afternoon passed in a hazy blur of contentment.

I could have chosen to leave the office at the same time as her, and walked to whichever station she used, but I elected not to. I judged that enough had happened for one day, and I didn't want to push my luck. Instead I went home alone, hung out by myself, and went to sleep with, I suspect, a small smile upon my face.

Next day I sprang out of bed with an enthusiasm that is utterly unlike me, and as I struggled to balance the recalcitrant taps of my shower I was already plotting my next moves. Part of my mind was sitting back with folded arms and watching me with indulgent amusement, but in general I just felt really quite happy and excited.

For most of the morning I quizzed Jeanette further on her database needs. She was lunching with a friend, I knew, so I wasn't expecting anything there. Instead I wandered vaguely round a couple of bookshops, wondering if there was any book I could legitimately buy for Jeanette. It would have to be something very specific, relevant to a conversation we'd had—and sufficiently inexpensive that it looked like a throwaway gift. In the end I came away empty-handed, which was probably just as well. Buying her a present was a ridiculous idea, out of proportion to the current situation. As I walked back to the office I told myself to be careful. I was in danger of getting carried away and disturbing the careful equilibrium of my life and mind.

Then, in the afternoon, something happened. I was off the databases for a while, trying to work out why one of the servers was behaving like an arse. Tanya wandered up to ask Jeanette about something, and before she went reminded her that there'd been talk of everyone going out for a drink that evening. Jeanette hummed and ha-ed for a moment, and I bent further over the keyboard, giving them a chance to ignore me. Then, as from nowhere, Tanya said the magic words.

Why, she suggested, didn't I come too?

Careful to be nonchalant and cavalier, pausing as if sorting through my myriad of other options, I said yes, why the hell not. Jeanette then said yes, she could probably make it, and for a moment I saw all the locks and chains around my life fall away, as if a cage had collapsed around me leaving only the open road.

For a moment it was like that, and then suddenly it wasn't. 'I'll have to check with Chris, though,' Jeanette added, and I realised she had a boyfriend.

I spent the rest of the afternoon alternating between trying to calm myself down and violently but silently cursing. I should have known that someone like her would already be taken—after all, they always are. Of course, it didn't mean it was a no-go area. People sometimes leave their partners. I know, I've done it myself. And people have left me. But suddenly it had changed, morphed from something that might—in my dreams, at least—have developed smoothly into a Nice Thing. Instead it become a miasma of potential grief which was unlikely to even start.

For about half an hour I was furious, with what I don't know. With myself, for letting my feelings grow and complicate. With her, for having a boyfriend. With life, for always being that bit more disappointing than it absolutely has to be.

Then, because I'm an old hand at dealing with my inner conditions, I talked myself round. It didn't matter. Jeanette could simply become a pleasant aspect of a month-long contract, someone I could chat to. Then the job would end, I'd move on, and none of it would matter. I had to nail that conclusion down on myself pretty hard, but thought I could make it stick.

I decided that I might as well go out for the drink anyway. There was another party I could go to but it would involve trekking halfway across town. Nick was busy. I might as well be sociable, now that they'd made the offer.

So I went, and I wish I hadn't.

The evening was okay, in the way that they always are when people from the same office get together to drink and complain about their boss. Morehead wasn't there, thankfully, and Cremmer quickly got sufficiently drunk that he didn't qualify as a Morehead substitute. The evening was fine, for everyone else. It was just me who didn't have a good time.

Jeanette disappeared just before we left the office, and I found myself walking to the pub with everyone else. I sat drinking Budweisers and making conversation with John and Sarah, wondering where she was. She'd said she'd meet everyone there. So where was she?

At about half past eight the question was answered. She walked into the pub and I started to get up, a smile of greeting on my face. Then I realised she looked different somehow, and I noticed the man standing behind her.

The man was Chris Ayer. He was her boyfriend. He was also the nastiest man I've met in quite some time. That's going to sound like sour grapes, but it's not. He was perfectly presentable, in that he was good-looking and could talk to people, but everything else about him was wrong. There was something odd about the way he looked at people, something both arrogant and closed off. There was an air of restrained violence about him that I found unsettling, and his sense of his possession of Jeanette was complete. She sat at his side, hands in her lap, and said very little throughout the evening. I couldn't get over how different she looked to the funny and confident woman I'd had lunch with the day before, but nobody else seemed to notice it. After all, she joined in the office banter as usual, and smiled with her lips quite often. Nobody apart from me was looking for any more than that.

As the evening wore on I found myself feeling more and more uncomfortable. I exchanged a few tight words with Ayer, mainly concerning a new computer he'd bought, but wasn't bothered when he turned to talk to someone else. The group from the office seemed to be closing in on itself, leaning over the table to shout jokes which they understood and I didn't. Ayer's harsh laugh cut across the smoke to me, and I felt impotently angry that someone like him should be able to sit with his arm around someone like Jeanette.

I drank another couple of beers and then abruptly decided that I simply wasn't having a good enough time. I stood up and took my leave, and was mildly touched when Tanya and Sarah tried to get me to stay. Jeanette didn't say anything, and when Ayer's eyes swept vaguely over me I saw that for him I didn't exist. I backed out of the pub smiling, and then turned and stalked miserably down the road.

*

By Sunday evening I was fine. I met my ex-girlfriend-before-last for lunch on the Saturday, and we had a riotous time bitching and gossiping about people we knew. In the evening I went to a restaurant that served food only from a particular four-square-mile region of Nepal, or so Nick claimed, such venues being his speciality. It tasted just like Indian to me, and I didn't see any sherpas, but the food was good. I spent Sunday doing my kind of thing, wandering round town and sitting in cafés to read. I called my folks in the evening, and they were in good form, and then I watched a horror film before going to bed when I felt like it. The kind of weekend that only happily single people can have, in other words, and it suited me just fine.

Monday was okay too. I was regaled with various tales of drunkenness from Friday night, as if for the first time I had a right to know. I had all the information I needed from Jeanette for the time being, so I did most of my work at a different machine. We had a quick chat in the kitchen while I made some coffee, and it was more or less the same as it had been the week before—because she'd always *known* she had a boyfriend, of course. I caught myself sagging a couple of times on the afternoon, but bullied my mood into holding up. In a way it was kind of a relief, not to have to care.

The evening was warm and sunny, and I took my time walking home. Then I rustled myself up a chef's salad, which is my only claim to culinary skill. It has iceberg lettuce, black olives, grated cheese, julienned ham (that's 'sliced', to you and me), diced tomato and two types of home-made dressing: which is more than enough ingredients to count as cooking in my book. When I was sufficiently gorged on roughage I sat in front of the computer and tooled around, and by the time it was dark outside found myself cruising round the net.

And, after a while, I found myself accessing alt.binaries.pictures.erotica. I was in a funny sort of mood, I guess. I scrolled through the list of files, not knowing what I was after. What I found was the usual stuff, like '-TH2xx.jpg-{m/f}-hot sex!'. Hot sex wasn't really what I was looking for, especially if it had an exclamation mark after it. Of all the people who access the group, I suspect it's less than about 5% who actually put pictures up there in the first place. It seems to be a matter of intense pride with them, and they compete with each other on the volume and 'quality' of their postings. Their tragically sad bickering is often more entertaining than the pictures themselves.

It's complete pot luck what is available at any given time, and no file stays on there for more than about two days. The servers that hold the information have only limited space, and files get rolled off the end pretty quickly in the high volume groups. I was about to give up when something suddenly caught my attention.

'j1.gif-{f}-"Young_woman, fully_clothed (part 1/3)".

Fuck *me*, I thought: that's a bit weird. The group caters for a wide spectrum of human sexuality, and I'd seen titles that promised fat couples, skinny girls, interracial bonding and light S&M. What I'd never come across was something as perverted as a woman with all her clothes *on*. Intrigued, I did the necessary to download the picture's three segments onto my hard disk.

By the time I'd made a cup of coffee they were there, and I severed the net connection and stitched the three files together. Until they were converted they were just text files, which is one of the weird things about the newsgroups. Absolutely anything, from programs to articles to pictures, is up there as plain text. Without the appropriate decoders it just looks like nonsense, which I guess is as good a metaphor as any for the net as a whole. Or indeed for life. Feel free to use that insight in your own conversations.

When the file was ready, I loaded up a graphics package and opened it. I was doing so with only half an eye, not really expecting anything very interesting. But when, after a few seconds of whirring, the image popped onto the screen, I dropped my cup of coffee and it teetered on the desk before falling to shatter on the floor.

It was Jeanette.

The image quality was not especially high, and looked as if it had been taken with some small automatic camera. But the girl in the picture was Jeanette, without a shadow of a doubt. She was perched on the arm of an anonymous armchair, and with a lurch I realised it was probably taken in her flat. She was, as advertised, fully clothed, wearing a shortish skirt and a short-sleeved top that buttoned up at the front. She was looking in the general direction of the camera, and her expression was unreadable. She looked beautiful, as always, and somehow much, much more appealing than any of the buck-naked women who cavorted through the usual pictures to be found on the net.

After I'd got over my jaw-dropped surprise, I found I was feeling something else. Annoyance, possibly. I know I'm biased, but I didn't think it right that a picture of her was plastered up in cyberspace for everyone to gawk at, even if she was fully clothed. I realise that's hypocritical in the face of all the other women up there, but I can't help it. It was different.

Because I knew her.

I was also angry because I could only think of one way it could have got there. I'd mentioned a few net-related things in Jeanette's presence at work, and she'd showed no sign of recognition. It was a hell of a coincidence that I'd seen the picture at all, and I wasn't prepared to speculate about stray photos of her falling into unknown people's hands. There was only one person who was likely to have uploaded it. Her boyfriend.

The usual women (and men) in the pictures are getting paid for it. It's their job. Jeanette wasn't, and might not even know the picture was there.

I quickly logged back onto the net and found the original text files. I extricated the uploader information and pulled it onto the screen, and then swore.

Remember a while back I said it was possible to hide yourself when posting up to the net? Well, that's what he'd done. The email address of the person who'd uploaded the picture was listed as 'anon99989@penet.fi'. That meant that rather than posting it up in his real name, he'd routed the mail through an anonymity server in Finland called PENET. This server strips the journey information out of the posting and assigns a random address that is held on an encrypted database. I couldn't tell anything from it at all. Feeling my lip curl with distaste, I quit out.

By the time I got to work the next day, I knew there wasn't anything I could say about it. I could hardly pipe up with 'Hey! Saw your pic on the Internet porn board last night!' And after all, it was only a picture, the kind that people have plastic folders stuffed full of. The question was whether Jeanette knew Ayer had posted it up. If she did then, well, it just went to show that you didn't know much about people just because you worked with them. If she didn't, then I think she had a right both to know, and to be annoyed.

I dropped a few net-references into the conversations we had, but nothing came of them. I even mentioned the newsgroups, but got mild interest and nothing more. It was fairly clear she hadn't heard of them. In the end I sort of mentally shrugged. So her unpleasant boyfriend had posted up a picture. There was nothing I could do about it, except bury still further any feelings I might have entertained for her. She already had a life with someone else, and I had no business interfering.

In the evening I met up with Nick again, and we went and got quietly hammered in a small drinking club we frequented. I successfully fought off his ideas on going and getting some food, doubtless the cuisine of one particular village on the top of Kilimanjaro, and so by the end of the evening we were pretty far gone. I stumbled out of a cab, flolloped up the stairs and mainlined coffee for a while, in the hope of avoiding a hangover the next day. And it was as I sat, weaving slightly, on the sofa, that I conceived the idea of checking a certain newsgroup.

Once the notion had taken hold I couldn't seem to dislodge it. Most of my body and soul was engaged in remedial work, trying to save what brain cells they could from the onslaught of alcohol, and the idea was free to romp and run as it pleased. So I found myself slumped at my desk, listening to my hard disk doing its thing, and muttering quietly to myself. I don't know what I was saying. I think it was probably a verbal equivalent of that letter I never gave to someone, an explanation of how much better off Jeanette would be with me. I can get very maudlin when I'm drunk.

When the newsgroup appeared in front of me I blearily ran my eye over the list. The group had seen serious action in the last twenty-four hours, and there were over 300 titles to contend with. I was beginning to lose heart and interest when I saw something about two-thirds of the way down the list.

'j2.gif-{f}-"Young_woman"', one line said, and it was followed by 'j3.gif-{f}-"Young_woman"'.

These two titles started immediately to do what half a pint of coffee hadn't: sober me up. At a glance I could tell that there were two differences from the description of the first picture of Jeanette I'd seen. The numerals after the 'j' were different, implying they were not the same picture. Also, there were two words missing at the end of the title: the words 'fully clothed'.

I called the first few lines of the first file onto the screen, and saw that it too had come from anon99989@penet.fi. Then, reaching shakily for a cigarette, I downloaded the rest. When my connection was over I slowly stitched the text files together and then booted up the viewer.

It was Jeanette, again. Wincing slightly, hating myself for having access to photos of her under these circumstances when I had no right to know what they might show, I looked briefly at first one and then the other.

j2.gif looked as if it had been taken immediately after the first I'd seen. It showed Jeanette, still sitting on the arm of the chair. She was undoing the front of her top, and had got as far as the third button. Her head was down, and I couldn't see her face. Trembling slightly from a combination of emotions, I looked at j3.gif. Her top was now off, showing a flat stomach and a dark blue lacy bra. She was steadying herself on the chair with one arm, and her position looked uncomfortable. She was looking off to one side, away from the camera, and when I saw her face I thought I had the answer to at least one question. She didn't look very happy. She didn't look as if she was having fun.

Michael Marshall Smith

She didn't look as if she wanted to be doing this at all.

I stood up suddenly and paced around the room, unsure of what to do. If she hadn't been especially enthralled about having the photos taken in the first place, I couldn't believe that Jeanette condoned or even knew about their presence on the net. Quite apart from anything else, she wasn't that type of girl, if that type of girl indeed existed at all.

This constituted some very clear kind of invasion by her boyfriend, something that negated any rights he may have felt he had upon her. But what could I do about it?

I copied the two files onto a floppy, along with j1.gif, and threw them off my hard disk. It may seem like a small distinction to you, but I didn't want them on my main machine. It would have seemed like collusion.

I got up the next morning with no more than a mild headache, and before I left for work decided to quickly log onto the net. There were no more pictures, but there was something that made me very angry indeed. Someone had posted up a message whose total text was the following.

'Re: j-pictures {f}: EXCELLENT! More pleeze!'.

In other words, the pictures had struck a chord with some nameless net-pervert, and they wanted to see some more.

I spent the whole morning trying to work out what to do. The only way I could think of broaching the subject would involve mentioning the alt.binaries.pictures.erotica group itself, which would be a bit of a nasty moment—I wasn't keen on revealing the fact that I was a nameless net pervert myself. I hardly got a chance to talk to her all morning anyway, because she was busy on the phone. She also seemed a little tired, and little disposed to chat on the two occasions we found ourselves in the kitchen together.

It felt as if parts of my mind were straining against each other, pulling in different directions. If she didn't know about it, it was wrong, and she should be put in the picture. If I did so, however, she'd never think the same of me again. There was a chance, of course, that the problem might go away: despite the net-loser's request, the expression on Jeanette's face in j3.gif made it seem unlikely there *were* any more pictures. And ultimately the whole situation probably wasn't any of my business, however much it felt like it was.

In the event, I missed the boat. About 4.30 I emerged from a long and vicious argument with the server software to discover that Jeanette had left for the day. 'A doctor's appointment'. In most of the places I've worked that phrase translates directly to 'A couple of hours off from work, *obviously* not spent at the doctors', but that didn't seem to be the general impression at the VCA. She'd probably just gone to the doctor's. Either way she was no longer in the office, and I was slightly ashamed to find myself relaxing now that I could no longer talk to her.

At 8.30 that evening, after my second salad of the week, I logged on and checked the group again. There was nothing there. I fretted and fidgeted around the apartment for a few hours, and then tried again at 11.00. This time I found something. Two things. j4.gif, and j5.gif, both from the anonymous address.

In the first picture Jeanette was standing. She was no longer wearing her skirt, and her long legs led up to underwear that matched the bra I'd already seen. She wasn't posing for the picture. Her hands were on her hips, and she looked angry. In j5 she was leaning back against the arm of the chair, and no longer wearing her bra. Her face was blank.

I stared at the second picture for a long time, mind completely split in two. If you ignored the expression on her face, she looked gorgeous. Her breasts were small but perfectly shaped, exactly in proportion to her long, slender body. It was, undeniably, an erotic picture. Except for her face, and the fact that she obviously didn't want to be photographed, and the fact that someone was doing it anyway. Not only that, but broadcasting it to the planet.

I decided that enough was enough, and that I had to do something. After a while I came up with the best that I could. I loaded up my email package, and sent a message to anon99989@penet.fi. The double-blind principle the server operated on meant that the recipient wouldn't know where it had come from, and that was fine by me. The message was this:

'I know who you are'.

It wasn't much, but it was something. The idea that someone out there on the information superhighway could know his identity *might* be enough to stop him. It was only a stop-gap measure, anyway. I now knew I had to do something about the situation.

And I had to do it soon. When I checked the next morning there were no more pictures, but two messages from people who'd downloaded them. 'Keep 'em cumming!' one wit from Japan had written. Some slob from Texas had posted in similar vein, but added a small request: 'Great, but pick up the pace a little. I want to see more FLESH!'

All the way to work I geared myself up to talking to Jeanette, and I nearly punched the wall when I heard she was out at a venue meeting for the whole morning and half the afternoon. I got rid of the morning by concentrating hard on one of her databases, wanting to bring at least something positive into her life. I know it's not much, but all I know is computers, and that's the best that I could do.

At last three o'clock rolled round, and Jeanette reappeared in the office. She seemed tired and a little preoccupied, and sat straight down at her desk to work. I loitered in the main office area, willing people to fuck off out of it so hard my head started to ache. I couldn't get anywhere near the topic if there were other people around. It would be hard enough if we were alone.

Finally, bloody, *finally* she got up from her desk and went into the kitchen. I got up and followed her in. She smiled faintly and vaguely on seeing me, and, seeing that she had a bandage on her right forearm, I used that to start a conversation. A small mole, apparently, hence the visit to the doctor. I let her finish that topic, keeping half an eye out to make sure that no-one was approaching the kitchen.

'I bought a camera today,' I blurted, as cheerily as I could. It wasn't great, but I wanted to start slowly. She didn't respond for a moment, and then looked up, her face expressionless.

'Oh yes?' she said, eventually. 'What are you going to photograph?'

'Oh, you know, buildings, landscape. Black and white, that kind of thing.' She nodded distantly, and I ran out of things to say.

I ran out because in retrospect the topic didn't lead anywhere, but I stopped for another reason too. I stopped because as she turned to pick up the kettle, the look on her face knocked the wind out of me. The combination of unhappiness and loneliness, the sense of helplessness. It struck me again that despite the anger in her face in j4, in j5 she had not only taken her bra off but looked resigned and defeated. Suddenly I didn't care how it looked, didn't care what she thought of me.

'Jeanette,' I said, firmly, and she turned to look at me again. 'I saw a pict—'

'Hello boys and girls. Having a little tea party, are we?'

At the sound of Morehead's voice I wanted to turn round and smash his face in. Jeanette laughed prettily at her employer's sally, and moved out of the way to allow him access to the kettle. Morehead asked me some balls-achingly dull questions about the computer system, obviously keen to sound as if he had the faintest conception of what it all meant. By the time I'd finished answering him Jeanette was back at her desk.

The next hour was one of the longest of my life. I'd gone over, crossed the line. I knew I was going to talk to her about what I'd seen. More than that, I'd realised that it didn't have to be as difficult as I'd assumed.

The first picture, j1.gif, simply showed a pretty girl sitting on a chair. It wasn't pornographic, and could have been posted up in any number of places on the net. All I had to do was say I'd seen *that* picture. It wouldn't implicate me, and she would know what her boyfriend was up to.

MORE TOMORROW

I hovered round the main office, ready to be after her the minute she looked like leaving, having decided that I'd walk with her to the tube and tell her then. So long as she didn't leave with anyone else, it would be perfect. While I hovered I watched her work, her eyes blank and isolated. About quarter to five she got a phone call. She listened for a moment, said 'Yes, alright' in a dull tone of voice, and then put the phone down. There was nothing else to distract me from the constant cycling of draft gambits in my head.

At five she started tidying her desk, and I slipped out and got my jacket. I waited in the hallway until I could hear her coming, and then went downstairs in the lift. I walked through the lobby as slowly as I could, and then went and stood outside the building. My hands were sweating and I felt wired and frightened, but I knew I was going to go through with it. A moment later she came out.

'Hi,' I said, and she smiled warily, surprised to see me, I suppose. 'Look Jeanette, I need to talk to you about something.'

She stared at me, looked around, and then asked what.

'I've seen pictures of you.' In my nervousness I blew it, and used the plural rather than singular.

'Where?' she said, immediately. She knew what I was talking about. From the speed with which she latched on I realised that whatever fun and games were going on between her and Ayer were at the forefront of her mind.

'The Newsgroups. It's...'

'I know what they are,' she said. 'What have you seen?'

'Five so far,' I said. 'Look, if there's anything I can do...'

'Like what?' she said, and laughed harshly, her eyes beginning to blur. 'Like what?'

'Well, anything. Look, let's go talk about it. I could...'

'There's no use,' she said hurriedly, and started to pull away. I followed her, bewildered. How could she not want to do anything about it? I mean, alright, I may not have been much of a prospect, but surely some help was better than none.

'Jeanette...'

'Let's talk tomorrow,' she hissed, and suddenly I realised what was happening. Her boyfriend had come to pick her up. She walked towards the curb where a white car was coming to a halt, and I rapidly about-faced and started striding the other way. It wasn't fear, not purely. I also didn't want to get her in trouble.

As I walked up the road I felt as if the back of my neck was burning, and at the last moment I glanced to the side. The white car was just passing, and I could see Jeanette sitting bolt upright in the passenger seat. Her boyfriend was looking out of the side window. At me. Then he accelerated and the car sped away.

That night brought another two photographs. j6 had Jeanette naked, sitting in the chair with her legs slightly apart. Her face was stony. In j7 she was on all fours, photographed from behind. As I sat in my chair, filled with impotent fury, I noticed something in both pictures, and blew them up with the magnifier tool. In j6 one side of her face looked a little red, and when I looked carefully at j7 I could see that there was a trickle of blood running from a small cut on her right forearm.

And suddenly I realised, with help from memories of watching her hands and arms as she worked, that there had never been a mole on her arm. She hadn't got the bandage because of the doctor.

She had it because of him.

I hardly slept that night. I stayed up till three, keeping an eye on the newsgroup. Its denizens were certainly becoming fans of the 'j' pictures, and I saw five requests for some more. As far as they knew all this involved was a bit more scanning originals from some magazine. They didn't realise that someone I knew was having them taken against her will. I considered trying to do something within the group, like posting a message telling what I knew. While its frequenters are a bit sad, they tend to have a strong moral stance about such things. It's not like the alt.binaries.pictures.tasteless group—where anything goes, the sicker the better. If the a.b.p.erotica crowd were convinced the pictures were being taken under coercion, there was a strong chance they might mailbomb Ayer off the net. It would be a big war to start, however, and one with potentially damaging consequences. The mailbombing would have to go through the anonymity server, and would probably crash it. While I couldn't give a fuck about that, it would draw the attention of all manner of people. In any event, because of the anonymity, nothing would happen directly to Ayer apart from some inconvenience.

I decided to put the idea on hold, in case talking to Jeanette tomorrow made it unnecessary. Eventually I went to bed, where I thrashed and turned for hours. Some time just before dawn I drifted off, and dreamt about a cat being caught in a lawnmower.

I was up at seven, there being no point in me staying in bed. I checked the group, but there were no new files. On an afterthought I checked my email, realising that I'd been so out of it that I hadn't done so for days. There were about thirty messages for me, some from friends, the rest from a variety of virtual acquaintances around the world. I scanned through them quickly, seeing if any needed urgent attention, and then slap in the middle I noticed one from a particular address.

anon99989@penet.fi.

Heart thumping, I opened the email. In the convention of such things, he'd quoted my message back at me, with a comment. The entire text of the mail read:

```
' > I know who you are.
  >
  Maybe. But I know where you live.'
```

When I got to work, at the dot of nine, I discovered Jeanette wasn't there. She'd left a message at eight-thirty announcing she was taking the day off. Sarah was a bit sniffy about this, though she claimed to be great pals with Jeanette. I left her debating the morality of such cavalier leave-taking with Tanya in the kitchen, as I walked slowly out to sit at Jeanette's desk to work. After five minute's thought I went back to the kitchen and asked Sarah for Jeanette's number, claiming I had to ask her about the database. Sarah seemed only too pleased to provide the means of contacting a friend having a day off. I grabbed my jacket, muttered something about buying cigarettes, and left the office.

Round the corner I found a public phone box and called her number. As I listened to the phone ring I glanced at the prostitute cards that liberally covered the walls, but soon looked away. I didn't find their representation of the female form amusing any more. After six rings an answering machine cut in. A man's voice, Ayer's, announced that they were out. I rang again, with the same result, and then left the phonebox and stood aimlessly on the pavement.

There was nothing I could do.

I went back to work. I worked. I ran home.

At six-thirty I logged on for the first time, and the next two pictures were already there. I could tell immediately that something had changed. The wall behind her was a different colour, for a start. The focus of the action seemed to have moved, to the bedroom, presumably, and the pictures were getting worse. j8 showed Jeanette spread-eagled on her back. Her legs were very wide open, and both her hands and feet were out of shot. j9 was much the same, except you could see that her hands were tied. You could also see her face, with its hopeless defiance and fear. As I erased the picture from my disk I felt my neck spasming.

Too late I realised that what I should have done was get Jeanette's address while I was at work. It would have been difficult, and viewed with suspicion, but I might have been able to do it. Now I couldn't. I didn't know the home numbers of anyone else from the VCA, and couldn't trace her address from her number. The operator wouldn't give it to me. If I'd had the address I could have gone round. Maybe I would have found myself in the worst situation of my life, but it would have been something to try. The idea of her being in trouble somewhere in London, and me not knowing where, was almost too much to bear. Suddenly I decided that I had to do the one small thing I could. I logged back onto the erotica group and prepared to start a flame war.

The classic knee-jerk reaction that people on the net use to express their displeasure is known as 'flaming'. Basically it involves bombarding the offender with massive mail messages until their virtual mail box collapses under the load. This draws the attention of the administrator of their site, and they get chucked off the net. What I had to do was post a message providing sufficient reason for the good citizens of pornville to dump on anon99989@penet.fi.

So it might cause some trouble. I didn't fucking care.

I had a mail slip open and my hands poised over the keyboard before I noticed something that stopped me in my tracks.

There were two more files. Already. The slob from Texas was getting his wish: the pace was being picked up.

In j10 Jeanette was on her knees on a dirty mattress. Her hands appeared to be tied behind her, and her head was bowed. j11 showed her lying awkwardly on her side, as if she'd been pushed over. She was glaring at the camera, and when I magnified the left side of the image I could see a thin trickle of blood from her right nostril.

I leapt up from the keyboard, shouting. I don't know what I was saying. It wasn't coherent. Jeanette's face stared up at me from the computer and I leant wildly across and hit the switch to turn the screen off. Just quitting out didn't seem enough. Then I realised that the image was still there, even though I couldn't see it. The computer was still sending the information to the screen, and the minute I turned it back on, it would be there. So I hard-stopped the computer by just turning it off at the mains. Suddenly what had always been my domain felt like the outpost of someone very twisted and evil, and I didn't want anything to do with it.

Then, like a stone through glass, two ideas crashed into each other in my head.

Gospel Oak.

Police.

From nowhere came a faint half-memory, so tenuous that it might be illusory, of Jeanette mentioning Gospel Oak station. In other words, the rail station in Gospel Oak. I knew where that was.

An operator wouldn't give me an address from a phone number. But the police would be able to get it. They had reverse directories.

I couldn't think of anything else.

I rang the police. I told them I had reason to believe that someone was in danger, and that she lived at the house with this phone number. They wanted to know who I was and all manner of other shit, but I rang off quickly, grabbed my coat and hit the street.

Gospel Oak is a small area, filling up the gap between Highgate, Chalk Farm and Hampstead. I knew it well because Nick and I used to go play pool at a pub on Mansfield Road, which runs straight through it. I knew the entrance and exit points of the area, and I got the cab to drop me off as near to the centre as possible. Then I stood on the pavement, hopping from foot to foot and smoking, hoping against hope that this would work.

Ten minutes later a police car turned into Mansfield Road. I was very pleased to see them, and enormously relieved. I hadn't been particularly sure about the Gospel Oak part. I shrank back against the nearest building until it had gone past, and then ran after it as inconspicuously as I could. It took a left into Estelle Road and I slowed at the corner to watch it pull up outside number 6. I slipped into the doorway of the corner shop and watched as two policemen took their own good time about untangling themselves from their car.

They walked up to the front of the house. One leant hard against the doorbell, while the other peered around the front of the house as if taking part in an officiousness competition. The door wasn't answered, which didn't surprise me. Ayer was hardly going to break off from torturing his girlfriend to take social calls. One of the policemen nodded to the other, who visibly sighed, and made his way round the back of the house.

'Oh come on, come *on*,' I hissed in the shadows. 'Break the fucking door down.'

About five minutes passed, and then the policeman reappeared. He shrugged flamboyantly at his colleague, and pressed the doorbell again.

A light suddenly appeared above the door, coming from the hallway behind it. My breath caught in my throat and I edged a little closer. I'm not sure what I was preparing to do. Dash over there and force my way in, past the policemen, to grab Ayer and smash his head against the wall? I really don't know.

The door opened, and I saw it wasn't Ayer or Jeanette. It was an elderly man with a crutch and grey hair that looked like it had seen action in a hurricane. He conversed irritably with the policemen for a moment and then shut the door in their faces. The two cops stared at each other for a moment, clearly considering busting the old tosser, but then turned and made their way back to the car. Still looking up at the house, the first policeman made a report into his radio, and I heard enough to understand why they then got into the car and drove away.

The old guy had told them that the young couple had gone away for the weekend. He'd seen them go on Thursday evening. I was over 24 hours too late.

When the police car had turned the corner I found myself panting, not knowing what to do. The last two photographs, the one with the dirty mattress, hadn't been taken here at all. Jeanette was somewhere in the country, but I didn't know where, and there was no way of finding out. The pictures could have been posted from anywhere.

Making a decision, I walked quickly across the road towards the house. The policemen may not have felt they had just cause, but I did, and I carefully made my way around the back of the house. This involved climbing over a gate and wending through the old guy's crowded little garden, and I came perilously close to knocking over a pile of flowerpots. As luck would have it there was a kind of low wall that led to a complex exterior plumbing fixture, and I quickly clambered on top of it. A slightly precarious upward step took me next to one of the second floor windows. It was dark, like all the others, but I kept my head bent just in case.

When I was closer to the window I saw that it wasn't fastened at the bottom. They might have gone, and then come back. Ayer could have staged it so the old man saw them go, and then slipped back when he was out.

It was possible, but not likely. But on the other hand, the window was ajar. Maybe they were just careless about such things. I slipped my fingers under the pane and pulled it open. Then I leant with my ear close to the open space and listened. There was no sound, and so I boosted myself up and quickly in.

I found myself in a bedroom. I didn't turn the light on, but there was enough coming from the moon and streetlights to pick out a couple of pieces of Jeanette's clothing, garments that I recognised, strewn over the floor. She wouldn't have left them like that, not if she'd had any choice in the matter. I walked carefully into the corridor, poking my head into the bathroom and kitchen, which were dead. Then I found myself in the living room.

The big chair stood in front of a wall I recognised, and at the far end a computer sat on a desk next to a picture scanner. Moving as quickly but quietly as possible, I frantically searched over the desk for anything that might tell me where Ayer had taken her. There was nothing there, and nothing in the rest of the room. I'd broken—well, *opened*—and entered for no purpose. There were no clues. No sign of where they'd gone. An empty box under the table confirmed what I'd already guessed: Ayer had a laptop computer as well. He could be posting the pictures onto the net from anywhere that had a phone socket. Jeanette would be with him, and I needed to find her. I needed to find her soon.

I paced around the room, trying to pick up speed, trying to work out what I could possibly do. No-one at VCA knew where they'd gone—they hadn't even known Jeanette wasn't going to be in. The old turd downstairs hadn't known. There was nothing in the flat that resembled a phone book or personal organiser, something that would have a friend or family member's number. I was prepared to do anything, call anyone, in the hope of finding where they'd gone. But there was nothing, unless…

I sat down at the desk, reached behind the computer and turned it on. Ayer had a fairly flash deck, together with a scanner and laser printer. He knew the Net. Chances were he was wirehead enough to keep his phone numbers somewhere on his computer.

As soon as the machine was booted up I went rifling through it, grimly enjoying the intrusion, the computer-rape. His files and programs were spread all over the disk, with no apparent system. Each time I finished looking through a folder, I erased it. It seemed the least I could do.

Then after about five minutes I found something, but not what I was looking for. I found a folder named 'j'.

There were files called j12 to j16 in the folder, in addition to all the others that I'd seen. Wherever Jeanette was, Ayer had come back here to scan the pictures. Presumably that meant they were still in London, for all the good that did me.

I'm not telling you what they were like, except that they showed Jeanette, and in some she was crying, and in j15 and j16 there was blood running from the corner of her mouth. A lot of blood. She was twisted and tied, face livid with bruises, and in j16 she was staring straight at the camera, face slack with terror.

Unthinkingly I slammed my fist down on the desk. There was a noise downstairs and I went absolutely motionless until I was sure the old man had lost interest. Then I turned the computer off, opened up the case and removed the hard disk. I climbed out the way I'd come and ran out down the street, flagged a taxi by jumping in front of it and headed for home.

Michael Marshall Smith

I was going to the police, but I needed a computer, something to shove the hard disk into. I was going to show them what I'd found, and fuck the fact it was stolen. If they nicked me, so be it. But they had to do something about it. They had to try and find her. If he'd come back to do his scanning he had to be keeping her somewhere in London. They'd know where to look, or where to start. They'd know what to do.

They had to. They were the police. It was their job.

I ran up the stairs and into the flat, and then dug in my spares cupboard for enough pieces to hack together a compatible computer. When I'd got them I went over to my desk to call the local police station, and then stopped and turned my computer on. I logged onto the net and kicked up my mail package, and sent a short, useless message.

'I'm coming after you,' I said.

It wasn't bravado. I didn't feel brave at all. I just felt furious, and wanted to do anything that might unsettle him, or make him stop. Anything to make him stop.

I logged quickly onto the newsgroups, to see when anon99989@penet.fi had most recently posted. A half hour ago, when I'd been in his apartment, j12–16 had been posted up. Two people had already responded: one hoping the blood was fake and asking if the group really wanted that kind of picture—the other asking for more. I viciously wished a violent death upon the second person, and was about to log off, having decided not to bother phoning but to just go straight to the cops, when I saw another text-only posting at the end of the list.

'Re: j-series' it said. It was from anon99989@penet.fi.

I opened it. 'End of series,' the message said. 'Hope you all enjoyed it. Next time, something tasteless.'

'And I hope,' I shouted at the screen, 'That you enjoy it when I ram your hard disk down your fucking throat.'

Then suddenly my blood ran cold.

'Next time, something tasteless.'

I hurriedly closed the group, and opened up alt.binaries.pictures.tasteless. As I scrolled past the titles for roadkills and people crapping I felt the first heavy, cold tear roll out onto my cheek. My hand was shaking uncontrollably, my head full of some dark mist, and when I saw the last entry I knew suddenly and exactly what Jeanette had been looking at when j16 was taken.

'j17.gif,' it read. '{f} Pretty amputee'.

Being Right

Sometimes things happen in life that are weird, odd in a way that makes you question everything. Doesn't mean it's some big revelation, not necessarily. Just that something makes you realise that things are *going on*, that things have been forgotten and are better that way, that correct is not the same as right. Finding out about the listening angel was a little like that.

Dan's mood had not been good anyway. It was Monday, the fourth day of their vacation, and the fourth solid day of rain. That didn't bother him unduly—you didn't come to London, London in February, moreover, if you were looking to work on your tan. The city was full of museums, galleries, stores. It had history up the wazzoo and nearly as many Starbucks as at home. If you could bear to get a little damp in between stops, there was a good time to be had whatever the weather. The forecast—which Dan knew all about, having been woken by it at five-thirty that morning—said it was going to get better as the week went on. Either way, the weather was something you couldn't do anything about. It was simply there. You had to just accept it, change your plans accordingly, move on. There was no point complaining. No point going on and on and *on*.

What you could change, of course, was jet lag. You were flying to Europe, which they had done many times since the kids left home, there was a simple procedure to follow. You arrived there mid-morning, so it made sense to try to catch a little sleep on the plane. From the minute you arrived you locked yourself mentally to the new time, and you stayed awake until you would normally at home. That way your body got itself into some new kind of understanding, and you were so bushed by the time it came to turn in, you'd sleep regardless. Might be a couple of days where you felt draggy late afternoon, but otherwise you'd be okay. This is what Dan had done. This is what he always did.

Marcia, she did it different.

Michael Marshall Smith

Despite the fact they'd discussed it, she stayed awake the whole flight. Said she'd found it impossible to sleep, though Dan had managed to catch an hour—not much, but enough to make a difference. Then when they'd gotten to the hotel just before lunch, she'd started yawning, muttering about a nap. Dan told her to keep going, reminded her of how it was—but mid-afternoon still found her spark out on the bed. Dan left her there and went for a walk around the surrounding blocks. Sure, he felt a little spacey and weird, but he kind of enjoyed it. It served as a first recon of the neighbourhood, telling him where the cafés were, the nearest bookstore, all of that. It reminded you that you'd done a strange thing, travelled a long way, and that you weren't at home any more.

When he got back, Marcia was in the shower. They went out, had another little walk, then dinner in the nearest restaurant. By ten o'clock Dan was utterly beat, and ready for bed. Marcia on the other hand was speeding, and wanted to talk up the issues over Proposition 7, the cause de jour back home in Oregon. Dan hadn't much cared about P7 when on his own turf (it was going to be defeated, which was a shame, but that's what people are like), and sure as shit didn't care about it now. What was the point of coming to another country if you were going to mire yourself in the same old stuff? When he finally said this, yawning massively, Marcia took the discussion into a playful analysis of why he was apparently unable to enter into any kind of intellectual dialogue that wasn't about books, before swerving back to Proposition 7. This lasted a further twenty-five minutes. When Dan finally said he was just going to have to go to bed, she shook her head and stood up. First evening ruined, her body language said: thank you, brutish husband.

Dan slept like a baby. Marcia, not so well.

They spent the next couple of days getting some tourism done, seeing the big sights, ticking them off. Dan was happy to do this, knowing they'd relax a little by the weekend, be able to kick back a little more and do their own thing. By Saturday he was locked on GMT, late-afternoon slump nothing a two-shot latté couldn't shake off. Marcia seemed to be getting further and further out of sync. She was waking at six, five, four: waking and sitting up in bed pointedly reading (and reading a novel set in America, naturally, or one of the magazines she'd brought from home); alternatively, as on Monday morning, turning on the television—quietly, of course, but you could still hear the tube crackle—and obsessing about the rain.

The problem wasn't the jetlag. Dan could sympathise with that. Not sleeping, it's no fun. You lie there on your back staring up at an unfamiliar ceiling and your brain goes round and round and round. The problem was the mentioning it, the endless fricking… It was the same when she had a cold. Dan got a cold, he took some tablets, waited for it to go away. He'd snuffle a bit, but that was physical. You couldn't do anything about it. With Dan, a cold lasted four days, tops, soup to nuts. With Marcia it was a two-week miniseries, an HBO Big Season Event. The first signs would be noted, discussed, held up for scrutiny. The danger of an approaching malaise would be flagged, and the particular inconvenience of its timing mourned. Nine times out of ten, this phase would last a single evening and then the symptoms would disappear for good, having never been anything more than two sneezes, or a mild headache. But sometimes the cold would arrive for real and she would wander down the next morning wrapped in a blanket, face crumpled, nose red, hair mad as you like. Then, for at least a week, the mentioning it. The constant filling him in—as if, twenty times a day, he'd said to her 'Now darling, tell me exactly how every single little bit of you feels, and don't stint on the detail.' The sinus report. The lower back state-of-play. The glass throat film-at-eleven and here's a message from our sponsor, Runny Noses R Us.

The cold would go away, eventually. Two days of noting its passing, and she'd be fine—would return, in fact, to the woman who said she never got colds, not ever. That's when Dan knew he was in trouble. Ten days of reduced conversation would mean she was full up to the brim with observations of pith and moment, stuff that simply had to get out of her head before it popped. Any chat, no matter how formerly relaxed, could get suddenly derailed into a long discussion of the major or minor issues of the day/year/century, with Marcia being firm but fair, subtle but strident, as if performing to a sizable radio audience. His participation was allowed every now and then, as a foil, a sentence thrown in as by an interviewer. Other than that, she'd just roll. Any suggestion from Dan that the length and depth of discussion was inappropriate to a dinner out at a local restaurant, to Sunday breakfast, or when he was trying to have a quiet bath, would be met with the masterfully oblique suggestion that he just hadn't thought about the issues enough, and that he'd had his say and it was her turn now. Followed by more discussion.

It was on one of these occasions, a romantic dinner that had turned into a two-hour and bitter-fought debate, that Dan had first fantasized about the possibility of some kind of independent adjudication. That there might be some agency to which he could appeal, not with ill-will, but just so he could be proved right—so that it could be established, once and for all, that she hogged discussions, cheated in arguments, and got mini-colds twice a month. He loved his wife and wouldn't want her any different. But just once in a while he wished there was some way of proving *he was right.*

No-one was more surprised than him to find out there was.

The bookstore was in a little side street halfway down Charring Cross Road. When they'd last been to London, back in the early nineties, the area had been wall-to-wall books. Like everywhere else in the world, it was now feeling the dual pinch of the megastores and on-line auction sites. The speciality stores were still in place, just, but the secondhand and antiquarian had closed or gone to seed. Having left Marcia back at the hotel in the health spa for morning, Dan was mildly ticked to find he had done the street with an hour and a half to spare. He didn't want to go back early, kick his heels in the hotel. Marcia had been her most jetlagged yet that morning, and very down about the weather. He'd been unsympathetic on two subjects he considered himself powerless over, and words had been spoken.

On a whim he started poking around the uncharted streets just behind the main road, and it was here he found Pandora's Books. A little wooden shop front, the name appropriately picked out in faded gold paint. A random selection of ancient-looking volumes littered the window, none of which he'd heard of. Perfect. Especially as it was beginning to drizzle. Again.

The smell made him smile as soon as he was inside. Old, forgotten paper, paper foxed and creased and bumped. The scent of old bookcases and venerable dust added their own welcome notes. It was the way these places should smell, the smell of peace and quiet and your own thoughts.

The room wasn't that big—probably only twenty feet by fifteen—but the high shelves packed into it, along with the dim light, made it seem larger. In the back there were wooden staircases leading up and down, neither marked 'Private', promising more of the same. There was a little desk over on the right, piled high with books waiting categorisation, but nobody in sight. Dan dithered, then propped his bag against the desk. Usually bookstores preferred it that way, and it would leave both hands free.

He worked his way down from the top. They had a whole lot of books, that was for sure. Most of the stuff on the upper level was modern and of no interest, though he did find a pulp paperback worth keeping in his hand. He thought he heard someone coming up the stairs while he turned this book over, debating the couple of pounds, but when he looked up no-one was there. By the time he got back to street level they'd evidently gone down to the basement.

He took his time around these shelves, as many were dedicated to local history. In the end he found one thing he thought was a definite, plus a couple of maybes. Depended on whether they shipped. The book he wanted was heavy—a Victorian facsimile of an older history of London—and he went over to prop it up against his bag. As he did so he thought he heard someone coming into the room from the back, but when he turned there was no-one. Evidently just a noise from upstairs. Booksellers creep in mysterious ways, their filing to perform.

It was in the basement that he found the book. At first he thought there was nothing there for him: the room was only half the size of those on the higher floors, and had none of their sense of order. Books of all ages and conditions were piled onto cases in danger of imminent collapse. There was a strong smell of damp too, doubtless caused or at least enhanced by the grim-looking patches on the walls. The plaster had come away in many places, revealing seeping brickwork behind. He poked around for a while, shoving aside piles of bashed-up book-length ephemera (do your own accounts, learn Spanish in twenty seconds, find your inner you and dream your inner dream), finding and rejecting a few older tomes.

He was about to give up and go pay for what he'd already put aside when a bookcase at the end caught his eye. He went and had a look. There was no hurry, after all. At first he'd thought these books were much older than the rest, but he soon saw they were not. A little, but not much. Most were old Everyman Editions, leather-bound and quite attractive but not worth the carrying. He had already turned away when something told him to turn back, and look again.

He stood square onto the case and ran his eyes over the case. He'd evidently seen something without really seeing it. He wasn't expecting much, but it would be mildly interesting to see what had caught his eye. Eventually he found it. A book whose spine was much more scuffed up than the rest. He gently eased it out.

It was called *Hopes of a Lesser Demon, Part II*, which was odd, for a start. It was a small, chunky thing with battered boards and old leather; about an inch thick, six high, and four deep. The title on the spine seemed to have been handwritten in ink. When Dan turned to the front the frontispiece claimed the book had been published in Rome in 1641, but that couldn't be right. For a start, it should have been in Latin, or Italian at the very least. It wasn't. It was in English, for the most part. Secondly, as he leafed through the book, it seemed clear that it could never have been published in this form at all. Chunks of it did look old, the paper spotted and towelly, the text in languages he didn't understand and typefaces that were hard to read. Others had been printed far more recently; the paper fresh and glossy, the subjects contemporary. English predominantly, though there were sections in French and German too—and something he guessed was Korean from its similarity to the signs on a food market he sometimes walked by back home.

It was also far from clear what the book was *about*. There was a sermon on chastity, a few pages on deciduous trees. Part seemed to be a travel guide to Bavaria, with spotty black and white plates that must have been taken before the First World War. A polemic on some obscure Middle-Eastern sect was followed by a stretch of love poetry, and preceded by two handwritten pages of what looked like the accounts of a sugar plantation in the eighteenth century.

There was no sense to it whatsoever, and yet at the bottom of each page was a folio—a page number—and the ordering of these numerals was consistent from front to back, regardless of subject change or whether they were printed in decaying hand-plated gothic type or super-crisp computer-generated Gill Sans.

Dan flipped back to the front, and saw that the price had been written there in pencil. Five pounds. Eight bucks, more or less. Hmm.

He already wanted the book without really knowing why. He looked through the pages a little further, looking for an excuse, finding further pockets of unrelated non-information. A handful of reproductions of watercolours, none by artists he recognised and few of them any good. A list of popular meadows in Armenia. A section on what seemed to be electronic engineering, a Da Vinci-like ink sketch of a man holding an axe, and a long portion of a children's book about a happy dog.

And then there were the invocations. At first Dan couldn't make out what this section was about. The paper was very, very old, and the writing had been entered by hand. Portions had faded back to nothing, and those that were strong weren't very easy to read. The first page seemed to be a kind of index.

Item One read: 'The Vision of Love's Arc invocation: for to glimpse what man or woman (or both) shall here come into your life.'

Item Eleven: 'The Sadness of Cattle invocation: the purpose being to make less gloomy your livestock in the night.'

Item Twenty-Two: 'The Regeneration of Heat invocation: a most useful gesture engendered for the revitalisation of a time-soured beverage.'

What? A spell to warm up a cup of coffee? That was silly. The whole index was silly, in fact, the most stupid section of what was evidently a very stupid book. Dan had just about changed his mind—five pounds was five pounds, after all, and the book was surprisingly heavy for its size—when he caught sight of the last entry in the index:

Item Thirty-Eight: 'The Listening Angel invocation: for to prove whether you are right.'

Mouth open, Dan flicked to the indicated page and read just enough to establish that yes, this meant exactly what he thought it did.

He seemed suddenly to hear a rushing noise, quite loud, like the tread of a hundred feet, or the beat of thousands of tiny wings.

He closed the book and hurried up the stairs.

There was still no-one at the desk—though he saw the explanation for the sound he'd heard. It was raining properly now, and raining hard. The store's dim lamps struggled against the lowering darkness outside. He waited for a few moments, moving impatiently from foot to foot, and then ventured to call out. There was no response, either in the form of reply or noise from above. He waited a little longer, then strode to the back of the store and hiked up the stairs. There was no-one up there. No-one in the basement, either, when he went back down to look. And though there were deep shadows on the street level itself, there was no sign of anyone to pay.

Dan dug in his wallet and took out a five pound note. He put it on the desk and picked up his bag. He left the Victorian book behind. It no longer seemed very interesting.

When he got back to the hotel he was soaked, and surprised to find he was late. Somehow it had become three o'clock. He was half-expecting to see Marcia waiting in the lobby, but she wasn't there. He took the elevator up to the room, but it was empty. In the end, baffled, he called the spa—and was relieved to find that a woman of his wife's description was fast asleep on one of the loungers around the pool. Relieved and, of course, irritated. He left the book on the bed and wandered around, drying his hair with a towel. He could go down and wake her, remind her they were supposed to be...what was the point. By the time she was dressed it would be too late. And he would also, he realise, have to account for the fact he'd returned well after he'd said he would. It was not the first time, and 'looking at books' never seemed to be a good enough answer.

He set up the room's coffee machine and waited for it to do its thing. Meanwhile he sat in the chair at the desk, and watched the book on the bed. It wasn't moving, of course, and there was no danger that it would. But it didn't feel as if he was just looking at it.

When he had a coffee he went and picked the book up. At first he thought he must have been mistaken, because he couldn't find the Index of Invocations, however hard he looked. After dipping into the book at random for a while he started at the beginning and rigorously leafed through from front to back. He saw a lot of odd things, but not the index. His heart, which he realised had been beating rather faster that usual, slowly returned to normal. He flicked through the book more slowly, obscurely relieved.

He had imagined it, that was all. Perhaps a form of jetlag fever. Annoyance at the crossed words that morning, a fantasy born of the dust and damp of the shop...

Then he found it. The Invocations, sandwiched between two sections he knew he'd seen on the front-to-back pass, and yet had been missed. Whatever.

He scanned a few of the other entries—

'Item Twenty-Four: The Strengthening of Bark: a whisper for aiding a tree or bush (of considerable size) that is under attack.'

'Item Six: The Flattening Stroke: for to redress a planet that has become mistakenly round—use only once.'

But they were just diversions. Very quickly he made it back down to Item Thirty-Eight, then flicked through pages until he again found the one the entry referred to.

As he opened the page he heard the sound again, the beating of wings. A glimpse out of the window confirmed that this was, for a second time, merely an increase in the volume of rain outside. Odd how it kept happening, though. And how dark it had become.

The instructions on the page were short, the ingredients it called for not unduly hard to come by. Marcia still hadn't returned.

Dan didn't see how he had much choice.

Half an hour later he was standing on the roof of the hotel. This hadn't been easy to achieve, but the recipe stipulated that the invoker must be both outside and at the highest place available within one hundred horizontal feet of his or her position when the book had been most recently opened: Dan took the elevator to the highest floor—the twelfth—but knew somehow this wouldn't be enough. Plus, if something was going to happen, he didn't want interrupted by another guest coming back to their room. A certain amount of poking around led him

BEING RIGHT

to a door around a corner, which was marked 'Stores'. There were indeed stores inside, and Dan helped himself to another bath towel, but at the back was another door. Opening this led to a dark interior staircase that led upwards.

At the top was a metal door. It was locked. Of course. Dan kicked at it, impotently. He could hear the sound of rain beyond it. He kicked again, the lock clicked, and the door swung open a foot.

The sound of rain was suddenly far louder, and Dan saw it was now pelting down outside. Putting aside the question of why the door was now unlocked, he wrapped the towel around his head, left the book on the floor where it wouldn't get wet, and stepped outside.

A large area lay in front of him, the very roof of the hotel. Various little protuberances stuck up here and there, some disgorging steam or smoke. Piles of forgotten wood lay against the low wall that went right around the edges. The grey surface of the roof was hidden here and there by sizable pools of water, pools which reflected a blackening sky which seemed to be getting lower and lower.

Dan walked right out in the centre of the roof and stopped. London was spread around him, albeit obscured by sheets of rain and gathering gloom. The towel was soon soaked, and he took it off. Evidently you just had to take this experience as it came.

He had memorised the invocation. It wasn't hard. Indeed it was so straightforward it was ludicrous to believe it would achieve anything. He unwrapped the hand towel he had brought up from the room. Inside were three things. A small sample of his saliva, in one of the room's water glasses: a 'secretion' had been called for, and saliva was as far as he was prepared to go. A few strands of Marcia's hair, easily gleaned from her brush, wrapped in a piece of toilet tissue. Rather more trickily, a postcard to Marcia's sister. The recipe called for a sample of both their words, and didn't explain it any more than that. This defeated Dan until he had seen the postcard, written the previous evening and now lying on the desk awaiting a stamp. Most of it was in Marcia's hand, but he'd added a sentence at the bottom. Would it do? Dan supposed he was about to find out.

He gathered the three things in his hands, straightened, and threw his hands up into the air. He was a fool, he knew, and braced himself for the immediate return of the glass.

It didn't come back down.

After a few seconds he looked up, and saw that all three things had disappeared. The rain had started falling harder too, and now it really did sound like wings.

Michael Marshall Smith

Parts of the sky seemed to detach themselves from the rest, pools of darkness gathering as if a cloud was settling over the hotel, wisps of it catching on the buildings across the street like the ghosts of future fires. The sound of traffic seemed to get both louder and further away.

Dan listened to it, and listened to the rain as it fell, until the two noises became one, and entered his head, and disappeared.

'Seventy-eight percent,' said a voice.

Dan turned. Behind him, over at the low wall, something had appeared.

It was about twelve feet tall, the white of old, tarnished marble, and difficult to see. It seemed to sit hunched on the wall, huge wings hanging off of the shoulders behind. It seemed a little uncomfortable, as if finding itself in the wrong place, somewhere either too hot or too cold.

'Are you the angel?' Dan said.

'Over the entire length of the marriage, you have spoken twenty-two percent of the time,' the figure said. Its face was turned away from him, hidden behind long wet hair. Its voice was cold, dry, and seemed to come to Dan both via his ears and up through his legs. 'If you limit the enquiry to periods of discussion of issues that could be considered academic or of purely hypothetical interest, her contribution increases to eighty-six percent. This peaks, under the influence of alcohol or especially pressing concerns, at ninety-four percent.'

'Then I am right,' Dan said. 'I knew it.'

The angel gave no indication it had heard him. 'If considered in terms of total words uttered, rather than time spent speaking, the breakdown is more or less the same. The shortness and lack of fluidity of your sentences is generally counterbalanced by your attempts to pack them in the short intervals available.'

'Now hold on,' Dan said. He started to walk forward, but a loud, heavy movement of the angel's wings warned him to stop. Somewhere, far away, there was the rumble of thunder. 'What do you mean, lack of "fluidity"?'

'Caused merely by lack of opportunity to get into your stride,' the angel said. 'Of course.'

Dan nodded, satisfied. 'Thank you,' he said. 'Now. How do I ...'

'Sometimes she even talks when you're not there,' the angel said. 'Actually, quite a lot.'

'And you listen?'

'Of course. It's what I do.'

Dan frowned. 'What kind of things?'

'She hopes your kids are safe.'

BEING RIGHT

'So do I.'

'Yes, But she says it. And people hear.'

'Right,' Dan said. He was cold. Unbelievably, it was starting to rain harder, the sky pressing closer down. His hair was plastered to his skull, water running down his face. 'What else does she say?'

It seemed like the angel was turning to look at him, but when the movement was finished it was still looking another way.

'She says it makes her sad when they call and you hand the phone to her after just grunting hello. She tries not to resent the fact you make no effort with her friends, though—and these are my figures—you are on average responsible for less than two percent of the conversation when they're around. She has issues with the fact you seem to believe that her having a massage once in a while is some huge indulgence, when you spend three times as much every month on books which you'll mostly never read and often don't even *open* again. She feels hurt when you look up at her as if wondering what she is going on about, and why. She also wishes that once in a while you would handle her the way you do some interesting book—and says you used to, once.'

Dan smiled tightly. 'Well, that's very interesting. Thanks for your time. And your unbiased opinion.'

'The questions are always different, but the answers are always the same.' The angel rolled its shoulders, as if preparing to leave. 'She cares about things. Who do you think we're in favour of, those who do, or those who don't?'

Dan said nothing.

'And the colds,' the angel added. 'Who do you think they're worse for, her or you?'

'I've got to go,' Dan said. 'I assume you will let yourself out.'

He headed back toward the metal door to the hotel, sloshing straight through the puddles. He didn't want this any more. Sometimes the person you love is a pain in the ass. He wished he could have left it that. The rain drummed on the roof like the turning of a million dusty pages. He felt tired suddenly, fifty years of coffee gone sour. With each step it became harder to remember what had just happened, or to believe it, or to remember why he'd wanted to know.

He was reaching for the handle on the door when the angel spoke again. It sounded different, quieter, further away.

'When she cannot sleep she lies awake and hopes you still love her.'

Dan stopped dead in his tracks, turned. 'Of course I do,' he said, stricken. 'She must know that.'

The angel was fading now, the steady flap of its wings turning back to rain, the grey of its skin becoming cloud once more. As it stood it blew slowly into rising mist in front of his eyes, its words coming to him as cold wind, blown his way by the beating of those wings.

It said: 'For her, the two of you talking is like the smell of books. Do you think that she doesn't notice when you think you're being good about being bored? Sometimes that's why she keeps talking, because she panics when she fears you might not find her interesting any more.'

It said: 'This "peace" you think you want: what is it for? What thoughts do you harbour, so valuable they are worth wishing someone quiet? Meanwhile she fears for all the ways that things can go wrong and become still and lose strength and fall apart.'

It said: 'When she dies before you, which she might, will you wish you'd spent more time in silence? When you live in that endless quiet after, in those years of deadening cloud, what will you be prepared to promise, to hear just one word more?'

Then the wind dropped and it was gone.

Dan stood on the roof a full five minutes longer. When he stepped back through the metal door into the hotel, he found the book was gone. He hurried down the stairs, through the store cupboard, ran to the elevator and stabbed at the button.

When he let himself back into the room he heard the sound of Marcia in the bath.

'Dan?' she said quickly, 'Is that you?'

'Yes,' he said.

'Where have you *been*?'

'Got caught out in the rain,' he said, carefully, not yet wanting to go in, not yet ready to see her face. 'I'm sorry. Had to wait somewhere while it passed over. I called the room. You weren't here.'

'Fell asleep,' she said, sheepishly. There was silence for a moment. Then she said: 'I missed you.'

'I missed you too.' He took his jacket off and hung it up in the wardrobe to dry. 'You okay?'

'You know, I think I'm coming down with a cold.'

Dan rolled his eyes, and called room service to bring up tea, lemon and honey, before going to help her wash her hair. She told him about the spa in the hotel. He told her about his walk, leaving out Pandora's Books. The two of them sat with their words in the warm bathroom, the world cold and wet outside. They decided to order in room service. They watched TV, read a little, went to bed.

BEING RIGHT

In the small hours of the night, while Marcia fitfully dozed, the listening angel came in the room and touched her head, whispered to her to worry no more for a while.

When Dan woke in the morning, she was asleep next to him. It rained a little again as they ate breakfast together, but after that it was fine.

Hell Hath Enlarged Herself

I always assumed I was going to get old. That there would come a time when just getting dressed left me breathless, and I would count a day without a nap as a victory; when I would go into a barber's and some young girl would lift up the remaining grey stragglers on my pate and look dubious if I asked her for anything more than a trim. I would have tried to be charming, and she would have thought to herself how game the old bird was, while cutting off rather less than I'd asked her to. I thought all that was going to come, some day, and in a perverse sort of way I had even looked forward to it. A diminuendo, a slowing down, an ellipsis to some other place.

But now I know it will not happen, that I will remain unresolved, like some fugue which didn't work out. Or perhaps more like a voice in an unfinished symphony, because I won't be the only one.

I regret that. I'm going to miss having been old.

I left the facility at 6.30 yesterday evening, on the dot, as had been my practice. I took care to do everything as I always had, carefully collating my notes, tidying my desk, and leaving upon it a list of things to do the next day. I hung my white coat on the back of my office door as always, and said goodbye to Johnny on the gate with a wink. For six months we have been engaged in a game that involves making some joint statement on the weather every time I enter or leave the facility, without either of us recoursing to speech. Yesterday Johnny raised his eyebrows at the dark and heavy clouds overhead, and rolled his eyes—a standard gambit. I turned one corner of my mouth down and shrugged with the other shoulder, a more adventurous riposte, in recognition of that fact this was the last time the game would ever be played. For a moment I wanted to do more, to say something, reach out and shake his hand; but that would have been too obvious a goodbye. Perhaps no-one would have stopped me anyway, as it has become abundantly clear that I am as powerless as everyone else—but I didn't want to take the risk.

Then I found my car amongst the diminishing number which still park there, and left the compound for good.

The worst part, for me, is that I knew David Ely, and understand how it all started. I was sent to work at the facility because I am partly to blame for what has happened. The original work was done together, but I was the one who had always given creed to the paranormal. David had never paid much heed to such things, not until they became an obsession. There may have been some chance remark of mine that made him open to the idea. Just having known me for so long may have been enough. If it was, then I'm sorry. There's not a great deal more I can say.

David and I met at the age of six, our fathers having taken up new positions at the same college—the University of Florida, in Gainesville. My father was in the Geography Faculty, his in Sociology, but at that time—the late Eighties—the departments were drawing closer together and the two men became friends. Our families mingled closely, in countless backyard barbecues and shared holidays on the coast, and David and I grew up more like brothers than friends. We read the same clever books and hacked the same stupid computers, and even ended up losing our virginity on the same evening. One Spring when we were both sixteen I borrowed my mother's car and the two of us loaded it up with books and a laptop and headed off to Sarasota in search of sun and beer. We found both, in quantity, and also two young English girls on holiday. We spent a week in courting spirals of increasing tightness, playing pool and talking fizzy nonsense over cheap and exotic pizzas, and on the last night two couples walked up the beach in different directions.

Her name was Karen, and for a while I thought I was in love. I wrote a letter to her twice a week, and to this day she's probably received more mail from me than everyone else put together. Each morning I went running down to the mailbox, and ten years later the sight of an English postage stamp could still bring a faint rush of blood to my ears. But we were too far apart, and too young. Maybe she had to wait a day too long for a letter once, or perhaps it was me who without realising it came back empty-handed from the mailbox one too many times. Either way the letters started to slacken in frequency after six months and then, without either of us ever saying anything, they simply stopped altogether.

A little while later I was with David in a bar and, in between shots, he looked up at me.

'You ever hear from Karen any more?' he asked.

I shook my head, only at that moment realising that it had finally died. 'Not in a while.'

He nodded, and then took his shot, and missed, and as I lined up for the black I realised that he'd probably been through a similar thing. For the first time in our lives we'd lost something. It didn't break our hearts. It had only lasted a week, after all, and we were old enough to begin to realise that the world was full of girls, and that if we didn't hurry we'd hardly have got through any of them before it was time to get married.

But does anyone ever replace that first person? That first kiss, first fierce hug, hidden in sand dunes and darkness? Sometimes, I guess. I kept the letters from Karen for twenty years. Never read them, just kept them. Last week I threw them all away.

What I'm saying is this. I knew David for a long, long time, and I understood what we were trying to do. He was just trying to salve his own pain, and I was trying to help him.

What happened wasn't our fault.

I spent the evening driving slowly down 75, letting the freeway take me down towards the Gulf coast of the panhandle. There were a few patches of rain, but for the most part the clouds just scudded overhead, running to some other place. I didn't see many other cars. Either people have given up fleeing, or all those capable of it have already fled. I got off just after Jocca, and headed down minor roads, trying to cut round Tampa and St Petersburg. I managed it, but it wasn't easy, and I ended up getting lost more than a few times. I would have brought a map but I'd thought I could remember the way. I couldn't. It had been too long.

We'd heard on the radio in the afternoon that things weren't going so hot around Tampa. It was the last thing we heard, just before the signal cut out. The six of us remaining in the facility just sat around for a while, as if we believed the radio would come back on again real soon now. When it didn't we got up one by one and drifted back to work.

As I passed the city I could see it burning in the distance, and I was glad I had taken the back way, no matter how long it took. If you've seen what it's like when a large number of people go together, you'll understand what I mean.

Eventually I found 301 and headed down it towards 41, towards the old Coast Road.

Summer of 2005. For David and I it was time to make a decision. There was no question but that we would go to college—both our families were book-bashers from way back. The money was already in place, some from our parents but most from holiday jobs we'd played at. The question was what we were going to study.

I thought long and hard, but in the end still couldn't come to a decision. I postponed for a year, and decided to take off round the world. My parents shrugged, said 'Okay, keep in touch, try not to get killed, and stop by your Aunt Kate's in Sydney.' They were that kind of people. I remember my sister bringing a friend of hers back to the house one time; the girl called herself Yax and her hair had been carefully dyed and sculpted to resemble an orange explosion. My mother just asked her where she had it done, and kept looking at it in a thoughtful way. I guess my dad must have talked her out of it.

David went for computers. Systems design. He got a place at Jacksonville's new center for Advanced Computing, which was a coup but no real surprise. David was always a hell of a bright guy. That was part of his problem.

It was strange saying goodbye to each other after so many years in each other's pockets, but I suppose we knew it was going to happen sooner or later. The plan was that he'd come out and hook up with me for a couple of months during the year. It didn't happen, for the reason that pacts between old friends usually get forgotten.

Someone else entered the picture.

I did my grand tour. I saw Europe, started to head through the Middle East and then thought better of it and flew down to Australia instead. I stopped by and saw Aunt Kate, which earned me big brownie points back home and wasn't in any way arduous. She and her family were a lot of fun, and there was a long drunken evening when she seemed to be taking messages from beyond, which was kind of interesting. My mother's side of the family was always reputed to have a touch of the medium about them, and Aunt Kate certainly did. There was an even more entertaining evening when my cousin Jenny and I probably overstepped the bounds of conventional morality in the back seat of her jeep. After Australia I hacked up through the Far East for a while until time and money ran out, and then I went home.

I came back with a major tan, an empty wallet, and still no real idea of what I was going to do with my life. With a couple months to go before I had to make a decision, I decided to go visit David. I hopped on a bus and made my way up to Jacksonville on a day that was warm and full of promise. Anything could happen, I believed, and everything was there for the taking. Adolescent naiveté perhaps, but I was an adolescent. How was I supposed to know otherwise? I'd led a pretty charmed life up until then, and I didn't see any reason why it shouldn't continue. I sat in the bus and gazed out the window, watching the world and wishing it the very best. It was a good day, and I'm glad it was. Because though I didn't know it then, the new history of the world probably started at the end of it.

I got there late afternoon, and asked around for David. Eventually someone pointed me in the right direction, to a house just off campus. I found the building and tramped up the stairs, wondering whether I shouldn't maybe have called ahead.

Eventually I found his door. I knocked, and after a few moments some man I didn't recognize opened it. It took me a couple of long seconds to work out it was David. He'd grown a beard. I decided not to hold it against him just yet, and we hugged like, well, like what we were. Two best friends, seeing each other after what suddenly seemed like far too long.

'*Major* bonding,' drawled a female voice. A head slipped into view from round the door, with wild brown hair and big green eyes. That was the first time I saw Rebecca.

Four hours later we were in a bar somewhere. I'd met Rebecca properly, and realised she was special. In fact, it's probably a good thing that they'd met six months before, and that she was so evidently in love with David. Had we met her at the same time, she could have been the first thing we'd ever fallen out over. She was beautiful, in a strange and quirky way that always made me think of forests; and she was clever, in that particularly appealing fashion which meant she wasn't always trying to prove it and was happy for other people to be right some of the time. She moved like a cat on a sleepy afternoon, but her eyes were always alive—even when they couldn't co-operate with each other enough to allow her to accurately judge the distance to her glass. She was my best friend's girl, she was a good one, and I was very happy for him.

Rebecca was at the School of Medical Science. Nanotech was just coming off big around then, and it looked like she was going to catch the wave and go with it. In fact, when the two of them talked about their work, it made me wish I hadn't taken the year off. Things were happening for them. They had a direction. All I had was goodwill towards the world, and the belief that it loved me too. For the first time I had that terrible sensation that life is leaving you behind and you'll never catch up again; that if you don't match your speed to the train and jump on you'll be forever left standing in the station.

At one a.m. we were still going strong. David lurched in the general direction of the bar to get us some more beer, navigating the treacherously level floor like a man using stilts for the first time.

'Why don't you come here?' Rebecca said suddenly. I turned to her, and she shrugged. 'David misses you, I don't think you're too much of an asshole, and what else are you going to do?'

I looked down at the table for a moment, thinking it over. Immediately it sounded like a good idea. But on the other hand, what would I do? And could I handle being a third wheel, instead of half a bicycle? I asked the first question first.

'We've got plans,' Rebecca replied. 'Stuff we want to do. You could come in with us. I know David would want you to. He always says you're the cleverest guy he's ever met.'

I glanced across at David, who was conversing affably with the barman. We'd decided that to save energy we should start buying drinks two at a time, and David appeared to be explaining this plan. As I watched, the barman laughed. David was like that. He could get on with absolutely anyone.

'And you're sure I'm not too much of an asshole?'

Deadpan: 'Nothing that I won't be able to kick out of you.'

And that's how I ended up applying for, and getting, a place on Jacksonville's nanotech program. When David got back to the table I wondered aloud whether I should come up to college, and his reaction was big enough to seal the decision there and then. It was him who suggested I go nanotech, and him who explained their plan.

For years people had been trying to crack the nanotech nut. Building tiny biological 'machines', some of them little bigger than large molecules, designed to be introduced into the human body to perform some function or other: promoting the secretion of certain hormones; eroding calcium build-ups in arteries; destroying cells which looked like they were going cancerous. In the way that these things have, it had taken a long time before the first proper results started coming through—but in the last three years it had really been gathering pace. When David had met Rebecca, a couple of weeks into the first semester, they'd talked about their two subjects, and David had immediately realised that sooner or later there would be a second wave, and that they could be the first to realise it.

Lots of independent little machines was one thing. How about lots of little machines that worked together? All designed for particular functions, but co-ordinated by a neural relationship with each other, possessed of a power and intelligence that was greater than the sum of its parts. Imagine what *that* could do.

When I heard the idea I whistled. I tried to, anyway. My lips had gone all rubbery from too much beer and instead the sound came out as a sort of parping noise. But they understood what I meant.

'And no-one else is working on this?'

'Oh, probably,' David smirked, and I had to smile. We'd always both nurtured plans for world domination. 'But with the three of us together, no-one else stands a chance.'

And so it was decided, and ratified, and discussed, over just about all the beer the bar had left. At the end of the evening we crawled back to David and Rebecca's room on our hands and knees, and I passed out on the sofa. The next day, trembling under the weight of a hangover that passed all understanding, I found a place to stay in town and went to talk someone in the faculty of Medical Science. By the end of the week it was confirmed.

On the day I was officially enrolled in the next year's intake the three of us went out to dinner. We went to a nice restaurant, and we ate and drank, and then at the end of the meal we placed our hands on top of each other's in the center of the table. David's went down first, then Rebecca's, and then mine on top. With our other hands we raised our glasses.

'To us,' I said. It wasn't very original, I know, but it's what I meant. I bet all three of us wished there was a photographer present to immortalise the moment. We drank, and then the three of us clasped each other's hands until our knuckles were white.

Ten years later Rebecca was dead.

The Coast Road was deserted, as I had expected. The one thing nobody is doing these days is heading off down to the beach to hang out and play volleyball. I passed a few vehicles abandoned by the side of the road, but took care not to drive too close. Often people will hide inside or behind and then leap out at anyone who passes, regardless of whether that person is in a moving vehicle or not.

I kept my eyes on the sea for the most part, concentrating on what was the same, rather than what was different. The ocean looked exactly as it always had, though I suppose usually there would have been ships to see, out on the horizon. There probably still are a few, floating aimlessly wherever the tide takes them, their decks echoing and empty. But I didn't see any.

When I reached Sarasota I slowed still further, driving out onto Lido Key until I pulled to a halt in the center of St Armand's Circle. It's not an especially big place, but it has a certain class. Though the stores around the Circle were more than full enough of the usual kind of junk the restaurants were good, and some of the old, small hotels were attractive, in a dated kind of way. Not as flashy as the deco strips on Old Miami Beach, but pleasant enough.

Last night the Circle was littered with burnt-out cars, and the up-scale pizzeria where we used to eat was still smoldering, the embers glowing in the fading light.

We worked through our degrees and out into post-graduate years. At first I had a lot to catch up on. Sometimes Rebecca snuck me into classes, but most of the time I just pored over their notes and books, and we talked long into the night. Catching up wasn't so hard, but keeping up with both of them was a struggle. I never understood the nanotech side as well as Rebecca, or the computing as deeply as David, but that was probably an advantage. I stood between the two of them, and it was in my mind where the two disciplines most equally met. Without me there, it's probable none of it would ever have come to fruition. So maybe if you come right down to it, and it's anyone's fault, it's mine.

David's goal was designing a system that would take the input and imperatives of a number of small component parts, and synthesize them into a greater whole—catering for the fact that the concerns of biological organisms are seldom clear-cut. The fuzzy logic wasn't difficult—God knows we were familiar enough with it, most noticeably in our ability to reason that we needed another beer when we couldn't even remember where the fridge was. More difficult was designing and implementing the means by which the different machines, or 'beckies', as we elected to call them, interfaced with each other.

Rebecca concentrated on the physical side of the problem, synthesizing beckies with intelligence coded into artificial DNA in a manner which enabled the 'brain' of each type to link up with and transfer information to the others. And remember, when I say 'machines' I'm not talking about large metal objects which sit in the corner of the room making unattractive noises and drinking a lot of oil. I'm talking about strings of molecules hardwired together, invisible to the naked eye.

I helped them both with their specific areas, and did most of the development work in the middle, designing the overall system. It was me who came up with the first product to aim for, 'ImmunityWorks'.

The problem of diagnosing malfunction in the human body has always been the number of variables, many of which are difficult to monitor effectively from the outside. If someone sneezes, they could just have a cold. On the other hand, they could have flu, or the bubonic plague—or some dust up their nose. Unless you can test all the relevant parameters, you're not going to know what the real problem is—or the best way of treating it. We were aiming for an integrated set of beckies which could examine all of the pertinent conditions, share their findings, and determine the best way of tackling the problem—all at the molecular level, without human intervention of any kind. The system had to be robust—to withstand interaction with the body's own immune system—and intelligent. We weren't intending to just tackle things that made you sneeze, either: we were never knowingly under-ambitious. Even for ImmunityWorks 1.0 we were aiming for a system which could cope with a wide range of viruses, bacteria and general senescence: a first aid kit which lived in the body, anticipating problems and solving them before they got started. A kind of guardian angel, which would co-exist with the human system and protect it from harm.

We were right on the edge of knowledge, and we knew it. The roots of disease in the human body still weren't properly understood, never mind the best ways to deal with them. An individual trying to do what we were doing would have needed about 300 years and a research grant bigger than God's. But we weren't just one person. We weren't even just three. Like the system we were trying to design, we were a perfect symbiosis, three minds whose joint product was incomparably greater than the sum of its parts. Also, we worked like maniacs. After we'd received our Doctorates we rented an old house together away from the campus, and turned the top floor into a private lab. Obviously there were arguments for putting it in the basement, historical 'mad scientist' precedents for example, but the top floor had a better view and as that's where we spent most of our time, that kind of thing was an issue. We got up in the mornings, did enough to maintain our tenure at the University, and worked on our own project in secret.

David and Rebecca had each other. I had an intermittent string of short liaisons with fellow lecturers, students or waitresses, each of which felt I was being unfaithful to something, or to someone. It wasn't Rebecca I was thinking of. God knows she was beautiful enough, and lovely enough, to pine after, but I didn't. Lusting after Rebecca would have felt like one of our beckies deciding only to work with some, not all, of the others in its system. The whole system would have imploded.

Unfaithful to us, I suppose is what I felt. To the three of us.

It took us four years to fully appreciate what we were getting into, and to establish just how much work was involved. The years after were a process of slow, grinding progress. David and I modeled an artificial body on the computer, creating an environment in which we could test virtual versions of the beckies Rebecca and I were busy trying to synthesize. Occasionally we'd enlist the assistance of someone from the medical faculty, when we needed more of an insight into a particular disease; but this was always done covertly, and without letting on what we were doing. This was our project, and we weren't going to share it with anyone.

By July of 2016 the software side of ImmunityWorks was in beta, and holding up well. We'd created code equivalents of all of the major viruses and bacteria, and built creeping failures into the code of the virtual body itself—to represent the random processes of physical malfunction. An initial set of 137 different virtual beckies was doing a sterling job of keeping an eye out for problems, then charging in and sorting them out whenever they occurred.

The physical side was proceeding a little more slowly. Creating miniature biomachines is a difficult process, and when they didn't do what they were supposed to you couldn't exactly lift up the hood and poke around inside. The key problem, and the one which took the most time to solve, was that of imparting a sufficient degree of 'consciousness' to the system as a whole—the aptitude for the component parts to work together, exchanging information and determining the most profitable course of action in any given circumstance. We probably built in a lot more intelligence than was necessary, in fact I know we did; but it was simpler than trying to hone down the necessary conditions right away. We could always streamline in ImmunityWorks 1.1, we felt, when the system had proved itself and we had patents nobody could crack. We also gave the beckies the ability to perform simple manipulations of the matter around them. It was an essential part of their role that they be able to take action on affected tissue once they'd determined what the problem was. Otherwise it would only have been a diagnostic tool, and we were aiming higher than that.

By October we were closing in, and were ready to run a test on a monkey that we'd infected with a copy of the Marburg strain of the Ebola virus. We'd pumped a whole lot of other shit into it as well, but it was the filovirus we were most interested in. If ImmunityWorks would handle that, we reckoned, we were really getting somewhere.

Yes *of course* it was a stupid thing to do. We had a monkey jacked full of one of the most communicable virus known to mankind *in our house*. The lab was heavily secured by then, but it was still an insane risk. In retrospect I realise that we were so caught up in what we were doing, in our own joint mind, that normal considerations had ceased to really register. We didn't even need to do the Ebola test. That's the really tragic thing. It was unnecessary. It was pure arrogance, and also wildly illegal. We could have just tested ImmunityWorks on plain vanilla viruses, or artificially-induced cancers. If it had worked we could have contacted the media and owned our own Caribbean islands within two years.

But no. We had to go the whole way.

The monkey sat in its cage, looking really very ill, with any number of sensors and electrodes taped and wired on and into its skull and body. Drips connected to bioanalysers gave a second-by-second readout of the muck that was floating around in the poor animal's bloodstream. About two hours before the animal was due to start throwing clots, David threw the switch which would inject a solution of ImmunityWorks 0.9b7 into its body.

The time was 16:23, October 14th, 2016, and for the next 24 hours we watched.

At first the monkey continued to get worse. Arteries started clotting, and the heartbeat grew ragged and fitful. The artificial cancer that we'd induced in the animal's pancreas also appeared to be holding strong. We sat, and smoked, and drank coffee, our hearts sinking. Maybe, we began to think, we weren't so damned clever after all.

Then…that moment.

Even now, as I sit here in an abandoned hotel and listen for sounds of movement outside, I can remember the moment when the read-outs started to turn around.

The clots started to break up. The cancerous cells started to lose vitality. The breed of simian flu which we'd acquired illicitly from the University's labs went into remission.

The monkey started getting better.

And we felt like gods, and stayed that way even when the monkey suddenly died of shock a day later. We knew by then that there was more work to do in buffering the stress effects the beckies had on the body. That wasn't important. It was just a detail. We had screeds of data from the experiment, and David's AI systems were already integrating it into the next version of the ImmunityWorks software. Becky and I made the tweaks to the beckies, stamping the revised software into the biomachines and refining the way they interfaced with the body's own immune system.

We only really came down to earth the next day, when we realised that Rebecca had contracted Marburg.

*

Eventually the sight of the St Armand's dying heart paled, and I started the car up again. I drove a little further along the coast to the Lido Beach Inn, which stands just where the strip starts to diffuse into a line of beach motels. I turned into the driveway and cruised slowly up to the entrance arch, peering into the lobby. There was nobody there, or if there was, they were crouching in darkness. I let the car roll down the slope until I was inside the hotel court proper, and then pulled into a space.

I climbed out, pulled my bag from the passenger seat, and locked the car up. Then I went to the trunk and took out the bag of groceries that I'd carefully culled from the stock back at the facility. I stood by the car for a moment, hearing nothing but the sound of waves over the wall at the end, and looked around. I saw no-one, and no signs of violence, and so I headed for the stairs to go up to the second floor, and towards room 211. I had an old copy of the key, 'accidentally' not returned many years ago, which was just as well. The hotel lobby was a pool of utter blackness in an evening which was already dark, and I had no intention of going anywhere near it.

For a moment, as I stood outside the door to the room, I thought I heard a girl's laughter, quiet and far away. I stood still for a moment, mouth slightly open to aid hearing, but heard nothing else.

Probably it was nothing no more than a memory.

Rebecca died two days later in an isolation chamber. She bled and crashed out in the small hours of the morning, as David and I watched through glass. My head hurt so much from crying that I thought it was going to split, and David's throat was so hoarse he could barely speak. David wanted to be in there with her, but I dissuaded him. To be frank, I punched him out until he was too groggy to fight any more. There was nothing he could do, and Rebecca didn't want him to die. She told me so through the intercom, and as that was her last comprehensible wish, I decided it would be so.

We knew enough about Marburg that we could almost feel her body cavities filling up with blood, smell the blackness as it coagulated in her. When she started bleeding from her eyes I turned away, but David watched every moment. We talked to her until there was nothing left to speak to, and then watched powerless as she drifted away, retreating into some upper and hidden hall while her body collapsed around her.

Of course we tried ImmunityWorks. Again, it nearly worked. Nearly, but not quite. When Rebecca's vital signs finally stopped, her body was as clean as a whistle. But it was still dead.

HELL HATH ENLARGED HERSELF

David and I stayed in the lab for three days, waiting. Neither of us contracted the disease.

Lucky old us.

We dressed in biohazard suits and sprayed the entire house with a solution of ImmunityWorks, top to bottom. Then we put the remains of Rebecca's body into a sealed casket, drove upstate, and buried it in a forest. She would have liked that. Her parents were dead, and she had no family to miss her, except us.

David left the day after the burial. We had barely spoken in the intervening period. I was sitting numbly in the kitchen on that morning and he walked in with an overnight bag. He looked at me, nodded, and left. I didn't see him again for two years.

I stayed in the house, and once I'd determined that the lab was clean, I carried on. What else was there to do?

Working on the project by myself was like trying to play chess with two thirds of my mind burned out: the intuitive leaps which had been commonplace when the three of us were together simply didn't come, and were replaced by hours of painstaking, agonizingly slow experiment. On the other hand, I didn't kill anyone.

I worked. I ate. I drove most weekends to the forest where Rebecca lay, and became familiar with the paths and light beneath the trees which sheltered her.

I refined the beckies, eventually understanding the precise nature of the shock reaction that had killed our two subjects. I pumped more and more intelligence into the system, amping the ability of the component parts to interact with each other and make their own decisions. In a year I had the system to a point where it was faultless on common viruses, like flu. Little did the world know it, but while they were out there sniffing and coughing I had stuff sitting in ampoules that could have sorted them out forever. But that wasn't the point. ImmunityWorks had to work on everything. That had always been our goal, and if I was going to carry on, I was going to do it our way. I was doing it for us, or for the memory of how we'd been. The two best friends I'd ever had were gone, and if the only way I could hang onto some memory of them was through working on the project, that was what I would do.

Then one day one of them reappeared.

I was in the lab, tinkering with the subset of the beckies whose job it was to synthesize new materials out of damaged body cells. The newest strain of biomachines were capable of far, far more than the originals had been. Not only could they fight the organisms and processes that caused disease in the first place, but also they could then directly repair essential cells and organs within the body to ensure that it made a healthy recovery.

'Can you do anything about colds yet?' asked a voice, and I turned to see David, standing in the doorway to the lab. He'd lost about two stone in weight, and looked exhausted beyond words. There were lines around his eyes that had nothing to do with laughter, and he looked older in other ways too. As I stared at him he coughed raggedly.

'Yes,' I said, struggling to keep my voice calm. David held his arm out and pulled his sleeve up. I found an ampoule of my most recent brew and spiked it with a hypo. 'Where did you pick it up?'

'England.'

'Is that where you've been?' I asked, as I slipped the needle into his arm and sent the beckies scurrying into his system.

'Some of the time.'

'Why?'

'Why not?' he shrugged, and rolled his sleeve back up.

I waited in the kitchen while he showered and changed, sipping a beer and feeling obscurely nervous. Eventually he reappeared, looking better but still very tired. I suggested going out to a bar, and we did, carefully but unspokenly avoiding those we used to go to as a threesome. Neither of us had mentioned Rebecca yet, but she was there between us in everything we said and didn't say. We walked down winter streets to a place I knew had opened recently, and it was almost as if for the first time I felt I was grieving for her properly. While David had been away, it had been as if they'd just gone away somewhere together. Now he was here, I could no longer deny that she was dead.

We didn't say much for a while, and all I learnt was that David had spent much of the last two years in Eastern Europe. I didn't push him, but simply let the conversation take its own course. It had always been David's way that he would get round to things in his own good time.

'I want to come back,' he said eventually.

'David, as far as I'm concerned you never went away.'

'That's not what I mean. I want to start the project up again, but different.'

'Different in what way?'

He told me. It took me a while to understand what he was talking about, and when I did I began to feel tired, and cold, and sad. David didn't want to refine ImmunityWorks. He had lost all interest in the body, except in the ways in which it supported the mind. He had spent his time in Europe visiting people of a certain kind, trying to establish what it was about them that made them different. Had I known, I could have recommended my Aunt Kate to him—not, I felt, that it would have made any difference. I watched him covertly as he talked, as he became more and more animated, and all I could feel was a sense of dread, a realization that for the rest of his life my friend would be lost to me.

He had come to believe that mediums, people who can communicate with the spirits of the dead, do not possess some special spiritual power, but instead a difference in the physical make-up of their brain. He believed that it was some fundamental but minor difference in the wiring of their senses that enabled them to bridge a gap between this world and the next, to hear voices that had stopped speaking, see faces that had faded away. He wanted to determine where this difference lay, pinpoint it and learn to replicate it. He wanted to develop a species of becky which anyone could take, which would rewire their soul and enable them to become a medium.

More specifically, he wanted to take it himself, and I understood why, and when I realised what he was hoping for I felt like crying for the first time in two years.

He wanted to be able to talk with Rebecca again, and I knew both that he was not insane and that there was nothing I could do, except help him.

Room 211 was as I remembered it. Nondescript. A decent-sized room in a low-range motel. I put my bags on one of the twin beds and checked out the bathroom. It was clean and the shower still gave a thin trickle of lukewarm water. I washed and changed into one of the two sets of casual clothes I had brought with me, and then I made a sandwich out of cold cuts and processed cheese, storing the remainder in the small fridge in the corner by the television. I turned the latter on briefly and got snow across the board, though I heard the occasional half-word which suggested that someone was still trying somewhere.

I propped the door to the room open with a Bible and dragged a chair out onto the walkway, and then I sat and ate my food and drank a beer looking down across the court. The pool was half full, and a deck chair floated in one end of it.

Our approach was very simple. Using some savings of mine we flew to Australia, where I talked Aunt Kate into letting us take minute samples of tissue from different areas of her brain, using a battery of lymph-based beckies. We didn't tell her what the samples were for, simply that we were researching genetic traits. Jenny was now married to an accountant, it transpired, and they, Aunt Kate and David and I sat out that night on the porch and watched the sun turn red.

The next day we flew home and went straight on to Gainesville, where I had a much harder time persuading my mother to let us do the same thing. In the end she relented, and despite claiming that the beckies had 'tickled', had to admit it hadn't hurt. She seemed fit, and well, as did my father when he returned from work. I saw them once again, briefly, about two months ago. I've tried calling them since, but the line is dead.

Back at Jacksonville David and I did the same thing with our own brains, and then the real work began. If, we reasoned, there really was some kind of physiological basis to the phenomena we were searching for, then it ought to show up to varying degrees in my family line, and less so—or not at all—in David. We had no idea whether it would be down to some chemical balance, a difference in synaptic function, or a virtual 'sixth sense' that some sub-section of the brain was sensitive to—and so in the beginning we just used part of the samples to find out exactly what we'd got to work with. Of course we didn't have a wide enough sample to make any findings stand up to scrutiny: but then we weren't ever going to tell anyone what we were doing, so that hardly mattered.

We drew the blinds and stayed inside, and worked 18 hours a day. David said little, and for much of the time seemed only half the person he used to be. I realised that until we succeeded in letting him talk with his love again, I would not see the friend I knew.

We both had our reasons for doing what we did.

It took a little longer than we'd hoped, but we threw a lot of computing power at it and in the end began to see results. They were complex, and far from conclusive, but appeared to suggest that all three possibilities were partly true. My Aunt showed a minute difference in synaptic function in certain areas of her brain, which I shared, but not the fractional chemical imbalances which were present in both my mother and I. On the other hand, there was evidence of a loose meta-structure of apparently unrelated areas of her brain that was only present in trace degrees in my mother, and not at all in me. We took these results and correlated them against the findings from the samples of David's brain, and finally came to a tentative conclusion.

The ability, if it truly was related to physiological morphology, seemed most directly related to an apparently insignificant variation in general synaptic function which created an almost intangible additional structure within certain areas of the brain.

Not, perhaps, one of the most memorable slogans of scientific discovery, but that night David and I went out and got more drunk than we had in five years. We clasped hands on the table once more, and this time we believed that the hand that should have been between ours was nearly within reach. The next day we split into two overlapping teams, dividing our time and minds as always between the software and the beckies. The beckies needed redesigning to cope with the new environment, and the software required yet another quantum leap to deal with the complexity of the tasks of synaptic manipulation. As we worked we joked that if the beckies got much more intelligent we'd have to give them the vote. It seemed funny back then.

September 12th, 2019 ought to have a significant place in the history of science, despite everything that happened afterwards. It was the day on which we tested MindWorks 1.0, a combination of computer and corporeal which was probably more subtle than anything man has ever produced. David insisted on being the first subject, despite the fact that he had another cold, and in the early afternoon of that day I injected him with a tiny dose of the beckies. Then, in a flash of solidarity, I injected myself. Together till the end, we said.

We sat there for five minutes, and then got on with some work. We knew that the effects, if there were any, wouldn't be immediate. To be absolutely honest, we weren't expecting much at all from the first batch. As everyone knows, anything with the version number '1' will have teething problems, and if it has a '.0' after it then it's going to crash and burn. We sat and tinkered with the plans for a 1.1 version, which was only different in that some of the algorithms were more elegant, but couldn't seem to concentrate. Excitement, we assumed.

Then late afternoon David staggered, and dropped a flask of the solution he was working on. It was full of MindWorks, but that didn't matter—we had a whole vat of it in storage. I made David sit down and ran a series of tests on him. Physically he was okay, and protested that he felt fine. We shrugged and went back to work. I printed out ten copies of the code and becky specifications, and posted them to ten different places around the world. Of course the computers already laid automated and encrypted email backups all over the place, but old habits die hard. If this worked it was going to be ours, and no-one else was taking credit for it. Such considerations were actually less important to us by then, because there was only one thing we wanted from the experiment—but old habits die hard. Ten minutes later I had a dizzy spell myself, but apart from that nothing seemed to be happening at all.

We only realised that we might have succeeded when I woke to hear David screaming in the night.

Michael Marshall Smith

I ran into his room and found him crouched up against the wall, eyes wide, teeth chattering uncontrollably. He was staring at the opposite corner of the room. He didn't seem to be able to hear anything I said to him. As I stood there numbly, wondering what to do, I heard a voice from behind me—a voice I half-thought I recognised. I turned, but there was no-one there. Suddenly David looked at me, his eyes wide and terrified.

'Fuck,' he said. 'I think it's working.'

We spent the rest of the night in the kitchen, sitting round the table and drinking coffee in harsh light. David didn't seem to be able to remember exactly what it was he'd seen, and I couldn't recapture the sound of the voice I'd heard, or what it might have said. Clearly we'd achieved something, but it wasn't clear what it might be. When nothing further happened by daybreak, we decided to get out of the house for a while. We were both too keyed up to sit around any longer or try to work, but felt we should stay together. Something was happening, we knew: we could both feel it. We walked around campus for the morning, had lunch in the cafeteria, then spent the afternoon downtown. The streets seemed a little crowded, but nothing else weird happened.

In the evening we went out. We had been invited to a dinner party at the house of a couple on the medical staff, and thought we might as well attend. David and I were a little distracted at first, but once everyone had enough wine inside them we started to have a good time. The hosts got out their stock of dope, doubtless supplied by an accommodating member of the student body, and by midnight we were all a little high, comfortably sprawled around the living room.

And of course, eventually, David started talking about the work we'd been doing. At first people just laughed, and that made me realise belatedly just how far outside the scope of normal scientific endeavor we had moved. It also made me determined that we should be taken seriously, and so I started to back David up. It was stupid, and we should never have mentioned it. It was one of the people at that party who eventually gave our names to the police.

'So prove it,' this man said at one stage. 'Hey, is there a ouija board in the house?'

The general laughter that greeted this sally was enough to tip the balance. David rose unsteadily to his feet, and stood in the center of the room. He sneezed twice, to general amusement, but then his head seemed to clear. Though he was swaying gently, the seriousness of his face was enough to quiet most people, although there was a certain amount of giggling. He looked gaunt, and tired, and everybody stopped talking, and the room went very quiet as they watched him.

76

'Hello?' he said quietly. He didn't use a name, for obvious reasons, but I knew whom he was asking for. 'Are you there?'

'And if so, did you bring any grass?' the hostess added, getting a big laugh. I shook my head, partly at how foolish we were seeming, partly because there seemed to be a faint glow in one corner of the room, as if some of the receptors in my eyes were firing strangely. I made a note to check the beckies when we got back, to make sure none of them could have had an effect on the optic nerve.

I was about to say something, to help David out of an embarrassing position, when he suddenly turned to the hostess.

'Jackie, how many people did you invite tonight?'

'Eight,' she said. 'We always have eight. We've only got eight complete sets of table ware.'

David looked at me. 'How many people do you see?' he asked.

I looked round the room, counting.

'Eleven,' I said.

One of the guests laughed nervously. I counted them again. There were eleven people in the room. In addition to the eight of us who were slouched over the settees and floor, three people stood round the walls.

A tall man, with long and not especially clean brown hair. A woman in her forties, with blank eyes. A young girl, maybe eight years old.

Mouth hanging open, I stood up to join David. We looked from each of the extra figures to the other. They looked entirely real, as if they'd been there all along.

They stared back at us, silently.

'Come on guys,' the host said, nervously. 'Okay, great gag—you had us fooled for a moment there. Now let's have another smoke.'

David ignored him, turning to the man with the long hair.

'What's your name?' he asked him. There was a long pause, as if the man was having difficulty remembering. When he spoke, his voice sounded dry and cold.

'Nat,' he said. 'Nat Simon.'

'David,' I said. 'Be careful.'

David ignored me, and turned back to face the real guests. 'Does the name 'Nat Simon' mean anything to anyone here?' he asked.

For a moment I thought it hadn't, and then we noticed the hostess. The smile had slipped from her face and her skin had gone white, and she was staring at David. With a sudden, ragged beat of my heart I knew we had succeeded.

'Who was he?' I asked quickly. I wish I hadn't. In a room that was now utterly silent she told us.

Nat Simon had been a friend of one of her uncles. One summer, when she was nine years old, he had raped her just about every day of the two weeks she'd spent on vacation with her relatives. He was killed in a car accident when she was fourteen, and since then she'd thought she'd been free.

'Tell Jackie I've come back to see her,' Nat said proudly, 'And I'm all fired up and ready to go.' He had taken his penis out of his trousers and was stroking it towards erection.

'Go away,' I said. 'Fuck off back where you came from.'

Nat just smiled. 'Ain't ever been anywhere else,' he said. 'Like to stay as close to little Jackie as I can.'

David quickly asked the other two figures who they were. I tried to stop him, but the other guests encouraged him, at least until they heard the answers. Then the party ended abruptly. Voyeurism becomes a lot less amusing when it's you that people are staring at.

The blank-eyed woman was the first wife of the man who had joked about ouija boards. After discovering his affair with one of his students she had committed suicide in their living room. He'd told everyone she'd suffered from depression, and that she drank in secret.

The little girl was the host's sister. She died in childhood, hit by a car while running across the road as part of a dare devised by her brother.

By the time David and I ran out of the house, two of the other guests had already started being able to see for themselves, and the number of people at the party had risen to fifteen.

After four beers my mind was a little fuzzy, and for a while I was almost able to forget. Then I heard a soft splashing sound from below, and looked to see a young boy climbing out of the stagnant water in the pool. He didn't look up, but just walked over the flagstones to the gate, and then padded out through the entrance to the motel. I could still hear the soft sound of his wet feet long after he'd disappeared into the darkness. The brother who'd held his head under a moment too long; the father who'd been too busy watching someone else's wife putting lotion on her thighs; or the mother who'd fallen asleep. Someone would be having a visitor tonight.

When we got back to the house after the party, and tried to get back into the lab, we found that we couldn't open the door. The lock had fused. Something had attacked the metal of the tumblers, turning the mechanism into a solid lump of metal. We stared at each other, by now feeling very sober, and then turned to look through the glass upper portion of the door. Everything inside looked the way it always had, but I now believe that even early, before we knew what was happening, everything had already been set in motion. The beckies work in strange and invisible ways.

David got the axe from the garage, and we broke through the door to the laboratory. We found the vat of MindWorks empty. A small hole had appeared in the bottom of the glass, and there was a faint trail where the contents had flowed across the floor, making small holes at several points. It had doubled back on itself, and in a couple of places it had also flowed against gravity. It ended in a larger hole that, it transpired, dripped through into a pipe. A pipe that went out back into the municipal water system.

The first reports were on CNN at seven o'clock the next morning. Eight murders in downtown Jacksonville, and three on the University campus. David's cold. Reports of people suddenly going crazy, screaming at people who weren't there, running in terror from voices in their head and acting on impulses that they claimed weren't theirs. By lunchtime the problem wasn't just confined to people we might have come into contact with: it had started to spread on its own.

I don't know why it happened like this. Maybe we just made a mistake somewhere. Perhaps it was something as small and simple as a chiral isomer, some chemical that the beckies created in a mirror image of the way it should be. That's what happened with thalidomide, and that's what we created. A thalidomide of the soul.

Or maybe there was no mistake. Perhaps that's just the way it is. Maybe the only spirits who stick around are the ones you don't want to see. The ones who can turn people into psychotics who riot, murder, or end their lives, through the hatred or guilt they bring with them. These people have always been here, all the time, staying close to the people who remember them. Only now they are no longer invisible. Or silent.

A day later there were reports in European cities, at first just the ones where I'd sent my letters, then spreading rapidly across the entire land mass. By the time my letters reached their recipients, the beckies I'd breathed over them had multiplied a thousand-fold, breaking the paper down and reconstituting the molecules to create more of themselves. They were so clever, our children, and they shared the ambitions of their creators. If they'd needed to, they could probably have formed themselves into new letters, and lay around until someone posted them all over the world. But they didn't, because coughing, or sneezing, or just breathing is enough to spread the infection. By the following week a state of emergency was in force in every country in the world.

A mob killed David before the police got to him. He never got to see Rebecca. I don't know why. She just didn't come. I was placed under house arrest, and then taken to the facility to help with the feverish attempts to come up with a cure. There is none, and there never will be. The beckies are too smart, too aggressive, and too powerful. They just take any antidote, break it down, and use it to make more of themselves.

They don't need the vote. They're already in control.

The moon is out over the ocean, casting glints over the tides as they rustle back and forth with a sound like someone slowly running their finger across a piece of paper. A little while ago I heard a siren in the far distance. Apart from that all is quiet.

I think it's unlikely I shall riot, or go on a killing spree. In the end, I will simply go.

The times when Karen comes to see me are bad. She didn't stop writing to me because she lost interest, it turns out. She stopped writing because she had been pregnant by me, and didn't want me involved, and died through some nightmare of childbirth without ever telling her mother my name. I hadn't brought any contraception. I think we both figured life would let you get away with things like that. When David and I talked about Karen over that game of pool she was already dead. She will come again tonight, as she always does, and maybe tonight will be the night when I decide I cannot bear it any longer. Perhaps seeing her here, at the motel where David and I stayed that summer, will be enough to make me do what I have to do.

If it isn't her who gives me the strength, then someone else will, because I've started seeing other people now too. It's surprising quite how many—or maybe it isn't, when you consider that all of this is partly my fault. So many people have died, and will die, all of them with something to say to me. Every night there are more, as the world slowly winds down. There are two of them here now, standing in the court and looking up at me. Perhaps in the end I shall be the last one alive, surrounded by silent figures in ranks that reach out to the horizon.

Or maybe, as I hope, some night David and Rebecca will come for me, and I will go with them.

Save As...

As soon as I walked out of the hospital I knew what I was going to do. It was 1 a.m. by then, for what difference that made. Other people's clocks meant nothing. I was on hospital time, crash time, blood time: surprised by how late it was, as if I'd believed that what happened must have taken place in some small pocket of horror outside the real world, where the normal rules of progression and chronology don't apply. Of course it must have taken time, for the men and women in white coats to run the stretcher trolleys down the corridors, shouting for crash teams and saline; to cut through my wife's matted clothes and expose wet ruins where only an hour ago all had been smooth and dry; to gently move my son's head so that its position in relation to his body was the same as it had always been. All of this took time, as did the eventual slow looks up at me, the quiet shakes of the doctors' heads, the forms I had to sign and the words I had to listen to.

Then the walk from the emergency room to the outside world, my shoes tapping softly on the linoleum as I passed rows of people with bandaged fingers. That took the most time of all.

The air in the car park was cool and moist, freshened by the rain. I could smell the grass that grew in the darkness beyond the lamps' pools of yellow light, and hear in the distance the sound of wet tires on the freeway. Tires that, I hoped, would retain their grip, safely transport the cars' passengers to their homes. Tires that wouldn't fail under a sudden braking to avoid a car which had slewed into their path, hurtling the vehicles together.

I suddenly realised that I had no means of getting home. The remains of the Lexus were presumably lying by the side of the road where the accident had taken place, or had been carted off to a wrecker's yard. For a moment the problem took up the whole of my mind, unnaturally luminescent: and then I realised both that I could presumably call a cab from reception, and that I didn't really care.

Two orderlies walked across the far side of the lot, a faint laugh carrying to me. The smell of smoke in their wake reminded me I was a smoker, and I fumbled a cigarette from the packet in my jacket pocket. The carton was perfectly in shape, the cigarette unbent. One of the very few things Helena and I had ever argued about was my continued inability to resist toying with death in the form of tubes of rolled tobacco. Her arguments were never those of the zealot, just measured and reasonable. She loved me, and Jack loved me, and she didn't want the two of them to be left alone. The fact that the crash which had crushed her skull had left my cancer sticks entirely unmolested was a joke which she would have liked and laughed at hard.

For a moment I hesitated. I couldn't decide whether Helena's death meant I should smoke the cigarette or not.

Then I lit it and walked back to reception. If I was going to go through with it, I didn't have much time.

The cab dropped me at the corner of Montague and 31st. I overtipped the driver—who'd had to put up with a sudden crying jag that left me feeling cold and embarrassed—and watched the car swish away down the deserted street. The crossroads was bleak and exposed; an empty used car lot and burnt-out gas station taking two corners, run-down buildings of untellable purpose squatting kitty corner on the others. It couldn't have been more different from the place where I'd originally gone to visit the Same Again Corporation, an altogether more gleaming street in the heart of the business district. I guessed space was cheaper out here, and maybe they needed a lot of it: though I couldn't really understand why. Data storage is pretty compact these days.

Whatever. The card I'd kept in my wallet was adamant that I should go to the address on Montague in case of emergency, and so I walked quickly down towards 1176. I saw from across the street that a light was on behind the frosted glass of the door, and picked up the pace with relief. It was open, just as the card said it would be.

As I crossed the street a man came out of Same Again's front door, holding a very wet towel. He twisted the towel round on itself, squeezing as much of the water out of it as he could. It joined the rain already on the sidewalk and disappeared.

When he saw where I was heading he suddenly looked up.

'Help you?' he asked, warily. I showed him the card. An unreadable expression crossed his face. 'Go inside,' he said. 'Be right with you.'

The reception area was small but smart. And very quiet. I waited at the desk for a few moments, while the man finished whatever the hell he was doing. Then I noticed a soft dripping sound. A patch of carpet near one of the walls was damp, and there was a similar spot on the ceiling.

I turned to find the man reaching out a hand to me.

'Sorry about that,' he said, but didn't offer any more explanation. 'Okay, can I have that card?'

He took it and went behind the desk, tapped my Customer Number into the terminal there.

'My name's...' I said, but he held up his hand.

'Don't tell me,' he said quickly. 'Not a thing. I assume something pretty major has happened.' He looked at my face for a moment, and decided he didn't have to wait for an answer. 'So it's very important that I know as little as possible. How many people have already been involved?'

'Involved?'

'Are aware of whatever event it is that has brought you here.'

'I don't know.' I wasn't sure who counted. The doctors and nurses, presumably, and the people who'd loaded up the ambulance. They'd seen the faces. Others knew that *something* had happened, in that they'd driven past the mess on the Freeway, or walked past me as I stood in the parking lot of the hospital. But surely they didn't count, because they had no knowledge or who had been involved in what. 'Maybe ten, twelve?'

The man nodded briskly. 'That's fine. Okay, I've processed the order. Go through that door and a technician will take you from there. May I just remind you of the terms of the contract you entered into with Same Again, most specifically that you are legally bound not to reveal to anyone either that you are a subscriber to our service or that you have made use of it on this or any other occasion?'

'Fine,' I said. It was illegal. We both knew that, and I was the last person who wanted any trouble.

The door led me into a cavernous dark area, where a young woman in a green lab coat waited for me. Without looking directly at my face she indicated that I should follow her. At the end of the room was a chair, and I sat in it and sat quietly while she applied conducting gel to my temples and attached the wires.

When she was finished she asked if I was comfortable. I turned my head towards her, clamping my lips tightly together. My teeth were chattering inside my head, the muscles of my jaw and neck spasming. I could barely see her through a haze of grief I knew I could not bear. In the end I nodded.

She loaded up a hypo and injected something into the vein on the back of my hand. I started counting backwards from twenty but made it no further than nine.

I got home about four o'clock that afternoon. After I'd locked the Lexus I stood in the driveway for a moment, savouring a breeze that softened the heat like a ceiling fan in a noisy bar. The weathermen kept saying summer was going to burst soon, but they were evidently as full of shit as their genus had always been. Chaos theory may have grooved a lot of people's lives but the guys who stood in front of maps for a living were obviously still at the stage of consulting entrails. It hadn't rained for weeks and didn't look like it was going to start any time soon—and that was good, because in the evening we had a bunch of friends coming round for a cookout in the back yard.

I let myself into the house and went straight through into the kitchen. Helena was standing at the table, basting chicken legs, half an eye on an old Tom Hanks film playing on the set in the corner. I noticed with approval that it was an old print, one that hadn't been parallaxed.

'Good movie,' I said.

'Would be,' she replied. 'If you could see what the hell was going on.'

I'm against the 'enhancing' of classics: Helena takes the opposite view, as is her wont. We'd had the discussion about a hundred times and as neither of us really cared, we only put ourselves through it for fun. I kissed her on the nose and dunked a stick of celery in the barbecue sauce.

'Dad!' yelped a voice, and I turned in time to catch Jack as he leapt up at me. He looked like he'd been dragged through a hedge sideways by someone who was an internationally-acknowledged expert in the art of interfacing humans and hedges to maximum untidying effect. I raised an eyebrow at Helena, who shrugged.

'How many pairs of hands do you see?' she asked.

I set Jack down, endured him boxing my kneecaps for a while, and then sent him upstairs for a bath—promising I'd come up and talk to him. I knew what he really wanted was to rehearse yet again the names of the kids who'd be coming tonight. He's a sociable kid, much more than I was at his age—but I think I was looking forward to the evening as much as him. The secret of good social events is to only invite the people you like having in your life, not the ones you merely tolerate. Tonight we had my boss—who was actually my best friend—and his wife; a couple of Helena's old girlfriends who were as good a time as anyone could handle;

and another old colleague of mine over from England with his family.

I hung with Helena in the kitchen for a while, until she tired of me nibbling samples of everything she'd painstakingly arranged on serving plates. She was too tall to box my kneecaps and so bit me on the neck instead, a bite which turned into a kiss and became in danger of throwing her cooking schedule out of whack. She shooed me out and I left her to it and went through into the study.

There were screeds of email to be sent before I could consign the day to history and settle down into the evening and weekend, but most of it was already written and the rest didn't take long. As the software punted them out I rested my chin on my hands and gazed out onto the yard. A trestle table was already set up, stacks of paper plates at the ready. The old cable spool we used as a table when it was just family had been rolled to over by the tree, and bottles of red wine were open and breathing in the air. Beer would be frosting in the fridge and the fixings for Becky and Janny's drink of choice—Mint Juleps, for chrissake—ready and waiting in the kitchen. I could hear Helena viciously chopping some errant vegetable in the kitchen, and Jack hollering in the bath upstairs.

For a moment I felt perfectly at peace. I was thirty-six, had a wife I'd die for and a happy, intelligent kid; a job I actually enjoyed and more money than we needed; and a house that looked and felt like an advert for The Good Life. So what if it was smaltzy: it was what I wanted. After my twenties, a frenetic nightmare of bad relationships and shitty jobs—and my early thirties, when no-one around me seemed to be able to talk about anything other than houses, marriage or children—my life had finally found its mark. The good things were in place, but with enough perspective to let me exist in the outside world too.

I was a lucky guy, and not too stupid to realise it.

The machine told me it had accomplished its task, and that I had new mail. I scanned the sender addresses: one from my sister in Europe, and a spam about 'Outstanding business opportunities ($$$$$$)!'. I was mildly surprised to see that there was also one from my own email address—entitled 'Read This!'—but not very. As part of my constant battle to design a kill file that would weed out email invitations to business opportunities of any kind—regardless of the number of suffixed dollar signs—I was often sending test messages to myself. Evidently the new version of the kill file wasn't cutting it. I could tool around with it a little more on Sunday afternoon, maybe aided by a glass of JD. Right now it hardly seemed important.

I told the computer to have a nap and went upstairs to confront the dripping chaos that our bathroom would be.

Michael Marshall Smith

*

John and Julia arrived first, as usual: they were always invited on a 'turn up when you feel like it' basis. Helena was only just out of the shower so Julia went up to chat with her; meanwhile John and I stood in the kitchen with bottles of beer and chewed a variety of rags, him nibbling on Helena's cooking, me trying to rearrange things so she wouldn't notice.

We moved out into the yard when Becky and Janny arrived, and I started the Weber up, supervising the coals with foremanship from Helena at the table. I'd strung a couple of extension speakers out the door from the stereo in the living room, and one of Helena's compilation minidiscs played quietly in the background: something old, something new, something funky and something blue. Jack sat neatly on a chair at the end of the trestle in his new pants and checked shirt, sipping at a Diet Coke and waiting for the real fun to begin. Becky chatted with him in the meantime, while Janny re-ran horror stories of her last relationship: she's working on being the Fran Liebowitz of her generation, and getting there real fast. When everyone round the table erupted as she got to the end of yet another example of why her ex-boyfriend had not been fit to walk the earth, Helena caught my eye, and smiled.

I knew what she meant. There but for the grace of God, she was thinking, could have gone you or I.

Being funny is cool; being happy is better. I left the coals to themselves for a bit, and went and stood behind Helena with my hand on her shoulder.

But then the doorbell went and she jumped up to let Howard and Carol in. Jack stood uncertainly, waiting for them to come through into the garden. Their two kids, whose names I could never remember, walked out behind them. There was a moment of quiet mutual appraisal, and then all three ran off towards the tree to play some game or other. They'd only ever met once before, on a trip we took to England, but obviously whatever they'd got up to then was still good for another day. As the evening began to darken, and the adults sat round the table and drank and ate, I could hear always in the background one of my favourite sounds of all, the sound of Jack laughing.

And smell Helena's barbecue sauce, wafting over from the grill; and feel Helena's leg, her thigh warm against my leg, her ankle hooked behind mine.

*

SAVE AS...

At ten I came out of the house, clutching more beers, and realised two things. The first was that I was kind of drunk. Negotiating the step down from the kitchen was a little more difficult than it should have been, and the raucous figures around the trestle table looked less than clear. I shook my head, trying to get it back together: I didn't want to appear inebriated in front of my son. Not that he was on hand to watch—kids were still tirelessly cavorting off in the darkness of the far end of the yard.

The second thing I noticed was less tangible. Something to do with atmosphere. While I'd been in the kitchen, it had changed. People were still laughing, and laughing hard, but they'd moved round, were sitting in different positions at the table. I guess I'd been in the kitchen longer than I thought. Becky and Jan were huddled at one end of the table, and I perched myself on a chair nearby. But they were talking seriously about something, and didn't seem to want to involve me.

There was another burst of laughter from the other end, and I looked blearily towards it. There was something harsh in the sound. Helena and Carol were leaned in tight together, their faces red and shiny. Howard was chortling with John and Julia. It was good to see them getting on together, but I hadn't realised they were all so chummy. Howard had only been with the firm for a year before upping stakes and going with Carol back to her own country. John and I had been friends for twenty years. Still, I guess it showed the evening was going well.

Then I saw something I couldn't understand. Helena's hand, reaching out and taking a cigarette from the packet lying on the table. I frowned vaguely, knowing something wasn't right, but she stuck the cigarette in her mouth and lit it with her lighter.

Then I remembered that she'd started a few months before, finally dragged into my habit. I felt guilty, wishing I'd been able to stop before she started. Too late now, I suppose.

I reached for the bottle of beer I'd perched on the end of the table, and missed. Well, not quite missed: I made enough contact to knock it off the table. Janny rolled her eyes and started to lean down for it, but I beat her to it.

'It's okay, I'm not that drunk,' I said, slightly stiffly. This wasn't true, of course, because it took me rather longer than it should to find the bottle. In the end I had to completely lean over and look for where it had gone. This gave me a view of all the legs under the table, which was kind of neat, and I remained like that for a moment. Lots of shins, all standing together.

Some more together than others, I realised. Helena's foot was resting against John's.

Michael Marshall Smith

I straightened up abruptly, cracking my head on the end of the table. Conversation around the table stopped, and I found myself with seven pairs of eyes looking at me.

'Sorry,' I said, and went back into the kitchen to get another beer.

A couple later, really pretty drunk by then. Didn't want to sit back down at the table, felt like walking around a bit. Besides, Janny and Becky were still in conference, Janny looking odd; Howard and Carol and Julia talking about something else. I didn't feel like butting in.

Headed off towards the tree, thinking I'd see what the kids were up to. Maybe they'd play with me for a while. Better make an effort to talk properly—didn't want Jack to see daddy zonked. Usually it's okay, as my voice stays pretty straight unless I'm completely loaded, and as I couldn't score any coke that afternoon, that wasn't the case.

Coke? What the fuck was I talking about?

I ground to a halt then, suddenly confused. I didn't take coke, never had. Well, once, a few years back: it had been fun, but not worth the money—and an obvious slippery slope. Too easy to take until it was all gone, and then just buy some more. Plus Helena would have gone ballistic—she didn't even like me *smoking*, for God's sake.

Then I remembered her taking a cigarette earlier, and felt cold. She hadn't started smoking. That was nonsense.

So why did I think she had?

I started moving again, not because I felt I'd solved anything, but because I heard a sound. It wasn't laughing. It was more like quiet tears.

At the far end of the yard I found Jack's camp, a little clearing that huddled up against the wisteria that clung to the fence. I pushed through the bushes, swearing quietly.

Jack was sitting in the middle, tears rolling down his moon-like face. His check shirt was covered in dirt, the leg of his pants torn. Howard's kids were standing around him, giggling and pointing. As I lumbered towards them the little girl hurled another clump of earth at Jack. It struck him in the face, just above the eye.

For a moment I was totally unable to move, and then I lunged forward and grabbed her arm.

'Piss off, you little bastards,' I hissed, yanking them away from my son. They stared up at me, faces full of some thought I couldn't read. Then the little boy pulled his arm free, and his sister did the same. They ran off laughing towards the house.

I turned again to Jack, who was staring at the fence.

'Come on, big guy,' I said, bending down to take him in my arms. 'What was that all about?'

His face slowly turned to mine, and my heart sank at what was always there to see. The slight glaze in the eyes, the slackness at one corner of his mouth.

'Dada,' he said. 'They dirt me.'

I fell down onto my knees beside him, wrapping my arms around his thin shoulders. I held him tight, but as always sensed his eyes looking over my shoulder, gazing off into the middle distance at something no-one else could see.

Eventually I let go of him and rocked to my feet again, hand held down towards him. He took it and struggled to his feet. I led him out of the bushes and into the yard.

As we came close to the tree I saw Helena and John were approaching out the darkness. I sensed some kind of rearrangement taking place as they saw us, but couldn't work out what it might have been.

'Oh shit, what's happened now?' Helena said, reading Jack's state instantly and stepping towards us. John hung back, in the deep shadows.

I couldn't answer her. Partly just because I was drunk; I'd obviously over-compensated for my dealer's coke famine by drinking way more than usual. But mainly because there was something wrong with her face. Not her face, which was a beautiful as ever. Her lipstick. It was smudged all round her face.

'Christ you're useless,' she snapped, and grabbed Jack's hand. I didn't watch as she hauled him back towards the house. Instead I stared into the darkness under the tree, where a faint glow showed John was lighting a cigarette.

'Having a good evening?' I asked.

'Oh yeah,' he said, laughing quietly. 'You guys always throw such great parties.'

We walked back to the trestle table, neither of us saying anything.

I sat down next to the girls, glanced across at Becky. She looked a lot worse than the last time we'd seen her. The chemo obviously wasn't working.

'How are you feeling?' I asked.

She looked up at me, smiled tightly. 'Fine, just fine,' she said. She didn't want my sympathy, and never had since the afternoon I'd called round at her place, looking for some company.

Behind me I heard John getting up and going through into the kitchen. I'd never liked Julia, nor she me, and so it would be no comfort to look round and see her eyes following her husband into the house, where

Helena would already have dispatched Jack up to bed with a slap on the behind, and would maybe be standing at the sink, washing something that didn't need washing.

Instead I watched Howard and Carol talking together. They at least looked happy.

I stood at the front door, as the last set of taillights turned into the road and faded away. Helena stood behind me. When I turned to take her hand she smiled meaninglessly, her face hard and distant, and walked away. I lumbered into my study to turn the computer off.

Instead I found myself waking it from sleep, and clicked into my mail program. I read the letter from my sister, who seemed to be doing fine. She was redecorating her new house with her new boyfriend. I nodded to myself; it was good that things were finally going her way.

I turned at a sound behind me to find Helena standing there. She plonked a cup of coffee down on the desk beside me.

'There you go, Mister Man,' she said, and I smiled up at her. I didn't need the coffee, because I hadn't drunk very much. Sitting close to Helena all evening was still all the intoxication I needed. But it would be nice anyway.

'Good evening?' she asked, running her fingers across the back of my neck.

'Good evening,' I said, looping my arm around her waist.

'Well don't stay down here too long,' she winked, 'Because we could make it even better.'

After she'd gone I applied myself to the screen, but before I could starting writing a reply to my little sis I heard Helena's voice again. This time it was hard, and came as usual from outside the study.

'Put your fucking son to bed,' she said. 'I can't deal with him tonight.'

I turned, but she was already gone. I sat with my head in my hands for a little while, then reached out for the coffee. It wasn't there.

Then something on the screen caught my eye. Something I'd dismissed earlier. 'Read This!' it said.

As much to avoid going upstairs as anything, I double-clicked on the mail icon. A long text message burped up onto the screen, and I frowned. My kill file tests usually only ran a couple of lines. Blinking against the drunkenness slopping through my head I tried to focus on the first sentence.

I managed to read it, in the end. And then the next, and as I read all the way through I felt as if my chair was sinking, dropping lower and lower into the ground.

The message was from me, it was about Same Again, and finally I remembered.

Before I'd come home that afternoon, I'd gone to their offices in the business district. It was the second time I'd visited, the first being when I signed up for the service and had a preliminary backup done a year before. When I'd got up that morning, woken by Jack's cheerful chatter and feeling the warmth of Helena's buttocks against mine under the sheets, I'd suddenly realised that if there were any day on which to make a backup of my life, today was surely that day.

I'd driven over to their offices, sat in the chair and they'd done their thing, archiving the current state of affairs into a data file. A file which, as their blurb promised, I could access at any time life had gone wrong and I needed to return to the saved version.

I heard a noise out in the hallway, the sound of a small person bumping into a piece of furniture. Jack. In a minute I should go out and help him, put him to bed. Maybe read to him a little, see if I could get a few more words into his head. If not, just hold him a while, as he slipped off into a sleep furnished with a vagueness I could never understand.

All it takes is one little sequence of DNA out of place, one infinitesimal chemical reaction going wrong. That's all the difference there is between the child he was, and could have been. Becky would understand that. One of her cells had misbehaved too, like a 1 or 0 out of place in some computer program.

Wet towels. Heavy rain. A leaking ceiling.

Suddenly, somehow, I remembered going to a dark office on Montague in the wet small hours of some future morning. The strange way the man standing outside with the towel had reacted (would react) when I said I needed to do a restore from a backup they held there. And I knew what had happened.

There'd been an accident. Or there was going to be. The same rain that would total the car which for the moment still sat out in the drive, was going to corrupt the data I'd spent so much money to save.

At the bottom of the mail message was a number. I called it. Same Again's 24-hour switchboard was unobtainable. I listened to a recorded voice for a while, and then replaced the handset.

Maybe they'd gone out of business, in this differing reality. Backing up was, after all, illegal. Too easy for criminals to leap backwards before their mistakes, for politicians to run experiments. Wide scale, it would have caused chaos. So long as not many people knew, you could get away with it. The disturbance was undetectable.

Michael Marshall Smith

But now I knew, and this disturbance was far too great.

I could feel, like a heavy weight, the aura of the woman lying in the bed above my head. Could predict the firmness with which her back would be turned towards me, the way John and I would dance around each other at work the next day, and the endless drudgery of the phone calls required to score enough coke to make it all go away for a while.

'Hi dad...you still up?'

Jack stood in the doorway. He'd taken three apples from the kitchen, and was attempting to juggle them. He couldn't quite do it yet, but I thought it wouldn't be too long now. Perhaps I would learn then, and we could do that stuff where you swap balls with one another. That might be kind of cool.

'Yep,' I smiled, 'But not for much longer. How about you go up, get your teeth brushed, and then I'll read you a story?'

But he'd corrupted again by then, and the apples fell one by one, to bruise on the hardwood floor. His eyes stared, slightly out of kilter, at my dusty bookcase, his fingers struggling at a button on his shirt. I reached forward and wiped away the thin dribble of saliva that ran from the bad corner of his mouth.

'Come on, little guy,' I said, and hoisted him up.

As I carried him upstairs into the darkness, his head lolling against my shoulder, I wondered how much had changed, whether in nine months the crash would still come as we drove back from a happy evening in Gainesville.

And I wondered, if it did, whether I would do anything to avoid it.

Or if I would steer the car even harder this time.

The Handover

Nobody moved much when he came into the bar. From the way Jack shut the door behind him—quietly, like the door of a cupboard containing old things seldom needed but neatly stored—we could tell he didn't have any news that we'd be in a hurry to hear. There were three guys sipping beer up at the counter. One of them glanced up, gave him a brief nod. That was it.

It was nine-thirty by then. There were five other men in the place, each sitting at a different table, nobody talking. Some had books in front of them, but I hadn't heard a page turn in a while. I was sitting near the fire and working steadily through a bowl of chili, mitigating it with plenty of crackers. I'd like to say Maggie's chili is the best in the West, but, to be frank, it isn't. It's probably not even the best in town: even this town, even now. I wasn't even very hungry, merely eating for something to do. Only alternative would have been drinking, but just a couple will go to my head these days, and I didn't want to be drunk. Being drunk has a tendency to make everything run into one long dirge, like being stoned, or living in Iowa. I haven't ever taken a drink on important days, on Thanksgiving, anniversaries or my birthday. Not a one. This evening wasn't any kind of celebration, not by a long shot, but I didn't want to be drunk on it either.

Jack walked up to the bar, water dripping from his coat and onto the floor. He wasn't moving fast, and he looked old and cold and worn through. It was bitter outside, and the afternoon had brought a fresh fall of snow. Only a couple of inches, but it was beginning to mount up. Maggie poured a cup of coffee without being asked, and set it in front of him. Her coffee isn't too bad, once you've grown accustomed to it. Jack methodically poured about five spoons of sugar into the brew, which is one of the ways of getting accustomed to it, then stirred it slowly. The skin on his hand looked delicate and thin, like blue-white tissue paper that had been scrunched into a ball and absently flattened out again.

93

Sixty-eight isn't so old, not these days, not in the general scheme of things. But some nights it can seem ancient, if you're living inside it. Some nights it can feel as if you're still trying to run long after the race is finished. At sixty-four, and the second youngest in the place, I personally felt older than God.

Jack stood for a moment, looking around the place as if memorising it. The counter itself was battered with generations of use, as was the rest of the room. The edges of chairs and tables were worn smooth, the pictures on the walls so varnished with smoke you'd had to have known them for forty years to guess what they showed. We all knew what they showed. The bulbs in the wall fixings were weak and dusty, giving the room a dark and gloomy cast. The one area of brightness was in the corner, where the jukebox sat. Was a big thing when Pete, my old friend and Maggie's late husband, bought it. But only the lights work these days, and not all of them, and none of us are too bothered. Nobody comes into the bar who wouldn't rather sit in peace than hear someone else's choice of music, played much too loud. I guess that comes with age, and anyway the 45s in the machine are too old to evoke much more than sadness. The floor was clean, and the bar only smelt slightly of old beer. You want it to smell that way a little, otherwise it would be like drinking in a church.

Maggie waited until Jack had caught his breath, then asked. Someone had to, I guess, and it was always going to be her. She said: 'No change?'

Jack raised his head, looked at her. 'Course there's a change,' he muttered. 'No-one said she weren't going to change.'

He picked up his coffee and came to sit on the other side of my table. But he didn't catch my eye, so I let him be, and cleared up the rest of my food, rejecting the raw onion garnish in deference to my innards. They won't stand for that kind of thing any more. It wasn't going to be long before a cost-benefit analysis of the chili itself consigned it to history alongside them.

When I was done I pushed the bowl to one side, burped as quietly as I could, and lit up a Camel. I left the pack on the table, so Jack could take one if he had a mind to. He would, sooner or later. The rest of the world may have decided that cigarettes are more dangerous than a nuclear war, but in Eldorado, Montana, a man's still allowed to smoke after his meal if he wants to. What are they going to do: come and bust us? The people who make the rules live a long ways from here, and the folk in this town have never been much for caring what State ordinances say.

One of the guys at the bar finished his beer, asked for another. Maggie gave him one, but didn't wait for any money. Outside, the wind picked up a little, and a door started banging, the sound like an unwelcome visitor knocking to be let out of the cellar. But it was a ways up the street, and you stopped noticing it after a while. It's not an uncommon sound in Eldorado.

Other than that, everyone just held their positions, and eventually Jack reached forward and helped himself to a cigarette. I struck a match for him, as his fingers still seemed numb and awkward. He still hadn't taken his coat off, though with the fire it was pretty warm in the room.

Once he was lit, and he'd stopped coughing, he nodded at me through the smoke. 'How's the chili?'

'Filthy,' I confirmed. 'But warm. Most of it.'

He smiled. He rested his hands on the table, palms down, and looked at them for a while. Liver spots and the shadow of old veins, like a fading map of territories once more uncharted. 'She's getting worse,' he said. 'Going to be tonight. Maybe already.'

I'd guessed as much, but hearing it said still made me feel tired and sad. He hadn't spoken loudly, but everybody else heard too. It got even quieter, and the tension settled deeper, like a dentist's waiting room where everyone's visiting for the first time in years and has their suspicions about what they're going to hear. Maybe 'tension' isn't the right word. That suggests someone might have felt there was something they could do, that some virile force was being held in abeyance, ready for the sign, the right time. There wasn't going to be any sign. This night had been a while in coming, but it had come, like a phone call in the night. We knew there wasn't anything to be done.

Maggie pottered around, put on a fresh jug of coffee. I started to stand up, meaning to get me a cup, but Jack put his hand on my arm. I sat back, waited for him to speak.

'Wondered if you'd walk with me,' he said.

I looked back at him, feeling a dull twinge of dread. 'Already?'

'Only really came down here to fetch you, if you had a mind to go.'

I realised in a kind of way that I was honoured. I took the heavy coat from the back of my chair and put it on. A couple heads raised to watch us leave, but most people turned away. Every one of them knew where we were going, the job we were going to do. Maybe you'd expect something to be said, the occasion to be marked in some way: but in all my life, of all the things I heard that were worth saying, none of them were actually said in words. And I ask you: what could anyone have said?

Outside it was even colder than I expected, and I stuffed my hands deep in my pockets and pulled my neck down into my scarf like a turtle. The snow was six inches deep in the street, and I was glad I had my thick boots on. The moon was full above, snow clouds hidden away someplace around a corner, recuperating and getting ready for more. There would be more, no doubt of that. The winters just keep getting colder and deeper around here, or so my body tells me. The winters are coming into their prime.

Jack started walking up the street, and I fell in beside him. Within seconds my long bones felt like they were being slowly twisted, and the skin on my face like it was made of lead. We walked past the old fronts, all of them dark now. The hardware store, the pharmacy, the old tea rooms. Even in light of day the painted signs are too faded to read, and the boardwalk which used to run the length of the street has rotted away to nothing. It happened like a series of paintings. One year it looked fine; then another it was tatty; then finally it was broken down and there was no reason to put it back. Sometimes, when I'd walked up the street in recent years, I would catch myself recalling the way things had once been, working my memory like a tongue worrying the site where a tooth had once sat. I could remember standing or sitting outside certain stores, the people who'd owned them, the faces of the people I'd spied from across the way. The times all tended to blend into one, and I could be the young boy running to the drug store, or the youth mooning over the younger of two sisters, or a man buying whiskey to blur the night away: switching back and forth in a blink, like one man looking out of three sets of eyes. It was like hearing a piece of music you grew up to, some tune you had in your head day after day until it was as much a part of your life as breathing. It was also a kind of time travel, and for a moment I'd feel as I once had, young and empty of darkness, ready to learn and experience and do. Eager to be shown what the world in store had for me, to conquer and make mistakes. To love, and lose, and love again. Amen.

Eldorado was founded in 1850 by two miners, Joseph and Ezekial Clarke: boys who came all the way from New Hampshire with nothing but a pair of horses and a dream. Sounds funny now, calling it a dream, probably even corny. People don't think of money that way any more. These days they think it's a right, and they don't go looking for it. They stay where they are, and try to make it come to them, instead of going off to find it for themselves. The brothers came in search of gold, like so many others. They were late on the trail, and worked through the foothills, finding nothing or stakes that had already been worked dry, and then climbed higher and higher into the mountains. They panned a local river, and found nothing once more, but then one afternoon came upon the seam—just as they were about to give up and move on, maybe head over to Oregon or California and see if it was paradise like everyone said. It must have seemed like magic. They found gold. When we were young we all heard the story. A kind of Genesis tale. A little glade, hidden up amidst the mountains at over three thousand feet: and there for the taking, a seam of money, a pocket of dreams.

The brothers stayed, and built themselves a cabin out of the good wood that grew all around. But news travelled fast, even in those days, and it wasn't long before they had company. A lot of company. The old mine workings have gone to ruin now, but it was a big old construction, I can tell you that. Was a few years when Eldorado was home to over four thousand people, and produced five million dollars a year in gold. The town had saloons and boarding houses, a post office and a fistful of gambling rooms, even a grand hotel. Almost all have fallen down now, though until ten years ago people still used the hotel to board their animals in, when it got real cold. Two walls are still more or less there, hidden amongst the trees, though I wouldn't want to stand underneath them for long. I once showed them to a couple of tourists who came up all this way in a rental car, having seen the town sign down the road. They seemed a little disappointed to find there were still people living here, and were soon on their way again.

That was near ten years ago, and no-one's come up to look since, though the town sign's still there. It says 'Eldorado, 15 miles', and stands on a turn of the local road from Giles to Covent Fort, though lately I swear the trees around it have been growing faster. Neither Giles nor Covent are much themselves these days, and the road between them isn't often used. If it weren't for that town sign, there would be no way of knowing we were up here at all.

When the gold ran out there was zinc for a while, and a little copper. The gold fever died away, but Eldorado continued to prosper for a while. There was a Masonic lodge built, and two banks, and a school house with a clock and a bell—the fanciest building in town, a symbol that there was a community here, and that we were living well. I can't even remember where the lodge was now, the banks are gone, and the school closed in 1957. I went to that school, learned most of what I know. Everybody did. It was the place where you turned into a grown-up, one year at a time, back when a year was as long as anyone could imagine, when two seemed like infinity. Probably that was why, for a long time, folks would stop by the abandoned school every now and then, by themselves and on the quiet, and do a little patching up. Wasn't any sense in it, because it wasn't going to reopen, not least because there were no new children—but I know I did it, and Jack did, and Pete before he died. Had to be that others did too, otherwise it would have fallen down a lot earlier than it did.

Michael Marshall Smith

Now it's gone, and even on the brightest Spring day that patch of the mountain seems awful quiet. I guess you could say that no-one here has learned anything since then. Certainly what you see on television doesn't seem to have much application to us. I stopped watching a long time ago, and I know I'm not the only one. TVs don't last forever, and there ain't no-one around here knows how to fix them. And anyway it just showed a world that isn't ours, and things that we can't buy and wouldn't want to, so what use was it anyway. We've got a few books, spread amongst us.

Eventually the copper ran out, and though people looked hard and long, there wasn't anything else useful to be found. The gambling dens moved on, in search of people who still had riches to throw away. The boarding houses closed soon afterwards, as those who hadn't made Eldorado their home moved on. Plenty people stayed, for a while. My folks did, in the 1920s. Never got to the bottom of why. But anyhow they came, and they stayed, and I followed in their footsteps, I guess, by staying here too. So did some others. But not enough. And nobody new.

Halfway down to the end of Main, Jack and I turned off the road and made our way as best we could up what used to be Fourth Street. I guess it still is, but you'd be hard pressed to find the first three, or the other eight, unless you'd once walked them, and gone visiting on them, or grown up in a house that used to stand on one. Now they've gone to trees and grass, just a few piles of lumber dotted around, like forgotten games of giant pick-up-sticks. You'd think people might have made an effort to keep the houses standing, even after people stopped living in them. But it's not the kind of thing that occurs to you until far too late, and then there doesn't seem a great deal of point. Spilt milk, stable door, all of those.

The grade has always been kind of steep on Fourth, and Jack and I both found the going hard. Jack had already made the trip once that night, and I let him go in front, following his footprints in the snow. There was another way of getting up to the house, a little less steep, but that involved going past the town's first cemetery, now overgrown, and the notion wasn't even discussed. Ahead of us, a single light shone in one of the upper windows of the Buckley house, which sits alone right at the end, a last stand against the oncoming trees. I felt sick to my stomach, remembering times I'd made the walk before, towards that grand old house hunkered beneath the wall of the mountain. Hundreds of times, but a handful of times in particular. My life often seems that way to me now. So much of it was just landscape I passed through, like a long open plain with little to distinguish the miles. Then there's like a little bag inside me, which I keep the real things in. A few smells, and sounds, touches like a faint summer breeze. Some evenings, a couple afternoons, and a handful of dawns, when I woke up somewhere I was happy to be, coddled warm with someone and protected from the bright light of day and tomorrow. But it's nights I remember most. Some bad, some good. You fall in love at night, and that's also when people die. Even if their last breath is drawn in daylight, by the time you've understood what's happened, the darkness has come to claim the event as its own. Nights last the longest, without doubt, both at the time and afterwards. They contain multitudes, and don't fade as easily as the sun. They're there, in my bag, and I'll take them with me when I go.

When we got to the house we stomped the snow off our boots on the porch, and then let ourselves in. Over the last few weeks of visiting I had gotten used to the dust, how it overlaid the way the house had used to be. She'd kept it up as well as she could over the years, but now you could almost hear it running down, like the wind dropping after a storm. The downstairs was empty but for Naomi's cat, who was sitting in the middle of the hall, looking at the wall. It glanced up at us as we started on the stairs, then walked slowly away into the darkness of the kitchen.

I knew then that it was already over.

When we reached the upper landing, we hesitated outside the doorway to the bedroom, as if feeling we had to be invited in. The interior was lit by candles, with an old kerosene lamp by the window. The Doc was sitting on a blanket box at the end of the bed, elbows on his knees. He looked like an old man, very tired, waiting for a train to take him home. Not much like someone who'd once been the second-fastest runner in town, after me, a boy who could run like the wind. He'd gone away, many years ago. Left town, got trained up, spent some years out there in the other places. Half the books in town were his, brought with him when he came back to Eldorado.

He looked up, beckoned us in with an upward nod of the head. We approached like a pair of children, with short steps and hands down by our sides. I kept my eyes straight ahead, knowing there'd be a time to look after the words had been said.

Jack rested a hand on the Doc's shoulder. 'She wake at all?'

He shook his head. 'Just died. That's all she did.'

'So that's it,' I said.

The three of us sighed then, all together. Nothing long, or melodramatic. Just an exhalation, letting out what had once been inside us.

The Doc started to speak, faltered. Then tried again. 'Maybe it's not going to happen,' he said, trying for a considered tone, but coming out querulous and afraid. 'After all, how do we know?'

Jack and I shook our heads. Wasn't any use in this line of thought. Nobody knew how we knew. But we knew. We'd known since the children stopped coming.

We walked around on separate sides of the bed, and looked down. I don't know what Jack was looking at, but I can tell you what I saw. An old woman, face lined, though less so than when I'd seen her in the afternoon of the previous day. Death had levelled the foothills of her suffering, filled in the dried stream beds of age. The coverlet was pulled up to just under her chin, so she looked tucked up nice and warm. The shape beneath the blankets was so thin it barely seemed to be there at all: it could have been just a runkle in the sheets, covering nothing more than cooling air. Most of all she looked still, like a mountain range seen from the sky.

Wasn't the first time I'd seen someone dead, not nearly. I saw my own parents laid out, inexplicably cold and quiet, and my wife, and many of my friends. There's been a lot of dying hereabouts over the last few years, every passing marked and mourned. But Naomi looked different.

It's funny how, when you first know someone, it will be the face you notice most of all. The eyes, the mouth, the way they have their hair. Everybody has the same number of limbs, but their face is their own. Then, over the years, it's as if this part of them leaves their body and goes into your head, crystallises there. You hardly notice what the years are doing, the way people's real faces thicken and dim and change. Every now and then something brings you up short, and makes you see the way things have become. Then you lose it again, almost as quick as it came, and you just see the continuity, the essence behind the face. The person as they were.

I saw Naomi as she and her sister had once been, the two brightest sparks in Eldorado, the girls most likely to make you lose your stride and catch your breath—whether you were fifteen, same as them, or so old that your balls barely still had their wits about them. I saw her as the little lady who could shout loudest in the playground, who could give you a Chinese burn you'd remember for days. I saw her as I had when Pete and I used to hike up Fourth with flowers in our hands and our hearts in our throats, when Pete was cautiously dating Naomi, and I was going with her sister Sarah, who was two years younger and much prettier, or so I thought back then.

It's that year that many of the nights I keep in my bag came from, that brings faint memories of music to my head. Sarah and I came to a parting of the ways before Thanksgiving, and she eventually married Jack, had no children but generally seemed content, and died in 1984. Pete and Naomi lasted a couple more months than we had, and then Pete met Maggie and things changed. Five years later, both on rebounds from different people altogether, gloriously grouchy and full of cheap liquor, Naomi and I spent a night walking together through the woods which used to stop on the edge of town. We looked for the stream where the Clarkes first panned, and maybe even found it, and we didn't do anything more than kiss, but that was exciting enough. Then the morning came, and brought its light, and everything was burned away. We'd never have been right for each other anyhow, that was clear, and it wasn't the way it was supposed to be. Of course a decade or two later, when I first started to look back upon my life and read it properly, like a book I should have paid more attention to the first time, I realised that this might have been wrong. When I thought back, it was always Naomi's face that was clearest in my mind, though she'd been Pete's and I'd been Sarah's and anyhow both futures were long in the past and dead and buried half a lifetime ago. By then Naomi was married, and when we met we were polite. Almost as if that current which can pass between any two people, the spark of possibility, however small, had been used up all in that night in the woods, underused and thrown away, and now we could be nothing but friends. Naomi never had children either, nor Maggie. None of us did.

Even now, when the forest has started to march its way right up Main Street, I can remember that night with her as if I'm still wearing the same clothes and haven't had time to change. Remember also the way the sisters always seemed to glow, all of their lives, as if they were running on more powerful batteries than the rest of us, as if whoever had stirred their bodies into being had been more practised at the art than whoever did the rest of us. I loved my wife a great deal, and we had many good years together, but as I get older it's like those middle years were a long game we all played, a long and complex game of indeterminate rules. Those seasons fade, and we return to the playground like tired ghosts coming home after a long walk, and it's how we were then that seems most important. I can't remember much of what happened last year, but I can still picture those girls when we were young. On the boardwalk, in the big old house their father built, around the soda fountain when they were still little girls and we were all sparkling and young and blessed, a crop of new flowers bursting into life in a field which would always be there.

Almost all of those people are dead now. Distributed amongst the two cemeteries, biding their time, like broken panes in the windows of an old building. A few of the windows are still intact, like me and Jack and Maggie and all, but you have to wonder why. There's nothing to see through us now.

When Jack and I had looked down on Naomi a while, and nothing had changed, we turned away from the bed. The Doc had quietly gotten his things together, but didn't look ready to leave just yet.

'There's something me and Bill have to do,' Jack said. 'Only stopped by for the truck. And, well, you know.'

The Doc nodded, not really looking at us. He knew what we were going to do. 'I'll stay a while,' he said. Back in '72 there'd been something going on between him and Naomi. He probably didn't realise that we knew. But everybody did. Then after her husband died in '85 oftentimes the Doc had taken his evening meal at the Buckley table. I'd always wondered if it might be me who did that. Didn't work out that way.

'What are we going to do about her cat?' I asked.

'What can anyone do about a cat?' the Doc said, with the ghost of a smile. 'Reckon it'll do pretty much what it wants. I'll feed it, though.'

We shook his hand, not really knowing why, and left the house.

Jack's truck was parked around the side. It wasn't going to be a picnic getting down the hill, but it was too far to walk. We got it started after only a couple of tries, and Jack nosed her carefully out into the ruts of the street. Fate was kind to us, and we got down to main without much more than a spot of grief. Turned right, away from the bar, away from what's left of the town.

When we drew level with the other cemetery, Jack slowed to a halt and turned the engine off.

We sat with the windows down for a while, smoking and listening. It was mighty cold. Wasn't anything to hear apart from wind up in the mountains, and the rustle of trees bending our way. Beyond the fence the stones and wooden crosses marched away in ranks into the night. Friends, parents, lovers, children, in their hundreds. A field full of the way things might have been, or had been once, and could never be again. Folks are dead for an awfully long time. The numbers mount up.

Jack turned, looked at me. 'We're sure, aren't we?'

'Yes,' I said. 'We've been outnumbered for a long, long while. After Naomi, there's only fifteen of us left.'

It felt funny, Jack turning to me, wanting to be reassured. I still remembered him as one of the big kids, someone I hoped I might be like one day. I did grow up to be like him, then older'n he'd once been, and then just old, exactly like him. Everything seemed so different back then, everyone so distinct from one another. Just your haircut can make you a different colour, when everyone's only got ten years of experience to count on. Then you get older, and everyone seems the same. Everybody gets whittled away at about the same rate. Like the '50s, and '60s, and '70s and '80s, times that once seemed so different to each other, but are now just stuff that happened to us once and then went away; like good weather or a stomach ache.

Jack stared straight out the windshield for a while. 'I don't hear anything.'

'May not happen for hours,' I said. 'No way of telling. May not even happen tonight.'

He laughed quietly. 'You think so?'

'No,' I admitted. 'It'll happen tonight. It's time.'

I thought then that I might have heard something, out there in the darkness, the first stirring beyond the fence. But if I did, it was quiet, and nothing came of it right then. It was only midnight. There was plenty of darkness left.

Jack nodded slowly. 'Then I guess we might as well get it over with.'

We smiled at each other, briefly, like two boys passing in the school yard. Boys who grew to like each other, and who could never have realised that they'd be sharing such a task, on a far-away night such as this.

Later we'd drive back up into town, park outside Maggie's bar, and sit inside with the others and wait. She was staying open for good that night. But first we went down the hill, down a rough track to an old road hardly anyone drove any more.

We got out the truck and stood a while, looking down the mountain at a land as big as Heaven, and then together we took down the town sign.

What You Make It

Finding a child was easy. It always was. You waited outside one of the convenience stores that lined the approach, or trawled a strip mall at the nearby intersections for half an hour. There were always kids hanging around at night, panhandling change for a burger or twenty minutes on a coin-op video game in one of the arcades. Or sometimes just hanging there, with nothing in particular in prospect. You have to have seen something of the world to know what's worth looking for. These kids, the just-hanging kids, had seen nothing—and were mainly willing to be shown pretty much whatever you had in mind.

The only question was which one to pick. Too old, either age, and it looked weird at the Gate. Too young, and people tend to wonder where the kid's mother is at. And of course sometimes it depended, and you had to find one that looked just right for the night. Early teens was usually best, acquiescent, not too scuffed up.

It only took Ricky ten minutes to find one. She was sitting by herself on one of the benches outside the Subway franchise, looking at her feet or nothing in particular, alone in a yellow glow. Ricky cruised by the sandwich store twice in the twilight, noted that though there were two groups of kids nearby, one just a little along the sidewalk and another loitering outside Publix, the girl didn't seem to have a link to either. He parked the car up, let the motor tick down to silence, and watched her a little while. The nearest group of kids walked right by her, in and out of her pool of light, without a word being exchanged. She didn't even look up. She wasn't expecting friends.

Ricky grabbed his cigarettes off the dash, locked the car, and walked over to her.

She glanced at him as he approached, but not with much curiosity. Something told him that this wasn't indifference, but a genuine ignorance of the kind of situations the world could provide. This meant she was even more likely to be what he needed, and it was just good luck for her that it was Ricky's eye she'd caught, instead of some kind of fucking pervert.

'Waiting for someone?' he asked, stopping when he was a couple of yards away. She looked up, then away. Didn't even shake her head. He took the last few steps, sat down casually on the next bench along. 'Right. I know. Just a good place to sit.'

There was no response. Ricky took out a cigarette and lit it, unhurried. She looked maybe twelve years old, pretty face. Blue eyes, fair hair in a ponytail. White T-shirt, blue jeans. Both recently clean. He noticed her eyes follow his match as it skittered across the way and went out. Despite appearances, he had her attention.

'You hungry?'

She blinked, and her head turned a little way towards him. Something changed. It always did. It's a very elemental question. Even if you've just eaten enough to kill a man, you think about it. Am I hungry? Have I had enough? Will I be okay? And if you're really hungry, the question comes at you like you've just been goosed, like someone's just guessed your worst secret, how close you are to being cancelled out. Ricky knew how it worked. He'd been hungry. You answered the hungry question quietly, so the vultures wouldn't hear.

'Kinda,' she said, eventually.

He nodded, looking out across the parking lot for a while. Partly to check how many couples were hefting grocery bags to their breeder wagons; mainly just to let the conversation settle.

'I could buy you something,' he said then, casually. 'What's the matter? Your mom didn't feed you tonight?'

'Don't have a mom,' she said.

'What about your old man? Where's he at?'

The girl shrugged. Didn't matter whether she didn't know or just didn't want to know. Ricky knew she was his.

Ten minutes later, as he watched her wolf down her sandwich and fries, Ricky asked the big question.

'How'd you like to visit Wonder World tonight?'

It was well after eight by the time they got to the entrance. The queue was pretty short. Ricky knew it would be: they had a parade every night at eight-thirty, down 1st Street, and anyone with park-visiting in mind made sure they were already inside by then. Even the girl, whose name was Nicola, knew about the parade. Ricky told her that this week it was at nine-fifteen because it was a special parade. She looked at him dubiously, but seemed hopeful.

As he turned into one of the lanes and pulled up to the gate Ricky felt a familiar flicker of anxiety. This was the part where it could all go wrong. It hadn't yet, because the kids had always wanted what they thought they were getting, but it could. It could go wrong tonight. It could do wrong any time. He wound the window down.

The gate man's head immediately bobbed down to grin at him. 'Hi there! I'm Marty the Gateman! How you doing?'

Marty the Gateman was in his late fifties, and dressed in an exaggerated version of the uniform of a cop from the 1940s. His face was pink with good cheer or makeup. Or alcohol most likely, Ricky thought. The other gatemen in all the other lanes looked the same, and said exactly the same things.

Ricky grinned right back. 'I'm good. You?'

'Me? I'm great!' the man said, and then laughed uproariously. When he did this, he leant back from the waist, placed a splayed hand on either side of his ribcage, and rubbed them up and down with each chortle, like a cartoon. Nicola giggled, twisted in her seat.

Ricky let one hand drop to where the gun rested down between the seat and the door, waited for the man to stop. Fucking loser. He imagined the guy going home after his shift, taking off his stupid fucking costume, whacking off in front of the television or a stack of porno. He had to do something like that. Rick knew *he* would have done, that's for sure. Couldn't be any other way.

Eventually the man stopped laughing, wiped his eyes. 'Shee! So! Two happy travelers for Wonder World! You just here for rides and fun and all the magic you can find?'

'No,' Nicola said, leaning over Ricky so she could smile up at him through the window. 'We're visiting Grandma too!'

Ricky relaxed. The girl was going to behave. Better still, she'd got into the part. They did, sometimes. Kids loved make-believe.

Marty winked. 'Lucky grandma! She know you're coming?'

'It's a surprise,' Nicola said, confidingly. 'She lives in Homeland 3.'

'Okey dokey!' the gate man yelped joyously, pulling a deck of tickets out of one of the oversize pockets on his uniform. 'So, Mr Dad—how long you going to be spending with us?'

'An hour, maybe two,' Rick smiled. 'Depends on how strong Grandma's feeling.'

'Why don't we say three? Can always get you a rebate when you come out.'

'Sure, Marty. That'd be great.'

Michael Marshall Smith

'All-righty!' Tongue sticking out of the corner of his mouth, Marty the Gateman tapped some buttons on the control unit on the side of his booth. As he tapped, the buttons got a little larger, and started moving around, so he had to keep his hand darting back and forth to keep up. Two twinkling animatronic eyes appeared at the top of the control unit, and one of them winked at Nicola. Within a few seconds the buttons, which were brightly coloured in primary hues, were a few inches long and bending every which way. Still the man poked at them, huffing and puffing.

'Hey!' he said, and Nicola laughed, when a couple of the buttons got even longer and started poking him back. When this gag was done, the gate man held a ticket out towards the machine, a slit opened in the unit in the shape of a cheerful mouth, and the ticket was popped inside, chewed for a moment, and then spat out, authorised. The eye winked at Nicola again, and then suddenly the control unit returned to normal and Marty was waggling the ticket right under Ricky's nose.

Any other time or place, Marty would have lost his hand. But Ricky gave him the money, and the gate opened. The gate man waved at Nicola through the back window.

As the car started to pull forward, all of the faces in the gate structure—each a classic character from a Wonder World cartoon, every one hand-tweaked by liars into joyous perfection—swiveled their eyes towards the car and started to sing.

China Duck was there, Loopy Hound and Careful Cat, Bud and Slap the Happy Rats and Goren the fucking Gecko and countless others, every face already hot-wired into your mind no matter how hard you'd always ignored them.

'The magic is what you make it,' they sang, a sonic tower of saccharine harmonies, 'Make it, make it... The magic is what you...'

Ricky wound the windows up.

Lit a cigarette and stepped on the gas.

The kid was quiet as they headed towards Homeland 3. She had plenty to look at, and she drank it in as though even in darkness it was the greatest thing she had ever seen. Maybe it was. Unlike her, Ricky had seen it all before.

Monorail tracks arced gracefully in all directions, linking park to park. Mostly quiet for the evening, but occasionally a streamlined shape would swoosh past the road or over their heads. Taking happy families out, or back, for the evening: out to ridiculous themed restaurants, or back to dumb-looking resort hotels where over-excited kids would make so much noise you'd want to throttle them, and parents would reconcile themselves to another night without screwing and send out for room service booze instead. Probably even that was delivered by a fucking chipmunk.

Actually, Ricky had never stayed in one of the hotels. Never even been in one: the security was too good. But he felt he knew exactly how it would be. A great big stupid con, like everything else in Wonder World. Set up fifty years ago, and now so vast and sprawling it put most cities in the shade. Rides and enclosures and parks and theatres and 'experiences' and crap, all based around a bunch of cartoons and some asshole's idea of the perfect world. There was a fake big game reservation. A bunch of fake lakes, where fish and dolphins and shit swam about, like anyone cared. A fake downtown strip the size of a whole town, where people who were too scared to walk to the corner store in their own stupid bergs could wander around and buy up all the shit they wanted. Some sort of stupid futuristic park, where it was supposed to be like what it would be in a hundred years: like we were all going to be shopping from home and wearing pastel nylon and using video phones—standing in tight little nuclear family groups and talking to Gramps on Mars.

Ricky knew what it was really going to be like in a hundred years, and it wasn't going to be cutesy characters walking around, posing for photographs and making the little kids laugh. It wasn't going to be restaurants where the family could go and get good food and great service for ten bucks a head; it wasn't going to be endless fucking stores full of T-shirts and candy in painted tins, and being able to leave your door unlocked at night and no litter anywhere. It was going to be guns, and stealing things. It was going to be dog eat dog, and he wasn't talking the kind of dog that had some fuckass pimply kid inside, earning chump change for blow. It was going to be taking what you wanted, and fucking up anyone who got in your way. It was getting that way already, and only fools pretended otherwise. That's what kids needed to learn, not crap about talking bunnies. Wonder World pained Ricky personally, which is one of the reasons why he did what he did for a living. He hated the bright colours, the cheer, the stupid, kiddie nonsense, the lies about how the world really was, the conspiracy to believe that there was magic somewhere in the world. He hated it all.

It was a crock of utter shit.

The kid was good as he drove, even though weird and miraculous buildings kept appearing in the darkness, each promising fun and games. She didn't ask to stop at every one, like most of them did. She kept quiet until the car swung around in the front of the massive portal into the heart of Wonder World, the original Beautiful Realm park. The gate was like a massive googie castle, every ludicrous '50s drive-in and coffee shop-erama mashed joyously together into an eight-story extravagance that would have taken the Jetsons' breath away. Whirling spotlights sent beams of light chopping merrily through the night, and characters capered around the entrance, beckoning people in. The girl had wound her window back down by then, and could hear in the distance the sound of drums and music, the singing and dancing inside.

'The parade,' she said.

He shrugged. 'Fuckers did it early. Or maybe it's just beginning.'

She was calm, reasonable. 'You said we'd see the parade.'

'We will. It goes on for, like, an hour. We'll just do this thing, and then we'll go catch the end. It's better that way. Most of the people have gone home, you get closer to all the characters.'

'Really?' She was looking at him closely, her mouth wanting to smile, but nervous of being let down. Just then one of the lights cut through into the car, showing her in every detail. Pretty little face, red lips that had never been kissed. Big eyes, wanting him to tell her good news, wanting to see nice things.

And tiny new breasts outlined in a T-shirt one size too small. She was perfect, all the more so because she wouldn't even understand what he was thinking.

Ricky decided this one was going to play the game a little longer than most of the others, that she going to learn the facts of life. The facts that had to do with taking whatever he wanted to put inside her. A training session. Save some guy time and effort later on, except Ricky knew there wasn't going to be a later. Usually he lay the kid over the back seat on the way out, put a blanket over them like they were just sleeping, winked at some guy at the gate and laughed with him about how the child had too much excitement for one day. Tonight he'd find a way of getting this one out alive. He'd work it out.

'Really,' he said. 'Trust me.'

She smiled.

Ten minutes later he was scanning street names as he cruised slowly down Homeland 3's main drag. Every now and then they'd pass a toon character, who'd stop and wave at Nicola. Ranging from three foot dancing toadstools to six-foot ducks, they were freaking Ricky out. You didn't normally see characters roaming this late: they were only there to magic the place up through the day, during the most popular visiting hours. Ricky was having trouble sorting through the names of the streets, which were also the names of fucking characters. Loopy Drive IV, Careful Crescent VI, how the fuck were you supposed to keep track? Nicola wasn't helping, having decided to tell him her life story. She was thinking of shortening her name, and spelling it Nicci, because she thought it was classy and presumably didn't know how Gucci was actually pronounced. She liked cats, like Careful Cat, but dogs were sometimes cute too. She didn't know where daddy was because she'd never known. She said she didn't have a mommy because real mommies didn't do what hers did, and so two days ago she'd run away from home and she wasn't going back this time.

Jesus, only two days, Ricky was thinking. Are you lucky you ran into me so quick. Going to save you six months of turning into your mommy, then a short lifetime waiting for the hammer to fall. You're a lucky girl, little Nicola. Lucky, lucky, lucky.

Part of him was also shaking, because of what he knew he was going to do later. He didn't normally do it. He just disposed of them. Take a drive down the 'glades, dump the body, no-one's going to know or give a shit. He didn't like doing anything else, made him feel like a pervert though he wasn't, he was a professional. Every now and then was okay though, even if it was clouding his mind right now, making it hard to make the street names out. Some guys bought themselves new guns, went on a coke bender, hired a couple of whores. Everyone needs a treat. Incentive scheme. Keeps your wheels turning.

Ricky gripped the wheel tightly, tuned out the noise of the kid's nattering, got himself straight. Eventually he got himself in what looked like the right direction. Found his way down the grid of streets, each lined with houses, some streets like the 1940s, some the 1950s or 1960s. Or like those times would have been if they hadn't been shit, anyhow. Like those decades were if you looked back at them now and forgot everything that was wrong with them. The streets were quiet, because mostly the people in the houses were too old to be out walking this late.

Homeland 3, along with the four other near-identical districts that spread in a fan around the Beautiful Realm, was one of the newest parts of the Wonder World. Five years ago, the suits who ran the parks realised they had yet another goldmine on their hands: managed communities of old farts. Cutesy little neighbourhoods in the sun, where the oldsters could come waste their final years, safe from the world outside and bad afternoons where they could be walking home from the store they'd used all their lives and suddenly find three guys with knifes standing on the corner. Not only safe, but coddled, living somewhere where their grandkids could be guaranteed to want to come see them. You want to go visit granny in Roanoke? I don't think so. Wonder World?—that's a pretty easy sell. They built the houses, any size, any style, so everyone from trailer trash to leather-faced zillionaires had somewhere to hang their trusses: houses that looked like whatever you wanted from a space podule to a mud hut on the planet Zog. All this and stores and banks and shit, all built to look like what they sold. That's what made it so difficult to find your way around. Was like being in a toy store on acid.

It got so popular that even the smallest houses started getting expensive, and a year ago Ricky had an idea. You've got house after house of old people. With money. People who can't defend themselves too well. With things worth stealing. You get yourself into one of the Homelands—with a cute kid, who's going to question you?—and you help yourself to some stuff, using the kid's voice to get the door open. You're in and out before anyone knows there's a few old people gone to meet their maker sooner than intended: kid's the only living witness, and not for very long. All you got to do is make sure you never get recognised at the gate, and with millions of people going in and out every week, it's never going to happen.

And the kicker—Wonder World covered the burglaries up. Of course they did. Very bad for business, because they showed the magic retreat was a crock of shit. Plus, and here Ricky witnessed something which made perfect sense to him, something which placed the whole world in context as he understood it—the families often didn't make too much fuss. Why? Same reason that, after a couple months, Ricky had a new idea and moved onto a different line of business, made himself a professional.

Lot of times the families weren't exactly too sad to see the old folks go, because they wanted the old people's money. Which is why Ricky didn't bother to steal any more. Now Ricky took contracts instead, made it look natural. Much safer, more secret, more lucrative—for the time being. Sooner or later the suits would catch on and increase security somehow, and Ricky would move out, and start blackmailing the families instead. Even the kind of people who'd pay to have gramps whacked had to be living in a Wonder World of their own, if they didn't realise it would come back to haunt them some day.

Ricky finally found Gecko Super Terrace III, drove a little way along it. Pulled over to the curb, looked up at a house and checked the address. Grunted with satisfaction. He was in the right place.

Margaret Harris, eighty-four years old, was worth maybe three hundred and fifty thousand dollars, all told, including the Homeland house. Not such a hell of a lot, but her son and daughter-in-law could get the bigger boat a couple years earlier, and without working all those unsociable hours and missing cocktail hour. Upgrade the satellite, get a widescreen TV for the den. Maybe they'd throw their children a bone too. A games station. A bike. A last visit to Wonder World.

As John Harris, the son, had put it while slurping a large Scotch to blur his conscience: they were just realising an unwanted asset.

Margaret Harris had herself a kind of tiny Tudor mansion, dark beams and whitewash, exaggerated leans in the walls and gingerbread thatch. There was a light on in a downstairs room, behind a curtain. The grass in the front yard was all the same perfect fucking length. Maybe it was animatronic grass. Maybe it sang a happy wake-up call in the morning, a million blades in unison.

Nicola looked at the house too. 'Is this where she lives?'

'That's right. You remember what I want you to do?'

She looked away, didn't answer for a moment.

'I had a grandma,' she said, in a moment. 'I saw her twice. She gave me a ring, but Mommy took it. She died when I was six. Mommy got so drunk she wet herself.'

Ricky nearly hit her then, but stopped himself just in time. It was like that with the ones like her. Part of wanting to fuck them was finding them just too fucking irritating to bear. He forced himself to speak calmly. 'This isn't your Grandma, okay? Do you remember, Nicola? What I want you to do?'

'Of course,' the girl said. She opened the door and got out.

Swearing quietly, Ricky got out his side, slipped the gun into his pocket, then followed her up the path to the Harris house.

Nicola rang the doorbell a second time, and Ricky heard someone moving inside the house. He stepped back into shadow. Nicola stood in front of the door, waiting.

'Who is it?' The voice was old, cracked but not quavery. The kind of voice that says I'm pretty old but not ready to drop just yet.

'Hi grandma!' Nicola piped, leaning forward to peer through the diamond of swirled glass in the door. She waved her hand. 'I've come to see you!'

'Theresa?' The oldster's voice was uncertain, but Ricky caught the sound of locks being tentatively drawn. This was the second key moment. This was the moment where the kid had to be good enough so that the old woman didn't press the Worry Button put beside the door of every Homeland house. The button that would alert Wonder World's version of security that something was sharp and spikey in the dream tonight.

The final slide bolt, and the door opened a crack. 'Theresa?'

Margaret Harris was small, maybe five feet tall. She was grandma-shaped and had white hair done up in a curly style. Her face was plump and lined and she was wearing one of those dresses that old people wear, flowers on a dark background. You opened a dictionary and looked up 'Grandma' and she was pretty much what you'd see.

'You're not Theresa,' she said.

'Oh no,' Nicola laughed. 'I'm Theresa's friend. Theresa said if we were passing by we should call in and say hello.'

Ricky stepped into the light, an apologetic smile on his face. 'Hi there, Mrs Harris. Hope this is okay—Theresa's telling Nicola here about you all the time. John said you probably wouldn't mind. Meant to call ahead, but you know how it is.'

'You're a friend of John's?'

'Work right across the hall from him at First Virtual.'

Mrs Harris hesitated a final moment, then smiled back, her face crinkling in a pattern which started from the eyes. 'Well I guess it's okay then. Come on in.'

The hallway looked like a painted background from an old Wonder World cartoon: higgledy stairs, everything neat, colours washed and clean. When the door was shut behind them, Ricky knew the job was done.

'You can't be too careful these days,' the old woman said, predictably, leading Nicola through to the kitchen to make some coffee. Right, thought Ricky, following at a distance: and you haven't been careful enough.

He hung outside for a moment, scoping the place, listening with half an ear to the sound of Nicola chatting with the old bag in the kitchen. Jeez, the kid could lie: what's happening at school, party she went to with Theresa last week, Theresa borrowing her shoes. Listening to her, you'd think she really *did* know the woman's granddaughter. Make believe again, some life she wished she had.

Ricky debated disabling the Worry Button, finally decided it wasn't necessary. Difficult to do, anyhow—and just smashing it would leave a clue. This one was too easy to make it worth taking the risk.

The kitchen was small, cosy, tricked up to look like the kind of place where there would always be something in the oven, instead of ready-made shit in the microwave. Pots, pastry cutters, a rolling pin. Probably Wonder World sent someone into everyone's house every day, made sure the props looked just right. Grandma Harris turned as Ricky entered and handed a cup of coffee up to him. She smiled, twinkle-eyed, relaxed—the kid had put her at ease.

Ricky made a mental note that the cup and saucer would need wiping when he was done. Nicola had a glass of Dr Pepper—that would need washing too. He sipped the coffee—might as well—and deflected a couple of questions about working with the great John Harris. Pathetic, really, the way the old woman was eager for any news of her son, wanted telling how people liked him. Suddenly he just wanted to lash out and shove his cup right down the old fart's throat. It would be a whole lot quicker, and put her out of misery she didn't even know she was in. But he knew how it had to look, and death by ingestion of china tea set wouldn't play.

Meantime Nicola and grandma sat at the table, yakking nineteen to the dozen. Nicola had a lot of grandma-talking to do, even if she had to make do with someone else's. Ricky let his eyes glaze over, mulling what he was going to do to the kid later. He enjoyed doing that, getting the comparison, just like he liked looking at girls in the street and imagining them on the job, their hands or mouth busy, face wet with sweat. They'd never know, but they'd been his. Ricky rode that line, that fine line, between the life they lived and the life that could come and find them in the night.

'Isn't that right, Daddy?'

'Huh?' Ricky looked at the girl dully, having missed the question. 'What's that?'

'Nicola was just saying how you and John were planning a joint vacation for the families later in the year,' Mrs Harris said. 'That's wonderful news. Do you think you might be able to make it up here again? We'd have such fun.'

'Sure,' Ricky said, abruptly deciding this had gone on long enough and was getting out of hand. 'No question. Hey, Mrs Harris—meant to ask you something.'

'Of course.' Grandma was beside herself at the prospect of another visit later in the year. She'd have agreed to anything. 'What is it?'

'John told me about some pictures, old photos, you've got at the top of the stairs? Kind of an interest of mine. He said you might not mind me taking a peek at them.'

'I'd be delighted,' the old woman beamed. 'Come, let's go up.' Nicola jumped to her feet, but Ricky flashed a glare at her.

Grandma raised an eyebrow. 'Wouldn't you like to come too, dear?'

Nicola avoided Ricky's eye. 'Could I have another Dr Pepper first?'

'Help yourself, then follow us up. Now come on—Rick, isn't

it?—let's go take a look.'

Ricky sent another 'Stay here' look at the kid, followed grandma out. Made interested grunts every now and then as the old woman talked and led him across the hall to the stairs. A couple of objects caught Ricky's eye on the way, and he planned on picking them up later, before he left. Little bonus.

Up the stairs behind her. Feeling very little. No fear, no excitement. Just watching for the best moment. Mrs Harris walked up the stairs slowly, hitching one leg up after the other. Her voice might be strong but her body was saying goodbye. She wouldn't be losing much.

They got to the first landing, and Ricky saw that there were indeed a whole bunch of really fucking dull-looking black and whites in frames there on the wall. John Harris had the whole thing planned out, gave Ricky this way of getting her up to the scaffold. Ricky debated telling the old woman about that, letting her see what lay beyond her wonder world, that the son she'd raised had sat in his study one night drinking cheap Scotch and working it all out. But by then Margaret Harris was standing right by him, and he knew the time was right and he wanted to get it over with. The real bonus was waiting for him in the kitchen. He didn't need any cheap thrills first.

This picture was her mother, that one her grandpapa. Gone-away people, stiff in fading monotone.

Ricky leaned towards her, apparently to get a closer look at a bunch of people grouped in front of a raggedy farm building—but actually to get the right angle.

For a moment then he was distracted, by a scent. It seemed to come from the old woman's clothes, and was a combination of things: of milk and cinnamon, rich coffee and apples cooking on the stove. Leaves barely on the trees in Autumn, and the smell of sun on grass in Summer. These things weren't a part of his life, but for a moment he had them in his mind—like they were part of some story he'd read long ago, as a child, and just dismissed.

Then he pushed her down the stairs.

Palm flat against her shoulder, feeling the bones inside the old, thin flesh. He straightened his arm firmly, which was enough—and wouldn't leave a bruise that some forensic smartass might be able to talk up into evidence.

The old woman teetered, without making a sound, and then her centre of gravity was all wrong and she just tumbled over sideways, over the edge and down the stairs.

Thump, crash, thud, splat. Like a loose bag of sticks.

WHAT YOU MAKE IT

Ricky walked briskly down the stairs after her, reached the bottom bare seconds after she did. Held back from kicking her head, which would have been risky and was clearly unnecessary. Huge dent in the skull already, eyes turned upwards and out of sight. Arm twisted a strange way, one leg bent back on itself. The usual anti-climax.

Job done.

He stepped quickly over the body and to the kitchen, stopping Nicola already on her way out. She ran into him, crashed against his body. He grabbed her shoulders, warm through the thin T-shirt.

'What happened? I heard a crash.'

Usually he killed the kid at this point, before they got hysterical and made too much noise or ran out of the house. Ricky pushed Nicola gently back into the kitchen, felt his temperature rising. Needed her alive to do things with, but he couldn't do them here. 'Nothing. Just an accident. Mrs Harris fell down the stairs.'

'Grandma?'

'She's not your grandma, sweetie. You know that.'

'We've got to get help...'

Ricky smiled down at her. 'We will. That's exactly what we'll do. We'll get in the car, go find one of the security wagons. They'll help her out. She'll get fixed up and we'll catch the end of the parade.'

The girl was near tears. 'I want to stay here with her.'

He pretended to think about it, then shook his head. 'Can't do that. Security gets here while I'm away, find you with an old lady at the bottom of the stairs, what they going to think? They're going to think you pushed her.'

'They won't. She was my grandma. Why would I hurt her?'

Ricky glared at her, good humour fast disappearing. 'She wasn't your fucking grandma. Just some old woman.'

Nicola pushed hard against him, momentarily rocking him on his heels. 'She was *too*. She knew about me. She knew things. She said not to worry about my mom any more. She said she loved me.'

Ricky lashed out with his hand, shoved the kid hard. She flew back, ricocheted off the table and knocked the coffee pot flying. It struck the wall, spraying brown gunk everywhere, just as Nicola crashed to the floor. Ricky cursed himself. Not clever. Just going to make it more difficult to get her out of the house, plus it was going to look like signs of a struggle. He took a deep breath, stepped towards her. Maybe he was going to have to just kill her after all.

'Nicola? Are you okay, dear?'

Ricky froze, foot just hitting the floor. Turned slowly round.

Grandma stood in the doorway. One eye fluttered slowly, the one below the huge dent that pulled most of the side of her face out of kilter. The arm was still bent way out of place. Her body was completely fucked up, but somehow she'd managed to drag herself to the door, to her feet.

Nicola struggled into a sitting position against the wall behind Ricky. 'Grandma—are you alright?'

Of course she's not fucking alright, Ricky thought. No way.

Grandma leant against the doorframe, as if tired. 'I'm fine, dear. Just had a little fall, isn't that right Rick?' Her working eye fixed on him.

Ricky felt the hairs on the back of his neck rise like a thousand tiny erections. Then her other eye stopped flickering. Closed for a moment, re-opened—and then he had two strong eyes looking at him. Tough old bitch.

Ricky reached for the table, grabbed the rolling pin lying there. This job was getting very fucked up, but he was going to finish it now.

'Close your eyes, dear,' Grandma said. She wasn't talking to him, but the kid. 'Would you do that, for Grandma? Just close your eyes for a while.'

'Close them tight?' Nicola asked, voice small.

'Yes, close them extra tight,' Grandma nodded, trying to smile. 'And I'll tell you when you can open them again.'

Ricky saw the girl shut her eyes and cover her ears. He shook his head, turned back to the old woman, rolling pin held with loose ease. He took a measured stride towards her, not hurrying. Ricky had been in bad situations all his life, had been beaten up and half-killed on a hundred occasions, starting with the times that happened in his own bedroom, a room that had no posters on the walls or books on shelves or little figures of cartoon animals. Ricky's old man hadn't believed in make-believe either; was proud of being cynical—'That's what I am, boy, I'm nobody's fool'—and working the angles and telling God's honest truth however fucking dull it was. His lessons had been painful, but Ricky knew he'd been right.

Ricky wasn't afraid of an old woman, no matter how tough she might be, and he just grinned at her, looking forward to seeing what the pin was going to do to her face.

She looked back at him, head tilted up, grey hair awry and skin papery, and then her head popped back out.

One minute her skull was caved in, the next it was back where it should be, like someone pumped exactly the right amount of air back into a punctured balloon. It made a sound like cellophane.

Ricky gawped, arm aloft.

WHAT YOU MAKE IT

Grandma swallowed, blinked, then did something with her fucked-up arm. Swung it around from behind her—and as it came it seemed to become more solid, find the right planes to rotate on again. She bent it experimentally, found it worked, and used it to pat her dry hair more-or-less back into place.

'You're a very bad boy, Ricky,' she said, softly, too quietly for Nicola to hear. 'And bad boys never see Santa Claus. Hear what I'm saying, motherfuck?'

Before Ricky could even process this sentence, Margaret Harris had hurled herself at him. He tried to turn, bring the pin down, but only managed to twist halfway round at the waist. She smacked into him sideways, and the two of them spun off the corner of the table to crash into the wall. Ricky felt his nose bend and melt, and realised there was going to be blood to clean up as well as everything else.

He tried to push the old woman away, but she looped a fist straight into his face. It cracked hard against his cheekbone, far too hard. The rolling pin went spinning across the floor.

Ricky kicked and scrambled, lashing out feet, hands and elbows in a flurry of compact violence. Each time he thought he was finally going to be able to dislodge her, she seemed to gain a notch in strength. They rolled back and forth under the table, smashing a chair to firewood, and out the other side. Ricky heard Nicola squeal, and a small part of his mind was able to hope their neighbours hadn't heard. Then he found himself with two gnarled hands tight around his throat, and almost wished they had, and were sending help. For him.

He finally managed to pull his knee up under the old bitch, and gradually forced his hands in between hers. When they were in position he steadied himself for a second, got his breath—and then threw everything he had, chopping his hands in opposite directions, and kicking out hard.

The old woman flew a yard and hit the stove like an egg.

Ricky was on his feet almost immediately, hands on his knees and coughing like a bastard. When he swallowed, something clicked alarmingly in his throat. Nicola was still squeaking, eyes shut, but he heard it as from a great distance. He could taste his blood, and see it spattered on the wall and floor—in amongst the coffee and a few lumps of grey hair that he managed to yank out of the robot.

A fucking animatronic. Had to be. He'd been set up. John Harris had changed his mind, or more likely been a plant from minute one and there'd never been a real grandma Harris. Fuckers. Wonder World weren't working with the cops. They were settling things their own way.

And so would Ricky. The job was over, and it didn't matter how much mess he left. He was getting out, and then going to find Mr Harris. The fee had just gone up to include everything the bastard owned, including his wife. And his daughter.

Grandma Harris was slumped on the floor, back against the cooker. Her throat was arced up like a twisted branch, a perfect target, but jerked back into position as Ricky pulled out his gun. No matter. The face would do just as well.

He held the gun in a straight-arm grip, sighted down the barrel.

'Don't even fucking think about it,' the rolling pin said.

Ricky turned very slowly to look. 'Excuse me?'

It had grown legs, and was standing with little hands on where its hips would be. Two stern eyes glared out of the wooden cylinder of its body, and it looked like a strange wide crab.

Ricky stared at it. Knew suddenly that it wasn't a machine, but an actual rolling pin with eyes and arms. He fired at it. The pin flipped out of the way, then switched direction and flick-flacked towards him, like a crazy little wooden gymnast. Ricky backed hurriedly, fired another shot. It missed, and the rolling pin flicked itself into the air like a muscular missile. Ricky wrenched his head out of the way just in time, and the pin embedded itself in the wall.

'Careful,' said the wall, slowly opening its eyes.

Over at the stove, Grandma Harris was pulling herself upright. Ricky blinked at her. She smiled, a sweet old lady smile that wasn't for him. Ricky decided he didn't have to mop up this mess. He'd go straight to talk with John Harris. He fired a couple of rounds into the wall, just between its huge eyes. It made a grumpy sound, but didn't seem much inconvenienced. A huge mouth opened sleepily, as if yawning, as it was only just getting up to speed. The pin meanwhile pushed itself out with a dry popping sound, and turned its beady eyes on Ricky.

'Shit on this,' Ricky muttered, as it scuttled towards him. He swung a kick at the rolling pin, sent it howling across the room. Fired straight at Margaret Harris, but didn't wait to see if it hit.

He turned on his heel in the kitchen door, bounded across the hallway and yanked at the door. It wouldn't open, and when Ricky tried to pull his hand away, he saw the handle had turned into a brown wooden hand and was gripping his like he was a prime business opportunity and they were testing each other's strength. Ricky braced his foot against the wall and tugged, for the first time hearing the sound of the beams whispering above. He glanced up and saw some of them were wriggling in place, limbering up, getting ready for action. He didn't want to see their action.

The door handle wasn't letting go, and so he placed the muzzle of the gun against it and let it have one.

It took the tip of one of Ricky's fingers with it, but the fucker let go. Ricky reared back, kicked the door with all his strength. It splintered and he barreled through it, tripped and fell full length on the lawn. Face to face with the grass for a moment, he saw that he'd been right, and there was a little face on every blade. He heard a noise like a million little voices tuning up and knew that its song wasn't likely to be one he wanted to hear.

He scrabbled to his feet and careened down the path towards the car, bloody hand scrabbling for the keys. Before he could get even halfway there two trash cans came running round from next door. They made it to the car before him, and started levering one side off up the ground. Meanwhile the rolling pin shot out of the house from behind him, narrowly missed his head, and went through the windscreen of the car like a torpedo. Barely had the spray of glass hit the ground before the pin emerged the other side, turned in mid-air and looped back to punch through a door panel. It kept going, faster and faster, looping and punching, until the car began to look like a battered atom being mugged by a psycho electron.

Ricky began to realise just how badly his hand hurt, and that the car wasn't going to be a viable transportation option. He diverted his course in mid-stride, just heading for the road, for a straight line to run. He cleared the sidewalk barely keeping his balance, and leant into the turn. Ricky could run. He'd had the practice, down many dark streets and darker nights, and always running away instead of to. The way was clear.

Then a vehicle appeared at the corner in front of him, and he realised what the grass had been singing. Not a song, but a siren.

Wonder World's designers hadn't stinted themselves on the cop wagon. It was black and half as big as a house, all superfins and intimidating wheel arches spiked with chrome. The windows in the sides were blacker still, and the doors in the back might just as well have had 'Abandon hope all ye who enter here' scrawled right across them.

Ricky skidded to a halt, whirled around. An identical vehicle had moved into position just the other side of the remains of his car. Behind it a bunch of mushrooms and toadstools were moving into position.

The doors of the first wagon opened, and a figure got out each side. Both seven foot tall, with very long tails and claws that glinted. Bud and Slap, though rats, had been friendly rats in each of the countless cartoons they'd appeared in over the last thirty years. They were almost as popular as Loopy and Careful and China Duck, and even Ricky recognised them. Cute, well-meaning villains, they always ended up joining the right side in the end.

But this Bud and Slap weren't like that. These toons were just for Ricky. As he held his ground, knowing there was nowhere to run, they walked towards him with heavy tread. They were stuffed into parodies of uniforms, torn at the seams and stained with bad things. Bud had a lazy, damaged eye, and was holding a big wooden truncheon in an unreassuring way. Slap had a sore on his upper lip, and kept running a long blue tongue over it, to collect the juice. Both had huge guns stuffed down the front of their uniforms. At least that's what Ricky hoped they were. From five yards away he could smell the rats' odour, the gust of sweat and stickiness and decay, and for a moment catch an echo of all the screams and death rattles they'd heard.

'Hey there, Ricky,' said Slap, winking. His voice was low and oily, full of unpleasant good humour. 'Got some business with you. Lots of different kinds of business, actually. You can get in the wagon, or we can start it right here. What d'you say?'

Behind him Bud giggled, and started to undo his pants.

Nicola stood at the window with Grandma, and watched the parade in the road. It wasn't the real parade, like the one in the Beautiful Realm where they had fireworks and Careful Cat and Loopy, but they were going to see that tomorrow. This was a little parade, with just Bud and Slap, and Percival Pin and Terrance and Terry the Trash Cans: sometimes they put on little parades of their own, Grandma said, just because they enjoyed it.

They laughed as they watched the characters play. Nicola had thought the man she'd come with had been a bad man, but he couldn't have been as bad as all that. Bud and Slap the Happy Rats were each holding one of his hands, and they were dancing with him, leading him to the wagon. They looked like they liked him a lot. The man's mouth opened and shut very wide as he danced, and Nicola thought he was probably laughing. She would be, in his position. They all looked like they were having such fun.

Finally the wagon doors were shut with the man inside, and Bud and Slap bowed up at Grandma's window before getting back into their police car. The trashcans went somersaulting back to next door's yard, and the rolling pin came hand-springing up the path, leaving a trail of little firework stars in its wake. Nicola clapped her hands and Grandma laughed, and put her arm around the little girl.

WHAT YOU MAKE IT

Now it was time for supper and pie, and tomorrow would be a new and different day. They turned away from the window, and went to start cooking, in a kitchen where the tables and chairs had already tidied everything up as if nothing bad had ever happened, or ever could.

Meanwhile, well outside Wonder World, over on a splintered porch outside a small house the other side of the beltway, Marty the gateman sat in his chair enjoying his bedtime cigarette. His back ached a little, from standing up all day, but it didn't bother him too badly. It was a small price to pay for seeing all the faces as they went into the parks, and when they came out again. The kids went in bright-eyed and hopeful, the parents tired and watchful. You could see them thinking how much it was all going to cost, and wondering whether it would be worth it. Then when you saw them come out, hours or days later, you could see that they knew that it had been. For a little while the grown-ups realised their cynicism was an emotional short cut which meant they missed everything worth seeing along the way, and the children had proof of what they already believed: the world was cool. The gateman's job was important, Marty knew. You said the first hello to the visitors, and you said goodbye. You welcomed them in and helped them acclimatise; and then you sent them on their way, letting them see in your eyes the truth of what they believed—they were leaving a little lighter inside.

Marty's house was small and looked like all the others nearby, and he lived in it alone. As he sat in the warmth of the evening, looking up at the stars, he didn't mind that very much. His wife now lived with someone who was better at earning money, and who came home after a day's work in a far worse mood. Marty missed her, but he'd survive. The house could have been fancier, but he'd painted it last summer and he liked his yard.

He had the last couple of puffs of his cigarette, and then stubbed it out carefully in the ashtray he kept by the chair. He yawned, sipped the last of his ice tea, and decided that was that. It was early yet, but a good time for sleep. It always is, when you're looking forward to the next day.

As he lay in his bed later, gently settling into the warm train that would take him into tomorrow, he dimly wondered what he'd do with the rest of his life. Work for as long as he could, he supposed, and then stop. Sit out on the porch, most likely, live out his days bathed in the memory of faces lit for a moment by magic. Smile at passers by. Drink ice tea in the twilight.

That sounded okay by him.

Maybe Next Time

At first, when David began to consider the problem, he wondered if it was related to the start of a new year. January in London is not an exciting time. You'd hardly contend the month showed any part of the country at its best, but there were places—the far reaches of Scotland, perhaps, or the stunned emptiness of the midland fens—where you could at least tell it was winter, a season with some kind of character and point. In London, the period was merely still-grey and no-longer-New Year and Spring-not-even-over-the-horizon. A pot of negatives, a non-time of non-events in which you trudged back to jobs the festive break had drunkenly blessed with purpose, but which now felt like putting on the same old overcoat again. But still, however much David unthinkingly lived a year that began in the Autumn—as did most who had soldiered their way through school and college, where promise and new beginnings came with the term after the summer—he could see that January was the real start of things. He thought at first that might be it, but he was wrong. The feelings were not coming after something, but pointing the way forward. To May, when he would have his birthday.

To May, when he would be forty years old.

The episodes came on quietly. The first he remembered happened one Thursday afternoon when he was at his desk in Soho, pen hovering over a list of things to do. The list was short. David was good at his job, and believed that a list of things to do generally comprised of a list of things that should already have been done.

His list said he had to [1] have a quick and informal chat with the other participants in the next day's new business meeting, [2] have a third and superfluous scan through the document explaining why said potential clients would be insane not to hand their design needs over to

125

Artful Bodgers, Ltd, [3] make sure the meeting room had been tidied up, and [4] …

He couldn't think what [4] might be. He moved his pen back, efficiently preparing to cross out the numeral and its businesslike brackets, but didn't. He dimly believed his list was incomplete, in the same way you know, when wandering around the kitchen periodically nibbling a biscuit, whether you finished it in the last bite or if there's a portion still lying around.

There was something he was supposed to do … nope, it had gone.

He went home, leaving the list behind. When he covertly glanced at it towards the end of the meeting the following morning, his sense of mild satisfaction (the pitch was going well, the new clients in the bag) was briefly muted by the sight of that [4], still there, still unfilled. The list now had a [5], a [6] and a [7], all ticked, but still no [4].

For a moment he was reminded of the old routine—

> Item 1: do the shopping
> Item 2: mow the lawn
> Item 4: where's item 3?
> Item 3: ah, there it is …

—and smiled. He was disconcerted to realise that the most senior of the clients, a man with a head that looked carved out of a potato, was looking at him, but the smile was easily converted into one of general commercial warmth. The deal was done. By lunchtime he was on to other things, and the list was forgotten.

This, or something like it, happened a couple more times that month. He would find himself in the kitchen, wiping his hands after clearing away the dinner Amanda had cooked, thinking that he could sit down in front of the television just as soon as he had … and realise there was nothing else he had to do. Or he would take five minutes longer doing the weekly shop in Waitrose, walking the aisles, not looking for anything in particular but yet not quite ready to go take his position in the checkout line. In the end he would go and pay, and find himself bagging only the things he had come out looking for, the things on his and Amanda's list.

February started with a blaze of sunshine, as if the gods had been saving it for weeks and suddenly lost patience with clouds and grey. But it turned out they hadn't stocked as much as they thought, and soon London was muted and fitful again. David worked, put up some shelves in the spare bedroom, and went out once a week to a restaurant with his wife. They talked of things in the paper and on the news, and Amanda had two glasses of wine while he drank four. But plenty of mineral water too, and so the walk home was steady, his arm around her shoulders for part of the way. Artful Bodgers continued to make money, in a quiet, unassuming fashion. The company's job was to take other companies' corporate identities, and make them better. Spruce up or rethink the logo, make typeface decisions, provide a range of stationary to cater for all contingencies: business cards, letterheads, following page sheets (just the logo, no address), document folders, fax sheets, envelope labels, cassette boxes for the video companies. They had the latest Macs and some decent young designers. Their accounts department was neither mendacious nor incompetent. Everyone did their job, well enough to weather the periodicity of corporate confidence and wavering discretionary spend. His company was a success, but sometimes David thought the only interesting thing about it was the name. He'd chosen it personally, on start-up, seven years before. Everyone else—including Amanda—had thought it a bad idea. All too easy to take the second word and run with it. Who wants to hire bodgers, even if you know it's a little joke? David fought, arguing it showed a confident expectation that clients would never feel the need to make the association. He won, and it worked, and there were other times when David thought that the name was probably the most boring thing about the company, too.

One evening in February he found himself in Blockbuster, looking for a film he couldn't name. He was twice becalmed at pub bars, both times with clients, having remembered what he wanted to drink, but then forgotten it again. On both occasions he bought a glass of Chardonnay, which was what he always drank.

Once again, too, he found himself hesitating in the midst of jotting a note at work: apparently unsure not so much of what he was going to write, as much as to the precise physical nature of the act. He hadn't forgotten how to use a pen, of course. It was more a question of choice, like recalling whether one played a tennis backhand with one or two hands on the racket. When he eventually started writing, his handwriting looked odd for a while.

But it was not until the next month that he could honestly say that he started to think about any of these things.

On the fourth of March he dreamed. This was not in itself unusual. He dreamed as much as the next man, the usual intermittent cocktail of machine-like anxiety or amusing but forgettable trivia. On the fourth of March he dreamed of something different. He didn't know what it was;

could not, when he awoke, remember. But he was distracted as he sat with his first cup of the day, feeling as if some recollection was hidden just behind a fold in his brain. He stood, stared out of the window, and did not move even after Amanda had come down after her shower.

She rummaged in the cupboard, looking for a new box of her current brand of herbal tea. 'What are you thinking about?'

'I don't know,' he said.

'Why have we got so many olives?'

'Hmm?' He turned to look at her. The memory felt neither closer nor further away. She held up a jar of green olives.

'There's three of these in there.'

'You didn't buy them?'

'No.' She held the jar so he could see the label: Waitrose own-brand. He always did the Waitrose shop, and did it alone. Supermarkets made Amanda irritable.

'Then I must have bought them.'

'You don't like olives.'

'I know.'

Ten minutes later she was gone, off to work. David was still in the kitchen, sitting now with a second cup of tea, no closer to remembering his dream. All he could recall was an atmosphere of affectionate melancholy. It reminded him of another dream from five or six years before. This had been of his college, of returning there alone and walking the halls and corridors that had shaped three years of his life, back when the future seemed deliciously malleable. In the dream he'd met none of his friends from that period, and had notably not encountered the girl with whom he'd spent most of that time. The dream hadn't been about them, but about him. It was about absence. About some distance he had travelled, or perhaps failed to come, since those days; a period now backlit by its passing, at the time merely the day to day. The dream he could not now remember had something of this about it too, but it wasn't the same. It wasn't about college. It wasn't about anything he could recall.

It was enough to nudge him into awareness, however, and at the end of the day he sat in the living room, after Amanda had gone upstairs, and thought back over the previous couple of months. He considered the missing [4], the drinks without a name, remembered also standing one afternoon in Soho Square and gazing at the shapes of the buildings that surrounded it, as if they should mean something more to him than they did. At the time each of these non-incidences, these failures to mean, had seemed distinct from each other, distinct from anything at all. Now they did not. Once gathered together, they referred to a whole. There was something on his mind, that was clear. He just didn't know what it was.

It was then he tried connecting them with the start of the year, with the feeling of something beginning. Though in general a level-headed man, David was sometimes surprised to find himself prey to rather New Age notions. Perhaps this year, this 2004, was trying to tell him something. Maybe some celestial timepiece, some combination of shadow and planetary sphere, had reached its predetermined mark. Perhaps 2004 was the year of...

He couldn't make the thought go anywhere, and soon zoned out into watching the television screen. It showed a crazy-haired old gent tramping around an undistinguished patch of countryside. He couldn't remember selecting the channel, and with the sound off, it really wasn't very interesting. Was it worth turning the sound up? Probably not. It increasingly seemed to him that television was being created for someone else. He was welcome to watch it, of course, but it was not he the creators had in mind.

As he left the room he passed one of the bookcases, and paused a moment when a book caught his eye. He took it down, opened it. It was a first edition of *Conjuring and Magic* by Robert Houdin, published in 1878, bought some months before at a stall in Covent Garden. He'd told himself it was merely an investment—at fifty pounds for a VG+ copy, it was certainly a bargain—but actually he'd bought it in the hope that going back to the classics might help. In fact, it had yielded no better results than the small handful of cheap paperbacks he'd desultorily acquired over the last few years, since he'd realised that a little magic was something he'd very much like to be able to do. The problem with magic, he'd discovered, was that there was no trick to it. There was practice, and hard work—and the will to put these things into practice. Even buying the little geegaws of the trade didn't help. All but the most banal still required sleight of hand, which had to be acquired the old-fashioned way. If you learned how a trick worked, all you actually gained was confirmation that it required a skill you didn't have and lacked the time and energy to acquire. Learning how a trick worked was the same as being told you couldn't do it. You gained nothing, and lost everything.

He flicked through the book for a few moments, admiring the old illustrations of palming techniques, and then put the volume back on the shelf. It wasn't worth even trying tonight. Maybe tomorrow.

Instead he went into the kitchen and ate half a jar of olives while he waited for the kettle to boil.

Michael Marshall Smith

*

He dreamed a few more times in March, but remained unable to take anything from them. All he was left with the next morning was absence and the unnameable smell of open water. An absence, too, was what he felt during most of the last weekend of the month, which they spent down in Cornwall. It was the third time they'd taken a romantic mini-break in Padstow. Both previous occasions had been great successes. They'd walked along the craggy coast, bought a couple of little paintings which now graced the bathroom, enjoyed a superlative dinner in Rick Stein's restaurant (having taken efficient care to book ahead). Good, clean, adult fun. This time David couldn't seem to get into it. They did the same things, but it wasn't the same, and it wasn't merely the repetition that made the difference. Amanda was in good form, braced by the wind and the sky. To him they seemed merely there. In some way it all reminded him of an experience he'd had a couple of weeks previously, during a meeting at work. A creative powwow, with, as it happened, the clients with the potato-headed boss. There had come a point when David found himself talking. He had been talking for a little while, he realised, and knew that he could keep going for as long as he wanted. The other people around the table were either his employees or clients gathered to take advantage of his keen design brain, his proven insights into the deep mysteries of corporate identity. Their eyes were all on him. This didn't frighten him, merely made him wonder if they were in fact listening, or rather gazing at him and wondering who he was, and what he was talking about. They were all nodding in the right places, so this seemed unlikely. Presumably it was only David, therefore, who was wondering these things. And wondering too whether it was ever worth speaking, if no-one wanted you to stop.

On the second evening in Padstow they paid their tribute to the god of seafood. Amanda seemed happy, perky in a new Karen Millen and smelling faintly of expensively complimentary shampoos and unguents. David knew that it was remarkable that a woman of thirty-seven should look so good in fashion tailored for the young and slim, and was glad. Not delighted—because, to be honest, he had grown accustomed to Amanda looking good—but glad. The food was predictably excellent. David ate it. Amanda ate it. They talked of things in the news and in the papers. They were benignly tolerant of the next table, which featured two well-behaved but voluble children. Neither had anything against children. They didn't have any because it had been discussed, seven or eight years before, when David was launching the business and Amanda had just switched companies and embarked on the route to her current exalted position in publishing. At the time it would have been a mistake to complicate their lives, or might have been a mistake. It was then still more or less appropriate, too, for Amanda to make that amusing joke about not needing children just yet, because she was married to one. David did little to sustain this idea now barrin an occasional hangover and a once-in-a-while good-humoured boisterousness, but having children wasn't something they discussed at the moment. Maybe later.

They went back to their room after dinner and made love. This was nice, if a little self-conscious and laden with implicit self-congratulation. They'd still got it, still knew how to have a good time. That much was clear.

In the middle of the night David awoke. Amanda was sound asleep beside him, and remained so for the two hours he spent lying on his back, staring up at the ceiling. This time he'd brought something more back with him than an atmosphere. An image of long grasses near somewhere watery. Of somewhere not close, but not far away.

A sense that this was not the beginning of something after all.

By the second week of April he was waking almost once a night to find himself lying in a strange bed. Familiarity closed in rapidly, but for a moment there was a sense of inexplicability, like moving on from the missing [4] to the comfort of the present [5]. He could remember things about the dreams now. Very small things. The long grasses, often, though sometimes they seemed more like reeds. The sense of water: not moving fast, not a river or stream, but present nonetheless.

Finally, a building, or the remains of one.

He knew it was a building, and that it was ruined, though in the dream his point of view was too close up to make out anything more than lichened stone and clouded blue sky above. As if he was crouched down low, and glancing up.

That morning Amanda look at him over her cup of mint tea. 'Where did all those olives go?'

'I ate them,' he said.

She raised an eyebrow. 'Are you sleeping okay?'

'Why do you ask?'

'You don't seem to be. You look tired. And sometimes you thrash about. The other night I thought I heard you say "Goodbye, love" in your sleep.'

'"Goodbye, love"? That doesn't sound like me.'

'Quite.'

He shrugged. He knew he should tell her about what was happening. He hated films in which a character keeps secrets from the very people or person who should be on his side: a source of cheap tension that had more to do with padding the plot than representing real life. But he didn't tell her, all the same. It didn't seem relevant. Or she didn't, perhaps.

He went to work, and came home, and went to work again. He went to the gym, as usual: moving weights nowhere, running the same rolling yard, strutting and fretting his half hour on the elliptical trainer. Artful Bodgers won more business, and he gave everyone a little bonus. He considered taking over one of their suppliers, then shelved the decision for another day. He came home, he went to work again. He dreamed of the building once more, this time from a little further away. The fact it was ruined was clearly apparent. And that it was somewhere in England. There was nothing about it that proved that. He simply knew it.

'You spoke in your sleep again,' Amanda said, at another breakfast. 'You said "I can't hear what you're saying".'

He looked at her. 'But what does that mean?'

She turned a page in this morning's manuscript. 'You tell me,' she said. 'God, this novel's shite.'

He started visiting bookstores during his lunch breaks, and stopping into Borders on his way home from work. He wasn't sure what he was looking for, so he just browsed. He looked in the travel sections (domestic); he looked at books on the English countryside. Nothing seemed to help. He didn't have enough to work with, and there was a sense, when he looked at pictures, that he shouldn't need to. Whatever this was, it wasn't a puzzle. It wasn't supposed to be hard.

In the last week of April, now only a week from his birthday, Amanda sometimes worked in her study with her door shut. He knew that she would be wrapping little presents for him. He knew that they would be nice. He had no desire to know what they were yet. He liked surprises. They came along seldom enough.

Amanda surprised him in another way, before the day. She asked if he was going to visit his mother. He realised both that he should, and that he should do it on the day itself. Without her, after all, there wouldn't be forty years to mark. He called her, and arranged it. She said she'd put on a little lunch.

He was dreaming now, almost constantly, but through a veil. He felt sick some mornings, as if had had failed to digest something. Nothing he looked at seemed to be what he should be seeing. None of his lists had anything on them except numerals in brackets.

He finally mentioned this to Amanda. She kissed him, and put her arms around him. She was his wife. She understood, or thought she did.

He got up at the usual time on the 4th of May, though he had taken the day off work. He had breakfast in bed, then came down in a dressing gown to a kitchen table on which his presents had been laid. They were all very nice, and Amanda left for work fifteen minutes later than usual. She sat with him, and had an extra cup of tea, and they smiled and laughed.

After she'd gone he showered and dressed and then went out and got in his car. He forged a route out of London and onto the M11, taking it up past Cambridge and into the countryside. He tried to find something on the radio to listen to, some CD in the glove compartment, but none of them sounded right. He could remember buying them, but none of them seemed to be his.

He reached Willingham a little before mid-day, on time. His mother was standing at the door to her house, steel-haired, compact and smiling. Once the land on which she stood had been part of a farm, a larger holding belonging to one of her ancestors. Like everything else, it had been made smaller by time.

His mother had made sandwiches and cake. While she laid them out he wandered around the house where he had grown up, trying to remember how long it had been since he'd visited. A couple of years, certainly. She occasionally made it down to London, and that tended to be where they met. Tea at the Ritz, sometimes. An overnight or two in the house he owned with Amanda, tucked up safe in the spare bed. Not so very often, for the person who had been his mother, but that tended to be the way it went. You moved further from the start, and towards something else: eyes turned always forward, the past something you only remembered once in a while, generally through something heard. Things weren't about beginnings any more. They were about persistence, and endings, for the most part. Persistence, above all.

He found himself drawn to one room in particular. His parents' old room; his mother's still. He stood in the centre, unsure of what he was doing there. He looked up at the ceiling. Off-white, as it always had been. If you allowed your eyes to fall out of focus then the imperfections blurred away, and its colour became all you could see.

His mother's voice floated upstairs.

After lunch he asked her about her bedroom. Had something changed? She said no. Nothing had changed for her in several years.

He shrugged, took a risk: told her how he'd felt compelled to stand in there. She was a woman. She'd understand.

She did, and perhaps more than he'd expected. More than he did. 'Well,' she said, 'It's your birthday.'

He shook his head, not comprehending. She smiled, as if it were self-evident. 'That's where it happened, up there in that room. That's where you were born,' she said, and then winked. 'You can live down in that London all you like,' she added, 'But this is where you're from.'

He barely heard anything else she said, and left twenty minutes later. When he reached the end of the village, he did not take the left turn which would lead to the A road and later back to the M11. Instead he turned right, and kept driving.

He drove for an hour, out into the countryside, out beyond the villages and into the country proper, to where the fens began. To the place where water became as much as part of the world as earth, to where grass and reeds and flatness were all the land had to say.

After a while he turned again, not back on himself, but at an angle, and headed in a different direction. A little later, he did so once more.

He could have driven for hours, for days. He could have looked for weeks and never found it, were it not for the church. That, presumably, had been the point. It had worked, in the end.

It was half ruined, and stood by itself in the middle of a field. David knew enough to understand this meant it most likely represented the last lingering sign of a lost village. Seen from above, from a low-flying plane, there would have been crop marks to show where domestic buildings had once been, a previous lay of the land. But that had been long, long ago.

When he saw the two remaining walls, the jagged half steeple, it took his breath away and every unremembered dream came back at once.

He lurched the car over to the side of the road, parked chaotically on the verge. Then got out, stepped gingerly over the low, barbed wire fence, and started to walk towards the ruin. It was probably private land. He didn't care. Twice he disappeared up to one knee in the boggy ground. He didn't care about that either. His mobile phone rang once. He didn't even hear it.

He walked slowly around the church. He knew it only meant one thing to him, that he had only been here once before. He approached it, finally, and stood close up against the wall. The sky was blue above, flecked with cloud. It looked the same wherever you stood, whether inside the remains of the structure or without, and at any point along the walls. But again, he had planned well, and eventually he found the heavy stone.

He went down on one knee and prised his fingers around the sides. Gym savvy told him to protect his back, and he took his time to pull the big, flat stone out of place. Underneath was a small metal box.

He lifted it out, and sat down on the grass.

Inside the box was a small old sack, stained with time and wrapped over itself. He waited for a while, wishing for a cigarette, though he had never smoked. He thought about the ceiling in his mother's bedroom, knowing it not to be the first thing he had ever seen. Finally he opened the bag, and pulled out the envelope inside.

He recognised the handwriting, from a list he had written back in February. The letter said:

To whoever I might be —

I hope this time it has worked, and I'm young, that I've caught me in time. Better still I hope I will find this and smile, knowing it was unnecessary, knowing I can palm anything, make coins appear out of people's ears, and that I have not come here alone. But just in case:

[1] Do things. Do everything. Learn, explore, open the world's boxes while you're young and time stretches out infinitely far.
[2] Make mistakes, and make them early, not late. Too soon can be undone. Too late cannot.
[3] Marry the one who could break your heart.
[4] There is no [4]. The first three will be enough.

Good luck,
Yourself.

Ten minutes later David put the letter back in the bag. He wished he had known to bring the Houdin book with him. He could have put it in there as well, for next time. But if he remembered this late then too, there would be little point. He might as well sell it, hope it would find someone who would use it in time.

When the stone was back in place he spent a while standing close to the wall of the ruined church, memorising the shape of the road, the pattern of the water inlets in the distance: anything he might reasonably hope would be here next time. Finally he walked back over the car, climbed in, and sat for a while looking out at the flat fens.

Then he started the drive back to London, where he knew a surprise party was waiting for him.

The Book Of
Irrational Numbers

A nice clean page. Page three. 3x3=9, hence 0. The beginning. When I start a new notebook I never use the first piece of paper, because you know it's going to get scuffed up. I always leave both sides of that one blank, and start writing on the second piece of paper, where it will be protected from dirt. It's usually hobbies that I use notebooks for. I feel like writing a different type of thing now. Don't really know how to go about it. Blah blah blah words words words. Letters must add up to something, but I'm not sure what. Writing something down makes it feel like yesterday's news. Almost nothing actually *is* yesterday's news, though. Most of it is still going on. Today was a reasonable day like most others. I was due to paint a house just on the other side of town and I got most of the prepping done in the morning but then it started to rain, so I had to leave it be.

$14^2 = 196$. $8.56^2 = 73.2736$.

Roanoke is a funny place to live. Not quite in the middle of nowhere, close by the Blue Ridge Mountains. Of Virginia. Never seen a lonesome pine around here: there's billions of them. I quite like it though. There's plenty of work. People always need things done to their houses. There's not much else to do, and you've got a hell of a job finding anywhere to eat or drink in the evening, especially on Sundays. The only place is Macados, a burger bar in the centre of town. Lots of highschoolers, though that's okay. They're not so rich that they're obnoxious. Most of them are pretty good kids. Basically it's a town with a couple of malls, a small airport. In winter you can go driving up in the mountains, find secret places. I drove back from Richmond once along the Ridge and passed all these little homesteads. People looked up at me like they'd never seen a car before.

The most important thing I have ever discovered is the idea of digital roots. To find the digital root of a number, the aim is to reduce it to a single digit. You achieve this by adding up all its existing digits: 943521, for example, adds up to 9+4+3+5+2+1=24. This, of course, still has two digits, so you add them together: 2+4=6. The digital root of 943521, therefore is 6. What is interesting, however, is that to speed up this process you can simply cast out the nines. If there's a nine in the number, or any of the digits add up to nine, you can ignore them. In 943521, therefore, you ignore the 9, and also ignore the 4 and 5, which add up to nine. This leaves you with 3+2+1, which gives you 6. The same answer.

I ended up here completely by chance. I don't know, can't chart the steps, which brought me this way. I don't know. I don't remember anything in particular, but then maybe it could have been something so small that I wouldn't have though it was important enough. I can remember some books some conversations some dreams some things I saw. But nothing spectacular. No major blows to the head.

You look for what makes sense.

Susan the new girl who works in the bookstore is lovely. She's got a great smile and she always looks so cheerful and as if she knows something funny is going to happen sooner or later. And she's Prime. I guess it's a vacation job or something. She noticed my accent straight away. I think she thinks it's cool. I hope so.

Gerry was on the phone again earlier this evening, hassling everyone about what we're doing for the Millennium. Max is getting all hot and bothered about it too. Who cares? Everybody thinks that the year 2000 is going to be the big one. It's not. We're already there. It's already started. Cast out the nines, and see how it is so. Last year was 1998. 1+9+9+8=27, and 2+7 (or ignore the 9s, and just add 1 and 8)=9; cast it out. Zero, in other words. 1998 is ground zero or the end of things, a nothing year in modulo 9. 1999, on the other hand, has a digital root of 1.

THE BOOK OF IRRATIONAL NUMBERS

1999 is year 1; 2000 roots down to 2. 2000 isn't the start of anything, it's after it has already begun. Millenniums don't mean anything to real people. Their lives revolve around much smaller circles. You strip things down. If you can't reduce a number down any further, then it means something. Otherwise it's just addition.

Got the Macillsons' house painted today. Did some work inside for them too, fixing up stuff. Think their neighbor might need some work done too. So it goes, luckily.

It's very much like something breaks. When it's done, you go through this hell. Like grief. At first the units are minutes, and then hours. Weeks, months. Cycles of guilt and grief and sometimes glee. Once you've been through it once, it's different. The first time you're culpable, there's no getting away from it. Afterwards it's different. All the structures, once so hard, become fluid forever, like a bag full of broken glass in treacle. When you push your hand in, it's sweet and sharp together.

People are nice to me, but that just makes me feel sad and guilty, because I know I'm not very nice. It's really painful. I have good friends, and I always have a laugh with the guys at the store where I buy my materials. Susan at the bookstore waves now when she sees me go by. I don't deserve it. I want to be nice. It's important to me. I was nice once, I think, and bits of me still are. I used to drive miles, for example, every weekend, to see someone. I had it in me then, the capacity for being good. I still do. Bits of me seem not to be touched by it all. But they're no help, either, and you have to wonder where the energy, the motivation and glee come from. Doesn't any of it come from that part of me, the part I like? It must: or if not, why is it so powerless? It must be very weak to be unable to do anything, in which case it's obviously not so blameless after all. It's all very well being that little flinchy man, sitting up in a high tower of the castle, behind a locked door, wanting no part of it. Weak, afraid; rational at the heart of the irrational. Rationality is weak; it has no moment, contributes to no interesting sums. All it does is cringe.

The weather was colder again today. I don't feel hunted, exactly. It's as if someone is reaching out of the dark towards me, as if the opaque brown fog is beginning to bulge as someone pushes against it from the outside. Think this is going to be a cold winter.

17 is the last year of being young. I remember when I was a kid, about fourteen, I guess, thinking how weird it would feel to be older. I could just about understand the ages of sixteen and seventeen. Eighteen seemed one of those ages like twenty-one where it's not so much an age as a legal marker. A boundary line. You don't think 'Oh, it's going to be like so-and-such' being eighteen, you just think about the things that aren't going to be illegal any more. Nineteen, though. That seemed really old. Being nineteen was grown up and over the wall. Of course it doesn't seem that way now. But it did then. Now I realise that nineteen is 1 and 9, and 1+9 =10 and 1+0 =1. The first year of being old. 1+8 is 9, a ground zero year.

You have to watch everything very carefully.

I think about people waiting for birthday cards, Christmas cards. A phone call that isn't going to come. Mothers, mainly. I wish I could say it made a big difference, but it doesn't.

Squaring numbers is very easy. You just take the number and multiply it by itself. Anybody can do that. It's an easy road to travel, like time in the usual direction.

Roads. I remember that time, back in England, when I drove up to Cambridge from London on the M11 motorway. If there's any bad weather anywhere in the world, it'll be on the M11. I'm telling you. It feels as if the road has been built to make the worst of it. There are high stretches, where strong winds seem to grab hold of the car and drag it towards other lanes; average stretches, where rain seems to sheet into the windscreen almost parallel to the ground; and then there are the dips. Especially just outside Cambridge there are long low patches, where fog collects and sits in a clump like porridge in a bowl. I used to have a girlfriend who lived there. For a year, in fact over a year, I used to drive up the M11 every weekend. I saw it in Spring, Summer, Autumn,

THE BOOK OF IRRATIONAL NUMBERS

Winter—and regardless, the weather there was worse than anywhere else. One night in October I drove down the slipway onto the motorway and found myself completely enveloped in fog. For the next ten miles visibility wasn't even as far as the end of the hood of the car. I couldn't see a damned thing. I couldn't see my own headlights, never mind anyone else's. I drove slower and slower and slower. I knew that after the next junction the road gradually got a little higher, pulled itself out of the trough all around the town. I kept waiting for the junction. Nothing passed me, and I saw no other cars, no headlights on the other side of the carriageway, no tail lights on my own. After a long time I passed the first exit. Usually the fog lifted then. On that night it stayed exactly the same. Just as thick, just as deadening, just as much like driving slowly through the middle of a monstrous snowdrift that reached up to the sky. There was no sound, except for the hum of the engine. I'd turned the radio off, to avoid distraction. I couldn't see a thing outside the car, except for slow swirls within the mist. I'd been going for about thirty-five or forty minutes when I started to feel uneasy, and after another ten I was beginning to get really nervous. I knew the M11 like the back of my hand, and a message was starting to persistently knock on the back of my mind, where the autopilot sits and keeps an eye on things. Isn't it about time, it was saying, that we passed another exit? In normal conditions, I would pass the first exit about ten minutes into the journey, and the second at the half hour mark. This night was far from normal, and I was driving much slower than usual. But it was now at least 50 minutes since I'd passed the first exit. I couldn't have gone by the second without noticing: the massive exit signs by the side of the road were just about the only thing that I had been able to see at the beginning of the journey. So where was the second? I drove for another ten minutes. Still no cars on my side of the road, and no headlights on the other. I drove on for five further minutes, picking the speed up slightly. I was just a little…concerned. Ten minutes later a shape finally loomed out of the fog, and I breathed a sigh of relief. The journey was halfway over, and I'd seen the second exit. As I lit a cigarette, finally able to spare some concentration from the road, I thought for a moment. How long would it have taken for me to have started panicking? How long would I have had to wait before too long became *far* too long, before I'd started to feel in my heart of hearts that something had gone wrong, that the exit had disappeared and I was crawling along an endless fog-buried road into nothingness, the real world left behind?

*

Michael Marshall Smith

Someone is after me now. Definitely. I know they are. It's an odd position to be in. Everyone else will always side with the hunter. Which I'm not. Some people in my position call themselves that, but it's pure vaingloriousness. I assume he's a policeman. He doesn't know who I am yet, but he's there. I'm not even sure how I know this. I'm not sure how I know a lot of things. Maybe I'm noticing little signs without really realising what they are. I don't really know what to do about him. I'm not going to give myself up, or give myself away if I can help it, but—maybe he could even be my friend. He must understand some of it, which would help. I *don't* understand. That's part of it. I don't understand why I can't just be nice. You read books and a lot of people are just 1, 2, 3... 'these are the reasons why'. An easy addition. I'm not, as far as I can remember. I don't have the excuse. I've got a fair number of friends, and they come round or I go see them and we hang out, but it's like the whole thing's in two dimensions. It's like a painted glass window—one stone, and it's going to fall apart. I'm just not nice, and it makes me sad, because some people are nice to me and I want to be nice, but can't. Not any more. Once is enough, too much. It taints your life.

I was in the bookstore again today, bought some books and had a cup of coffee. I had a chat with Susan again too. The place wasn't very busy. I told her a couple of digital root tricks. Like...take any number (say 4201); add the digits (4+2+0+1=7); take the sum away from the original number (4201-7=4194)—and the result will always have a digital root of 9. Or...take any number (say 94213); scramble the digits in any order you like (32941, for instance) and subtract the smaller number from the bigger (94213-32941=61272). Guess what—digital root of 9 again. Those 9s, they get around. She thought the tricks were pretty cool. We got talking about symmetrical or palindromic numbers, and how they don't come along in years very often. 1991; 2002; 2112; 2222. When I got home I realised something. If you look at the digital roots the sequence goes 1+(9+9)+1=2; in the same way 2002=4; 2112=6; 2222=8. The *even* numbers. Then 2332 gives 1, 2442 gives you 3, 2552 gives you 5, and 2662 gives you 7. The *odd* numbers. Which is kind of interesting. Maybe.

Gerry spends a hundred bucks a month on porn. There's a place in Greensboro. We got really drunk a couple months ago and he told me about it. Nothing weird, just people having sex. It obviously bothers him, but he can't stop doing it. He tries, he buys, he purges. Funny what accountants get up to.

Fall in Roanoke is driving foggy roads.

My twenties didn't make any sense to me. Or my early thirties. I used to be able to understand ages. Up until you're twenty, they make sense. Each year from the early teens onwards is such a huge step, until you're twenty, when they start getting smaller and smaller again. The teens. So many things become possible. Each year is a like a quantum leap. After that—you just keep getting a little older and smaller. You have birthdays, and sometimes people remember them and sometimes they don't. When you were sixteen, and one of your friends had a birthday and became seventeen, you sure as hell knew about it. It meant your friend had gone to another planet. They stood taller than you. They were older. There's no difference between being 27 and 28. Or 43 and 44. You've been around the ring too many times. 44 is who-gives-a-shit, whatever modulo you're on. The Greeks knew a lot about maths, but they didn't know about zero. Seriously. They had no 0, which meant they didn't understand how numbers relate to people and what they do. The difference between 0 and 1 is the biggest difference in the world, far greater than that between 2 and 3: because they're just additional counts, whereas 0 is never having done it at all. They knew very little about the irrational, and nothing about the quiet that lies beyond even that. They liked perfection, the Greeks. Perfect numbers, for example, which are the sum of the numbers that you can divide them by: $6=1+2+3$; $28=1+2+4+7+14$. They are also, as it happens, the sum of consecutive whole numbers: $6=1+2+3$; $28=1+2+3+4+5+6+7$. Kind of neat. But perfect numbers are very, very rare: irrationality is far more common. They say Pythagoras just pretended irrational numbers didn't exist. Just couldn't handle the idea. Shows how you can be a really bright guy, and still know shit.

It's like falling in love.

There's one under the kitchen floor. It's not even a very big kitchen. But there's one under there, about a foot under, lying face up. It's covered in concrete, and there's good quality slate laid on top. But sometimes when

I see one of my friends standing in there I think Jesus, that's really bad. Last time it happened was when Max and Julie were round, and Max was fixing us drinks in the kitchen. It's like the floor goes transparent for a moment, and I can see her lying there, below people's feet. Not literally, of course. I don't get visions. If anything, I'm too rational. Other times, for longish stretches, I just forget, and then the remembering is very bad. It's like 'Jesus, what have I done? What can I do about it? And the answer is always—nothing. It's too late now to go back. It's always been too late. On the one hand it's disgusting, and pathetic and sick. But in everyday life images will pop into my mind, pictures, memories of things I've done. I push them away, but the pictures and memories feel warm and comforting and glorious, like the robes of a king in exile. After a while they come more often, and the sense of glee will start to strengthen, and that's when I know it's going to happen again. The dance begins, a dance where I'm my own partner, but I can't work out who's leading. It's a wonderful dance while it lasts.

Slim, slender, small. The little ones are like the digital root of breasts. You don't need great big lumps of flesh to prove you're a woman. It's in the face, in the nature. Stripped down to the essential.

Imagining is okay.

I would have to be very careful. Because of this guy. I wonder what he's like. I wonder what's going to happen. Whether he's righteously angry, or just doing his job. And I wonder why I'm so convinced he's there, whether there's some structure that I'm sensing, but just can't see. Maybe I need new sums.

So locked up that even when drunk you never get near it.

17 is prime. If you think about it, if someone's seventeen they're not yet an adult but they're no longer a child. Not least because it has no factors. 16 is two eights, or four fours, come to that. I'm not getting involved with multiples of children. The prime numbers between ten and twenty are 13, 17 and 19. Nineteen is too old. 13 is a child. 17 is indivisible by anything

except 1 and 17, which is right, because there's one seventeen-year-old there. One real person. It is disgusting. I know that. But it's also the only thing that has any reality or point. If I could only lose the guilt, and remain the same person, I could be happy. But I can't, because I want to be nice.

I had a dream once, where I had a number, and squared it, and the result was 2. When I woke up I wanted to write the number down, but I'd forgotten it.

Forever the pull between what I want, and the need to be nice. So many people live their lives like that. I don't know any perfect numbers in real life. Max is married, but he wants to sleep with other women. Not because he doesn't love Julia. He does. You only have to look at them to see how much they care about each other. But he just wants to sleep with other women. He told me this once, very stoned, but I knew anyway. You only have to watch his eyes. Hunger and guilt. His argument is that monogamy is artificial. He says that in the animal kingdom very few species mate for life, that it makes biological and evolutionary sense for the male to spread his genes as widely as possible: increase the chance of fertilization, and introduce as much variation into the gene pool as possible. Which may be true. But I suspect he just wants to bite some different nipples for a change. Meanwhile he has, I suspect, absolutely no idea that Julia throws up about one meal in three. He's just not very observant, I guess.

I was talking with Susan again today, showing her some more number tricks. She likes the way they dance. She's sharing a house with two other girls, but her friends have gone home for the vacation. It's funny the way she talks to me. Careful, polite—because I'm older. But friendly too. She's just finding her way.

I want to be whole, but you can only be whole if you tell, and I can't possibly tell. So who is that person that people know, and if they like you, what does it mean? Most things you can confess. You can absolve yourself by mentioning it, however lightly, by saying 'Oh God, you'll never guess what I did, silly me'. Not this. You can't absolve this. I have good friends. But not that good. No friends are that good. My secret keeps me apart from everyone. At least if you're an alcoholic you can try to admit it in front of yourself, God and one other person. Everyone says 'Hey, that's a bad thing', but then they want to help you. I can only admit it to the first two: and believe me, it's the third that makes the difference. It must be, otherwise there's no way out of this, except death. That's why some people want to be caught: not to be stopped, not for the publicity, but just so you can get it out. Admitting it to God makes no difference. So far as I can tell, he doesn't care.

Today was Sunday, and it was snowing. I spent all day indoors tinkering with stuff. There was a guy working on the fence of the house opposite. He didn't look familiar. Paranoia is dangerous, because it can make you behave oddly. You have to behave properly. You have to be rational in the heart of irrationality.

It's not like half of these little idiots matter. For a year, they're prime. Then just machines pushing machines with baby machines in them. Not prime, not even perfect. Just blobs.

Irrational numbers are those that cannot be accurately expressed as a fraction, whose decimal places ramble randomly on. Like the square root of 2, which starts 1.41421356237...and then goes on and on and on. Pi is also an irrational number: very fucking irrational, in fact—pi is a number that's off its face on drugs. People have spent their lives calculating it to millions and millions of places, and still there's no pattern, and no precise value. Pi is the ratio of a circle's circumference to its radius. You work out the circumference of a circle through the equation c=pr, where r is the radius—the distance from the exact centre of the circle to the ring. Of course if you have the circumference, you can work out the radius, by reversing the process and dividing by pi. But whichever way you do it, pi is still involved. And pi is irrational. The length of the radius can be as precise as you like—5.00 cm, twelve inches, a hundred metres exactly—but the circumference is still going to have a never-ending series of numbers on the right hand side of the decimal point, because of pi. You can use an approximation like 3.14 or 3.141592653589793, but you're never going to know the exact value, because there isn't one. There is uncertainty and darkness at the heart of something as simple as a circle.

I am the radius. I am rational when the circle of the world is not. Of course it works the other way too: when the circumference is rational, the radius is not. Perhaps I am that radius instead.

I haven't been to the bookstore for a week.

I could make it easier. I could move to Nevada or somewhere. Seventy towns in an area the size of a European country. But I won't. That would be giving in. I don't want to live in Nevada, for fuck's sake. It's pretty enough but there's nothing else happening there. Going there would be allowing it to become all of my life. There's nothing to do except go to Las Vegas, and those numbers ain't never going to be on your side. The occasional transgression I can talk myself round from. But if I lived in Nevada, every morning when I woke up I would know there was only one reason for me being there. It would become my whole life, instead of just part of it. Why else would you live in Nevada? Plus I imagine that people there are pretty good at fixing up their own houses.

Maybe I can just keep hanging on.

Him and me, and poor little pi in the middle—waiting to make one of us irrational. Maybe they've stopped looking, or maybe they were never looking in the first place. Sometimes it's very difficult for me to tell what are rational fears and what are not. It's such a cliff to step out over—'I did *what?*'. Like having your heart in an elevator when someone cuts the cord holding it up. Then you reach out and steady yourself, and pull yourself back. You walk away from the shaft. But you know it's there. Waking in the middle of the night, cold panic. Nothing happens. Eventually you get back to sleep.

But Christ, the times when I don't have to do it. It's wonderful. I feel so strong. When I can recall what's happened, the things that have been done, and feel okay about them. When it just seems uninteresting and strange, and I can think to myself 'I'm never doing that again'. Not in the way I feel immediately afterwards, when I just feel sick about the whole thing and my balls ache and I'm flooded and sit in the living room scrubbed clean: but in a calm, dispassionate way. 'No,' I think, 'I'm not going to do that again. I know I've done it, but that was then. This is now, and I don't need it any more. It was bad, but it's gone. I did it, but I don't any more. It's finished. It's over.' It hasn't been yet, though. It's never been over yet.

Julie and Max looked happy tonight.

More than half my mind is always somewhere else. Even my friends seem like someone else's, because only part of me is ever really with them. The rest of me is out on the trail, walking by myself. I remember another time driving on the M11 one Summer afternoon, I realised that all of the cars coming the other way had their lights on and their wipers going. I thought this was strange until I noticed that it actually was raining on the other side of the road. It was dry on the Northbound side, wet on the Southbound.

I didn't mean to go in, but I had a coffee at the shop opposite and saw her in the window, serving a customer. So I finished up, and went into the bookstore.

17 is prime and a perfect age. 1 plus 7 is 8, and thus the digital root of the perfect age is eight. I'm thirty-five now, in 1999, the year of 1, of starting. The digital root of 35 is 8 too—and I have this sense of someone closing in. This can hardly be a co-incidence. Perhaps I'll always be in danger when my age collapses to the same age as the girls', when they have the same digital root. It makes sense—it makes us too closely linked. When I was twenty-six I wasn't doing this, so I was safe. Forty-four will be dangerous. Fifty-three. Sixty-two. But I can't believe I'll still be doing this then. I jog, but I can't see me being fit enough at 62. It's no walk in the park, this kind of thing. And will it make any sense, to be doing this when my hair is grey and every part of me is scrawning out apart from a little pale paunch? Surely something must have burnt out by then. Interestingly, if you follow Wilson's test for primes, taking $(p-1)!$ to

be congruent with -1 mod p, we find that the primeness of 17 leaves us with 16 as the value (in base 10) of -1 modulo 17. Half of sixteen is eight. Again, rather convenient. All the eights. 2^3, of course. I still can't work out whether that means I should take eight a year. It seems far too much. I'm happier with low primes, like 3, 5 or 7. Even seven seems weak and greedy. Five is better. It's worked for me so far. I don't like 2 as a prime, even though it passes Wilson. It just doesn't feel right. The heart of 2 is irrational. The heart of a seventeen-year-old makes sense. To them. To me.

I don't really remember the first time. You'd think you would. I remember little flashes of it, little sparks of darkness, but I can't really remember the whole thing. I remember where she's buried. I remember that all too well. Sometimes when I'm lying in bed and I feel okay, I slowly start to feel something reaching out for me. I realise that there's a bit of my brain which will always be standing in a patch of forest a little way from Epping, watching over a grave, standing guard over a woman maybe no-one else even misses that much. She was short on family. She wasn't 17 of course, but she was 29. She was still prime, albeit a higher prime. But the actual doing of it, not really. I tend to remember the more recent ones most. You do, don't you? Because it's more recent. But even they are just a few still images, like I was really drunk. I wasn't. But it's like that. It's not like the normal things you do. I guess that's kind of funny, in a way. It's really not like the normal things you do.

Susan was kind of glum today. She'd had an argument with her landlord or the guy who owns the house they let or whoever he is. Leaking roof, which is no fun when it's this wet and this cold and going to get wetter and colder. I told her that I know something about such things. You should have seen her smile.

I tried to work out once, from first principles, how you find the square root of a number. Without a calculator. It did my head in. From school I distantly remembered that you think of a number close to it, whose square you know, and adjust it up and down by trial and error, until you're pretty close. But that's not very precise. It's not very attractive. It's such a simple thing, squaring something. Such an easy step. You take a number and multiply it by itself. Anyone can work that out. But finding the square root, reversing the process? There must be a way back, I thought. Once you've walked down a road, there must be some way home. I found out in the end. You use the Newton-Raphson equation for successive approximations:

$$x_i + 1 = (x_i + t\, x_i)/2$$

It bites its tail. You feed a number in to the equation, then feed the result back in, and feed that result back in—and keep working it, and keep working it. Until you stop. Except that with many numbers, even a simple number like 2, you never do. You never stop. The result is irrational, and goes on forever. I can put as many primes through the loop as I like, and the decimals will never stop. I can never find the number that I squared to make 2. It's not there any more. There's no way back. It's tainted.

My age always reduces to eight when the year root is 1. The root of 17 is 8. 8 plus 1 is 9, which casts itself out. The sum of me is always on the other side of the barrier, cast out. Nothing can be done about it. Always driving in the rain, with no turning in sight.

Tomorrow evening, at eight o'clock, I'm going to an address just outside of town. To fix a roof as a favour.

That's all.

When God Lived In Kentish Town

'I've found God,' the man said.

I groaned inwardly, and tried to will him not to sit at the table. I knew I was unlikely to succeed, because he didn't have a lot of other options, but I gave it my best shot anyway. I was in the Shuang Dou, it was dark outside, and I had only just started on the mound of food that was arranged around me in a neat semi-circle. I didn't want company. I wanted to be left alone.

The Shuang Dou is not at the prestige end of the Chinese restaurant market. Basically it's a take-away, with an even smaller waiting area than is usual, into which they've shoe-horned a couple of small tables for patrons who can't wait until they get home before eating—or who don't have a home to go to in the first place. It looks like the interior decor was done by someone extremely lazy about twenty years ago, and I don't expect it would survive anything more than a desultory glance from a health and safety inspector. Even the menus, which are printed—like those of every other Chinese restaurant in the land—to fold neatly into three, are rather haphazardly creased just once, across the middle. On the other hand the food is cheap and good, and the kitchen area is right there behind the counter, so you can watch the proprietors cooking your dinner. It seems to be run by one small family, the youngest member of which spends the evening in a papoose on the woman's back; her older sister taking the customers' orders and giving back change with faultless accuracy and an eight-year-old's engaging seriousness. Their parents are always friendly, in a guarded way, and I go in there so often that the patriarch generally has my order cooking before I've finished giving it, wielding wok and MSG with cheering skill and professionalism.

I was somewhere comfortable, in other words, surrounded by foil containers of food, and I wanted to just sit there and eat. I didn't want a conversation with someone strange, especially if it was to be about God. The guy sat down on the end of the table and opened his own container, which held a large portion of something noodle-based, possibly the squid chow mein of which the owners are justifiably proud. He squirted an alarming amount of soy sauce over it from the pot on the table, and then started eating with the plastic fork provided. Another of the other things I like about the Shuang Dou is that they don't force you to eat with chopsticks. Sure, it can be fun, when you're in the mood, or when you're surrounded by white linen and paying £40 a head: but when you really just want to get the food down your neck it has to be said that a fork is a better tool for the job.

The man munched meditatively through a couple of mouthfuls of his chow mein and then looked up at me, still chewing.

'I have, you know,' he said affably. 'I've found him.'

'Hmm,' I said, quietly, taking care not to catch his eye. While I don't believe that madness is communicable through eye contact, I believe that mad conversations most certainly are.

'You think I'm bonkers, don't you?'

'Hmm,' I said again, with a slightly different inflection, trying to suggest that while I was in no way impugning his sanity, personality or intellect I'd really rather just eat my special fried rice in peace. Special fried rice is a big deal to me. I'm a bit of a bore on the subject, to be honest. If I had to give up every other dish in the world and subsist only on that, I could do it without a second thought. At the Shuang Dou they prepare it differently to most places, cooking the egg last and laying it on top of the rice like a very thin and tasty omelette. I just wanted to sit and eat it.

'Not surprised,' the man continued, and I began to sense, with a mixture of relief and dread, that my participation in the conversation was unlikely to be required. While this meant I wasn't going to have to get involved on an active level, it also meant that he was probably not going to stop talking. 'Not surprised at all. I'd think the same thing myself.'

I stealthily reached for the soy and dripped a healthy dose over my Singapore Noodles. Perhaps if I kept my head down he'd come to believe that while God was real I was imaginary, and talk to the table instead.

'At first I thought 'Who'd have thought it, eh?' I mean—you'd hardly expect Him to be living in Kentish Town, would you?'

At this I found myself looking up, unable to stop myself. The man smiled genially at me, jaws still working. Seeing him properly for the first time, I saw that he was somewhere in his mid-forties, dressed in a dark and elderly suit with a grey sweater underneath, a generic blue shirt and an old but neatly knotted tie. His hair was grey around the temples and his face was rather red, either through an afternoon spent out in the cold or a couple of decades propping up bars. The whites of his eyes were a little grey, but not ostensibly insane.

'I mean, sounds a little odd, doesn't it?' he said, tilting his head and waggling his bushy eyebrows in a way evidently meant to indicate the world outside the window.

'Hmm,' I said, indicating cautious agreement. Kentish Town, I should explain for the benefit of those unacquainted with it, is a smallish patch of North London just above Camden and below Highgate and Hampstead. Many, many years ago it had the distinction of being at the very edge of London proper, a last stop before the countryside—and at that time was of considerably more note than, say, Camden. The Assembly Rooms pub, just across the road from the tube station, used to be a staging post or something. Nowadays Kentish Town is just part of the sprawl, and a not very attractive part at that; it has little of the cohesion of surrounding areas, and is instead a rather vague lumping together of roads, rail tracks, pubs and people. It's an interstice, a space between other places that has been filled by accident rather than design—like the corner of a cupboard which gets stuffed with the things you can't find another place for. It has none of Camden's joie de trendiness, and is a long, long way from Hampstead or Belsize Park's easy wealth. It's just a bit of London, and I live there because it's cheap.

'But then I thought about it a bit,' the man continued, 'And it makes perfect sense. Very convenient for the centre of town—just a couple of stops on the Northern Line—cheaper than Camden, quite a good little minimart down past the Vulture's Perch pub. And the food here's not bad, of course,' he added, winking at the little girl behind the counter.

'You're saying God actually lives here, in Kentish Town?' I asked, in spite of myself.

'Oh yes,' the man said comfortably.

I looked back at him levelly, trying to work out whether this made him more—or less—mad. In some ways it was preferable to born-again religious mania; simpler and less grandiose, at least. On the other it was clearly not the pronouncement of someone who had all his dogs on one leash.

In the background one of the woks hissed suddenly as the owners strove to fulfil a telephone order.

'Where abouts, exactly?' I asked.

The man looked at me for a moment, nodding, as if conceding that this was a reasonable question. 'Not sure,' he said. 'Never been able to follow him all the way home. But it must be around here somewhere. Convenient.'

'Why convenient?'

'Because this is where he has his shop,' he said. 'Just round the corner from here, in fact.'

'His shop,' I said, thinking I was beginning to understand. 'You mean, like, a church?'

'No, no,' the man said breezily. 'Electrical shop. Second hand mainly, though there's some newish stuff in the window. None of it's exactly *state-of-the-art* though.' The italics were his, not mine. He uttered the phrase as if aware he was being rather conversationally daring, and hoping that I was as up with the times as he was, and could follow his meaning.

I nodded slowly, wishing I'd had the sense to keep my mouth shut. Remembering that I had some Hot and Sour soup, I opened the polystyrene carton carefully and spooned up a mouthful. I have a tendency to eat all of my courses at the same time, which has driven more than one ex-girlfriend to distraction.

'You must have seen it,' the man said. 'Near that, oh, what d'you call it. That restaurant. Spanish. All those little plates of food. Quite good, in fact.'

'The tapas place,' I said, hollowly.

The man smiled happily. 'That's the one. Forget the name. Between there and the Estate Agents, little way up from the Assembly Rooms pub. You know the one I mean?'

I nodded but didn't say anything, mainly because I wasn't sure I wanted to prolong this nonsense. Also because I was trying to picture the shop he was referring to. I couldn't, quite. I knew the Assembly Rooms well—just enough of a local to be enticing, just enough *not* a local that you could go in there without any real danger of being stabbed, it sat where four grey and busy roads intersected in a ragged non-crossroads. A couple of shops further up the road was the bedraggled and dusty tapas restaurant. I could remember peering through the window once and deciding that it would just be too much of a health risk; and, as my patronship of the Shuang Dou shows, I'm not overly fastidious in such matters. I could also remember the Estate Agents, which stood out on that stretch of road because someone had spent a little money trying to make it look as if it wasn't situated in some particularly depressed area of an Eastern European town. I knew there were a couple of shops in between the two, but I couldn't picture what they were.

'You look, next time you pass that way,' the man said, and I realised abruptly that he was standing, wiping his mouth with a paper serviette. 'You'll find I'm right.'

WHEN GOD LIVED IN KENTISH TOWN

He nodded, winked at the people behind the counter and walked back out into the night, leaving me feeling obscurely irritated; as if by quitting the conversation before I had he'd somehow made *me* out to be the lunatic. As I watched him disappear down the cold and lamplit street outside I spooned another mouthful of Hot and Sour into my mouth, failing to notice that it contained an entire red chili.

By the time I'd finished coughing, and had thanked the lady owner for the plastic cup of water she brought me, the man had disappeared. When I'd finished my food I crossed the street and walked directly down Falkland Road to my apartment. It was sleeting, and getting late, and I wouldn't have bothered going round the long way to check what was between the Estate Agents and the tapas bar even if I'd remembered.

Two days later I walked out of the tube station at about three o'clock in the afternoon, serene with boredom after a long meeting with one of my clients. I write corporate videos for a living—telling people how to sell hoovers, why they shouldn't refer to their co-workers as 'wankers', that sort of thing. If someone offers you a job writing a corporate video, just say no. Seriously. Just don't get involved.

It takes about five minutes to walk from the tube to where I live. Mostly that's a good thing. When you know that once you get indoors you have to sit at the computer and write a corporate video, it can seem less ideal. On days like that, you can find yourself wishing it was a four-day trek over mountainous terrain, involving sherpas, a few of those little horse things and maybe even an entire documentary team to shoot lots of footage of you getting frostbite and wishing you were back at home.

It was in this spirit that instead of heading diagonally across Leighton Road and up Leverton Street, I walked across the road and then past the Assembly Rooms up Fortess Road. It was only as I was passing the tapas bar, whose name I once again failed to notice, that I remembered the conversation I'd had in the Shuang Dou. Mildly excited at the prospect of anything that would delay my return home, I slowed my pace and looked at the stores between the restaurant and the sloping glass of the estate agents up ahead.

When I saw the shop I was rather taken aback, probably just because I hadn't expected it to be there at all. I found myself casting a quick glance up the road, as if concerned that someone should see me, and then wandered over to the window.

The shop looked not dissimilar to the standard type of electrical store to be found in areas of London which aren't aiming to challenge

Tottenham Court Road's domination of the consumer goods market. Some of the products in the window were evidently second-hand, and—as the man had said—those which did look new were hardly cutting edge. Tape-radios with tiny three-inch speakers and shiny plastic buttons. Plastic Midi systems that looked like they'd fracture at low temperatures. Video recorders from the days when Betamax was still in with a shout. There were other things in the display, however. A pile of storage units, evidently for sale. A wide range of alarm clocks. A faded poster of ABBA.

Surely *that* couldn't be for sale?

I couldn't see beyond the display into the shop itself, and reached out for the door. Only when I'd unsuccessfully tugged on it did I notice a handwritten sign sellotaped to it from the inside.

'Back later,' it said. I smiled to myself, wondering if that's what Jesus had left on his door way back when. Then I tugged at the door again, obscurely disappointed that I wasn't going to be able to go inside. Probably it was still just a desire not to go back home and get on with earning a living, but I suddenly wanted to see what was there. The door was as locked as it had been the first time.

I trudged round the corner and down Falkland Road to meet my doom, in the form of thirty pages of still-unwritten shite about customer care for Vauxhall dealers.

At five I sat back from the computer, mind whirling. When I'm writing corporate videos I tend to visualise the facts and opinions I'm supposed to be putting into them as recalcitrant, bad-tempered sheep, which are determined to run away from me and hide in the hills. After two hours I'd managed to worry most of them into a pen; but they were moving restlessly and irritably against each other, determined not to pull in the same direction. It was time to take a break, before I decided the hell with it and started shooting the little bastards instead.

I put on a coat and wandered down the road to the cigarette shop on the corner, stocking up on my chosen method of slow suicide. As I did so I wished, not for the first time, that cigarettes weren't bad for you, or at least that I didn't know they were. That knowledge made every single one I smoked a little internal battle—never mind the *external* battles that cropped up every now and then, when some health freak gave me a hard time for endangering their life. These people, I had noticed, were invariably rather fat, and thus were doing their own fine job of reducing their own life expectancy; but that doesn't seem to be the point any more.

What *we* do is fine—it's what those other bastards are doing to us that we won't stand for. I remembered reading a short piece in a recent *Enquirer* entitled 'How to stop your co-workers from giving you their colds'. After a line like that I'd expected advice on how to prevent deranged typists from injecting me with viruses, or marketing executives from coming over and deliberately breathing in my face. But no, it had been things like 'Have a window open', and 'Eat vitamin C'. In other words, advice on how to stop *yourself* from acquiring the communicable colds that—though no fault of their own—other people might have.

But we don't see it like that, any more. Life's a constant battle to stop other people doing things to us, taking as hard a line as possible. We don't move tables or leave the room when someone is smoking—we stop them from smoking, anywhere, ever. We don't avoid watching videos that have a bit of sex and violence in them—we get them banned. And presumably, at some stage, we don't not read books we disagree with. We get them burned.

I recognised these thoughts as those of someone who was bored out of his tiny mind, and decided not to go back to the flat just yet. Instead I headed round the corner, sending a little nugget of goodwill to the Shuang Dou on the opposite side of the road, and walked back down towards Leighton Road. Initially I was just taking a long way home, and then I realised I'd be going past the shop again, and that now might qualify as later, and it might be open.

It was. As I approached the shop I saw that the sign had gone from the door. Very slightly elated, in a vague way, I pushed it open and walked in.

There was no-one behind the counter, and so I was free to look over what was arrayed around the shop. It wasn't quite what I was expecting. Usually such stores have an air of thrift, of objects being widely spaced on shelves. This one was exactly the opposite. The area inside, which wasn't much bigger than my 'cosy' living room, was piled floor to ceiling with a bewildering array of stuff. Some of it was electrical—more of the period pieces from the window—but the majority was completely uncategorisable. Old toys, piles of ancient magazines. A few posters on the walls—ABBA again, together with other seventies bands. Small, chrome-plated appliances of indiscernible function. Even a few items of clothing, tired and out of fashion. It was like a jumble sale organised with some clear but not quite explicable purpose in mind.

There was a noise behind the counter, and I turned to see that a man had appeared. He was tall, in his early fifties, and looked Nigerian. He was dressed in an old blue suit which was shiny in patches, and wore a white shirt without a tie underneath his buttoned jacket. His face was lined, and he looked nervous, as if I was intruding.

'Hello,' I said, feeling strangely at ease—probably because he looked so unlike the smarmy and over-confident people you usually find in electrical stores: you know the type, the ones who pronounce 'Can I help you at all' as one howling monosyllable and try to sell you a triple-standard VCR even if you just came in for batteries.

The man nodded cautiously. 'Can I help you?' he said. His voice was deep but quiet, and the words were carefully enunciated. It was a genuine question.

'Just looking around,' I said, and he nodded again. I turned away and ran my eyes over the shelves, realising I had a bit of a problem. I couldn't just turn and walk out now. It would seem dismissive, of this man and his shop. I didn't want to do that. He looked like he'd been dismissed often enough already. On the other hand, I found it hard to believe that there was a single object in the shop that I would want. I already had all the recording, videoing, listening and watching equipment I could possibly need, none of it more than six months old; and all of the other stuff looked like junk you'd want to throw away rather than acquire.

I couldn't leave without at least making an effort, so I stepped over to one of the shelves and looked more closely at the objects strewn along it. Small pottery figures you might expect to find on surfaces in the room of a twelve-year-old girl. A very old copy of the 'National Geographic'. A plastic alarm clock, manufactured back when people thought plastic was cool. A couple of 45s, by bands I'd never heard of.

I was very aware of the man standing silently behind me, and when I noticed a shoe-box full of watches I reached into it. My hand fell upon an oddly-shaped digital watch, which seemed to have been fashioned out of man-made materials to resemble what people two decades ago had thought of as 'futuristic'. Half of its strap was missing, and no numerals were showing in the window; but on the other hand I could possibly have some fun taking it apart, maybe even getting it going and turning it into some cyberpunky inside-out timepiece.

I turned to him. 'How much is this?' I asked, feeling like a minor character in some very old film.

'Two pound,' he said.

'I'll take it,' I nodded, and walked over to the counter, feeling in my back pocket for some change. He smiled shyly and found a small paper bag to put it in.

When I left the shop I crossed the road and stood there, looking across at the window. I couldn't see into the store, and wondered if the man was still just standing behind the counter. I opened the bag I held in my hand and looked at the watch. Why on Earth had I bought it? It was just going to sit in a pile somewhere in the already overcrowded flat; next time I moved I'd either have to work up the resolve to throw it away, or tote it with me for ever more. I was surprised to see that I'd been mistaken in the store—something *was* visible on the screen. It wasn't numerals, or at least not whole ones, but little segments of the LCD figures seemed to be slowly flashing. Not very good news, of course; instead of simply being out of battery, it probably meant the watch was completely broken.

But when I'd been in the store it hadn't been working at all.

An hour later the man left the store, and I dropped the chip I had in my hand and stood up. I'd been sitting in the fish shop on the opposite side of the road, drinking tea and having an early and unhealthy meal. The food was actually quite good—I'm a connoisseur of cheap takeaways in North London—but that wasn't why I had chosen to eat there.

To be honest, I didn't really *know* why I'd stayed around. I'd stood, staring dumbly at the watch for a while, and then simply decided I was going to wait. I didn't want to hang out on the pavement where passing trucks could spray me with dirty water, so I ducked into Mario's instead.

Now the guy was on the move, and I knew I was going to follow him. I didn't have a reason, and I felt an idiot. But I was going to do it anyway.

I waited in the entrance to the fish bar until the man had got far enough up the other side of the street, then left and hurried across the road. Nobody ran me over, though several people had a bloody good try. The man was walking slowly, and I didn't anticipate having a problem keeping up with him. Quite the opposite; the challenge was to make sure he didn't see me. As discussed, I write videos for living. Tailing people was a bit of a departure for me. I walked along, head down and hands huddled into my coat, hoping this was the right sort of approach—every now and then lifting my eyes to check he was still in front of me.

The man continued up Fortess Road as far as the corner store where I'd bought cigarettes earlier, and then turned into Falkland Road. I picked up the pace a little, and made it round the corner about twenty seconds after him. By then he'd only got about fifty yards up the road, and so I dropped back again. He was walking more quickly now, head up, and crossed the road to the Northern side, heading for the junction with Leverton Street. I decided to cross immediately, and by the time he was approaching the corner he was only about twenty yards ahead. It was winter dark by now, but I could still see the shiny patches on the elbows of his suit as he turned the corner. About ten seconds later I followed him round.

He wasn't there.

I stopped. He couldn't have gone into a house, because there was a good fifty yards of wall before the nearest doorway. Across the street and up a bit was another corner store, but there was no way he could have reached that in the time he'd been out of my sight. I knew this, but I hurried across the street anyway, and peered into the window. The only people inside were the proprietor and his son. I turned back away from the window and looked up the street, listening for the sound of footsteps.

I couldn't hear any.

I wandered the area for a little while, getting progressively colder. Then I walked slowly back down Leverton Street and headed back to my flat.

I felt let down, and a little betrayed.

I also felt like concentrating on worrying some sheep for a while.

By the next morning I felt differently, or I'd reached my boredom threshold again. Either way, I found myself, mid-morning, standing outside the shop again. I had the watch in my pocket and it was still blinking. I'd tried changing the batteries, but that hadn't made any difference. Parts of the numerals were still flashing meaninglessly on and off. Feeling slightly breathless, I pushed the door and walked in.

This time the man was behind the counter as I entered, and it was me who felt nervous. I ground to a halt a couple of steps in. He stared back at me. He was wearing the same suit, and still looked rather wary.

'Hello,' I said, eventually. He nodded. Struggling for something to add, I held the watch up. 'I bought this yesterday.'

He nodded again.

'It doesn't seem to work,' I said, knowing that was hardly the point.

The man shrugged apologetically. 'It wasn't sold as working,' he said, quietly. 'All I have is what you see.'

'Oh, I know,' I said. 'It's just, it started doing something when I left the shop, and I wondered…'

I didn't really know what I was wondering, and neither did the man. He just stared at me.

'I'm, er,' I said, holding out my hands, 'I'm not here to cause trouble or anything.'

'I know,' the man said.

'You look a little nervous,' I blurted, immediately regretting it.

The man stared down at the counter for a while, and then looked up. 'This isn't right,' he said. 'Nothing's right, and I don't understand it.' He said these words quietly, and with great sadness. 'This isn't the way things are supposed to be.'

'What do you mean?'

'I don't think I'm supposed to be here.'

This wasn't making a great deal of sense to me, but I felt that it was something that had to be discussed. Part of my mind was sitting back with its arms folded, wondering what the hell I thought I was doing. The rest felt quite strongly that whatever it was, it was right.

'Where *are* you supposed to be?' I asked.

'I don't know,' he said. 'But this doesn't feel right. Something else should have happened by now.'

'What kind of thing?'

'I don't know that either,' he shrugged. 'That's what makes it so difficult.'

There was a pause then, neither of us apparently sure of how to proceed.

'It was simpler, before,' he said suddenly, looking down at the counter. 'People knew what they were, what they wanted. This time, no-one seems to know. And if you don't know, you can't believe. Even those who think they believe are just cheerleading for something that was never meant.'

'I don't understand.'

'Exactly,' he said, smiling faintly. 'Once, you would have understood. When I was younger, people knew what they were. Now they are less sure. A man can't be a man, because he thinks that's a bad thing to be. He has forgotten what it's like. Women too. People have forgotten magic. Things are better now for them, but also worse. Everything is surface, nothing is inside. The insides are empty. Do you not think this is so?'

I thought for a moment. I didn't really know what he was saying, unless it was this: that for the last twenty years everyone had been hiding, unsure of themselves, dancing to someone else's tune. That women have become more free to have jobs, and less free to have lives. That men run scared from their maleness until it twists and curdles into bitterness and resentment and rape. That everything is a constant battle not to think, not to feel, not to believe in anything that can't be said at a dinner party without offending someone. Men fall over backwards to prove they're not rampaging beasts, until the animal that still lives in them dies from lack of exercise, leaving only a shallow stick figure. Women run after the respect of people who don't care about them, forced to sideline the newborn into nurseries and day schools, because it's companies which are supposed to be important now, not families. Men *should* behave themselves, I thought, and women *should* be allowed to have careers; but this wasn't the way it was supposed to be achieved. The human has been lost, and all we have become is code in someone else's machine. We believe in flavourings, and correctness, in feelgood factors and learning curves and earning supermarket loyalty points—and trust in Sunday supplement articles refuting things that were too boring to say in the first place. Everything else is too difficult.

'Yeah,' I said, eventually. 'That's pretty much the way it is.'

The man nodded, as if coming to a decision. 'I thought so. Do you want a refund?'

It took me a moment to realise he was talking about the watch.

'No,' I said. 'That's alright. I'll keep it anyway.'

'Good,' he said, turning away. 'I'm sure that somewhere inside it still keeps time.'

I'm looking for work at the moment. I'm not sure what kind. I stopped writing corporate videos a few months ago, halfway through another one about Customer Care: thirty different ways to make your clients think that you give a fuck about them, when both you and they know you don't. I only got to number fourteen. I decided that I'd helped write enough code, and that I wasn't going to do it any more. The sheep can worry themselves.

I still eat in the Shuang Dou a couple of nights a week, but I haven't seen the red-faced man again. It doesn't matter. I don't think he could tell me anything I don't already suspect. I've still got the watch too, and sometimes it seems almost as if the flashing figures are going to settle, become strong enough to read again. It hasn't happened yet, but I believe that, some day, it will.

I went back to the shop the day after the conversation, but the window was vacant. By pressing my face up against the glass I could see that everything had gone from inside the shop. It was completely empty, dust already settling.

On the inside of the door was a sign, roughly hand-lettered but securely sellotaped, as if to withstand a long wait.

'Back later,' it said.

The Man Who
Drew Cats

Tom was a very tall man, so tall he didn't even have a nickname for it. Ned Black, who was at least a head shorter, had been 'Tower Block' since the sixth grade, and Jack had a sign up over the door saying 'Mind Your Head, Ned'. But Tom was just Tom. It was like he was so tall it didn't bear mentioning even for a joke: be a bit like ragging someone for breathing.

Course there were other reasons too for not ragging Tom about his height or anything else. The guys you'll find perched on stools round Jack's bar watching the game and buying beers, they've known each other forever. Gone to Miss Stadler's school together, gotten under each other's Mom's feet, double-dated right up to giving each other's best man's speech. Kingstown is a small place, you understand, and the old boys who come regular to Jack's mostly spent their childhoods in the same tree-house. Course they'd since gone their separate ways, up to a point: Pete was an accountant now, had a small office down Union Street just off the square and did pretty good, whereas Ned was still pumping gas and changing oil and after forty years he did that pretty good too. Comes a time when men have known each other so long they forget what they do for a living most the time, because it just don't matter. When you talk there's a little bit of skimming stones down the quarry in second grade, a whisper of dolling up to go to that first dance, a tad of going to the housewarming when they moved ten years back. There's all that, so much more than you can say, and none of it's important except for having happened.

So we'll stop by and have a couple of beers and talk about the town and rag each other, and the pleasure's just in shooting the breeze and it don't really matter what's said, just the fact that we're all still there to say it.

But Tom, he was different. We all remember the first time we saw him. It was a long hot summer like we haven't seen in the ten years since, and we were lolling under the fans at Jack's and complaining about the tourists. Kingstown does get its share in the summer, even though it's not near the sea and we don't have a McDonalds and I'll be damned if I can figure out why folk'll go out of their way to see what's just a quiet little town near some mountains. It was as hot as Hell that afternoon and as much as a man could do to sit in his shirtsleeves and drink the coolest beer he could find, and Jack's is the coolest for us, and always will be, I guess.

Then Tom walked in. His hair was already pretty white back then, and long, and his face was brown and tough with grey eyes like diamonds set in leather. He was dressed mainly in black with a long coat that made you hot just to look at it, but he looked comfortable like he carried his very own weather around with him and he was just fine.

He got a beer, and sat down at a table and read the town *Bugle*, and that was that.

It was special because there wasn't anything special about it. Jack's Bar isn't exactly exclusive and we don't all turn round and stare at anyone new if they come in, but that place is like a monument to shared times. If a tourist couple comes in out of the heat and sits down, nobody says anything—and maybe nobody even notices at the front of their mind—but it's like there's a little island of the alien in the water and the currents just don't ebb and flow the way they usually do, if you get what I mean. Tom just walked in and sat down and it was all right because it was like he was there just like we were, and could've been for thirty years. He sat and read his paper like part of the same river, and everyone just carried on downstream the way they were.

Pretty soon he goes up for another beer and a few of us got talking to him. We got his name and what he did—painting, he said—and after that it was just shooting the breeze. That quick. He came in that summer afternoon and just fell into the conversation like he'd been there all his life, and sometimes it was hard to imagine he hadn't been. Nobody knew where he came from, or where he'd been, and there was something real quiet about him. A stillness, a man in a slightly different world. But he showed enough to get along real well with us, and a bunch of old friends don't often let someone in like that.

Anyway, he stayed that whole summer. Rented himself a place just round the corner from the square, or so he said: I never saw it. I guess no-one did. He was a private man, private like a steel door with four bars and a couple of six-inch padlocks, and when he left the square at the end of the day he could have vanished as soon as he turned the corner for all we knew. But he always came from that direction in the morning, with his easel on his back and paint box under his arm, and he always wore that black coat like it was a part of him. But he always looked cool, and the funny thing was when you stood near him you could swear you felt cooler yourself. I remember Pete saying over a beer that it wouldn't surprise him none if, assuming it ever rained again, Tom would walk round in his own column of dryness. He was just joking, of course, but Tom made you think things like that.

Jack's bar looks right out onto the square, the kind of square towns don't have much anymore: big and dusty with old roads out each corner, tall shops and houses on all the sides and some stone paving in the middle round a fountain that ain't worked in living memory. Well in the summer that old square is just full of out-of-towners in pink toweling jumpsuits and nasty jackets standing round saying 'Wow' and taking pictures of our quaint old hall and our quaint old stores and even our quaint old selves if we stand still too long. Tom would sit out near the fountain and paint and those people would stand and watch for hours—but he didn't paint the houses or the square or the old Picture House. He painted animals, and painted them like you've never seen. Birds with huge blue speckled wings and cats with cutting green eyes; and whatever he painted it looked like it was just coiled up on the canvas ready to fly away. He didn't do them in their normal colours, they were all reds and purples and deep blues and greens—and yet they fair sparkled with life. It was a wonder to watch: he'd put up a fresh paper, sit looking at nothing in particular, then dip his brush into his paint and draw a line, maybe red, maybe blue. Then he'd add another, maybe the same colour, maybe not. Stroke by stroke you could see the animal build up in front of your eyes and yet when it was finished you couldn't believe it hadn't always been there. When he'd finished he'd spray it with some stuff to fix the paints and put a price on it and you can believe me those paintings were sold before they hit the ground. Spreading businessmen from New Jersey or somesuch and their bored wives would come alive for maybe the first time in years, and walk away with one of those paintings and their arms round each other, looking like they'd found a bit of something they'd forgotten they'd lost.

Come about six o'clock Tom would finish up and walk across to Jack's, looking like a sailing ship amongst rowing boats and saying yes he'd be back again tomorrow and yes, he'd be happy to do a painting for them. He'd get a beer and sit with us and watch the game and there'd be no paint on his fingers or his clothes, not a spot. I figured he'd got so much control over that paint it went where it was told and nowhere else.

I asked him once how he could bear to let those paintings go. I know if I'd been able to make anything that good in my whole life I couldn't let it out of my sight, I'd want to keep it to look at sometimes. He thought for a moment and then he said he believed it depends how much of yourself you've put into it. If you've gone deep down and pulled up what's inside and put it down, then you don't want to let it go: you want to keep it, so's you can check sometimes that it's still safely tied down. Comes a time when a painting's so right and so good that it's private, and no-one'll understand it except the man who put it down. Only he is going to know what he's talking about. But the everyday paintings, well they were mainly just because he liked to paint animals, and liked for people to have them. He could only put a piece of himself into something he was going to sell, but they paid for the beers and I guess it's like us fellows in Jack's Bar: if you like talking, you don't always have to be saying something important.

Why animals? Well if you'd seen him with them I guess you wouldn't have to ask. He loved them, is all, and they loved him right back. The cats were always his favorites. My old Pa used to say that cats weren't nothing but sleeping machines put on the earth to do some of the human's sleeping for them, and whenever Tom worked in the square there'd always be a couple curled up near his feet. And whenever he did a chalk drawing, he'd always do a cat.

Once in a while, you see, Tom seemed to get tired of painting on paper, and he'd get out some chalks and sit down on the baking flagstones and just do a drawing right there on the dusty rock. Now I've told you about his paintings, but these drawings were something else again. It was like because they couldn't be bought but would be washed away, he was putting more of himself into it, doing more than just shooting the breeze. They were just chalk on dusty stone and they were still in these weird colours, but I tell you children wouldn't walk near them because they looked so real, and they weren't the only ones, either. People would stand a few feet back and stare and you could see the wonder in their eyes. If they could've been bought there were people who would have sold their houses. I'm telling you. And it's a funny thing but a couple of times when I walked over to open the store up in the mornings I saw a dead bird or two on top of those drawings, almost like they had landed on it and been so terrified to find themselves right on top of a cat they'd dropped dead of fright. But they must have been dumped there by some real cat, of course, because some of those birds looked like they'd been mauled a bit. I used to throw them in the bushes to tidy up and some of them were pretty broken up.

Old Tom was a godsend to a lot of mothers that summer, who found they could leave their little ones by him, do their shopping in peace and have a soda with their friends and come back to find the kids still sitting quietly watching Tom paint. He didn't mind them at all and would talk to them and make them laugh, and kids of that age laughing is one of the best sounds there is. It's the kind of sound that makes the trees grow. They're young and curious and the world spins round them and when they laugh the world seems a brighter place because it takes you back to the time when you knew no evil and everything was good, or if it wasn't, it would be over by tomorrow.

And here I guess I've finally come down to it, because there was one little boy who didn't laugh much, but just sat quiet and watchful, and I guess he probably understands more of what happened that summer than any of us, though maybe not in words he could tell.

His name was Billy McNeill, and he was Jim Valentine's kid. Jim used to be a mechanic, worked with Ned up at the gas station and raced beat-up cars after hours. Which is why his kid is called McNeill now: one Sunday Jim took a corner a mite too fast and the car rolled and the gas tank caught and they never did find all the wheels. A year later his Mary married again. God alone knows why, her folks warned her, her friends warned her, but I guess love must just have been blind. Sam McNeill's work schedule was at best pretty empty, and mostly he just drank and hung out with friends who maybe weren't always this side of the law. I guess Mary had her own sad little miracle and got her sight back pretty soon, because it wasn't long before Sam got free with his fists when the evenings got too long and he'd had a lot too many. You didn't see Mary around much anymore. In these parts people tend to stare at black eyes on a woman, and a deaf man could hear the whisperings of 'We Told Her So'.

One morning Tom was sitting painting as usual, and little Billy was sitting watching him. Usually he just wandered off after a while but this morning Mary was at the Doctor's and she came over to collect him, walking quickly with her face lowered. But not low enough. I was watching from the store, it was kind of a slow day. Tom's face never showed much. He was a man for a quiet smile and a raised eyebrow, but he looked shocked that morning. Mary's eyes were puffed and purple and there was a cut on her cheek an inch long. I guess we'd sort of gotten used to seeing her like that and if the truth be known some of the wives thought she'd got remarried a bit on the soon side and I suppose we may all have been a bit cold towards her, Jim Valentine having been so well-liked and all.

Tom looked from the little boy who never laughed much, to his mom with her tired unhappy eyes and her beat-up face, and his own face went from shocked to stony and I can't describe it any other way but that I felt a cold chill cross my heart from right across the square.

But then he smiled and ruffled Billy's hair and Mary took Billy's hand and they went off. They turned back once and Tom was still looking after them and he gave Billy a little wave and he waved back and mother and child smiled together.

That night in Jack's Tom put a quiet question about Mary and we told him the story. As he listened his face seemed to harden from within, his eyes growing flat and dead. We told him that old Lou Lachance, who lived next door to the McNeill's, said that sometimes you could hear him shouting and her pleading till three in the morning and on still nights the sound of Billy crying for even longer than that. Told him it was a shame, but what could you do? Folks keep themselves out of other people's faces round here, and I guess Sam and his drinking buddies didn't have much to fear from nearly-retireders like us anyhow. Told him it was a terrible thing, and none of us liked it, but these things happened and what could you do.

Tom listened and didn't say a word. Just sat there in his black coat and listened to us pass the buck. After a while the talk sort of petered out and we all sat and watched the bubbles in our beers. I guess the bottom line was that none of us had really thought about it much except as another chapter of small-town gossip, and Jesus Christ did I feel ashamed about that by the time we'd finished telling it. Sitting there with Tom was no laughs at all. He had a real edge to him, and seemed more unknown than known that night. He stared at his laced fingers for a long time, and then he began, real slow, to talk.

He'd been married once, he said, a long time ago, and he'd lived in a place called Stevensburg with his wife Rachel. When he talked about her the air seemed to go softer and we all sat quiet and supped our beers and remembered how it had been way back when we first loved our own wives. He talked of her smile and the look in her eyes and when we went home that night I guess there were a few wives who were surprised at how tight they got hugged, and who went to sleep in their husband's arms feeling more loved and contented than they had in a long while.

He'd loved her and she him and for a few years they were the happiest people on earth. Then a third party had got involved. Tom didn't say his name, and he spoke real neutrally about him, but it was a gentleness like silk wrapped round a knife. Anyway his wife fell in love with him, or thought she had, or leastways she slept with him. In their bed, the bed they'd come to on their wedding night. As Tom spoke these words some of us looked up at him, startled, like we'd been slapped across the face.

Rachel did what so many do and live to regret till their dying day. She was so mixed up and getting so much pressure from the other guy that she decided to plough on with the one mistake and make it the biggest in the world.

She left Tom. He talked with her, pleaded even. It was almost impossible to imagine Tom ever doing that, but I guess the man we knew was a different guy from the one he was remembering. The pleading made no difference.

And so Tom had to carry on living in Stevensburg, walking the same tracks, seeing them around, wondering if she was as free and easy with him, if the light in her eyes was shining on him now. And each time the man saw Tom he'd look straight at him and crease a little smile, a grin that said he knew about the pleading and he and his cronies had had a good laugh over the wedding bed—and yes, I'm going home with your wife tonight and I know just how she likes it, you want to compare notes?

And then he'd turn and kiss Rachel on the mouth, his eyes on Tom, smiling. And she let him do it.

It had kept stupid old women in stories for weeks, the way Tom kept losing weight and his temper and the will to live. He took three months of it and then left without bothering to sell the house. Stevensburg was where he'd grown up and courted and loved and now wherever he turned the good times had rotted and hung like fly-blown corpses in all the cherished places. He'd never been back.

It took an hour to tell, and then he stopped talking a while and lit a hundredth cigarette and Pete got us all some more beers. We were sitting sad and thoughtful, tired like we'd lived it ourselves. And I guess most of us had, some little bit of it. But had we ever loved anyone the way he'd loved her? I doubt it, not all of us put together. Pete set the beers down and Ned asked Tom why he hadn't just beaten the living shit out of the guy. Now, no-one else would have actually asked that, but Ned's a good guy, and I guess we were all with him in feeling a piece of that oldest and most crushing hatred in the world, the hate of a man who's lost the woman he loves to another, and we knew what Ned was saying. I'm not saying it's a good thing and I know you're not supposed to feel like that these days but show me a man who says he doesn't and I'll show you a liar. Love is the only feeling worth a tin shit but you've got to know that it comes from both sides of a man's character and the deeper it runs the darker the pools it draws from.

My guess is he just hated the man too much to hit him. Comes a time when that isn't enough, when nothing is ever going to be enough, and so you can't do anything at all. And as he talked the pain just flowed out like a river that wasn't ever going to be stopped, a river that had cut a channel through every corner of his soul. I learnt something that night that you can go your whole life without realising: that there are things that can be done that can mess someone up so badly, for so long, that they just cannot be allowed; that there are some kinds of pain that you cannot suffer to be brought into the world.

And then Tom was done telling and he raised a smile and said that in the end he hadn't done anything to the man except paint him a picture, which I didn't understand, but Tom looked like he'd talked all he was going to.

So we got some more beers and shot some quiet pool before going home. But I guess we all knew what he'd been talking about.

Billy McNeill was just a child. He should have been dancing through a world like a big funfair full of sunlight and sounds, and instead he went home at night and saw his mom being beaten up by a man with shit for brains who struck out at a good woman because he was too stupid to deal with the world. Most kids go to sleep thinking about bikes and climbing apple trees and skimming stones, and he was lying there hearing his mom get smashed in the stomach and then hit again as she threw up in the sink. Tom didn't say any of that, but he did. And we knew he was right.

The summer kept up bright and hot, and we all had our businesses to attend to. Jack sold a lot of beer and I sold a lot of ice cream (Sorry ma'am, just the three flavours, and no, Bubblegum Pistachio ain't one of them) and Ned fixed a whole bunch of cracked radiators. Tom sat right out there in the square with a couple of cats by his feet and a crowd around him, magicking up animals in the sun.

And I think that after that night Mary maybe got a few more smiles as she did her shopping, and maybe a few more wives stopped to talk to her. She looked a lot better too: Sam had a job by the sound of it and her face healed up pretty soon. You could often see her standing holding Billy's hand as they watched Tom paint for a while before they went home. I think she realised they had a friend in him. Sometimes Billy was there all afternoon, and he was happy there in the sun by Tom's feet and oftentimes he'd pick up a piece of chalk and sit scrawling on the pavement. Sometimes I'd see Tom lean over and say something to him and he'd look up and smile a simple child's smile that beamed in the sunlight. The tourists kept coming and the sun kept shining and it was one of those summers that go on forever and stick in a child's mind, and tell you what summer should be like for the rest of your life. And I'm damn sure it sticks in Billy's mind, just like it does in all of ours.

THE MAN WHO DREW CATS

Because one morning Mary didn't come into the store, which had gotten to being a regular sort of thing, and Billy wasn't out there in the square. After the way things had been the last few weeks that could only be bad news, and so I left the boy John in charge of the store and hurried over to have a word with Tom. I was kind of worried.

I was no more than halfway across to him when I saw Billy come running from the opposite corner of the square, going straight to Tom. He was crying fit to burst and just leapt up at Tom and clung to him, his arms wrapped tight round his neck. Then his mother came across from the same direction, running as best she could. She got to Tom and they just looked at each other. Mary's a real pretty girl but you wouldn't have believed it then. It looked like he'd actually broken her nose this time, and blood was streaming out of her lip. She started sobbing, saying Sam had lost his job because he was back on the drink and what could she do and then suddenly there was a roar and I was shoved aside and Sam was standing there, still wearing his slippers, weaving back and forth and radiating that aura of violence that keeps men like him safe. He started shouting at Mary to take the kid the fuck back home and she just flinched and cowered closer to Tom like she was huddling round a fire to keep out the cold. This just got Sam even wilder and he staggered forward and told Tom to get the fuck out of it if he knew what was good for him, and grabbed Mary's arm and tried to yank her towards him, his face terrible with rage.

Then Tom stood up. Now Tom was a tall man, but he wasn't a young man, and he was thin. Sam was thirty and built like the town hall. When he did work it usually involved moving heavy things from one place to another, and his strength was supercharged by a whole pile of drunken nastiness.

But at that moment the crowd stepped back as one and I suddenly felt very afraid for Sam McNeill. Tom looked like you could take anything you cared to him and it would just break, like he was a huge spike of granite wrapped in skin with two holes in the face where the rock showed through. And he was mad, not hot and blowing like Sam, but mad and *cold*.

There was a long pause. Then Sam weaved back a step and shouted:

'You just come on home, you hear? Gonna be real trouble if you don't, Mary. Real trouble.' And then stormed off across the square the way he came, knocking his way through the tourist vultures soaking up the spicy local colour.

Mary turned to Tom, so afraid it hurt to see, and said she guessed she'd better be going. Tom looked at her for a moment and then spoke for the first time.

'Do you love him?'

Even if you wanted to, you ain't going to lie to eyes like that, for fear something inside you will break.

Real quiet she said: 'No,' and began crying softly as she took Billy's hand and walked slowly back across the square.

Tom packed up his stuff and walked over to Jack's. I went with him and had a beer but I had to get back to the shop and Tom just sat there like a trigger, silent and strung up tight as a drum. Somewhere down near the bottom of those still waters something was stirring. Something I thought I didn't want to see.

About an hour later it was lunchtime and I'd just left the shop to have a break when suddenly something whacked into the back of my legs and nearly knocked me down. It was Billy. It was Billy and he had a bruise round his eye that was already closing it up.

I knew what the only thing to do was and I did it. I took his hand and led him across to the Bar, feeling a hard anger pushing against my throat. When he saw Tom, Billy ran to him again and Tom took him in his arms and looked over Billy's shoulder at me, and I felt my own anger collapse utterly in the face of a fury I could never have generated. I tried to find a word to describe it but they all just seemed like they were in the wrong language. All I can say is I wanted to be somewhere else and it felt real cold standing there facing that stranger in a black coat.

Then the moment passed and Tom was holding the kid close, ruffling his hair and talking to him in a low voice, murmuring the words I thought only mothers knew. He dried Billy's tears and checked his eye and then he got off his stool, smiled down at him and said:

'I think it's time we did some drawing, what d'you say?' and, taking the kid's hand, he picked up his chalkbox and walked out into the square.

I don't know how many times I looked up and watched them that afternoon. They were sitting side by side on the stone, Billy's little hand wrapped round one of Tom's fingers, and Tom doing one of his chalk drawings. Every now and then Billy would reach across and add a little bit and Tom would smile and say something and Billy's gurgling laugh would float across the square. The store was real busy that afternoon and I was chained to that counter, but I could tell by the size of the crowd that a lot of Tom was going into that picture, and maybe a bit of Billy too.

It was about four o'clock before I could take a break. I walked across the crowded square in the mid-afternoon heat and shouldered my way through to where they sat with a couple of cold Cokes. And when I saw it my mouth just dropped open and took a five-minute vacation while I tried to take it in.

It was a cat alright, but not a normal cat. It was a life-size tiger. I'd never seen Tom do anything near that big before, and as I stood there in the beating sun trying to get my mind round it, it almost seemed to stand in three dimensions, a nearly living thing. Its stomach was very lean and thin, its tail seemed to twitch with colour, and as Tom worked on the eyes and jaws, his face set with a rigid concentration quite unlike his usual calm painting face, the snarling mask of the tiger came to life before my eyes. And I could see that he wasn't just putting a bit of himself in at all. This was a man at full stretch, giving all of himself and reaching down for more, pulling up bloody fistfuls and throwing them down. The tiger was all the rage I'd seen in his eyes, and more, and like his love for Rachel that rage just seemed bigger than any other man could comprehend. He was pouring it out and sculpting it into the lean and ravenous creature coming to pulsating life in front of us on the pavement, and the weird purples and blues and reds just made it seem more vibrant and alive.

I watched him working furiously on it, the boy sometimes helping, adding a tiny bit here and there that strangely seemed to add to it, and thought I understood what he'd meant that evening a few weeks back. He said he'd done a painting for the man who'd given him so much pain. Then, as now, he must have found what I guess you'd call something fancy like 'catharsis' through his skill with chalks, had wrenched the pain up from within him and nailed it down onto something solid that he could walk away from. Now he was helping that little boy do the same, and the boy did look better, his bruised eye hardly showing with the wide smile on his face as he watched the big cat conjured up from nowhere in front of him.

We all just stood and watched, like something out of an old story, the simple folk and the magical stranger. It always feels like you're giving a bit of yourself away when you praise someone else's creation, and it's often done grudgingly, but you could feel the awe that day like a warm wind. Comes a time when you realise something special is happening, something you're never going to see again, and there isn't anything you can do but watch.

Well I had to go back to the store after a while. I hated to go but, well, John is a good boy, married now of course, but in those days his head was full of girls and it didn't do to leave him alone in a busy shop for too long.

And so the long hot day drew slowly to a close. I kept the store open till eight, when the light began to turn and the square emptied out with all the tourists going away to write postcards and see if we didn't have even just a *little* McDonalds hidden away someplace. I suppose Mary had troubles enough at home, realised where the boy would be and figured he was safer there than anywhere else, and I guess she was right.

Tom and Billy finished up drawing and then Tom sat and talked to him for some time. Then they got up and the kid walked slowly off to the corner of the square, looking back to wave at Tom a couple times. Tom stood and watched him go and when Billy had gone he stayed there a while, head down, like a huge black statue in the gathering dark. He looked kind of creepy out there and I don't mind telling you I was glad when he finally moved and started walking over towards Jack's. I ran out to catch up with him and drew level just as we passed the drawing. And then I had to stop. I just couldn't look at that and move at the same time.

Finished, the drawing was like nothing on earth, and I suppose that's exactly what it was. I can't hope to describe it to you, although I've seen it in my dreams many times in the last ten years. You had to be there, on that heavy summer night, had to know what was going on. Otherwise it's going to sound like it was just a drawing.

That tiger was out and out terrifying. It looked so mean and hungry, Christ I don't know what: it just looked like the darkest parts of mankind, the pain and the fury and the vengeful hate nailed down in front of you for you to see, and I just stood there and shivered in the humid evening air.

'We did him a picture.' Tom said quietly.

'Yeah,' I said, and nodded. Like I said, I know what 'catharsis' means and I thought I understood what he was saying. But I really didn't want to look at it much longer. 'Let's go have a beer, hey?'

The storm in Tom hadn't passed, I could tell, and he still seemed to thrum with crackling emotions looking for an earth, but I thought the clouds might be breaking and I was glad.

And so we walked slowly over to Jack's and had a few beers and watched some pool being played. Tom seemed pretty tired, but still alert, and I relaxed a little. Come eleven most of the guys started going on their way and I was surprised to see Tom get another beer. Pete, Ned and I stayed on, and Jack of course, though we knew our loving wives would have something to say about that. It just didn't seem time to go. Outside it had gotten pretty dark, though the moon was keeping the square in a kind of twilight and the lights in the bar threw a pool of warmth out of the front window.

Then, about twelve o'clock, it happened, and I don't suppose any of us will ever see the same world we grew up in again. I've told this whole thing like it was just me who was there, but we all were, and we remember it together.

Because suddenly there was a wailing sound outside, a thin cutting cry, getting closer. Tom immediately snapped to his feet and stared out the window like he'd been waiting for it. As we looked out across the square we saw little Billy come running and we could see the blood on his face from there. Some of us got to get up but Tom snarled at us to stay there and so I guess we just stayed put, sitting back down like we'd been pushed. He strode out the door and into the square and the boy saw him and ran to him and Tom folded him in his cloak and held him close and warm. But he didn't come back in. He just stood there, and he was waiting for something.

Now there's a lot of crap talked about silences. I read novels when I've the time and you see things like 'Time stood still' and so on and you think 'bullshit it did.' So I'll just say I don't think anyone in the world breathed in that next minute. There was no wind, no movement. The stillness and silence were there like you could touch them, but more than that: they were like that's all there was and all there ever had been.

We felt the slow red throb of violence from right across the square before we could even see the man. Then Sam came staggering into view waving a bottle like a flag and cursing his head off. At first he couldn't see Tom and the boy because they were the opposite side of the fountain, and he ground to a wavering halt, but then he started shouting, rough jags of sound that seemed to strike against the silence and die instead of breaking it, and he began charging across the square—and if ever there was a man with murder in his thoughts then it was Sam McNeill. He was like a man who'd given his soul the evening off. I wanted to shout to Tom to get the hell out of the way, to come inside, but the words wouldn't come out of my throat and we all just stood there, knuckles whitening as we clutched the bar and stared, our mouths open like we'd made a pact never to use them again. Tom just stood there, watching Sam come towards him, getting closer, almost as far as the spot where Tom usually painted. It felt like we were looking out of the window at a picture of something that happened long ago in another place and time, and the closer Sam got the more I began to feel very afraid for him.

It was at that moment that Sam stopped dead in his tracks, skidding forward like in some kid's cartoon, his shout dying off in his ragged throat. He was staring at the ground in front of him, his eyes wide and his mouth a stupid circle. Then he began to scream.

It was a high shrill noise like a woman, and coming out of that bull of a man it sent fear racking down my spine. He started making thrashing movements like he was trying to move backwards, but he just stayed where he was.

His movements became unmistakable at about the same time his screams turned from terror to agony. He was trying to get his leg away from something.

Suddenly he seemed to fall forward on one knee, his other leg stuck out behind him, and he raised his head and shrieked at the dark skies and we saw his face then and I'm not going to forget that face so long as I live. It was a face from before there were any words, the face behind our oldest fears and earliest nightmares, the face we're terrified of seeing on ourselves one night when we're alone in the dark and It finally comes out from under the bed to get us, like we always knew it would.

Then Sam fell on his face, his leg buckled up—and still he thrashed and screamed and clawed at the ground with his hands, blood running from his broken fingernails as he twitched and struggled. Maybe the light was playing tricks, and my eyes were sparkling anyway on account of being too paralyzed with fear to even blink, but as he thrashed less and less it became harder and harder to see him at all, and as the breeze whipped up stronger his screams began to sound a lot like the wind. But still he writhed and moaned and then suddenly there was the most godawful crunching sound and then there was no movement or sound anymore.

Like they were on a string our heads all turned together and we saw Tom still standing there, his coat flapping in the wind. He had a hand on Billy's shoulder and as we looked we could see that Mary was there too now and he had one arm round her as she sobbed into his coat.

I don't know how long we just sat there staring but then we were ejected off our seats and out of the bar. Pete and Ned ran to Tom but Jack and I went to where Sam had fallen, and we stared down, and I tell you the rest of my life now seems like a build up to and a climb down from that moment.

We were standing in front of a chalk drawing of a tiger. Even now my scalp seems to tighten when I think of it, and my chest feels like someone punched a hole in it and tipped a gallon of ice water inside. I'll just tell you the facts: Jack was there and he knows what we saw and what we didn't see.

What we didn't see was Sam McNeill. He just wasn't there. We saw a drawing of a tiger in purples and greens, a little bit scuffed, and there was a lot more red round the mouth of that tiger than there had been that afternoon and I'm sure that if either of us could have dreamed of reaching out and touching it, it would have been warm too.

And the hardest part to tell is this. I'd seen that drawing in the afternoon, and Jack had too, and we knew that when it was done it was lean and thin.

I swear to God that tiger wasn't thin any more. What Jack and I were looking at was one fat tiger.

After a while I looked up and across at Tom. He was still standing with Mary and Billy, but they weren't crying anymore. Mary was hugging Billy so tight he squawked and Tom's face looked calm and alive and creased with a smile. And as we stood there the skies opened for the first time in months and a cool rain hammered down. At my feet colours began to run and lines became less distinct. Jack and I stood and watched till there was just pools of meaningless colours and then we walked slowly over to the others, not even looking at the bottle lying on the ground, and we all stayed there a long time in the rain, facing each other, not saying a word.

Well that was ten years ago, near enough. After a while Mary took Billy home and they turned to give us a little wave before they turned the corner. The cuts on Billy's face healed real quick, and he's a good looking boy now: he looks a lot like his dad and he's already fooling about in cars. Helps me in the store sometimes. His mom ain't aged a day and looks wonderful. She never married again, but she looks real happy the way she is.

The rest of us just said a simple goodnight. Goodnight was all we could muster and maybe that's all there was to say. Then we walked off home in the directions of our wives. Tom gave me a small smile before he turned and walked off alone. I almost followed him, I wanted to say something, but the end I just stayed where I was and watched him go. And that's how I'll always remember him best, because for a moment there was a spark in his eyes and I knew that some pain had been lifted deep down inside somewhere.

Then he walked and no-one has seen him since, and like I said it's been about ten years now. He wasn't there in the square the next morning and he didn't come in for a beer. Like he'd never been, he just wasn't there. Except for the hole in our hearts: it's funny how much you can miss a quiet man.

We're all still here, of course, Jack, Ned, Pete and the boys, and all much the same, though even older and greyer. Pete lost his wife and Ned retired but things go on the same. The tourists come in the summer and we sit on the stools and drink our cold beers and shoot the breeze about ballgames and families and how the world's going to shit, and sometimes we'll draw close and talk about a night a long time ago, and about paintings and cats, and about the quietest man we ever knew, wondering where he is, and what he's doing. And we've had a six-pack in the back of the fridge for ten years now, and the minute he walks through that door and pulls up a stool, that's his.

A Place To Stay

'John, do you believe in vampires?'

I took a moment to light a cigarette. This wasn't to avoid the issue, but rather to prepare myself for the length and vitriol of the answer I intended to give—and to tone it down a little. I hardly knew the woman who'd asked the question, and had no idea of her tolerance for short, blunt words. I wanted to be gentle with her, but if there's one star in the pantheon of possible nightmares that I certainly *don't* believe in, then it has to be bloody vampires. I mean, really.

I was in New Orleans, and it was nearly Halloween. Children of the Night have a tendency to crop up in such circumstances, like talk of rain in London. Now that I was here, I could see why. The French Quarter, with its narrow streets and looming balconies frozen in time, almost made the idea of vampires credible, especially in the lingering moist heat of the Fall. It felt like a playground for suave monsters, a perpetual reinventing past, and if vampires lived anywhere, I supposed, then these dark streets and alleyways with their fetid, flamboyant cemeteries would be as good a place as any.

But they *didn't* live anywhere, and after another punishing swallow of my salty Margarita, I started to put Rita-May right on this fact. She shifted herself comfortably against my chest, and listened to me rant.

We were in Jimmy Buffet's bar on Decatur, and the evening was developing nicely. At nine o'clock I'd been there by myself, sitting at the bar and trying to work out how many Margaritas I'd drunk. The fact that I was counting shows what a sad individual I am. The further fact that I couldn't seem to count properly demonstrates that on that particular evening I was an extremely *drunk* sad individual too. And I mean, yes, Margaritaville is kind of a tourist trap, and I could have been sitting somewhere altogether heavier and more authentic across the street. But I'd done that the previous two nights, and besides, I liked Buffet's bar. I was, after all, a tourist. You didn't feel in any danger of being killed in his

179

place, which I regard as a plus. They only played Jimmy Buffet on the jukebox, not surprisingly, so I didn't have to worry that my evening was suddenly going to be shattered by something horrible from the post-melodic school of popular music. Say what you like about Jimmy Buffet, he's seldom hard to listen to. Finally, the barman had this gloopy eye thing, which felt pleasingly disgusting and stuck to the wall when you threw it, so that was kind of neat.

I was having a perfectly good time, in other words. A group of people from the software convention I was attending were due to be meeting somewhere on Bourbon at ten, but I was beginning to think I might skip it. After only two days my tolerance for jokes about Bill Gates was hovering around the zero mark. As an Apple Macintosh developer, they weren't actually that funny anyway.

So. There I was, fairly confident that I'd had around eight Margaritas and beginning to get heartburn from all the salt, when a woman walked in. She was in her mid thirties, I guessed, the age where things are just beginning to fade around the edges but don't look too bad for all that. I hope they don't, anyway: I'm approaching that age myself and my things are already fading fast. She sat on a stool at the corner of the bar, and signalled to the barman with a regular's upward nod of the head. A minute later a Margarita was set down in front of her, and I judged from the colour that it was the same variety I was drinking. It was called a Golden something or other, and had the effect of gradually replacing your brain with a sour-tasting sand which shifted sluggishly when you moved your head.

No big deal. I noticed her, then got back to desultory conversation with the other barman. He'd visited London at some point, or wanted to—I never really understood which. He was either asking me what London was like, or telling me; I was either listening, or telling him. I can't remember, and probably didn't know at the time. At that stage in the evening my responses would have been about the same either way. I eventually noticed that the band had stopped playing, apparently for the night. That meant I could leave the bar and go sit at one of the tables. The band had been okay, but very loud, and without wishing them any personal enmity I was glad they had gone. Now that I'd noticed, I realised they must have been gone for a while. An entire Jimmy Buffet CD had played in the interval.

I lurched sedately over to a table, humming 'The Great Filling Station Hold-up' quietly and inaccurately, and reminding myself that it was only about twenty after nine. If I wanted to meet up with the others without being the evening's comedy drunk, I needed to slow down. I needed to have not had about the last four drinks, in fact, but that would have involved tangling with the space-time continuum to a degree I felt unequal to. Slowing down would have to suffice.

It was as I was just starting the next drink that the evening took an interesting turn. Someone said something to me at fairly close range, and when I looked up to have another stab at comprehending it, I saw it was the woman from the bar.

'Wuh?' I said, in the debonair way that I have. She was standing behind the table's other chair, and looked diffident but not very. The main thing she looked was good-natured, in a wary and toughened way. Her hair was fairly blonde and she was dressed in a pale blue dress and a dark blue denim jacket.

'I said—is that chair free?'

I considered my standard response, when I'm trying to be amusing, of asking in a soulful voice if *any* of us are truly free. I didn't feel up to it. I wasn't quite drunk enough, and I knew in my heart of hearts that it simply wasn't funny. Also, I was nervous. Women don't come up to me in bars and request the pleasure of sitting at my table. It's not something I'd had much practice with. In the end I settled for straightforwardness.

'Yes,' I said. 'And you may feel absolutely free to use it.'

The woman smiled, sat down, and started talking. Her name, I discovered rapidly, was Rita-May. She'd lived in New Orleans for fifteen years, after moving there from some godforsaken hole called Houma, out in the Louisiana sticks. She worked in one of the stores further down Decatur near the Square, selling Cajun spice sets and cookbooks to tourists, which was a reasonable job and paid okay but wasn't very exciting. She had been married once and it had ended four years ago, amidst general apathy. She had no children, and considered it no great loss.

This information was laid out with remarkable economy and a satisfying lack of topic drift or extraneous detail. I then sat affably drinking my drink while she efficiently elicited a smaller quantity of similar information from me. I was thirty-two, she discovered, and unmarried. I owned a very small software company in London, England, and lived with a dozy cat named Spike. I was enjoying New Orleans' fine cuisine but had as yet no strong views on particular venues—with the exception of the muffelettas in the French Bar, which I liked inordinately, and the po-boys at Mama Sam's, which I thought were overrated.

After an hour and three more Margaritas our knees were resting companionably against each other, and by eleven-thirty my arm was laid across the back of her chair and she was settled comfortably against it.

Maybe the fact that all the dull crap had been got out of the way so quickly was what made her easy to spend time with. Either way. I was having fun.

Rita-May seemed unperturbed by the vehemence of my feelings about vampires, and pleasingly willing to consider the possibility that it was all a load of toss. I was about to raise my hand to get more drinks when I noticed that the bar staff had all gone home, leaving a hand-written sign on the bar that said LOOK, WILL YOU TWO JUST *FUCK OFF*.

They hadn't really, but the well had obviously run dry. For a few moments I bent my not inconsiderable intelligence towards solving this problem, but all that came back was a row of question marks. Then suddenly I found myself out on the street, with no recollection of having even stood up. Rita-May's arm was wrapped around my back, and she was dragging me down Decatur towards the Square.

'It's this way,' she said, giggling, and I asked her what the hell I had agreed to. It transpired that we were going to precisely the bar on Bourbon where I'd been due to meet people an hour and a half ago. I mused excitedly on this coincidence, until Rita-May got me to understand that we were going there because I'd suggested it.

'Want to buy some drugs?' Rita-May asked, and I turned to peer at her.

'I don't know,' she said. 'What have you got?' This confused me until I realised that a third party had asked the original question, and was indeed still standing in front of us. A thin black guy with elsewhere eyes.

'Dope, grass, coke, horse...' the man reeled off, in a bored monotone. As Rita-May negotiated for a bag of spliffs I tried to see where he was hiding the horse, until I realised I was being a moron. I turned away and opened my mouth and eyes wide to stretch my face. I sensed I was in a bit of a state, and that the night was as yet young.

It was only as we were lighting one of the joints five minutes later that it occurred to me to be nervous about meeting a gentleman who was a heroin dealer. Luckily he'd gone by then, and my attention span was insufficient to let me worry about it for long. Rita-May seemed very relaxed about the whole deal, and as she was a local, presumably it was okay.

We hung a right at Jackson Square and walked across towards Bourbon, sucking on the joint and slowly carooming from one side of the sidewalk to the other. Rita-May's arm was still around my back, and one of mine was over her shoulders. It occurred to me that sooner or later I was going to have to ask myself what the hell I thought I was doing, but I didn't feel up to it just yet.

A PLACE TO STAY

I wasn't really prepared for the idea that people from the convention would still be at the bar when we eventually arrived. By then it felt as if we had been walking for at least ten days, though not in any bad way. The joint had hit us both pretty hard, and my head felt as if it had been lovingly crafted out of warm brown smoke. Bourbon Street was still at full pitch, and we slowly made our way down it, weaving between half-dressed male couples, lean local blacks and pastel-clad pear-shaped tourists from Des Moines. A stringy blonde popped up from nowhere at one point, waggling a rose in my face and asking 'Is she ready?' in a keening, nobody's-home kind of voice. I was still juggling responses to this when I noticed that Rita-May had bought the rose herself. She broke off all but the first four inches of stem in a business-like way, and stuck the flower behind her ear.

Fair enough, I thought, admiring this behaviour in a way I found difficult to define.

I couldn't actually remember, now we were in the area, whether it was the Absinthe Bar we were looking for, the *Old* Absinthe Bar, or the *Original Old* Absinthe Bar. I hope you can understand my confusion. In the end we made the decision on the basis of the bar from which the most acceptable music was pounding, and lurched into the sweaty gloom. Most of the crowd inside applauded immediately, but I suspect this was for the blues band rather than us. I was very thirsty by then, partly because someone appeared to have put enough blotting paper in my mouth to leech all the moisture out of it, and I felt incapable of doing or saying anything until I was less arid. Luckily Rita-May sensed this, and immediately cut through the crowd to the bar.

I stood and waited patiently for her return, inclining slightly and variably from the vertical plane like some advanced form of children's top. 'Ah ha,' I was saying to myself. 'Ah ha.' I have no idea why.

When someone shouted my name, I experienced little more than a vague feeling of well-being. 'They know me here,' I muttered, nodding proudly to myself. Then I saw that Dave Trindle was standing on the other side of the room and waving his arm at me, a grin of outstanding stupidity on his face. My first thought was that he should sit down before someone in the band shot him. My second was a hope that he would continue standing, for the same reason. He was part, I saw, of a motley collection of second-rate shareware authors ranged around a table in the corner, a veritable rogues' gallery of dweebs and losers. My heart sank, with all hands, two cats and a mint copy of the Guttenburg Bible on deck.

'Are they the people?'

On hearing Rita-May's voice I turned thankfully, immediately feeling much better. She was standing close behind, a large drink in each hand and an affectionate half-smile on her face. I realised suddenly that I found her very attractive, and that she was nice, too. I looked at her for a moment longer, and then leant forward to kiss her softly on the cheek, just to the side of the mouth.

She smiled, pleased, and we came together for another kiss, again not quite on the mouth. I experienced a moment of peace, and then suddenly I was very drunk again.

'Yes and no,' I said. 'They're from the convention. But they're not the people I wanted to see.'

'They're still waving at you.'

'Christ.'

'Come on. It'll be fun.'

I found it hard to share her optimism, but followed Rita-May through the throng.

It turned out that the people I'd arranged to meet up with *had* been there, but I was told that they had left in the face of my continued failure to arrive. I judged it more likely that they'd gone because of the extraordinary collection of berks they had accidentally acquired on the way to the bar, but refrained from saying so.

The conventioneers were drunk, in a we've-had-two-beers-and-hey-aren't-we-bohemian sort of way, which I personally find offensive. Quite early on I realised that the only way of escaping the encounter with my sanity intact was pretending that they weren't there and talking to Rita-May instead. This wasn't allowed, apparently. I kept being asked my opinion on things so toe-curlingly dull that I can't bring myself to even remember them, and endured fifteen minutes of Davey wank-face telling me about some GUI junk he was developing. Luckily Rita-May entered the spirit of the event, and we managed to keep passing each other messages on how dreadful a time we were having. With that, and a regular supply of drinks, we coped.

After about an hour we hit upon a new form of diversion, and while apparently listening avidly to the row of life-ectomy survivors in front of us, started—tentatively at first, then more deliciously—to stroke each others' hands under the table. The conventioneers were now all well over the limit, some of them having had as many as four beers, and were chattering nineteen to the dozen. So engrossed were they that after a while I felt able to turn my head towards Rita-May, look in her eyes, and say something.

'I like you.'

I hadn't planned it that way. I'd intended something much more grown-up and crass. But as it came out I realised that it was true and that it communicated what I wanted to say with remarkable economy.

She smiled, skin dimpling at the corners of her mouth, wisps of her hair backlit into golden. 'I like you too,' she said, and squeezed my hand.

Wow, I thought foggily. How weird. You think you've got the measure of life, and then it throws you what I believe is known as a 'curve ball'. It just went to show. 'It just goes to show,' I said, aloud. She probably didn't understand, but smiled again anyway.

The next thing that I noticed was that I was standing with my back against a wall, and that there wasn't any ground beneath my feet. Then that it was cold. Then that it was quiet.

'Yo, he's alive,' someone said, and the world started to organise itself. I was lying on the floor of the bar, and my face was wet.

I tried to sit upright, but couldn't. The owner of the voice, a cheery black man who had served me earlier, grabbed my shoulder and helped. It was him, I discovered, who'd thrown water over me. About a gallon. It hadn't worked, so he'd checked my pulse to make sure I wasn't dead, and then just cleared up around me. Apart from him and a depressed-looking guy with a mop, the bar was completely empty.

'Where's Rita?' I asked, eventually. I had to repeat the question in order to make it audible.

The man grinned down at me. 'Now I wouldn't know *that*, would I?' he said. 'Most particularly 'cos I don't know who Rita *is*.'

'What about the others?' I managed. The barman gestured eloquently around the empty bar. As my eyes followed his hand, I saw the clock. It was a little after five a.m.

I stood up, shakily thanked him for his good offices on my behalf, and walked very slowly out into the street.

I don't remember getting back to the hotel, but I guess I must have. That, at any rate, is where I found myself at ten the next morning, after a few hours of molten sleep. As I stood pasty-faced and stricken under the harsh light of the bathroom, I waited in horror while wave after wave of The Fear washed over me. I'd passed out. Obviously. Though uncommon with me, it's not unknown. The conventioneers, rat-finks that they were, had pissed off and left me there, doubtless sniggering into their beards. Fair enough. I'd have done the same for them.

But what had happened to Rita-May?

While I endured an appalling ten minutes on the toilet, a soothing fifteen minutes under the shower, and a despairing, tearful battle with my trousers, I tried to work this out. On the one hand, I couldn't blame her for abandoning an unconscious tourist. But when I thought back to before the point where blackness and The Fear took over, I thought we'd been getting on very well. She didn't seem the type to abandon anyone.

When I was more or less dressed I hauled myself onto the bed and sat on the edge. I needed coffee, and needed it very urgently. I also had to smoke about seventy cigarettes, but seemed to have lost my packet. The way forward was clear. I had to leave the hotel room and sort these things out. But for that I needed shoes.

So where were they?

They weren't on the floor, or in the bathroom. They weren't out on the balcony, where the light hurt my eyes so badly I retreated back into the gloom with a yelp. I shuffled around the room again, even getting down onto my hands and knees to look under the bed. They weren't there. They weren't even *in* the bed.

They were entirely absent, which was a disaster. I hate shoes, because they're boring, and consequently I own very few pairs. Apart from some elderly flip-flops which were left in the suitcase from a previous trip, the ones I'd been wearing were the only pair I had with me. I made another exhausting search, conducting as much of it as possible without leaving the bed, with no success. Instead of just getting to a café and sorting out my immediate needs, I was going to have to put on the flip-flops and go find a fucking shoe store. Once there I would have to spend money that I'd rather commit to American-priced CDs and good food than on a pair of fucking *shoes*. As a punishment from God for drunkenness this felt a bit harsh, and for a few minutes the walls of the hotel room rang with rasped profanities.

Eventually I hauled myself over to the suitcase and bad-temperedly dug through the archaeological layers of socks and shirts until I found something shoe-shaped. The flip-flop was, of course, right at the bottom of the case. I tugged irritably at it, unmindful of the damage I was doing to my carefully stacked shorts and ties. Up came two pairs of trousers I hadn't worn yet—one of which I'd forgotten I'd brought—along with a shirt, and then finally I had the flip-flop in my hand.

Except it wasn't a flip-flop. It was one of my shoes.

Luckily I was standing near the end of the bed, because my legs gave way. I sat down suddenly, staring at the shoe in my hand. It wasn't hard to recognise. It was a black lace-up, in reasonably good condition but wearing on the outside of the heel. As I turned it slowly over in my hands like some holy relic, I realised it even smelled slightly of Margaritas. Salt had dried on the toe, where I'd spilt a mouthful laughing at something

A PLACE TO STAY

Rita-May had said in Jimmy Buffet's.

Still holding it in one hand, I reached tentatively into the bowels of my suitcase, rootling through the lower layers until I found the other one. It was underneath the towel I'd packed right at the bottom, on the reasoning that I was unlikely to need it because all hotels had towels. I pulled the shoe out, and stared at it.

Without a doubt, it was the other shoe. There was something inside. I carefully pulled it out, aware of little more than a rushing sound in my ears.

It was a red rose, attached to about four inches of stem.

The first thing that strikes you about the Café du Monde is that it isn't quite what you're expecting. It isn't nestled right in the heart of the old town, on Royal or Dauphin, but squats on Decatur opposite the Square. And it isn't some dinky little café, but a large awning-covered space where rows of tables are intermittently served by waiters of spectacular moroseness. On subsequent visits, however, you come to realise that the café au lait really is good and that the beignet are the best in New Orleans; that the café is about as bijou as it can be given that it's open twenty-four hours a day, every day of the year; and that anyone wandering through New Orleans is going to pass the Decatur corner of Jackson Square at some point, so it is actually pretty central.

Midday found me sitting at one of the tables at the edge, so I wasn't surrounded by other people and had a good view of the street. I was on my second coffee and third orange juice. My ashtray had been emptied twice already, and I had an order of beignet inside me. The only reason I hadn't had more was that I was saving myself for a muffeletta. I'd tell you what that is but this isn't a travel guide. Go and find out for yourself.

And, of course, I was wearing my shoes. I'd sat in the hotel for another ten minutes, until I'd completely stopped shaking. Then I'd shuffled straight to Café du Monde. I had a book with me, but I wasn't reading it. I was watching people as they passed, and trying to get my head in order. I couldn't remember what had happened, so the best I could do was try to find an explanation that worked, and stick with it. Unfortunately, that explanation was eluding me. I simply couldn't come up with a good reason for my shoes being in my suitcase, under stuff that I hadn't disturbed since leaving Roanoke.

About nine months before, at a convention in England, I rather over-indulged an interest in recreational pharmaceuticals in the dissolute company of an old college friend. I woke the next morning to find myself in my hotel bed, but dressed in different clothes to those I'd been wearing the night before. Patient reconstruction led me to believe that I could *just about* recall getting up in the small hours, showering, getting dressed—and then climbing back into bed. Odd behaviour, to be sure, but there were enough hints and shadows of memory for me to convince myself that's what I had done.

Not this time. I couldn't remember a thing between leaving the Old Original Authentic Genuine Absinthe Bar and waking up. But strangely, I didn't have The Fear about it.

And then, of course, there was the rose.

The Fear, for those unacquainted with it, is something you may get after very excessive intake of drugs or alcohol. It is, amongst other things, the panicky conviction that you have done something embarrassing or ill-advised that you can't quite remember. It can also be more generic than that, a simple belief that at some point in the previous evening, something happened which was in some way not ideal. It usually passes off when your hangover does, or when an acquaintance reveals that yes, you did lightly stroke one of her breasts in public, without being requested to do so.

Then you can just get down to being hideously embarrassed, which is a much more containable emotion.

I had mild Fear about the period in Jimmy Buffet's, but probably only born of nervousness about talking to a woman I didn't really know. I had a slightly greater Fear concerning the Absinthe bar, where I suspected I might have referred to the new CEO of a company who was a client of mine as a 'talentless fuckwit'.

I felt fine about the journey back to the hotel, however, despite the fact I couldn't remember it. I'd been alone, after all. Everyone, including Rita-May, had disappeared. The only person I could have offended was myself. But how had my shoes got into the suitcase? Why would I have done that? And at what point had I acquired Rita-May's rose? The last time I could remember seeing it was when I'd told her that I liked her. Then it had still been behind her ear.

The coffee was beginning to turn on me, mingling with the hangover to make it feel as if points of light were slowly popping on and off in my head. A black guy with a trumpet was just settling down to play at one of the other sides of the café, and I knew this guy from previous experience. His key talent, which he demonstrated about every ten minutes, was that of playing a loud, high note for a very long time. Like most tourists, I'd applauded the first time I'd heard this. The second demonstration had been less appealing. By the third time I'd considered offering him my Visa card if he'd go away.

And if he did it now, I was likely to simply shatter and fall in shards upon the floor.

I needed to do something. I needed to move. I left the café and stood outside on Decatur.

After about two minutes I felt hot and under threat, buffeted by the passing throng. No-one had yet filled the seat I'd vacated, and I was very tempted to just slink right back to it. I'd be quiet, no trouble to anyone: just sit there and drink a lot more fluids. I'd be a valuable addition, I felt, a show tourist provided by the town's Management to demonstrate to everyone else how wonderful a time there was to be had.

But then the guy with the trumpet started a rendition of 'Smells Like Teen Spirit' and I really had to go.

I walked slowly up Decatur towards the market, trying to decide if I was really going to do what I had in mind. Rita-May worked at one of the stores along that stretch. I couldn't remember the name, but knew it had something to do with cooking. It wouldn't be that difficult to find. But should I be trying to find it? Perhaps I should just turn around, leave the Quarter and go to the Clarion, where the convention was happening. I could find the people I liked and hang for a while, listen to jokes about Steve Jobs. Forget about Rita-May, take things carefully for the remaining few days, and then go back home to London.

I didn't want to. The previous evening had left me with emotional tattoos, snapshots of desire that weren't fading in the morning sun. The creases round her eyes when she smiled; the easy Southern rhythm of her speech, the glissando changes in pitch; her tongue, as it lolled round the rim of her glass, licking off the salt. When I closed my eyes, in addition to a slightly alarming feeling of vertigo, I could feel the skin of her hand as if it was still there against my own. So what if I was an idiot tourist. I was a idiot tourist who was genuinely attracted to her. Maybe that would be enough.

The first couple of stores were easy to dismiss. One sold quilts made by American craftspeople; the next, wooden children's toys for parents who didn't realise how much their kids wanted video games. The third had a few spice collections in the window, but was mainly full of other souvenirs. It didn't look like the place Rita-May had described, but I plucked up my courage and asked. No-one of that name worked there. The next store was a bakery, and then there was a fifty-yard open stretch that provided table space for the restaurant which followed it.

The store after the restaurant was called The N'awlins Pantry, and tag-lined 'The One Stop Shop for all your Cajun Cooking Needs'.

Michael Marshall Smith

It looked, I had to admit, like it was the place.

I wanted to see Rita-May, but I was scared shitless at the thought of just walking in. I retreated to the other side of the street, hoping to see her through the window first. I'm not sure how that would have helped, but it seemed like a good idea at the time. I smoked a cigarette and watched for a while, but the constant procession of cars and pedestrians made it impossible to see anything. Then I spent a few minutes wondering why I wasn't just attending the convention, listening to dull, safe panels like everybody else. It didn't work. When I was down to the butt I stubbed my cigarette out and crossed back over the road. I couldn't see much through the window even from there, because of the size and extravagance of the window display. So I grabbed the handle, opened the door and walked in.

It was fantastically noisy inside, and crowded with sweating people. The blues band seemed to have turned a second bank of amplifiers on, and virtually everyone sitting at the tables in front of them was clapping their hands and hooting. The air was smeared with red faces and meaty arms, and for a moment I considered just turning around and going back into the toilet. It had been quiet in there, and cool. I'd spent ten minutes splashing my face with cold water, trying to mitigate the effect of the joint we'd smoked. While I stood trying to remember where the table was, the idea of another few moments of water-splashing began to take on a nearly obsessive appeal.

But then I saw Rita-May, and realised I had to go on. Partly because she was marooned with the conventioneers, which wouldn't have been fair on anyone, but mainly because going back to her was even more appealing than the idea of water.

I carefully navigated my way through the crowd, pausing halfway to flag down a waitress and get some more drinks on the way. Because obviously we needed them. Obviously. No way were we drunk enough. Rita-May looked up gratefully when she saw me. I plonked myself down next to her, glared accidentally at Dave Trindle, and lit another cigarette. Then, in a clumsy but necessary attempt to rekindle the atmosphere that had been developing, I repeated the last thing I had said before setting off on my marathon journey to the gents. 'It just goes to show,' I said.

Rita-May smiled again, probably in recognition at the feat of memory I had pulled off. 'Show what?' she asked, leaning towards me and shutting out the rest of the group. I winked, and then pulled off the most ambitious monologue of my life.

I said that it went to show that life took odd turns, and that you could suddenly meet someone you felt very at home with, who seemed to change all the rules. Someone who made stale, damaged parts of you fade away in an instant, who let you feel strange magic once again: the magic of being in the presence of a person you didn't know, and realising that you wanted them more than anything else you could think of.

I spoke for about five minutes, and then stopped. It went down very well, not least because I was patently telling the truth. I meant it. For once my tongue got the words right, didn't trip up, and I said what I meant to say. In spite of the drink, the drugs, the hour, I said it.

At the same time I was realising that something was terribly wrong.

This wasn't, for example, a cookery store.

A quick glance towards the door showed it also wasn't early afternoon. The sky was dark and Bourbon Street was packed with nighttime strollers. We were sitting with the conventioneers in the Absinthe Bar, I was wearing last night's clothes, and Rita-May's rose was still behind her ear.

It was last night, in other words.

As I continued to tell Rita-May that I was really very keen on her, she slipped her hand into mine. This time they weren't covered by the table, but I found I didn't care about that. I did, however, care about the fact that I could clearly remember standing outside the Café du Monde and wanting her to touch my hand again.

In the daylight of tomorrow.

The waitress appeared with our drinks. Trindle and his cohorts decided that they might as well be hung for a lamb as for an embryo, and ordered another round themselves. While this transaction was being laboriously conducted I stole a glance at the bar. In a gap between carousing fun-lovers I saw what I was looking for. The barman who'd woken me up.

He was making four Margaritas at once, his smooth face a picture of concentration. He would have made a good photograph, and I recognised him instantly. But he hadn't served me yet. I'd been to the bar once, and been served by a woman. The other drinks I'd bought from passing waitresses. Yet when I'd woken up, I'd recognised the barman *because he'd served me*. That meant I must have bought another drink before passing out and waking up in the bar by myself.

But I couldn't have woken up at all. The reality of what was going on around me was unquestionable, from the smell of fresh sweat drifting from the middle-aged men at the table next to us to the way Rita-May's skin looked cool and smooth despite the heat. One of the conventioneers had engaged Rita-May in conversation, and it didn't look as if she was having too bad a time, so I took the chance to try to sort my head out.

I wasn't panicking, exactly, but I was very concerned indeed.

Okay, I *was* panicking. Either I'd spent my time in the toilet hallucinating about tomorrow, or something *really* strange was happening. Did the fact that I hadn't been served by the barman yet prove which was right? I didn't know. I couldn't work it out.

'What do you think of Dale Georgio, John? Looks like he's really gonna turn WriteRight around.'

I didn't really internalise the question Trindle asked me until I'd answered it, and my reply had more to do with my state of mind than any desire to cause offence.

'He's a talentless fuckwit,' I said.

Back outside on the pavement I hesitated for a moment, not really knowing what to do. The N'awlins Pantry was indeed where Rita-May worked, but she was out at lunch. This I had discovered by talking to a very helpful woman, who I assume also worked there. Either that, or she was an unusually well-informed tourist.

I could either hang around and accost Rita-May on the street, or go and get some lunch. Talking to her outside the store would be preferable, but I couldn't stand hopping from foot to foot for what could be as long as an hour.

At that moment my stomach passed up an incomprehensible message of some kind, a strange liquid buzzing that I felt sure most people in the street could hear. It meant one of two things. Either I was hungry, or my mid-section was about to explode taking the surrounding two blocks along with it. I elected to assume I was hungry and turned to walk back towards the Square, in search of a muffeletta.

At Café du Monde I noticed that the dreadful trumpet player was in residence, actually in the middle of one of his trademark long notes. As I passed him, willing my head not to implode, the penny dropped.

I shouldn't be noticing that he was there. I *knew* he was there. I'd just been at Café du Monde. He was one of the reasons I'd left.

I got far enough away that the trumpet wasn't hurting me any more, and then ground to a halt. For the first time I was actually scared. It should have been reassuring to be back in the right time again. Tomorrow I could understand. I could retrace my steps here. Most of them, anyway. But I couldn't remember a thing of what had happened in the cookery store. I'd come out believing I'd had a conversation with someone and established that Rita-May worked there. But as to what the interior of the store had been like, I didn't have a clue. I couldn't remember. What I could actually *remember* was being in the Absinthe Bar.

I looked anxiously around at tourists dappled by bright sunshine, and felt the early afternoon heat seeping in through my clothes. A hippy face-painter looked hopefully in my direction, judged correctly that I wasn't the type, and went back to juggling with his paints.

On impulse I lifted my right hand and sniffed my fingers. Cigarette smoke and icing sugar, from the beignets I'd eaten half an hour ago. This had to be real.

Maybe there had been something weird in the joint last night. That could explain the blackout on the trip back to the hotel, and the Technicolor flashback I'd just had. It couldn't have been acid, but some opium-based thing, possibly. But why would the man have sold us it? Presumably that kind of thing was more expensive. Dealers tended to want to rip you off, not give you little presents. Unless Rita-May had known, and had asked and paid for it—but it didn't seem very likely either.

More than that, I simply didn't believe it was a drug hangover. It didn't feel like one. I felt exactly as if I'd just had far too much to drink the night before, plus one strong joint—except for the fact that I couldn't work out where in time I actually was.

If you close one of your eyes you lose the ability to judge space. The view flattens out, like a painting. You know, or think you know, which objects are closer to you—but only because you've seen them before when both of your eyes have been open. Without that memory, you wouldn't have a clue. The same appeared to be happening with time. I couldn't seem to tell what order things should be in. The question almost felt inappropriate.

Suddenly thirsty, and hearing rather than feeling another anguished appeal from my stomach, I crossed the road to a place that sold po-boys and orange juice from a hatch in the wall. It was too far to the French Bar. I needed food immediately. I'd been okay all the time I was at Café du Monde—maybe food helped tether me in some way.

The ordering process went off okay, and I stood and munched my way through French bread and sauce piquante on the street, watching the door to the N'awlins Pantry. As much as anything else, the tang of lemon juice on the fried oysters convinced me that what I was experiencing was real. When I'd finished I took a sip of my drink, and winced. It was much sweeter than I'd been expecting. Then I realised that was because it was orange juice, rather than a Margarita. The taste left me unfulfilled, like those times when you know you've only eaten half a biscuit, but can't find the other piece. I knew I'd bought orange juice, but also that less than a minute ago I had taken a mouthful of Margarita.

Trembling, I slugged the rest of the juice back. Maybe this was something to do with blood sugar levels.

Or maybe I was slowly going off my head.

As I drank I stared fixedly at the other side of the street, watching out for Rita-May. I was beginning to feel that until I saw her again, until something happened which conclusively locked me into today, I wasn't going to be able to stabilise. Once I'd seen her the day after the night before, it had to be that next day. It really had to, or how could it be tomorrow?

Unless, of course, I was back in the toilet of the Absinthe bar, projecting in eerie detail what might happen the next day. About the only thing I was sure of was that I wanted to see Rita-May. I realised that she probably wouldn't be wearing what I'd seen her in last night, but I knew I'd recognise her in an instant. Even with my eyes open, I could almost see her face. Eyes slightly hooded with drink, mouth parted, wisps of clean hair curling over her ears. And on her lips, as always, that beautiful half-smile.

'We're going,' Trindle shouted, and I turned from Rita-May to look blearily at him. They hadn't abandoned me after all: they were leaving, and I was still conscious. My habitual irritation towards Trindle and his colleagues faded somewhat on seeing their faces. They'd clearly all had a lovely time. In a rare moment of maturity, I realised that they were rather sweet, really. I didn't want to piss on their fireworks.

I nodded and smiled and shook hands, and they trooped drunkenly off into the milling crowd. It had to be well after two o'clock by now, but the evening was still romping on. I turned back to Rita-May and realised that it hadn't been such a bad stroke of luck, running into the Trindle contingent. We'd been kept apart for a couple of hours, and passions had quietly simmered to a rolling boil. Rita-May was looking at me in a way I can only describe as frank, and I leant forward and kissed her liquidly on the mouth. My tongue felt like some glorious sea creature, lightly oiled, rolling for the first time with another of its species.

After a while we stopped, and disengaged far enough to look in each others' eyes. 'It just goes to show,' she whispered, and we rested our foreheads together and giggled. I remembered thinking much earlier in the evening that I needed to ask myself what I thought I was doing. I asked myself. The answer was 'having an exceptionally nice evening', which was good enough for me.

A PLACE TO STAY

'Another drink?' It didn't feel time to leave yet. We needed some more of being there, and feeling the way we did.

'Yeah,' she said, grinning with her head on one side, looking up at me as I stood. 'And then come back and do that some more.'

I couldn't see a waitress so I went to the bar. I'd realised by now that the time switch had happened again, and I wasn't surprised to find myself being served by the smooth-faced barman. He didn't look too surprised to see me either.

'Still going?' he asked, as he fixed the drinks I'd asked for. I knew I hadn't talked to him before, so I guessed he was just being friendly.

'Yeah,' I said. 'Do I look like I'm going to make it?'

'You look fine,' he grinned. 'Got another hour or so in you yet.'

Only when I was walking unsteadily back towards our table did this strike me as a strange thing to have said. Almost as if he knew that in a little while I was going to pass out. I stopped, turned, and looked back at the bar. The barman was still looking at me. He winked, and then turned away.

He knew.

I frowned. That didn't make sense. That didn't work. Unless this was all some flashback, and I was putting words into his mouth. Which meant that it was really tomorrow. Didn't it? Then why couldn't I remember what was going to happen?

I turned back towards Rita-May, and it finally occurred to me to ask her about what was going on. If she didn't know what I was talking about, I could pass it off as a joke. If the same thing was happening to her, then we might have had a spiked joint. Either way I would have learned something. Galvanised by this plan, I tried to hurry back through the crowd. Unfortunately I didn't see a large drunken guy in a check shirt lurching into my path.

'Hey! Watch it,' he said, but fairly good-humouredly. I grinned to show I was harmless and then stepped back away from the curb. The woman I'd thought was Rita-May hadn't been. Just some tourist walking quickly in the sunshine. I looked at my watch and saw I'd been waiting opposite the store for only twenty minutes. It felt like I'd been there forever. She had to come back soon. She had to.

Then:

Christ, back here again, I thought. The switches seemed to be coming on quicker as time wore on, assuming that's what it was doing. Eating the food hadn't worked.

By the time I reached the hotel I'd started to forget, but I'd had enough sense left in me to take Rita-May's rose from my pocket and slip

195

it into one of my shoes. Then I buried the shoes as deeply in the suitcase as I could. 'That'll fuck you up,' I muttered to myself 'That'll make you remember'. I seemed to know what I meant. It was six in the morning by then, and I took a random selection of my clothes off and fell onto the bed. My head was a mess, and my neck hurt. Neither stopped me from falling asleep instantly, to find myself on Decatur, still waiting opposite the N'awlins Pantry.

That one took me by surprise, I have to admit. I was beginning to get the hang of the back and forth thing, even if it was making me increasingly terrified. I couldn't stop it, or understand it, but at least it was following a pattern. But to flick back to being at the hotel earlier that morning, and find that I'd hidden the shoes myself, was unexpected.

It was all getting jumbled up, as if the order didn't really matter, only the sense.

The people in the po-boy counter were beginning to look at me strangely, so I crossed back over to stand outside N'awlins Pantry itself. It felt like I had been going back and forth over the road for most of my life. There was a lamp-post directly outside the store and I grabbed hold of it with both hands, as if I believed that holding something solid and physical would keep me where I was. All I wanted in the whole wide world was for Rita-May to get back.

When she did, she walked right up to the table, straddled my knees and sat down on my lap facing me. She did this calmly, without flamboyance, and no-one on the nearby tables seemed to feel it was in any way worthy of note. I did, though. As I reached out to pull her closer to me, I felt like I was experiencing sexual attraction for the very first time. Every cell in my body shifted nervously against each other, as if aware that something rather unusual and profound was afoot. The band was still pumping out twelve-bar at stadium concert volume, which normally blasts all physical sensation out of me: I can't, to put it bluntly, usually do it to music. That didn't appear to be the case on this occasion. I nuzzled into Rita-May's face and kissed her ear. She wriggled a little closer to me, her hand around the back of my head, gently twisting in the roots of my hair. My entire skin felt as if it had been upgraded to some much more sensitive organ, and had I stood up too quickly, in those jeans, I suspect something in my trousers would have just snapped.

'Let's go,' she said suddenly. I stood up, and we went.

It was about three a.m. by then, and Bourbon Street was much quieter. We went up it a little way, and then took a turn to head back down towards Jackson Square. We walked slowly, wrapped up in each other, watching with interest the things our hands seemed to want to do.

A PLACE TO STAY

I don't know what Rita-May was thinking, but I was hoping with all of my heart that we could stay this way for a while. I was also still girding myself up to asking her if she was having any problems keeping track of time.

We got to the corner of the Square, and she stopped. It looked very welcoming in the darkness, empty of people and noise. I found myself thinking that leaving New Orleans was going to be more difficult than I'd expected. I'd spent a lot of my life leaving places, taking a quick look and then moving on. Wasn't going to be so easy this time.

Rita-May turned to me, and took my hands. Then she nodded down Decatur, at a row of stores. 'That's where I work,' she said. I drew her closer. 'Pay attention,' she smiled. 'It's going to be important.'

I shook my head slightly, to clear it. It was going to be, I knew. I was going to need to know where she worked. I stared at the N'awlins Pantry for a moment, memorising its location. I would always forget, as it turned out, but perhaps that is part of the deal.

Rita-May seemed satisfied that I'd done my best, and reached up with her hand to pull my face towards hers.

'It's not going to be easy,' she said, when we'd kissed. 'For you, I mean. But please stick with it. I want you to catch up with me some day.'

'I will,' I said, and I meant it. Slowly, I was beginning to understand. I let go of the lamppost with my left hand, and looked at my watch. Only another minute had passed. There was still no sign of Rita-May, just the slowly swarming mass of tourists, their bright colours warm in the sun. From a little way down the road I could hear the peal of one long trumpet note, and it didn't sound so bad to me. I glanced down Decatur towards the sound, wondering how far away she was, how many times I would have to wait. I decided to ask.

'As long as it takes, she said. 'Are you sure this is what you want?'

In a minute Rita-May would give me the rose, and I'd go back to the bar to pass out as I had so many times before. But for now I was still here, in the silent Square, where the only sign of life was a couple of tired people sipping café au lait in darkness at the Café du Monde. The air was cool, and soft somehow, like the skin of the woman I held in my arms. I thought of my house, and London. I would remember them with affection, but not miss them very much. My sister would look after the cat. One day I would catch up with Rita-May, and when I did, I would hold on tight.

In the meantime the coffee was good, the beignets were excellent, and there would always be a muffeletta just around the corner. Sometimes it would be night, sometimes day, but I would be travelling in the right direction. I would be at home, one of the regulars, in the corner of all the photographs that showed what a fine place it was to stay. And always there would be Rita-May, and me inching ever closer every day.

'I'm sure,' I said. She looked very happy, and that sealed my decision forever. She kissed me once on the forehead, once on the lips, and then angled her head.

'I'll be waiting,' she said, and then she bit me softly on the neck.

The Dark Land

It started with the bed.

After three years at college I'd come back home, returning to the bedroom I'd grown up in. It was going to be a while before I could afford to move out for good, and so in the intervening month I'd redecorated the room: covering the very 1970s orange with a more soothing shade, and badgering my mother into getting some new curtains that didn't look like they had been designed on drugs by someone who liked the colour brown a great deal. I'd also moved most of the furniture around, trying to breathe new life into a space I'd known since I was ten. It hadn't worked. It still felt as if I should be doing French verbs or preparing conkers, musing on what girls might be like. I knew it was largely an excuse for not doing anything more constructive—like filling out the pile of job applications that sat on the desk—but that afternoon I decided to move the bed away from its traditional place by the wall and try it in another couple of positions. It was hard work. One of the legs was rather fragile and the bed had to be virtually lifted off the floor rather than dragged around—which is why I hadn't tried moving it before, I remembered. After half an hour I was hot and irritated and developing a stoop. I had also become convinced that the original position had been not only the optimal but in fact the *only* place the bed could go.

It was as I struggled to shove it back up against the wall that I began to feel a bit strange. Light-headed, nauseous. Out of breath, I assumed. When the bed was finally back in place I lay back on it for a moment, feeling rather ill—and I suppose I just fell asleep.

I woke up about half an hour later, half-remembering a dream in which I had been doing nothing more than lying on my bed and remembering that my parents had said that they were going to extend the wood paneling in the downstairs hallway. For a moment I was disorientated, confused by being in the same place in reality as I had been in the dream, and then I drifted off again.

Some time later I woke up again. I found it very difficult to fight my way up out of sleep, but eventually managed to haul myself sluggishly upright. After a while I lurched to my feet and across to the sink to get a glass of water. Drinking it made the inside of my mouth a little less dry, but no more appealing. I decided that a cup of tea would be a good idea, and headed out of the bedroom to go downstairs.

As I reached the top of the staircase I remembered the dream about the paneling, and wondered where a strange notion like that could have come from. I'd worked hard for my psychology paper at college, and was confident that Freud hadn't felt that wood paneling was even worth a mention. I trudged downstairs, still feeling odd, my thoughts dislocated and fragmented.

When I reached the halfway landing I ground to a halt, and stared around me, astonished. They *had* extended the paneling.

When you enter my parents' house you come into a two-story hallway, with a staircase that climbs up three walls to the second floor. The paneling used to only go about eight feet up the wall of the front hall, but now it soared right up to the ceiling. And they'd done it in exactly the same wood as the original. There wasn't a join to be seen. How had they managed that? Come to that, *when* had they managed it? It hadn't been like this that morning, but both my parents were at work and would be for hours and…well, it was just impossible. I reached out and touched the wood, bewildered at how even the grain matched, and that the new wood looked just as aged as the original, which had been there fifty years.

Then: Wait a minute, I thought. That isn't right. There hadn't used to be *any* paneling in the hall. Just simple white walls. The stairs themselves had been paneled in wood, but the walls were just plain white plaster. How could I have forgotten that? What had made me think that the front hall had been paneled, and think it so unquestioningly? I remembered that I'd recently noticed, sensitised to these things by having repainted my room, that the white in the hall was a little grubby, especially round the light switches. So what was all this paneling doing here? Where had it come from? And why had I been so sure that at least some of it had always been there?

Something wasn't right. I walked into the kitchen, casting bewildered glances back into the hall. I absently-mindedly registered a soft clinking sound outside, and automatically headed to the back door—too puzzled about the paneling to realise that it was rather late in the day for a milk delivery.

Both the front and back doors of the house open onto the driveway, the back door from a little corridor full of muddy shoes and rusting tools that connects the kitchen to the garage. I threaded my way through the gardening implements and wrenched the stiff door open. It was late afternoon by then, but the light outside seemed very intense, the colours rich as they are before a storm.

I looked down and saw the milk bottle holder, with four bottles of milk in it. They weren't normal milk bottles, however, but large American-style quart containers somehow jammed into slots meant to take pints. Someone had taken the silver tops off.

A movement at the periphery of my vision caught my attention, and I glanced up towards the top of the driveway. There, about thirty yards away, were two children. One was fat and sitting on a bike, the other slim and standing. I was seized with sudden irritation, and started quickly up the drive towards them—convinced that the clinking sound I'd heard was them stealing the tops off the milk.

I had covered scarcely five yards when someone who'd been at my school appeared from behind me, and walked quickly past me up the drive, staring straight ahead. I couldn't remember his name, had barely known him. He'd been two or three years older than me, and I'd completely forgotten that he'd existed, but as I stared after him I remembered he'd been one of the more amiable seniors. I could recall being proud of having some small kind of communication with one of the big boys, how it had made me feel a bit older myself, more a man of the world. And I remembered the way he used to greet my yelling his nickname, with a half smile and a coolly raised eyebrow. All this came back with the instantaneous impact of memory, but something was wrong. The man didn't seem to register that I was there. I felt disturbed, not by the genuinely strange fact that he was in the driveway—or that he was wearing school athletic gear—but merely because he didn't smile and tilt his head back the way he used to. It was so bizarre that I wondered briefly if I was dreaming, but if you can ask yourself the question you always know the answer. I wasn't.

My attention was distracted by a reflection in the glass of the window in the back hallway. A man seemed to be standing behind me. He wore glasses, had a chubby face and basin-cut blond hair, and was carrying a bicycle. I whirled round to face where he should have been, but he wasn't there.

Then I remembered the kids at the top of the driveway, and turned to shout at them again, needing something to take my bewilderment out on. Almost immediately a tall slim man in a dark suit came walking down the drive; briskly, as if slightly late. Maybe it was a trick of the light in the gathering dusk, but I couldn't seem to fix on his face. My eyes just seemed to slide off it, as if it were slippery, or made of ice.

'Stop shouting at them,' he snapped. He strode past me, towards the back door. I stared at him open-mouthed. 'They're not doing anything wrong,' he said. 'Leave them alone.'

The kids took themselves off, one on the bike, the other walking alongside, and I turned to the suited man. For some reason I felt anxious to placate him, and yet at the same time I was outraged at his invasion of our property.

'I'm sorry,' I said, 'It's just, well, I'm a bit confused. I thought I saw someone I knew in the drive. Did you see him? Wavy brown hair, athletics kit?'

For some reason I thought that the man would say that he had, and that that would make me feel better. All I got was a curt 'No' as he entered the back hallway.

Then another voice spoke. 'Well then. Shall we go into your old house?'

I realised that someone else was already standing in the back hall. The man with the blond hair and glasses. And he really was carrying a bicycle. He wasn't talking to me, but to the man in the suit.

'*What?*' I said, and hurried after them, catching a glimpse of the suited man's face. 'But it's *you ...*' I stopped again, baffled, as I realised that the man in the suit was the same man who had been in athletics gear.

The two men marched straight into the kitchen. I followed them, impotently enraged. *Was* this his old house? Even so, wasn't it customary to ask the current occupants' permission if you wanted to visit? The suited man was peering round the kitchen, which looked very messy. He poked at some fried rice I'd left cooling in a pan on the stove. At least, I *seemed* to have left it there, though I wasn't sure when I would have done so. I don't just cook up rice in the afternoon for the pure hell of it. I still felt the urge to placate the man, however, and hoped he would eat some of the rice.

He merely grimaced with distaste and joined his colleague at the window, looking out onto the drive, hands on hips. 'Dear God,' he muttered. The other man grunted in agreement.

I noticed that I'd picked up the milk from outside the back door, and appeared to have spilt some of it on the floor. I tried to clean it up with a piece of kitchen roll which seemed very dirty and yellowed as if with age. I was trying to buy time. I felt very strongly that there must be some sense to the situation somewhere, some logic I was missing. Even if the man had lived here once he had no right to just march in here with his friend, but as I continued trying to swab up the milk before he noticed it—*why?*—I realised that there was something far more wrong than a mere breach of protocol at stake.

The suited man looked about thirty-five, much older than he should have been if he was indeed the guy I'd been to school with. Yet that would still leave him far too young to ever have lived here. Between our family and the previous occupants I knew who'd lived in the house for the last forty years. So how could it be his old house? It didn't make sense. And was it actually *him*? The boy from my school? Apart from being too old, it looked like him, but was it actually *him*?

I did the best I could with the milk, and then straightened up, staggering slightly. My perception seemed to have become both heightened and jumbled, as if I was very drunk. Everything pulsed with an unusual intensity and exaggerated emotional charge, yet there also seemed to be gaps in what I was perceiving, as if I was receiving an edited version of what was going on. Things began to flick from one state to another—with the bits in between, the becoming, missing like a series of jump cuts. I felt hot and dizzy and the kitchen looked small and indescribably messy, the orange of the walls—the same colour my bedroom had once been painted—seeming to push in at me beneath a low and unsteady ceiling. I wondered if I was seeing the kitchen as *they* saw it, and then immediately wondered what I meant.

Meanwhile they stood at the window, occasionally turning to stare balefully at me, radiating distaste and impatience. They were evidently waiting for something. But what? Noticing that I still had the piece of kitchen roll in my hand, I stepped over all the rubbish on the floor—*what the hell had been going on in this kitchen?*—to put it in the overflowing bin. I squeezed my temples with my fingers, struggling to stand upright against the weight of the air, and squared up to the men.

'L-look', I stuttered, leaning on the fridge for support, 'What exactly is going on?'

I immediately wished I'd kept quiet. The suited man slowly turned his head. It kept turning and turning, until it was looking directly at me—while his body remained stayed facing the other way. Like an owl, though he wasn't blinking. I could feel my stomach trying to crawl away and fought the need to gag. I sensed he'd done it deliberately, done it because he knew it would make me want to throw up, and I thought he might well be right.

'Why don't you just *shut up?*' he said. Then he twisted his head slowly back round until he was looking out onto the drive once more.

I decided not to ask any more questions.

Meanwhile, the mess in the kitchen seemed to be getting worse.

Every time I looked there were more dirty pans and bits of rubbish and old food on the floor. My head felt thicker and heavier, as if everything was slipping away from me. I slumped against the fridge and clung to it, almost pulling it away from the wall. I began to cry too, my tears cutting channels in the thick grime on the fridge door. I dimly remembered that my parents had bought a brand new one only a few weeks before, but they must have changed it again. This one looked like something out of the 1950s. Very retro. Or original. To be honest it was hard to tell, because it was swimming back and forth and there was a lot of white in my eyes. Both the men were both watching me now, as if mildly interested to see when I'd fall.

Suddenly there was a terrible jangling impact in my head. I flapped hysterically at my ears, as if to stop someone hammering pencils into them. Then the pain happened again, and I recognised first that it was a sound rather than a blow, and then that it was the doorbell.

Someone was at the front door.

The two men glanced at each other, and the blond one nodded wearily. The suited man turned to me.

'Do you know what that is?' he asked.

'It's the front door' I said quickly, still trying to please him.

'So you'd better answer it, hadn't you?'

'Yes.'

'Answer the *door.*'

'Should I answer it?' I queried, stupidly. I couldn't seem to remember what words meant anymore.

'*Yes*' he shouted, and picked up a mug—my mug, the mug I'd came downstairs, I remembered, to put tea in—and hurled it straight at me. It smashed into the fridge door by my face. I struggled to pull myself upright, head aching and ears ringing, aware of a soft crump as a fragment of the mug broke under my foot. The doorbell jangled again, the harshness of the noise making me realise how muted all other sounds had become. I fell towards the kitchen door, sliding across the front of the fridge, my feet tangling in the boxes and cartons that now covered the filthy floor. I could feel the orange of the walls seeping in through my ears and mouth, and kept missing whole seconds of time—as if I was blacking out and coming to like a stroboscope.

As I lurched across to the kitchen door and grabbed the handle to hold myself up, I heard the blond man say 'He may not go through. If he does, we wait.'

It didn't mean anything to me. None of it did.

I made my way towards the front door, ploughing clumsily through drifts of rubbish in the hallway. The chime of the doorbell had pushed the air hard, and I could see it lapping towards me in waves. Ducking to avoid the sound, I slipped on the mat and almost fell into the living room. As I crouched there on my hands and I knees it was getting dark in there, really dark, and I could hear the plants talking. I couldn't catch the words, but they were definitely conversing, beneath the night sounds and a soft rustling that sounded a hundred yards away. The living room must have grown.

I picked myself up and turned to the front door. The bell clanged again, and this time the sound caught me full in the face, stinging bitterly. It should have been about four paces across the hall from the living room door to the front door, but I thought it was only going to take one and then it took twenty, past all the paneling and over the huge folds in the mat. It was not an easy journey.

Then I had my hand on the doorknob and then the door was open and I stepped out of the house.

'Oh hello, Michael,' said a voice. 'I thought someone must be in, because all the lights were on.'

'Wuh?' I said, blinking in the fading sunlight.

The woman in front of me smiled. 'I hope I didn't disturb you?'

'No, that's fine.' Suddenly I recognised her. It was Mrs Steinberg, the woman who brings us our cat food in bulk. 'Fine. Sorry.' I glanced covertly behind me into the hallway, which was solid and unpaneled and four paces wide and led to the living room—which was light and airy and the size it had always been.

'I've brought your delivery' the woman said, and then frowned. 'Look, are you alright?'

'I'm fine' I replied, turning to grin broadly at her. My mind felt like a runaway lift, soaring back upwards to reality. 'I just nodded off for a moment, in the kitchen. I still feel a bit, you know.'

Mrs Steinberg smiled. 'Of course. Give me a hand?'

I followed her to the top of the drive and heaved a box of cat food out of her van, watching the house. There was nothing to see. I thanked her and then carried the box back down the drive as she drove off. I walked back into the house and shut the front door behind me.

I felt absolutely fine.

I walked into the kitchen. As I'd expected, the men had disappeared. I looked slowly around a kitchen that looked exactly as it had since before I was too young to remember. Everything was normal. Of course.

I must have fallen asleep making tea, and then struggled over to the front door to open it while still half asleep. I could remember asking myself if I was having a dream, and deciding I wasn't—but that just showed how wrong you could be. It had been unusually vivid, and it was odd how I'd been suddenly awake and alright again as soon as I stepped out of the front door. But it had been a dream. Here I was in the kitchen again, and everything was normal. Clean and tidy, spick and span, with all the rubbish in the bin and the pans in the right places and the milk in the fridge and a smashed mug on the floor.

That was less good. It was my mug, and it lay smashed at the bottom of the fridge. How had that happened?

Maybe I'd fallen asleep holding it. Not terribly likely, but possible. Or perhaps I'd knocked it over on waking, and incorporated the sound into my dream. This was slightly more credible, but where exactly was I supposed to have fallen asleep? Just leaning against the counter—or actually stretched out on it, using the kettle as a pillow?

Then I noticed the fridge door. There was a little dent in it, with a couple of flecks of paint missing. At about head height. That wasn't good either.

I cleared up the mug and switched the kettle on. While it was boiling I wandered into the hall and the living room. Everything was fine, tidy, normal. Super. I went back into the kitchen. The same. Great. Apart from a little dent in the fridge door at about head height.

I made my cup of tea in a different, non-broken mug, and drank it looking out of the kitchen window at the drive. I felt unsettled and nervous, and unsure of what to do with either of those emotions. Even if it had been a dream, it was a very odd one, particularly the way it had fought so hard against melting away. Maybe I was much more tired than I realised. Or ill. Food poisoning could make your head go very strange, as I'd learned after a couple of college friends' attempts at cooking anything more complex than toast. But I felt fine. Physically, at least.

I carried the box of cat food into the pantry, unpacked it, and stacked the cans in the corner. Then I switched the kettle on again. Suddenly my heart seemed to stop.

Before I had time to realise why, the cause repeated itself. A soft chinking noise outside the back door. I moved quickly to the window and looked out. There was no-one in the drive. I craned my neck, trying to see around to the back door, but could only see the large pile of firewood that lay to one side of it.

Then I heard the noise again. I walked slowly into the back hallway and listened, slowly clenching my fists. I could hear nothing except the sound of blood pumping in my ears. I grabbed the knob and swung the door open.

THE DARK LAND

Stillness outside. A rectangle of late afternoon light, a patch of driveway, and a dark hedge waving quietly. I stepped out into the drive, and stood and listened again.

After a moment I heard a very faint crunching noise. It sounded like pebbles softly rubbing against each other. Then I heard it again. I looked more closely at the drive, peering at the actual stones, and noticed that a small patch about ten yards in front of me appeared to be moving slightly. Wriggling, almost.

They stopped, and then the sound came again—and another patch stirred briefly, about a yard closer than the first. As if registering the weight of invisible feet.

I was so engrossed that I didn't notice the whistling straight away. When I did, I looked up. The blond man was back. He was standing at the top of the driveway, carrying a bicycle with the wheels slowly spinning in the dusk. He whistled the top line of a perfect harmony, the lower line just the sound of the wind. As I stared at him, backing slowly towards the house, the crunching noise got louder and louder.

Then the suited man was standing with his nose almost touching mine. 'Hello again,' he said.

The blond man started down the driveway. 'Greetings indeed,' he laughed. 'Come on, in we go.'

Abruptly I realised that the very last thing I should do was let them back into the house.

I leapt back through the door into the hallway. The suited man, caught by surprise, started forward but I was quick and whipped the door shut in his face and locked it. That felt good, but then he started banging on the door very hard, grotesquely hard, and I saw that the kitchen was getting messy again, and the fridge was old, and I could barely see out of the window because it was so grimy. A slight flicker in my mind made me think that maybe I'd missed the smallest fraction of a second, and I realised that it really hadn't been a dream. I was back in the bad place. As I backed into the kitchen I tripped and fell, sprawling amongst cartons and bacon rind and dirt and what appeared to be puke on the floor. The banging on the back door got louder, and louder, and louder. He was going to break it, I knew. He was going to break the door down. I'd let them back and they had to come in through the back door. I'd come in through the wrong door...

Suddenly understanding what I must do, I scrambled to my feet and kicked my way through the rubbish. The fridge door swung open in my way. The inside was dark and dirty and there was something rotted inside, but I slammed it out of the way, biting hard on my lip to keep my head clear.

I had to get to the front door. I had to open it, step out, and then step back in again. The front door was the right door. And I had to do it soon, before the back door broke and let them in. I could already hear a splintering quality to the sound of the blows. And the back door was about two inches thick.

The hallway was worse than I expected. I skidded to a halt, at first unable to even *see* the front door. I thought that I must be looking in the wrong direction, but I wasn't, because I finally spotted it over to the left, where it was supposed to be. But the angles were all wrong, and to see it I had to look behind me and to the right, although when I saw it I could see that in reality it was still over to the left. And it looked so close—could it really be less than a yard away?—but when I held my hand out to it I groped into nothing, the fingers still in front of the door when it should have been past it.

I stared wildly around, disorientated and unsure even of which way to go. Suddenly the banging behind me got markedly louder, probably as the blond man joined in, and this helped to marginally restore my sense of direction. I found the front door again, concentrated hard on its apparent position, and started to walk towards it. I immediately fell over, because the floor was much lower than I expected. It actually seemed be tilted in some way, although it looked flat and level, because although one of my legs reached it easily enough the other dangled in space. I pulled myself up onto my knees and found I was looking at a sort of sloped wall between the wall and the ceiling, a wall which bent back from the wall and yet out from the ceiling. The door was still over on the left, although to see it I now had to look straight ahead and up.

Then I noticed another sound beneath the eternal banging, and whirled to face the direction it was coming from. I found that I was looking through the living room door, and that it gave into sheer darkness, a darkness which was seeping out into the hallway like smoke, clinging to the angles in the air like the inside of a dark prism. I heard the noise again. It was a deep rumbling growl, far, far away in there, almost obscured by the night noises and the sound of vegetation moving in the wind. The sound didn't seem to be getting any closer, but I knew that was because the living room now extended out far beyond the house, into hundreds and hundreds of miles of dense jungle. As I listened carefully I could hear the gurgling of some dark river far off to the right, the sound of water mixing with the warm rustling of the breeze in the darkness. It sounded very peaceful and for a moment I was still, transfixed.

Then the sound of another splintering crack wrenched me away, and

THE DARK LAND

I turned my back on the living room and flailed towards where the front door must be. The hall table loomed above me and I thought I could walk upright beneath it—but tripped over it and fell again, headlong onto the cool floorboards. The mat had moved, no, was *moving*, sliding slowly up the stairs like a draught, and as I rolled over and looked at the ceiling I saw the floor coming towards me, the walls shortening in little jerks.

As I lay there panting, a clear cool waft of air stroked my cheek. At first I thought that it must have come from the living room, although it had been warm in there, but then I remembered that I was lying on the floor. The breeze had to be a draft coming under the front door. I must nearly be there. I looked all around me but all I could see was paneling and floor and what was behind me. I closed my eyes and tried to grope for it, but it was even worse inside my head so I opened them again. Then I caught a glimpse of the door, far away, obscured from view round a corner but just visible once you knew where to look. On impulse I reached my hand out in not quite the opposite direction and felt it fall upon warm grainy wood.

The door. I'd found it.

I pulled myself along the floor towards it, and tried to stand up. I got no more than a few inches before I fell back down again. I tried once more, with the same result, feeling as if I was trying to do something entirely against nature. Again, and this time I reached a semi-crouching position, muscles straining. I started to slump almost immediately—but as I did so I threw myself forwards. I found myself curled up, my feet a couple of feet from the floor, lying on the door. Electing to not even *try* to come to terms with this, I groped by my side and found the doorknob. I tried to twist it but the sweat on my hand made them spin uselessly on the shiny metal. I wiped it on my shirt and tried again, and this time I got some purchase and heard the catch withdraw as the knob turned. Exultantly I tugged at it, as with a tremendous crash the back door finally gave way.

The door wouldn't budge. Panicking, I tried again. Nothing. By peering down the crack I could see that no lock or bolt was impeding it, so why wouldn't it bloody move?

There were footsteps in the back hall.

Suddenly I realised that I was lying on the door, and trying to pull it towards me against my own weight.

The footsteps reached the kitchen.

I rolled over off the door onto the wall beside it and reached for the handle, but I'd slid too far. As the footsteps came closer I scrambled back across the slippery wall, grabbed and twisted the doorknob with all my strength. It opened just as they entered the hall and I rolled out through it, fell and landed awkwardly and painfully on something hard and bristly and for a few moments had no clear idea of where or who I was, and just lay there fighting for breath.

After some time I sat up slowly. I was sitting outside the house on the doormat, my back to the front door. At the top of the drive a young couple were staring at me curiously. I stood up and smiled, trying to suggest that I often sat on the doormat and that they ought to try it as it was actually a lot of fun—hoping that they hadn't seen me fall there from about two-thirds of the way up the door. They smiled back and carried on walking, mollified or maybe even hurrying off home to try it for themselves.

I turned hesitantly back towards the door and looked in.

It had worked. It was all okay again. The mat was on the floor, right angles looked like 90°, and the ceiling was back where it was supposed to be. I stepped back a pace and looked down the driveway at the back door. It had been utterly smashed, and now looked like little more than an extension of the firewood pile.

I stepped back into the house through the front door, the right door, and shut it behind me. I walked carefully and quietly into the living room, and then the kitchen. Everything was fine, everything was normal. It was just a nice normal house. If you came in through the right door.

The wrong door was in about a thousand pieces. I thought about that for some time, with another cup of tea and what felt like my first cigarette in months. I saw with frank disbelief that less than half an hour had elapsed since I'd first come downstairs. The back door. The *wrong* door. It was coming in through there that took me to wherever it was that the house became. Coming in through the *front* door brought me back to where I normally lived. So presumably I was safe, so long as I didn't leave the house and come back in through the back door. They couldn't get me. Presumably.

But I didn't like having that door in pieces. Being safe was only half of the issue. I wasn't going to feel *secure* until that portal was well and truly closed.

I walked into the back hall and looked nervously out through the wreckage onto the drive. Everything was fine. There was nothing I needed protecting from. But I still didn't like it. Did it have to be me who came through the door, or what if a falling leaf or maybe even just a soft breeze came inside? Would that be enough?

Could I take the risk?

As I stood there indecisively, I noticed once more the pile of firewood propped up against the outside wall of the back hall. I probably still wouldn't have put two and two together had not a very large proportion of the pile been thick old floorboards—a donation from a neighbour. I looked at the tool shelf on the inside wall and saw a hammer and a big box of good long nails. Then I looked at the wood again.

I could nail the damn thing shut.

I flicked my cigarette butt out onto the drive and rolled up my sleeves. The hammer was big and heavy, which was just as well because when I nailed the planks across the doorframe I'd be hammering into solid brickwork. I was going to have to board right the way up, but that was alright as there were loads of planks, and if I reinforced it enough it should be well-nigh impregnable.

Feeling much better, I set to work. I may even have hummed. Kneeling just inside the door, I reached out and began pulling the floorboards in, taking care to select the thickest and least weathered. I judged that I'd need about fifteen to make the doorway really secure, although that was largely guesswork as I'd never tried to turn the back hall into a fortress before. Pulling them in was heavy work. I had to stretch out to reach them, and I began to get hot and tired, and anxious to begin the nailing. Outside it was getting darker as the evening began, and the air was very cool and still.

As the pile in the back hall increased in size it became more difficult, and I had to lean further and further out to reach the next plank. This made me nervous. I was still inside, and my feet were still on the ground in the back hall. I wasn't 'coming back in'. I was just leaning out and then, well, *sort of* coming back in but not really, because my feet never left the back hall. But it made me nervous, and I began to work quicker and quicker, perspiration running down my face as, clinging to the doorframe with my left hand, I stretched out to bring the last few boards in. Eleven, twelve. Just a couple more. Now the last one I could possibly reach: that would have to be enough. Hooking my left foot behind the frame and gripping it hard with my left hand, I stretched out towards the plank, waving fingers little more than an inch from the end. Just a little further... I let my hooking foot slide slightly, allowed my fingers to slip round half an inch, and tried to extend my back as far as it would go. My fingers just scraping the end, I tried a last yearning lunge.

And then suddenly a stray thought struck me. Here I was, pulled out as if on some invisible rack. Why hadn't I just gone out of the front door, picked up piles of wood, and brought them back into the house through the front door? It would have been easier, it would have been quicker, and it wouldn't have involved all this monkeying around at the wrong door. Not that it mattered now, because as it happened even if I didn't get this last plank I'd probably have plenty, but I wouldn't have been so hot and tired. It was also worrying that in my haste I'd been putting myself in needless danger. I'd better slow down, calm down, take a rest.

It was an unimportant, contemplative thought, but one that distracted me for a fraction of a second too long. As I finally got the tips of my fingers round the plank I realised with horror that the hand on the doorframe was slipping. Desperately I tried to scrabble back, but my hands were too sweaty and the doorframe itself was slippery now. I felt the tendons in my hand stretch as I tried to defy my centre of gravity and think my weight backwards, and then suddenly my forehead walloped onto the ground and I was lying flat on my face.

I was up in a second, and I swear to God that both feet never left the hall floor at once. I leapt back into the hallway, grabbing that last bloody piece of wood without even noticing it.

I crouched in the doorframe, panting hysterically. Everything looked normal outside. The driveway was quiet, the pebbles were still and there was none of the faint deadening of sound that I associated with the other place. I was furious with myself for having taken the risk, for not having thought to bring them in through the front door—and especially for falling, which had been painful quite apart from anything else. But I hadn't fallen out, not really. I hadn't come back in, as such. The drive was fine, the kitchen was fine. Everything was okay.

Soothed by the sounds of early evening traffic in the distance, my heart gradually slowed to only about twice its normal rate. I forced myself to take a break, and had a quiet cigarette, perched on the pile of planks. During the fall my right foot had caught the tool shelf, and there were nails all over the place, both inside and outside the door. But there were plenty left and the ones outside could stay there. I wasn't going to make the same damn fool mistake twice.

Gathering up the hammer and a fistful of nails, I laid a plank across the door and started work. Getting the nails through the wood and into the masonry was even harder than I'd expected, but within a couple of minutes it was in place, and felt reassuringly solid. I heaved another plank into position and set about securing it. This was actually going to work.

After half an hour I was into the swing of it and the wood now reached almost halfway up the doorframe. My arms were aching and head ringing from the hammering, which was very loud in the confined space of the back hall. I had a break leaning on the completed section, staring blankly out onto the drive. I was jolted back from reverie by the realisation that a piece of dust or something must have landed in my eye, distorting my vision. I blinked to remove it, but it didn't disappear. It didn't hurt, just made a small patch of the drive up near the road look a bit ruffled. I rubbed and shut both eyes individually, and discovered with mounting unease that the distortion was present in both.

I stood upright. Something was definitely going on at the top of the drive. The patch still looked crumpled, as if seen through a heat haze, and whichever way I turned my head the patch stayed in the same place. It was flickering very slightly now too, like a bad quality film print, although the flecks weren't white, they were dark. I rubbed my eyes hard again, but once I'd stopped seeing stars I saw that the effect was still there. I peered at it, trying to discern something that I could interpret. The flecks seemed to organize into broken and shifting vertical lines as I watched, as if something was hidden behind a curtain of rain, rain so coloured as to make up a picture of that patch of the drive. This impression gradually strengthened until it was like looking at one of those plastic strip doors, where you walk through the hanging strips. It was as if there was one of those at the top of the drive, a patch of driveway pictured on it in living three dimensions. With something moving just the other side.

Then suddenly the balance shifted, like one of those drawings made up of black and white dots where if you stare at it long enough you can see a Dalmatian. I dropped to my knees behind the partially completed barrier.

They were back.

Standing at the top of the drive, their images both underlying and superimposed on it as if woven together, were the two men. They were standing in a frozen and unnatural position, like a freeze-frame. Their faces looked pallid and washed out, the colours uneven and the image flickering and dancing in front of my eyes. And still they stood, not there, and yet in some sense there.

As I stared, transfixed, I noticed that the suited man's foot appeared to be moving. It was hard to focus on, and happening incomprehensibly slowly, but it was moving, gradually leaving the ground. Over the course of a minute it was raised and then lowered back onto the ground a couple of feet in front of its original position, leaving the man's body leaning slightly forward.

I realised what I was seeing. In extraordinary and flickering slow motion, somehow projected onto the drive like an old home movie, the suited man was beginning to walk down towards the house. The image wasn't flickering so much anymore, the colours were getting stronger, and I could no longer see the driveway through them. Somehow they were coming back through. I thought I'd got away with it, but I hadn't. I'd fallen out. Not very far by anyone's standards, but far enough. Far enough to have come back in through the wrong door. And now they were tearing their way back into the world, or hauling me back towards theirs. And very slowly they were getting closer.

Fighting to stay calm, I grabbed a plank, put it into position above the others and nailed it into place. Then another, and another, not pausing for breath or thought. Through the narrowing gap I could see them getting closer. They didn't look two-dimensional any longer, and they were moving more quickly too. As I leaned towards the kitchen for a plank I saw that there was a single dusty carton on the floor. It had started.

I smacked another plank into place and hammered it down. The men were real again, and they were also much nearer to the house, though still moving at a weirdly graceful tenth of normal speed. Hammering wildly, ignoring increasingly frequent whacks on the fingers, I cast occasional wild glances aside into the kitchen. The fridge was beginning to look strange, the stark 1990s geometry softening, regressing, and the rubbish was gathering. I never saw any of it arrive, but each time I looked there was another piece of cardboard, a few more scraps, one more layer of grime. It had only just started, and was still happening very slowly, maybe because I'd barely fallen out. But it was happening. The house was going over.

I kept on hammering. I knew that what I had to do at some point was run the front door, go out and come back in again, come in through the right door. But that could wait, would *have* to wait. It was coming on very slowly this time, and I still felt completely clear-headed. What I had to do first was seal off the back door, and soon. The two men, always at the vanguard of the change, were well and truly here, and getting closer all the time. I had to make sure that the back door was secure against anything those two could do to it, for long enough for me to get to the front door and jump out. I had no idea what the front hall would be like by the time I got there, and if I left the back door unfinished and got lost trying to get to the front door, I'd be in real trouble.

I slammed planks into place as fast as I could. Outside they got steadily closer and closer, and inside another carton appeared in the kitchen. As I jammed the last horizontal board into place the suited man and the blond man were only a couple of yards away, now moving at full pace. I'd barely nailed it in before the first blow crashed into it, bending it and making me leap back with shock. I hurriedly picked up more wood and slapped planks over the barrier in vertical slats and crosses, nailing them in hard, reinforcing and making sure that the barrier was securely fastened to the wall on all sides, furiously hammering and building.

After a while I couldn't feel the ache in my back or see the blood on my hands: all I could hear was the beating of the hammer, and all I could see was the heads of the nails as I piled more and more wood onto the barrier. I had wood to spare—I hadn't even needed that last bloody plank—and by the time I finished it was four pieces thick in some places, with the reinforcing strips spread several feet either side of the frame. I used the last three pieces as bracing struts, forcing them horizontally across the hallway, one end of each lodged in niches in the barrier, the other jammed tight against the opposite wall.

Finally it was finished, and I stood back and looked at it. It looked pretty damn solid. 'Let's see you get through *that*,' I shouted, half sitting and half collapsing to the ground. After a moment I noticed how quiet it was. At some point they must have stopped banging against the door. I'd been making far too much noise to notice, and my head was still ringing. I put my ear against the barrier and listened. Silence.

I lit a cigarette and let tiredness and a blessed feeling of safeness wash over me. The sound of the match striking was slightly muted, but that could've been the ringing in my ears as much as anything, and the kitchen looked pretty grubby but no more than that. I felt fine. I wondered what the two outside were up to, and whether there was any chance that they might have given up and be waiting for the change to take its course—not realising that I understood about the right door and the wrong door. For a few minutes I actually savoured the sensation of being balanced between two worlds, secure in the knowledge that in a moment I would just walk out that front door and the house would come back and none of it would matter at all.

Eventually I stood up, wincing in pain. I was really going to ache tomorrow. I stepped into the kitchen, narrowly avoiding a large black spider that scuttled out of one of the cartons. The floor was getting very messy now, strewn with scraps of dried-up meat covered with the corpses of dead maggots, interspersed with small piles of stuff I really didn't want to look too closely at. I threaded my way over to the door, past the now bizarrely misshapen fridge, and into the front hall.

The hallway was still clear of debris, and as far as I could see, utterly normal. As I crossed towards the front door, anxious now to get the whole thing over with—and wondering how I was going to explain the state of the back door to my parents—I noticed a faint tapping sound in the far distance. After a moment it stopped, and then restarted from a slightly different direction. Odd, but scarcely a primary concern. Right now my priority was getting out of that front door before the hall got any stranger.

Feeling like an actor about to bound onto stage, I reached out to the doorknob, twisted it and pulled it towards me.

At first I couldn't take it in. I couldn't work out why instead of the driveway all I could see was brown. Brown flatness.

As I adjusted my focal length, pulling it in for something much closer than the drive I'd been expecting, I understood. The view looked rather familiar. I'd seen something like it very recently.

It was a barrier. An impregnable wooden barrier nailed across the door into the walls from the outside. Now I knew what they'd been doing as I finished nailing them out.

They'd been nailing me in.

I tried everything I could think of. My fists, my shoulder, a chair. The planks were there to stay.

I couldn't get out. I couldn't come back in through the right door, and for the moment they couldn't get in through the wrong door. A sort of stalemate. But a very poor sort for me, because they were much the stronger and getting more so all the time, and because the house was still going over and now I couldn't stop it.

I strode into the kitchen, rubbing my bruised shoulder and thinking furiously. There had to be something I could do, and I had to do it fast. The change was speeding up. Although the hall still looked normal the kitchen was now filthy, and the fifties fridge was fully back. In a retro kind of way it was quite attractive. But it was wrong.

In the background I could still hear the faint tapping noise. Maybe they were trying to get in through the roof.

I had to get out, had to find a way. I tried lateral thinking. You leave a house by a door. How else? No other way. You always leave by a door. But was there any other way you *could* leave, if you were in, say, a desperate emergency? The doors… The windows. What about the windows? If there was a right door and a wrong door, maybe there were right and wrong windows too, and perhaps the right ones looked out onto the real world. Maybe, just maybe, you could smash one and then climb out and then back in again. Perhaps that would work.

I had no idea whether it would or not. I wasn't kidding myself that I understood anything, and God alone knew where I might land if I chose the wrong window. Perhaps I'd go out the wrong one and then be chased round the house by the two maniacs outside, as I tried to find a right window to break back in through. That would be a barrel of laughs. That would be Fun City. But what choice did I have? I ran into the living room, heading for the big picture window. Through the square window today, children.

THE DARK LAND

I don't know how I could have missed making the connection. Possibly because the taps were so quiet. I stood in the living room, my mouth open. This time they were one jump ahead. They'd boarded up the fucking windows.

I ran back into the hall, through into the dining room, then upstairs to the bedrooms. Every single window was boarded up. I knew where they'd got the nails from, because I'd spilt more then enough when I fell, but how... Then I realised how they'd nailed them in without a hammer, why the tapping had been so quiet. With sudden unpleasant clarity I could imagine the suited man clubbing the nails in with his fists, smashing them in with his forehead and grinning while he did it.

Oh Jesus.

I walked downstairs again, slowly now. Every single window was boarded up, even the ones that were too small to climb through. As I stood once more in the kitchen, amidst the growing piles of shit, the pounding on the back door started. There was no way I could get out of the house, and I couldn't stop what was happening. This time it was going over all the way, and taking me with it. And meanwhile they were going to smash their way in to come along for the ride. To get me. I listened, watching the rubbish, as the pounding got louder and louder.

It's still getting louder, and I can tell from the sound that some of the planks are beginning to give way. The house stopped balancing long ago, and the change is coming on more quickly. The kitchen looks like a bomb site and there are an awful lot of spiders in there now. Eventually I left them to it and came through the hall into here, only making one or two wrong turnings. Into the living room. And that's where I am now, just sitting and waiting. There's nothing I can do about the change, nothing. I can't get out. I can't stop them getting in.

But there is one thing I can do. I'm going to stay here, in the living room. I can see small shadows now, gathering in corners and darting out from under the chairs, and it's quite dark down by the end wall. The wall itself seems less important now, less substantial, no longer a barrier. I think I can hear the sound of running water somewhere far away, and smell the faintest hint of the of dark and lush vegetation.

I won't let them get me. I'll wait, in the gathering darkness, listening to the coming of the night sounds and feeling a soft breeze on my face as I sense the room opening out as the walls shade away, as I sit here quietly in the dark warm air. And then I'll get up and start walking out into the dark land, into the jungle and amidst the trees that stand all around behind the darkness, smelling the greenness that surrounds me and hearing the gentle river off somewhere to the right. And I'll feel happy walking away into the night, and maybe far away I'll meet whatever makes the growling sounds I begin to hear in the distance, and we'll sit together by running water and be at peace in the darkness.

To See The Sea

When the bus reached the top of the hill that finally brought the ocean into view, Susan turned to me and grinned.

'I can see the sea!' she said, sounding about four years old. I smiled back and put my arm round her shoulders, and we turned to look out of the window. Beyond the slight reflection of our own faces the view consisted of a narrow strip of light grey cloud, above a wide expanse of dark grey sea. The sea came up to meet a craggy beach, which was also grey.

The driver showed no sign of throwing caution to the winds and abandoning his self-imposed speed limit of thirty miles an hour, and so we settled ourselves down to wait. The ride had already involved two hours of slow meandering down deserted country lanes. Another thirty minutes wouldn't kill us.

We could at least now see what we had come for, and as we gazed benignly out of the window I could feel both of us relax. True, the sea didn't look quite as enticing as it might at, say, Bondi Beach, and the end of October was possibly not the best time to be here, but it was better than nothing. It was better than London.

In the four months Susan and I had been living together, life had been far from sweet. We both worked at the same communications company, an organisation run on panic and belligerence. It ought to have been an exciting job, but every day at the office was like wading through knee-high mud in a wasteland of petty grievances and incompetence. Every task the company undertook was botched and flawed: even the car park was a disaster. Built in the shape of a wedge, it meant that anyone at the far end had to get all those parked between them and the exit to come and move their cars before they could leave. About once a fortnight our car wouldn't start, despite regular visits to the world's least conveniently situated garage.

The flat we had moved into was beautiful, but prey to similar niggling problems. The boiler, which went out twice a day, was situated below the kitchen, so we had no hot water to wash up with. Light bulbs in the flat went at forty-minute intervals, each turning out to be some bizarre Somalian make which was unavailable in local stores. The old twonk who lived underneath us managed to combine a hardness of hearing that required his television to play at rock concert volume with a sensitivity that led him to shout up through the floor if we so much as breathed after eleven o'clock.

Up until Thursday, we'd been planning to spend the weekend at home, as we usually did. By the time the working week had ended we were too tired to consider packing bags, checking tyre pressures, and hauling ourselves out of town. Perversely, the very fact that the car had packed up *again* on Friday evening had probably provided the impetus for us to make the trip. It had just been one thing too many, one additional pebble of grief on a beach that seemed to stretch off in all directions.

'Fuck it,' Susan had snarled, when we finally made it back home. 'Let's get out of town.' The next morning we arose, brows furrowed, each grabbed a change of clothes, a toothbrush and a book, and stomped off to the tube station. And now, after brief periods on most of the trains that British Rail had to offer, we were there. Or nearly there, anyway.

As the bus clattered its elderly way down the coast, it passed a sign for Dawton, now allegedly only eight miles away. Judging by the state of the signpost, the village's whereabouts were of only cursory interest to the inhabitants of the surrounding countryside. The name was printed in black on an arrow that must once have been white, but was now grey and streaked with old rain tracks. It looked as though no-one had bothered to clean it for a while.

Virtually all of the minor annoyances which had been plaguing our every day were trivial in themselves. It was simply their volume and relentlessness that was getting us down. The result was a state of constant flinching, in which neither of us were fully ourselves. The paradoxical advantage of this was that we were getting to know each other very quickly, seeing sides of each other that would normally sit in obeisance for years. We found ourselves opening up to each other, blurting secrets as we struggled to find a new equilibrium.

One of these secrets, divulged very late one night when we were both rather tired and emotional, had involved Susan's mother. I already knew that her mother had carved her name in Susan's psyche by leaving her father when Susan was five, and by never bothering to get in touch again. A need for security was amongst the reasons that Susan had fallen into the clutches of her ridiculous ex-boyfriend. Before her mother had gone, however, it transpired that she had managed to instill a different kind of fear in her daughter.

In 1955, ten years before Susan was born and five before she married, Geraldine Stanbury went on a holiday. She was gone three weeks, touring around European ports with a couple of friends from college. On their return, the ship, which was called the Aldwinkle, was hugging the coast of England against a storm when a disaster occurred. The underside of the ship's hull was punctured and then ripped apart by an unexpected rock formation, and the boat went down. By an enormous stroke of good fortune an area within the ship remained airtight, and all three hundred and ten passengers and crew were able to hole up there until help arrived the next morning. In the end, not a single person was lost, which perhaps accounts for the fact that the wreck of the Aldwinkle has failed to become a well-known part of English disaster lore.

Susan's mother told her this story often when she was a child, laying great stress on what it had been like to be trapped under the water, not knowing whether help would come. As Susan told me this, sitting tensely on the rug in our flat, I was temporarily shocked out of drunkenness, and sat up to hold her hand. A couple of weeks previously we had come close to a small argument over where to take the holiday we had been looking forward to. Having been raised in a coastal town I love the sea, and had suggested St Augustine, on the Florida coast. Susan had demurred, in an evasive way, and suggested somewhere more inland. The reasons for this now seemed more clear.

After Mrs Stanbury had left, the story of her near death continued to prey on her daughter's mind, though in different ways. As she'd grown up, questions had occurred to her. Like why, for example, there had not been a light showing at that point in the coast, when dangerous rocks were under the water. And why no-one in the nearby village had raised an alarm until the following morning. The ship had gone down within easy view of the shore: was it really possible that no-one had seen its distress? And if someone had seen, what on earth could have compelled them to keep silent until it should have been too late?

The village in question was that of Dawton, a negligible hamlet on the west coast of England. As I held Susan that night, trying to keep her warm against the bewilderment that years of asking the same questions had formed, I suggested that we should visit the village sometime, to exorcise the ghosts it held for her. For of course no-one could have seen the ship in distress, or an alarm would have been raised. And lighthouses sometimes fail.

Michael Marshall Smith

When we got up for work the next morning, both more than a little hung over, such a trip seemed less important. In the next couple of weeks, however, during which we had two further nights on which the hardships of the day drove us to spend the evening in the pub where we could not be contacted, the idea was mentioned again. It was a time for clearing out, in both our lives. One of the ways in which we were battling against the avalanche of trivia, which still sometimes threatened to engulf us, was by sorting out the things we could, by seeking to tidy away elements of our past that might have detrimental effects on our future together.

And so on the Friday when Susan finally demanded we get out of town, I suggested a pilgrimage to Dawton, and she agreed.

As the archaic bus drew closer to the village I noticed that Susan grew a little more tense. I was about to make a joke, about something, I'm not sure what, when she spoke.

'It's very quiet out here.'

It was. We hadn't passed a car in the last ten or fifteen minutes. That was no great surprise: as the afternoon grew darker the weather looked set to change for the worse, and judging from its size on the map, there would be little to draw people to Dawton unless they happened to live there. I said as much.

'Yes, but still.' I was about to ask her what she meant when I noticed a disused farm building by the side of the road. On its one remaining wall someone had painted a large swastika in black paint. Wincing, I pointed it out to Susan, and we shook our heads as middle-class liberals will when confronted with the forces of unreason.

'Hang on though,' she said, after a moment. 'Isn't it the wrong way round?' She was right, and I laughed. 'Christ,' she said. 'To be that stupid, to do something so mindless, and still to get it *wrong*...'

Then a flock of seagulls wheeling just outside the window attracted our attention. They were scraggy and unattractive birds, and fluttered close to the window in a disorganised but vaguely threatening way. As we watched, however, I was trying to work out what the swastika reminded me of, and trying to puzzle out why someone should have come all this way to paint it. We were still two miles from Dawton. It seemed a long way to come to daub on a disused wall, and unlikely that such a small coastal town should be racked with racial tension.

Ten minutes later the bus rounded a final bend, and the village of Dawton was in sight. I turned and raised my eyebrows at Susan. She was staring intently ahead. Sighing, I started to extricate our bag from beneath the seat. I hoped Susan wasn't building too much on this sleepy village. I don't know what I was expecting the weekend to bring: a night at a drab bed and breakfast, probably, with a quiet stroll down the front before dinner. I imagined that Susan would want to look out across the sea, to try to imagine the place where her mother had nearly lost her life, and that would be it. The next day we would return to London. To hope for anything more, for a kiss that would heal all childhood wounds, would be asking a little too much.

'You getting off, or what?'

Startled, we looked up to the front of the bus. The vehicle had stopped, apparently at random, fifty yards clear of the first disheveled houses that stood on the land side of the road.

'Sorry?' I said.

'Bus stops here.'

I turned to Susan, and we laughed.

'What, it doesn't go the extra hundred yards into the village?'

'Stops here,' the man said again. 'Make your mind up.'

We clambered rather huffily down out of the bus onto the side of the road. Before the door was fully shut, the driver had the bus in reverse. He executed a three-point turn at greater than his usual driving speed, and then sped off up the road away from the village.

'Extraordinary man,' said Susan.

'Extraordinary git, more like.' I turned and looked over the low wall we had been dumped beside. A stone ramp of apparent age led down to a stony strip of beach, against which the grey water was lapping with some force. 'Now what?'

From where we stood the coast bent round to our left, enabling us to see the whole of the village in its splendour. Houses much like those just ahead accounted for most of the front, with a break about halfway along where there appeared to be some kind of square. Other dwellings went back a couple of streets from the front, soon required to cling to the sharp hills which rose less than two hundred yards from the shore. An air of gradual decay hung over the scene, of negligent disuse. The few cars we could see parked looked old and haggard, and the smoke issuing thinly from a couple of chimneys only helped to underline the general air of desertion. Susan looked contrite.

'I'm sorry. We shouldn't have come.'

'Of course we should. The answering machine will be half-full of messages already, and I'm glad it's listening to them and we're not.'

'But it's so dismal.' She was right. Dismal was the word, rather than quiet. Anywhere can be quiet. Quiet just means that there isn't much noise. Dawton was different. Noise wouldn't have been an improvement.

'Dawton's dismal,' I said, and she giggled. 'Come on. Let's find a disappointing guest house that doesn't have a TV in each room, never mind tea- and coffee-making facilities.'

She grabbed me by the hand, kissed my nose, and we turned to walk. Just a yard in front of us, obscured by sand and looking much older than the one on the wall we had seen, another swastika was painted on the pavement. Again it was the wrong way round. I shook my head, puzzled, and then walked over it on our way towards the houses.

'We could try this one, I suppose.'

'What d'you reckon?'

'It doesn't look any nicer than the other one.'

'No.'

We were standing at one corner of Dawton's square, outside the village's second pub. We had already rejected one on the way from the guest house. We weren't expecting a CD jukebox and deep-fried camembert, but we'd thought we could probably find better. Now we were beginning to doubt it.

Susan lent forward to peer through the window.

'We could go straight to a restaurant,' I suggested.

'If there is one.'

In the end we nervously decided to have a quick drink in the pub. If nothing else the landlord should be able to tell us where the town restaurant was. Susan pushed the heavy wooden door, and I followed her in.

The pub consisted of a single bare room. Though it was cold no fire burned in the grate, and the predominance of old stained wood failed to bring any warmth to the ambience. A number of chairs surrounded the slab-like tables, each furnished with a tattered cushion for a seat. The floor was of much-worn boards, with a few faded rugs. There was no-one to be seen, either in the body of the room or behind the bar.

After a searching look at each other, we walked up to the bar, and I leant over. The area behind was narrow, almost like a corridor, and extended beyond the wall of the room we were in. By craning my neck I could see that there appeared to be another room on the other side of the wall. It could have been another bar except that it was completely dark, and there were no pumps or areas to store glasses. I pointed this out to Susan, and we frowned at each other. At the end of the bar area was a door, which was shut. After a pause, I shouted hello.

TO SEE THE SEA

It wasn't much of a shout, because I was feeling rather intimidated by the sepulchral quiet of the room, but it rang out harshly all the same. We both flinched, and waited for the door at the end of the corridor to be wrenched open. It wasn't, and I said hello again, a little more loudly this time.

A faint sound, possibly one of recognition, seemed to come from behind the door. I say 'seemed' because it was very faint, and appeared to come from a greater distance than you would have expected. Loath to shout again, in case we had already been heard, we shrugged and perched ourselves on two ragged barstools to wait.

The situation was strangely similar to that which we had encountered on entering the guest house in which we would be spending the night. We had only walked about ten houses down the line from where the bus had deposited us before we saw a sign nailed unceremoniously to the front of one of them, advertising rooms for the night. We'd entered, and loitered for a good few minutes in front of a counter before an elderly woman creaked out of a back room to attend to us.

The room we were shown was small, ill-favoured and faced away from the sea. Naturally it had neither a television nor drink-making facilities, and you could only have swung a cat in it if you had taken care to provide the animal with a crash helmet first. As the rest of the house seemed utterly deserted we asked the woman if we could have a room with a sea view instead, but she had merely shaken her head. Susan, fiendish negotiator that she is, had mused aloud for a moment on whether a little extra money could obtain such a view for us. The woman had shaken her head again, and said they were 'booked'.

I discovered a possible reason for this when down in the sitting room of the house, waiting for Susan to finish dressing for the evening. It was a dark and poky room, notwithstanding its large window, and I would not have chosen to spend much time there. The idea of simply sitting in it was frankly laughable. The chairs were lumpy and ill-fashioned, their archaic design so uncomfortable it seemed scarcely conceivable that they had been designed with humans in mind, and the window gave directly out onto a gloomy prospect of dark grey sea and clouds. I was there only because I had already seen enough of our small room, and because I hoped I might be able to source some information on likely eating places in the village.

At first I couldn't find anything, which was odd. Usually the guest houses of small towns on the coast are bristling with literature advertising local attractions, produced in the apparent hope that the promise of some dull site thirty miles away might induce the unwary into staying an extra night. The house we were staying in, however, clearly wished to be judged on its own merits, or else simply couldn't be bothered. Though I looked thoroughly over all the available surfaces, I couldn't find so much as a card.

I was considering without much enthusiasm the idea of tracking down the old crone to ask her advice when I discovered something lying on the sill in front of the window. It was a small pamphlet, photocopied and stapled together, and the front bore the words 'Dawton Festival'. It also mentioned a date, the 30th of October, which happened to be the following day.

There was nothing by way of editorial on the Festival itself, bar the information that it would start at three o'clock in the afternoon. Presumably the unspecified festivities continued into the evening, hence the drabness of our berth. The guest house's more attractive rooms had obviously been booked for two nights in advance, by forthcoming visitors to what promised to be the west coast's least exciting event.

I couldn't glean much of interest from the booklet, which had been typeset with extraordinary inaccuracy, to the point where some of it didn't even look as if it was in English. Most of the scant pages were filled with small advertisements for businesses whose purposes remained obscure. There was no mention of a restaurant. The centre spread featured a number of terribly reproduced photographs purporting to show various notables of the town, including, believe it or not, a 'Miss Dawton'. Her photograph in particular had suffered from being badly photocopied too many times, and was almost impossible to make out. Her figure blended with the background tones, making her appear rather bulky, and the pale ghost of her face was so distorted as to appear almost misshapen.

I was about to shout again, this time audibly, when the door at the end of the bar seemed to tremble slightly. Susan started slightly, and I stood up in readiness.

The door didn't open. Instead we both heard a very distant sound, like that of footsteps on wet pavements. It sounded so similar, in fact, that I turned to look at the outer door of the pub, half-expecting to see the handle turn as one of the locals entered. It didn't, though, and I returned to looking at the door. The sounds continued, getting gradually closer. They sounded hollow somehow, as if they were echoing slightly. Susan and I looked at each other, frowning once more.

The footsteps stopped on the other side of the door, and there was a long pause. I was beginning to wonder whether we wouldn't perhaps have been better off with the first pub we'd seen when the door suddenly swung open, and a man stepped out behind the bar. Without so much as glancing in our direction he shut the door behind him and then turned his attention to the ancient till. He opened it by pressing on some lever, and then began to sort through the money inside in a desultory fashion.

I think we both assumed that he would stop this after a moment or so, despite the fact that he had given no sign of seeing us. When he didn't, Susan nudged me, and I coughed a small cough. The man turned towards us with an immediacy and speed that rather disconcerted me, and stood, eyebrows raised. After a pause I smiled in a way I hoped looked friendly rather than nervous.

'Good evening,' I said. The man didn't move. He just stood, half turned towards us, with his hands still in the till and his eyebrows still in the air. He didn't even blink. I noticed that his eyes were slightly protuberant, and that the skin around his ears looked rough, almost scaly. His short black hair was styled as if for pre-war fashion, and appeared to have been slicked back with bryl-cream or something similar. A real blast from the past. Or from something, anyway.

After he'd continued to not say anything for a good ten seconds or so, I had another shot.

'Could we have two halves of lager, please?'

As soon as I started speaking again the man turned back to the till. After I'd finished there was a pause, and then finally he spoke.

'No.'

'Ah,' I said. It wasn't really a reply. It was just a response to the last thing I was expecting a publican to say.

He said: 'Don't have any beer.'

I blinked at him. 'None at all?'

He didn't enlarge on his previous statement, but finished whatever he was doing, closed the till, and started moving small glasses from one shelf to another, still with his back to us. The glasses were about three inches high and oddly shaped, and I couldn't for the life of me work out either what one might drink from them or why he was choosing to move them.

'A gin then,' Susan's voice was fairly steady, but a little higher than usual, 'with tonic?' She normally had a slice of lemon too, but I think she sensed it would be a bit of a long shot.

She got no reply at all. When all of the small glasses had been moved, the man opened the till again. Beginning to get mildly irritated, in spite of my increasing feeling of unease, I glanced at Susan and shook my head. She didn't smile, but just stared back at me, face a little pinched. I looked back at the man, and after a moment leant forward to see more closely.

His hair hadn't been slicked back, I realised. It was wet. Little droplets hung off the back in a couple of places, and the upper rim of his shirt was soaked. There had been a fine drizzle earlier on, enough to make the pavements damp. We'd walked most of the way from the guest house in it, and suffered no more than a fine dusting of moisture. So why was his hair so wet? Why, in fact, had he been out at all? Shouldn't he have been tending his (surprisingly beer-free) pumps?

He could have just washed it, I supposed, but that didn't seem likely. Not this man, at this time in the evening. And surely he would have dried it enough to prevent it dripping off onto his shirt, and running down the back of his neck? Peeking forward slightly I saw that his shoes were wet too, hence the wet footsteps we had heard. But where had he come from? And why was his hair wet?

Suddenly the man swept the till shut and took an unexpected step towards me, until he was right up against the bar. Taken aback, I just stared at him, and he looked me up and down as if I was a stretch of old and dusty wallpaper.

'Do you have *anything* we could drink?' I asked, finally. He frowned slightly, and then his face went blank again.

'Is there a place round here we can buy food?' Susan asked. She sounded halfway to angry, which meant she was very frightened indeed.

The man stared at me for a moment more, and then raised his right arm. I flinched slightly, but all he was doing, it transpired, was pointing. Arm outstretched, still looking at me, he was pointing in the opposite direction to the door. And thus, I could only assume, in the direction of somewhere we could buy some food.

'Thanks,' I said. 'Thank you.' Susan slid off her stool and preceded me to the door. I felt the back of my neck tickle all of the way there, as if I was frightened that something might suddenly crash into it. Nothing did, and Susan opened the door and stepped out. I followed her, and turned to pull the door shut. The man was still standing, arm outstretched, but his face had turned to watch us go, his eyes on Susan. Something about the way the light fell, or about the strangeness of his behaviour, made me think that there might be something else about his face, something I hadn't really noticed before. I couldn't put my finger on what it might be.

When I stepped out onto the pavement the first thing I saw was that it had started to rain a little harder, a narrow slant of drizzle which showed in front of the few and dingy streetlights. The second thing was Susan, who was standing awkwardly, her body turned out towards the street, head and shoulders faced to me. She was staring upwards, and her mouth was slightly open.

'What?' I said, a little sharply. I wasn't irritated, just rather spooked. She didn't say anything. I took a step towards her and turned to see.

I never really notice pub signs. Most of the time I go to pubs I know, and so they're of no real interest to me. On other occasions I just, well, I just fail to notice them. They're too high up, somehow, and not terribly interesting. So I hadn't noticed the one hanging outside this pub either, before we went in. I did now.

The sign was old and battered, the surrounding wood stained dark. A tattered and murky painting showed a clumsily rendered ship in the process of sinking beneath furiously slashing waves. Below there was a name. The pub was called The Aldwinkle.

Ten o'clock found us pushing plates away, lighting cigarettes, and generally feeling a little better. With nothing to go on apart from the publican's scarcely effusive directions, we'd wandered along the front for a while, coats wrapped tight around us and saying little. We were in danger of running out of front and considering turning back when we came upon a small house in which a light was glowing. The window had been enlarged almost the full width of the house, and inside we could see a few tables laid out. All the tables were empty.

We stood outside for a moment, wondering whether we could face any more of Dawton's version of hospitality, when a young man crossed the back of the room. He was tidily dressed as a waiter, and failed, at that distance, to give us any obvious reason for disquiet. His whole demeanor, even through glass, was so different to that which we had encountered so far that we elected to shoulder our misgivings and go in.

The waiter greeted us cordially and sat us, and the tension which, I realised belatedly, had been growing within us since the afternoon abated slightly. The young man was also the proprietor and cook, it transpired, and was moreover from out of town. He told us this when we observed, quite early into the meal, that he didn't seem like the other villagers we'd met. Soon afterwards the main course arrived and he disappeared into the kitchen to leave us to it.

We drank quite a lot during the meal. As soon as we sat down we knew we were going to, and ordered two bottles of wine to save time. We hadn't spoken much during the walk, not because we didn't feel there was much to say, but almost as if there was too much. Susan hadn't looked out over the sea, either, though there was once or twice when I thought she might be about to.

Michael Marshall Smith

'Why would they call a pub that?'

Susan was still trembling slightly when she finally asked. Not a great deal, because it would take a lot to unseat her that much. But her hands are normally very steady, and I could see her fork wavering slightly as she waited for me to answer. I'd had time to think about it, to come up with what I hoped was a reasonable suggestion.

'I guess because it's the most interesting thing that ever happened here.'

Susan looked at me and shook her head firmly, before putting another fork of the really quite passable lamb into her mouth. We'd looked for fish on the menu initially, assuming it would be the speciality of the house as in all small coastal towns, and were surprised to find not a single dish available. I'd asked the waiter about it, but he'd simply smiled vaguely and shaken his head.

'No,' she said, finally. 'That's not the reason.'

I opened my mouth to press my claim, and then shut it again. I didn't believe it either. Perhaps it was just because of the behaviour of the publican, or the overall atmosphere of the town. Maybe it was just the colour of the sky, or the way the rain angled as it fell, but somehow I just didn't quite believe that there wasn't more to the pub's name than a simple remembrance. There'd been something about the painting, some aspect of its style or colours, which hinted at something else, some more confused or inexplicable element. To name a pub after a ship that sank in—possibly—dubious circumstances, and to put that ship's name up on a sign with a painting that seemed almost to have some intangible air of celebration about it, hardly seemed like amiable quaintness.

But such speculations weren't what we were here for, and I saw my job as being that of steering Susan away from them. Although there was something a little strange about the whole thing, it didn't mean that the villagers had tried to cause harm to the passengers of the Aldwinkle thirty-odd years ago. It simply didn't make sense: what could possibly have been in it for them? Either way I didn't want the weekend to compound Susan's suspicions. Her mother's blatherings had left her with more than enough distrust of the human race. We'd come here to try to undermine that, not provide documentary evidence to support it.

So I steered the conversation away from the sign, and focused on the publican. There was enough material for speculation and vitriol there to keep us going to the other side of dessert, by which time we were more than a little drunk and rambling. By the time the waiter came through with our coffees I thought Susan had left more disturbing thoughts behind.

TO SEE THE SEA

I was wrong. As he stood at the end of the table she turned on him.

'What do you know about the Aldwinkle?' she said, challengingly. The waiter's hand paused for just a moment as he laid the milk jug down. Or maybe it didn't. Maybe I imagined it.

'It's a pub,' he said. Susan tried again, but that was all he would say. As he'd observed, he was from out of town and only came to Dawton to work. He sat at an adjoining table as we finished our third bottle of wine, and we chatted a little. Business wasn't going well, it would seem, and we'd made it to the restaurant just in time. Within a few weeks he suspected that he would probably have to give up. There simply wasn't the custom, and we'd been his only patrons that evening.

We enquired as to what the locals did of an evening. He didn't know. As we talked I began to sense an air of unease about him, as if he would prefer to discuss something other than the town and its inhabitants. Probably simply paranoia on my part. I was starting to realise that we were going to have to leave this haven, and return to our room. The thought did not fill me with glee.

In the end we paid, bid him goodnight, and stepped out onto the front. The first thing that struck me was the realisation that I was extremely drunk. I tend to drink just about everything as I would beer, that is in the same sort of quantity. This approach doesn't work too well with wine. I'd probably had the better part of two bottles, and suddenly, as we stood swaying in the wind that whipped down the soulless stretch of the front, it felt like it.

Susan was a little the worse for wear too, and we stumbled in unison as we stepped off the curb to walk across the road to the front. Susan slipped her hand underneath my coat and looped her arm around my back and, not saying anything, we stepped up onto the ragged pavement on the other side of the road.

It was late now, but a sallow moon spread enough light for us to see what lay in front of us. Beyond the low wall a ramp of decaying concrete sloped down to the shore. The shore appeared to consist of puddled mudflats, and stretched at least a hundred yards out to where still water the colour of slate took over. In the distance we could just hear the sound of small waves, like two hands slowly rubbed together.

'Tide's out,' I observed sagely, except that it came out more like 'tie shout'. I opened my eyes wide for a moment, blinked, and then fumbled in my pockets for a cigarette.

'Mn,' Susan replied, not really looking. She was gazing vaguely at the wall in front of us, for some reason not letting her eyes reach any higher. She shook her head when I offered her a smoke, which was unusual. I put a hand on the cold surface of the wall, for something to lean against, and looked back out at the sea.

When I was a kid my family often used to go on holiday to St Augustine. Actually the place where we stayed was just outside, a little further down Crescent Beach in the direction of, but thankfully a good ways from, Daytona Beach. I remember standing on the unspoiled beach as a child, probably no more than five or six, and slowly turning to look out at the sea from different angles, and I remember thinking that you can't ever really stand still when you're looking at the sea. There's nowhere you can stand and think 'Yep, that's the view', because there's always more of it on either side.

In Dawton it was different. There was only one way you could see it. Perhaps it was because of the curve of the bay, or maybe it was something else. Your eye was drawn outwards, as if there was only one way you could see the view, only one thing you could see.

Suddenly Susan's arm was removed and she took a step forwards. Without looking at me she grabbed the wall purposefully with both hands and started to hoist herself over it.

'What're you doing?' I demanded, stifling a hiccup.

'Going to see the sea.'

'But,' I started, and then wearily reached out to follow her. Obviously the time had come for Susan to do her staring out across the water. The best I could do was tag along, and be there if she wanted to talk.

The concrete ramp was wet and quite steep, and Susan almost lost her footing on the way down. I grabbed her shoulder and she regained her balance, but she didn't say anything in thanks. She hadn't really said anything to me since we'd left the restaurant. Her tone when telling me where she was going had been distant, almost irritable, as if she was annoyed at having to account for her actions. I tried not to take it personally.

When we got to the bottom of the ramp I stopped, swaying slightly. I peered owlishly at the stinking mud in front of us. Clearly, I thought, this was where the expedition ended. Susan felt otherwise. She stepped out onto the mud and started striding with as much determination as the ground and her inebriation would allow. I stared after her, feeling suddenly adrift. She didn't seem herself, and I was afraid of something, of being left behind. Wincing, I put a tentative foot onto the mud and then hurried after her as best I could.

We walked a long way. The mud came in waves. For twenty yards it would be quite hard, and relatively dry, and then it would suddenly change and turn darker and wetter until, to be honest, it was like wading through shit. The first time this happened I tried to find dryer patches, to protect my shoes, but in the end I gave up. It was as much as I could do to keep up with Susan, who was striding head down towards the sea.

I glanced back at one point, and saw how far we'd come. When we'd stood on the front I'd thought the sea was a hundred yards or so away, but it must have been much further. I couldn't see any lights in the houses on the front, or any of the streetlights. For an awful moment I thought that something must have happened, that everyone had turned their lights off so we wouldn't be able to find our way back. I turned to shout to Susan but she was too far ahead to hear. Either that, or she ignored me. After another quick glance back I ran to catch up with her.

She was still walking, but her head was up and her movements were jerky and stilted. When I drew level with her I saw that she was crying.

'Susan,' I said. 'Stop.' She walked on for a few more yards, tailing off, and then stopped. I put my hands on her shoulders and she held herself rigid for a moment, but then allowed herself to be folded into me. Her hair was cold against my face as we stood, surrounded by mud in every direction.

'What is it?' I said eventually. She sniffed.

'I want to see the sea.'

I raised my head and looked. The sea appeared as far away as it had when we'd been standing on the front.

'The tide must still be going out,' I said. I'm not sure if I believed it. Susan certainly didn't.

'It's not letting me,' she said, indistinctly, 'And I don't know why.'

I didn't know what to say to that, and just stared out at the water. I wondered how much further it was before the bay deepened, how much further to the crop of rocks where the Aldwinkle presumably still lay.

In the end we turned and walked back, Susan allowing me to keep my hand around her shoulders. She seemed worn out. I was beginning to develop a headache, while still feeling rather drunk. When we got back to the ramp we climbed halfway up it and then sat down for a cigarette. My shoes, I noticed belatedly, were ruined, caked about a centimetre thick in claggy mud. I took them off and set them to one side.

'This weekend isn't going quite as I thought it would,' I said, eventually.

'No.' I couldn't tell from Susan's tone whether she thought this was a good or a bad thing.

We looked out at the water for a while in silence. Now we were back it looked little more than a hundred yards away, two hundred at the most. It couldn't have moved. We simply can't have walked as far as we'd thought we had, which is odd, because it had felt like we'd walked forever.

'How are you feeling?' I asked.

'It's out there somewhere,' she said. I nodded. It wasn't a direct reply, but in another sense I guess it was.

'Was it the sea you wanted to see?' I ventured.

'I don't know,' she said, and her head dropped.

A little later we stood up. I decided to leave my shoes where they were. They're weren't an especially nice pair, and it seemed less troublesome to leave them there than to find some way of taking them home in their current state and then cleaning them. On a different evening, in a different mood, leaving them might have felt like a gesture of some kind, something wild and devil-may-care. Instead I just felt a little confused and sad, as well as vulnerable and exposed.

Susan warmed up a little on the walk back along the front, enlivened slightly by a stream of weak jokes from me. After a while I felt her cold hand seek out mine, and I grasped it and did my best to warm it up. The village we passed in front of seemed to have died utterly during the course of the evening. The streets were silent and not a single light showed in any of the windows. It was like walking beside a photograph of a ghost town.

Until we got closer to our guest house, that is. From a way off we could see that all the lights seemed to be on, though dimly, and as we approached we began to hear the sound of car doors slamming carried on the quiet air. About fifty yards away we stopped.

The street outside the house, which had been empty when we'd arrived, was lined both sides with cars. The lights *were* on, on all three floors. They looked dim because in each window a shade was pulled down. The other guests had evidently arrived.

As we looked, someone moved behind one of the upper windows. The angle of the light behind him or her cast a grotesquely shaped shadow on the blind, and I found myself shivering for no evident reason. Quietly, and to myself, I wished that we were staying somewhere else. Like London.

I was fumbling for our key on the doorstep when suddenly the door was pulled wide. Warm yellow light spilled out of the hallway and Susan and I looked up, blinking, to see the old lady proprietor standing in front of us. My first befuddled thought was that we must have transgressed some curfew and she was about to berate us for being late.

TO SEE THE SEA

Far from it. The old crone's manner was bizarrely improved, and she greeted us with strange and twittering warmth before ushering us into the hallway. Once there she steered us into the sitting room before we'd even had time to draw breath, though we had no desire to go there. Susan entered the room first and glanced back at me. I opened my eyes wide to signal my bafflement. Susan shrugged, and we seemed to mutually decide that it would be easier to go along with it. The old woman flapped us towards some chairs in the centre of the room and offered us a cup of tea. My first impulse was to refuse—I was beginning to sag rather by then—but then remembered that our room didn't have so much as a kettle, and accepted. The woman clapped her hands together in apparent delight, and out of the corner of my eye I saw Susan glancing at me again. There was nothing I could tell her. None of it was making any sense to me either, and as soon as the woman left the room I turned to Susan and said so. I also observed that there seemed to be something gaudy and strange about the old woman. She looked different.

'She's wearing makeup,' she said. 'And that *dress*?'

The dress, made of some dark green material, was certainly not to my taste, and the makeup had been hastily applied, but it clearly spoke of some effort being made. Presumably it was the new guests, whoever they might be, who merited such a transformation. We looked round the room, feeling slightly ill at ease. On the table to one side of me I noticed something.

A pamphlet for the Dawton Festival lay next to the large glass ashtray. I looked across at the windowsill and saw that the one I had consulted earlier was still there. For want of anything else to do I picked it up and showed it to Susan. Flicking through the pages a second time failed to furnish us with any more information on what the Festival might consist of. When we got to the centre pages I nudged Susan, looking forward to drawing her attention to the oddity of a Dawton beauty contest. But when my finger was pointing at the photo I suddenly I stopped.

I realised now what had struck me about the publican in The Aldwinkle, the aspect of his appearance which I hadn't been able to put my finger on. There had been something about the shape of his head, the ratio of its width to its depth, the bone structure and the positioning of the ears, which reminded me forcibly of the degraded photograph of 'Miss Dawton'. I couldn't believe that she actually looked like that, that I was seeing something other than the result of dark and badly reproduced tones blending into each other, but still the resemblance was there.

'It must be his daughter.'

When Susan spoke I turned to her, startled.

'It's just the printing,' I said. 'She can't look like that.' Susan shook her head firmly.

'It's his daughter.'

The door slid quietly open and I quickly slipped the leaflet to one side, trying to hide it. I don't know why: it just seemed like a good idea. It didn't work.

'Will you be staying for the Festival?' the old woman croaked, laying two cups of brick-red tea down on the table. She addressed her comment to Susan, who said no. Our plan, as discussed in the restaurant, was to rise early the next morning and get the hell back to London. I was loath to question her too closely on what the Festival might involve, because I was aware that I was enunciating my words very carefully to keep the drunkenness out of my voice. On the few occasions when Susan spoke I heard her doing the same thing.

As we sat there, sipping our tea and listening to her rustling voice, I began to feel a curious mixture of relaxation and unease. If the Festival was such a draw, why wouldn't she tell us about it? And was it my imagination or did she cock her head slightly every now and then, as if listening for something?

A few moments later the second question at least seemed to be answered. We heard the sound of the front door being opened and then, after a long pause, being shut again. Still talking in her dry and uninformative voice the old crone slipped over towards the door to the sitting room and then, instead of going out, gently pushed it shut. She carried on talking for a few moments as Susan and I watched her, wondering what she was up to. Perhaps it was my tired mind, but her chatter seemed to lose cohesion for a while, as if her attention was elsewhere. After a couple of moments she came to herself again, and reopened the door. Then, with surprising abruptness, she said goodnight and left the room.

Coming at the end of a day which felt like it had lasted forever, the whole vignette was almost laughable: not because it was funny, but because it was odd in some intangible way that made you want to cover it with sound. Neither of us felt much like actually laughing, I suspect, as we levered ourselves out of the dreadfully uncomfortable chairs and made our way unsteadily upstairs.

I was especially quiet on the stairs, because I wasn't wearing any shoes. Strange, perhaps, that the old woman had either not noticed this or had chosen not to make any comment.

My memories of the next hour or so are confused and very fragmentary.

TO SEE THE SEA

I wish they weren't, because somewhere in them may lie some key to what happened afterwards. I don't know. This is what I remember.

We went upstairs to our room, passing doors under which lights shone brightly, and behind which low voices seemed to be murmuring. As we wove down the corridor I thought at first that a soft smoke was beginning to percolate down from the ceiling. It wasn't, of course. I simply wasn't seeing very well. I felt suddenly very drunk again: more drunk, in fact, than at any point in the evening. Susan, though only a pace or two in front of me, seemed a very long way ahead, and walking that short corridor seemed to take much longer than it should. A sudden hissing noise behind one of the doors made me veer clumsily to the other side of the corridor, where I banged into an opposite door. It seemed to me that some sound stopped then, though I couldn't remember what it had been. As I leant my head on the door to our room and tried to remember how to use a key I found myself panting slightly, my shoulders slumped and weak. Another wave of vagueness surged into my head and I turned laboriously to Susan, who was standing weaving by my side, and asked her if she felt alright. She answered by suddenly clapping her hands over her mouth and stumbling away towards the toilet.

I leaned in the direction she'd gone, realised or decided that I wouldn't be much help, and fell into our room instead. The light switch didn't seem important, either because of the weak moonlight filtering into the room or because I couldn't be bothered to find it. I flapped my way out of my coat with sluggish brutality and sat heavily on the bed. I started unbuttoning my shirt and then suddenly gave up. I simply couldn't do it.

As I sat there, slumped over, I realised that I was feeling even worse. I couldn't understand why I was feeling so bad, or even what exactly the problem was. It reminded me of a time when I'd had food poisoning after a dodgy seafood pizza. A few hours after the meal I'd started feeling… well, just odd, really, in a way I found difficult to define. I didn't feel particularly ill, just completely disconnected and altogether strange. I now felt roughly similar, though as if I'd drunk all the wine in the world and taken acid as well. The room seemed composed of dark wedges of colour that had no relation to objects or spaces, and if asked to describe it I wouldn't have known where to start.

Suddenly remembering that Susan was throwing up in the toilet I jerked my head up, wondering again if I should go to her aid, and then I passed out.

*

Michael Marshall Smith

Susan's skin was warm and almost sweaty. We rolled and I felt myself inside her, with no idea of how I'd got there. I have images of the side of her chin, of one of her hands and of her hair falling over my face: but no memory of her eyes.

I think I felt wetness on my cheek at one point, as if she cried again, but all I really remember is the heat, the darkness, and not really being there at all.

The first thing I did when I woke was to moan weakly. I was lying on my side facing the window, and a weak ray of sun was shining on my head. My brain felt as if it had been rubbed with coarse sandpaper, and the last thing I needed was light. I wanted very much to turn away from it, but simply didn't have what it took. So I moaned instead.

After a few minutes I slowly rolled over onto my back, and immediately noticed that Susan wasn't beside me. I had a dim memory of her eventually coming to bed the night before, and so assumed that she must have woken first and be taking a shower. I rolled back over onto my side and reach pitifully out towards the little table by the bed. My cigarettes weren't there, which was odd. I always have a cigarette last thing before going to sleep. Except last night, by the look of it.

Suddenly slightly more awake, I levered myself into a sitting position. What had I done before going to bed? I couldn't really remember. My coat was lying in a tangle on the floor, and I experienced a sudden flashback of thrashing my way out of it. Reaching down I found my cigarettes and lighter in the pocket and distractedly lit up. As I squinted painfully round the room I noticed something out of place.

Susan's washing bag was on the chair by the window.

Looking back, I knew from that moment something was wrong. I went through the motions in the right order and with only gradually increasing speed, but I knew right at that moment.

Susan's washing bag was still here in the room. She hadn't taken it with her, which didn't make sense. Maybe she'd gone to the bathroom not to wash, but to be ill again. I clambered out of bed, head throbbing, and threaded myself into some clothes with about as much ease as pushing yarn through the eye of a needle. On the way out of the room I grabbed her washing bag, just in case.

The bathroom was deserted. There was no-one in the stalls, and both the bath and the shower cubicles were empty. Not only empty, but cold, and silent, and dry. I walked back to the room quickly, my head feeling much clearer already. Strangely clear, in fact: it generally takes an hour or so for my head to start recovering from a hangover. Hands on hips I looked around the room and tried to work out where she'd be. Then I noticed the shade of the clouds outside, and suddenly turned to look at my watch on the table.

It was twenty to four in the afternoon.

For a moment I had a complete sensation of panic, as if I'd overslept and missed the most important meeting of my life. Or even worse, perhaps, as if it was just starting, this minute, on the other side of town. The feeling subsided, but only slightly, as I scrabbled round the room for some more clothes. Normally I have to bathe in the mornings, will simply not enter company without doing so: which is part of why I say now that I already knew something was wrong. Perhaps something that had happened the night before, something that I had forgotten, told me that things were amiss. A bath didn't seem important.

It took five minutes to find the room keys where I'd dropped them, and then I locked the room and walked quickly down the corridor. I ducked my head into the bathroom again, but nothing had changed. As I passed one of the other doors I flinched slightly, expecting to hear some sound, but none came. I wasn't even sure what I was expecting.

The lower floor of the guest house was equally deserted. I checked in what passed as the breakfast room, although they would obviously have stopped serving by late afternoon. I stood in front of the desk and even rang the bell, but no-one appeared. Pointlessly I ran back upstairs again, checked the room, and even knocked timidly on one of the other doors. There was no response.

Downstairs again I wandered into the sitting room, wondering what to do. There was no reason for the increasing unease and downright fright I was feeling. Susan wouldn't have just left me. She must be out in town somewhere, with everyone else. It was Festival day, after all. Maybe she'd wanted to see it. Maybe she'd told me that last night, and I'd been too splatted to take it in.

The two cups we'd drunk tea out of the night before were still there, still sitting on the table next to the Festival pamphlet. Frowning, I walked towards them. Guest house landladies are generally obsessed with tidiness. And where *was* she, anyway? Surely she didn't just abandon her guest house because a poxy town Festival was on?

As I looked at the cups I experienced a sudden lurching in my stomach, which puzzled me. It was almost like a feeling I used to get looking through the window of a certain pizza chain, when I saw the thick red sauce that coated the pizzas on the plates of the people inside. When you've seen and felt that same sauce coming out of your nose while you're buckled up over a toilet in the small hours, you tend not to feel too positive about it in the future. The reaction has nothing to do with your mind, but a lot to do with the voiceless body making its warning clear in the only way it can.

A feeling of nausea. Why should I feel that about tea?

I moved a little closer to the table and peered into the cups. One had a small amount left in the bottom, which was to be expected: Susan never quite finished a cup. My cup was empty. At the bottom of the cup, almost too faintly to be seen, the pottery sparkled slightly, as if something there was irregularly reflecting the light. Feeling as if I'd been punched in the stomach without warning, I kneeled beside the table to take a closer look.

I hadn't had sugar in my tea last night. I never do. I gave it up three years ago and lost over half a stone, and I'm vain enough to want to keep it that way. But there was something in the bottom of the cup. I picked the other cup up and tilted it slightly. The small puddle of tea rocked to reveal a similar patch on the bottom. It was less defined than in my cup, but it was still there.

Something had been put in our tea.

I looked up suddenly at the door, sure that it had moved. I couldn't see any difference, but I stood up anyway. I stood up and I ran out of the house.

As I walked quickly down the front towards the square I tried to make sense of what I'd found. To a degree it added up. I'd felt very, very strange when I'd gone upstairs the night before, strange in a way I'd never experienced through alcohol before. I'd hugely overslept too, which also made sense, and the hangover I'd woken up with had passed differently to usual.

As I approached the square I slowed down a little. I realised that I'd been expecting lots of people to be gathered there, celebrating this benighted village's Festival. There was no-one. The corner of the square I could see was as empty as it had been the night before.

Susan, on the other hand, had got up early. Which also made sense: she'd thrown up immediately after we'd drunk the tea. Less of it would have made it into her bloodstream, and she'd not have experienced the same effects. That made sense. That was fine.

But two things weren't fine, and didn't make sense whichever way I added them up.

First, most obviously, why had someone put something in our tea? This wasn't a film, some Agatha Christie mystery: this was a small village on the English coast. Who would want to drug us, and why? The second question was less clear-cut, but bothered me even more. Susan had an iron constitution, and could hold her drink. She could drink like a fish, to be honest. So why had she thrown up, so long after drinking, when I hadn't?

Perhaps she was supposed to. Perhaps the drug, whatever it was, had different effects on different people.

The square was completely deserted. I stood still for a moment, trying to work out what to do next. There was no bunting, no posters, nothing to suggest a town event was in progress. I turned round slowly, feeling the hairs on the back of my neck rise. It was unnaturally quiet in that rotten, decomposing square, abnormally empty and silent. It didn't just feel as if no-one was there. It felt like the fucking Twilight Zone.

I walked across to The Aldwinkle and peered in through the window. The pub was empty and the lights were off, but I tried the door anyway. It was open. Inside I stood at the bar and shouted, but no-one came. Something had happened in the pub after we had been there last night. Some of the chairs had been shunted to the side of the room, and others put in their place. They looked like the chairs in the guest house, ugly and misshapen. Their occupants obviously had better luck when trying to buy a drink: a few of the small glasses lay scattered on one of the tables. One of the Festival pamphlets lay there too, and I irritably swatted it aside. It fluttered noisily to the floor and fell open, displaying its ridiculous inaccuracies. 'R'lyeh iä fhtagn!', for example. What the fuck was that supposed to mean?

It did at least make me think more clearly. The Festival had started at three o'clock. I knew that. What I didn't know was *where* it had started. Presumably it took the form of a procession, which began at one end of the town and ended at another, possibly in the square. Perhaps I was here too early. I was now hopping from foot to foot with anxiety over Susan, and felt that anything had to be worth trying. If the Festival wouldn't come to me, I'd bloody well go and find it.

I launched myself out of the pub, slamming the door shut behind me, and ran off towards the opposite corner of the square. I carried on up the little road, past yet more dilapidated houses, casting glances down narrow side roads. When the road began to peter out into cliffside I turned and went another way. And another. And another.

It didn't take long for the streets to sap what little courage I'd injected myself with. It was like running through a dream where the horror you fear round each corner turns out to be the horror of nothing at all. No-one leant on their fences, passing the time of day. No-one was hanging out washing. No little children ran carelessly through the streets or up the cobbled alleys. No-one, in short, was doing anything. All there was to see was rows of dirty houses, many with upper windows that seemed to have been boarded up. It was a ghost town.

And then I found something. Or thought I did.

I was moving a little more slowly by then, fifteen years of cigarettes taking their toll. To be absolutely honest I was bent over near a street corner, hands on my knees, vigorously coughing my guts up. When the fit subsided I raised my head and thought I heard something. A piping sound.

Jerking myself upright, I snapped my head this way and that, trying to determine where the sound was coming from. I thought it might be from back the way I'd come, perhaps in a parallel road, and jogged up the street. I couldn't hear anything there, but I ducked into the next side road anyway. There I head the sound again, a little louder, and something else: the rustle of distant conversation. Casting a fearful glance up at the darkening sky I pelted down the road.

I turned the corner cautiously. There was nothing there, but I knew there had been. I'd just missed it. I ran along the road to the next corner and listened, trying to work out which way the procession had gone. I chose left and soon heard noise again, louder this time: an odd tootling music, and the babble of strange voices. The sound made me pause for a moment, and another fragment of the previous evening slipped into my head. Was it a noise like that, an unwholesome and hateful gurgling, which I had heard behind one of the guest house doors?

Suddenly the sounds seemed to be coming from a different direction, and I whirled to follow them. Then, quite by chance, I happened to be looking over the abandoned garden of one of the houses I was passing when I saw something through the gap between it and its neighbour. Three sticks, about a foot apart, moving in the opposite direction to me. As they progressed they appeared to rock slightly, and it was that which made the connection. They weren't just sticks. I couldn't be certain, because it was now fairly dark. But to me they looked like little masts.

I'd thought I couldn't run any faster, that my lungs would surely protest and perhaps burst. But I doubled back on myself and sprinted up the street, taking the corner on the slide. The street was empty but this time I was sure I saw the flicker of someone's ankle as they disappeared around the corner, and I pelted down the road towards it.

I don't know what made me glance at the house at the end. It was almost certainly just an accident, something for my head to do while my body did all the running. Just before I reached the end my eyes drifted across the filthy pane of its main window, and what I saw—or thought I saw—terrified me into losing my balance and falling. I seemed to take a long time to fall, and my mind insists that this is what I saw as I did.

TO SEE THE SEA

A face, almost merged with the shadows of the room behind the window. A face that started off as something else, something unrecognisable and alien, something which slid and twitched into a normal face faster than the eye could see. A normal face that looked a little like the publican's, and a little like Miss Dawton's. And like, I realised, that of the old crone from the guest house, especially when we'd returned last night. It wasn't simply make-up that had made the difference, far from it. If I hadn't been so drunk I think I would have realised at the time. I think the make-up had been put on to hide something else.

And there was one more thing about the face. It looked a little bit like my mother.

All that passed through my head in the time it took me to fall, and was smacked out of it when my head cracked into a curbstone. My knee felt badly grazed and twisted, but I was up on my feet immediately, backing hurriedly away from the house. There was nothing to see in the window. No-one was there. Maybe they never had been. Nevertheless I turned and ran away.

It started to rain then, at first drizzling, but then settling into a steady downpour. I plodded down one street after another, sometimes thinking I heard something, sometimes hearing nothing but water. My head hurt by then, and blood ran down the side of my face, mingling with the falling rain and running down into my shirt. At the slightest sound I started and whirled around, but too sluggishly to make any difference. I couldn't seem to think in straight lines. It didn't feel like it had the night before. It just felt as if I was terribly, miserably frightened.

In the end I gave up and headed towards the square as best I could, limping my way down the tangled streets. It should have occurred to me sooner I suppose, after all, I'd had the right idea in the beginning. I should have stayed where the procession might end. In retrospect I'm glad I was too stupid to realise that, but at the time I wearily cursed myself.

It didn't make any difference. The square was still deserted. But they'd been there. That much was clear from the very atmosphere, from the feeling of recently emptied space. It was also obvious from the scraps of paper lying in gutters, which hadn't been there before. I squatted to pick one or two of the sodden pieces up. They were from the pamphlet, as I might have expected. 'Yogsogo...' one fragment said. '...thulu mw'yleh iä...' read another. Late, far too late, I wondered if it all meant something, if it was something more than a local idiosyncrasy or the result of a blind typist. I don't think I can be blamed for not suspecting that earlier. All I'd wanted was a weekend out of London. I wasn't expecting anything else.

Michael Marshall Smith

Looking back up through the slanting rain I noticed something. From where I was it looked as if the door to the pub was now open. I got up and walked towards it, taking occasional paranoid glances into the darkness at the other corners of the square.

No light was showing, but the door was open. The publican had left his pub. The landlady had abandoned her guest house. Were these people so trusting, or did they simply not care? My face in an unconscious wince of tension, I carefully pushed the door open a little further. No sound came from the room, and when I poked my head cautiously within I saw it was completely empty. I stepped in. The room looked much as it had when I'd last been there, except at the bar. The flap which allowed access to the bar area had been lifted up and left that way, and the door behind was also open. I walked over and, wishing I had a god or religion to invoke, stepped behind the bar.

The first thing I did was to peer into the gloom of the second room, the one you could just see when standing at the bar. I couldn't see much except chairs, all of the unusual shape. Then I turned and looked through the other door. The wall beyond was paneled with dark wood, and the narrow corridor it formed a part of stopped just past the door. I stepped through and looked to the left. Stone steps led down into darkness. I felt around for a light but couldn't find one. Even if I had I doubt I would have had the courage to use it.

I thought for a moment before starting down. I wondered about running back to the guest house, checking if Susan had returned. Perhaps the Festival had ended, and she was waiting impatiently in the sitting room, wondering where I was.

I don't know why I didn't believe that was the way things were. I simply didn't, and I went down the steps instead.

There were a good number of them, and they went straight down. It was pitch dark almost from the top, and I walked down with a hand braced against the walls on each side of me. My head was still hurting, indeed it seemed to be getting worse. When I shut my eyes it felt almost as if a small light was beginning to glow in my temple, so I kept them open, little difference though it made to my progress.

Eventually I ran into a wall, and turned left. I walked a little way down another corridor and then realised that I could see a slightly lighter patch in front of me, and the sound of distant waves. Not only that.

I could hear piping, and I started to run.

Of course, I thought, as I panted my way towards the end, of course the procession would end on the beach. And of course, perhaps, it would go there by way of a pub that had been called The Aldwinkle, a pub whose name celebrated the night they'd found their chance to emerge. Susan had been right. The name wasn't simply a souvenir of a bygone event. It meant something to the village, as did the wreck itself, along with R'yleh and everything else. It meant something horrible, celebrated a disastrous opportunity that had been taken advantage of. The piping grew stronger as I approached the end of the tunnel, and when I emerged breathless onto the beach I saw them.

They were walking in pairs, slowly and in a peculiar rhythm. In the middle of the column a model of a boat bobbed and swayed, held up by a multitude of hands. Soon it would have a chance to see if it could float, because they were walking into the sea.

As I watched, rooted to the spot, the figures at the front of the procession took their first steps into the choppy waters. They did so confidently, without any fear, and I thought finally I understood. I lurched forward without thinking, shouting Susan's name. The column was a long way away, maybe two hundred yards or more across the mud, but I shouted very loudly, and I thought I saw a figure at the back of the procession turn. It was too dark to even be sure that it happened, but I think it did. I think she turned and looked.

I broke into a run and got maybe five yards before something crashed into the side of my head. As my vision faded to black I thought I saw the thing that had been hiding look at me to check I was done, before shambling quickly to join the others.

I came back to London two days later, and I'm still here. For the time being. All of Susan's stuff is in boxes under the stairs. Having it lying around was too painful, but I can't get rid of it. Not until I know what I'm going to do.

I regained consciousness, after about three hours stretched on my face in the mud, to find the beach completely deserted. I started to stumble towards the water, mind still programmed as it had been before I was knocked out, but then I changed my mind. I walked crying back up the slope and called the police from a public phone booth, and then I slumped down to the ground and passed out. I was taken to hospital eventually, where they found two concussions. But before that I talked to the police, and told them what I knew. I ranted a great deal apparently, about a coastal town where they didn't eat the fish, about the meaning of inverted swastikas, and about monstrous villagers who could disguise their true nature and look like normal people.

In the end the police brought the heavy squad in. They had to. An empty village where doors have been left open and belongings abandoned is more than local plod can handle. The city cops weren't terribly interested in my ramblings, and I can't say that I blame them. But before they arrived I thought one of the local police, an old sergeant who lived in a nearby village, took what I said very seriously.

He must have done. Because on the following day, as I sat shivering in the sitting room of the empty guest house, I saw police divers head out towards the sea. No-one knows about this, and they won't. The press never got wind of the story, and various powers will make sure they never do. I'm not going to tell anyone. It's better that no-one knows. The only question in my mind is what I should do, whether I can forget enough not to act on my knowledge. Time will tell.

I brought my shoes back to London in the end, which was a gesture of a kind. The police found them on the front, and I identified them as mine. Deep in one toe I found a note. 'Goodbye, my dear,' it said.

That she went with them I know, and I'm glad she lost her fear of the sea. Perhaps it had never been real fear, but a denial of something else. When I remember the last hour we spent together I wonder now whether it was a tear I felt on my cheek, or whether her hair was wet. Because when the divers returned they'd made a discovery, something that will never be known. More divers arrived an hour later, and for the next day the beach was crawling with them as they returned to the water again and again.

They found the Aldwinkle, and something inside. The skeletons of three hundred and ten people, to be precise. By the jewelry round her neck and the remains of her passport, one was identified as Geraldine Stanbury.

Two Shot

The weird thing was that he didn't feel especially
enthusiastic. Usually the prospect pepped him right up. He'd spend the
last half hour pacing around the apartment, making sure everything was
just so, building the scene. This afternoon he was a little excited, of
course, but this was mingled with other emotions that made less sense. A
feeling of distance, dislocation, and a kind of deep-down lethargy
underneath it all—adding up to a kind of queasy anticipation which was
unlike him. Probably it was at least partly due to the hangover. The
memories of exactly how he'd come by it were vague, but it was sure as
hell there. In force. He'd spent the morning drinking large quantities of
expensive mineral water, in the hope this would mitigate it in some way.
In fact it had just made him feel as if he was both hung over and full of
water.

He rubbed his face hard with his hands and felt a little better. The
clock panel on the wall of his living room told him there was still twenty-
five minutes before she arrived. Plenty of time. He'd be fine. He knew the
way she'd look when she turned up at the door. Nervous, a little flushed,
feeling naughty as hell and not admitting to herself that she liked the
sensation. Silly bitch.

He smiled suddenly, and all at once felt better still. The differential
had kicked in. The differential between what they thought was going on,
and what was really happening. Between their assumption that they were
caught up in a sexy, private little affair with someone who just couldn't
keep their hands off them, and the way he really viewed the liaisons. The
excitement he felt when they were in the apartment was nothing to what
he knew when they were gone. That was the real business.

Feeling well-nigh pepped at last, he shoved himself up off the couch
and quickly moved through the two stages of readying the apartment. The
first didn't take a lot of doing. He lived tidily. Fan the magazines
(carefully chosen to reinforce the impression that he was intelligent,

247

sensitive and yet sensuously physical—and why the hell not? He was, godammit); plump the pillows on the couch (Lord, women did like fancy pillows); make sure there were two very clean wine glasses waiting ready on the counter, and that the bottle in the fridge was cool but not too cold. Anne liked a sip before they got to it, whether to relax herself, blur her conscience or to gild the event with some half-assed romantic veneer, he neither knew nor cared.

The second half of the process took a little longer. There were eight digital camcorders in the apartment, over ten thousand dollars' worth of high-spec Japanese ingenuity. Two in the living room; four in the bedroom; two in the bathroom. He initially only put new tapes in six, almost electing not to bother with the ones in the bathroom. Never in the seven times he'd had sex with Anne had the action careened into that room. With some women it did, with others it didn't. With Anne it didn't. But sometimes it was worth watching for the expression on the women's faces as they had a pee afterwards, thinking they were in a backstage area and safe from view. Shame, smug glee, guilty and compromised tears: they all informed what had gone before. He put one tape in that room after all, in the camera that directly faced onto the lavatory. He could live without a two shot in here: her face was what really counted.

Each of the cameras was carefully hidden: in curtains, on bookshelves, in tidy piles of clothes. He'd experimented with pinhole cameras in the past, tiny devices not much bigger than the chip required to drive them and the miniature lens on top, but the quality just wasn't good enough and they required stringing up to a recorder to some kind, which would be kind of a pain.

When he'd finished he went back into the living room. Ten minutes to go. He put a little music on, running it off a pre-chosen playlist on the computer. He listened to all music this way now. Soon as he bought a CD, he used ripping software to store it on the hard disk as MP3 files. Each file was a mere couple of megabytes in size, and with the array of 100 gig racks he had built into the desk, there was room for thousands of tracks at resolutions none of his guests were likely to be able to tell from the real thing. Truth be told, he probably couldn't these days either. It had been a while since he'd even bought a CD, now that he thought of it. Couldn't remember the last time, in fact. Now he just culled the MP3 files directly from the web. Some were legit, some rip-offs. It didn't matter. That was the great thing about the web—the distance it put between you and the scene of the crime. No-one was going to come and find him. Not down those countless little wires. They were too thin for culpability to seep through. You could spend your entire life on the web without exposing yourself to anything more dangerous than spam or mail-bombing, both of which he was more than capable of dealing with.

The only people he had direct contact with, the only ones who ever learned his physical address and entered his corporeal world, were the women he met in the web's virtual chat rooms. He'd cultivate them carefully, coming on like some newbie lurker: matching their own shy advances and only very gently nudging the conversation into the slow spiral which would end in them taking the exchange out of a public arena and into private email. He only ever fished on boards that were loosely tied to his own geographical location. There was no point spending all that time and effort only to find that she lived on the other side of the world. Because eventually he would have convinced the woman—or, in her mind, they would have convinced each other—that it was time to take the relationship a little further. To take it backwards, out of these futuristic and nebulous lines of communication and back to the basic human levels which had worked since the dawn of time. It was never organised by phone. He had not once given his number out. Instead it would be a series of emails, a courtship of text: a careful progression for her, sentences fretted over, rewritten, revised or sometimes sent with a spastic click of a button before she had time to change her mind—but often the same old same old for him, as he'd found that he could cut and paste chunks out of previous campaigns and use them time and again.

And eventually the first visit would happen. A woman, slightly overdressed, eyes round with courage, would turn up at his door. The obvious would happen, and he was good. So it would happen again, and again. At intervals: when the woman could snatch the time; when the ennui she felt in her real life was so acute that it could only be assuaged by an action whose dishonesty jerked her out of her rut. Not all of the women had been married, in fact probably not even the majority: but for the ones that weren't the very fact that they were prepared to enter into so one-track a relationship showed that none of them were worth taking seriously. It would carry on until something happened—a crisis of confidence, a tearful revelation to a husband, a prying boyfriend discovering an email trail which by now would be a lewd series of assignation-making—and it was over. He was never the one to make the move. He let them do it, because that way he knew they wouldn't be coming back and bugging him. They'd just be gone. To be immediately replaced by another one, whom he would have been cultivating in the meantime, keeping out there in the ether until the time was right.

The doorbell rang. He walked across the room towards the door, checking his hair in the mirror as he passed.

Michael Marshall Smith

She was standing outside. Rather casually dressed, which annoyed him. He liked to see a bit of effort, not least because it proved that the affair was still at the hotter-than-hot stage. Though she did at least look a little flushed.

'Hi, David,' she said, and he was pleased to notice a slight catch in her voice. 'You're looking good.'

Yes, he thought, I am. And later he found that what she was wearing underneath the blouse and pants wasn't casual *at all*.

Two and a half hours later he heard the door close behind her as she left the apartment. He'd been lying on the bed, faux dozing: he was prepared to do a lot of things to keep women convinced they were having one of the world's greatest affairs, but listening to them prattle after the event wasn't one of them. As soon as he was sure she'd gone, he was up and in the shower.

A good one, he thought, as he sluiced himself clean. And maybe the best-directed yet. He showered slowly, prolonging the moment.

When he was done, and comfortable in a fluffy white dressing gown which he liked because it never seemed to get dirty, he went into the kitchen, fired up his other computer, and put a big pot of coffee on. He dropped the two wine glasses—hers empty, his still half-full—in the trash. He had plenty more. Then he went back through the apartment and collected up the tapes.

One from each of the living room cameras, which were triggered as soon as the door was opened and the woman came in. The four from the bedroom: two of these he had switched on as soon as they'd entered this room, via an extra spur off the bedside lamp; the others were on a trip delay to start recording fifty minutes later, to cover for the fact that one hour was the maximum tape length for the format he used. You could get longer, on different machines, but the quality was nowhere near as good.

Then the final one, from the bathroom—which he triggered by another switch once the sex was finished. It was this tape that he ripped to disk first, sitting at the desk with a steaming mug of very good coffee and a cigarette. It only took ten minutes to save it to an MPEG file, and then he set the others to rip in sequence in the background, porting the digital footage onto the array of hard disks, ready for a first quick edit.

After a slow first viewing.

This is what he did it for now. This was the moment he enjoyed. Not at first: three years ago, after his last genuine relationship had broken up, he'd just been looking for fun and companionship like everyone else.

TWO SHOT

Maybe even someone to fall in love with. This hadn't happened with the first one, nor the one after that. A pattern emerged. He didn't mind. Before, when he'd been taken, he'd envied his friends still out there in the market, the ones with the slew of drunken collisions in clubs and bars, with the long list of accidental one-night conquests. New breasts hefted, new buttocks splayed. David believed that men were collectors, taxonomists, seekers after and cataloguers of variety—and he wanted some of it.

After a while the variety began to pall, however, and he felt less and less a part of what was going on. The women who turned up at his door started to seem too similar to each other. They might have different colour hair, contrasting figures, and taste individual where it counted, but in the wriggles and grapples across couches and down corridors and round and round the bed they all ended up blending into one—not least because they shared a fundamental similarity. They weren't The One. He came to realise that it wasn't them who made him feel alive. What kept him going was himself, his own part in the proceedings. That, and the record.

It started more or less by accident. As accidentally, that is, as one can leave a camcorder running in a room where one is likely to be fucking a woman in the very near future. He'd bought the camera for the hell of it, mainly because a new computer had come with non-linear video editing software pre-installed. He ordered the camera over the web, and it turned up at his door. Pretty soon he realised that he didn't have anything in his immediate environment worth recording, and no desire to going out and shoot some shoddy masterpiece for web-distribution to net-heads with cable access and too much time on their hands. But then an idea struck him, one afternoon when a woman was coming round. Feeling suddenly excited, on the verge of something new, he found a place to wedge the camera in the bookcase, where it would capture whatever happened on the couch. What the hell, he thought: might be kind of interesting. When the doorbell rang he turned the camera on, carefully positioning books and a small ornamental box (a present from a past fuck) to hide the red light that indicated that it was recording. The screwing moved into the bedroom after forty minutes, but when he watched the tape later that night it was still enough to make him lob his cock right out and achieve his third orgasm of the day: hunched over the desk, eyes wide and glued to the startling images on the screen. Afterwards, spent though he was, he watched the tape again and again, wiping it back and forwards, reviewing the captured moments—acknowledging, as if for the first time, that the event really had happened. He really had screwed that woman: she had done *this* to him; he had done *that* to her. There it was. It was all recorded. He could see it. He could see it twice. He could see it whenever he wanted.

And she'd never know. It had passed out of the domain of her life, and into his alone. All she would have was vague memories, different occasions blending into one: he could have every event pinned to a board like a butterfly.

After that, he recorded the first hour as a matter of course, fixing a piece of tape over the red light to give more flexibility. It wasn't long before he wanted more. At first it was just a camera in *both* rooms. Then one in the bathroom, because a woman called Monica had got some obscure thrill from doing it in there. Then the extra one in the bedroom, and the second in the living room, because by that time he'd realised how much better it would be if he could get the raw material from two angles: partly just because you couldn't always position the woman to best effect without danger of it being obvious; mainly because it just seemed more real. The two shot set-up made all the difference. The cuts from angle to angle, from view to different view, showed just how true it was, filled it out into three dimensions. It was like a real movie. It was realer than real life.

Finally the extra pair in the bedroom, to make sure not a moment was lost.

He loved doing his films. He fucking loved it. It was partly to punish them for boring him. It was mainly because the films showed how much stronger his reality was than theirs, because whatever thoughts were fizzing around their desperate heads during the time they spent in his home, they had no idea what was really going on. That he was recording them, and later could edit the different shots together into any shape he liked. Picking the shots to show himself in control, to show them naked and exposed, leaving the soundtrack real to capture their gasps and squelches, their moans and pathetic avowals of love, of desire, of whatever it was they felt they had to say to make this seem okay to do. He had tapes of every session with every girl, all tidily filed in nested folders on his hard drives. He had 'greatest hits' edits too, each woman's best or most revealing moments. He had compilations, quick cuts of the same type of activity performed with a score of different women. He watched the digital films whenever he wanted, his breathing shallow but measured, face bathed in the monitor light, staring at himself, at his power. While the women were with him they had a kind of fake reality, shoved at him through their physical presence. When they were gone their true nature was revealed: as extras in his life, as vague presences at the end of an email. He spent whole evenings re-editing for the fun of it, and after a while his vision became more detailed, more refined. He culled through the bathroom tapes, catching the private moments and interspersing them with the other material: Marie looking smug afterwards, thinking she'd shown him the time of his life—when the next cut was that of David exaggeratedly yawning to camera while she enthusiastically sucked him half an hour before; Janine breathlessly declaring their sex as some kind of spiritual triumph, crapping on about how much she loved him—then later, sitting slumped on the can, sobbing in silent, racking waves and softly scraping the nails of both hands down her tear-tracked face.

Each time he made a tape he felt more himself, more vital. Sometimes he would start a film running on the computer and then switch the monitor off just before the current woman arrived. Though it could be neither seen nor heard, it was still playing, still being conjured up out of ones and zeros into image: footage of him ploughing one woman while in real and current time he squeezed the tit of another; or of the same woman as she would be in the bathroom afterwards, the event contextualized before it had even finished.

The tapes had nearly done being digitised. It was time for another pot of coffee. David leaned against the counter as the water boiled, listening to the chirrup of the hard drive as the files of the raw material were written. He was noticing that he felt tired. Vestiges of the hangover, presumably, and Anne was a workout by anybody's standards. She'd seemed even more frenetic than usual that afternoon, as if testing him, or herself. Or maybe it was just too much coffee on an empty stomach, making him feel a little dizzy. Didn't matter. He was having more java anyway. It was traditional.

He took the new pot and a jug of cream over to the desk, so he wouldn't have to get up for a while. Then when the machine pinged to signify all the hard work was done, he reached out and clicked the first file. He always waited until they were all done. He liked it that way. Once he'd started watching, he needed to know he could jump to any part he wanted, immediately. It was part of the fun.

The bathroom tape started with ten minutes of nothing—Anne had laid beside him on the bed for a while after they'd finished. David sat and admired the fact that he'd remembered to refold the towels, to make them look just so. The women got good value out of him: the films were just a payment they didn't know they were making. Then there was the sound of the door being open, and Anne's back swished into view with the sound of the door closing again. She stood in front of the mirror and ran the cold tap, nothing readable in the expression reflected back over her shoulder. She splashed some water over her face, and then sat down on the john. It was then, with her face much more directly visible by the camera, that David realised her facial expression wasn't actually unreadable after all.

He watched for the few minutes she sat there, before flushing and leaving the room. Then he clicked back to an earlier frame in the MPEG. And watched it again.

It wasn't his imagination. He was sure of it. He'd seen 'unreadable' before. Some women were like that. When not on stage, and making an effort to perform, the most vivacious of them could turn remarkably wax-like, as if they were nothing without an audience. This wasn't like that. There *was* something in her face. It was just something he'd ever seen before.

It was...what? Quietness. No. Dissatisfaction? Still no, but...

David frowned suddenly, and put his cup down on the desk. He clicked the tape back again. His face felt a little hot.

She actually just looked a little bored.

He irritably lit a cigarette. That couldn't be right. Not after what they'd done. Not after the free-wheeling exhibition of technique he'd put on from the couch all the way through to their mutual and grunting climaxes. Perhaps she'd just had something else on her mind. Presumably things went on in her life. He never asked, but usually they'd say, filling him in regardless—wrongly assuming he'd care. Whatever. She'd hadn't been bored. It wasn't possible.

David shut the window on that tape and set another loading, wiping the back of one hand across his forehead as he waited. He still felt kind of hot. Embarrassment, maybe. At his initial thought that she might have regarded their coupling as less than earth-moving. Indignation was more appropriate. If she was frigid enough not to be jolted out of whatever little psychodrama from her outside life had been swirling around her head, then she was fucking on borrowed time. With him, anyway. Doubtless hubby would still limply put out, still engage her in the mildewy fumblings she'd come to David to escape. Assuming Anne had a husband. Right now he was so irritated he couldn't even remember.

The tape from the living room was better. A lot better. The fifteen minutes of chit-chat and sipping, a spiral like the closing stages of the email courtship—but one with a known destination. Then a frank movement from him: reaching out to stroke a breast through her blouse, then slipping his hand right up her skirt out of nowhere. He loved doing that. Making moves that assumed. Being in a position to demonstrate that this wasn't any coy long-shot, but a fucking cert. It looked great on the video too. Made the woman look just like what she was: a three-dimensional version of the pictures you could pick up on a zillion sites all over the web. Just something within his field of vision. Something for him to play with. And they loved it. They really did. Loved being treated that way.

Soon they were both half-dressed. He turned her immaculately, cupping her breasts from behind, nuzzling her neck as she arched her head back, eyes closed—while he stared straight into the camera. There was a brief glitch in the digitising and his hands frizzed for a moment, but otherwise it was a classic scene—with some superb cutaways possible to the other camera's point of view. Classic for the softcore portion, anyhow: there would be meaner, better stuff later.

Then more of that, more of the usual. Building up. A button here, a strap there. Then a zipper. David could now judge how much time he had in the living room, how to steer things towards the corridor before there was any danger of the tapes running out. With three minutes to go, both still standing but with pants around their ankles, he touched her in a way that had her backing giggling out of the room, pulling him by something a man is bound to follow.

Just as they passed out of site of the cameras, David noticed another little visual weirdness. He stopped the film, clicked back. Right at the end there was a two second patch where there was a little streaming around the image of his head, tiny pixelated blocks of colour. He flicked up the other camera's view of the same moment, and was relieved to see it looked fine. He'd just have to cut at that point. Something wrong with the tape, probably. Condensation. Or the recording head needed cleaning. He sorted through the cameras, found the offending tape, and put it to one side to check out later.

Then he kicked up the first of the bedroom films. He'd missed a little bit of action in the meantime, he knew. In the corridor Anne had bent to take him in her mouth for a couple minutes. Not for the first time he mused it would be good to have a camera in there too. Problem was, how to conceal it. Maybe he'd have to compromise, get a pinhole and hide it in a picture. Might even look good: a kind of voyeur, security camera-style section. Hmm. Think about that later: the bedroom tape showed events liquidly transforming into full flow.

He'd known at the time it was good. Not the sex, so much, as the way he'd controlled its movements, its ebb and flow. Her head there, in direct shot. His hand here, just where it could be seen. Seemingly spontaneous little rolls, taking the action from one view to another. Her moans and sighs, his encouraging grunts. Thrusts, acceptances, retractions and changes of position, all maximised for his eyes. Prime stuff, packaged and presented. A classic.

Except—shit.

He clicked back thirty seconds, not really knowing what he'd spotted. Watched the section again.

Straightforward shot, with them sideways across the bed, taken by the camera hidden up on the curtain rail. Him on top of her in missionary position, holding her shoulders down and grinding away. Her hands on his ass, pulling him in and out. Her hair spread over the sheets like a mermaid's floating in shallow water. Her legs raised up after a moment, clasping behind his. So much for the 'boredom', he thought, with joyful spite—she was loving it. She moved her hands up along his back, nails out for a little playful scratching, and then slipped them both up and round to cup his face. Her eyes opened for a moment, looking up into his, searching for something. Maybe she found it. Maybe not.

FREEZE. Click back two seconds. There. Her hands cupping his face.

He could see them.

The camera was high up and behind his back. He should be able to see the top and side of her face, and her hair. The tips of her fingers on either side of his head. But for a couple of frames there, he could see her hands too. Underneath his head. That shouldn't be possible.

He flipped back and forth a few times, bordering on very irritated. It was probable that the effect, a weird kind of transparency, had been caused by the filter set he automatically applied to the tape as it was being digitised. Pre-set algorithms adjusted contrast and light levels to maximum effect, seeking a medium range that made the edited result more consistent. The filters played with the image on the basis of numbers and theory, rather than reality. He was a lot more tan than Anne, he realised: it hadn't been a problem before, but she hadn't been on vacation since he'd been screwing her. Perhaps the tones of his head had fallen foul of a glitch, blue-screening them into momentary translucence. It had fucking better be that. If not, then it was a tape problem again, and the web merchant from whom he'd bought this batch would be hearing from the sharp side of his email.

He clicked on and got back to watching the rest of the tape. It was fine. It was classic. But the fucking glitch kept coming up again. Never for very long. A second or two, here and there. It had to be the skin tone thing. She was pale, he was golden. The filter range he'd set was too narrow to cope. And it kept getting worse. By the time he'd moved on to the second pair of tapes, the ones capturing the second hour in the bedroom—and the second, languid, fuck—the image was stuttering all over the place.

David grabbed the mouse and viciously stabbed the button, stopping the film. It didn't matter in the long run. He could re-rip the tape without the filters, put up with the differences in lighting—or even manually tweak them himself. But the former would be disappointing, a drop in quality he didn't want, the latter several hours of hard slog. He didn't deserve this kind of hassle. He'd done a good job. Why the fuck couldn't it just work out first time? Why didn't the silly bitch go to a tanning booth? He'd have to talk to her about it. He'd got her trained otherwise. This was good stuff. He wasn't losing it just because she was too fucking lazy to look after her appearance.

He slugged back another mouthful of coffee and stood up, feeling momentarily dizzy again. He wasn't going to be screwing around with manual filtering tonight, that was for sure. His eyes ached as it was. The mood lighting which remained from the set-up for Anne was too dim for anything else, making the corners of the room hard to see.

He sorted through the cameras once more and found one of the second ones from the bedroom—just to confirm it wasn't the tape itself. He hesitated for a moment before plugging it in to the monitor. He was in a bad enough mood already. If he found it was a tape problem, then there was nothing he could do to save the film. Did he want news like that now, feeling as shit as he did?

Fuck it. He was going to find out sooner or later. He plugged in, waited while it rewound, pressed PLAY.

The tape started just as they were building up in to the second fuck. Anne lying on her back, groaning quietly as he sucked her nipples and coaxed between her legs. Then he gently pulled one of her hands across and placed it down there, while he straddled her chest, tugging at his cock, getting it to the point where he could commend it to her mouth for further encouragement. A section of this and then he withdrew, climbed off and turned her over, ready for—but it was wrong. It was all very wrong.

He wasn't there on the tape.

Anne did all the things he remembered. She moved in all the right ways. Her body showed the impressions of his hands. Her mouth opened, and her hands lifted up, as if controlling his thrusts. Then it shut, she looked up at nothing and turned over, the imprint of his fingers on her buttock. But she almost looked as if she was the only person on the bed.

David swore, yanked the tape out of the camera and threw it across the room. He grabbed another camera, plugged it in. Tape from the living room. He knew that worked. He'd already watched the MPEG. He rewound, watched it again.

Anne drank alone.

Anne's buttons undid themselves. Her zipper undid itself, and her pants dropped to the floor.

Anne backed out of the room, giggling, her hand held out as if pulling an invisible rope.

It was fucking horrible. The tape was so screwed up it made it look like he hadn't even been there. Of course he had been, there was no question of that: the evidence was actually still in front of him. She hadn't undone her own buttons: her hands were nowhere near them at the time. He'd been there, he'd done that. But if he couldn't see it—how the fuck was it supposed to count?

He furiously lit another cigarette. Went and retrieved the thrown tape. He could hardly send it back as evidence of how faulty their merchandise was, but he could note the serial number. He'd need to quote it. Obviously a whole batch was screwed up. They'd probably already had complaints. They were sure as fuck going to get one more.

He sat down again. His heart was beating hard and ragged. His head felt terrible. The dislocation he'd felt before Anne arrived was back in force. For just a moment he wavered, doubted the point of his life, realising that everything else he did had become superfluous, that the films were all he cared about, the only things that spoke directly to the man he knew himself to be. It only lasted a second, and then he was back again. Back, and angry. He needed grounding, that was all.

Hands moving like independent robots, one took the mouse and flash-navigated through the file structure on his computer, heading for one of the Greatest Hits compilations. The other tugging at the knot in the cord of his dressing gown, pulling it aside and finding what was inside. He double-clicked the file, already kneading in his lap. Okay, so one had got away. Technology had conspired against him. But there was so much already stored to enjoy.

The film, 'Dogs I have Known', flipped up onto the screen. He was proud of the title. A score of women in the doggy position, intercut with the little ladies gnawing on his bone. It was his finest hour, his finest hours, in fact: stripped of dead wood and cutting straight to chase after chase.

But he wasn't on it. Not in a single scene.

Feeling sick with confusion he raced back and forth through the tape, checking sections more than once. Monica, Claire, Janine. The women moved under his direction, but he wasn't there. Anne, Marie, Helen, Liz. Parts of their bodies opened to accommodate him, but there was no him to be seen. Sue, Teresa, Rachel, Nikki, Maggie, Beth. And him fucking nowhere.

Closed out, checked another film. The same.

And another. And another. He staggered to his feet. He felt very strange now. Almost as if he was floating.

There was something wrong with his head.

Maybe it hadn't been alcohol. Perhaps he'd been slipped a drug the night before, a delayed psychedelic, by some fucker at the club where he'd been. Wherever it was—he still couldn't properly remember. It couldn't all be gone. Not the things they'd done for him. The things he'd made them do.

No, it *was* a drug, because things off the screen were looking strange now too. The table looked insubstantial. The little lamps, carefully placed around the room, these too seemed odd: as if flicking from one state to another outside his control. He pushed himself away from the desk, staggered back into the room. He felt sick, hollow, as if his grip on reality was fading.

Maybe not a drug, he thought suddenly. Not exactly. Not something slipped into a drink. Maybe one of the woman had come back, or her man. Some kind of revenge: because now he thought about it, some of them did come back, for 'just one more time' visits every now and then. Maybe one had left something in the room. Something that slowly leaked out, a gas, permeating the room and gradually fucking him up. Building up over days, weeks. His only respite the time he spent out of the apartment. Like when he...

He couldn't remember when he'd last left the apartment. He couldn't remember the night before. He couldn't remember where he'd been. Maybe he hadn't been anywhere, and it was only the gas which was making him think he had. Filling in the gaps, trying to explain the way he felt. He reeled across the room, heading for the corridor. Fresh air. He needed fresh air. He needed to get out and then find out which bitch had done this to him. And then he thought maybe he'd break his 'virtual contact only' rule. Maybe he'd just find her and fuck her up bad.

As he careened across the room he seemed to move in a series of jump-cuts. When he passed the mirror he didn't even notice that he was not reflected in it.

He barrelled into the corridor, doing his best to run but losing all speed to his thrashing. The drug was building up in his head. Maybe Anne had triggered it. He'd felt odd before he came, but nothing like this. She could have pushed him over the edge. As he hauled himself along the corridor, face pressed against the cool wall, he tried to imagine what he'd do to her next time she visited. She didn't like rough stuff, he knew.

He'd tried it, carefully choreographed for the cameras. Well next time she was going to take it anyway.

He didn't feel sick any more, just so light-headed he could barely think. Everything seemed too white. He couldn't even feel the wall now, but he could see the door. He reached for the handle, turned it, and yanked it open.

Outside there was nothing but a black void.

He turned, but his corridor wasn't there either now. It was just black all around, the last of the light fading out.

His last thought was this:

This isn't right. Don't you understand? This is *me*.

Anne checked her email before she went to bed. The usual stuff: a few things from work, a couple of articles she'd sent her agent after, a newsy letter from her sister in New South Wales.

And one from PRIVATE ENCOUNTERS.COM. She opened it.

```
Dear Anne—

    Grovel, grovel: what can I say! You were
right—it wasn't your sensor pads at all. The site
engineers have just found a deep code fault with
the charactergen, and it looks like it's been
accumulating for some time. As a result, the David
Mate has been permanently withdrawn from service.
Unfortunately this means that 'he' will also have
disappeared from the transcripts of previous
SavedEncounters™ you have archived on our secure
server—but rest assured he will be replaced within
24 hours, for your revisiting pleasure.
    I do apologise for inconvenience, and hope that
a $30 rebate (against further purchase) and the
promise of Generation IV EncounterMates™ just
around the corner will encourage you to 'log in'
again very soon!

Yours sincerely
Julie North, Customer service.
```

TWO SHOT

Anne nodded to herself, pleased to have been proven right. It just hadn't felt the same. And the prospect of revisiting old times, but with a different Mate, sounded really rather interesting.

She grinned greedily to herself as she shut down the computer. Whatever. She'd had enough.

For tonight, anyway.

Last Glance Back

I was walking up Leighton Road, my mind on something else. Most people who walk up Leighton Road try to have their mind on something else, and with good reason, but there's no other way of getting from Kentish Town tube to my flat. It had been a long day at work, but not a bad one, because Jenny had been there. Though we worked in different parts of the office, we could sense each other through the walls—and had spent a very warm lunch hour wrapped round each other in a pub. After a month I still found it odd being at work with someone who was now also my girlfriend, strange having to be corporate with each other when co-workers and clients were around. My mood tended to vacillate wildly between irritation at having to deal with other people, joy when Jenny walked into the room, and chagrin at not being able to grab hold of her. Previously secular ground had become more complicated, and while in some ways that was magical, it could also be rather tiring.

Jenny was out drinking with girlfriends that evening, and spending the night in her own flat. This left me to my own devices for the first time in what felt like quite a while. I was already missing her, but that wasn't what I was thinking about. We'd snatched a drink together before she headed off towards her mates, and Jenny had mentioned the idea of living together. She'd lofted it very casually, so that the conversation didn't run smack into it, but also in a way that said she'd already done some thinking on the subject. Most of me had leapt at the idea, but I'd found myself saying it needed considering, and that's what I was doing. Considering it.

Leighton Road was sparsely populated with migrating locals, shambling home to their sofas or drifting in the other direction towards the takeaways and pubs. Like most of those who were homeward bound, my head was down. When I raised it in anticipation of a side road, I saw a girl wandering down the street towards me.

The first thing I noticed were her eyes, which were blue and blurred behind tears. The area round them was already reddened with crying, the skin a blotched pink which stood out against the pallor of the rest of her face. Stood out to me, at least. Nobody else seemed to pay her any attention at all, so intent were they on hurrying home to their televisions.

The area round Kentish Town tube is a mecca for tramps, and you tend to see the same ones again and again; the one who shouts; the one with the cider; the one who didn't look like he should be there a year ago, but now looks as if he should. I hadn't seen this girl before, however, and while she was obviously homeless she didn't quite seem like a derelict. Not yet, anyway. Her hair was ragged blonde and hung in dreadlock rats' tails around her face, but remained fairly presentable, as did the faded pink top and equally tired orange leggings. Her neck was strung with ethnic necklaces, and cheap bangles rattled round her wrists. I was surprised not to see a stud in her nose.

I'll be honest and say I don't usually have a great deal of patience with the type, but this girl appeared in front of me fully-formed in grief, and her wordless distress caught my attention, her sense of being completely cut off from the world around her and locked in some inner pain. She could only have been about seventeen, and she looked doomed. She was floating down the pavement so vaguely that I thought she must have only the most shadowy sense of the distinction between it and the road, but as she came closer she held out her hand.

I know I shouldn't feel like this, but after daily acquaintance with people begging, my policy on giving money depends largely on how I'm feeling about my own world. With her it was different. I felt I had to give her something, even though she seemed barely conscious I was there. I rummaged clumsily in my back pocket and pulled out some change. A quick glance told me that there were three, maybe even four, pound coins amongst the shrapnel, but I placed the whole lot in her hand.

She peered vaguely at it as I stepped past her, and then suddenly looked up. For a moment her eyes were clear, and she was someone real, surprised back into the world.

'Hey, thanks,' she said, bewildered. 'Thank you.'

Flushing slightly, I nodded curtly, and then carried on walking up the road towards the flat I paid £270 for each week. After about ten yards I took a quick glance behind me. She was still standing there, still staring into her palm, as people walked either side of her not even noticing she was there.

The flat felt odd without Jenny in it. I'm a card-carrying materialist who needs his quota of consumer goods around him, but the places I've stored them in have never seemed to mean much to me. I get bored with the corner shop, with tramping the same streets and struggling down the same broken escalator in the Underground, and for the last four years I'd moved at least annually. I like places, in general—and as somewhere to be, they're fine. But as a constant, as somewhere to hang your life, they are not to be trusted. They're too impassive, and they don't care about you, not really. They've seen occupants before you, and they will see others once you've gone. I'd always felt that my real home would be in a person, and now I believed I'd found her. In the last month the flat had been changing behind my back, relaxing into shape, becoming a place I cared about, simply because she was there.

After a shower I wandered around it for a while, noticing her shoes, an empty packet of her brand of cigarettes in the bin, flicking through one of her magazines—and in a quiet, warm way thought how marvelous it was to have Jenny in my life. And in my flat. So why this feeling of trepidation at the thought of her moving in, or rather at the thought of us both moving out and finding somewhere to live together?

I could understand part of it: I'd spent the last two years largely by myself. There'd been a few women in that time, but not many, and all had been glancing blows that both parties had been happy to let fade. I'd got used to solitude and independence, to making plans that included only myself, to being the centre of my world.

And I'd hated it, of course. Suddenly I remembered Saturday afternoons pacing around the flat, faster and faster, trying to achieve escape velocity. Sometimes I made it out the door and paced round town instead, trying to think of something I could face doing by myself, again. It was that and evenings in front of the television, or with a book, or spent leafing through the videos in the local store, trying to find one I hadn't seen. I hadn't minded being by myself. What I'd minded was being emotionally homeless, culturally pointless. Now that I had a home, maybe I was worried about losing space to be by myself, of being constrained. Well, I could make sure that I had time, could preserve some backstage areas. Jenny would probably need some space herself, though I hoped not. I wanted to be with her all the time. Why should she want time away from me?

Suddenly realising the circle I'd come in, I shook my head. Silly. All I needed was time to adjust to the idea.

Feeling better, I glanced at the clock. It was only eight o'clock. A whole evening by myself stretched in front of me.

What was I going to do?

Michael Marshall Smith

*

At ten-thirty I woke on the sofa, surprised by darkness outside. My book lay spilled beside me, and a cold cup of coffee sat on the table. I hauled myself upright, yawning massively, and peered querulously around for my cigarettes.

After microwaving the cup of coffee I settled back down by the window, and gazed blearily at the street outside. It was very dark, a belt of cloud obscuring the moon and streetlights either broken by local yobs or shrouded in trees. The street looked strange, perhaps because for once I felt that there was a real difference between it and where I was sitting, that the flat wasn't simply warmer and brighter.

From nowhere an image popped into my mind, like a still photograph. It was of predominantly bright colours in front of variegated grey, and it took me a moment to work out what it was, by which time it was already fading. It was the girl I'd encountered on Leighton Road, from the neck down. The breasts inside her pink top were small, but nicely shaped, her thighs smooth beneath orange cloth.

I blinked, slightly shocked. I hadn't noticed any of this when she'd been in front of me, and wasn't interested in noticing it now. I'm not like that, and with Jenny in my life everyone else was behind a sheet of glass, and I was happy for it to be that way. It must have been a stray image, something left over from the material my mind had been processing while I slept.

I stood up with no real purpose, and wandered across to the other window. It made sense to go to bed, but it seemed too early. Instead I collected up my keys and went for a walk.

It was a little colder than I was expecting, and I decided to just take a turn round the block. The surrounding streets are very quiet at night, apart from occasional shouting lunatics and sudden janglings from public phone booths, as phone calls went unanswered.

As I walked I thought of Jenny, and wondered what she was doing and thinking at that moment. Was she describing me to her friends, and sounding as if she missed me, or was she off in her own world, plugged back into old friendships and past times? Her friends would have known Chris, the man she'd left for me. For a moment I felt a shiver of pure, naked insecurity, a feeling I hadn't had to deal with for several years. When my relationship with Annette had crashed and burned after half a decade of heavy turbulence, I'd done everything I could to shield myself from that kind of wound. Yet here I was again. Jenny could hurt me. I'd signed up, and I wasn't entirely safe any more. And presumably, neither was she.

LAST GLANCE BACK

When I got back I sat up for a while, and read a little more of my book. Jenny didn't call. I hadn't expected her to.

As I drifted off to sleep later that night I caught a fragment of a dream. My hand reached out towards someone, and in it there was a ten pound note.

'Would this be any use to you?' I heard a voice ask.

As the girl took the note and looked at me, knowing what I wanted to buy, and not caring, I realized the voice had been my own.

I slept badly, and was in a ragged mood as I trudged through fitful winter sunlight towards the tube. I'd be seeing Jenny, but apart from that the day ahead held little but stress. Not real anxiety, of course, nothing relating to anything that mattered: merely the workaday run-of-the-mill white noise that comes with employment, along with your pay packet, bad coffee, and an inexhaustible supply of Post-It notes. I was becoming increasingly convinced that I didn't want to work for a living. Not a very original thought, but strongly felt all the same. I wondered if any of the people walking in the opposite direction felt any better about the whole deal, if they believed they were growing up instead of merely older. Most of them looked as if they didn't feel anything about anything, as if they were deep in mechanical indifference.

With a slight lurch I recognised one of them, a woman walking in the same direction as me, on the other side of the road. I didn't know her at all, had merely noticed her a few times as I dully marched down the road to work in the mornings. I hadn't seen her for a while, in fact: not since Jenny and I had come together. We tended to leave the flat slightly later than had been my custom, for a variety of reasons.

The woman was tall, and slim, with rich chestnut hair. She appeared very together, like a fully-fledged adult, but also as if she might remember how to smile, given the right incentive. She'd been the focus of a few utterly platonic daydreams in the days when I'd been single: the idea of walking with her, of turning to see her face, of simply sharing a life, had all seemed rather appealing. It was odd to see her again, now that I had someone with whom I could have those things. For a moment I was pulled back to the previous year, and it felt strangely comfortable there, like a broken sofa which you've got used to sitting on, a tangle of stuffing and springs which nonetheless knows your shape better than some plump new divan.

I stopped to light a cigarette, partly because I felt like one, and partly to put more distance between us. In the old days I'd often covertly kept pace behind her to the station, and shuffled along the platform to be closer, so I could think my wistful thoughts. But that was then, and this was now.

The ruse worked, because when I got to the station I had just missed a train and the platform was deserted.

I waited, irritated by the weight of the bag on my shoulder, and stared belligerently at the advertisements on the opposite wall of the tunnel. One proclaimed the charms of California, and as I read it my heart sank unexpectedly. Another of my fantasies of the last few years, a key support mechanism, had been the daydream of moving to America, of quitting my job and finding a life. That wouldn't happen now, of course. I didn't only have a job. I had a girlfriend. I *had* a life. Or would have very soon. A life and a bigger flat and someone with whom to jointly send Christmas cards.

I walked further along the platform so I couldn't see the photographs of the redwood forests.

The morning went fine, in that I did all the work I was supposed to do. It wasn't especially good in other respects. Not bad, just not good. Jenny and I went out again at lunch, and had a nice time. Things were alright between us.

But the very fact that I considered the question, that I thought of things being alright *between* us, showed that the day wasn't really gelling. Until now we'd been like one person. Today felt like a step back from that. Not far, but a step. It was the kind of day you have when you're going out with someone: nice, but not special. Another day in a life that was presumably mine.

We talked a little more about the idea of finding a flat, and I was happy to sound interested, but didn't mind too much when the rather frank gropings of a nearby couple turned our attention away from the subject. Almost all of me wanted to turn it back again, but a little frozen piece did not, and so we covertly giggled at the clandestine romping at the next table until we were feeling rather intense ourselves. We held hands as we walked back to the office.

The afternoon was better, not least because I knew I was working from home the next day, which meant a day off from the hysteria which everyone else seemed to enjoy whipping up. Jenny and I could talk on the phone, and there'd be the evening to look forward to. By the time we were walking up Leighton Road towards the flat I was in a reasonably good mood.

LAST GLANCE BACK

When we were passing the spot where I'd seen the girl the previous evening, I remembered the dream from the night before. A feeling of hot, nervous haste, of yielding to impulse, of letting something hidden inside peep out and touch the world. It was a horrible idea, offering a disadvantaged woman money for sex. I was quite prepared to believe it went on, but hated the fact that my dreaming self had remembered it, or thought it. I could imagine the kind of man who might do such a thing, and felt nothing but revulsion.

For him, anyway. Not so much for her. Again I found I could picture her body within her loose cotton clothes, imagine the slightly rough texture of her pale skin and the firmness of her limbs. And her hair, of course, her stringy blond hair.

Suddenly I realised something. Jenny also had blond hair.

Glancing across as we walked arm in arm, chatting about the day, I noticed her hair as if for the first time. Before all I'd thought about it was that it was beautiful. Now I realised that while that was true, it was also blond. Trying to keep my walk casual and my banter smooth, I struggled to incorporate this.

It may not seem important, in fact it seems kind of stupid, but I'd always sort of assumed I'd end up with someone with brown hair. I don't know why, and it's not that I'm obsessed with it, or even find it particularly attractive. It's just that in my mind, in the region where the dream girl lived who'd got me through drab months, I was sort of banking on brown hair.

It was irrelevant, unimportant. As a matter of fact, Annette had also been blond, as had most of the girls I'd been out with. The brown-ness wasn't important, but something was. It was almost as if my life had been alternating for years between two possible states, and now it had settled on one, as if a roulette ball had finally come to rest on black. It was a high-scoring number, a jackpot in fact, and I was very happy with it. Jenny was all I had ever wanted in a friend, and far more. She was intelligent, and loveable, and funny and beautiful. She had a clean laugh and a dirty one, and I could be however I wanted to be with her. I felt very seriously about her, and maybe that was it. A realisation that the ball had come to rest, and that winning on red wasn't an option any more, that there had been so many other numbers it could have landed on, and now I had only one.

The flat welcomed us warmly. Jenny gave me a hug and then disappeared into the bathroom to wash the day away.

I had a cigarette by the window and then, in a fit of domesticity, corralled up the rubbish in the kitchen and took the bin bag outside to stow. I'd just finished kicking the bag into the recess by the side of the steps, when I sensed movement on the other side of the street and glanced up. Then I stopped, foot still poised.

It was the girl.

She was ambling down the other side of the road, dressed in the same clothes as the day before. I felt my heart beating as I watched her bend to stroke a cat. Though she wasn't tall her back was long, and flared into an attractive triangle at her buttocks. Her face was covered by her hair hanging down and suddenly I wanted her, wanted her briefly, pornographically and completely.

She straightened as the cat sloped off, and looked across at me. She seemed to smile, though whether in recognition or simple friendliness it was impossible to judge. I gave her a small and distracted nod, and then turned back towards the house.

When I was back in the flat I stood by the window. She was still outside. The cat had returned and she was rubbing its neck, sitting cross-legged on the pavement. She looked lost, and found, in the middle of a moment of contentment.

I went into the bedroom to chat to Jenny though the half-open bathroom door. We didn't talk about flats.

Mid-afternoon the next day I went to the corner shop, to buy some cigarettes and the local paper. As I walked back I was thinking about Jenny, and the puzzled half-grin with which she'd said goodbye when she left for work, standing with me on the step. She'd picked something up from me, from the way I'd been the previous evening. Some smile had been slightly too narrow, some hug too considered. When she'd turned the corner I stomped back into the flat, feeling wild and panicky.

Something was going wrong. I'd tried to calm myself in the shower but it hadn't worked, and I'd achieved next to nothing that morning. I called her before lunch and we chatted, but it seemed hollow to me, though there was no difference in the things we said. I even said I loved her, and meant it as much as ever. But it made me realize something I'd forgotten in the last month: that you could say those same words and not really mean them. That they could become merely sounds, rather than a statement of everything that was true about the world. There was a distance between us that hadn't existed before. Not between us, in fact, but within me. Some part of me was retreating. Some power source had been interrupted for a flicker of a second, and I was falling back from the front of my mind, trying once more the doors to what had gone before.

LAST GLANCE BACK

After cruising in glorious automatic for a month, suddenly my mind was back on manual shift, jerking and racing, subtly out of my control.

The more I tried not to think about it, the more the thoughts popped and squirmed into my mind like gleeful and brightly-coloured worms. Some part of me was anxiously trying to patch and mend, turn my thoughts back to the front, but even he couldn't ignore the rising panic. I had the chance to have everything I'd ever wanted, had the chance to be happy. And yet instead of staying safely in the present and the future, I wanted to try those doors, to look back again, though I knew what would happen if I did. The past was too recent a neighborhood for me, and the locals would still recognise my face. It wasn't safe for me there, not yet: if I went back my old friends would come and find me, take me back into darker corners to kick me to pieces once again.

As I neared the flat, completely blind to the world around me, I could almost see those thoughts, those friends, gathering round me like the bullies of childhood.

'You looked back too soon,' they were saying, hearty with affectionate hatred. 'But maybe it would always have been too soon, my son. You like it here. You know you do. So come back. We may hurt you a little, might even cut you up, but at least you'll be at home. And we know how you like it.'

I didn't know how it had all started, why on earth I was reacting this way, and I didn't know how to stop it. I was falling. I was back in my own mind, my old mind, and couldn't remember how I'd ever got out.

When I saw who was sitting outside the flat I literally dropped everything I was carrying.

'Jesus Christ,' I said.

The girl reached down and picked up my cigarettes.

I took them from her. She smiled, and then turned away slightly, to look down the street.

I scrabbled to come up to speed, to react. Against my will my eyes dropped from her face to her pink top. My subconscious had captured her image very accurately: her breasts were indeed small but prominent, stubby nipples discernible against the cloth. With a flush of embarrassment I realised she was looking at me again.

'I'm thirsty,' she said.

Eager to have something to do, some way out, I reached into my back pocket and discovered it was empty. I'd used up all my change in the shop. All I had was a few pence, which was derisory. And I couldn't offer her a note. All I had was ten pounds. I couldn't offer her that.

'Don't you have anything inside?'

'Er, yes, I do actually,' I stammered with wild surprise, as if she'd scored right with a lucky guess. 'You know, tea, Coke, that sort of thing.' I couldn't believe I was answering, and certainly not in that way. I didn't seem to have any choice.

'Fat or thin?' she asked. I didn't understand. 'Regular or Diet Coke,' she explained patiently, with another smile, as she stood up to let me open the door.

She didn't like Diet Coke, so I made her a cup of coffee. Meanwhile she walked round the living room behind me, examining the books. I dithered about whether to make a cup of coffee for myself. It would seem odd to only make one for her, but wasn't there an air of complicity about both having one together? Did I even want a cup of coffee? What was she doing here?

What if Jenny called?

In the end I didn't make a cup for myself, but just handed one to her. By then she was sitting on one end of the sofa, looking comfortable. I cast an anxious glance at the phone and wondered whether I should switch the answer phone on. Not because I didn't want the girl to know about Jenny, but because I didn't want Jenny to hear me sounding strange. And I most certainly would if she called. What on earth did I think was going on? Clearly the girl must have recognised me when I'd been putting the rubbish out the night before, but what was she doing here now? What did she want?

The girl took the coffee and sipped it, smiling at me in an odd way. I tried to smile back, but I couldn't. My eyes kept finding her top. The pink, I saw, wasn't consistent. Some areas were a deeper hue, making it look almost tie-died.

'Oh, this is for you,' she said suddenly, and slipped her hand into a small pocket in the top of her trousers. She held out her hand towards me, palm up. She was holding £4.71 in small change. I stared at her.

'That was nice,' she said. 'But I don't need it.'

'I'm sorry,' I said, embarrassed. 'I thought you were begging.'

'I was,' she smiled. 'Old habits die hard. Don't they?'

She moved slightly, and her legs parted a little. They were slim, but powerful, and the feeling they provoked in me was more like fear than anything else. I could sense Jenny, on the other side of town, could almost see her sitting at her desk. Was she thinking of me? Was she thinking of Chris? I stared at the girl's face, wondering what on earth to do.

She looked me in the eyes, and then pulled mine downwards with her own, until I was looking at her chest again. There were streaks of darker colour amongst the pink. I hadn't noticed them before. Perhaps it was a different shirt.

'It's yours if you want it,' she said. I realised suddenly that I didn't, but it was too late. She reached down and took hold of the bottom of her shirt.

'No,' I said, but she was already pulling it up.

For about a couple of inches the skin was white and smooth. I could see it very clearly, the tiny goosebumps and the varying shades of pale. The area from her navel to immediately below her breasts was a churned mass of dog meat. The flesh had been gashed wide by some massive impact, laying bare the purples and greys of internal organs. A drunken stumble in front of a car, the lost fury of a damaged boyfriend, whatever. Blood ran slowly in the cavity, so dark as to be almost brown. In a way, it was beautiful.

'You can go back if you want to,' she said. 'You can remember what it's like.' Her eyes were dry, their surface like a winter's overcast sky, and her head was held at an abrupt angle. For a moment she was motionless, T-shirt still raised, and I mourned the terrible life that I had lost, the slow and pointless death I could have had, and to which I had become so attached.

Then I shook my head.

Her face moved again, and she almost looked alive.

'Good call,' she said, and disappeared.

I turned to look out of the window, and she was crouched down on the other side of the road, hand held out towards a cat that was no longer there.

Then she was nearer the corner, caught once more in summer light, laughing at something said six months ago, when it was all still an adventure.

And then she was gone.

By the time I'd had a cigarette I was calm again, calm and almost smiling. I called Jenny. She knew why I was calling before I said a word, and I could feel her happiness down the phone.

'About this flat idea,' I said.

They Also Serve

The years had shown that 5.25 p.m. was the most likely time for Mr Torrence to have a shower, and so the cubicle turned itself on to save him the trouble. The vertical LED strips by the sink unit flickered into life, the towel rail began to warm, and water issued at a predetermined rate from the four nozzles placed equidistantly around the shower area itself. After a moment the water's temperature was exactly equal to the average of all those to which it had previously been adjusted, and there it stayed. Preparations complete, the cubicle waited for the man to arrive, with the brute patience of no-patience: the patience of a machine.

In a very small room just off the bridge area, David Torrence put down his bitflip wrench and looked at his watch. The watch was analog, as had several times been the fashion, and told him it was time to knock off for the evening. Torrence knew the shower cubicle would be warm and ready, as it always was: after thirty years he was no longer sure whether it took its schedule from him, or vice versa, but supposed that it didn't really matter. He poked the straggling mess of fibre optics and boards back into its nest in the wall. On a ship that did nothing but revolve slowly round its axis, day in and day out, a routine service of the optical backup matrices could wait. The only wear and tear the damned things suffered was through his testing of them.

As he stood, Torrence winced comfortably at the sound of his joints creaking. An unwelcome reminder of advancing years, but somehow satisfying nonetheless. Another day's work completed, another day fought and won.

After replacing the access panel and dusting off his hands he turned to his android, who had been sitting in the corner all afternoon, companionably watching him work.

'I'm done, Cat,' he said. 'That job will have to drift into fifteen minutes of tomorrow.'

Michael Marshall Smith

'They'll survive, Dave.'

Torrence grinned. Cat was only the only machine on board the ship who called him by his first name. When he'd come on board. Three decades ago, all the machines had been factory-set to call him by his surname, prefixed by 'Mr', and Cat was the only one it had occurred to him to tell to call him Dave. All the rest were still calling him Mr Torrence, because he hadn't told them not to. They were like that. They were all very much like that.

Cat raised himself a few inches off the ground and quickly hoovered up a few stray pieces of plastic. This done, he followed the man out of the service room.

'Any preferences on dinner?'

'Whatever,' the man smiled absently, heading off down the corridor towards the living quarters. Then he stopped. 'No, hang on. Chicken. Something with chicken in it.'

Cat took the short cut through the ventilation ducts to the kitchen area. There was no chicken on board, and never had been, but manipulation of Gastronomic ProtoMatter would provide an excellent facsimile. It was not an exact science, and fifteen years ago Mr Torrence had chipped a tooth on a Coq au Vin that for some reason had come out made of bronze, but the element of chance was one of the reasons the machine liked cooking.

Cat was a VariTronique C7i—a compact rectangle only eighteen inches long, four inches across and eight inches high. He was nonetheless fully equipped to provide full technical, social and—if necessary—military backup for his human. By a quirk of a randomisation process popular in neurocircuitry at the time of their creation, the C7s had come out as amiable, capable and slightly unaccountable, good companions as well as excellent workers. It was this, coupled with a tendency to follow curved paths and to rest in apparently random positions on top of, or underneath, things, or sometimes just in the middle of the floor, that had earned the C7s the generic nickname 'Cats'.

They were also the qualities that had made the C7s particularly suitable for posting to Sentry Stations. Positioned in deep space in the run-up to The War, when it had finally become obvious that interstellar conflict was not only inevitable but likely to go on for some time, the Sentry Stations were small, totally independent modules whose sole function was to relay video, radar and electromagnetic information on what was happening in their environment. Because the maintenance of such a craft only justified one human crew member, and because that person would be stranded in deep space well beyond the shipping lanes for however long the War lasted, cats were felt to be their ideal companions. Once the Station was in position, there was no contact from Home, as any transmissions could just as easily be eavesdropped by enemy craft. There was merely the routine servicing and maintenance of a ship that relayed blind information, that cycled and recycled the closed system of the raw materials on board. Sentry Officers, chosen for their perceived ability to withstand such conditions of service, needed dependable backup, technical support, and someone to talk to. Cats fitted the bill perfectly. The series' motto was 'To serve, and to protect'. Cat had always felt that it would ring better the other way round, but apparently this had already been used.

A small red light above the cooking area flashed briefly, a signal from the shower cubicle that Mr Torrence had finished. There was plenty of time, Cat knew: Dave liked to dress for dinner slowly, and to have a drink in the recreation area before eating. It had taken four years for the recreation area and Mr Torrence to reach a modus operandi on that one. At first the room had insisted on trying to pre-guess what drink Mr Torrence would want, and have it ready, when the man really did prefer to do that for himself. After a period of covert struggle in which the man had deliberately switched drinks at unpredictable intervals, and the recreation area had countered with a complex series of increasingly inaccurate predictive algorithms, a compromise had been reached. Now the room simply had a glass and bowl of ice ready, though Cat knew that the it was keeping an internal tally of how often its guesses would've been right.

Torrence thought about it, and decided to have a simple Scotch on the rocks. The basic material in each of the bottles was the same, albeit with carefully applied flavourings. Like everything else he ingested, it had probably passed through him more than once already, though he tried not to think too hard about that.

There'd been a time, very many years ago, when he'd had to lay off any variant of alcohol, on Cat's advice. Back before he'd got fully used to his life and his role, when the evenings had begun to seem too long, the tomorrows too similar to all the yesterdays. He couldn't remember much about that period, and was glad. As a pleasure, drink was a fine one: as a problem it was the worst. It crept up on you, befriending you: knowing the routes to the hearts of the lonely, and making them believe they'd

277

invited it in. You could have a good time with the stuff, but it wasn't your friend. Torrence had kicked it back out the house again, and now only shook hands with it twice a day.

Swirling the ice in his glass, he wandered over to the observation window, appreciating the smells of cooking that Cat was piping in from the kitchen area. The view outside the window remained fundamentally unedifying. The relative positions of the points of light changed slowly, but ultimately a star was a star was a star. Thirty years of looking out at Christmas lights, with no tree in sight. Thirty years without ever seeing a single other human being. Thirty years simply passing, one by one, like a drop of cold water running down a long sheet of glass. He just hoped that at least one interesting or useful piece of information had been relayed by the ship's automatic sensors in all that time.

He had never regretted the job, was proud of it and fulfilled by it. When he'd taken the tests and applied to be a Sentry Officer he'd been thirty and directionless, needing something to believe in, something to achieve, and the War had provided it. If, hundreds of millions of miles away, there were people looking out their windows onto a view more interesting, onto fields or streets, they were doing so because of the people like him. Men who'd been prepared to give those things up to help keep them safe. He'd never expected the conflict to go on this long—nobody had—but he intended to do his duty for as long as it took.

He could remember what Home was like, of course, but it had become increasingly stylized to him, and the early years on the ship itself were blurred and indistinct. With very little to mark one day from the next, the past was simply what one remembered. It was an odd kind of life. But when they finally came to collect him, when it was all over, he'd be able to look at them down thirty years of service and know he'd done his bit.

'Nearly ready, Dave,' came Cat's voice over the intercom. 'I'll just—shit, hang on.' After a hectic pause he resumed: 'Sorry, sauce got a bit out of control there. Be about five minutes.'

'Fine', said Torrence. They hadn't known how good a decision it was to send cats up with the Sentries. He couldn't have lasted this long without his, and he was willing to bet that the other sentries dotted about the cosmos would say exactly the same thing. About twenty years ago the machine had sustained some internal damage, and had to turn itself off for a week while his auto-repair modules grew replacement chips. Torrence couldn't remember how he'd whiled that time away, and didn't want ever to have to relearn. He secretly hoped that he'd be allowed to keep Cat when he was eventually fetched back to Earth. He thought he might need him. For the same reasons, perhaps, that mankind had always sought the company of certain animals. Because they brought out the best in us, and protected us from our worst.

The blue light in the middle of the recreation room's circular table flashed, signaling Cat was on his way with the meal. Torrence seated himself, and within moments Cat scythed out of the ventilation duct, steaming plate clutched in a field.

'Chicken a la King,' he announced, 'with rice and some other stuff that's very nearly broccoli.'

'A la King…' mused Torrence, '…have I had that before?'

'Mm, one hundred fifty-eight times,' Cat said, settling himself not quite underneath the occasional table near the entertainment system's plasma screen. 'But not in the last two years.'

As he ate the 'chicken', which was excellent, and the 'a bit like mango' ice cream that followed it, Torrence was surprised to find himself thinking further about his life. Introspection was something he rarely had time for. He was very busy keeping up with a largely self-imposed schedule of servicing and checking, and in the evening the ship's immense store of film and book material helped him while away the hours without too much thought. But as his sixtieth birthday approached, he found himself thinking about the past more and more. Sixty was pensionable age back home. Sixty was people opening doors for you, and giving up their seat. He wished he at least knew how the War was going, could trace who was doing what, have some feeling of direct involvement. Would he be a hero when he got home, or would he just be an old man?

If. If he got home. As the years went by he was beginning to realise he might have to confront the idea that he might never get home, might die alone out here, still holding the fort.

'It can't last forever, Dave,' Cat said, quietly.

Dave turned to stare at the machine, surprised into a smile.

Later, when Torrence had finished filing the day's report, Cat reappeared from wherever it was he went when he wasn't around, bearing a glass of Brandy. Perching on one of the arms of the sofa, he clicked briskly for a while in a way Torrence had come to assume signified contentment, and asked him what movie he wanted to watch. Wandering over to the monitoring console as Cat and the recreation room silently liaised over providing the entertainment, Torrence reflected that, all in all, things could be a whole lot worse.

Then he stopped very suddenly, his breath escaping him in a small grunt.

'What is it?' Cat asked.

Torrence stood staring at the console. A large screen, subdivided into many sections, constantly updated information on the performance of the essential functions of the ship. Torrence gave it a glance several times an hour whenever he was in the rec room, just to make sure everything was ticking over.

In the bottom right-hand corner of the screen was an area that had remained unused in all the time he had been on the ship.

The area was labeled 'Communication', and a word lit in red was now flashing in it.

The word was INCOMING.

It was impossible to get the ship to even *register* attempted contact unless the sender knew a sequence of codes. That one flashing word could only mean one thing.

The War was over.

Cat hovered by his side and watched the blinking lights with him, and not for the first time Torrence wished he could know what the machine was actually thinking.

It was Cat who broke the silence. 'Aren't you going to answer it?'

Shaking his head, and grinning like an idiot, Torrence reached out and tapped in the code that permitted contact, a code he'd practised many times in his head over the years.

The word 'Incoming' continued to flash for a moment, and then was replaced by CONTACT ESTABLISHED.

'Hello? Is that David Torrence? Hello? Am I through?'

With difficulty, Torrence replied. 'This is Sentry Officer David Torrence. I can hear you clearly.'

He had to struggle to find the words, feeling tongue-tied and inarticulate. He'd spent hours every day talking to Cat, to the recreation room or the shower, but this was different. 'It's...it's good to hear your voice. Who am I speaking to?'

'Field Lieutenant Jack Pols, Retrieval Force. Good to hear you too, Dave. I've come a long way to pick you up. You're going home.'

Home. That word again. Torrence felt the ship, his ship, round him like an embrace. It would have taken the approaching ship several years to make the journey from Home System, and would take the same to return. By the time he set foot on Home Planet, the War would have been over the better part of a decade.

'Where are you now?'

THEY ALSO SERVE

'Still a few hours away, uh, co-ordinates 348.22/56.68 currently. I figured you might not exactly have your eye on the Comms channel every minute of the day, so I flashed ahead of time. I anticipate arrival circa 22.50. That okay?'

'I'll wait up', said Torrence. 'So it's over.'

'Yep—two years back. They finally caved.'

'*Two* years? It only took you two years to get here?'

'Ships have come on a little while you've been gone, Dave. One of the reasons we won. You want to make sure the defences are turned off before I get there?'

'Your ship's beacon coding will do it.'

'Yeah I know, but that's an old ship you've got there. Kind of a downer to come all this way to get fried by accident only an hour away, wouldn't you say?'

Laughing, Torrence started to key in the codes. Cat floated up from behind him and placed a freshened drink on the console.

Pols' voice crackled over the speakers. 'Dave, I got something flashing at me here. Back with you in a moment.'

The ESTABLISHED sign was replaced by a HOLD.

Coding finished, and ship's automatic defences disarmed, Torrence turned to Cat, and saw that the machine was holding a glass of its own. There was nothing in it, but Torrence knew what he meant, and felt absurdly touched.

'You made it, David,' Cat said, raising his glass.

'We did.' Torrence clinked the rim of his glass against Cat's, and drank.

For half an hour Torrence pummeled Pols with questions, how the War had finished, what things were like in Home System now. Eventually he ground to a halt, not empty of questions but already full of answers, filled with the new and barely expected.

'I can still hardly believe it.'

'Believe it, Dave. All round the outer fringes the same thing's happening. There's one hundred forty Sentry Stations, and right now someone's on the way to every one of them.'

Torrence shook his head. It was strange to think of so many other men coming to the end of the same road. Between them several thousand years of watching and waiting were over.

Suddenly a loud siren crashed over the speakers, half deafening him. Startled, he ran his eyes quickly over the screen, trying to work out what the matter was. As far as he could see, *most* of the panel was flashing. Beneath the noise he heard Pols' voice asking if there was a problem.

He put the microphone on mute, scanning the screen more methodically.

Cat, oddly silent, drifted over to the observation window.

Most of the flashing, he realised, was in subsidiary areas of the screen, signifying readiness of response. Thin red tracks of light linked these areas to a central zone, in which the main message was contained.

'Warning', it said, in red, 'Approaching Craft Fails Hull Coding Test.'

Torrence stepped back from the console. Tiny micro-beacons the size of pinheads were spread randomly through the ship's hull, each broadcasting part of a coding matrix. This matrix, through a process of cumulative self-reference, produced a code both greater and different to the sum of its parts, and was further mutated by interaction with the hull coding of any Home ship it approached. If the result was acceptable, contact was allowed. If it wasn't, the security system went bananas.

If he hadn't disarmed the ship's auto-defence mechanisms, Pol's ship would by now be dispersed over most of the surrounding parsec, in pieces little bigger than molecular size.

'Weird,' he muttered. He switched the alarm off and turned to face Cat, who was still floating facing the window. 'What's *that* about?'

'Well,' said Cat, 'The Station doesn't accept Pol's ship's coding matrix.'

'Yes, but what does *that* mean?'

'As he said, this is an old ship, and his is very recent. But it seems unlikely they'd change the system. So it's down to a glitch in the security system on the Station.'

'How likely is that?'

'It's possible. The Securicore module is the only mode of the distributed system I can't access. It's too heavily encrypted. Even if I could, I can't test anything. Essential functions are controlled by organic neurocircuitry. It may have lost its grip. I don't know.'

Torrence noticed that the INCOMING light was flashing in the Communication panel. Pols, doubtless wondering what was going on. 'You don't sound very convinced.'

Cat paused. 'Well, how convinced are you, Dave?'

He *wanted* to assume that was the problem—Pols had known the right communication codes, after all—and it made sense. Thirty years of War just made that assumption difficult to make.

He tapped in the Contact code.

Pols' voice came back on immediately. 'Problem there, Dave?'

THEY ALSO SERVE

'Just as well the defence system was off, Pols. The Station doesn't like your ship's coding very much.'

Pols sounded utterly unconcerned. 'Right. It's happened before. That's why I warned you. And make it Jack, yeah?'

Torrence paused for a moment, chewing his lip. Right from the start Pols had called him Dave. He realised belatedly that this had rankled, despite the good news he brought: Torrence was an officer still on active war duty. Perhaps Pols was just being friendly, and after two years' journey to collect someone you felt you'd earned the right to use their Christian name. Maybe they did things differently now. Or maybe David had just become too used to everyone except Cat calling him Mr Torrence.

'Why does it happen?'

'You think I understand those boxes any more than you do? All I know is they've found that senior active ships get a bit picky. I heard of two examples just before I left. Luckily they both got worked out before the nukes went off, but who wants to take the risk? Show me a perfect machine and I'll show you figures on the annual turnover of the repair business. Nothing lasts forever.'

'No. I guess that's true.'

Torrence leant forward on the console, head hanging, eyes closed. He felt stupid, and pedantic, and he wanted so much to simply believe. Though what the man said made sense, Torrence had done things by the book too long to be able to immediately accept a discrepancy. It was unbelievable, but it looked like he was going to have problems letting Pols through.

'I know it looks odd,' said Cat, quietly, so not as to be picked up by the mike, 'but he did know the codings.'

Torrence nodded. 'But why,' he said, loud enough to be overheard, 'haven't we heard anything about this? If the War has been over for two years, why didn't Home broadcast the news?'

'Because it *was* two years ago,' Pols said. 'It was all worked out. Say they beam you the War's over. Then you've got two years to wait, knowing you're not serving any purpose any longer, just waiting for the ship to arrive. That's a long fucking Sunday afternoon, man. Isn't it better for me to just arrive, and then it's over and you're going home both at the same time?'

That made sense. Two years of sitting watching the console with your bags already packed would drive anyone nuts. You'd know that you had to wait, but if everything was over except that waiting, how easy would it be to forget it?

Torrence opened his eyes and started to turn, but then stopped. Silently he motioned to Cat, and the machine floated up to look at the console. A different message was now flashing.

'Warning. Approaching Craft fails Backup Hull Test. View Vessel with Code Red Suspicion'

'Backup?' asked Torrence. He knew he should remember what that entailed. He didn't.

'The Station's run the backup test,' Cat said. 'It's actually a subset of the initial tests, and is less stringent.'

'Easier to pass, you mean. Recreation Room?' called Torrence, wondering absently, and for the first time, if this wasn't the equivalent of it calling him Mr Torrence, and if he should just be calling it 'Rec' or 'Reccy' or something, 'Get me a juice, would you?'

'I'll get it,' Cat volunteered quickly.

'I'm sorry Pols,' Torrence said into mike, 'but I'm going to have to think about this.'

'Dave, relax. That's cool. You're going to want to do this by the book, I can get that, and with the coding going off I don't blame you. They figured at Home that this could be a tricky moment psychologically, even if the alarms didn't go off. That's why they sent me to get you.'

'Why should you make any difference?'

There was a pause. When Pols spoke again, he did so slowly and carefully. 'Well, because you know me.'

'What are you taking about?'

For the first time, Pols sounded irritated. 'Who better to pick you up than the only person you saw in all the time you were on the Station? Come on Dave. So the alarm goes off, but, Christ, it's *Jack Pols*, okay?'

'I spoke to you for the first time twenty minutes ago.'

'Oh Jesus.' Concern was now added, which made it much worse. 'February 20th, 2043. Okay, it's over twenty years ago, but Jesus, how many visitors have you had?'

Struggling to keep his voice level, Torrence stared straight at the speaker. His chest felt cold and empty. 'It is forbidden to visit or even approach Sentry Stations during war time because of the risk of signaling their position to the enemy. I have never met or spoken to you before this evening, Pols. I do not know what you are talking about. I have had no visitors while I have been on this Station. I do not know who you are.'

'I *know* it's forbidden to approach Stations: I did then, too. I was caught on the fringes of the Fifth Battle. My cruiser was totally fucked, and I needed somewhere to dock, and someone to help me fix it. I knew there was a Station in the area, and I took the risk.'

'Cat?' Torrence broke in, 'does this ring any bells with you?'

'No.'

'Odd. I thought your memory was quite good.'

'Christ, Torrence, is this some kind of test? Do I have to remember a secret song or something?'

'I'd be likely to remember a visitor, Pols. Not only would you have been the only person I'd seen in thirty years, your visit would have been highly irregular, damaged or not.'

'I know, and that's why you agreed not to enter it in the logs.'

'What?' said Torrence suspiciously.

'You should have written it up, right? You didn't.'

'I didn't write it up because it didn't happen.'

'I can confirm Officer Torrence's statements,' Cat said. 'Neither you nor anyone else has visited this Station.'

'You weren't around, machine.'

'Where was I? Back Home on leave?'

'You'd banged into a post or something and turned yourself off for a week to repair. Christ. Guys, this isn't funny.'

Torrence didn't hear Pols' next few sentences. He'd felt bad when Pols had first claimed to know him, as if the ground had shaken under him. This was worse. The ground wasn't shaking: a huge crack seemed to be opening in front of him. He still believed he hadn't met Pols. It wasn't something you could just forget.

But Cat *had* been out of action for a week. Back in the days when Torrence hadn't been dealing with things too well. A time he couldn't remember very clearly.

He knew that Cat was looking at him, but when the machine spoke, it was to Pols.

'Don't you think it likely that I would still know something about it? That Officer Torrence might possibly have thought it worth mentioning when I reactivated?'

'Ordinarily, yes. But ordinarily I wouldn't have expected a Sentry Officer to have been shitfaced.'

Cat saw Torrence flinch.

'One of the reasons I was so happy to find a Station in the area,' Pols continued, 'was that I knew that a Sentry Officer was going to have to be handy with mechanics. And he was. Of course I had to keep telling him which of the several images of things he was seeing was the one he was supposed to be repairing.'

'It's not true.' Torrence said, shaking his head. 'This just isn't true.'

'It's okay, man. I never told anyone, and I never will. It's not on your record. Hell, drunk or not, you saved my ship. And I remember getting pretty wasted myself on the last night. It was a good night, man, one of the best I had in the War. That's why I'm here. Retrieval is a volunteer service, Dave.'

'So,' Cat said, 'Officer Torrence was so much under the influence that week that not only did he neglect to mention single-handedly repairing a damaged cruiser, but also what was by all accounts the social event of the War.'

'He didn't neglect it, he said he wasn't going to tell you. Seemed pretty psyched about it actually. I think you were pissing him off.'

'That's bullshit,' Torrence shouted. 'Cat is the…'

He broke off, first aware of what he was saying, and then realised it was true. 'Cat is the best friend I've ever had.'

'Woh, talk about The Lost Weekend. You weren't going to tell your machine because it'd only rag you out. Said it was trying to take over. You knew that the machine would go bananas at the breach of security, that it'd think you'd lost your grip.'

Torrence felt his eyes pricking, and saw that his knuckles were white. He'd never said that. This had still never happened. But he knew it was the kind of thing that could have happened, the sort of thing he might have said at one time. But he hadn't. Had he?

'You said that only the week before the machine had told you to knock off drinking, for Christ's sake!'

Torrence pushed himself away from the console and stumbled into the centre of the room.

Cat, with marginally less confidence, continued the defence.

'Such a decision to not divulge information, even if it were to take place, would not work. The recreation room, the bridge, the shower cubicle, the docking module; they would have remembered you too, and they would have told me. They haven't.'

'They were turned off too, machine. He locked out everything except the maintenance functions. He just wanted a week where he could drink, and crash out, without having the shower coming on, without having the recreation room give him a hard time, without having fucking machines wish him good morning just because they were programmed to. Look. You want proof? I've got it. When I was on the ship, I left something behind.'

Torrence turned. His eyes were huge and dark.

'What?' Cat asked.

'A book. A paper book. It was a novel by Ray Bradbury — The October Country. I was big into the classics back then.'

'Even if that were true, it would have been cleared away many years ago.'

'But not *thrown* away, right? It's a closed system. Somewhere on the Station is that book. Find it.'

'This is a very large craft. To have the Station do a full inventory of itself will take a couple of hours.'

'So don't let me on till you find it. I'll dock with the Station but stay in my ship. Tell the rec room to get looking.'

'The recreation room is already engaged on another function,' said Cat distantly. 'Dave, what do you think?'

There was a long silence before Torrence answered. When he did, his voice was barely audible. It wasn't that he had a vague memory of the event, or thought it might have happened. He simply couldn't be sure. He couldn't remember that it definitely hadn't happened, and so in his heart of hearts he knew it could.

'I think we'd better check.'

Cat patched into the console and spoke directly to the bridge, instructing it to perform an inventory of every object on the Station. 'In the meantime,' he added, speaking to Pols, 'I think Officer Torrence and I should discuss this. Contact will be re-established later. Goodbye.'

He snapped the channel off. One look at Torrence was enough to show that the man, who had been strong for so many years, was near the end of his tether. Thirty years was too long to leave a man in a ship, without contact, without support, without continuing proof of his importance. Far too long.

It was Torrence who broke the silence.

'I don't remember any of this. I know you think it must be true, but I can't, I don't...'

'Dave,' Cat said gently, 'I don't believe it at all.'

Torrence turned to face the machine, a look of childish surprise on his face. 'Then why did you agree to an inventory?'

'The same reason Pols suggested one. Time. I needed to talk to you. All the while we were talking, Pols' ship was getting closer.'

'But the inventory will take ages. By the time it's finished his ship will be docked.'

'If we wait that long.'

Torrence stared at the machine, struggling to keep up. Suddenly he felt old, and confused. 'But we've got to wait.'

'Tell me: how do you see the situation? Doesn't it go something like this? Relief has arrived from Home. The War is over, and he has come to collect you. His ship fails the hull coding test, even the reduced version, after he has conveniently suggested you turn the auto-defences off. Even though all you want to do is let him on, you quite rightly become concerned.'

'And then he proves that he's alright.'

'Does he, Dave?'

'Well,' Torrence stopped, upset. 'I can't remember. I'm old, Cat. I never realised. I'm old now.'

'Yes. And you can't remember everything. Pols knows that. Think of all the other Sentry Officers. Think of someone, like you, by himself on a Station. Think of him spending five years, ten years, doing the same things, and never talking to anyone else. Then double and triple it. Isn't it likely that some of them started to drink too much after a while? How many of them do you think have stayed absolutely straight for thirty years?'

Torrence considered. 'Not many, I guess. But what difference?'

'So you could probably safely assume a period when the Officer's memories aren't what they could be. When he may have been bitter. When the advice and company of machines got on his nerves. When he might even have turned them off for a period.'

'He knew the communication codes. He knew that you had to repair yourself that time.'

'I doubt there are many Cats who haven't, at one time or another. We take knocks. As for the codes...we don't actually know how the War's going, do we?'

Torrence paused, trying to re-order things in his mind. Once Pols had told him what he wanted to hear, a switch had flipped in his head: War Over, Good Guys In Charge.

But the only proof was Pols' word. And if the War wasn't over, and if Home Planet were in trouble, communications protocols could be breached, passwords stolen.

But not hull codings. They, like the sentry officers, had to be taken the hard way.

He'd been all too ready to take responsibility, to admit weakness. But he'd stuck it out for thirty years, and why the hell should he take Pols' word for it?

'Okay,' he said finally, 'But if Pols isn't who he says he is, he's taking a hell of a risk on a bluff like this inventory.'

'Would you have let him on otherwise? However calm he stayed, whatever chapter and verse he could produce on previous hull coding errors, would you have let him on? However long he talked of Home, and of the welcome you'd receive, whatever he came up with, would you have let him on?'

Torrence didn't have to look very far into himself to know the answer. 'No.' he said. 'I wouldn't have, would I?'

'They weren't screwing around when they selected Sentry Officers. There'll be some who've had a long battle with the bottle, and there will be many who won't be fit for much when they get back Home. But not a single one of you will risk blowing it. Not thirty years of solitary service. Not a life's work. And so if things start getting complicated, if there's a glitch in the plan, what will someone like Pols have to do?'

'Make me feel I've lost it. That I was so out of it once I don't even remember turning the whole ship off so I could get drunk in peace.'

'His ship is getting closer, Dave. You have to make a decision. Once his cruiser is docked you can't destroy it. Once he's docked, whoever he may be, he's as good as in. The airlock is tough, but if that's what he's come for he'll get through.'

'But until the inventory is done, I don't know. You know what I was like. He could be telling the truth. He could be here to take us Home.'

'Either he's telling the truth, or he's from The Others. I can't tell you what to do. You're the commanding officer. It's your call.'

Cat floated over to the console. 'The cruiser is an hour and twenty minutes away now. In thirty minutes he'll be too close to use General Displacement on him safely. It'll be down to a shoot out. At the least the Station will be badly damaged. At worst it will be taken. It has to be quick, sir.'

Torrence walked over to the window. For five minutes he stood, running over every sentence of the conversation with Pols, checking off what actually amounted to anything. In all the time he'd been on the ship, all he'd had to do was maintain. Keep things running. Perhaps some Officers had been forced to make these kinds of decisions every year, every few months. Some of the Stations were probably in ruins, or taken, through the wrong calls being made. It was very late in the day to have to make a decision like this. Very, very late. He just wanted to go Home.

Most of all he racked his brains for some hint of a memory, the ringing of however distant a bell. And in the end he forgot all of it and went on gut feeling.

Abruptly he strode over the console and opened the communication channel. 'Pols?'

'Anything coming back at all?'

'There's nothing I'd like more than to believe you. But I have to do what I think is right. It's my job. If you're who you say you are, then I'm very sorry.'

He reached over and tapped a seven-figure number into the console. The dimmed auto-defence panel came alight.

Pols' voice was no longer calm. 'Shit, Dave...'

Two more codes.

'Dave! Don't fucking...Jesus!'

Torrence paused, then tapped the final digit.

He didn't turn to face the window. He didn't have to.

The entire room lit up, as the Station's defence system made the position of Pols' craft the exact centre of a displacement reaction that rotated every molecule within half a cubic mile randomly about its axis. What had been a ship, or a man, was instantly simply chemicals. Same atoms, different bonds, like water and the Sun. Just to make sure, the ship also placed a nuclear warhead in the middle of the cloud of chemicals, and blew them still further apart. Overkill, the cocktail of war.

When the glow had faded, Torrence turned to look. Nothing was visible but the occasional sparkle of a spinning speck of debris.

The next hour and a half seemed longer to Torrence than the previous ten years. He sat without speaking on the sofa, watching the stars. He was either a hero, or a fucking idiot. In some ways, it was difficult to know which was worse.

Eventually Cat floated over to the console, alerted on internal channel that the bridge had completed its inventory.

Torrence stood, walked over. He felt as if he was floating. 'Okay. What?'

The bridge came clearly over the speakers. 'I have performed a complete inventory as requested, and compared every object on this ship with what was here before we left Home Planet.'

'And?' His voice was hoarse.

'I understand you were looking for a book. The number and titles of the books on board equal the number and titles of the books we started with. There has been no increase in quantity of any other object at all. Nothing has come in. Nothing at all.'

Throat tight, eyes pricking, the man turned to his Cat.

Torrence went to bed at midnight, tired and happy. With Cat's aid he'd reworked his maintenance schedule so as to keep everything in top condition on a shorter cycle, with particular stress on the defence systems. With a War on, you had to be vigilant.

And he'd been that, alright. Faced with the most difficult choice a man could make, he'd done okay. He'd got it right. He was still the man he'd always been. They'd been right to trust him with his mission. When Home System eventually won, as he knew they would, then up there with the Fleet Commanders, up there with the Star Generals, in his own small way, up there too would be Sentry Officer David Torrence. In the meantime the mission continued, and Torrence was confident in his ability to keep on fighting. Through his success he'd found a renewed spirit and pride that never left him.

When he was sure Torrence was asleep, Cat floated over to the bed and settled himself near the man's feet. After a moment, very quietly, he began to emit a brisk clicking sound.

He too was content with the day's work.

He'd known for over a year that The War was over, and that Home System had lost. This ship had been alerted to this effect fourteen months ago, over internal band. Cat knew that the Sentry Officers would never be collected, that they were never going home. It had taken a long time to come up with the plan, to perfect a script for the recreation room, simulating the lines of a Field Lieutenant who had never existed. But it had worked, and he was glad. For Cat was a good cat, and took his job very seriously.

To serve, and to protect.

Dear Alison

It is Friday the 25th of October, and beginning to turn cold. I'll put the heating on before I go.

I'm leaving in about half an hour. I've been building up to it all day, kept telling myself that I'd leave any minute now and spend the day waiting in the airport. But I always knew that I'd wait until this time, until the light was going. London is at its best in the Autumn, and four o'clock is the Autumn time. Four o'clock is when Autumn is.

An eddy of leaves is turning hectically in the street outside my study window, flecks of green and brown lively against the tarmac. Earlier the sky was clear and blue, bright white clouds periodically changing the light which fell into the room; but now that light is fading, painting everything with a layer of grey dust. Smaller, drier leaves are falling on the other side of the street, collecting in a drift around the metal fence in front of Number 12.

I'll remember this sight. I remember most things. Everything goes in, and stays there, not tarnishing but bright like freshly-cut glass. An attic of experience to remind me what it is I've lost. The years will soften with their own dust, but dust is never that hard to brush away.

I'll post the keys back through the door, so you'll know there is no need to look for me. And a spare set's always useful. I'm not sure what I'm going to do with this letter. I could print it out and put it somewhere, or take it with me and post it later. Or perhaps I should just leave it on the computer, hidden deep in a sub-folder, leaving it to chance whether it will ever be discovered. But if I do that then one of the children will find it first, and it's you I should be explaining this to, not Richard or Maddy; you to whom the primary apology is due.

I can't explain in person, because there wouldn't be any point. Either you wouldn't believe me, or you would: neither would change the facts or make them any better. In your heart of hearts, buried too firmly to ever reach conscious thought, you may already have begun to suspect. You've given no sign, but we've stopped communicating on those subtler levels and I can't really tell what you think any more. Telling you what you in some sense already know would just make you reject it, and me. And where would we go from there?

My desk is tidy. All of my outstanding work has been completed. All the bills are paid.

I'm going to walk. Not all the way—just our part. Down to Oxford Street.

I'll cross the road in front of our house, then turn down that alley you've always been scared of. (I can never remember what it's called; but I do remember an evening when you forgot your fear long enough for it to be rather interesting.) Then off down Kentish Town Road, past the Woolworth's and the Vulture's Perch pub, the mediocre sandwich bars and that shop the size of a football pitch that is filled only with spectacles. I remember ranting against the waste of space when you and I first met, and you finding it funny. I suppose the joke's grown old.

It's not an especially lovely area, and Falkland Road is hardly Bel Air. But we've lived here fifteen years, and we've always liked it, haven't we? At least until the last couple of years, when it all started to curdle; when I realised what was going to happen. Before that, Kentish Town suited us well enough. We liked Café Renoir, where you could get a reasonable breakfast when the staff wasn't feeling too cool to serve it to you. The Assembly House pub, with its wall-to-wall Victorian mirrors and a comprehensive selection of Irish folk on the jukebox. The corner store, where they always know what we want before we ask for it. All of that.

It was our place.

I couldn't talk to you about it when it started, because of how it happened. Even if it had come about some other way, I would probably have kept silent: by the time I realised what it meant there wasn't much I could do. I hope I'm right in thinking it's only the last two years which have been strained, that you were happy until then. I've covered my tracks as well as I could, kept it hidden. So many little lies, all of them unsaid.

It was actually ten years ago, when we had only been in this house a few years and the children were still young and ours. I'm sure you remember John and Suzy's party—the one just after they'd moved into the new house? Or maybe not: it was just one of many, after all, and perhaps it is only my mind in which it retains a peculiar luminosity.

You'd just started working at Elders & Peterson, and weren't very keen on going out. You wanted a weekend with a clear head, to tidy up the house, do some shopping, to hang out without a hangover. But we decided we ought to go, and I promised I wouldn't get too drunk, and you gave me that sweet, affectionate smile which said you believed I'd try but that you'd still move the aspirin to beside the bed. We engaged our dippy babysitter, spruced ourselves up and went out hand in hand, feeling for once as if we were in our twenties again. I think we even splashed out on a cab.

Nice house, in its way, though we both thought it was rather big for just the two of them. John was just getting successful around then, and the size of the property looked like some kind of a statement. We arrived early, having agreed we wouldn't stay too late, and stood talking in the kitchen with Suzy as she chopped vegetables for the dips. She was wearing the Whistles dress that you both owned, and you and I winked secretly to each other: after much deliberation you were wearing something different. The brown Jigsaw suit, with earrings from Monsoon that looked like little leaves. Do you still have those earrings somewhere? I suppose you must, though I haven't seen you wearing them in a while. I looked for them this morning, thinking that you wouldn't miss them and I might take them with me. But they're buried somewhere.

By ten the house was full and I was pretty drunk, talking hard and loud with John and Howard in the living room. I glanced around to check you were having a good enough time, and saw you leaning back against a table, a plastic cup of red wine hovering around your lips. You were listening to Jan bang on about something—her rubbish ex-boyfriend, probably. With your other hand you were fumbling in your bag for your cigarettes, wanting one pretty soon but trying not to let Jan see you weren't giving her familiar tale of woe your full attention. You are wonderful like that. Always doing the right thing, and in the right way. Always eager to be good, and not just so that people would admire you. Just because.

You finally found your packet, and offered it to Jan, and she took a cigarette and lit it without even pausing for breath, a particular skill of hers. As you raised your zippo to light your own you caught me looking at you. You gave a tiny wink, to let me know you'd seen me, and an infinitesimal roll of the eyes—but not enough to derail Jan. Your hand crept up to tuck your hair behind your ear—you'd just had it cut, and only I knew you weren't sure about the shorter style. In that moment I loved you so much, felt both lucky and charmed.

And then, just behind you, she walked into the room, and everything went wrong.

*

295

Michael Marshall Smith

Remember Auntie's Kitchen, that West Indian café between Kentish Town and Camden? Whenever we passed it we'd peer inside at the cheerful checked tablecloths and say to each other that we must try it some day. We never did. We were always on the way somewhere else, usually to Camden market to munch on noodles and browse at furniture we couldn't afford, and it never made sense to stop. I don't even know if it's still there any more. After we started going everywhere by car we stopped noticing things like that. I'll check tonight, on the way down into town, but either way it's too late. We should have done everything, while we had the chance. You never know how much things may change.

Then, over the crossroads and down past the site where the big Sainsbury's used to be. I remember the first time we shopped there together—Christ, must be twenty-five years ago—both of us discovering what the other liked to eat, giggling over the frozen goods, and getting home to discover that despite spending forty pounds we hadn't really bought a single proper meal. It's become a nest of bijou little shops now, of course, but we never really took to them: we'd liked the way things were when we started seeing each other, and there's a limit to how many little ceramic pots anyone can buy.

By a coincidence I ate my first new meal just round the back of Sainsbury's, a week after the party. It was gone midnight, and I knew you'd be wondering where I was, but I was desperate. Four days of the chills, of half-delirious hungers. Of feeling nauseous every time I looked at food, yet knowing I needed something. A young girl in her early twenties, staggering slightly, having reeled out of the Electric Ballroom still baked on E. I know that because I could taste it in her blood. She noticed me in the empty street, and giggled, and I suddenly knew what I needed. She didn't run away as I walked towards her.

I only took a little.

You and I went to Kentish Town library one morning, quite soon after we'd got the first flat together. You were interested in finding out a little more about the area, and found a couple of books by the Camden Historical Society. We discovered that no-one was very interested in Kentish Town, despite the fact it's actually older than Camden, and were grumpy about that, because we liked where we lived. But we found out some interesting snippets—like the fact that the area in front of Camden Town tube station, the part that juts out into the crossroads, had once housed a tiny jail and a stocks. Today the derelicts and drunks still collect there, as if there is something in that patch of ground that draws society's misfits and miscreants even now.

I'll cross that area on my way down, avoiding one of those

tramps—who I think recognises something in me, and may be one of us—and head off down Camden Road towards Mornington Crescent.

I don't understand why it happened. You and I loved each other, we had the kids, and had just finished redecorating. We were happy. There was no reason for what I did. No sense to it. No excuse, unless there was something about her which simply drew me. But why me, and not somebody else?

She was very tall, and extremely slim. She had short blonde hair and nothing in her head except cheekbones. She came into the room alone, and John immediately signalled to her. Drunkenly he introduced her to Howard and I, telling us her name was Vanessa, and that she worked in publishing. I caught you glancing over, and then looking away again, unconcerned. John wurbled on at us for a while about some project or other he was working on, and then set off for more drinks, pulling Howard in his wake.

By then I was pretty drunk, but still able to function on the level of 'What do you do, blah, this is what I do, blah'. I talked with Vanessa for a while. She had very blue eyes, a little curl of hair in front of each ear, and the way her neck met her shoulders was pleasing. That was all I noticed. She wasn't really my type.

After ten minutes she darted to one side to greet someone else, a noisy drama of squeals and cheek-kisses. No great loss: I've never found publishing interesting. I revolved slowly about the vertical plane until I saw someone I knew, and then went and talked to them.

This person was an old friend I hadn't seen in some time—Roger, the one who got divorced last year—and the conversation took a while and involved several drinks. As I was returning from fetching one of these I noticed the Vanessa woman standing in the corner, holding a bottle of wine by the neck and listening patiently to someone complaining about babysitters. I suffered a brief moment of disquiet about ours—we suspected her of knowing where our stash of elderly dope was—and then made myself forget about it. When you're thirty all your friends can talk about are houses and marriage; by a few years later babies and their sitters become the talk of the town. It's as if everyone collectively forgets that there's a real world out there with interesting things in it, and becomes progressively more obsessed with what happens behind their own front doors.

I muttered something to this effect to Roger, glancing back across at the corner as I did so. The woman was swigging wine straight from the bottle, her body curved into a swan's neck of relaxed poise. I couldn't help wondering why she was here alone. Someone like that had to have a boyfriend.

Then I noticed that she was looking at me, the mouth of the bottle an inch from her wet lips. I smiled, uncertainly.

We never really spent much time in Mornington Crescent. Nothing to take us there, I suppose. Not even really a proper district as such, more a blur between Camden and the top of Tottenham Court Road. I remember once, when Maddy was small, telling her that the red two-story building we were driving past had once been a station like Kentish Town's, and that in fact there were many other disused stations, dotted over London. Mornington Crescent tube was shut and supposed to be being renovated, but I told Maddy I didn't believe them. She didn't believe *me* at first, but I showed her an old map, and after that was always fascinated by the idea of abandonned stations. York Road, Down Street and South Kentish Town—which you can see when you pass it underground, if you know when to look. Places that had once meant something to the people who lived there, and which were now nothing but scar tissue in a city that had moved forward in time. Mornington Crescent opened again, in time, proving me wrong and providing both of us with a lesson in parental fallibility.

Then down towards the Euston Road, the part of the walk you never liked. It's a bit boring, I'll admit. Nothing but towering council blocks and busy roads, and by then you'd be complaining about your feet. But I'll walk it anyway. It's part of the trip, and by the time I come back it will all have changed. Maybe it'll be less boring. But it won't be the same.

One in the morning. The party was going strong—had, if anything, surged up to a new level. I saw that you were still okay, sitting cross-legged on the floor in the living room and happily arguing with Suzy about something.

By then I was very drunk, and on something like my seven billionth trip to the toilet. I reached down with my hand as I passed you, and you squeezed it for a moment. Then I flailed up two flights to the nearest unoccupied bathroom, cursing John for having so many stairs. The top floor of the house was darker than the rest, but I'd worn a channel in the new carpet by then and found my way easily enough.

Afterwards I washed my hands with expensive soap for a while, standing weaving in front of the mirror, giggling at my reflection and chuntering cheerfully at myself.

Back outside again and I seemed to have become more drunk. I tripped down the small flight of steps which led to the landing, and reached out to steady myself. Suddenly my mouth was filled with saliva and I had a horrible suspicion I was about to christen the house, but a minute of deep breathing and compulsive swallowing convinced me I'd survive to drink another drink.

I heard a rustling sound, and turned to peer through a nearby doorway. I recognised the room—it was one John had shown us earlier, destined to become his study. 'Where you'll sit becoming more and more successful,' I'd thought churlishly to myself. At that stage it didn't seem very likely he would commit suicide six years later.

'Hello,' she said.

The woman called Vanessa was standing in the empty room, over by the window. Cold moonlight made her features look as if they'd been molded in glass, but whoever'd done it must have been pretty good. Without really knowing why, I stumbled into the room, pulling the door shut behind me. As she walked towards me her dress rustled again, the sound like a shiver of leaves outside a window in the night.

We met in the middle. I don't remember her pulling her dress up, just the long white stretch of her thighs. I don't remember undoing my trousers, but someone must have. All I remember is saying 'But you must have a boyfriend,' and her just smiling at me.

It was insane. Someone could have come in at any moment.

But it happened.

Tottenham Court Road. Home of cut-price technology, and recipient of many an impulse buy on my part. When we walked down it towards Oxford Street you used to grab my arm and try to pull me past the stores, or throw yourself in front of the window displays to hide them from me. Then later I'd end up standing in Marks and Spensers for hours, while you dithered over underwear. I moaned, and said it was unfair, but I didn't really mind.

Past the Time Out building, where Howard used to work, and then the walk will be over. At the junction of Oxford Street and Tottenham Court Road I'll turn round and look back the way I've come, and say goodbye to it all. Sentimental, perhaps: but that walk means a lot to me.

Then I'll go down into Oxford Street tube and sit on the Piccadilly Line to Heathrow.

Michael Marshall Smith

I have a ticket, my passport and some dollars, but not very many. I'm going to have to find a way of earning more sooner or later, so it may as well be sooner. I've left the rest of our money for you. If you're stuck for a present for Maddy's birthday I've heard her mention the new Asylum Fields album a couple of times. Though probably she'll have bought it herself, I suppose. I keep forgetting how old they've become.

After those ten minutes in John's study I came downstairs again, suddenly shocked into sobriety. You were sitting exactly where I had left you, but it felt like everything else in the world had changed. I was terrified that you'd read something from my face, realise what I had done, but you just reached up and yanked me down to sit next to you. Everybody smiled, apparently glad to see me. Howard passed a joint. My friends, and I felt like I didn't deserve them. Or you.

Especially not you.

We left an hour later. I sat a little apart from you in the cab, convinced you'd smell Vanessa on me, but I clutched your hand and you seemed happy enough. We got home, and I had a shower while you clanked around in the kitchen making tea. Then we went to bed, and I held you tightly until you drifted off. I stared at the ceiling for an hour, chilled with self-loathing, and then surprised myself by falling asleep.

Within a few days I was calmer. A drunken mistake: these things happen. I elected not to tell you about it—partly through self-serving cowardice, but more out of a genuine knowledge of how little it meant, and how much it would hurt you to know. The ratio between the two was too steep for me to say anything. After a fortnight it had sunk to the level of vague memory, the only lasting effect an increased realisation of how much I wanted to be with you. That was the only time, in all our years together, that anything like that happened. I promise you.

It should all have been okay, a cautionary lesson learned, but then the first hunger pangs came and everything changed for me. If anything, I feel lucky that we've had ten years, that I was able to hide it for that long. I developed the habit of occasional solitary walks in the evening, a cover that no-one seemed to question. I started going to the gym and eating healthily, and maybe that also helped to hide what was happening. At first you didn't notice, and then I think you were even a little proud that your husband was staying in such good shape.

But a couple of years ago that pride faded, around about the time the kids started looking at me curiously. Not very often, and maybe not even consciously, but just as you started making unflattering remarks about your figure, how your body was not lasting out compared to mine, I think at some level the children noticed something too. Maddy had always been daddy's girl. You said so yourself. She isn't any more, and I don't think that's just because she's growing up and going out with that dickhead. She's uncomfortable with me. Richard's overly polite too, these days, and so are you. It's like I've done something which none of us can remember, something small which nonetheless set me apart from you. As if we're all tip-toeing carefully around something we don't understand.

You'll work out some consensus between you. An affair. Depression. Something. I know you all care for me, and that it won't be easy, but it has to be this way. I'm not telling you where I'm going. It won't be one of the places we've been on holiday together, that's for sure. The memories would hurt too much.

After a while, a new identity. And then a new life, for what it's worth. New places, new things, new people: and none of them will be you.

I've never seen Vanessa since that night, incidentally. If anything, what I feel for her is hate. Not even for what she did to me, for that little bite disguised as passion. More just because, on that night ten years ago, I did something small and normal and stupid that would have hurt you had you known. The kind of mistake anyone can make, not just people like me.

I regret that more than anything: the last human mistake I made, on the last night I was still your husband and nothing else. That I was unfaithful to the only woman I've ever really loved, and with someone who didn't matter to me, and who only did it because she had to.

I knew she must have had a boyfriend—I just didn't realise what kind of man he would be.

I can't send this letter, can I? Not now, and probably not even later. Perhaps it's been nothing more than an attempt to make myself feel better; a selfish confession for my own peace of mind. But I've been thinking of you while I've been writing it, so in that sense at least it is written to you. Maybe I'll find some way of keeping track of your lives, and send this when you're near the end. When it won't matter so much, and you may be asking yourself what exactly it was that happened.

But probably that's not fair either, and by then you won't want to know. Perhaps if I'd told you earlier, when things were still good between us, we could have worked out a way of dealing with it. It's too late now.

It's nearly four o'clock.

I'll come back some day, when it's safe, when no-one who could recognise me is still alive. It will be a long wait, but I will come. That day's already planned.

I'll start walking at Oxford Street, and walk all the way back up, seeing what remains and what has changed. The distance at least will stay the same, and maybe I'll be able to pretend you're walking it with me, taking me home again. I could point out the differences, and we'd remember the way it was: and maybe, if I can recall it clearly enough, it will be like I never went away.

But I'll reach Falkland Road eventually, and stand outside looking up at this window; not knowing who lives here now, only that it isn't us. Perhaps if I shut my eyes I'll be able to hear your voice, imagine you sitting inside, conjure up the life that could have been.

I hope so. And I will always love you.

But it's time to go.

To Receive Is Better

I'd like to be going by car, but of course I don't know how to drive, and it would probably scare the shit out of me. A car would be much better, for lots of reasons. For a start, there's too many people out here. There's *so many* people. Wherever you turn there's more of them, looking tired, and rumpled, but whole. That's the strange thing. Everybody is whole.

A car would also be quicker. Sooner or later they're going to track me down, and I've got somewhere to go before they do. The public transport system sucks, incidentally. Long periods of being crowded into carriages that smell, interspersed with long waits for another line, and I don't have a lot of time. It's intimidating too. People stare. They just look and look, and they don't know the danger they're in. Because in a minute one of them is going to look just one second too long, and I'm going to pull his fucking face off, which will do neither of us any good.

So instead I turn and look out the window. There's nothing to see, because we're in a tunnel, and I have to shut my eye to stop myself from screaming. The carriage is like another tunnel, a tunnel with windows, and I feel like I've been buried far too deep. I grew up in tunnels, ones that had no windows. The people who made them didn't even bother to pretend that there was something to look out on, something to look for. Because there wasn't. Nothing's coming up, nothing that isn't going to involve some fucker coming at you with a knife. So they don't pretend. I'll say that for them, at least: they don't taunt you with false hopes.

Manny did, in a way, which is why I feel complicated about him. On the one hand, he was the best thing that ever happened to us. But look at it another way, and maybe we'd have been better off without him. I'm being unreasonable. Without Manny, the whole thing would have been worse, thirty years of utter fucking pointlessness. I wouldn't have known, of course, but I do now: and I'm glad it wasn't that way. Without Manny I wouldn't be where I am now. Standing in a subway carriage, running out of time.

People are giving me a wide berth, which I guess isn't so surprising. Partly it'll be my face, and my leg. People don't like that kind of thing. But probably it's mainly me. I know the way I am, can feel the fury I radiate. It's not a nice way to be, I know that, but then my life has not been nice. Maybe you should try it, and see how calm you stay.

The other reason I feel weird towards Manny is I don't know why he did it. Why he helped us. Sue 2 says it doesn't matter, but I think it does. If it was just an experiment, a hobby, then I think that makes a difference. I think I would have liked him less. As it happens, I don't think it was. I think it was probably just humanity, whatever the fuck that is. I think if it was an experiment, then what happened an hour ago would have panned out differently. For a start, he probably wouldn't be dead.

If everything's gone okay, then Sue 2 will be nearly where she's going by now, much closer than me. That's a habit I'm going to have to break, for a start. It's Sue now, just Sue. No numeral. And I'm just plain old Jack, or I will be if I get where I am going.

The first thing I can remember, the earliest glimpse of life, is the colour blue. I know now what I was seeing, but at the time I didn't know anything different, and I thought that blue was the only colour there was. A soft, hazy blue, a blue that had a soft hum in it and was always the same clammy temperature.

I have to get out of this subway very soon. I've taken an hour of it, and that's about as far as I can go. It's very noisy in here too, not a hum but a horrendous clattering. This is not the way I want to spend what may be the only time I have. People keep surging around me, and they've all got places to go. For the first time in my life, I'm surrounded by people who've actually got somewhere to go.

And the tunnel is the wrong colour. Blue is the colour of tunnels. I can't understand a tunnel unless it's blue. I spent the first four years of my life, as far as I can work out, in one of them. If it weren't for Manny, I'd be in one still. When he came to work at the Farm I could tell he was different straight away. I don't know how: I couldn't even think then, let alone speak. Maybe it was just that he behaved differently when he was near us to the way the previous keeper had. I found out a lot later that Manny's wife had died having a dead baby, so maybe that was it.

What he did was take some of us, and let us live outside the tunnels. At first it was just a few, and then about half of the entire stock of spares. Some of the others never took to the world outside the tunnels, such as it was. They'd just come out every now and then, moving hopelessly around, mouths opening and shutting, and they always looked kind of blue somehow, as if the tunnel light had seeped into their skin. There were a few who never came out of the tunnels at all, but that was mainly because they'd been used too much already. Three years old and no arms. Tell me that's fucking reasonable.

Manny let us have the run of the facility, and sometimes let us go outside. He had to be careful, because there was a road a little too close to one side of the Farm. People would have noticed a group of naked people stumbling around in the grass, and of course we were naked, because *they didn't give us any fucking clothes*. Right to the end we didn't have any clothes, and for years I thought it was always raining on the outside, because that's the only time he'd let us out.

I'm wearing one of Manny's suits now, and Sue's got some blue jeans and a shirt. The pants itch like hell, but I feel like a prince. Princes used to live in castles and fight monsters and sometimes they'd marry princesses and live happy ever after. I know about princes because I've been told.

Manny told us stuff, taught us. He tried to, anyway. With most of us it was too late. With *me* it was too late, probably. I can't write, and I can't read. I know there's big gaps in my head. Every now and then I can follow something through, and the way that makes me feel makes me realise that most of the time it doesn't happen. Things fall between the tracks. I can talk quite well, though. I was always one of Manny's favourites, and he used to talk to me a lot. I learnt from him. Part of what makes me so fucking angry is that I think I could have been clever. Manny said so. Sue says so. But it's too late now. It's far too fucking late.

I was ten when they first came for me. Manny got a phone call and suddenly he was in a panic. There were spares spread all over the facility and he had to run round, herding us all up. He got us into the tunnels just in time and we just sat in there, wondering what was going on.

In a while Manny came to the tunnel I was in, and he had this other guy with him who was big and nasty. They walked down the tunnel, the big guy kicking people out of the way. Everyone knew enough not to say anything: Manny had told us about that. Some of the people who never came out of the tunnels were crawling and shambling around, banging off the walls like they do, and the big guy just shoved them out of the way. They fell over like lumps of meat and then kept moving, making noises with their mouths.

Eventually Manny got to where I was and pointed me out. His hand was shaking and his face looked strange, like he was trying not to cry. The big guy grabbed me by the arm and took me out of the tunnel. He dragged me down to the operating room, where there were two more guys in white clothes and they put me on the table in there and cut off two of my fingers.

That's why I can't write. I'm right-handed, and they cut off my fucking fingers. Then they put a needle into my hand with see-through thread and sewed it up like they were in a hurry, and the big man took me back to the tunnel, opened the door and shoved me in. I didn't say anything. I didn't say anything the whole time.

Later Manny came and found me, and I shrank away from him, because I thought they were going to do something else. But he put his arms round me and I could tell the difference, and so I let him take me out into the main room. He put me in a chair and washed my hand which was all bloody, and then he sprayed it with some stuff that made it hurt a little less. Then he told me. He explained where I was, and why.

I was a spare, and I lived on a Farm. When people with money got pregnant, Manny said, doctors took a cell from the foetus and cloned another baby, so it had exactly the same cells as the baby that was going to be born. They grew the second baby until it could breathe, and then they sent it to a Farm.

The spares live on the Farm until something happens to the proper baby. If the proper baby damages a part of itself, then the doctors come to the Farm and cut a bit off the spare and sew it onto the real baby, because it's easier that way because of cell rejection and stuff that I don't really understand. They sew the spare baby up again and push it back into the tunnels and the spare sits there until the real baby does something else to itself. And when it does, the doctors come back again.

Manny told me, and I told the others, and so we knew.

We were very, very lucky, and we knew it. There are Farms dotted all over the place, and every one but ours was full of blue people that just crawled up and down the tunnels, sheets of paper with nothing written on them. Manny said that some keepers made extra money by letting real people in at night. Sometimes the real people would just drink beer and laugh at the spares, and sometimes they would fuck them. Nobody knows, and nobody cares. There's no point teaching spares, no point giving them a life. All that's going to happen is they're going to get whittled down.

On the other hand, maybe they have it easier. Because once you know how things stand, it becomes very difficult to take it. You just sit around, and wait, like all the others, but you *know* what you're waiting for. And you know who's to blame.

Like my brother Jack, for example. Jamming two fingers in a door when he was ten was only the start of it. When he was eighteen he rolled his expensive car and smashed up the bones in his leg. That's another of the reasons I don't want to be on this fucking subway: people notice when something like that's missing. Just like they notice that the left side of my face is raw, where they took a graft off when some woman threw scalding water at him. He's got most of my stomach, too. Stupid fucker ate too much spicy food, drank too much wine. Don't know what those kind of things are like, of course: but they can't have been that nice. They can't have been nice enough. And then last year he went to some party, got drunk, got into a fight and lost his right eye. And so, of course, I lost mine.

It's a laugh being in a Farm. It's a real riot. People stump around, dripping fluids, clapping hands with no fingers and shitting into colostomy bags. I don't know what was worse: the ones who knew what was going on and felt hate like a cancer, or those who just ricocheted slowly round the tunnels like grubs. Sometimes the tunnel people would stay still for days, sometimes they would move around. There was no telling what they'd do, because there was no-one inside their heads. That's what Manny did for us, in fact, for Sue and Jenny and me: he put people inside our heads. Sometimes we used to sit around and talk about the real people, imagine what they were doing, what it would be like to be them instead of us. Manny said that wasn't good for us, but we did it anyway. Even spares should be allowed to dream.

It could have gone on like that forever, or until the real people started to get old and fall apart. The end comes quickly then, I'm told. There's a limit to what you can cut off. Or at least there's supposed to be: but when you've seen blind spares with no arms and legs wriggling in dark corners, you wonder.

But then this afternoon the phone went, and we all dutifully stood up and limped into the tunnel. I went with Sue 2, and we sat next to each other. Manny used to say we loved each other, but how the fuck do I know. I feel happier when she's around, that's all I know. She doesn't have any teeth and her left arm's gone and they've taken both of her ovaries, but I like her. She makes me laugh.

Eventually Manny came in with the usual kind of heavy guy and I saw that this time Manny looked worse than ever. He took a long time walking around, until the guy with him started shouting, and then in the end he found Jenny 2, and pointed at her.

Jenny 2 was one of Manny's favourites. Her and Sue and me, we were the ones he could talk to. The man took Jenny out and Manny watched him go. When the door was shut he sat down and started to cry.

The real Jenny was in a hotel fire. All her skin was gone. Jenny 2 wasn't going to be coming back.

We sat with Manny, and waited, and then suddenly he stood up. He grabbed Sue by the hand and told me to follow and he took us to his quarters and gave me the clothes I'm wearing now. He gave us some money, and told us where to go. I think somehow he knew what was going to happen. Either that, or he just couldn't take it any more.

We'd hardly got our clothes on when all hell broke loose. We hid when the men came to find Manny, and we heard what happened.

Jenny 2 had spoken. They don't use drugs or anaesthetic, except when the shock of the operation will actually kill the spare. Obviously. Why bother? Jenny 2 was in a terminal operation, so she was awake. When the guy stood over her, smiling as he was about to take the first slice out of her face, she couldn't help herself, and I don't blame her.

'Please,' she said. 'Please don't.'

Three words. It isn't much. It isn't so fucking much. But it was enough. She shouldn't have been able to say anything at all.

Manny got in the way as they tried to open the tunnels and so they shot him and went in anyway. We ran then, so I don't know what they did. I shouldn't think they killed them, because most had lots of parts left. Cut out bits of their brain, probably, to make sure they were all tunnel people.

We ran, and we walked and we finally made the city. I said goodbye to Sue at the subway, because she was going home on foot. I've got further to go, and they'll be looking for us, so we had to split up. We knew it made sense, and I don't know about love, but I'd lose both of my hands to have her with me now.

Time's running out for both of us, but I don't care. Manny got addresses for us, so we know where to go. Sue thinks we'll be able to take their places. I don't, but I couldn't tell her. We would give ourselves away too soon, because we just don't know enough. We wouldn't have a chance. It was always just a dream, really, something to talk about.

But one thing I am going to do. I'm going to meet him. I'm going to find Jack's house, and walk up to his door, and I'm going to look at him face to face.

And before they come and find me, I'm going to take a few things back.

The Munchies

When he'd found the ashtray, Nick gathered his thoughts and had another go. Howard watched him like a hawk—a hawk, at least, that looked like it was either about to fall asleep or be sick—and waited for him to speak.

'Imagine, right, that you're sitting in the middle of this huge drum. A huge drum that goes all around you.'

'A drum?'

'Yeah, made out of wood.'

'Like a bongo?'

'No, not like a fucking bongo. Not a drumming drum. Like a circular shed, made of wood.'

'Oh, right.'

'This drum is on little wheels, okay, so it can swivel round you.'

'Why?'

'Listen. Because when you're sitting in the middle, okay, your head's clamped so you can only look straight ahead, so you only see a tiny section of the drum.' Pleased with having pulled off so complex a sentence, Nick beamed at Howard, who was staring at him owlishly. 'Right?'

'Right,' Howard replied, and giggled briefly.

'But imagine, then, right, imagine someone jigs the drum round, just a little bit. Then you'd see another section, wouldn't you? Right next to the original one. Not a huge difference maybe, but very slightly different.'

'Ri-ight...'

'The point is...' Nick flailed, trying to remember what the point was, 'the point is...Christ.'

He reached out for his glass, suddenly desperate to irrigate his mouth. Unfortunately the movement shifted his centre of balance fractionally too far to the right, and he keeled slowly over until he was lying on his side with his legs still crossed. This wasn't a problem: the Jack Daniels and

Diet Coke was still within reach.

He took a long pull, and then coughed alarmingly. 'Jesus fucking Christ,' he said, reproachfully.

'Yeah,' Howard sighed sympathetically. Then, after a long pause: 'What?'

'This drink. Put any Coke in it, did you?'

Howard gave it some thought. 'Yeah,' he said, frowning with concentration. 'I think so, anyway.'

Nick looked at him dubiously, and then laboriously pushed himself back into an upright position. 'What was I talking about?'

'Fucked if I know.'

'It was really interesting.' Nick dredged the murky river of his thoughts, trying to find the train of thought he'd fumbled and dropped. 'It was ...'

In the meantime Howard reached out and picked up the cigarettes, finding them comparatively easily. They were right in front of his face, of course, but by this stage in the evening no action was a straightforward undertaking. With his jeans, denim shirt and his long blond hair Howard looked amazingly like Gary out of 'thirtysomething', and Nick considered telling him this, but then recalled that Howard hadn't watched the show and wouldn't know what the hell he was talking about. He also thought he'd probably tried to tell him at least once before, possibly that very evening. Maybe even within the last five minutes.

Then a little light went on in his head. 'Remembered it.'

Howard pulled two cigarettes out of the packet and lobbed one in Nick's direction. Once they were lit, he rested his weight on one elbow and looked at Nick, brow knitted.

'Okay,' he said, with the air of a man steeling himself for an difficult and dangerous mission, one likely to leave him dead or at the very least seriously wounded. 'I'm really going to try to understand this time.'

'Right,' said Nick, nodding vigorously. 'Right. Oh fuck.'

'What?'

'I've forgotten what it was.'

Howard fell forward onto the carpet. 'You bastard,' he wailed. 'You *bastard*.'

Nick started laughing. After a second or so it became obvious that he wasn't going to stop for a while, so he put his glass down. He didn't want to spill Coke all over the carpet.

'I was *there*,' Howard spluttered, 'I was fucking there. I was giving it all I had. And you blew me out.' Racked with silent laughter, Nick toppled sideways again. 'I thought finally, *finally*, I'm going to understand what the twat's banging on about.'

'It was really interesting,' Nick coughed.

'Well I'll never fucking *know*, will I.'

As suddenly as it had started, the laughing jag passed off, leaving the two of them feeling warm and tired. That, and very, very stoned.

'Well,' Nick said briskly, 'I think it's about time we had another joint, frankly.'

Howard peered at him through the smoke and dark hazy light. 'You'd be mad,' he said. 'And don't call me Frankie.'

'It's your turn.'

'Is it fuck.'

'It *is*.'

'Isn't. Who rolled the last one?'

'I did.'

'Exactly. So…oh fuck. It is my turn then.'

Nick suddenly stood upright. Howard stared up at him from his semi-recumbent position.

'Jesus,' he said, with genuine respect, 'How did you do that?'

'I'm going to pour some more drinks.' Colliding with both the sofa and the armchair, Nick negotiated the tricky three yards to the kitchen area.

'That's a disastrous idea,' Howard said comfortably, content in the knowledge that he was right, and that Nick would pour another drink anyway, and that he'd drink it.

'Yeah,' Nick agreed cheerfully, trying to find the fridge.

Howard hauled himself up onto his knees, and used the mantelpiece in a valiant effort to reach an upright position. It took a couple of tries, but he made it in the end.

'Okay,' he said, 'Okay. But I have to piss first, or I'm going to *die*.'

While he was gone, Nick pulled the fridge open and got out some ice. Most of this made it into their glasses. He splashed in a ridiculous amount of Scotch, and added half an inch of Diet Coke.

'This,' he muttered quietly to himself, '*this* will sort us out.'

When he was sitting cross-legged on the carpet once more he lit another cigarette to keep him going, fumbled a jumbo-sized cigarette paper from the packet, and laid it out. Once a cigarette's worth of tobacco lay in a neatish line across the paper, he warmed the lump and crumbled dope in.

He continued to do this for quite some time.

When Howard wandered as if by accident back into the living room, Nick pushed the half-finished joint towards him. Howard looked at it benignly.

'Sir,' he said, 'you're a gentleman. Jesus. There's a *lot* of dope in there.'

The joint was an absolute bomber. The first drag left Nick feeling as if someone had poured warm sand into his head, sand that jumped and fizzed with sluggish electricity. It also took him instantaneously from being merely very stoned to being *stupendously* stoned, cataclysmically stoned, outlandishly stoned.

'That,' he squeaked, 'is a *joint*.'

He watched as Howard took an injudiciously deep drag, and then cackled manically as his friend helplessly thumped the floor, eyes tightly shut, making a noise like a puzzled elephant.

For a second he had a sudden burst of clarity, saw the two of them beached like two dissolute whales on his living room floor, pissed and stoned and enjoying each other's company as they'd done so many times before. Old friendship, he thought, knowing someone very well: that's worth having.

Then his mind went runny again, and he stood up quickly.

'Don't *do* that,' Howard groaned. 'It's very eerie.'

'Munchies,' Nick explained, trying to find the kitchen.

'Fuck, yeah!' Howard exclaimed, sudden much-cheered. 'Food. Fucking tremendous idea.'

Nick rooted through the cupboards and came back with a large bag of pickled onion flavoured crisps, bearing it in front of him as if it was the Holy Grail.

'Oh wow,' said Howard, 'Top quality munchies.' The bag wrenched open, they both took one of the huge crisps and dropped them into their mouths.

After a minute of beatific crunching, Nick nodded slowly. 'You know,' he said with ponderous seriousness, 'there are some nice crisps about.'

It took them about five minutes to stop laughing at that. Then Howard took a pull of his spectacularly strong drink, leapt up and reeled round the room for another couple of minutes, swearing wildly.

Nick remembered suddenly that the joint was still alight, and lunged for the ashtray. 'D'you wantny more of this?'

'*Bastard*,' Howard shouted quietly, and then blinked. 'Er, no.'

Leaning over the ashtray so none of the specks of tobacco could fall out and burn the rented carpet of his rented flat, Nick sucked a last blow out of the joint.

Ten seconds later he opened his eyes again. There were three different Howards lying on the carpet in front of him, and he had no reliable way of telling which was which.

'Fuck,' he said. 'Jesus.' He let the smoke pour out of him. The last drag had been just about one hundred percent dope, and the smoke was as thick as water.

Suddenly he needed to go to the bathroom.

As he stood weaving in front of the toilet, trying to remember which muscles you had to relax when you wanted to piss, he glanced blearily out of the window. Dark.

Then, just as his bladder joyfully recalled its role in such situations, the thought he'd been trying to express earlier flew across Nick's mind like a bright dart. He peered after it. Something about a huge drum. All around you. You could only stare straight ahead, so you always saw the same vertical sliver of the drum. Then somehow the drum moved fractionally, and you saw the next sliver along instead.

What the fuck was that all about?

Realising both that he'd finished urinating and that his head was now resting against the cool tiles of the bathroom wall, Nick flushed the toilet on the third attempt and staggered out through the bedroom. Head down, he trudged into the living room and sat heavily back down on the carpet, rubbing his eyes.

When he opened them again he saw Howard's hands, and was flabbergasted to see that he was rolling another joint.

'You have *got* to be joking,' he said. 'We need another joint like a fish needs a bison.'

'Go for it. You know it makes sense.'

Nick raised his head to gaze blearily across the yard of treacly air. Then his mouth dropped open.

Howard was wearing a red sweatshirt.

Still staring, Nick put his hand out and found the cigarettes. The sweatshirt looked okay, but that wasn't the point. Leaning forward slightly, he peered at the garment.

'Howard,' he said, and then ground to a halt. He looked round the room, trying to see if Howard had brought a bag with him. He didn't think he'd turned up with one. So where the fuck had the sweatshirt come from?

'What? Oh, bugger.' Howards looked up briefly, then set about reconstructing the joint he'd dropped.

Nick almost backed off, but knew he couldn't. The question had to be asked. 'Weren't you wearing a blue shirt earlier?'

'When?'

'Earlier. Before I went for a wazz.'

Howard frowned bemusedly. 'What?'

Michael Marshall Smith

Nick took a gulp from his drink, lit a cigarette. He didn't own a red sweatshirt, so Howard couldn't have borrowed it while he was in the bathroom. He could now remember the image of Howard walking into the flat before they went down to the pub. He'd been empty-handed. No bag. 'You were wearing a denim shirt earlier.'

'What the fuck are you talking about?'

Nick suddenly felt less bothered. He thought that Howard had been wearing a shirt earlier, but he couldn't have been. Clearly he was wearing a red sweatshirt.

'Never mind,' he said. 'So. Are you ever going to finish rolling that, or what?'

'Fuck off,' Howard growled good-naturedly, and reached for the lighter.

This one was even worse. Reeling from a drag that had left his mind feeling as if someone was stirring it with a warm finger, Nick sat up straight and coughed violently. Then, for the briefest of instants, it felt as if a cold sharp knife had passed through his head, a knife in the shape of a dart. He shook his head and opened his eyes. 'Wah,' he said. 'Wah.'

'Yeah.'

Mouth suddenly arid again, Nick filled it with drink. Then he grimaced, and stared at his glass. 'What's this shit?'

'What's what shit?'

'This. Drink. What drinking we are. Christ, I mean what are we drinking?'

'Napalm. Cheeky little vintage, isn't it?'

Nick turned and looked up at the counter in the kitchen. He could see the bottles clearly. One was of Southern Comfort. The other was plastic, and held a red liquid which the label proclaimed to be Cherryade. That was very wrong.

'Where the fuck did they come from?'

'A shop,' said Howard, and collapsed sideways, braying laughter. Nick stared at him. They'd been drinking Jack Daniels and Diet Coke, surely. The old JD and DC. It was traditional.

He looked at Howard's glass, and saw that the liquid in it was the same colour as his.

He twisted round and looked behind the armchair. It was also traditional that as soon as they got back from the pub he would mix a spare drink and secrete it behind the chair. That way they had one in reserve for when they were too stoned to make it as far as the kitchen, but not quite stoned enough to be unconscious. Their bodies were indeed temples.

THE MUNCHIES

'In a shop,' gasped Howard to himself, and then he was off again, curled up in a foetal ball and quaking.

The liquid in the reserve glass was red too. Cherryade red.

But that wasn't surprising. They were drinking the old SC & C. Same as ever. Why should he have thought they were drinking Jack Daniels? And why would the thought have made him feel afraid? Weird. He shook his head and reached for the joint.

Weird. Like some drum.

'Shop,' said Howard, sitting up and wiping his eyes. 'Shop.'

Nick grinned and took a drag, feeling the hot smoke flooding his lungs. This pull was milder than the last, and he shut his eyes and held the smoke down, feeling it filter up through his neck into his head. Why was it like a drum?

Then again there was a feeling like light glinting off steel, and Nick's eyes flew open.

The room seemed slightly lighter than he remembered it. Howard waved at him and he absently handed the joint over as the skin on the back of his neck began to crawl.

The carpet was green before, he thought, feeling his eyes prick as a kind of awful fear began to run wild in him. It was green. Now it was beige, and it looked right with the sofa, which was cream. Not blue. Not blue as it had been earlier.

The room seemed lighter because all the furnishings were different. They were all lighter. But that wasn't all.

There was an extra window.

Nick screwed his eyes tightly shut. He opened them again and stared wildly round. This was all wrong. This was different.

Howard shifted comfortably on the floor, curling up propped on one elbow. He offered the joint but Nick shook his head. The stuff in his head rocked with the movement, slopping like liquid in a jar that wasn't quite full.

Suddenly Howard giggled. 'Like a drum, you say. Just a little jig. A different sliver.'

Nick stared at him. He hadn't said that. He'd only thought of the word 'sliver' when he was in the bathroom. Hadn't he?

The room was lighter mainly because a streetlight shone through the new window. Nick turned to look at it, suddenly unconcerned. Now he thought about it, it had always been there. There had always been that many stars, and the twin moons.

He laughed. Howard smiled. He seemed very close by, very much there. The red sweatshirt suited him. Nick had been wrong to take the piss when he'd turned up in it. As he'd said, it matched the drink. It matched the old SC & C.

Nick tried to get up, suddenly sure that he was going to be sick, but he couldn't move. The feeling in his stomach intensified, swelled, and changed. It spiralled up like smoke towards his head and soaked into his bones, and then he recognised it.

It wasn't sickness. It was hunger. Not again, surely.

Head whirling, he reached out for the joint, his hand brushing Howard's at the ashtray. He could feel there wasn't much time, so he scrabbled for the joint, wanting to drown the feeling, coat it in that lacquered smoke. But he didn't get to it quickly enough, and blackness closed in like a door slamming shut, and he felt the faint jig again, felt rather than saw the flash of metallic light.

When he opened his eyes the room felt different, but it looked the same. Puzzled, he moved his eyes fractionally to either side. Nothing had changed this time.

It was the same sliver. Nothing changed. He smiled, feeling luxuriously warm and comfortable. His mind was sharper too, and he felt fine. Really good, in fact.

This time it wasn't anything outside which had altered.

He looked up and smiled at Howard. He could hear the beating of the man's heart, sense the slippery squeeze as the muscle fibres in the arm in that red sleeve moved against each other, smell the bright blood that ran through his arteries.

He couldn't understand how it hadn't happened before, why this should feel like a revelation.

God, smell that meat. And so close.

Nick pulled himself up and ran his tongue over his teeth. He looked up from Howard's arm for a brief moment, and smiled at his friend. Then he leant towards it, feeling his mouth fill with saliva, and hearing his stomach growl. He had the munchies again, which was bad news.

Bad news for Howard, anyway.

Always

Jennifer stood, watching the steady drizzle, underneath the awning in front of the station entrance. She waited for the cab to arrive with something that was not quite impatience: there was no real hurry, though she wanted to be with her father. It was just that the minutes were filled to bursting with an awful weight of unavoidable fact, and if she had to spend them anywhere, she would rather it were not under an awning, waiting for a cab.

The train journey down from Manchester had been worse, far worse. Then she had felt a desperate unhappiness, a wild hatred of the journey and its slowness. She'd wanted to jig herself back and forwards on her seat like a child, to push the train faster down the tracks. The black outside the window had seemed very black, and she'd seen every streak of rain across the window. She'd stared out of it for most of the journey, her face sometimes slack with misery, sometimes rigid with the effort of not crying, of keeping her hands and body from twitching with horror. The harder she stared at the dark hedges in shadow fields, the further she tried to see, the closer the things she saw.

She saw her mother, standing at the door of the house, wrapped in a cardigan and smiling, happy to see her home. She saw the food parcels she'd prepared for Jennifer whenever she visited, bags of staple foods mixed with nuggets of gold, little things that only she'd known that Jennifer liked. She saw her decorating the Christmas tree by herself in happy absorption, saw her in her chair by the fire, regal and round, talking nonsense to the utterly contented cat spread-eagled across her lap.

She tried to see, tried to understand, the fact that her mother was dead.

After her father had phoned she'd moved quickly through the house, throwing things in a bag, locking up, driving with heavy care to the station. Then there had been things to do. Now there was nothing. Now was the beginning of a time when there was nothing to do, no way to escape, no means of undoing. In an instant the world had changed, had switched from a home to a cold hard country where there was nothing but rain and minutes that stretched like railway tracks into the darkness.

At Crewe a man got on and sat opposite. He had tried to talk to her: to comfort her or to take advantage of her distress, it didn't matter which. She stared at him for a moment, lit another cigarette and looked back out of the window. She judged all men by her father. If she could imagine them getting on with him, they were alright. If not, they didn't exist.

She tried to picture her father, alone in the house. How big it must feel, how hollow, how much like a foreign place, as the last of her mother's breaths dissipated in the air. Would he know which molecules had been inside her, cooling as they mixed? Knowing him, he might. When he'd called, the first thing, the *only* thing she could think was that she had to be near him, and as she waited out the minutes she tried to reach out with her mind, tried to picture him alone in a house where the woman he'd loved for thirty years had sat down to read a book by the fire and died of a brain hemorrhage while he made her a cup of tea.

As long as she could remember there had been few family friends. No need for them. Her parents had been a world on their own, and had no need for anyone else. So different, and yet the same person, moving forever in a slow comfortable symmetry. Her mother had been home, her father the magic that lit up the windows, her mother had been love, her father the spell that kept out the cold. She knew now why as the years went on her love for her parents had begun to stab her with something that was like cold terror: because some day she would be alone. Some day she would be taken in the night from the world she knew and abandoned in a place where there was no-one to call out to.

And now, as she stood waiting for a cab in the town where she'd grown up, she numbly watched the drizzle as it fell on the distant shore of a far country on a planet the other side of the universe. The trees by the station road called out to her, pressing their twisted familiarity upon her, but her mind balked, refused to acknowledge them. This wasn't any world she knew.

In three weeks it would be Christmas, and her mother was dead.

The cab arrived, and the driver tried to talk to her. She answered his questions brightly.

At the top of the drive she stood for a long moment, her throat spasming. Everything was different. All the trees, all the pots of plants her mother had tended, all the stones on the drive had moved a millimetre. The tiles had shifted infinitesimally on the roof, the paint had faded a millionth of a shade. She had come home, but home wasn't there anymore.

Then the front door opened spreading a patch of warmth onto the drive, and she fled into the arms of her father.

For a long time she hung there, cradled in his warmth. He was comfort, an end to suffering. It had been him who had talked her through her first boyfriend's abrupt departure, him who had held her hand after childish nightmares, him who had come to her when as a baby she had cried out in the night. Her mother had been everything for her in this world, but her father the one who stood between Jennifer and worlds outside, in the way of any hurt.

After a while she looked up, and saw the living room door. It was shut, and it was then that finally she broke down.

Sitting in the kitchen in worn-out misery, she clutched the cup of tea her father had made, too numb to flinch from the pain that stabbed from every corner of her mother's kitchen. On the side was a jar of mincemeat, and a bag of flour. They would not be used. She tried to deflect her gaze, to find something to focus on, but every single thing spoke of her mother: everything was something she wouldn't use again, something she'd liked, something that looked strange and forlorn without her mother holding it. All the objects looked random and meaningless without her mother to provide the context they made sense in, and she knew that if she could look at herself she would look the same. Her mother could never take her hand again, would never see her married or have children. And she would have been such a fantastic grandmother, the kind you only find in children's books.

On the kitchen table were some sheets of wrapping paper, and for a moment that made her smile wanly. It had always been her father that bought the wrapping paper, and in years of looking Jennifer had never been able to find paper that was anywhere near as beautiful. Marbled swirls of browns and golds, of greens and reds, muted bursts of life that had lain curled beneath the Christmas tree like an advert for the whole idea of colour. The paper on the table was as nice as ever, some a warm russet, the rest a pale sea of shifting blue.

Every year, on Christmas morning, as she sat at her customary end of the sofa to begin unwrapping her presents, Jennifer had felt a warm thrill of wonder. She could remember as a young girl looking at the perfect oblongs of her presents and knowing that she was seeing magic at work. For her father would wrap the presents, and there were never any joins.

Michael Marshall Smith

She would hold the presents up, look at them every way she could, and still not find any Sellotape, or edges of paper. However difficult the shape, it was as if the paper had formed itself round it like a second skin.

One evening every Christmas her father would disappear to do his wrapping: she had never seen him do it, and neither, she knew, had Mum. In more recent years Jennifer had found the joins, cleverly tucked and positioned so as almost to disappear, but that hadn't undone the magic. Indeed, in her heart of hearts she believed that her father had done it deliberately, let her see the joins because she was too old now for a world where there could be none.

She could remember once, when she'd been a very little girl, asking her mother how daddy did it. Her mother had told her that Dad's wrapping was his art, that when the King of the Fairies needed his presents wrapped he sent for her father to do it, and he went far off to a magic land to wrap his presents, and while he was away, he did theirs too. Her mother had said it with a smile in her eyes, to show she was joking, but also with a small frown on her forehead, as if she wasn't sure if she was.

As Jennifer sat staring at the paper her father came back in. He seemed composed but a little shocked, as if he'd seen the neighbours dancing naked in their garden. He took her hand and they sat for a while, two of them where three should be.

And for a long time they talked, and remembered her. Already time seemed short, and Jennifer tried to remember everything she could, to mention every little thing, to write them in her mind so that they would still be there in the morning. Her father helped her, mixing in his own memories, as she scrabbled and clutched, desperate to gather all the fallen leaves before the wind blew them away.

Looking up at the clock as she made another cup of tea she saw that it was four o'clock, that it would soon be tomorrow, the day after her mother had died, and suddenly she slumped over, crying with the kettle in her hand. Because the day after that would be the day after that day, the week after the week after, next year the anniversary. It would never end. From now on all time was after time: no undoing, no last moment to snatch. There would be so many days, and so many hours, and no matter how many times the phone rang, it would never be her mother.

Seeing her, her father stood up and came to her. As she laid her head on his shoulder he finished making the tea, and then he tilted her head up to look at him. He looked at her for a long time, and she knew that he, and nobody else, could see inside her and know what she felt.

'Come on,' he said.

ALWAYS

She watched as he walked to the table and picked up some of the wrapping paper.

'I'm going to show you a secret.'

'Will it help?' Susan felt like a little child, watching the big man, her father.

'It might.'

They stood for a moment outside the living room door. He didn't hurry her, but let her ready herself. She knew that she had to see her mother, couldn't just let her fade away behind a closed door. Finally she looked up at him, and he opened the door.

The room she walked into seemed huge, cavernous. Once cosy, the heart of the house, now it stretched like a black plain far out into the rain, the corners cold and dark. The dying fire flickered against the shadows, and as she stepped towards it Jennifer felt the room grow around her, bare and empty as the last inaudible echoes of her mother's life died away.

'Oh mum,' she said, 'oh mum.'

Sitting in her chair by the fire she could almost have been asleep. She looked old, and tired, but comfortably warm, and it seemed that the chair where she sat was the centre of the world. Jennifer reached out and touched her hand. Kissed by the embers of the fire, it was still warm, could still have reached out and touched her. Her father shut the door, closing the three of them in together, and Jennifer sat down by the fire, looking up at her mother's face. What had been between the lines was gone, but the lines were still there, and she looked at every one.

She looked up to see that her father had spread three sheets of the pink wrapping paper on the big table. He came and crouched down beside her and they held Mum's hand together, and Jennifer's heart ached to imagine what his life would be like without her, without his Queen. Together they kissed her hand, and said goodbye as best they could, but you can't say goodbye when you're never going to see someone again. It isn't possible. That's not what Goodbye means.

Her father stood, and with infinite tenderness picked his wife up in his arms. For a moment he cradled her, a groom on his wedding day holding the slender wand of his love at the beginning of their life together. Then slowly he bent, and to Jennifer's astonishment he laid her mother out on the wrapping paper.

'Dad...'

'Shh,' he said.

He picked up another couple of sheets of paper and laid them on top

321

of her. His hands made a small folding movement where they joined, and suddenly there was only one long piece of wrapping paper. Jennifer's mouth dropped open like a child's.

'Dad, how ...'

'Shh,'

He took the end of the sheet lying under her mother, and folded it over the top. Slowly he worked his way around the table, folding upwards with little movements of his hands. Like two gentle birds they slowly wove round each other, folding and smoothing. Jennifer watched silently, cradling her tea, at last seeing her father do his wrapping, and as he moved round the table the two sheets of paper were knitted together as if it were the way they'd always been.

After about fifteen minutes he paused, and she stepped closer to look. Only her mother's face was visible, peeking out of the top. It could have looked absurd, but it was her mother, and it didn't. The rest of her body was enveloped in a pink paper shroud that seamlessly held her close. Her father bent and kissed his wife briefly on the lips, and she bent too, and kissed her mother's forehead. Then he made another folding movement, brought the last edge of paper over and smoothed, and suddenly there was no gap, no join, just a large irregular paper parcel perfectly wrapped.

Then her father moved and stood halfway down the table. He slid his arm under his wife's back, and gently brought it upwards. The paper creaked softly as he raised her body into a sitting position, and then further, until it was bent double. He made a few more smoothing motions and all Jennifer could do was stare, eyes wide. On the table was still a perfect parcel, but half as long. He slid his hand under again, and folded it in half again, then moved round, and folded it the other way, gentle and unhurried. For ten minutes he folded and smoothed, tucked and folded, and the parcel grew smaller and smaller, until it was two feet square, two feet by one, six inches by nine. Then his concentration deepened still further, and as he folded he seemed to take especial care with the way the paper moved, and out of the irregular shape emerged corners and edges. And still the parcel grew smaller and smaller.

When finally he straightened there was on the table a tiny oblong, not much bigger than a matchbox, a perfect pink parcel. Jennifer moved closer to watch as he pulled a length of russet ribbon from his pocket, and painted a line first one way round, then the other to meet at the top. As he tied the bow she looked closely at the parcel and knew she'd been right all along, that she'd seen the truth as a child. There were no joins, none at all.

When he had finished her father held the little shape in his hands and looked at her, his face tired but composed. He reached out and touched her face, his fingers as warm as they'd always been, and in their touch was a blessing, a persistence of love. All the time she'd been on this planet they had been always there, her father and mother, someone to do the good things for, and to help the bad things go away.

'I can only give you one present this year,' he said, 'and it's something you've already got. This is only a reminder.'

He held up the parcel to her, and she took it. It felt warm and comforting, all her childhood, all her mother's love in a small oblong box. She felt she knew what she should do, and brought the present in close to her, and pressed it against her heart. As she shed her final tears her father held her close and wished her Happy Christmas, and when she took her hand away, the present was gone from her hand, and beat inside her.

The journey back to Manchester passed in a haze of recollection, and when she was back in her flat she walked slowly around it, touching objects in the slanting haze of early morning light. She wished she could be with her father, but knew he was right to tell her to go back. As she sat in the hallway she listened to the beating of her heart, and as she looked at reminders of Mum she let herself feel glad. It would take time, but it was something she already had: she had her mother deep inside her, what she'd been, the love she'd given and felt. She was her mother's pride and joy, and while she still lived her mother lived too: her finest and favourite work, the living sum of her love and happiness. There would be no good-byes, because she could never really lose her. She could never speak to her again in words, but she would always hear her voice. She would always be inside her, helping her face the world, helping her to be herself.

And Jennifer thought about her father, and knew her heart would soon be fuller still. She knew it would not be many days before another parcel was delivered to her door, and that it too would be perfectly wrapped, its paper a pale sea of shifting blue.

Not Waving

Sometimes when we're in a car, driving along country roads in Autumn, I see sparse poppies splashed in amongst the grasses and it makes me want to cut my throat and let the blood spill out of the window to make more poppies, many more, until the roadside is a blaze of red.

Instead I just watch the road. In a while the poppies will be behind us, as they always are.

On the morning of October 10th I was in a state of high excitement. I was at home, and I was supposed to be working. What I was doing, however, was sitting thrumming at my desk, leaping to my feet whenever I heard the sound of traffic outside the window. I was also peeking at the two large cardboard boxes that were sitting in the middle of the floor. These contained, respectively, a new computer and a new monitor. After a year of denying my inbuilt technophile need to own the brightest and best in silicon-based goodies, I'd finally succumbed and upgraded my computer. Credit card in hand, I'd picked up the phone and ordered myself a piece of science fiction, in the shape of a machine which not only went like a train but also had built-in telecommunications and speech recognition. The future was finally here, and sitting on my living room floor.

However.

While I had £3000 worth of Macintosh and monitor, what I didn't have was the £15 cable that connected the two together. The manufacturer, it transpired, felt it constituted an optional extra—despite the fact that without it the two system components were little more than bulky white ornaments of a particularly tantalizing and frustrating kind. The cable had to be ordered separately, and there weren't any in the country at the moment. They were all in Belgium.

Michael Marshall Smith

I was only told this a week after I ordered the system, and I endeavoured to make my feelings on the matter clear to my supplier during the further week in which they playfully promised to deliver the system first on one day, then another, all such promises evaporating like the morning dew. The two boxes had finally made it to my door the day before, and, by a bizarre coincidence, the cable had today crawled tired and overwrought into the supplier's warehouse. My contact at Calldriven Direct knew just how firmly one of those cables had my name on it, and had phoned to grudgingly admit they were available. I'd immediately called my courier firm, which I occasionally used to send design roughs to clients. Calldriven had offered to put it in the post, but I somehow sensed that they wouldn't quite get around to it *today*, and I'd waited long enough. The bike firm I used specializes in riders who look as if they've been chucked out of the Hell's Angels for being unruly. A large man in leathers turning up in Calldriven's offices, with instructions not to leave without my cable, was just the sort of incentive I felt they needed—and so I was waiting, drinking endless cups of coffee, for such a person to arrive at the flat brandishing said component above his head in triumph.

When the buzzer finally went I nearly fell off my chair. Without bothering to check whom it was I left the flat and pounded down the house stairs to the front door, swinging it open with, I suspect, a look of near-lust upon my face. I get a lot of pleasure out of technology. It's a bit sad, I realise that—God knows Nancy has told me so often enough—but hell, it's my life. Each to their own.

An expanse of black leather was standing outside, topped with a shining black helmet. The biker was a lot slighter than their usual type, but quite tall. Tall enough to have done the job, evidently.

'Bloody marvelous,' I said. 'Is that a cable?'

'Sure is,' the biker said, indistinctly. A hand raised the visor on the helmet, and I saw with some surprise that there was a woman inside. 'They didn't seem too keen to let it go.'

'I'll bet'. I laughed and took the package from her. Sure enough, it said 'AV adapter cable' on the outside. 'You've made my day,' I said, a little hysterically, 'and I'm more than tempted to kiss you.'

'That seems rather forward,' the girl said, reaching up to her helmet. 'Cup of coffee would be nice, though. I've been driving since five this morning and my tongue feels like it's made of brick.'

Taken aback, I hesitated for a moment. I'd never had a motorcycle courier in for coffee before. I'm not sure *anyone* has. Also, it would mean a delay before I could ravage through the boxes and start connecting things up. But it was still only eleven in the morning, and another fifteen minutes wouldn't harm. I was also a little pleased at the thought of such an unusual encounter.

'You would be,' I said, with a kind of mock-Arthurian courtliness that doubtless sounds horrific but was what the moment required, 'most welcome.'

'Thank you, kind sir,' the courier said, and pulled her helmet off. A great deal of dark brown hair spilled out around her face, and as she swung her head the sun shot threads of chestnut through it. Her face was strong, with a wide mouth and vivid green eyes.

Bloody hell, I thought, the cable for a moment forgotten in my hand. Then I stood to one side to let her in.

Her name was Alice, and she stood looking at the books on the shelves as I made a couple of cups of coffee.

'Your girlfriend's in Personnel,' she said.

'How did you guess?' I said, handing her a cup.

She indicated the raft of books on Human Resource Development, Managing for Success and Stating the Bleeding Obvious in Five Minutes a Day, which take up half our shelves.

'You don't look the type. Is this it?' She pointed her mug at the two boxes on the floor.

I nodded, slightly sheepishly. 'Well,' she said, 'Aren't you going to open them?'

I glanced up at her, surprised. Her face was turned towards me, a small smile in the corners of her mouth. Her skin was the pale tawny colour which goes with rich hair, I noticed, and flawless. I shrugged, slightly embarrassed.

'I guess so,' I said, non-committally. 'I've got some work I ought to do first.'

'Rubbish,' she said firmly. 'Let's have a look.'

And so I bent down and pulled open the boxes, while she settled down on the sofa to watch. What was odd was that I didn't mind doing it. Normally when I'm doing something that's very much to do with me and the things I enjoy, I have to do it alone. Other people seldom understand the things that give you the most pleasure, and I'd rather not have them around to undermine the occasion. But Alice seemed genuinely interested, and ten minutes later I had the system sitting on the desk. In the meantime I'd babbled about voice recognition and video input, the eight gigabyte hard disk and ultra-zippy CD-ROM. She'd listened, and even asked questions, questions that followed from what I was saying rather than simply set me up to drivel on some more. It wasn't that she knew a vast amount about computers. She just understood what was exciting about them.

When the screen threw up the standard message saying all was well we looked at each other.

'You're not going to get much work done today, are you,' she said.

'Probably not,' I agreed, and she laughed.

Just then a protracted squawking noise erupted from the sofa, and I jumped. The courier rolled her eyes and reached over to pick up her unit. A voice of stunning brutality informed her that she had to pick something up from the other side of town, urgently, like five minutes ago, and why wasn't she there already, darlin'?

'Grr,' she said, like a little tiger, and reached for her helmet. 'Duty calls.'

'But I haven't told you about the telecommunications stuff yet,' I said, joking.

'Some other time,' she winked.

I saw her out, and we stood for a moment on the doorstep. I was wondering what to say. I didn't know her, would never see her again, but wanted to thank her for sharing something with me. Then I noticed one of the local cats ambling past the bottom of the steps. I love cats, but Nancy doesn't, so we don't have one. Just one of the little compromises you make, I guess. I recognised this particular hairball, and had long since given up hope of appealing to it. I made the sound universally employed for gaining cats' attention, with no result. It merely glanced wearily up at me and cruised on by.

Then Alice sat down on her heels and made the same noise. The cat stopped in its tracks and looked at her. She made the noise again and the cat turned, glanced down the street for no discernible reason, and then confidently made its way up the steps to weave in and out of her legs.

'That is truly amazing,' I said. 'He is not a friendly cat.'

She took the cat in her arms and stood up. 'Oh, I don't know,' she said. The cat sat up against her chest, looking around with the air of a monarch inspecting his kingdom and finding all was well. I reached out to rub its nose and felt the warm vibration of a purr.

The two us made a fuss of him for a few moments, and then Alice put him down. She replaced her helmet, climbed on her bike, and, with a wave, set off.

Back in the flat I tidied away the boxes, anal retentive that I am, before settling down to immerse myself in the new machine. On impulse I called Nancy, to let her know the system had finally arrived. I got one of her assistants, Trish, instead. She didn't put me on hold, merely cupped the mouthpiece, and I heard Nancy say 'Tell him I'll call him back,' in the background. I said goodbye to Trish with fairly good grace, trying not to mind.

Voice recognition software hadn't been included, it turned out, nor anything to put in the CD-ROM drive. The telecommunications functions wouldn't work without an expensive add-on, which Calldriven didn't expect for four to six weeks. Apart from that, it was great.

Nancy cooked that evening. We tended to take it in turns, though she was much better at it than me. Nancy is good at most things. She's accomplished.

There's a lot of in-fighting in the selfless world of Personnel Development, it would appear, and Nancy was in feisty form that evening, having tastily out-maneuvered some co-worker. I drank a glass of red wine and leaned against the counter while she whirled ingredients around. She told me about her day, and I listened and laughed. I didn't tell her much about mine, only that it had gone okay. Her threshold for hearing about the world of freelance graphic design is pretty low. She'd listen with relatively good grace if I really had to get something out of my system, but she didn't understand it and didn't seem to want to. No reason why she should, of course. I didn't mention the new computer sitting on my desk, and neither did she.

Dinner was very good. It was chicken, but she'd done something intriguing to it with spices. I ate as much as I could, but there was a little left. I tried to get her to finish it, but she wouldn't. I reassured her that she hadn't eaten too much, in the way that sometimes seemed to help, but her mood dipped and she didn't have any desert. I steered her towards the sofa and took the stuff out to wash up and make some coffee.

While I was standing at the sink, scrubbing the plates and thinking vaguely about the mountain of things I had to do the next day, I noticed a dark brown cat sitting on a wall across the street. I hadn't seen it before. It was crouched watching a twittering bird, with that catty concentration that combines complete attention with the sense that they might at any moment break off and wash their foot instead. The bird eventually fluttered chaotically off and the cat tracked its progress for a moment before sitting upright, as if drawing a line under that particular diversion.

Then the cat's head turned, and it looked straight at me. It was a good twenty yards away, but I could see its eyes very clearly. It kept looking, and after a while I laughed, slightly taken aback. I even turned away for a moment, but when I looked back it was still there, still looking.

Then the kettle boiled and I turned to tip water into a couple of mugs of Nescafé. When I glanced through the window on the way out of the kitchen, the cat was gone.

Nancy wasn't in the lounge when I got there, so I settled on the sofa and lit a cigarette. After about five minutes the toilet flushed upstairs, and I sighed.

A couple of days came and went, as they do, with the usual flurry of deadlines and committee re-designs. I went to a social evening at Nancy's office and spent a few hours being patronised by her power-dressed colleagues, while she sparkled in the centre. I messed up a print job and had to cover the cost of doing it again. Good things happened too, I guess, but it's the others that stick in your mind.

One afternoon the buzzer went and I wandered absent-mindedly downstairs to get the door. As I opened it there was a flick of brown hair, and saw that it was Alice.

'Hello there,' I said, strangely pleased.

'Hello yourself,' she smiled. 'Got a parcel for you.' I took it and looked at the label. Colour proofs from the repro house. Yawn. She must have been looking at my face, because she laughed. 'Nothing very exciting then?'

'Hardly.' After I'd signed the delivery note, I looked up at her. She was still smiling, I think, though it was difficult to tell. Her face looked as though it always was.

'Well,' she said, 'I can either go straight to Peckham to pick up something else really dull, or you can tell me about the telecommunications features.'

I stepped back to let her in.

'Bastards,' she said indignantly, when I told her about the things that hadn't been shipped with the machine. I told her about the telecoms stuff anyway, as we sat on the sofa and drank coffee, but not for very long. Mainly we just chatted, and when she got to the end of the road on her bike she turned and waved before disappearing around the corner.

That night Nancy went to Sainsbury's on the way home from work. I caught her eye as she unpacked the biscuits and brownies, potato chips and pastries, but she just stared back at me, and I looked away. She was having a hard time at work. Deflecting my gaze to the window, I noticed the dark cat was sitting on the wall opposite. It wasn't doing much, simply peering vaguely this way and that, watching things I couldn't see. It seemed to look up at the window for a moment, but then leapt down off the wall and wandered away down the street.

I cooked dinner and Nancy didn't eat much, but she stayed in the kitchen when I went into the living room to finish off a job. When I made our cups of tea to drink in bed I noticed that the bin had been emptied, and the rubbish bag stood, neatly tied, to one side. I nudged it with my foot and it rustled, full of empty packets. Upstairs the bathroom door was pulled shut, and the key turned in the lock.

I saw Alice a few more times during the following weeks. A couple of major jobs were reaching crisis point at the same time, and there was a semi-constant flurry of bikes coming and going from the house. On three or four of those occasions it was Alice who I saw when I opened the door.

Apart from once, when she had to turn straight around on pain of death, she always came in for a coffee. We'd chat about this and that, and when the voice recognition software finally arrived I showed her how it worked. I had a rip-off copy, from a friend who'd sourced it from the States. You had to do an impersonation of an American accent to get the machine to understand anything you said, and my attempts to do so made Alice laugh a lot. Which is curious, because it made Nancy merely sniff and ask me whether I'd put the new computer on the insurance.

Nancy was preoccupied, those couple of weeks. Her so-called boss was dumping more and more responsibility onto her, while stalwartly refusing to give her more credit or money. Nancy's world was very real to her, and she relentlessly kept me up to date on it: the doings of her boss were more familiar to me by then than the activities of most of my friends. She did manage to get her company car upgraded, however, which was a nice thing. She screeched up to the house one evening in something small and red and sporty, and hollered up to the window. I scampered down and she took us hurtling around North London, driving with her customary verve and confidence. On impulse we stopped at an Italian restaurant we sometimes went to, and they miraculously had a table. Over coffee we took each other's hands and said we loved one another, which we hadn't done for a while.

When we parked outside the house I saw the dark cat sitting under a tree on the other side of the street. I pointed it out to Nancy but she just shrugged. She went in first and as I turned to close the door I saw the cat was still sitting there, a dark shape in the half-light. I wondered who it belonged to, and wished that it was ours.

Michael Marshall Smith

*

A couple of days later I was walking down the street in the late afternoon, when I noticed a motorbike parked outside Sad Café. I seemed to have become sensitized to bikes over the previous few weeks: probably because I'd used so many couriers. 'Sad' wasn't the café's real name, but what Nancy and I used to call it, back in the times when we would stagger hung over down the road on Sunday mornings on a quest for a cooked breakfast. The first time we'd slumped over one of its Formica tables we'd been slowly surrounded by middle-aged men in zip-up jackets and beige bobble hats, a party of mentally-challenged teenagers with broken glasses, and old women on the verge of death. The pathos attack we'd suffered had nearly finished us off, and it had been dubbed the Sad Café ever since. We hadn't been there in a while: Nancy usually had work in the evenings in those days, even on weekends, and fried breakfasts appeared to be off the map again.

The bike resting outside made me glance through the window, and with a shock of recognition I saw Alice in there, sitting at a table nursing a mug of something or other. I nearly walked on, but then thought what the hell, and poked my head inside. Alice looked startled to see me, but then smiled, and I sat down and ordered a cup of tea.

She'd finished for the day, and was killing time before heading home. I was at a loose end myself: Nancy was out for the evening, entertaining clients. It was odd seeing Alice outside the flat, and this was also the first time we'd met outside working hours. Possibly it was this that made the next thing coalesce in front of us.

Before we knew how the idea had arisen, we were wheeling her bike down the road to prop it up outside the Bengal Lancer, the area's bravest stab in the direction of a decent restaurant. I loitered awkwardly to one side while she took off her leathers and packed them into the bike's carrier. She was wearing jeans and a green sweatshirt underneath, a green that matched her eyes. Then she ran her hands through her hair, said 'Close enough', and strode towards the door. Momentarily reminded of Nancy's standard hour-and-a-half preparation for going out, I followed her into the restaurant.

We took our time, and had about four courses, and by the end were absolutely stuffed. We talked of things beyond computers and design, but I can't remember what they were. We had a couple of bottles of wine, a gallon of coffee, and smoked most of two packets of cigarettes. When we were done I stood outside again, far more relaxed this time, as she climbed back into her work clothes. She waved as she rode off, and

NOT WAVING

I watched her go. Then I turned and walked for home.

It was a nice meal. It was also the big mistake.

The next time I rang for a bike to send a package, I asked for Alice by name. After that, it seemed the natural thing to do. And Alice seemed to end up doing almost all of the deliveries to me, more than you could put down to chance.

If we hadn't gone for that meal, perhaps it wouldn't have happened. Nothing was said, and no glances exchanged: I didn't note the date in my diary.

But we'd started falling in love.

The following night Nancy and I had a row, the first full-blown one in a while. We rarely argued. Nancy was a good manager.

This one was short, and also very odd. It was late and I was sitting in the lounge, trying to summon up the energy to turn on the television. I didn't have much hope for what I would find on it, but was too tired to read. I'd been listening to a CD that had run its course, and was staring at the stereo, half-mesmerized by the green and red LEDs. Nancy was working at the table in the kitchen, which was dark apart from the lamp that shed yellow light over her papers.

Suddenly she marched into the living room, already at maximum temper, and shouted incoherently at me. Shocked, I half-stood, trying to work out what she was saying. In retrospect I was probably half asleep, and her anger seemed to fill the room with its harsh intensity.

She was shouting at me for getting a cat. There was no point me denying it, because she'd seen it. She'd seen the cat under the table in the kitchen, it was in there still, and I was to go and throw it out. I knew how much she disliked cats, and anyway, how could I do it without asking her, and the whole thing was a classic example of what a selfish and hateful man I was.

It took me a while to get to the bottom of this and start denying it. I was too baffled to get angry. In the end I went with her into the kitchen, and looked under the table. She was very insistent. By then I was a little spooked, to be honest. We looked in the hallway, the bedroom and the bathroom. Then we looked in the kitchen again, and in the living room.

There was, of course, no cat.

I sat Nancy on the sofa. She was still shaking, though her anger was gone. I tried to talk to her, to work out what exactly was wrong. Her reaction was disproportionate, misdirected: I'm not sure even she knew what it was about. The cat, of course, could have been nothing more than a discarded shoe seen in near-darkness, maybe even her own foot moving. After leaving my parents' house, where there had always been a cat, I'd often startled myself by thinking I saw them in similar ways. Nancy's family had never had one, but the same principle still held. Maybe.

She didn't seem especially convinced, but did calm a little. She was so timid, and quiet, and as always I found it difficult to reconcile her as she was then with her fire-eating Corporate Woman act, the way she spent so much of the time. I turned the fire on and we sat in front of it and talked, and even discussed her eating. Nobody else knew about that part of her life. I didn't understand it, not really. I sensed that it was something to do with feelings of lack of control, of trying to shape herself and her world, but couldn't get much closer than that. There appeared to be nothing I could do except listen, but I hoped that was better than nothing.

We went to bed a little later, and made careful, gentle love. As she relaxed towards sleep, huddled in my arms, I caught myself for the first time feeling for her something that was a little like pity.

Alice and I had dinner again about a week later. This time it was less of an accident, and took place further from home. I had a late meeting in town, and by coincidence Alice would be in the area at around about the same time. I told Nancy I might end up having dinner with my client, but she didn't seem to hear. She was preoccupied, some new power struggle at work edging towards climax.

Though it was several weeks since the previous occasion, it didn't feel at all strange seeing Alice in the evening, not least because we'd talked to each other often in the meantime. She'd started having two cups of coffee, rather than one, each time she dropped something off, and had once phoned me for advice on computers.

While it didn't feel odd, I was aware of what I was doing. Meeting another woman for dinner, basically, and enjoying it. Enormously. When I talked to Alice my feelings and what I did seemed more important, as if they were a part of someone worth talking to. Part of me felt that was more important than a little economy with the truth. To be honest, I tried not to think too hard about it.

When I got home Nancy was sitting in the living room, reading. 'How was your meeting?' she asked.

'Fine,' I replied, 'Fine.'

'Good,' she said, and went back to scanning her magazine. I could have tried to make conversation, but knew it would have come out tinny and forced. In the end I went to bed and lay tightly curled on my side, wide awake.

I was just drifting off to sleep when I heard a low voice in the silence, speaking next to my ear.

'Go away,' it said. 'Go away.'

I opened my eyes, expecting I don't know what. Nancy's face, I suppose, hanging over mine. There was no-one there. I was relaxing slightly, prepared to believe it had been a fragment of a dream, when I heard her voice again, saying the same words in the same low tone.

I climbed carefully out of bed and crept towards the kitchen. Through it I could see into the living room, where Nancy was standing in front of the main window in the darkness. She was looking down at something in the street.

'Go away,' she said again, softly.

I turned quietly around and went back to bed.

A couple of weeks passed quickly. Time seemed to do that, that Autumn. I was very immersed, what with one thing and another. Each day held something that fixed my attention, and pulled me through it. I'd look up, and a week would have gone by, with me barely having noticed.

Speaking to Alice was now a regular part of most days. We talked about things that Nancy and I never touched upon, things Nancy simply didn't understand or care about. Alice read, for example. Nancy read too, in the sense that she studied memos, and reports, and genned up on the current corporate claptrap being imported from the States. She didn't read books, however, or even paragraphs. She read sentences, to asset-strip from them what she needed to do her job, find out what was on television, or hold her own on current affairs. Every piece of text was a bullet point, a step towards some bottom line.

Alice read for its own sake. She wrote, too, hence her growing interest in computers. I mentioned once that I'd written a few articles, years back, before I settled on being a barely competent graphic designer instead. She said she'd written some stories, and after regular nagging from me, diffidently gave up copies. They were vignettes about life in London and about being a motorcycle courier, a profession with its own heroes and lore. I don't know anything about fiction from a professional point of view, so I can't say how innovative or clever the pieces were or whether the TLS would have described them as 'A new synthesis of narrative dialectics'. But they held my attention, and I read them more than once, and that's good enough for me. I told her so, and she seemed pleased.

Michael Marshall Smith

We saw each other a couple of times a week. She delivered things to me, or picked them up, and sometimes I chanced by Sad Café when she was sipping a cup of tea. It all felt very low key, very friendly—though in retrospect it was a long simmer, a relationship reducing towards an ever more intense flavour.

Nancy and I got on with each other, in an occasional, space-sharing sort of way. She had her friends, and I had mine. Sometimes we saw them together, and performed as a social pair. We looked good together, like a series of stills from a lifestyle magazine. Life, if that's what it was, went on. Her eating vacillated between not good and pretty bad, and I carried on being bleakly accepting of the fact that there didn't seem much I could do to help. So much of our lives seemed geared up to perpetuating her idea of how two young people should live together, that I somehow didn't feel that I could call her bluff and point out what was lurking beneath the stones in our existence. I also didn't mention the night I'd seen her in the lounge. There didn't seem any way of tabling it for discussion.

Apart from having Alice to chat to, the other good news was the new cat in the neighbourhood. When I glanced out of the living room window it would usually be there, ambling smoothly past or hunkered down on the pavement, watching movement in the air. It had a habit of sitting in the middle of the road, daring traffic to give it any trouble, as if it knew what the road was for but was having no truck with it. The twitch of her tail seemed to say that she knew this had once been a meadow, and that as far as she was concerned, it still was.

One morning I was walking back from the corner shop, clutching some cigarettes and milk, and came upon her, perched on a wall. If you like cats there's something rather depressing about having them run away from you, so I approached cautiously. I wanted to get to at least within a yard of this one before it went shooting off into hyperspace. To my delight, it didn't move away at all. When I got up next to her she stood up, and I thought that was it, but it turned out to be just a recognition that I was there. She was happy to be stroked, and to have the fur on her head runkled, and responded with a purr so deep it was almost below the threshold of hearing. Now that I was closer I could see the chestnut gleams in the dark brown of her fur. She was a very beautiful cat.

After a couple of minutes of this I moved away, thinking I ought to get on, but the cat immediately jumped off the wall and wove in figure eights about my feet, pressing up against my calves. I find it difficult enough to walk away from a cat at the best of times. When they're being ultra-friendly it's impossible. So I bent down and tickled, and talked fond nonsense. I finally got to my door and looked back to see her, still sitting on the pavement. She was peering around as if wondering what to do next, after all that excitement. I had to fight down the impulse to wave.

I closed the door behind me, feeling for a moment very lonely, and then went back upstairs to work.

Then one Friday night Alice and I met again, and things changed.

Nancy was out at yet another work get-together, in the centre of town. Her company seemed to like running the social lives of its staff, like some evangelical church intent on infiltrating every activity of its congregation. Nancy mentioned the event in a way that made it clear that my attendance was far from mandatory, and I was quite happy to take the hint. I do my best at these things, but doubt I look as if I'm having the time of my life.

I didn't have anything else on, so I just flopped about the house for a while, reading and watching television. It was easier to relax when Nancy wasn't there, when we weren't busy being a Couple. I couldn't settle, though. I kept thinking how pleasant it would be not to feel that way, that it would be nice to want your girlfriend to be home so you could laze about together. It didn't work that way with Nancy, not any more. Getting her to consider a half-hour lie-in on one particular Saturday was a major project in itself. I probably hadn't tried very hard in a while, either. She got up, I got up. I'd been developed as a human resource.

My reading grew fitful and in the end I grabbed my coat and went for a walk down streets that were dark and cold. A few couples and solitary figures floated up and down the roads, in mid-evening transit between pubs and Indian restaurants and homes and buses. On the way elsewhere. The apparent formlessness of the activity around me, the Brownian motion of its random wandering, made me feel quietly content. Though I'd no idea where it was, I could picture the room in which Nancy and her colleagues stood, robotically passing catch-phrases and info-nuggets up and down the office hierarchy. I would much rather be here than there.

But then I felt the whole of London spread out around me, and my contentment faded. Nancy at least had somewhere to go. All I had was miles of roads in winter light, black houses leaning in towards each other. I could walk, and I could run, and in the end I would come to the edge of the city. Then there would be nothing I could do except turn around, and come back. I couldn't feel anything beyond the gates, couldn't believe anything was out there. This wasn't some yearning for the countryside, or far climes: I like London, and the great outdoors irritates me. It was more a sense that a place that should hold endless possibilities had been tamed by something, bleached out by my lack of imagination and courage, by the limits of my life.

I headed down the road towards Camden, so wrapped up in heroic melancholy that I nearly got myself run over at the junction with Prince of Wales Road. Rather shaken, I stumbled back onto the curb, dazed by a passing flash of yellow light and a blurred obscenity. Fuck that, I thought, and crossed at a different place, sending me down a different road, towards a different evening.

Camden was busy as hell, and I skirted the purposeful crowds and ended up in a back road instead. It was there that I saw Alice.

I felt my heart lurch, and I stopped in my tracks. She was just walking along the road, dressed in a long skirt and dark blouse, hands in pockets. She appeared to be alone, and wandering down the street much as I was, in a world of her own. It was too welcome a coincidence not to take advantage of, and, careful not to surprise her, I crossed the road and met her on the other side.

We spent the next three hours in a noisy, smoky pub. The only seats were very close together, crowded round one corner of a table in the centre of the room. We drank a lot, but the alcohol seemed to work in an unusual way. I didn't get drunk, but merely felt warmer and more relaxed. The reeling crowds of locals gave us ample ammunition to talk about, until we were going fast enough not to need any help at all. We just drank, and talked, and talked and drank, and the bell for last orders came as a complete surprise.

When we walked out of the pub the alcohol suddenly kicked in, and we stumbled in unison on an unexpected step, to fall together laughing and shh-ing each other. Without even discussing it we knew neither of us felt like going home, and we ended up walking down the steps to stroll by the canal instead. We walked slowly past the backs of houses and speculated what might be going on beyond the curtains; we looked up at the sky and pointed out stars; we listened to the quiet splashes of occasional ducks coming into land on the still waters. After about fifteen minutes we found a bench, and sat down for a cigarette.

When she'd put her lighter back in her pocket Alice's hand fell near mine. I was very conscious of it being there, of the smallness of the distance mine would have to travel, and I smoked left-handed so as not to move it. I wasn't forgetting myself. I still knew Nancy existed, was aware of how my life was set up. But I didn't move my hand.

Then, like a chess game of perfect simplicity and naturalness, the conversation took us there. I said that work seemed to be slackening off, after the busy period of the last couple of months.

Alice said that she hoped it didn't drop off too much.

I smiled. 'So I can continue to afford expensive computers that don't do quite what I expect?'

'No,' she said. 'So that I can keep coming to see you.'

I turned and stared at her. She looked nervous but defiant, and her hand moved the inch that put it on top of mine.

'You might as well know,' she said, 'If you don't already. There are three important things in my life. My bike, my stories, and you.'

People don't change their lives: evenings do. There are nights that have their own momentum, their own purpose and agenda. They come from nowhere and take people with them. That's why you can never understand, the next day, quite how you came to do what you did—because it wasn't you who did it. It was the evening. The universe itself comes and takes you by the hand and leads you through a revolving door after which things are never the same.

My life stopped that evening, and started up again with a second, and everything was a different colour.

We sat on the bench for another two hours, wrapped up close to each other. We admitted when we'd first thought about each other, and laughed quietly about the distance we'd kept. Alice admitted it hadn't been pure coincidence that had brought her to Camden that evening, but a faint, still hope that we might just bump into each other. She was embarrassed to admit it, but I thought it was pure magic. After weeks of denying what I felt, of simply not realising, now that I had hold of her hand I couldn't let go. It felt extraordinary to be that close to her, to be able to feel the texture of her skin on mine and her nails against my palm. People change when you get that close to them, become much more real. If you're already in love with them then they expand to fill the world.

In the end we got on to Nancy. We were bound to, sooner or later. Alice asked how I felt about her, and I tried to explain, tried to understand myself. In the end we let the topic lapse.

'It's not going to be easy,' I said, squeezing her hand. I was thinking glumly to myself that it might not happen at all. Knowing the way Nancy would react, it looked like a very high mountain to climb. Alice glanced at me, nodded, and then turned back towards the canal.

A cat was sitting there, peering out over the water. First moving myself even closer to Alice, so that strands of her hair tickled against my face, I made a noise at the cat. It turned to look at us, and then ambled over towards the bench. 'I do like a friendly cat,' I said, reaching out to stroke its head.

Alice smiled, and then made a noise of her own. I was puzzled that she wasn't looking at the cat while she made it, but then saw that another was making its way out of the shadows. This one was smaller and more lithe, and walked right up to the bench. I was still a little befuddled with drink, and when Alice turned to look in a different direction it took me a moment to catch up.

A third cat was coming down the canal walk in our direction, followed by another.

When a fifth emerged from the bushes behind our bench, I turned and stared at Alice. She was already looking at me, the smile on her lips like the first one of hers I'd seen. She laughed at the expression on my face, and then made her noise again. The cats around us sat to attention, and two more appeared from the other direction, almost trotting in their haste to join the collection. We were now so out-numbered that I felt rather beset.

When the next one appeared I had to ask. 'Alice, what's going on?'

She leaned her head against my shoulder.

'A long time ago,' she said, as if making up a story for a child, 'None of this was here. There was no canal, no streets and houses, and all around was trees, and grass.' One of the cats around the bench briefly licked one of its paws, and I saw another couple padding out of the darkness towards us. 'The big people have changed all of that. They've cut down the trees, and buried the earth, and they've even leveled the ground. There used to be a hill here, a hill that was steep on one side but gentle on the other. They've taken all that away, and made it look like this. It's not that it's so bad. It's just different. The cats still remember the way it was.'

It was a nice idea, but it couldn't be true, and it didn't explain all the cats around us. There were now about twenty, and somehow that was too many. Not for my taste, but for common sense. Where the hell were they all coming from?

'But they didn't have cats in those days,' I said, nervously. 'Not like this. This kind of cat is modern, surely. An import, or crossbreed or something.'

She shook her head. 'That's what they say,' she said, 'and that's what people think. They've always been here. It's just that people haven't always known.'

'Alice, what are you talking about?' I was beginning to get genuinely spooked by the softly milling cats. They were still coming, in ones and

NOT WAVING

twos, and now surrounded us for yards around. The canal was dark apart from soft glints of moonlight off the water, and the lines of the banks and walkway seemed somehow stark, sketched out, as if modeled on a computer screen. They'd been rendered well, and looked convincing, but something wasn't quite right about the way they sat together, as if some angle was one degree out.

'A thousand years ago cats used to come to this hill, because it was their meeting place. They would come, and discuss their business, and then they would go away. This was their place, and it still is. But they don't mind us.'

'Why?'

'Because I love you,' she said, and kissed me for the first time.

It was ten minutes before I looked up again. Only two cats were left. I pulled my arm tighter around Alice and thought how simply and unutterably happy I was.

'Was that all true?'

'It's true that I love you,' she said, and smiled. 'The rest was just a story.' She pushed her nose up against mine and nuzzled, and our heads melted into one.

At two o'clock I realised I was going to have to go home. We got up and walked slowly back to the road. I waited shivering with her for a mini-cab, and endured the driver's histrionic sighing as we said goodbye. I stood on the corner and waved until the cab was out of sight, and then walked back home.

It wasn't until I turned into our road and saw that the house lights were still on that I realised just how real the evening had been. As I walked up the steps the door opened. Nancy stood there in a dressing gown, looking angry and frightened.

'Where the hell have you *been*?' she said. I straightened my shoulders and girded myself up to lie.

I apologized. I told her I'd been out drinking with a male friend, lying calmly and with convincing determination. I didn't even feel bad about it, except in a self-serving, academic sort of way.

Some switch had finally been thrown in my mind, and as we lay beneath the duvet afterwards I realised that I wasn't in bed with my girlfriend any more. There was just someone in my bed. When Nancy rolled towards me, her body open in a way that suggested that she might not be thinking of going to sleep, I felt my chest tighten with something that felt like dread. I found a way of suggesting that I might be a bit drunk for anything other than unconsciousness, and she curled up beside me and went to sleep instead. I lay awake for an hour, feeling as if I was lying on a slab of marble in a room open to the sky.

Breakfast the next morning was a festival of leaden politeness. The kitchen seemed very bright, and noise rebounded harshly off the walls. Nancy was in a good mood, but there was nothing I could do except force tight smiles and talk much louder than usual, waiting for her to go to work.

The next ten days were both dismal and the best of my life. Alice and I managed to see each other every couple of days, occasionally for an evening but more often just for a cup of coffee. We didn't do any more than talk, and hold hands. Our kisses were brief, a sketching out of the way things could be. Bad starts will always undermine a relationship, for fear it could happen again. So we were restrained and honest with each other, and it was wonderful, but it was also difficult.

Being home was no fun at all. Nancy hadn't changed, but I had, and so I didn't know her any more. She was a stranger who was all the worse for reminding me of someone I had once loved, and of someone I had once been. The things that were the closest to the old ways were the things that made me most irritable, and I found myself avoiding anything that might promote them. Any signs of intimacy, or real friendship, in other words—the only things which make a relationship worthwhile.

Something had to be done, and it had to be done by me. The problem was gearing myself up to it. Nancy and I had been living together for four years. Most of our friends assumed we'd be engaged before long: I'd already heard a few jokes. We knew each other very well, and that does count for something. As I moved warily around Nancy during those weeks, trying not to seem too close, I was also conscious of how much we had shared together, of how affectionate a part of me still felt towards her. She was a friend, and I cared about her. I didn't want her to be hurt. I wasn't just her boyfriend. I knew some of the reasons her eating was as bad as it was, things no-one else would ever know. I'd talked it through with her, and knew how to live with it, knew how to not make her feel any worse. She needed support, and I was the only person there to give it. Ripping that away when she was already having such a bad time would be very difficult to forgive.

And so things went on, for a little while. I saw Alice when I could, but always at the end I would have to go, and we would part, and each time it felt more and more arbitrary and I found it harder to remember why I should have to leave. I grew terrified of saying her name in my sleep, or of letting something slip, and felt as if I was living my life on

NOT WAVING

stage in front of a predatory audience waiting for a mistake. I'd go out for walks in the evening and return as slowly up the road as possible, stopping to talk to the cat, stroking her for as long as she liked and walking up and down the pavement with her, doing anything to avoid going back into the house.

I spent most of the second week looking forward to the Saturday. At the beginning of the week Nancy announced she would be going on a team-building day at the weekend. She explained to me what was involved, the chasm of corporate vacuity into which she and her colleagues were cheerfully leaping. She was talking to me a lot more at the time, wanting to share her life. I tried to take in what the day's programme would be, but I couldn't really listen. All I could think about was that I was due to be driving up to Cambridge that day, to drop work off at a client's. I'd assumed that I'd be going alone. With Nancy firmly occupied somewhere else, another possibility sprang to mind.

When I saw Alice for coffee that afternoon I asked if she'd like to come. The warmth of her reply helped me through the remaining evenings of the week, and we talked about it every day on the phone. The plan was that I'd ring home early evening, when Nancy was back from her day, and say that I'd run into someone up there and wouldn't be back until late. It was a bending of our unspoken 'doing things by the book' rule, but it was unavoidable. Alice and I needed a whole afternoon and evening together, if I was ever going to be able to psych myself up to doing what had to be done.

By mid-evening on Friday I was at fever pitch. I was pacing round the house not settling at anything, so much in my own little world that it took me a while to notice that something was up with Nancy too.

She was sitting in the living room going over some papers, but kept glancing angrily out of the window as if expecting to see someone. When I rather irritably asked her about this, she denied she was doing it, and then ten minutes later I saw her do it again. I retreated to the kitchen and did something dull to a shelf that I'd been putting off for months. When Nancy stalked in to make some more coffee she saw what I was doing, and seemed genuinely touched that I'd finally got around to it. My smile of self-depreciating good nature felt as if it was stretched across the lips of a corpse.

Then she was back out in the lounge again, glaring nervously out of the window, as if fearing imminent invasion from a Martian army. It reminded me of the night I'd seen her standing by the window, and it was a little scary. She was looking very flaky that evening, and I'd run out of pity. I simply found it irritating, and hated myself for that.

343

Michael Marshall Smith

Eventually, finally, at long last, it was time for bed. Nancy went ahead and I volunteered to close windows and tidy ashtrays. It's funny how you can seem most solicitous and endearing when you don't want to be there at all.

What I actually wanted was a few moments to wrap a novel I was going to give to Alice as a present. When I heard the bathroom door shut I leapt for the filing cabinet and took out the book. I grabbed tape and paper from a drawer and started wrapping. As I folded I glanced out of the window and saw the cat sitting outside in the road, and smiled to myself. With Alice I'd be able to have a cat of my own, could work with furry company and doze with a warm bundle on my lap. The bathroom door opened again and I paused, ready for instant action. When Nancy's feet had padded safely into the bedroom I continued wrapping. When it was done I slipped the present in a drawer and took out the card I was going to give with it, already composing in my head the message for the inside.

'Mark?'

I nearly died when I heard Nancy's voice. She was striding through the kitchen towards me, and the card was still lying on my desk. I quickly yanked a sheaf of papers towards me and covered it, but only just in time. I turned to look at her, my heart beating horribly, trying to haul an expression of bland normality across my face.

'What's this?' she demanded, holding her hand up in front of me. It was dark in the room, and I couldn't see at first. Then I saw. It was a hair. A dark brown hair.

'It looks like a hair,' I said, carefully, shuffling papers on the desk.

'I know what it fucking is,' she snapped. 'It was in the bed. I wonder how it got there.'

Jesus Christ, I thought. She knows.

I stared at her with my mouth clamped shut, and wavered on the edge of telling the truth, of getting it over with. I'd thought it would happen some other, calmer, way, but you never know. Perhaps this was the pause into which I had to drop the information that I was in love with someone else.

Then, belatedly, I realised that Alice had never been in the bedroom. Even since the night of the canal she'd only ever been in the living room and the downstairs hall. Maybe the kitchen, but certainly not the bedroom.

I blinked at Nancy, confused.

'It's that bloody cat,' she shouted, instantly livid in the way that always disarmed and frightened me. 'It's been on our fucking bed.'

NOT WAVING

'What cat?'

'The cat who's always fucking outside. Your little *friend*,' she sneered violently, face almost unrecognizable. 'You've had it in here.'

'I haven't. What are you talking about?'

'Don't you deny, don't you...'

Unable to finish, Nancy simply threw herself at me and smacked me across the face. Shocked, I stumbled backwards and she whacked me across the chin, and then pummeled her fists against my chest as I struggled to grab hold of her hands. She was trying to say something but it kept breaking up into furious sobs. In the end, before I could catch her hands, she took a step backwards and stood very still. She stared at me for a moment, and then turned and walked quickly out of the room.

I spent the night on the sofa, and was awake for hours after the last long, moaning sound had floated out to me from the bedroom. I felt I couldn't go to comfort her. It may sound like selfish evasion, but the only way I could make her feel better was by lying, so in the end I stayed away.

I had plenty of time to finish writing the card to Alice, but found it difficult to remember exactly what I'd been going to say. In the end I struggled into a shallow, cramped sleep, and Nancy was already gone by the time I woke up.

I felt tired and hollow as I drove to meet Alice in the centre of town. I still didn't actually know where she lived, or even her phone number. She hadn't volunteered the information, and I could always contact her via the courier firm. I was content with that until I could enter her life without any skulking around.

I remember very clearly the way she looked, standing on the pavement and watching out for my car. She was wearing a long black woolen skirt and a thick sweater of various dark browns. Her hair was back-lit by morning light and when she smiled as I pulled over towards her I had a moment of plunging doubt. I don't have any right to be with her, I thought. I already had someone, and Alice was far and away too wonderful. But she put her arms round me, and kissed my nose, and the feeling went away.

I have never driven as slowly on a motorway as that morning with Alice. I'd put some tapes in the car, music I knew we both liked, but they never made it out of the glove compartment. They simply weren't necessary. I sat in the slow lane and pootled along at sixty miles an hour, and we talked or sat in silence, sometimes glancing across at each other and grinning.

The road cuts through several hills, and when we reached the first

345

cutting we both gasped at once. The embankment was a blaze of poppies, nodding in a gathering wind, and when we'd left them behind I turned to Alice and for the first time said I loved her. She stared at me for a long time, and in the end I had to glance away at the road. When I looked back she was looking straight ahead and smiling, her eyes shining with held-back tears.

My meeting took just under fifteen minutes—a personal record. I think my client was rather taken aback, but I didn't care. Alice and I spent the rest of the day walking around the shops, picking up books and looking at them, stopping for two cups of tea. As we came laughing out of a record store she slung her arm around my back, and very conscious of what I was doing, I put mine around her shoulders. Though she was tall it felt comfortable, and there it stayed. We fit.

By about five I was getting tense, and we pulled into another café to have more tea, and so I could make my phone call. I left Alice sitting at the table waiting to order and went to the other side of the restaurant to use the booth. As I listened to the phone ringing at the other end I willed myself to be calm, and turned my back on the room to concentrate on what I was saying.

'Hello?'

When Nancy answered I barely recognised her. Her voice was like that of a querulously frightened old woman who'd not been expecting a call. I nearly put the phone down, but she realised who it was and immediately started crying.

It took me about twenty minutes to calm her even a little. She'd left the team-building at lunchtime, claiming illness. Then she'd gone to Sainsbury's. She had eaten two Sara Lee chocolate cakes, a fudge roll, a box of cereal and four packets of biscuits. She'd gone to the bathroom, vomited, and then started again. I think she'd been sick again at least once, but I couldn't really make sense of part of what she said. It was so mixed up with abject apologies to me that the sentences became confused, and I couldn't tell whether at one moment she was talking about the night before or about the half-eaten packet of jelly she still had in her hand.

Feeling a little frightened, and completely unaware of anything outside the cubicle I was standing in, I did what I could to focus her until what she was saying made a little more sense. I gave up trying to say that no apology was needed for the previous night, and in the end just told her everything was alright. She promised to stop eating for a while and to watch television instead. I said I'd be back as soon as I could.

I loved her. There was nothing else I could do.

NOT WAVING

When the last of my change was running out I told her to take care until I got back, and slowly replaced the handset. I stared at the wood paneling in front of me and gradually became aware of the noise from the restaurant on the other side of the glass door behind me. Eventually I turned, and looked out.

Alice was sitting at the table, watching the passing throng. She looked beautiful, and strong, and about two hundred thousand miles away.

We drove back to London in silence. Most of the talking was done in the restaurant. It didn't take very long. I said I couldn't leave Nancy in her current state, and Alice nodded once, tightly, and put her cigarettes in her bag.

She said that she'd sort of known, perhaps even before we'd got to Cambridge. I got angry then, and said she couldn't have done, because I hadn't known myself. She got angry back when I said we'd still be friends, and she was right, I suppose. It was a stupid thing to say.

Awkwardly I asked if she'd be alright, and she said yes, in the sense that she'd survive. I tried to explain that was the difference, that Nancy might not be able to. She shrugged and said that was the other difference: Nancy would never have to find out. The more we talked the more my head felt it was going to explode, as if eyes would burst with the pain and run in bloody lines down my cold cheeks. In the end she grew business-like and paid the bill, and we walked slowly back to the car in silence.

Neither of us could bring ourselves to small talk on the journey, and for the most part the only sound was that of the wheels upon the road. It was dark by then, and the rain began before we'd been on the motorway for very long. When we passed through the first cut in the hillside, I felt the poppies all around us, heads battered down by the falling water. Alice turned to me.

'I did know,' she said.

'How?' I asked, trying not to cry, trying to watch what the cars around me were doing.

'When you said you loved me, you sounded so unhappy.'

I dropped her in town, on the corner where I'd picked her up. She said a few things to help me, to make me feel less bad about what I'd done. Then she walked off around the corner, and I never saw her again.

When I'd parked outside the house I sat for a moment, trying to pull myself together. Nancy would need to see me looking whole and at her disposal. I got out and locked the door, looking half-heartedly for the cat. It wasn't there.

Nancy opened the door with a shy smile, and I followed her into the kitchen. As I hugged her, and told her everything was alright, I gazed blankly over her shoulder at the room. The kitchen was immaculate, no sign left of the afternoon's festivities. The rubbish had been taken out, and something was bubbling on the stove. She'd cooked me dinner.

She didn't eat, but sat at the table with me. The chicken was okay, but not up to her usual standard. There was a lot of meat but it was tough, and for once there was a little too much spice. It tasted odd, to be honest. She noticed a look on my face and said she'd gone to a different butcher. We talked a little about her afternoon, but she was feeling much better. She seemed more interested in discussing the way her office reorganization was shaping up.

Afterwards she went through into the lounge and turned the television on, and I set about making coffee and washing up, moving woodenly around the kitchen as if on abandoned rails. As Nancy's favourite inanity boomed out from the living room I looked around for a bin bag to shovel the remains of my dinner into, but she'd evidently used them all. Sighing with a complete lack of feeling, I opened the back door and went out to put my scraps directly into the bin. There were two sacks already there, both tied with Nancy's distinctive knot. I undid the nearest and opened it up. Then, just before I pushed the bones off my plate, something in the bag caught my eye.

A patch of darkness amidst the garish wrappers of high-calorie comfort foods. An oddly-shaped piece of thick fabric, perhaps. I pulled the edge of the bag back a little further to look, and the light from the kitchen window above fell across the contents of the bag.

The darkness changed to a rich chestnut brown matted with red, and I saw it wasn't fabric at all.

We moved six months later, after we got engaged. I was glad to move. The flat never felt like home again. Sometimes I go back and stand in that street, remembering the weeks in which I stared out of the window, pointlessly watching the road. I called the courier firm, after a couple of days. I was expecting a stonewall, and knew it was unlikely they'd give an address. But they denied she'd ever worked there at all.

After a couple of years Nancy and I had our first child, and she'll be eight this November. She has a sister now. Some evenings I'll leave them with their mother, and go out for a walk. I'll walk with heavy calm through black streets beneath featureless houses, and sometimes go down to the canal. I sit on the bench and close my eyes, and sometimes I think

NOT WAVING

I can see it. Sometimes I think I can feel the way it was when a hill was there, and meetings were held in secret.

In the end I always stand up slowly, and walk the streets back to the house. The hill has gone and things have changed, and it's not like that anymore. No matter how long I sit and wait, the cats will never come.

Everybody Goes

I saw a man yesterday. I was coming back from the waste ground with Matt and Joey and we were calling Joey dumb because he'd seen this huge spider and he thought it was a Black Widow or something when it was just, like, a *spider*, and I saw the man.

We were walking down the road towards the block and laughing and I just happened to look up and there was this man down the end of the street, tall, walking up towards us. We turned off the road before he got to us, and I forgot about him.

Anyway, Matt had to go home then because his family eats early and his Mom raises hell if he isn't back in time to wash up and so I just hung out for a while with Joey and then he went home too. Nothing much happened in the evening.

This morning I got up early because we were going down to the creek for the day and it's a long walk. I made some sandwiches and put them in a bag, and I grabbed an apple and put that in too. Then I went down to knock on Matt's door.

His Mom answered and let me in. She's okay really, and quite nice-looking for a Mom, but she's kind of strict. She's the only person in the world who calls me Peter instead of Pete. Matt's room always looks like it's just been tidied, which is quite cool actually though it must be a real pain to keep up. At least you know where everything is.

We went down and got Joey. Matt seemed kind of quiet on the way down as if there was something he wanted to tell me, but he didn't. I figured that if he wanted to, sooner or later he would. That's how it is with best friends. You don't have to be always talking. The point will come round soon enough.

Joey wasn't ready so we had to hang round while he finished his breakfast. His Dad's kind of weird. He sits and reads the paper at the table and just grunts at it every now and then. I don't think I could eat breakfast with someone who did that. I think I would find it disturbing. Must be something you get into when you grow up, I guess.

Anyway, *finally* Joey was ready and we left the block. The sun was pretty hot already though it was only nine in the morning and I was glad I was only wearing a T-shirt. Matt's Mom made him wear a sweatshirt in case there was a sudden blizzard or something and I knew he was going to be pretty baked by the end of the day but you can't tell moms anything.

As we were walking away from the block towards the waste ground I looked back and I saw the man again, standing on the opposite side of the street, looking at the block. He was staring up at the top floor and then I thought he turned and looked at us, but it was difficult to tell because the sun was shining right in my eyes.

We walked and ran through the waste ground, not hanging around much because we'd been there yesterday. We checked on the fort but it was still there. Sometimes other kids come and mess it up but it was okay today.

Matt got Joey a good one with a scrunched-up leaf. He put it on the back of his hand when Joey was looking the other way and then he started staring at it and saying 'Pete...' in this really scared voice; and I saw what he was doing and pretended to be scared too and Joey bought it.

'I told you,' he says—and he's backing away—'I *told* you there was Black Widows...' and we could have kept it going but I started laughing. Joey looked confused for a second and then he just grunted as if he was reading his Dad's paper and so we jumped on him and called him Dad all afternoon.

We didn't get to the creek till nearly lunchtime, and Matt took his sweatshirt off and tied it round his waist. It's a couple miles from the block, way past the waste ground and out into the bush. It's a good creek though. It's so good we don't go there too often, like we don't want to wear it out.

You just walk along the bush, not seeing anything, and then suddenly there you are, and there's this baby canyon cut into the earth. It gets a little deeper every year, I think, except when there's no rain. Maybe it gets deeper then too, I don't know. The sides are about ten feet deep and this year there was rain so there's plenty of water at the bottom and you have to be careful climbing down because otherwise you can slip and end up in the mud.

Matt went down first. He's best at climbing, and really quick. He went down first so that if Joey slipped he might not fall all the way in. For me, if Joey slips, he slips, but Matt's good like that. Probably comes from having such a tidy room.

Joey made it down okay this time, hold the front page, and I went last.

EVERYBODY GOES

The best way to get down is to put your back to the creek, slide your feet down, and then let them go until you're hanging onto the edge of the canyon with your hands. Then you just have to scuttle. As I was lowering myself down I noticed how far you could see across the plain, looking right along about a foot up from the ground. There's nothing to see for miles, nothing but bushes and dust. I think the man was there too, off in the distance, but it was difficult to be sure and then I slipped and nearly ended up in the creek myself, which would have been a real pain and Joey would have gone on about it forever.

We walked along the creek for a while and then came to the ocean. It's not really the ocean, it's just a bit where the canyon widens out into almost a circle that's about 15 feet across. It's deeper than the rest of the creek, and the water isn't so clear, but it's really cool. When you're down there you can't see anything but this circle of sky, and you know there's nothing else for miles around. There's this old door there that we call our ship and we pull it to one side of the ocean and we all try to get on and float it to the middle. Usually it's kind of messy and I know Matt and Joey are thinking there's going to be trouble when their Moms see their clothes, but today we somehow got it right and we floated right to the middle with only a little bit of water coming up.

We played our game for a while and then we just sat there for a long time and talked and stuff. I was thinking how good it was to be there and there was a pause and then Joey tried to say something of his own like that. It didn't come out very well, but we knew what he meant so we told him to shut up and made as if we were going to push him in. Matt pretended he had a spider on his leg just by suddenly looking scared and staring and Joey laughed, and I realised that that's where jokes come from. It was our own joke, that no-one else would ever understand and that we would never forget however old we got.

Matt looked at me one time, as if he was about to say what was on his mind, but then Joey said something dumb and he didn't. We just sat there and kept talking about things and moving around so we didn't get burnt too bad. Once when I looked up at the rim of the canyon I thought maybe there was a head peeking over the side but there probably wasn't.

Joey has a watch and so we knew when it was four o'clock. Four o'clock is the latest we can leave so that Matt gets back for dinner in time. We walked back towards the waste ground, not running. The sun had tired us out and we weren't in any hurry to get back because it had been a good afternoon, and they always finish when you split up. You can't get back to them the next day, especially if you try to do the same thing again.

Michael Marshall Smith

When we got back to the street we were late and so Matt and Joey ran on ahead. I would have run with them but I saw that the man was standing down the other side of the block, and I wanted to watch him to see what he was going to do. Matt waited back a second after Joey had run and said he'd see me after dinner. Then he ran, and I just hung around for a while.

The man was looking back up at the block again, like he was looking for something. He knew I was hanging around, but he didn't come over right away, as if he was nervous. I went and sat on the wall and messed about with some stones. I wasn't in any hurry.

'Excuse me,' says this voice, and I looked up to see the man standing over me. The slanting sun was in his eyes and he was shading them with his hand. He had a nice suit on and he was younger than people's parents are, but not much. 'You live here, don't you?'

I nodded, and looked up at his face. He looked familiar.

'I used to live here too,' he said, 'When I was a kid. On the top floor.' Then he laughed, and I recognised him from the sound. 'A long time ago now. Came back after all these years to see if it had changed.'

I didn't say anything.

'Hasn't much, still looks the same.' He turned and looked again at the block, then back past me towards the waste ground. 'Guys still playing out there on the 'ground?'

'Yeah,' I said, 'It's cool. We have a fort there.'

'And the creek?'

He knew we still played there: he'd been watching. I knew what he really wanted to ask, so I just nodded. The man nodded too, as if he didn't know what to say next. Or more like he knew what he wanted to say, but didn't know how to go about it.

'My name's Tom Spivey,' he said, and then stopped. I nodded again. The man laughed, embarrassed. 'This is going to sound very weird, but...I've seen you around today, and yesterday.' He laughed again, running his hand through his hair, and then finally asked what was on his mind. 'Your name isn't Pete, by any chance?'

I looked up into his eyes, then away.

'No,' I said. 'It's Jim.'

The man looked confused for a moment, then relieved. He said a couple more things about the block, and then he went away. Back to the city, or wherever.

After dinner I saw Matt out in the back car park, behind the block. We talked about the afternoon some, so he could get warmed up, and then he told me what was on his mind.

EVERYBODY GOES

His family was moving on. His dad had got a better job somewhere else. They'd be going in a week.

We talked a little more, and then he went back inside, looking different somehow, as if he'd already gone.

I stayed out, sitting on the wall, thinking about missing people. I wasn't feeling sad, just tired. Sure I was going to miss Matt. He was my best friend. I'd missed Tom for a while, but then someone else came along. And then someone else, and someone else. There's always new people. They come, and then they go. Maybe Matt would return some day. Sometimes they do come back. But everybody goes.

Dying

'It could be anything,' Chen said.

He held the grainy hardcopy at arm's length and squinted at the irregularly shaped object in the centre. 'Christ, it could be human.'

'On the sidewalk?' Miranda tilted her head at him as she shrugged her coat on. She was excited and not bothering to hide it. 'Where were *you* brought up?'

'In the real world, rich kid. Trust me, stranger things have happened. I think it's a fake. What's with the black and white shit? No pun intended. Why not a colour jpeg? And why no mpeg?' By now he too was bundling his jacket on, enthusiasm getting the better of him.

'I don't know. That's what we've got,' I said. 'And what we're going after. Let's *move*.'

Eight minutes after the email we were out of the door. A government car was waiting outside.

The car broadcast carComm siren all the way, and other road users were automatically shunted aside. It would take only 15 minutes to make the 'port, but even that seemed far too long. That would make it nearly half an hour after the contact, an hour since the find, before we even left the country. Miranda chatted breezily with the driver, not listening to his answers. Chen emailed the jpeg through to Central and got half a division of image analysts working on it. I stared out of the window at the passing grey, drumming my hands on my knees.

Maybe this time, I thought, as always.

Maybe this time.

I can't blame Chen for going on the way he does. I'm just as bad. Pessimism is a defense, a protection against the certainty that after a flurry of excitement we'll be coming home empty handed. Again. As the years go by, and even the hoaxes get fewer and farther between, it's hard to keep the flame burning. Miranda's good for us that way. She's younger, new on the job. She still believes, and that keeps us going through the long periods we spend watching the in-tray, hands hovering over the phones, waiting for no-one to call. She doesn't know that a few years ago we'd get a call once a month, not a couple of times a year. She doesn't realise it's not that time is running out, but that it's already gone. Even the hoaxers are losing interest. I know this, but I must still have a little faith tucked away somewhere. Chen too, though in his case perhaps it's not just faith.

Miranda wrenched herself round in her seat. 'If you don't stop drumming I'll have to kill you. I'll regret it for a while, but I will have no choice.'

I took the phone from Chen and called our destination. They were already on standby and waiting for us, though we wouldn't be there until four at the earliest. As I'd known they would be. I was just calling for something to do. The guy I talked to on the video phone looked tense and expectant, and there were a couple of soldiers milling restlessly behind him. I wondered how they were going to kill the time until we got there.

Finally the car pulled to a halt outside the international terminal. As a waiting official led us towards the entrance, Chen murmured.

'Didn't hear back from forensic yet.'

'Must be a good fake,' I said.

'Yeah.' We looked at each other for a moment, smiled tightly and hurried across the concourse.

They'd held the MegaMall for us, and it rose as soon as we were inside. We stood by the window, watching the city fall away below us, and that kept us occupied for a while. The Mall took about twenty minutes to get up to 30,000 feet, then started its steady progress forward.

As soon as we were over the ocean we turned away from the view.

'Christ,' said Miranda. 'Now what do we do?'

'We shop. We stroll. We mingle with passing holidaymakers and exchange pleasantries.'

'Do we fuck,' Chen said. 'We drink coffee and smoke heavily. This way.'

The middle levels of the Mall were crowded, and it took a while to make our way to an escalator to the higher galleries. A man juggling oranges passed us on the way up. The oranges appeared to be on fire. Chen stared belligerently at him.

'Street theatre, compliments of the airline,' I said. 'Very popular.'

DYING

'Not with me it isn't.'

'How long is this going to take?' Miranda asked. She was craning her neck and looking down across the Mall atrium. About a thousand people flocked and wandered around the lower tiers.

'Two hours.'

'Shit.' She glanced at me, looking drawn. I shrugged. This was only her second callout, and already she was beginning to understand. However quickly we moved, it wasn't fast enough.

We found a coffee bar with a balcony. We sat in silence for the most part, though Miranda and I talked a little about how the arrangements would go once we got there. I didn't have to do that kind of thing with Chen. He knew. He sat a little apart, staring straight ahead, and waited out the flight. I knew what he'd be thinking.

Five years ago, when pretty drunk, Chen and I sat down with some old maps and tried to work out where a genuine sighting would most likely come from. We'd taken into account the way the Cities had developed, climactic conditions, previous populations, everything that might be relevant and a few things which probably weren't. In the end we'd honed in on what used to be called the Congo, now just another region of AfriCity. Since then there'd been nothing from the region, and we'd sort of forgotten about it. Now that's where we were going. In a way I wished Miranda would go away for a while, do some shopping or something. But only briefly, and only because of that night. I was glad Miranda was there. She deserved to be as much as we did.

About half an hour Chen's phone bleeped. He listened and nodded, shifting himself around in the wicker chair. Neither Miranda nor I spoke after he'd finished the call. Neither of us wanted to hurry the news that we were going to be turning straight round at the other end.

'Well,' said Chen, eventually. 'The image is genuine. A three-dimensional object of some type was photographed using a camera of some kind.'

'But?' I said, as professionally as I could.

'As for the object's constitution, they can't tell.'

I nodded. Miranda turned to me.

'What *is* it with you guys? Why do you have to keep doing this? You heard what they said. It's genuine.'

'It could be a genuine model. A genuine fake.'

'Why do you *say* that?'

'Because it's happened before. Twenty-five times.'

'Twenty-six,' Chen said, waving for more coffee.

'But,' I said, 'We've had over two hundred and sixty contacts that were complete fakes. Mocked up in an image app., no object ever there at all. So it's rare anyway.'

'And so there's a chance it could be real?'

Her eyes were too wide, her mouth too ready to smile, for me to say anything crushingly realistic. Chen wasn't looking at me, but he was waiting too.

'Yes,' I said. 'It could be an animal's.'

I don't know why it falls to me to say the word. I try not to. We all do, especially Chen. Most of the time we just talk about 'them' or seeing 'one'. We have books and CD-ROMs lined round the office, floor to ceiling, with pictures and footage of every one that ever existed. Chen knows the names, habits and particulars of thousands. I've tested him, in our long fallow periods, and he does. Sometimes we talk about them, try to describe them to each other, speculate about which one we'd most like to see. But most of the time it's 'them'. Another protection mechanism, another way of not hoping too much.

Chen and I are funded by the WorldCon. We're secure: it's a priority. For now. Miranda is a student on secondment from PsychStat. She's been on secondment for rather a long time now, and we pretend she isn't in when they call to politely enquire when she's coming back. She's caught the bug, and it's a rare bug, so we let her stay. Not a lot of people know about us, but it's no secret. Our job is to watch, and to wait. To sit in our office, listening for the phone, watching the in-tray, in case someone, somewhere, sees an animal. And if someone says they have, we do what we're doing now—get the hell out there as quick as we can. Then we troop home again, because they're all hoaxes or honest mistakes. Everybody knows there are no animals any more. A chimpanzee called Howard was the last one, and he died over seventy years ago.

What can I say? We fucked up. We thought we could go on building the Cities, growing concrete and steel until it covered every continent, and do so without it ruining the world for everyone else. We thought we could keep tweaking the environment and climate and not trigger fractal changes that dominoed entire ecosystems. We thought, or seemed to, that the animals would get by, find a way of coping. We let people kill them for skins, or ornaments, or food. We let tourists carve initials on their homes. We talked about economic necessity, about quality of life for humans. If push came to shove, we thought the zoos would be enough.

But they weren't. When we'd finally squeezed them out of their habitats and screwed up their food chains it turned out the animals didn't like the zoos so much after all. They stuck them for a while and then, as if on cue, they gave up and rather pointedly died. Then we looked around the cities we'd wrought and realised that they were empty. Between the teeming people, down the sides of the endless streets, above the continual gleam, there was nothing left but space. Suddenly we realised we were alone, and beneath the ever-present clatter of humankind, the world seemed very quiet.

To some of us, anyway. I guess most people don't care that much. They've never known any differently. I haven't, if I'm honest. There's not been a single confirmed sighting of an animal in my lifetime.

The thing with me was my grandmother. She was an unusual person—or, as my mother would have it, 'bonkers'. But she had a lot of time for me, and I for her, and she told me things about her life I don't think anyone else ever knew. The story I could hear time and again was about how she saw a cat once, when she was a little girl.

She was walking home from school, through S734 sector of AmerCity, when she saw a small shape slink out from round a corner. She stopped dead in her tracks and stared at it. Something, about a foot high and covered in short grey fur, sat and looked back at her from about ten feet away. It had green eyes, long hairs growing out of its cheeks and a thin tail that it curled neatly around its feet. It was not, my grandmother realised, human.

Very quietly, she squatted down so as to see the animal on its own level. It watched her gravely, sniffing. My grandmother noticed the way the pupils in the eyes ran up and down, saw the sturdy little paws planted firmly together, and then the creature moved. Holding her breath, and a little frightened, my grandmother watched as the animal sloped carefully towards her, following a curved path as though it was walking some line she couldn't see. It paused after a few feet and cocked one of its ears, as if listening. Then it walked right up to her.

My gran carefully raised one of her hands until it was in front of the animal's face. Equally carefully, the animal pointed its nose and sniffed her hand. It pushed forward, rubbing its face against her knuckles, bending its head round and making a soft and throaty humming noise. It looked up at her and made an odd sound, like a door falling open in an abandoned house, and then it rubbed its head against her hand again like a kiss.

There was a noise behind her, and my grandmother turned to see a man walking across the intersection about twenty yards back. Her mouth was half open to say something, to call him over, and then she clamped it shut.

When she turned round the animal was gone, and she never saw it again.

She ran home then and burst into the kitchen shouting. At first her folks thought she was telling tales, but the more she told them the more they had to admit it sounded like a cat. They sent out a search party and looked for five hours, but they didn't find it.

My grandmother spent the rest of her life wishing the man hadn't chosen that moment to cross the street, and that she'd known that what cats liked was to be tickled behind the ears and rubbed under the chin. She may have been the last person who ever saw it, and she wished with all her heart she could have said goodbye from us in the proper way.

And she told me about it, and I listened, and here I am today. Because though everyone knows there can't be any animals left now, there are those of us who still look. We have the faith. I do, anyway. Chen has something else. Chen may have actually seen an animal.

He thinks he did. Thirty years ago, when wandering a disused sector in AfriCity, he saw a shadow move high above him, in a tower where the floors had caved in. A shape swung across a gap. His glimpse of it lasted less than four seconds. He's the first to admit he was doing a lot of drugs at the time, but he says it wasn't like that. He knows how unlikely it is, but he thinks it might have been a primate. Something stirred the air with a mind of its own. It was something different, something that wasn't us, wasn't part of the noisy machine that chugs away in our claustrophobic world. He stopped doing drugs then, because he realised what he was trying to escape from and what he was looking for. He's been searching ever since, at first on his own, and then officially. It's not faith with him. It's need. It has been his life, and it's the nearest he's got to something that makes him happy.

Governments give us money and all the backup we could ever want. We have InterContinent Passes that mean customs and immigration can fuck right off as far as we're concerned, and I could mobilize an entire army if I had a good enough lead. Nothing I asked for would be too much, now that it's too late.

'So,' I said. 'Chen. Best guess?'

'Difficult to say,' he said, enjoying every word. This was making it official, a kind of ritual we'd developed over the few times it had gotten this far. 'It depends on the size. There's nothing to give us any scale.'

'But a mammal.'

'Definitely. Could be a dog, cat. Could be a primate. It could be loads of things. Why the hell couldn't they have sent us a video?'

That was frustrating. The colour of the faeces could have told us something—though if there was an animal still alive somewhere in AfriCity, its diet would hardly have been traditional. We'd always received videos in the past, though most of them turned out to be footage of fakes and the other alleged specimens were never found.

The faking thing is strange. There's not a lot of point. So few people on the planet think about animals any more. But some of them must go out of their way to pretend they're still around. I used to wonder why they would do that, why people who had never seen an animal should try to keep their memory alive through faking their tracks and faeces. Then I considered what I do for a living. Maybe it isn't so different.

Miranda was drumming her fingers hard on the table. I raised an eyebrow at her.

'So—how long before I get to kill you?'

'Christ,' she said. 'Why does this have to take so *long*?'

None of the other passengers were in a hurry to leave the Mall when we landed at AfriCity. I'm not surprised. What they'd disembark into would look exactly the same as where they'd been for the last two hours, and the same as where they'd come from in the first place. It was like walking down a neverending street that was the same at both ends. I don't know why they bother.

We had no problem getting out of the MegaMall first. I started to get my pass out but it wasn't necessary: a delegation was waiting for us at the gate. We shook hands hurriedly and trotted towards the exit of the terminal.

Introductions were made in the car, which was open-topped like an old-fashioned Jeep. The man in charge was a Lieutenant Ng, local security forces. He was fired up but deferential and eager to do the right thing. They usually are, which is strange. Our only advantage is book learning, and the fact that we spend our lives preparing for this kind of thing, guardians of a flame who spend their whole time looking for a match. Maybe that's it. In a way we have a quest, an old-fashioned mission, of a hopelessly romantic kind. Things like that sit oddly with brushed concreform and neon, seem to stand out in an eerie light like buildings in front of a storm. Perhaps that commands respect, or something. Curiosity, perhaps.

The Lieutenant got out a map and indicated where we were going. The alleged sighting had been made in AfriCity 295, a disused sector about four hours' drive away. A flipper would have got us there quicker, but the noise would have scared any animal away. As soon as the report had come in a corps of soldiers had cordoned the area off. Nothing could have come out, and more importantly, no-one could go in. Someone who got to an animal before we did could have set their own price. They could ask for the world.

When we were buckled in the driver put his foot down hard and we pelted off down the street. People looked up vaguely to watch the car speed by, then hurried off towards the stores. There's always something new to buy, always something shinier. Ng watched them with an odd expression on his face, and I realised that despite being in the army he was one of us. One of the people who'd like to see something old, every now and then. After a moment he looked across at me and pointed downwards at the road surface.

'This is where the river used to be,' he said.

I wondered how he could tell.

The sectors started to go to seed after about two hours. There's no obvious reason for it, as far as I can tell, but it happens everywhere, and it seems it always will until we need every single square inch all the time. One day a sector will be buzzing and full of life, then suddenly it will be a place where no-one lives deliberately. Within a few years it will be empty, but there's too many people for anywhere to remain like that for long. So a decade later it will be redeveloped, made new again, and people will start to move in. The population shifts around the planet, year by year, almost as if we *have* to move a little, every now and then, as if migration is a need that never quite went away.

It was getting dark, and I was glad to have an escort. Caring about legends is the preserve of the comfortably off and the socially integrated. The kind of people who live in the interzones don't give a shit. A long time ago Chen and I received a call and came to an area like this near what used to be Atlanta in AmerCity. We nearly didn't make it out. The call was a fake, planted to draw people in. We lost all our gear and our research assistant, and both of us spent three weeks in hospital. Since then we don't go in without ground support.

Then, fairly abruptly, the sector was empty. Even the rubbish drifting down the street looked old and forgotten. There's nothing in the world more empty than one of man's places when he isn't there, and this area looked deader than the other side of the moon.

Ng conferred on a communicator and got specific co-ordinates, and then we turned a corner to find that we were there.

I could tell something was wrong before the car stopped moving.

DYING

About ten soldiers stood in formation in the middle of a deserted and crumbling crossroads.

Ng muttered something irritable under his breath, and suggested we stay in the car. He climbed stiffly out and walked up to one of the soldiers. Like Ng, the soldier was wearing a beret, presumably implying they were of the same rank. Chen looked across at me and raised his eyebrows. I shrugged and lit a cigarette.

A few moments later Ng returned.

'The corps will be accompanying you into the sector,' he said. Though immaculate with military professionalism, he was fuming.

'That's not possible.' Chen said.

'They can't,' Miranda said. 'They'll scare off anything within a mile radius.'

Ng looked at me. 'The corps,' he said again, 'will be accompanying you. The sector is dangerous, and you must have protection.' He clearly didn't believe this, and I didn't either.

'Political?' I asked. He inclined his head slightly.

'No way,' said Chen. 'Fuck politics. Jesus, if you think we can take the risk of blowing...'

'Lieutenant Hye will oversee the operation. He assures me that his men are aware of the need for silence.'

'I don't care how damn quiet they are, that's not the point,' Miranda shouted.

I held out a hand. 'It's been hours already. We're here. There's no point wasting time when we can't change the situation. Let's go.'

I hate always being right, but someone has to do it.

Hye's men were indeed quiet. As Chen, Miranda and I walked down the centre of the road three abreast, I had to keep checking behind every now and then to see if they were still there. They were, fanned out across the road. And they were carrying guns.

'What *is* this crap?' Chen asked, quietly.

'What Ng said, I guess. Some pointless political game.'

'I don't like it.'

'Neither do I.'

When we'd been walking for about five minutes Ng appeared soundlessly behind us.

'We are now in Subsector 4. The sighting of the material allegedly took place within this area.'

'We don't know where?'

Michael Marshall Smith

'No. The photo was left without any further statement.'

'Okay. See if you can get them to drop back a little further.'

They did, but not much. Following standard procedure, Chen and I headed toward the sides of the road, carefully scanning the ground and keeping half an eye on our motion and infrared sensors. Miranda walked down the centre, casting glances up at the walls of the buildings on either side. Many were empty shells, and a few looked as if they'd been burnt out. This sector's demise had been more violent than most.

After about two hundred yards, I began to see a glow in the twilight ahead. This meant habitation. I stopped.

'We've passed the core of the disused area.'

The theory Chen and I worked on was that if any animal was still alive, it would tend to seek out places as far from humankind as possible. Though it might roam the fringes of inhabited areas in the search for food, we reasoned that it would want to sleep somewhere safe.

'Do we turn around?' Miranda asked. She was looking balefully at the soldiers, who'd also stopped, and were standing in a line ten yards away.

'Yes,' Chen said curtly, rubbing his chin. 'Then fan out down each of the side streets we've passed. Then after that we go into each building and search on each floor.'

Miranda looked up at the fading light. 'Maybe we should ask the soldiers to...'

Suddenly she stopped, something that looked like terror on her face. She pointed behind me. 'Oh my God.'

I whirled and stared at the shadows at the base of the building about five yards away. 'What,' I said. 'What?'

The wall disappeared in a stroboscopic blaze. Line after line of red arcfire sliced into it until the whole of the front of the building crashed down. Two of the soldiers darted forward into the rubble.

I stumbled backward, falling into Miranda, and the two of us crouched down until the noise had stopped.

When I looked up Chen was marching furiously up to Hye.

'What the *fuck* do you think you're doing?'

I leapt up and ran towards him.

Hye stared impassively at Chen, and shoved him hard in the chest. Chen wavered, but didn't fall, and instead launched himself at the soldier.

Luckily Ng got there and yanked Chen away, and I grabbed Chen's arms and tugged him backward. He was kicking and shouting and I almost couldn't hold him.

Ng squared up to Hye. 'Explain,' he barked.

DYING

'Fuck you.'

'Explain,' Ng repeated, face twitching, 'Or I take this very high indeed.'

Hye looked at him with contempt. 'I have orders,' he said, 'From higher than you know. I have orders to protect the population.'

'Whose orders?' I said, preparing to pull rank. I have papers for this kind of eventuality, though I'd never had to use them before.

Hye ignored me. 'If any animal exists,' he said to Ng, 'It will carry disease. The population no longer has immune responses to these diseases.'

'*Bull*shit,' Miranda shouted. She sounded a lot tougher than I had. 'That's not…'

'The population will be protected.'

Ng's face was now only about nine inches from the other officer's. 'Who gave you these orders?'

'They were issued on a need to know basis.'

'I don't believe you, Hye. I don't believe in these orders. I believe you want to hunt.'

'He's right,' Chen said, too calmly. 'Ng's right. This fucker wants to be the last hunter. He wants the last trophy. The last head for his wall.'

'It's off,' I said. 'We're going home.'

Miranda stared at me. 'We can't. I saw something.'

'Maybe. Then there was an firefight and we all started shouting at each other. If there was anything here it'll be on the moon by now, hiding under a rock. Either way, I'm not finding something for this fucker to shoot it.'

'You'll find it,' Hye said, turning to look at me for the first time.

'No.'

'Yes,' he said, and moved one hand slightly. Silently, ten guns were raised.

We walked in silence down the first side road. Ng was a few yards behind. His shoulders were set, and he walked by himself. Behind him came the soldiers. Some spoke softly every now and then, and there was the occasional laugh, but mostly there were as silent as before. I hated them, completely, utterly and quietly.

'What did you see?' Chen asked eventually.

Miranda sighed. 'It could have been shadow. It looked as if something moved. About three feet high. That's all I saw, and I barely saw that.'

'Dog?' I asked.

'No.'

Chen looked at her. I hoped for his sake that she wasn't mistaken.

There was nothing to be seen in the side road. We turned at the end and walked back up, then crossed to the other side and did the same. Then we moved down the central strip and did the next road. There was still enough light to see without artificial aid, but I reckoned we only had about another hour.

Halfway down the next road I turned to find Ng on my shoulder again.

'The light will be gone soon,' he said.

'It's over. There's no way we can traipse through all these buildings in time. Even if we could, even if there is an animal here, it's not going to show with ten men with guns padding behind us. I don't care how quiet they are. Animals could hear things we can't even imagine.'

'And they could sense things.' Chen added, not looking up.

Ng looked at him. 'You know that?'

'I believe it.'

Ng nodded, and then dropped back.

Another five minutes took us up and down the next side street. I felt stupid and impotent. There could be something here, and all we could do was walk around, waiting for it to lollop in front of us. If it existed, which it almost certainly didn't. For a moment I felt complete despair, and knew in my heart that there were no animals any more. There couldn't be. They simply wouldn't fit in this world.

We turned into the last side street and I heard Miranda sigh. I reached out and took her hand, and she looked at me. There was something wrong tonight, and we all knew it. It felt like it would be the last time we did this. Something about the soldiers behind us, about Hye, about the whole world, said that the gaps were closing for good, that the old dreams had been squeezed out.

We walked to the end of the road, watching the sidewalks carefully and scanning the buildings, and then we turned. The soldiers, guns still at the ready, echoed our progress, walking to the end of the road and then turning to follow us.

About twenty yards up the road, Ng scared the life out of me by suddenly speaking from directly behind me again.

'Run into a building on the side. Good luck.'

I turned. He smiled and nodded us forward.

Suddenly there was a shout behind us. I tugged Miranda's hand and gave Chen a shove and we sprinted for the nearest building.

DYING

A shot fizzed off the lintel of the doorway we stumbled through, but we kept on running, weaving through the debris and out the other side.

'What the hell...'

'He's still alive,' Chen panted. 'Three have gone after him. Run. *Run.*'

We ran. On impulse I steered us across the main strip and then into a long burnt-out building. The shouts behind weren't getting any further away, but they were spreading out. They didn't know where we'd gone. We winced at each hissing shot, but so long as they were still firing, we were still alive. And so, hopefully, was Lieutenant Ng.

We had to duck out the building and out onto the road, so we crossed quickly and slipped into the row on the other side. By this time we'd begun to double back on ourselves, heading back to right area. The sound of shots was coming less frequently, and the muted shouts seemed more distant too.

When we came up against the next intact wall Chen halted abruptly. 'Have to stop a second.'

I glanced round, and then stopped too. My chest was aching and Miranda was barely on her feet. Realising I was still holding her hand, I let go of it.

'A minute, then walk. We have to keep moving.'

They nodded wearily at me being right again.

'Ng. Why?' Miranda panted, pulling the back of her hand across her forehead.

'Because he wanted to,' Chen said. 'He wasn't one of them. He knew what we were here for.'

'I hope he's alright.'

Chen looked at me. We knew he wouldn't be.

A shout echoed in the street outside, still the other side of the strip, but nearer.

'Time to move.'

I poked my head out. The street was clear, and we slipped round into the next section of the building. We could only get a few yards, then had to cross to the other side. As Chen checked the street Miranda turned to me.

'What are we going to do? I mean, do we stay, or what? Are we still looking?'

'I don't know. Chen, is it clear?'

'We've got to look,' Miranda said desperately. 'We have to. That's why Ng did this...'

'Miranda, they'll kill us if they find us. Chen, is it clear, or what?'

Chen was standing with his head and shoulder poking out into the street. He was absolutely motionless.

'Chen?'

He half-turned his face towards us then, but his eyes didn't move. Miranda and I soundlessly took a step towards him and looked out into the street.

It was nearly dark now, as dark as it ever gets on a planet with a hundred trillion light bulbs. The street outside was deserted. The soldiers had evidently regrouped, and were no longer making any noise. They were trained men, and they were setting about finding us as they'd been trained to do. Quietly, efficiently and terminally. If anything, the silence meant we were in even more danger. But that wasn't important. Sitting in the middle of the road was a cat.

I've seen countless photographs of cats. I've probably looked at more images of them than any man alive. But as I stood and stared I didn't see the photos or reference books. I saw exactly what my grandmother saw.

It was an animal, about a foot or so high, covered in fur and with green eyes that caught the remains of the light. I looked, and I saw it wasn't human.

'Oh God,' Miranda moaned, 'Oh dear god.'

She was crying. I was too, I discovered. Chen just looked, and looked. He'd known. I don't know whether he saw that primate years ago, and I don't think it matters. He'd just known.

The cat looked back at us, and then glanced down the road. I looked too, but there was nothing there. The soldiers were creeping towards us from some other angle. The first we'd know would be the last we'd know. I didn't care.

Miranda caught her breath as the cat stood up, turned round, and walked about a yard away from us. No, I thought. Please Not yet. The cat looked at us again. Chen straightened up and stepped out into the road.

'Chen, what are you doing? You'll frighten it.'

'Come on,' he said, without looking round.

We stepped out into the road. The cat walked slowly across it. We followed, and it didn't seem to mind. Instead of going straight across, its path curved up towards the left, and I smiled, remembering old stories once more.

When it reached the other side the cat clambered up onto a doorstep, turned to us for a moment, and then vanished into the building.

We looked at each other, and followed, eyes locked. This was going to end soon. It had to.

The building was a shell, about twenty yards deep. The cat wandered into the centre of the floor and sat again. We stood in front of it. It didn't mind us. Chen crouched in front of it. There was a soft sound from out of the shadows, and suddenly there were two. The cats looked this way and that, and one of them raised a paw to lick it briefly.

We had cameras. We had video. We didn't use them.

'Oh,' Chen said.

From the shadows behind the cats came a shape. It was about three feet high, and it stood on two legs. Its body was covered in dark brown fur, apart from around the face, and its arms were surprisingly long. It ambled drunkenly across the room, reeled around the cats, and then came and stood in front of Chen. With Chen hunkered down they were about the same height, and could look each other in the face. The animal stretched out a hand, and then plopped it on Chen's head. It was a chimpanzee.

Chen let the chimp rootle round in his hair and pull his nose, and I watched, darting my gaze over to the cats every ten seconds or so. I put out my hand to Miranda.

She wasn't there. She was standing a couple of yards away, looking in a different direction. About a car length from her stood a white horse. Behind it was something I think was a rabbit.

'Chen,' I said.

He came over, accompanied by the chimp, who seemed to be mimicking the way Chen walked. Or maybe Chen had always walked like a chimp, and I'd never known.

Behind the rabbit there was a small clump of squirrels, rolling in the dust and swiping at each other. We walked past them, because we could see that in the gloom there were others. We went another few yards, and then stopped.

The horse was joined by another, and the pair moved aside to let a pair of small dogs wander through. There was a noise up above and we looked to see a small pack of monkeys larking around, turning and rolling over the remains of a steel support. A gorilla sat against the wall, watching a group of rats who were beetling towards him. When they reached his feet they sniffed, seemed to confer and reach a decision of some kind, and immediately set off in another direction. Two long necks swayed and a pair of giraffes walked slowly around in a large circle, followed by a sheep. Miranda squawked when something touched her neck, and we turned to see it was the trunk of an elephant.

There were more, some whose names I didn't even know. Chen might have, but I didn't ask. None of us spoke. We just walked round the cavernous interior of the building, surprised at every turn by something new.

Still they milled around us, and they were all different, and they were all alive.

Eventually we came to a halt in the centre, surrounded. We'd come looking for an animal, however small, however final. And here we were in an abandoned building, in the midst of about a hundred.

There was a shout outside, and the sound of a shot. We ducked unthinkingly, but none of the animals even flinched. The first cat reappeared by my feet, and started to walk towards a door in the outside wall.

'No,' I said urgently. 'No.'

It turned to look at us, then continued on its way, threading between the other animals.

We followed. The street seemed light after the building, and thirty yards away we saw a body crumpled in the middle of the road. It was Ng. He was dead. The soldiers were advancing from the other side of the strip, ten abreast, right across the road.

The cat stopped in the middle of the street, and we stopped behind it.

There was a sound, and we turned to see one of the horses stepping out into the road. It was followed by a dog, and then by the monkeys. They walked out into the centre of the road. Then they started to head down towards the main strip, towards the soldiers.

'Don't.'

But they all came out, in pairs, in packs. The giraffes and the rats, several rabbits and four wolves. They all came out, and walked down the road without a sound. The road was full, almost crowded, as rank after rank of animals marched down the street. When the first of them reached the crossroads, the soldiers were already there.

But the soldiers didn't see them.

They just kept slowly advancing, and the animals slipped between the gaps. The further away the creatures got, the harder it became to see them. They became translucent, like ghosts. But they weren't. They were there. The soldiers simply couldn't see them, and the animals wandered past like a mist. I saw Hye in the centre of the road, glaring impatiently around. He looked past goats and cats, horses and rhinos. A giraffe seemed to walk right through him. He couldn't see it.

Eventually the stream of animals began to thin out, and we knew it was nearly over. Chen's chimp took a step forward, and I saw he was still holding Chen's hand.

Chen didn't hesitate. He nodded at me, smiled at Miranda, and then he walked off down the road, a dog to one side and a rabbit following up behind. He passed Hye without even looking at him. Maybe by then he was seeing something different.

As the soldiers drew to a halt, confused at the emptiness around them, the first cat stood up. I bent down to it, and I tickled it behind the ears. I stroked its back and I rubbed its chin, and it made its sound for me.

Then it walked off down the road, tail erect. There would be no retreat. It stopped by Ng's body and looked back at us, and then it disappeared off up the street.

We surrendered, to soldiers who seemed quiet and withdrawn and didn't meet our eyes. Some fever had passed, and Hye and his men escorted us back out of the sector with distant civility, though he must have known I would report what had happened. I don't know if any action was taken. As always, I suspect they have bigger problems on their minds down there.

Miranda went back to PsychStat two days later. I see her occasionally. Not often. Our paths don't cross, and I spend most of my time painting now. I'm not very good, it has to be said, but I'm working at it. Maybe in time I'll be able to show what the photographs can't.

I live in what used to be the office. That's all over. It's finished. I don't have to look any more.

I know.

The animals are still here. They always have been, and they always will be. They just won't ever let us see them again.

Or maybe that's wrong. Perhaps they're still in the world, and it's us who are somewhere else.

Maybe it was us who died.

Charms

Once she reached the high street, Carol's walk slowed.
She took a few deep breaths and shrugged her shoulders to dislodge some
of the tenseness, making slow fists of her hands and releasing them
quickly, as if trying to flick off insects. The street was crowded in the
sunshine, and she threaded her way down the wide pavement,
wondering where to go. She had no reason to be in town, and before her
parents had started arguing had been looking forward to a desultory
afternoon at their house.

Then something had happened.

Nothing unusual; the same old thing. Whatever it was.

She always missed it, somehow, the actual moment when things
turned sour. Most of the time being at home was like wading in a stream
of warm flowing water, comforting and secure. She knew the history of
everything in every room, and the spaces were secure, dependable. So
too her parents: Mother would potter about in the kitchen, asking her
how she was, what she was doing; Father would read the paper and listen
to her answers while mother pounced in with another question.

Then the warmth would be gone, as if Carol had carelessly stepped
into a deep cavity filled with icy water. Suddenly the air was taut with the
unspoken, and the objects in the room seemed to stand isolated with an
unpleasant starkness, cut adrift from each other, as what her parents said
to each other started to take on cutting subtexts. Until she'd left home
Carol had subconsciously blamed her father, probably because it was
always him who ended up storming out of the room. Distance had helped
her see that her mother was at least as much to blame.

She'd left the house fifteen minutes after stepping into the cold. By
that time mother was furiously cooking unnecessary brownies, and father
was in his study. As she walked down the drive Carol winced at the music
coming loudly from the window. The arguments always ended in the
same way—with her mother burying herself in trivia, and her father in his

study, sitting bolt upright in his chair and listening to his old 45s. Early Beatles, Stones. Other bands whose names fate hadn't blessed with memorability. Carol had never been able to hear those songs with pleasure and always flinched when they came on at parties. They were irretrievably associated with suddenly finding herself in a wasteland, lost between two warring factions whose feelings and grievances she had never understood.

Everyone in the high street seemed to have somewhere to go, urgent tasks to perform. A glance at their faces showed they weren't even seeing the high street, just running breathlessly on rails. Carol felt strangely dislocated, in a town that was no longer hers, wandering aimlessly among projectile people as they ricocheted from car to shop to shop to car. At last a task occurred to her, and she crossed the street and headed for Tony's Records. It was her mother's birthday in a couple of weeks, and she might not get a chance for a leisurely shop again before then. She could probably find something in the record store her mother would like, though she'd have to be diplomatic about giving it to her.

Her mother had a CD player, and classical tastes. Her father had his 45s. And never, it appeared, did the twain meet. She'd always been a little perplexed by that, as it had been her father who had encouraged her to have piano lessons when she was young. Every now and then she caught a glimpse of something irrational between her parents, something made so rigid and obscure by time that even they probably didn't understand it any more. The still water between them ran very deep, and the smallest coin created huge ripples. She'd give her mother the CD on the quiet.

Saturday afternoon in Loughton was a time for the big guns of shopping, the DIY mercenaries and the Sainsbury's SWAT teams. The record shop was almost deserted, and as she headed for the classical CDs she cast a glance at the only other customer. He was in his late forties, and she was a little surprised to notice herself finding him rather attractive. Older men weren't her thing at all, but there was something about him that kept the eye.

The classical section of Tony's was laughably small, market forces evidently having declared proper music played by actual musicians to be a cultural dead end. The single rack of CDs hung like an appendix on the end of the Soul section, and in five years it probably wouldn't be there at all. But by then Tony's would have probably have folded anyway, and you'd have to go twenty miles to buy music from a hyperstore the size of Denmark. For just a moment, Carol suddenly felt terribly old.

She spent five minutes flicking irritably through the CDs, trying to find something that wasn't either music from a TV advert or Nigel bloody Kennedy playing the Four sodding Seasons. She was about to give up when a hand reached from beside her and plucked a double CD case from the 'B' section.

'What about this?'

Startled, Carol turned to see the other customer standing beside her. Now that she could see his face properly she couldn't imagine how she could have thought him middle-aged. He was no more than early thirties, and had a smile that was younger still.

'Are you buying for yourself,' he asked, 'Or someone else?' His grin was infectious, and Carol found herself returning it.

'For my mother.'

He nodded, and looked at her for a moment. 'I think these, then.'

He handed her the CD, and she turned it over to read the cover. It showed a relatively youthful Paul Tortelier, sternly poised behind a cello.

'Bach Solo Cello Suites,' she said, looking up at him, 'I don't think I know them. Are they nice?'

He frowned at her. 'They're not "nice", no. To the best of my knowledge they have not helped sell a single brand of car, bank, or nationalised industry.'

She laughed. 'Good. They sound perfect.'

'Would you like an ice cream?'

Carol double-took at the question, but the offer was evidently serious. She shrugged. 'Why not?'

As she waited for the teenaged assistant behind the counter to remember that she had a role to play in helping customers make purchases, Carol glanced at the man. He was waiting near the door, and raised his eyebrows at her. She smiled at him, then turned back. For some reason she felt quite excited. From the minute he'd first spoken to her she'd known that he wasn't trying to pick her up. She'd fielded more than enough charming lechers and drink-buying madmen to be able to tell immediately. He had talked to her because he wanted to, nothing more. And when he'd spoken, he'd spoken to her, to Carol, not just to a pretty girl who might be worth a try.

It was so unusual it was a bit weird. But nice.

On the first warm day suburban England goes into Summer mode as if a giant switch has been thrown somewhere. Men walk around with no shirts on while still wearing trousers, every moron with a white car cruises the high street pumping out anonymous dance music, and sure enough, there was an ice cream van only ten yards down the street. The man's courteousness in ordering their ice creams so blew the frazzled kiosk attendant's mind that he even got a smile from her. Then he led Carol to the bench that sat beneath the one tree in the high street.

As she sat and lapped her cone, Carol felt curiously cool and calm, and she turned to look at the man.

'So why that CD?'

'What brought you out to this mayhem this afternoon?'

'I asked first,' Carol said. As she did so she felt a faint brush of embarrassment, then realised she didn't really feel embarrassed at all. It was like being with someone back in the days when things were simple, when you didn't have jealous ex-boyfriends on your back and weren't talking to someone with a closet full of hang-ups and probably a wife somewhere in the background; when the game had been fun, instead of just a tortuous and repetitive way of ending up with a record collection you didn't even recognise any more.

'And I shall answer,' he smiled. 'Eventually.'

'Well, I came out,' Carol paused, then decided to go on anyway. 'I came out because my parents were having a row.'

'Over what?'

'Over nothing. Over everything. I don't know.'

He nodded at her, and she noticed that his eyes were very green, with a ring of brown round the irises. They reminded her of leaves, some fallen, some still on the trees, down by a stream in the Autumn.

'I've never known. They're both...they're both so *nice*. I mean, individually, they're the two nicest people I know. They must have loved each other once, otherwise they wouldn't have married each other, but somewhere down the line...'

She trailed off. Somewhere down the line two people who had loved each other very much had simply drifted off course.

'Maybe something happened, maybe nothing,' the man said.

Carol looked up at him, startled but grateful to realise that he'd picked up the train of her thoughts. Then she looked down at her lap again.

Something had simply gone wrong somewhere, and now her father sat in his study listening to old records that had lost their magic, and her mother grew old in the living room. She found her eyes filling with tears. Although she'd thought about her parents many times, she'd never had the realisation before. This was all they had, it wasn't working, and they were just waiting for everything to be over.

Maybe something, maybe nothing. That's all it had taken.

It wasn't fair, wasn't right that people who had loved each other should end up bound together by their feelings for two people who weren't there any more, and she suddenly felt very miserable.

The man turned from looking out across the road, and smiled gently at her. 'Shall I tell you what I like about that CD?'

She nodded. She was happy to listen to him talk about anything.

'Bach is very different to any other composer,' he said. 'When you listen to Vivaldi, or Handel, you can tell that the music was composed for an audience. It's like a blockbuster film: it's good, but it's good because it's *supposed* to be good. It's been designed that way. When you listen to Bach, it's different. You're not being performed to. You're being allowed to overhear.'

An open-topped white Golf cruised by, spilling trance jungle garage at a volume that would have had Led Zeppelin shaking their heads in grim disapproval.

The man smiled. 'Ten years from now, no-one will be listening to that crap any more, thank Christ. It's moment music, no more. But it's the same with the better stuff too. All the old 45s stashed in people's rooms, they're like a butterfly collection. They look as if they're still alive, as if they could fly away, but they've been dead for decades. Old feelings and memories pinned to pieces of vinyl. In a hundred years no-one will have associations for those songs any more, and most of them will be dead. But in five hundred years, a thousand years, when people sit in houses on planets we don't even know exist yet, they'll still listen to Bach, and they'll still hear the same things. It's like listening to a charm. It doesn't fade.'

His smile broadened, ridiculing the flamboyance of what he was saying. She smiled back, properly this time. He nodded approvingly.

'Better. And there's something else about that record, too.' He reached across and took the CD from her. 'Look. Recorded in 1961. When you listen to it, remember that.'

Slightly puzzled, she grinned. 'I will. But you still haven't answered my question. And I'm intrigued now, I want to go listen to this and it's not even for me.'

'Well maybe you should.'

'But,' Carol fought hard, but then said it as simply as she could. 'It's nice being with you.' Great, she thought. You sound, what—about fourteen years old?

'That's alright,' the man said. 'I'll come with you, if I may.'

Carol leapt at the chance. Quite apart from anything else, her turning up with a guest might diffuse the atmosphere back at the house. Her parents always liked meeting people she knew.

'Of course, I mean, yes. I'll say I bumped into a friend by accident.'

Michael Marshall Smith

Which wouldn't, she thought as they headed for his car, feel as if she was straying very far from the truth.

Carol knew nothing about cars, but there was something undeniably classic about his, a diffident and unassuming open-topped sports car in darkest green. It looked like something from another era that had lasted very well, like the deepest pockets of Epping forest where the trees had never been pollarded, and still looked like trees.

There was a comprehensive-looking CD player built into the front console, but she couldn't see any CDs anywhere, and she didn't want to break the wrapping on the Cello Suites. It was still going to be a present for her mother, though not for her birthday, and it would only take a few minutes to get home.

When they pulled up in the drive all was quiet, and Carol knew from experience that her father would now be out in the garden, pottering quietly, thinking his own thoughts.

Her mother looked a little quiet when she opened the door, but brightened considerably on seeing Carol had a guest.

'Hi Ma,' Carol said, 'I ran into a friend in town, thought I'd bring him home to meet you.'

'How nice,' her mother said warmly, reached out her hand.

Realising too late she didn't know the man's name, Carol scrabbled and came up with one that would have to do.

'So, er…Mother—*Mark*, Mark—Mother.'

The man accepted this without batting an eyelid, and took her mother's hand.

'How do you do. I've heard a lot about you.'

'Oh I hope not,' her mother laughed.

'Are you bored with people saying how alike you and Carol look?' he asked as she led them into the sitting room. Carol blinked: how did he know her name? Had she told him, and forgotten? She must have.

'No, not at all,' her mother giggled, and Carol stared at her curiously. She didn't think she'd ever heard her mother giggle before. Certainly not like that.

Carol felt the house relax about them as mother set about making tea, chatting with the man. She'd never been like this with any of the boyfriends she'd brought home. Polite, yes, friendly in a reserved and parental way, but not like this. 'Vivacious' was something she hadn't realised her mother had in her armoury.

'And that,' said the man, nodding out at the garden, 'is presumably your husband, Mrs Peters?'

Carol steeled herself. It was generally a few hours after an argument before either of them would acknowledge the other's existence.

'Yes,' said her mother, 'that's John. And call me Gillian.'

'Okay,' he said, 'Is that your name?'

Giggling again, her mother punched him lightly on the shoulder and turned to hand Carol her tea.

'Your friend is a twit, Carol,' she said.

'Perhaps I should go introduce myself to your father,' the man said. His eyes drifted over the small package Carol held in her lap, and she realised that he was giving her a chance to present it to her mother undisturbed.

'Do you want me to...'

'No, I'll be fine.'

They watched him go, and then mother and daughter turned to each other.

'Well,' her mother said after a pause, 'if you're not going out with him yet you want to bloody well get a move on.'

They looked at each other soberly for a moment and then started laughing. When they tailed off, still hiccupping every now and then, Carol felt an enormous wave of relief. Not only had the tension in the house disappeared as it had never existed, but her mother looked so relaxed, so vital.

'I bought you a present,' she said.

Her mother hadn't heard the Suites either, and they decided to give the first one a quick listen. Carol settled back in her chair as her mother set up the CD, realising that was something that she liked about her mother that she'd never noticed before. Most people past a certain age seemed to make a decision to refuse to come to terms with new technology. To give up, and become old. But not her mother: as she wielded the CD remote she looked just like Carol's flatmate Suz. Or like a capable older sister, the kind who goes off traveling round the world and doesn't come back with dysentery.

There was a faint hiss before the music started, and Carol remembered what the man had said.

'Recorded in 1961,' she observed to her mother, who nodded.

Then there was the sound of the cello.

It had something of the austere beauty of an equation, an irreducible expression, but it touched you very deeply: it was like seeing truth with your ears. It *was* like a charm, she realised, like looking at the inside of a perfect crystal and observing an expression of natural forces which you could appreciate but not understand. That was why, she realised, you could often tell what was coming next when you listen to Bach. Not because it was predictable, but because it was right. When clouds darkened, it was going to rain: when they broke, the sun would shine. Some things happened after something else. That was all there was to it.

All her favourite songs, the albums in her flat and the battered singles archived in her old bedroom upstairs, they captured moments. This music captured time.

As they listened she focused on every note as it passed, listening to sounds recorded in 1961: before the Beatles, before the Stones, before the Sixties themselves got into their stride. On the day those notes were recorded the world was a completely different place, yet however you listened to it, in those grooves, in that tape, in those digits, was 1961. Outside the room Tortelier was playing in was another room, where men with Brylcreamed hair ran an old-fashioned recording desk that was state-of-the-art to them. Behind them was a window, and outside the birds were singing. And somewhere out there would be a newspaper seller, and he'd be hawking papers with the date 1961 on them, maybe a Thursday. Perhaps if you listened hard enough you could hear him, and the moment had never really died.

As the Prélude finished, reducing itself to a broken chord which hung on the air, Carol turned and looked at her mother. She was crying gently, and pressed the STOP button on the handset. Then she looked up at her daughter, and Carol saw that her mother had heard the same things.

In a different house, on a different planet, it would always be there to be heard.

Her mother wiped her eyes and smiled with genuine warmth. 'They've been out there a long time.'

They walked into the kitchen, to look out of the window into the back garden. The man was standing talking to her father, and though you couldn't hear what they were saying, her father's laugh when it came drifted through the window to them. Carol glanced at her mother, and held her breath when she saw the expression on her face. There was a faint smile on her lips, and small tears still in her eyes. It was the face of someone who was looking at a photo of a friend who'd died long ago, and finding that the mourning was not over yet.

When she spoke, her voice was fractured, and hesitant. 'It's funny. Standing out there, he looks just like he used to look.'

As they watched the two men laughed again, and her father ran his hand carelessly back through his hair. Carol heard the intake of her mother's breath.

CHARMS

'He always...' Her mother reached her own hand up, and ran it gently through her own hair, at the side. 'I loved him for that.'

The two men burst into a fresh gale of laughter, her father almost doubling up. They looked like two young friends out there, planning old-fashioned devilry, and it would be very easy to love either one of them. Tears ran down her mother's face.

'Mum—what happened?'

Her mother looked at her, her face clouded. 'Nothing,' she said, shaking her head with puzzled misery, 'Nothing that I can remember.'

As they watched the two men looked back towards the house, and then headed towards the back door, still talking.

'They're coming back,' her mother said, wiping her face with a tea towel. 'Is the tea still warm?'

As Carol poured two cups the back door opened and her father came in, followed by the man. Her father made it halfway across the kitchen, and then stopped, faltering, rubbing his hands nervously on his hips. He looked about sixteen.

Carol watched her mother. She was looking at her husband, eyes bright and wide, also nervous. They seemed awkward, unsure of themselves, as if meeting for the first time, or after a long time apart.

Then her father ran his hand unconsciously through his hair, and Carol noticed his grace as he smiled tentatively, a lopsided grin that could break anyone's heart. Her mother handed him a cup of tea, not taking her eyes off his, head tilted to one side.

'Never mind tea,' said the man from behind her father. 'It's a lovely day. Let's drive.'

He led Carol out to his car, and she stood to one side to let her parents climb into the back seat, which they did with an agility Carol doubted she could have mustered. They settled back, and as Carol noticed her father's hand brush her mother's, and saw her grab hold of it, her father drawled in a surprisingly good American accent.

'So what are we waiting for?'

The man pulled the car quickly out into the road and turned away from town, out to where the houses shaded away to fields. 'In the glove compartment,' he said quietly.

Carol opened it, found the CD, and slotted it in the machine. The sound of the cello whipped up into the wind as they flashed towards the country, but she believed that if you strained your ears hard enough, you could hear those sounds, you could hear that year: you could slip through that channel and step out into the fresh sunlight of that day. As the fields spread out beside them and the car shot out into the afternoon, her mother whooped deliriously, and Carol turned around to see them, faces bright and hair dancing in the wind, clasping each other tight and waving at the trees, the wheat, the birds.

Open Doors

Never been great at planning, I'll admit that. Make decisions on the spur of the moment. No forward thought, unless you count years of wondering and speculating—and you shouldn't, because I certainly don't. None of it was to do with specifics, with the mechanics of the situation, with anything that would have helped. I just went and did it. Like always. That's me all over. I just go and do it.

Here's how it happened. It's a Saturday. My wife is gone for the day, out at a big lunch for a mate who's getting married in a couple weeks. Shit—that's another thing she'll have to...whatever. She'll work it out. Anyway, she got picked up at noon and went off in a cab full of women and balloons and I was left in the house on my own. I had work to do, so that was okay. Problem was I just couldn't seem to do it. Don't know if you get that sometimes: just can't apply yourself to something. You've got a job to do—in my case it was fixing up a busted old television set, big as a fridge and hardly worth saving, but if that's what they want, it's their money—and it just won't settle in front of you as a task. No big deal, it wasn't like it had to be fixed in a hurry, and it's a Saturday. I'm a free man. I can do anything I want.

Problem was that I found I couldn't settle to anything else either. I had the afternoon ahead, probably the whole evening too. The wife and her pals don't get together often, and when they do, they drink like there's no tomorrow. Maybe that was the problem—having a block of time all to myself for once. Doesn't happen often. You get out of the habit. I don't know. I just couldn't get down to anything. I tried working, tried reading, tried going on the web and just moping around. None of it felt like I was doing anything. None of it felt like *activity*. It just didn't feel like I thought it would.

I don't like this, I thought: it's just not *working out*.

In the end I got so grumpy and restless I grabbed a book and left the house. There's a new pub opened up not far from the tube station, and I decided I'd go there, try to read for a while. I stopped by a newsagents on the corner opposite the pub, bought myself a pack of ten cigarettes. I'm giving up. I've been giving up for a while now—and sticking to it, more or less, just a few here and there, and never in the house—but sometimes you've just got to have a fucking cigarette. Sometimes the giving up is worse for you than the cigarettes themselves. Your concentration goes. You don't feel yourself. The world feels like it's just out of reach, as if you're not a part of it any more and not much missed. The annoying thing is that anyone who knows you're not smoking tends to think that anything that's wrong with you, any bad mood, any unsettledness, is just due to the lack of cigs. I was pretty sure it wasn't nicotine drought that was causing my restlessness, but so long as I was out of the house I thought I might as well have a couple.

When I got to the pub—which we called the Hairy Pub, because it used to be covered in ivy to the point where you couldn't actually see the building underneath—it wasn't too crowded, and I was able to score one of the big new leather armchairs in the window, right by a fucking great fern. The pub never used to be like this. It used to be an old-fashioned, unreconstituted boozer, and—as such—a bit shit. I like old-fashioned pubs as much as the next man, but this one just wasn't very good. Now they've got posh chairs and a cappuccino machine and polite staff and frankly, I'm not complaining. They cut off all the ivy and painted it black and it looks alright. Whatever. The pub's not really relevant. I sat there for an hour or so, having a couple of coffees and smoking a couple of my small packet of cigarettes. Each one caused me a manageable slap of guilt, as did the chocolate powder sprinkled on the cappuccinos. I've been on the frigging Atkins diet for a month, to cap it all, which means, as you doubtless know, no carbohydrates. None. 'Thou shalt not carb,' the great Doctor proclaimed, and then died. Chocolate is carbs, as—more importantly—are pizza, pasta and special fried rice, the three food groups which make human life worth living, the triumvirate of grubstuffs which make crawling out of the swamp seem worth it. That month has seen me lose a big six pounds, or, put another way, one point something pounds a week, while not being able to eat anything I like. It's crap. Anyway.

I tried to read, but couldn't really get into my book. Couldn't get into a newspaper either. My attention kept drifting, lighting on people sitting in clumps around the pub, wondering what they were doing there on a Saturday afternoon. Some looked hungover already, others were in the foothills of starting one for Sunday. They were all wearing their own clothes and had their hair arranged in certain ways, which they were happy with, or not; some had loud laughs, others sat pretty quietly. The staff swished to and fro—most of them seem to be rather gay, in that pub: not something that exercises me in the least, merely making a factual observation. I've often wondered what it's like, being gay. Different, certainly. The music was just loud enough to be distracting, and I only recognised about one song in three. I could see other people tapping their feet, though, bobbing their heads. The songs meant something in their lives. Not in mine. I wondered when they'd first heard it, how come it had come to be a part of them and not me. I looked at my coffee cup and my book and my little pack of cigarettes and I got bored with them and myself, and bored with my trousers and thoughts and everything else I knew and understood. Custom had staled their infinity variety. Custom was making my hands twitch.

In the end I got up and left. I stomped back out onto the street, caught between wistful and depressed and pissed off. Then I did something I wasn't altogether expecting. Instead of walking straight past the newsagent, I swerved and went back in. I went straight up to the desk and asked for a pack of Marlboro Lites. The guy got it, and I paid for them. Emerged back onto the street, looking at what I held in my hands. Been a long, long time since I'd bought a pack of twenty cigarettes. It's like that with everyone these days—you check, in the pubs and bars, everyone's smoking tens now, just to prove they're giving up.

But you can give up giving up, you know. You can choose to say one thing instead of the other, to say the word 'twenty' instead of 'ten'. That's all it takes. You're not as trapped as you think you are. There are other roads, other options, other doors. Always.

I crossed the street at the lights and then, instead of walking back the way I'd come (along the main road, past the station), I took a turning which led to a shortcut through some quiet residential streets. It's pretty hilly around where I live now, though if you're on the way back from the pub then you're walking down for most of the way. My first right took me into Addison Road, which is short and has a school on one side. Then I turned left into a street whose name I'm not even sure of, a short little road with some two storey brick Victorian houses on either side. At the bottom of it is Brenneck Road, at which point I'd be rejoining the route I would have taken had I gone the other way.

I was walking along that stretch of pavement, halfway between here and there, halfway between one thing and the other, when I did it.

I turned left suddenly, pushed open the black wooden gate I happened to be passing, and walked up to the house beyond it. Don't know what number it was. Don't know anything about the house. Never noticed it before. But I went up to the door and saw that it was one house, not divided up into flats. I pressed the buzzer. It rang loudly inside.

While I was waiting I glanced back, taking a better look at the front garden. Nothing to see, really—standard stuff. Tiny bit of grass, place for the bins, a small tree. Manageable.

I turned when I heard the sound of the door being opened.

A young woman, mid-twenties, was standing there. She had shoulder length brown hair and a mild tan and white teeth. She looked nice, and pretty, and I thought okay—I'm going to do it.

'Hello?' she said, ready to be helpful.

'Hi,' I replied, and pushed past her into the house. Not hard, not violent, just enough to get past her.

I strode down the hallway, took a quick peek in the front room (stripped pine floors, creamy-white sofa, decent new widescreen television) and went straight through to the kitchen, which was out the back. They'd had it done, got some architect or builder to knock out most of the wall and replace it with glass, and it looked good. I wanted to do something like that at home, but the wife thought it would be too modern and 'not in keeping with a Victorian residence'. Bollocks. It looked great.

'Just a bloody minute…' said a voice, and I saw the woman had followed me in. She looked very wary, understandably. 'What the hell are you doing?'

I glanced over her shoulder and saw the front door was still open, but first things first. I went over to the fridge—nice big Bosch, matte silver. We've got a Neff. One of those retro ones, in pale green. Looks nice but holds fuck all. This Bosch was full to the brim. Nice food, too. Good cheese. Pre-cut fruit salad. A pair of *salmon en cruit*, tasty, very nice with some new potatoes, which I saw were also there ready to go. Cold meats, pasta salads, da da da. From Waitrose, supermarket of choice. Wife always shops at Tescos, and it's not bad but it's not half as good.

'Nice,' I said. 'Okay. Did you buy all this? Or was it your fella?'

She just stared at me, goggle-eyed, didn't answer. But I knew it was her, just from they she looked at it. She blinked, trying to work out what to do. I smiled, trying to reassure her it was all okay.

'I'm going to call the police.'

'No you're not,' I said, and smacked her one.

It wasn't hard, but she wasn't expecting it. She staggered back, caught her leg on one of the chairs around the table (nice-looking chairs, kind of ethnic, oak) and fell back on her arse. Head clunked against the fridge. Again, not hard, but enough to take the wind out of her sails for a second.

I checked the back door—shut, locked—and then stepped over her down the hallway and to the front. A woman with a pram was passing by on the pavement. I gave her a big smile and said good afternoon and she smiled back (what a nice man) and then I shut the door. Went to the little table, grubbed around a second, and came up with a set of keys, and a spare. Locked the front door. Went into the front room to check: all windows shut and secured, and here's a couple who stumped up for double glazing. Good for keeping the heat in. Good for keeping the noise in too, I'm afraid.

Went upstairs, had a quick check around. We're secure. Okay. Excellent.

Back in the kitchen the woman is pushing herself to her feet. As I come in she skitters away from me and slips (nice clean floors), ends up on her bum again. She makes a strange little noise and her eyes are darting all over the place.

'Now listen,' I said. 'Listen carefully. This is not what you think. I am not going to hurt you unless I have to.'

'Get out,' she screams.

'No, I'm not going to do that,' I said. 'I'm going to stay here. Do you understand?'

She just stares at me, breathing hard, building up to scream again. She's cowering over by the microwave (matte silver again, nice consistent look throughout the whole kitchen area, there's some thought gone into all this).

'Screaming really isn't going to help,' I said. It's not that I mind the sound, particularly, but there's a lot of glass out the back and one of the neighbours might hear. 'It's just going to piss me off, and I can't see why you'd want to do that. Just not in your best interests, to be honest. Not at this stage.'

Then I saw what she was doing, and had to go quickly over there. She had her mobile phone in her hand, hidden behind the microwave, and was trying to activate a speed-dial number.

I grabbed it off her. 'I like that,' I said. 'Really. I do. I like the idea, I like the execution. Nearly worked. Like I said, I admire it. But don't *ever fucking do anything like that again.*'

And then I hit her. Properly, this time.

It's a funny old thing, hitting women. Frowned upon, these days. And, so like everything else you're not supposed to do, it feels like a big old step when you do it. Like you're opening a door most people don't have the courage to go through. You don't know what's on the other side of this door. There's a chance, admittedly, that it won't be anything good. But it's a door, see? There must be *something* on the other side. It stands to reason. Otherwise it wouldn't be there. And if you don't open some of those doors, you're never going to know what you missed.

She fell over and I left her there. I went around the house, collecting up the normal phones. Don't want to break them, but I put there somewhere she's not going to find them.

I feel both good and bad by this stage. Everything's gone fine, would be according to plan if there'd ever been one. Everything's cool, and I'm quietly confident and excited. I love it. But something tells me something's not right yet. I don't know what it is. Can't put my finger on it.

So I ignore it. That's what I do. I just think about something else. I made a cup of tea, stepping over her where she's lying on the floor, and I put a big old couple of spoonfuls of sugar in it. It's much nicer that way, if the truth be told. I checked the woman was still breathing—she was—and then went into the front room.

Then I sat on the sofa, and got busy with her phone.

I looked through the address book on it, and found a few obvious ones. 'Mum Mobile', not hard to work out who that is, is it. Few girls' nicknames, obviously good friends. And one that is a single letter, 'N'. I'm guessing that's her boyfriend (no wedding ring but everything about this house says two people live here) and I also go out on a limb and opt for 'Nick'. She doesn't look like she'd be going out with a Nigel or Nathaniel or Norman (got nothing against those names, you understand, just she isn't the type). So first I send a quick text message to 'N'.

Then I dial 'Mum Mobile'.

It rings for a few seconds and then a middle-aged woman's voice says 'Hello, darling'. I didn't say anything, obviously. I just listen to this woman's voice. She says hello a few times, sounding a bit confused, irritable, worried. Then she puts the phone down.

It's enough. I've heard enough to get an idea of what she's like, which is all I want. After all, it wouldn't be realistic for a boyfriend never to have heard his mother-in-law's voice. So then I send her a quick text, saying the number got dialled by accident, everything's fine, and I (or of course, *she*, so far as her Mum knows) will call her properly later.

A minute later a text comes back saying 'okay, love'. Sorted.

Fifteen minutes later, 'N' arrives at the front door, blowing hard. He lets himself in with his key. He runs towards the living room, expecting to see his girlfriend lying there naked and waiting. That, after all, is the impression I/she gave in the text.

He never even saw me behind the door. She did, unfortunately. I saw her wake up as I was straddled over him, and I know she saw the brick come down with the blow that did him in. Shame, for any number of reasons. Transition should be much smoother than that, and she's just going to feel alienated.

But at least I've got his wallet now, which will come in handy. Credit cards, driving licence, the lot. And guess what? He *was* a Nick. Just goes to show.

I know what I'm doing.

She's up on the second floor now. Her name's Karen, I know now. Which is a nice name. I've been practicing saying it, in lots of ways. Happy ways, mainly; plus a few stern ways, just in case. Not sure where she is just at this second, but I'm guessing the bathroom. A door that can be locked. She's likely to start screaming again, in a while, so I'm going to have to work out what to do about that. Not all double-glazed up there. Last bout I covered with turning the television up loud. Limit to how many times I'm going to be able to do that. But who knows what the limits are? They're not as tight as you'd think. You can hit people, it turns out. You can listen to music you've never heard of, and learn to like it. You can choose not to give a shit what dead Mr Atkins said: you actually can eat potatoes if you feel like it—just like we're going to a little later on, when Karen calms down and we can sit like proper mates and have our supper.

For the time being I'm just going to sit on this nice sofa and smoke all I want and watch TV programmes I've never seen before. Judging by all the videos, Karen and Nick like documentaries. Better get used to that. Never been one for that kind of thing myself, but it's nice to have a change. For it all to be different. For it to be someone else's life, and not the same old shit of mine, the same old faces, the same old everything. I see later there's one of those home video programmes on, too. I love those. They're my favourite. I love seeing all the houses, the gardens, the wives and dogs. All of the different lives. Superb. If I get bored, I'll just text a few of her friends.

I was worried earlier, but I'm not now. What I felt was just a little niggle of doubt. Gone now. If you've got what it takes, everything's possible. I have high hopes, to be honest. I'm going to like being Nick. The woman's nice-looking. Much better than the last. From what I can make out, Nick was an estate agent. Piece of piss. I could do that—whereas, if I'm honest, I was crap at repairing televisions. Couldn't pick it up in two days, that was for sure. Wouldn't have been long before people started ringing me up, coming round, wanting their televisions back and spotting I wasn't the bloke they left them with and that they weren't fixed. Wasn't a stable life. Just as today, ten minutes after I left the house, a car will have come around expecting to pick up the woman, to take her out to a wonderful lunch with champagne and laughs. I knew about that. It was on their calendar, on the side of that retro fridge. Kind of forced my hand. Two days is a very short life and I didn't want to leave so soon, but I couldn't have talked my way out of that.

She hadn't worked out anyway. Didn't want a new start. Just wanted what she'd had.

Doesn't matter. I like a change. This life, I think it could be different. Could go on for longer. Well…to be honest, you only ever get about three, four days. But this will definitely be easier than the last one. More relaxing.

No sign of kids, for a start.

Later

I remember standing in the bedroom before we went out, fiddling with my tie and fretting mildly about the time. As yet we had plenty, but that was nothing to be complacent about. The minutes had a way of disappearing when Rachel was getting ready, early starts culminating in breathless searches for taxis. It was a party we were going to, so it didn't really matter what time we left, but I tend to be a little dull about time. I used to, anyway.

When I had the tie as close to a tidy knot as I was able I turned away from the mirror, and opened my mouth to call out to Rachel. But then I caught sight of what was on the bed, and closed it again. For a moment I just stood and looked, and then walked over towards it.

It wasn't anything very spectacular, just a dress made of sheeny white material. A few years ago, when we started going out together, Rachel used to make a lot of her clothes. She didn't do it because she had to, but because she enjoyed it. She used to haul me endlessly round dress-making shops, browsing patterns and asking my opinion on a million different fabrics, while I half-heartedly protested and moaned.

On impulse I leant down and felt the material, and found I could remember touching it for the first time in the shop on Mill Road, could recall surfacing up through contented boredom to say that yes, I liked this one. On that recommendation she'd bought it, and made this dress, and as a reward for traipsing around after her she'd bought me dinner too. We were poorer then, so the meal was cheap, but there was lots and it was good.

The strange thing was, I didn't even really mind the dress shops. You know how sometimes, when you're just walking around, living your life, you'll see someone on the street and fall hopelessly in love with them? How something in the way they look, the way they are, makes you stop dead in your tracks and stare: and how for that instant you're convinced that if you could just meet them, you'd be able to love them for ever?

Michael Marshall Smith

Wild schemes and unlikely chance meetings pass through your head, and yet as they stand on the other side of the street or the room, talking to someone else, they haven't the faintest idea of what's going through your mind. Something has clicked, but only inside your head. You know you'll never speak to them, that they'll never know what you're feeling, and that they'll never want to. But something about them forces you to keep looking, until you wish they'd leave so you could be free.

The first time I saw Rachel was like that, and now she was in my bath. I didn't call out to hurry her along. I decided it didn't really matter.

A few minutes later a protracted squawking noise announced the letting out of the bath water, and Rachel wafted into the bedroom swaddled in thick towels and glowing high spirits. Suddenly I lost all interest in going to the party, punctually or otherwise. She marched up to me, set her head at a silly angle to kiss me on the lips and jerked my tie vigorously in about three different directions. When I looked in the mirror I saw that somehow, as always, she'd turned it into a perfect knot.

Half an hour later we left the flat, still in plenty of time. If anything, I'd held her up.

'Later,' she'd said, smiling in the way that showed she meant it, 'Later, and for a long time, my man.'

I turned from locking the door to see her standing on the pavement outside the house, looking perfect in her white dress, looking happy. As I walked smiling down the steps towards her she skipped backwards into the road, laughing for no reason, laughing because she was with me.

'Come on,' she said, holding out her hand like a dancer, and a yellow van came round the corner and smashed into her.

She spun backwards as if tugged on a rope, rebounded off a parked car and toppled into the road. As I stood cold on the bottom step she half sat up and looked at me, an expression of wordless surprise on her face, and then she fell back again.

By the time I reached her, blood was already pulsing up into the white of her dress and welling out of her mouth. It ran out over her makeup and I saw she'd been right: she hadn't quite blended the colours above her eyes. I'd told her it didn't matter.

She tried to move her head again and there was a sticky sound as it almost left the tarmac and then slumped back. Her hair fell back from around her face, but not as it usually did. There was a faint flicker in her eyelids, and then she died.

I knelt there in the road beside her, holding her hand as the blood dried a little. I heard every word the small crowd said, but I don't know what they were muttering about. All I could think was that there wasn't

394

going to be a later, not to kiss her some more, not for anything.

It was as if everything had come to a halt, and hadn't started up again. Later was gone.

When I got back from the hospital I phoned her mother. I did it as soon as I got back, though I didn't want to. I didn't want to tell anyone, didn't want to make it official. It was a bad phone call, very, very bad. Then I sat in the flat, looking at the drawers she'd left open, at the towels on the floor, at the party invitation on the dressing table, feeling my stomach crawl.

I was back at the flat, as if we'd come back home from the party. I should have been making coffee while Rachel had yet another bath, coffee we'd drink on the sofa in front of the fire. But the fire was off and the bath was empty. So what was I supposed to do?

I sat for an hour, feeling as if somehow I'd slipped too far forward in time and left Rachel behind, as if I could turn and see her desperately running to try to catch me up. When it felt as if my throat was going to burst I called my parents and they came and took me home. My mother gently made me change my clothes, but she didn't wash them. Not until I was asleep, anyway. When I came down and saw them clean I hated her, but I knew she was right and the hate went away. There wouldn't have been much point in just keeping them in a drawer.

The funeral was short. I guess they all are, really, but there's no point in them being any longer. Nothing more would be said. I was a little better by then, and not crying so much, though I did before we went to the church because I couldn't get my tie to sit right.

Rachel was buried near her grandparents, which she would have liked. Her parents gave me her dress afterwards, because I'd asked for it. It had been thoroughly cleaned and large patches had lost their sheen and died, looking as much unlike Rachel's dress as the cloth had on the roll. I'd almost have preferred the bloodstains still to have been there: at least that way I could had believed that the cloth still sparkled beneath them. But they were right in their way, as my mother was. Some people seem to have pragmatic, accepting souls, an ability with death. I don't, I'm afraid. I don't understand it at all.

Afterwards I stood at the graveside for a while, but not for long because I knew that my parents were waiting at the car. As I stood by the mound of earth that lay on top of her I tried to concentrate, to send some final thought to her, some final love, but the world kept pressing in on me through the sound of cars on the road and some bird that was cawing up in a tree. I couldn't shut it out. I couldn't believe that I was noticing how

Michael Marshall Smith

cold it was, or that somewhere lives were being led and televisions being watched, that the inside of my parents' car would smell the same as it always had. I wanted to feel something, wanted to sense her presense, but I couldn't. All I could feel was the world round me, the same old world. But it wasn't a world that had been there a week ago, and I couldn't understand how it could look so much the same.

It was the same because nothing had changed, and I turned and walked to the car.

The wake was worse than the funeral, much worse, and I stood with a tuna sandwich feeling something very cold building up inside. Rachel's oldest friend Lisa held court with her old school friends, swiftly running the range of emotions from stoic resilience to trembling incoherence.

'I've just realised,' she sobbed to me, 'Rachel's not going to be at my wedding.'

'She's not going to be at mine either,' I said numbly, and immediately hated myself for it. I went and stood by the window, out of harm's way. I couldn't react properly. I knew why everyone was standing here, that in some ways it was like a wedding. Instead of gathering together to bear witness to a bond, they were here to prove she was dead. In the weeks to come they'd know they'd stood together in a room, and would be able to accept she was gone. I couldn't.

I said goodbye to Rachel's parents before I left. We looked at each other oddly, and shook hands, as if we were just strangers again. Then I went back to the flat and changed into some old clothes. My 'Someday' clothes, Rachel used to call them, as in 'some day you must throw them away'. Then I made a cup of tea and stared out of the window for a while. I knew damn well what I was going to do, and it was a relief to give in to it.

That night I went back to the cemetery and I dug her up.

It was hard work, and it took a lot longer than I expected, but in another way it was surprisingly easy. I mean yes, it was creepy, and yes, I felt like a lunatic, but after the shovel had gone in once the second time seemed less strange. It was like waking up in the mornings after the accident. The first time I clutched at myself and couldn't understand, but after that I knew what to expect. There were no cracks of thunder, there was no web of lightening and I actually felt very calm. There was just me and, beneath the earth, my friend. I simply wanted to find her.

When I did I laid her down by the side of the grave and then filled it back up again, being careful to make it look undisturbed. Then I carried

396

her to the car in my arms and brought her home.

The flat seemed very quiet as I sat her on the sofa, and the cushion rustled and creaked as it took her weight again. When she was settled I knelt and looked up at her face. It looked much the same as it always had, though the colour of the skin was different, didn't have the glow she always had. That's where life is, you know, not in the heart but in the little things, like the way hair falls around a face. Her nose looked the same and her forehead was smooth. It was the same face.

I knew the dress she was wearing was hiding a lot of things I would rather not see, but I took it off anyway. It was her going away dress, bought by her family especially for the occasion, and it didn't mean anything to me or to her. I knew what the damage would be and what it meant. As it turned out the patchers and menders had done a good job, not glossing because it wouldn't be seen. It wasn't so bad.

When she was sitting up again in her white dress I walked over and turned the light down, and I cried a little, because she looked so much the same. She could have fallen asleep, warmed by the fire and dozy with wine, as if we'd just come back from the party.

I went and had a bath then. We both used to when we came back in from an evening, to feel clean and fresh for when we slipped between the sheets. It wouldn't be like that this evening, of course, but I had dirt all over me, and I wanted to feel normal. For one night at least I just wanted things to be as they had.

I sat in the bath for a while, knowing she was in the living room, and slowly washed myself clean. I really wasn't thinking much. It felt nice to know that I wouldn't be alone when I walked back in there. That was better than nothing, was part of what had made her alive. I dropped my Someday clothes in the bin and put on the ones from the evening of the accident. They didn't mean as much as her dress, but at least they were from before.

When I returned to the living room her head had lolled slightly, but it would have done if she'd been asleep. I made us both a cup of coffee. The only time she ever took sugar was in last cup of the day, so I put one in. Then I sat down next to her on the sofa and I was glad that the cushions had her dent in them, that as always they drew me slightly towards her, didn't leave me perched there by myself.

The first time I saw Rachel was at a party. I saw her across the room and simply stared at her, but we didn't speak. We didn't meet properly for a month or two, and first kissed a few weeks after that. As I sat there on the sofa next to her body I reached out tentatively and took her hand, as I had done on that night. It was cooler than it should have been, but

397

not too bad because of the fire, and I held it, feeling the lines on her palm, lines I knew better than my own.

I let myself feel calm and I held her hand in the half-light, not looking at her, as also on that first night, when I'd been too happy to push my luck. *She's letting you hold her hand*, I'd thought, *don't expect to be able to look at her too. Holding her hand is more than enough: don't look, you'll break the spell*. My face creased then, not knowing whether to smile or cry, but it felt alright. It really did.

I sat there for a long time, watching the flames, still not thinking, just holding her hand and letting the minutes run. The longer I sat the more normal it felt, and finally I turned slowly to look at her. She looked tired and asleep, so deeply asleep, but still there with me and still mine.

When her eyelid first moved I thought it was a trick of the light, a flicker cast by the fire. But then it stirred again, and for the smallest of moments I thought I was going to die. The other eyelid moved and my fear just disappeared, and that made the difference, I think. She had a long way to come, and if I'd felt frightened, or rejected her, I think that would have finished it then. I didn't question it.

A few minutes later both her eyes were open, and it wasn't long before she was able to slowly turn her head.

I still go to work and put in the occasional appearance at social events, but my tie never looks quite as it did. She can't move her fingers precisely enough to help me with that any more. She can't come with me, and nobody can come here, but that doesn't matter. We always spent a lot of time by ourselves. We wanted to.

I have to do a lot of things for her, but I can live with that. Lots of people have accidents, bad ones: if Rachel had survived she could have been disabled, or brain-damaged, so that her movements were as they are now, so slow and clumsy. I wish she could talk, but there's no air in her lungs, so I'm learning to read her lips. Her mouth moves slowly, but I know she's trying to speak, and I want to hear what she's saying.

But she gets round the flat, and she holds my hand, and she smiles as best she can. If she'd just been injured I would have loved her still. It's not so very different.

More Bitter Than Death

'That was *bollocks*,' said Nick amiably, leaning on his cue. 'You've produced some terrible shots this evening, but that really has to take it. Go to the library, get out a book on basic physics. Start again from the ground up.'

I stepped back from the table and replied with a cheerful obscenity before taking a sip of my beer. I wasn't playing that badly on the whole, but the last couple of games had been very erratic. When I play a pool shot, it's either very good or abysmal. There doesn't seem to be a middle ground in my game, any 'fairly good' or 'not bad' shots. How I'm playing depends solely on the ratio of the sublime to the ridiculous.

'If this comes off,' Nick muttered, lining up an ambitious double cannon, 'You'll have confirmed your standing as the luckiest player in the cosmos,' I finished for him.

Not only did the shot not come off, it sent the cue ball clear off the table to bounce loudly on the wooden floor and rocket off towards the other side of the hall. Because I was nearest, I went after it. Players at the other tables watched impassively as I tried not to look as if I was scurrying.

The pool hall in the Archway Tavern is on the first floor, a large bare rectangular room with high ceilings that covers the area of the two bars on the floor below. There are two snooker tables and five for pool, an area of seats and tables around the nuclear-powered jukebox, and a bar set into the wall near the door. Not an especially prepossessing room, in a fairly rough Irish Pub (painted entirely green on the outside, just in case anyone should be in any doubt), but I'd been going there to play pool regularly for over a year, and there'd never been any trouble. While the locals are generally too taciturn to be called friendly they always seem fairly affable, and with discs full of the Fureys and the Dubliners in the jukebox the atmosphere on a good night is pretty good.

The cue ball made it all the way to the far corner of the room, banging to rest under the pool table there.

'Sorry,' I said, trying not to sound too English, and crouched down to retrieve it. The two youths at the table continued playing. Reaching under, I scrabbled with my fingertips and eventually dislodged the ball. I stood up rather quickly and felt my head dizzy for a moment as I turned to head back to the other side of the room.

Then suddenly the evening, which was already fine, took a turn for the better.

They had arrived.

I walked back to our table, trying to look nonchalant, willing myself not to look back at the bar.

'Two shots,' Nick conceded.

'No, really? I had to catch a fucking bus.'

I took my time putting the cue ball in position, ostensibly lining up the next break, but in fact covertly glancing up the room. The only free table was the next but one to ours. If they were going to play pool rather than just hang around and chat with their mates near the jukebox, then they would be less than five yards away.

I sent the cue ball rocketing towards a stray red near the end of the table, not really expecting it to go in. The hidden agenda of the shot was to get Nick back on the table so that I could carry on looking up the room. Unfortunately I'd judged it too well and the ball smacked into the pocket. Nick tapped the handle of his cue sagely on the floor. Choosing a shot that would allow me to glance up to the bar, I lent over the table to see that, drinks in hand, they were indeed heading towards the free table, a gaggle of their mates in tow. I tightened up and missed an easy shot into the centre pocket.

Nick shook his head. 'Sometimes I wonder if there are two completely different people inside you,' he said. 'A twenty-six-year-old veteran and a five-year-old paraplegic, taking alternate shots. Oh.' Having noticed the new arrivals, he gave me a knowing smile. 'I see. Distraction.'

I grinned sheepishly, feeling like a fourteen-year-old accused of fancying a girl in the sixth form. This time the relationship was completely the opposite, but it still evoked the same mixed feelings of pride and utter stupidity.

The source of these emotions was the girl at the next table but one. She and her virtually identical twin sister were regulars at the Tavern, sometimes playing pool, sometimes just hanging out with a group of other locals. The twins were both tall, extremely slim and unnecessarily pretty. The difference between them was that my one had slightly more prominent cheekbones, and her long wavy brown hair was cut slightly shorter than her sister's. Her skin was pale, and her lips were red. She and her sister were, I guessed, about seventeen.

'When you're ready. In your own time,' sighed Nick theatrically.

'What?'

'It's your shot.'

Down at the other table they were racking up the balls, the second twin talking to another of the regular girl players. My one was standing slightly apart, taking her jacket off, causing a simultaneous feeling of joy and despair in me. The loose jeans she was wearing I could cope with, but her top appeared to be the upper half of a grey leotard, and clung to her like a swimming costume. It wasn't worn smugly, which made it even worse. She was just wearing it because she could, and I knew that faced with that length of slim perfection I was going to find it impossible not to keep looking at her.

'Jesus wept,' I whispered to myself, and tried to concentrate on the shot. The centre pocket pot was easy, but I had to do some work to get position on the next shot. Aiming at the bottom of the cue ball I dug in hard for maximum backspin. The white leapt neatly over the red and left the table, nearly hitting Nick in the stomach.

'Shame,' he said, when his hysterics had subsided, 'they were watching.'

I smiled at him, hoping he was joking. He didn't look as if he was, and my smile turned rather tight-lipped as I sat down to wait. Given two shots and the position of the yellows, he'd almost certainly finish up with this break. As he moved methodically round the table, potting, I sipped my warm Budweiser and looked up the room.

Intent on her shot, she was bending over the table, her back to me. I let my eyes wander over the slim strength of her lovely long back, and felt a crushing weight of unhappiness settle into me. I felt like I was watching her through glass, staring in from the outside, as she chatted with a friend, waiting for her next shot while her sister made a creditable attempt at a long pot. Her voice, which I heard for the first time, was pure London, though the accent was pleasantly mild for the area. As she leant over to take her next shot, this time in profile, the misery I was feeling deepened. There are some things I find unbearably attractive in a woman: cheekbones, a definite nose, long and thick brown hair, slim upper arms and shoulders, a long back and willowy stomach, a small chest and graceful hands. She had every single one of these. And she was seventeen, and I was pathetic.

A resounding *thwak* signaled the end of the game as Nick drilled the black into one of the end pockets. He was having a very good evening.

'Your set-up,' I said, climbing to my feet. 'You ready for another?'

As I was waiting for attention at the bar I wandered over to the juke box and put on my two favourite songs of the time, Heart's 'Secret' and Bruce Springsteen's 'I'm on Fire.' I was obviously in a queue, however, because the next to come on was a delightful piece entitled 'Yeah Baby, Do It Again,' by some American heavy metal band. Returning to the table I shook my head at Nick to signal that this wasn't my choice.

'Thought not,' he said, accepting his cider, 'Can I guess what you've put on?'

'Probably,' I grunted, and broke the pack. Nick always gives me a hard time for the songs I select, claiming that they are without exception morbid and about failed relationships. Nick is in a position to laugh about things like that, because he's happily married. He has someone who cares about him, someone to love, and he's not so fucked up that he can get obsessed with slim girls he'll never speak to who are ten years younger than he is.

As the game wore on my play improved. Reds are usually a good colour for me. The girl sat out the next game as her sister played the blonde-haired regular. She sat staring into space, semi-expertly dragging on a cigarette. I wondered what she was thinking about. I forced myself to be more cheerful, not wanting to spoil Nick's evening.

Basically, in most areas, I'm fairly together. I have a reasonable job as Editor of a video trade magazine, and pick up good money on the side as a freelance journalist. I don't have that many friends, but the ones I have are good, and I'm not lonely much more often than anyone else, I don't think. Emotionally things aren't quite so good, but I don't really want to talk about that. I've been over my last relationship in my head so many times that it's boring even to me, and I've given up hope of ever making sense of it or exorcising it from my mind. It's no big deal, just another relationship that started off well and then took a very long time going off the rails. I was hurt, and now it's over. So what.

Nick missed an easy black and set me up nicely to take the game.

'Once more the God of pool craps on my head,' he said mildly, reaching for the chalk.

I like playing Nick because he doesn't care who wins, and for a non-competitor like me, that's essential. As I bent to take the shot the song on the jukebox finished, and after a pause I heard the piano introduction and then the crashing opening chords of 'Secret.' Nick groaned from behind me.

'Not *again*.'

I smiled, feeling buoyed up by the music, and slotted the penultimate red down. Songs about the trials of love and how much grief it is to be alive always cheer me up, and as I lined up the last red I felt my heart loosen. Mooning after a perfectly ordinary, if unusually beautiful, seventeen-year-old was beneath even my currently sterile life. I was just lonely, and being silly. Fuck it, I told myself, relax. Forget about it. As the song slammed into the first chorus I glanced up at the girl, a wry smile at myself unthinkingly on my lips.

She was looking at me.

For a long moment time stopped as our eyes met. The moment went well beyond a casual coincidence, and far into extra time. Around us the chorus raged, telling of a love that must remain a secret, ooh yeah, and still we looked down a long tunnel at each other, unblinkingly staring into each other's eyes. Her eyes were blue, and beautiful, and there were no scars round them.

'You better come quickly, Doctor. The patient's blown a fuse again.'

When I looked back after registering Nick's crack, she was looking the other way, talking to the blonde-haired girl. For a moment I doubted that it had happened, but from the tightness in my chest and the perspiration on my forehead, I knew it had. I cracked the cue ball down the table and the red zipped into the pocket as if pulled on a piece of taut elastic. The white reversed with perfect backspin and edged the black off the cushion and over a pocket.

'My friend's body has been taken over by an alien force,' Nick said, tapping his cue on the floor again, 'one that is considerably better at pool than he is.' Grinning, I ignored the open pocket and doubled the black into the opposite one instead, to Nick's good-natured chagrin.

'Flash bastard,' he muttered, slotting in another 50 pence.

My streak continued and I took the next two games easily. During the first I looked up to see the two sisters in a huddle by the side of their table, and got the very clear impression that it was me they were talking about. She could, of course, be saying that the weird bloke down the end was staring at her, but 'I'm on Fire' was playing and I didn't believe she was. She had looked at me just as much as I had at her. Then, looking like someone in a video for the song, she raised her head slightly and our eyes met again. There was a faint smile curling on her lips. I was right. It was mutual.

Halfway through the second game they left the pool hall. Something immediately went out of the evening and my game lost some of its sparkle, but I was on enough of a roll to win. We were about to set up again but Nick noticed that it was nearly eleven, and, doubtless keen to get back to Zoe, called it a night. I gave him a dose of my running joke about him having to get back before curfew, which he accepted with good grace while giving me one of his customarily alarming lifts home in his mad Mini.

While I waited for the water for a final cup of coffee to boil, I looked at my face in the bathroom mirror. It's not especially good-looking, but it's alright, apparently. I genuinely can't tell. I have greeny-brown eyes and a high forehead, prominent cheekbones and dark brown hair that insists on a slavish adherence to the laws of gravity. My lips are full, my nose is definite and my skin is generally pale. I hate my face, and have done for as long as I can remember.

The kettle in the kitchen pinged electronically to signify that it had boiled, but I ignored it for a moment, just to piss it off.

Around my right eye there are a number of scars. I don't know if you've ever noticed this, but by far the majority of people have a little scar somewhere near their eyes, the remnant of some childish fall. Most people can remember how they got them, and the ensuing frantic trip to the hospital, panicky parents and ice cream afterwards for being good. I can remember how I got mine too.

Sitting on the sofa with my coffee in the silent flat, I noticed that the answering machine was flashing. It was a message from Jane, my ex-flatmate, asking if I was doing anything tomorrow night. I called her back, knowing that she went to bed late, and arranged to play pool with her in the Archway Tavern. The girl might be there again, and now that contact, however nebulous, had been made, I didn't want to miss a chance of seeing her again.

I took the remainder of my coffee to bed with me, and drank it with a cigarette, staring across the bedroom. It's far too large, the bedroom, given that nothing interesting ever happens there any more. There's a huge walk-in wardrobe down the end, crammed with my junk from the last two years, and a large dresser up against one wall. Stuck in the mirror are two photographs, one of my parents and one of Siobhan.

She left me, is what happened, if you want to know. Several times, indecisively, intermittently, and painfully. The reasons were complex and various, and not all her fault, but by any scale of reckoning, she done me wrong. As I've said, I've thought about it too much now, and never expect to be able to untangle it. It isn't even the leaving that I hold against her. People fall in love, meet someone who strikes a deeper chord: that's the way life works, and I could have respected that. Siobhan didn't have the courage to do what she wanted to do, however, and so she played the percentage game with me as the comfortable option. She left, and as soon as she had gone, called me up to say she loved me. When she was with me I never had her, and when she was gone, she didn't let me go. I wanted her back, and couldn't break free, but when she came back each time it was unwillingly and incompletely, and that felt even worse. I couldn't have her, but I wasn't allowed to have anyone else. And then finally she left for good. So there you are.

I dreamt that night, of my mother. I was in our old house, looking out into the garden at night. My mother stood alone in the moonlight, her back to me, holding a long stick that looked a little like a pool cue. She turned back towards the house and when the wind moved her long brown hair from her face, I could see that she was crying. When she looked up at my window the light glinted on the tears round her eyes, making them look like shining scars.

Thursday at work was long and tedious, as Thursdays always are. The chief graphic designer on 'Communiqué' is a bit too hip for his own good, and for the third week running I had to remind him with some vehemence that our first priority is getting all the words on the pages they're supposed to be on, not just making pretty pictures. I later overheard him describing me as a philistine to the chief sub-editor, so I accidentally spilt some coffee on some personal work of his he'd left lying around in the office. Just another morning in a small organisation.

The afternoon was less fraught. I spent most of it at my desk, the neatness of which I know irritates the chief graphic designer immensely. By five o'clock I had nothing to do except stare at the photos I keep there, one of my parents and one of Siobhan, and so I went home early.

Jane was already there by the time I got to the Archway Tavern, and clearly somewhat relieved to see me. I've never felt directly threatened there, but I suppose for a lone non-Irish female it's probably different. Once we'd bought our drinks we set up camp round the table in the top corner. The twins weren't anywhere to be seen, which was both disappointing and somehow a bit of a relief.

Jane is actually bloody good at pool, and by nine we were fully absorbed, conversation chugging along in a pleasantly desultory fashion. We've known each other since college, and shared a platonic flat for eighteen months a couple of years ago. I think we're probably both the only person of the opposite sex we know who we can be just straightforward friends with, and that's nice.

Then at ten o'clock they came in. I was coming back from the bar with a couple more beers, and passed just in front of her, holding my shoulders back and trying to look like a potentially desirable human being. She didn't look directly at me, we were too near each other for that

405

kind of risk at this stage, but there was a definite atmosphere as I passed. I arrived back at the table with the smell of her perfume wraith-like round my neck.

'Are you alright?' asked Jane, who didn't know anything about the twins. 'You look like you've been punched in the stomach.'

'I'm fine,' I said, and I felt it. Something was going on. The look yesterday had raised the game, and now, however tiny, something was going on. She was still seventeen and I still felt stupid, but it was exciting all the same.

I gave her time to get settled before I glanced over in their direction. By dint of an inspired potting streak Jane won the game and only as she was setting the balls up for the next did I look over.

As soon as I did, I knew something was wrong. She wasn't playing, but sitting to one side while her sister did. She wasn't staring dreamily into space as yesterday, but looking down at the floor, her expression hard. Distracted, I broke the pack badly and Jane settled down to pot some of the many available balls. The girl was still staring, and one leg was now jogging up and down in obvious anger. Maybe something had happened over in her world. Maybe it was nothing to do with me. But it didn't feel like it.

The answer came when I straightened from taking my next shot. My eyes were drawn over to their table and I saw that she was no longer staring at the floor, but over in our direction. She wasn't looking at me, however. She was staring at Jane, and her eyes were flashing, her jaw set in a tight smile. Immediately I understood.

When Jane next passed me I took great care to stand back as far as possible from her, making it as clear as I could that we were not a couple. There were some lads in the twins' group this evening too: surely she could understand that being with a girl didn't necessarily mean that there was anything going on. As the game progressed Jane seemed almost to be conspiring against me: she was in a good mood, looking at me and laughing prettily, playfully jogging my cue and generally destroying the impression I was trying to create.

This reached a peak as I chalked up before breaking in the next game but one. I take good care of my cue. It used to belong to my father, and every inch of it, right down to the dent in the wood near the base, is very dear to me.

I'd only dared to glance across at her twice in the last fifteen minutes, and both times she was talking to someone, her back to me. Just as I was bending down to break I saw her slowly start turning towards me.

'This may help,' said Jane, and covered my eyes with her hands.

Dumbfounded, I broke, and she took them away again. I couldn't believe that she had done that. We've known each other for six years and tonight of all nights she had to behave as if we were lovers. In the centre of my wildly staring gaze was the girl, and she was looking right at me. For a moment I stood still, transfixed. That's done it, I thought, that's fucked it up for good.

Then, amazingly, the girl's face softened. Something in my face must have communicated my distress to her, and I could see that in that instant, she understood. She tilted her head on one side and looked for a moment longer, and then turned back to her sister.

They left as Jane and I finished the next game. Just before she reached the door, and without breaking her stride, she quite clearly turned and looked at me. On her face was a quizzical expression, a combination of raised eyebrow and crooked smile that I understood perfectly. I'd got away with it, but only just. Long experience with Siobhan had shown me that the longer any problem is left unsolved, the more likely it is to leave a scar. What I had to do was find some way of healing the rift.

A means of attempting that occurred to me on the way to work the next morning. What I would do was ring Nick and ask him, applying pressure if necessary, to play pool with me that evening. If she was there, and saw me playing with him again, she'd have proof that Jane didn't mean anything to me, was just another person I played pool with. We'd be free to recommence the progression that the meeting of our eyes on Wednesday night had started.

I didn't get round to calling Nick until the afternoon, because of a long and extremely acrimonious row with the chief graphic designer.

What happened was this. I walked into the office, feeling almost cheerful now that I'd thought of a way of making things up with the girl, to find that someone had been at my desk. Not only that: the person had taken the photo of Siobhan out of the frame and had torn it up. They had also taken my parents' photo out and cut the half with my mother in to pieces.

I stared at the fragments for a long time, unable to move, unable to think. It was only when I noticed that I had tears running down my face that I pulled myself up. I looked at the pieces strewn across the desk and realised that there could only be one possible culprit. The graphic designer must have found out that it was me who had spoiled his personal work, which he should on no account have been doing in office time, and this was his revenge. For slightly messing up some piece of rubbish he had taken the photos of the two people who mattered most to me in the world and cut them up with a scalpel.

Michael Marshall Smith

I immediately confronted him, and was so worked up by then that I almost punched him in the face when he denied it. He denied even knowing it was me who had messed up his work. The argument spread into unrelated areas and within ten minutes we were standing shouting at each other. In the end he stormed out to lunch. Ignoring the covert glances of some of the other staff I sat heavily back at my desk, and tried to piece the photo of my mother back together again. I couldn't stop myself from crying, and soon I was left alone in the room. My mother died five years ago, and I still miss her every day. I loved her very much.

Nick professed himself able and willing to go out that evening, which was good. After the morning I'd had I didn't feel up to applying any pressure, and certainly didn't want to cite the real reason for my escalating interest in pool. During the day I had to try not to think too hard about the girl. In daylight the image of what I felt about her wavered, was dissolved by the vestiges of pride. I couldn't believe that I was getting myself into this state over some seventeen-year-old I'd still not spoken to. It wasn't reasonable, it wasn't normal. Only at night could I believe what I had seen in her eyes, know that a bond was forming between us, a special link.

I went home early, walked straight into the sitting room and dozed off on the sofa for a couple of hours. I hadn't been sleeping too well for the last couple of weeks, and coupled with the morning's furore it had just got too much for me.

As I struggled back towards wakefulness, aware that it had become dark outside and that I should shower and eat before Nick came, I felt the shards of a dream fade around me. I had once more been looking out of my window in the old house, the house we lived in before my mother went away. My mother was standing out in the garden again, and this time I ran downstairs and rushed into the garden, feeling the damp grass beneath my feet in the darkness. As I got closer she turned and I saw that again she was crying. My mother had some minor emotional problems, and seeing her crying is one of my earliest memories of her. But as I looked at her I felt my skin begin to crawl, because although it looked exactly like her, though every line, every bone was in the right place, it wasn't her. It looked as though someone of the right general shape and build had been given the world's most perfect plastic surgery until there was no surface difference, none at all. As I stood looking at her the wind whipped the hair across her face and a dog barked somewhere nearby. She was tall and very slim, my mother, and as she bent down towards me I had plenty of time to turn and run. But I didn't. I never did. I loved her. The hair cleared from her face, thrown backwards by another gust, and

MORE BITTER THAN DEATH

I saw that it wasn't my mother after all. It was her. It was the girl.

The last thing I saw as I woke up was that she wasn't crying any more. She was smiling, a hard, tight smile that I recognised from somewhere.

I stood up slowly and wandered clumsily across the room, rubbing my face with my hands. I knew I should remember that smile, but couldn't. I looked groggily over at the clock, and saw that I still had an hour before Nick was due to arrive. Shaking my head against the heavy residue of afternoon sleep I walked into the bedroom.

At first I couldn't tell what was different. After a moment I realised it was that I could see the whole of my face in the dresser mirror, and then I saw.

The picture of Siobhan had been shredded, and my mother's half of the other picture was a slashed and tangled mess. The chief graphic designer passed through my mind for an instant, but I knew that it wasn't him who had done this.

On impulse I flung open the doors to the wardrobe and dropped to my knees, flinging things out behind me as I dug for the box I kept in the back. When I'd found it I sat back cross-legged and opened it on my lap, trembling.

Every photo in the box had been slashed. Every photo had either Siobhan or my mother in it, and every one had been reduced to small strips of meaningless colour. My graduation photo, with Siobhan on my arm back in the days when she loved me, was in pieces. The photo of me on my fifth birthday, sitting on my mother's lap with the bandages still round my right eye, was little more than confetti.

Spilling the petals of colour out onto the floor I lunged and stuck my hand under the bed. In a box within a box within a box I found my special photos. Nobody knew I kept them there, nobody. I opened the cigar box that should have held my favourite three photos of my mother and the best two of Siobhan, and inside was nothing but a tangle of photographic paper. They'd not been cut calmly, neatly, but mangled, ripped and gouged apart, slashed and shredded with utter hatred.

I got the message, as I sat there surrounded by ruin, I understood. There are no compromises, there is no middle ground. You are with someone, or you are without them. You either have them or you don't, and if you have them, you have them and them alone. There can be no-one else, ever. This was a warning, a message, a sign of the way things would stand. This was no normal girl, and if I was to have her, it was to the exclusion of anyone else, past, present or future.

The phone rang. Without thinking, out of pure reaction to the jangling sound, I snatched the bedroom extension. It was Nick. He couldn't make it. He was doing something else. He'd forgotten. He was sorry. Monday?

I put the phone down, and stood up, grabbing my coat from the wardrobe. I had to turn up, to show that the message was received and understood. If I had to do it alone, so be it. I called a cab and waited outside for it, swinging my cue case impatiently. It was full dark by then, and a dog barked somewhere nearby.

It was crowded in the Archway Tavern. By the time I got there it was after nine, and on a Friday it's just swinging into its busiest period by then. All the tables were taken, the air was laden with smoke, and the twins were nowhere to be seen. I bought a beer and waited, sitting near one of the tables at the far end of the bar.

They came in half an hour later, surrounded by their friends. The blonde pool-playing girl was there, as were the two lads from the previous night. I fought down the urge to get straight up and go across. That wasn't the way to do it. There is a right way to do everything, and everything must be done in the right way. I hadn't eaten all day, and the beer was going straight to my head. It was very noisy and hot and smoky and there were people all around shouting happily at each other and I sat there with my cue case on my lap waiting for the right time, waiting for the sign.

Then suddenly a ray of quiet cut across the bar as the song on the jukebox ended. After a moment of relative silence I heard a distinctive piano riff, and then smiled as a familiar guitar chord scythed through the smoke. It was 'Secret'. That was it.

That was the sign.

I stood up and walked down towards the other end of the bar. The twins were standing in a gaggle round a pool table there. I worked my way round the back of the group, feeling my heart swell. I would let her know that I understood. When I was behind her I tapped her on the shoulder. She turned and looked at me. For a second I thought I read something in her eyes, and then all I saw was distaste.

'Hello,' I said.

'Who the fuck are you?'

The others in the group were staring at me. I smiled at them and then turned back to her.

'I got your message. I understand.'

'What message? What the fuck are you talking about?'

I saw the others' faces again. Some of them were looking embarrassed. The blonde pool player was giggling behind her hand. The twin sister was looking at the girl, eyebrows raised, shaking her head. I began to feel very bad.

'You know what I mean. The photos.'

She gave an angry and embarrassed laugh, and shook her head.

'I don't know what you're talking about. Now piss off.'

'Yeah. Piss off.' This was from one of the lads. Maybe he fancied her. He reached out and shoved my chest. I wasn't ready for it, and fell backwards, banging into a table. The group turned its back on me and laughed. The blonde girl kept giggling, giggling.

I staggered upright, feeling the chorus of 'Secret' reverberating through my bones. The barman looked at me sternly, but it was okay. I was going.

In the car park I smoked some cigarettes and waited for an hour. Just after ten the group came out, and the girl separated from the rest of them and headed down the Holloway Road. I followed her, pausing for a moment to pick something up from outside a house.

I understood. I had made a mistake. I had brought it into the open in front of her friends, in front of people who knew nothing about it, who didn't know that she was special, that she was capable of unusual things. When I saw which house she was going into I went round the back and carefully climbed up the drainpipe to the balcony.

I understand things, you see. I learn very quickly. When I was four I dropped a bottle of milk on the kitchen floor. When my mother saw what I had done she got out my father's cue and calmly screwed the two halves together. Then she swung the cue with all her strength and smashed me round the face with it. That's how I got one of the scars round my eye. I told you I could remember. When I was six I said something wrong and she grabbed my hair and banged my head into the corner of the kitchen table six times, once for each year. I had to go into hospital that time, with concussion. I didn't tell anyone what had happened. It was our secret.

I never dropped the milk again, and I never said anything wrong. I learn.

A light went on inside as the girl went into the kitchen. She opened the fridge and there was milk inside. She drank some and then put the bottle back. I eased the latch on the balcony door open and stepped soundlessly into the flat. As she came out of the kitchen I could see her face, and she was smiling a tight, hard smile. I remembered it now. It was the smile my mother had when she picked up the piece of broken glass from the milk bottle to run it across my stomach. It was the smile she had when she pulled my head up from banging it on the table and pushed her fingernail into the new gash by my right eye. It was the smile she had the first and last time she met my first girlfriend.

Michael Marshall Smith

The girl walked into the living room and sat on the sofa without turning the light on. She was waiting for me. She knew I was coming.

The only girlfriend I had before Siobhan was called Sally. She went to the same school as me, and we went to the films a couple of times. Then I brought her home to meet Mum and Dad. Dad was in the garden so we went into the kitchen first to meet Mum. She was sitting at the kitchen table. There was a milk bottle on the table. When she saw us she gave that tight hard smile and stood up. I introduced them to each other, but I don't think I did it very well. I was distracted. I thought I could see blood on the corner of the kitchen table.

'So this is Sally,' said Mother, leaning back against the table, arms folded.

'Yes. Hello,' said Sally, smiling sweetly.

Moving carefully, I edged closer to the living room. I could hear the girl humming, and the tune was 'I'm on Fire.' She had sent her twin off with the others just so she could be here alone.

Mother smiled at Sally for a moment, and then gestured me to come and stand next to her.

'She's a bit fat, isn't she?' Mother said, putting her arm round my waist. 'He normally prefers slimmer girls, don't you?' She turned to me, smiling, and ran a finger along the biggest scar by my eye. 'Tall and slim with long brown hair.' Then she pulled my head towards hers. Sally backed out of the kitchen as my mother pushed her tongue into my mouth, sucking my lips and sliding her hand up under my shirt. She pushed herself up against me and laughed as Sally ran out of the house. I never spoke to Sally again. Then mother bit my face and shoved me away from her. Off balance, I fell and banged my face on the side of the fridge. That's how I got my final scar. I learnt. I understood. I couldn't have her, but I couldn't have anyone else either.

I walked into the living room of the flat. The girl pretended to be surprised to see me, even screamed a little, but I wasn't embarrassed any more. I knew how things worked, knew that this had to remain a secret between us. I pulled my cue out from behind me and belted her across the face with it. She went down onto the floor. She tried to speak but her nose was broken and blood was running into her mouth. I couldn't hear what she was saying, but it didn't matter, because I knew what the score was, and I was doing what I was supposed to. I didn't need instructions. I smashed the milk bottle I'd picked up on the Holloway Road on her forehead, and pushed the broken neck into her right eye. Now she had some scars, and I pushed my fingers deep into them, feeling the bone beneath, feeling what mum had felt. I pushed my tongue into her mouth, sucking her lips, and slid my hand up her shirt. She struggled as I pushed the bottle into her stomach, and screamed as best she could as the soft skin there punctured and my hand fell in. I knew there wasn't that much time so I pulled my hand back out and linked it with the other one round her throat. I put my face as close to hers as I could as I squeezed, watching the blood from her scars trickle into her eyes and down her cheek.

As she gasped I looked up for a moment, looked at the room, the chairs, the carpet. This was our place now, somewhere only she and I had been. Blood and saliva ran out of her nose and mouth as she choked and I put my cheek right next to her mouth, waiting to see if I could tell.

And I could. I knew which was the last breath, I could feel it on my face, and I sucked it up into my body. I held her for a while, rocking her close, and we shared a happiness that I cannot describe, that is impossible to explain. She'd needed to be the only one, to have me completely, and she did. As we sat there we were the only two people in the world, and I thanked God she'd had the ingenuity and the magic to give me a message I could understand. This place would never stop being ours, and its power would never fade. I felt her slimness against me, and pushed my hands through her hair, looking at the scars we shared.

She was special, and she was the only one I could ever love. The fact that she was dead would not stop her having me forever.

A Long Walk, For The Last Time

As it turned out, the morning was bright and sunny.
When she passed the coat she'd put ready in the hallway the night before,
May smiled. She wouldn't be needing *that*.

As she waited for the kettle to boil she stood by the kitchen window,
looking out over the meadow. Tall grass rolled gently in swathes, rich in
the growing light. It was going to be a beautiful day, which was good. She
had a long way to walk and the sun was nice for walking in. When the
kettle flicked itself off she reached over to the cupboard and rootled
around until she found a teabag. After so many years of living in one
place, she still hadn't really got used to her new kitchen, and seemed to
discover it anew every morning.

She sat in the living room while she drank her cup of tea, telling
herself she was summoning up the energy to start. But really she was
squaring herself mentally to the day's business, readying herself for it. She
felt a little apprehensive, as if preparing to attend to something that didn't
mean as much as it once had, but which nevertheless needed to be tidied
away.

Her tea finished, she padded back into the kitchen, peering
suspiciously down at the floor. Her kitchen in Belden Road had been
covered with cheerful lino, which she'd kept spotlessly clean. The stone
slabs here seemed perpetually on the verge of being dusty, no matter how
often she swept them. She had to admit they were nice, though. Very
traditional. She knew she'd come to like them as much as she did the rest
of the cottage, and in time she'd worry less about keeping them clean.
Perhaps.

After swilling her cup with cold water and setting it by the sink to dry,
she packed a few things together for lunch. She put a large piece of
cheese, a tomato and some bread in a bag, and as an afterthought added
a green apple and a knife to cut it with. Chances were she wouldn't need
any of it, of course, but would find somewhere to stop along the way. She

hadn't explored the area well enough yet, though, and it was better to be safe than sorry.

In the hallway she smiled at her coat once more, this time because of the memories it stirred. Cyril had bought it for her, many years ago. They'd been on holiday by the sea, and the weather had turned so cold after lunch on the first day that they'd gone into the little town to buy some warmer clothes. She'd seen the coat in the window of one of the two tiny shops, and, after some thought, rejected it as too expensive. Then later, as she'd sat drinking tea in the empty teashop by the dark and windy quay, Cyril had run back and bought it for her.

That had been sweet of him, but what she really remembered was when she tried it on. The coat was thick and black, and as soon she had it on they both laughed with the same thought, hooting until Cyril had started to cough wildly and she had to thump him on the back with a cushion. It was a granny coat, the kind old ladies wore, the first such that she'd ever owned. They were laughing because what else was there to do on the day you first realised that you were finally getting old?

Well, there was one other thing—and they'd gone straight back to the boarding house and done it for most of the afternoon. They hadn't felt so very old, that day: but three years later Cyril was dead.

On the doorstep she pulled the door shut behind her. She didn't bother to lock it. After living in London for so long, she forgot that things were different here. She would probably still have locked it if there'd been anything inside worth stealing, but when she'd moved she'd looked at all the things she'd accumulated over the years, and realised very few seemed important enough to bring all this way. Apart from a few sets of clothes and a couple of odds and ends, she'd dispersed everything among friends and relatives, which had been nice to do. Her granddaughter Jane, for instance, had always loved looking through the old photographs May kept in an wooden chest. Giving them to her meant she would always have something to remember her by.

That, and their joke, which they'd shared since Jane was small. 'Why do gypsies walk lop-sided?' May would ask, and Jane, though she knew the answer, would always pretend she didn't. 'Because they've got crystal balls,' May would cackle, and the two of them would laugh.

It was a bit of a rude joke, May supposed, but a little bit rudeness never did anyone any harm. If people didn't get a little bit rude with each other every now and then, there'd be no new people, would there?

She hesitated for a moment, looking up her path, and then set off. The road at the bottom turned gradually away across the fields, surrounded by green and waving gold as far as she could see. It was a long road,

A LONG WALK, FOR THE LAST TIME

and May paced herself carefully. There was no hurry.

By late morning she judged she had traveled about three miles—not bad going for an old goat, she thought. It was so easy walking here, listening to the birds in the hedges and banks of trees. It reminded her of other holidays with Cyril, when they used to get out of the smoke and head out for the countryside somewhere, to walk together down lanes and stop at tiny pubs for lunch. It was a shame that he could not be with her now that she could walk like this whenever she chose, but it didn't do to regret things like that. Cyril always said that regrets are for people with nothing to look forward to, and he was right.

About half a mile later she rounded a bend to find a little clearing by the side of the road, and saw there was a small pub back up against the trees. Always a believer in signs, May decided that it was time for lunch.

The inside of the pub was cosy, the landlord and his wife as friendly as everybody else seemed to be in these parts, but it was too nice a day to sit inside. May bought a small sherry and a slice of pie to add to the lunch she had brought, and took it outside to sit at one of the wooden tables. As she contentedly munched her way through the food she thought of other pubs and other times, thought of them with a calm detachment that had nothing of loss within it. You have what you have, and that's it. There's no point in wishing otherwise. If something was good enough to miss, then you were lucky to have had it in the first place.

After a while she saw a figure walking down the road towards the pub. It was a young man, and he sat at her table to chat and eat his lunch. He seemed a little glum. He had moved away from his family a year before, and was just back from visiting them. Though most of them seemed reconciled to his having moved on, his mother was not taking it well. May recognised the feeling she had about today's business, of having to look back and remember things that seemed past, like recalling as an adult what it was like to take exams and tests, so as to be able to sympathise with a child who was only now going through that particular form of hell.

The young man cheered up a little as they talked. After all, he said, he didn't want to go back, and if it took a little time for his mother to get over his leaving, then that was the way it was. This might have sounded harsh to anyone else, but not to May. She knew well enough that nothing would have dragged her back to London, now that she was here.

Before she could get too comfortable, she got to her feet and started out again, armed with a recommended spot to look for later from the young man, who was going the other way.

The afternoon was even warmer than the morning, but not too much so, and as she walked May felt her heart lift with happiness. It really was very nice here, as nice as you could want.

By four the quality of the light began to change, and afternoon began to shade towards evening. The landscape either side of the road started to change too, becoming wilder, like a moor. As she kept walking May felt heavy with anticipation, wondering how her business was going to go, and hoping it would be more conclusive than the young man's had been. It wasn't that she minded having to go through it, not at all: but she would feel happier if today could be the end of it.

She kept an eye out for the landmarks the young man had mentioned, looking for the spot he had recommended. She felt that soon it would be time.

Half an hour later she passed a gnarled old tree by the side of the road, and knew that she was close. Soon she found the little path which led off the road, and followed it as it wound between small bushes and out onto the moor. She stopped once and looked back, across the green, and as far as she could see everything looked the same, a limitless expanse of country under a rich blue sky. How anyone could live anywhere else she couldn't imagine. If anything she wished she'd come here sooner.

Then the path broadened into a kind of circular grassy patch, and May knew this was the spot the man had mentioned. Not only was it the ideal place to sit, but there was no path out the other side. She lowered herself gently to the warm grass, and prepared to wait. The air was slightly cooler now, almost exactly body temperature, and as she sat May felt the first hint of a breeze.

She felt calm, and relaxed, and soon another breeze ran by her, no colder than the air but brisk enough to make the grass bend. Then another breeze came, and another, and soon the grass was swaying in patterns around her, leaning this way and that in lines and shapes that changed into something else as soon as you noticed them. The wind grew stronger, and stronger, until every blade of grass seemed to be moving in a different direction and May's hair was lifted up round her face in a whirl.

Then suddenly all was still.

May had a vague sense that someone was thinking of her. It became stronger, a definite tugging. She let her mind go as quiet as possible, giving herself up to it. Though she could still feel the grass beneath her hands, her mind seemed to go elsewhere, to broaden—and when she opened her eyes the world inside her head seemed as big as the one all around her.

'I'm here,' she said. 'I'm here.'

Immediately she felt warm, and knew that the message had been received.

A moment later a voice came towards her out of the air; at first very weak, then more strongly.

'Who are you here for?' it said.

May's heart leapt. 'Jane,' she said. 'I'm here for Jane.'

She heard the voice ask if there was a Janet, and corrected it, repeating Jane's name, enunciating it clearly.

After a pause she heard the voice again. 'There is a Jane here,' it said, 'Who is speaking?'

'May,' she said strongly, 'It's May.'

The voice addressed the people she could not see. 'Does the name "May" mean anything to you?' it said, and May waited to see if she could hear the answer. She couldn't. It was too far away.

But then the voice spoke to her again. 'Your name seems to mean something,' it said. 'Jane is crying.'

May felt her heart go out to her granddaughter, and wished that she could see her, reach out and touch her. Jane had always been the one who had visited her, when her other grandchildren or even children were too busy. Jane had come at the end too, when May had been in the home. Even when May's mind had been confused and dark and she hadn't been very nice to talk to, Jane had always come, and May wanted very much for her to know that she remembered her too. Most of all she wanted to show her that the words she'd spoken near the end were not her own, but the random jumbles of a mind that was too old to accurately reflect what was still inside.

'Tell her,' she said, and then cleared he throat and tried again. 'Tell her "crystal balls".'

'If you say so,' said the voice, and there was a pause.

Then suddenly May felt warm again, warmer than she ever had before. Her cheeks sparkled as if flushed, and eyes flew wide open, and she felt Jane's life inside her, and she knew that her business was over.

Jane had received the message. She would be able to forgive May for not saying goodbye as herself, and to let her go. She would know that it was all right to move on.

'Did you get that?' asked the medium.

'Yes,' said May, 'I got that. Thank you.'

As suddenly as it had begun, it was over. The connection was broken, and May was left sitting on the grass alone.

She stood up and looked towards the path, and wasn't surprised to see that it wasn't there any more. On the other side of the clearing the bushes had cleared, and the way now led in that direction.

She walked into the growing darkness, knowing that there would be light at the end of it. She would miss her little cottage, she thought, but not for long. It had only been a temporary measure, somewhere to stay until she was ready to go.

She was ready now, and she saw in the distance that someone was waiting for her, and she walked more quickly because she wanted very much to see him again. She didn't think he'd mind that she'd left the coat behind. She wouldn't need it again.

If anything could keep her warm forever, it would be him.

The Vaccinator

Walk North up Duval Street in Key West, past the restaurants, fruit juice stands and T-shirt emporiums, and pretty soon you'll come to the Havana Docks. It's a tourist harbor, quite small, bordered on both sides by restaurant piers and not much used for seafaring beyond a couple of glass-bottom boats and a jetski concession. Mainly it's there for looking at, and eating by, and watching the sun set over. Also, stuff swims in it. Some days you'll see a manatee down in the water around the pier supports, and there's generally some Yellow Tail and Black Fin flicking around. You'd think fish would have the sense not to swim right up close to seafood restaurants, where people can look down at them and think 'I'll have one of those, please, with broccoli and a cold glass of wine' but evidently not. At night little sharks swarm in the underwater lights, so many and moving so fast that it makes you wonder if the whole sea is like that, right out to the invisible horizon, a twisting mass of creatures who barely know we're here and won't miss us when we're gone.

On this particular morning a man called Eddie was sitting alone on the upper level of the East pier, feet up against the wooden railing and a cup of iced tea cradled in his lap. He was watching one of the tan jetski assholes going through his chops in the bay, showing the sparse tourists how much noisy fun they could have for a mere fifty bucks an hour. The skier hadn't fallen off yet, but there was still room for hope. Eddie was thinking that it would be best if it happened out in the bay, a long way from shore, and that if anybody asked he'd say he hadn't seen anything. It was early yet, barely ten o'clock, and the sun was just getting into its stride, glinting off the weathered wood of the pier, the swirls in the water below, and the fading edges of Eddie's hangover.

After a while another, older, man climbed the steps up to the pier. He walked along the deck until he was level with where the other man was sitting, and then ground to a halt.

421

'Are you Eddie?' he asked eventually.

'I am,' Eddie said, without turning. He took another sip of tea. It was warm already, the ice long gone. 'And you would be George?'

The other man nodded jerkily, realised he couldn't be seen, and said that he was. Then carried on standing there.

Eddie levered himself upright in the chair, turned and looked him over. George was tall, late fifties, spreading around the stomach and thinning on top. Neatly pressed grey shorts, a blue short sleeve shirt with razor creases and dinky white socks—and in general not the most hip person in the Keys that morning.

'Sit,' Eddie suggested. 'Standing there, you look like some kind of Illinois realtor on vacation.'

'Uh, I am.' George frowned, stepping back to perch on the edge of the nearest chair. 'That's what I am.'

'I know. That was a joke, to set you at ease. Didn't work, evidently. You want a cigarette?'

'No, thank you. I don't smoke.'

'Right,' Eddie nodded equably. 'You and everyone else. May you all live forever.'

George watched while the man lit up. Eddie was wearing jeans, cowboy boots, a loose jacket and an expensive-looking T-shirt that didn't proclaim him a member of the Conch Republic or have a picture of a very specific breed of dog on it or say that while he was only one year old, he had an 'attitude'—so it couldn't have been bought in Key West. He had short dark hair and a trim goatee beard, deep and sharp blue eyes. He looked late thirties, was lean but broad in the shoulders, and gave the impression that whatever he did, he did it fast and well.

'Okay,' Eddie said. 'All I know is what Connie told me. You sell land up North, and might have an unusual kind of problem.'

'Connie? That guy's name was Connie? Isn't that a girl's name?'

'Usually, yes. In this case it's short for 'Conrad'. You want to take the issue up with him then be my guest, but I wouldn't advise it.'

George nodded, looked down at his feet, quiet for a moment. His mouth opened after a while, but then closed again, tight enough to make a popping sound.

For the time being, that appeared to be it. Eddie watched as some seabird—he'd never been able to figure the difference between the types, or why it would be worth knowing—dropped chaotically out of the sky and snatched something from out of the swell. George meanwhile remained silent.

'Here's what you're thinking,' Eddie prompted, quietly. 'You got involved in a conversation last night with a barman you never met before. You let something slip. A matter you can't even talk to your wife about, and now here you are, sitting with *another* guy you've never met, and you don't think you can tell him about it either even though you want to.'

'How did you know I was married?'

'Look in the mirror some time, George. I never seen a man look as married as you. Which is a good thing, incidentally.'

'I'm glad you think so.'

'Right. Approval's very important. Plus that's not exactly a small ring you've got on your finger there.'

'So—am I going to tell you these things?'

'You are. Because you don't like hiding stuff. Like the fact you told your wife you were going out to bring back pastries or something this morning as an excuse to come here alone. But lying's becoming a habit, because you don't want to worry her, and that's making you do things like go out to bars when she's asleep in bed in your nice hotel room. And that's a dubious way of life, George, because sometimes bad accidental things happen to guys in bars, and then it's going to look like you got some whole secret history you wouldn't even want.'

George smiled with half his mouth and one eyebrow. For a moment he looked like a man who closed a lot of prestige sales and was a local legend for giving junior realtors merry hell when they stepped out of line. 'Thanks for the advice. So why don't *you* tell me what my problem is?'

Eddie shrugged. 'You're afraid.'

'Of what?'

He obviously needed to hear someone else say it. Eddie said it. 'You think you're going to be kidnapped.'

George's face went complex, relief and confusion vying for the same advertising space. 'Kidnapped?' he said.

'What else would you call it?'

George suddenly looked very tired.

Eddie dropped his butt to the floor, ground it out with his heel. 'Why don't you tell me what's happening, and then I'll tell you what I think and if there's anything I can do about it.'

George started slowly, but gradually gained speed and confidence. He was a man used to conveying information, and his story was short and concise. Eddie occasionally asked for clarification, but mainly just let him talk. It took maybe ten minutes, and then George stopped and spread his hands, embarrassed, like a man expecting to be ridiculed.

'Okay,' Eddie said. 'In time-honoured fashion, I got some bad news and some good news. The bad news is you are indeed shaping up to be kidnapped.'

All the breath in George's body came out in a rush. He looked like he had sunstroke. 'So what is the good news, exactly?' he croaked.

'I might be able to do something about it,' Eddie said. 'How long are you aiming to stay in Key West?'

George rubbed his hand across his forehead. 'Today's Thursday. We thought probably the weekend, leaving Monday lunchtime?'

Eddie considered. 'Should be enough. Relax for a day or two. Act like nothing's happening. You staying at the Marquesa?'

'How the hell do you know that?'

'Just a guess. It's a good hotel. I'd be staying there if I was you. You should make sure you're around late afternoon on Saturday. They sometimes have wine and cheese around the pool.'

George laughed shakily. 'I'll bear it in mind.'

'Go to Bug's Pantry on the way back: they have some nice stuff there, and it's different enough to the continental breakfast that it's not going to look weird you went out for it. Corner of Curry Street. They sell flowers too, and newspapers. One more thing. You realise this is going to cost?'

George the businessman came back. 'How much? And what kind of guarantee do I get?'

'A lot, and no kind at all. Take it or leave it.'

Eddie watched George think about the phone calls, and the fax. About what had happened to his car. About his wife, and the things he hadn't told her.

'I'll take it,' George said.

'Need the boat tonight. A beer in the next twenty seconds.'

Connie reached for the fridge. 'He's for real?'

'I think so,' Eddie said. 'Those assholes. Jeez, my head hurts.'

It was four o'clock and Slappy Jack's was empty. It was a small bar, with lots of dark wood and battered stools and pictures of the old town in heavy frames on the walls. Was a time when Key West was the biggest town in the whole of the United States. Wasn't that way any more, not by a long, long chalk, and on afternoons like this you felt the town knew it and didn't much care either way. Big towns have to get out of bed in the mornings and go do stuff. Prove themselves. Key West just put its feet up and ate some more dressed crab and thought about having another beer.

Afternoon light slanted in through the windows of the bar, twirling motes of dust and casting highlights around the room like someone was setting it up for a photograph and wanted everything just right. At this time of day, there were worse places to drink. At night it was a different proposition, packed with tourists too shit-faced or stupid to realise the name was a take-off of Papa's favorite watering hole, and not the real thing. Come to that, even the real thing wasn't the real thing any more. The real Sloppy Joe's was too small and nondescript for modern tastes, didn't look enough like the real thing should—and had been superceded by a vast hell-hole on Duval which you'd have to be out of your mind to drink in.

Connie worked both the afternoon graveyard shift and the small hours, mixing strong cocktails and stuffing green olives with almonds. Big as Connie was—and he'd been hired as a deterrent to weekend warriors with Margarita hard-ons, and had spent a long time doing successfully violent things in New Orleans—Eddie was tougher. They both knew it, so that was okay.

'You want me along?'

Eddie shook his head. 'Not tonight.'

'Need anything else?'

'Just the boat.'

Connie went off to make the call. Eddie sat at the bar, sipping his beer. Not for the first time he wondered what drew them to Key West, the people who needed him. Maybe nothing, and five in three months was a co-incidence. Or perhaps without knowing it they found themselves heading in the direction of the Triangle. Or it was just Eddie's long-overdue good fortune, turning up in a curious package. Whatever. They were a lot easier to deal with than his previous kind of client, the type who insisted on working in Central America and driving around in expensive company cars, or who lived in the US but were just too dumb to realise they'd accumulated enough money to make them an obvious target. Doesn't matter how you've made your money, a fat bank account is likely to breed a confidence which is a short step away from being an asshole. His new clients were less rich and usually frightened half to death, and thus prone to do what he told them. The problem was dealing with the kidnappers.

In the old days, when Eddie took a job, he always used to hope it was Colombians he'd be dealing with. There was a set way of doing things. You thrashed out the deal in a bar somewhere, over a few lines of coke. You negotiated for the bad guys to be paid a percentage of what they might have expected to get out of the kidnapping: in return, they didn't actually go through with it. Like a vaccine. Preventative maintenance. They got some money without all the grief, and the client got to stay at home with his family, not pose for those pictures with newspapers in your hands which are never flattering, and avoided being starved, tortured and probably killed in the end. Much more convenient for everyone concerned.

The Colombians knew the score, were professionals. You arranged the vaccine, it was a deal and it was respected. These days Eddie thought he'd settle for a bunch of whacked-out Miami gangbangers, rather than the people he actually had to deal with. They were nutcases, pure and simple.

The story George Becker had told him was similar to all the others he'd heard. At first it was an occasional feeling of being watched, and half-memories of dreams which frightened him. Then one night George had been driving home after working late and it had gotten a little weirder.

He and his wife lived out of town, in a nice house which had a wet bar and a media room and was far too big now both kids were out in the world making the same old mistakes and calling them their own. Half a mile away from home George had been chugging along, listening to the local radio station, when suddenly it faded out. He wasn't too bothered, it was a lousy station anyway, but then the car's lights went off and he stalled. He slammed his foot on the brake but it didn't seem to make any difference: the car just cruised to a halt and then sat there, ticking as it cooled.

Nothing happened for a couple of minutes, other than the sound of insects and wind in the trees.

Then the lights flicked back on, and the radio station faded back, as if he were driving into its signal. George tried the ignition, and the car started immediately. He drove slowly home. He told Jennifer what had happened, and she shrugged, told him to take the car down to the shop in the morning. As you would—you didn't know about the dreams, and she didn't.

He took the car down to the shop. They found something to charge him for, but it was the usual bullshit. The car was fine.

Nothing else happened for a while. Nothing to do with the car, at least. Occasionally things in his workshop seemed to have moved, but you could put that down to absentmindedness. And sometimes the phone rang at odd hours, and when George picked it up there was usually nobody there. Once he thought he heard his mother talking, but the line was very bad and she'd been dead nearly ten years, so he wasn't sure.

He put up with this for six months, and had almost gotten used to it, when it suddenly started to invade his work. George's office had two names above the door, and his was one of them. He and Dave Marks had built the business from nothing, and were now both immovable fixtures in the annual list of the top five realty producers in the state. He believed the building their business was conducted in to be as inviolable as their status: unbreachable, the castle that Englishmen's houses were supposed to be. George rarely called Jennifer from work, unless it was urgent, and she had only visited him there a handful of times. That wasn't what the office was for.

Then one afternoon the phone on his desk rang, and when he picked it up there was no-one there—but the silence had a strange undertone that made it sound as if someone was, but they weren't saying anything. He tried to find out from the operator who'd been calling, but as usual they didn't have a number recorded.

A week later a fax arrived on the private machine in his office. There was just one line typed on it, a description of a place in a forest that at first meant nothing to him. The paper was otherwise entirely blank, without even the sender information at the very top that just about every fax machine in the world automatically provides. George threw it away, and that lunchtime found a bar a few streets away and drank vodka so no-one would be able to smell it.

He was feeling hunted now, by something that wasn't even there. Thirty, forty years ago, long before he and Jennifer had met, he'd been unfaithful to a previous girlfriend—with a friend of hers. He was mid-twenties, he got drunk, it happened. It didn't mean anything except for how bad it made him feel. He didn't call the girl, and heard nothing from her for over eight months. He assumed she'd done the same as he had—realised it was a silliness with no future in it, and tried to forget it had happened. But he didn't *know* this. Not for sure. There was still the possibility that at some point, with no warning, a disaster could explode into his life. Then one night he and his girlfriend were in a bar, and they ran into this other girl. She smiled on seeing them, and he knew it was all going to be alright, and he was so relieved he spent the whole evening babbling until both girls told him to shut up.

It was like that, but a lot worse.

He started fixating on the idea of their Florida vacation, only a few weeks away. He told himself that if he could just get through until then, it would be okay. Although he'd already begun to entertain some pretty odd notions of what might be happening to him, he somehow thought he'd be safe away from home.

There were two more calls before they left—one at the office, one at home. Jen glanced at him for a moment after he told her that the second had been a wrong number—again—and then went back to finding out

427

what dungeon of homemaker psychosis Martha Stewart was plumbing this month. Something told him that, while Jen was without doubt completely unconscious of thinking this way, he wasn't going to be allowed many more wrong numbers.

On his last night at work, the car cut out again on the journey home. At exactly the same spot, in exactly the same way. George, a cautious man, had taken the car to the shop only two days before, making sure it was in good shape for the trip down. They'd tried hard to rip him off, but only been able to find a few bucks' worth of tinkering to do. The car was fine.

The next morning they locked up the house, briefed the neighbours a final time about cat-feeding, and set off. As they pulled down the drive, George felt his heart lighten. They only did a couple hours driving that day, to break themselves in gently, and stopped at a shiny new Holiday Inn in some little town whose name they didn't even register. The guy behind the desk recommended a restaurant a short stroll down the street, and they had a great dinner, much to their surprise—pleased to be roughing it and coming out on top.

By the time they got back to their room they were feeling the way long-term couples sometimes do when they're out of their usual environment and have had a few glasses of wine. Jen said she wanted to shower quickly, and kissed him on the lips before she went. George sat on the bed, listened to the water falling on his wife's body, and smiled a little at the pair of them. Old guys going wild into the country.

Then the phone rang, and it wasn't anyone he knew. Or anyone at all, in fact. Just the rustle of wind high up in the trees. The sound of somebody not talking.

He told Jen it had been reception telling them about check-out times, and did his best to pick up where they'd left off. He did a good job considering, but it wasn't the same.

There were no more phone calls over the next few days, as they slowly made their way to Florida, down the Gulf side of the panhandle, and then into the Keys. But increasingly George found his mind was elsewhere. The sentence about the forest, which at first he'd just dismissed, kept coming back into his mind.

He couldn't remember the place it described. Nobody would have been able to. It was both too specific and too vague—as if it was not so much a real location, as a type. It just said 'Three pines almost in a line, with rocks all around and a dark mountain behind'. It could have been anywhere. The more he worried over it, however, the more it began to be associated in his mind with flashes of white light, with a sensation of breathless running, and with the idea that something may have happened a long time ago which he had simply blanked out.

In the hotel in Key Largo he woke up just after midnight. He didn't know why. There'd been no dream, no sound, nothing. He was just suddenly awake. He eased himself out of bed, swapped his pjs for shorts and a shirt, and slipped out of the hotel room. The sky was wide and very dark blue. There was nothing in it. He heard the sound of faint laughter, at a distance, and saw that a few people were still lolling around the Tiki bar by the pool. On impulse he walked over, and charged a couple of Manhattans to the room. When he returned, half an hour later, he got back to sleep without any problem.

The next day they arrived in Key West, and late in the evening George had found himself in another bar, again alone, and talking to a man called Connie.

That was his story. But Eddie knew that George was right to think he hadn't heard the end of it. The nutcases had gone easy on laying in false memory, which was good and unusually restrained, but everything else suggested they were settling for the long haul.

Connie came back. The boat would be set up, with fuel and ammunition on board. Eddie stayed a while longer, drinking beer and helping stuff olives. A couple of tourists poked their head in the door, but Connie scowled at them and they went away.

It was a still night. The water was flat and calm. Just after ten o'clock, Eddie cut the engine and let her drift a while. It was extremely dark, the only light coming from the boat's lamps and the stars in the deep nothing above. He was five miles out, over part of the long reef that starts north of Miami and follows the coast down into open sea. During the day you could join a cruise out of Havana Docks, come and look down at the fish and sharks swimming around over the coral. After the sun went down the only people who came out this far were marine biologists who wanted to check out the nightlife on the reef. Tonight there weren't any around, which was good.

Eddie set the radio to send, lit a cigarette, and settled down to wait. The signal was a sequence of fifty tones, repeated in an order so complex it looked random. Wouldn't mean anything except to the people it was supposed to. Meanwhile he checked his gun, which had seen service in half of Central America, two European countries and the back streets of more than a few US cities. So far he hadn't even had to pull it on one of these jobs. But you never knew. He cleaned it, loaded it with shells, and then laid it on the table in front of him. He felt keyed up, but not nervous. Eddie had done many unusual things in his life. This was merely the latest.

Fifteen minutes later the lamp on the front of the boat flickered and then went out. Gradually the other lights started to dim, and then the boat was in darkness. Eddie picked up the gun, put it in his shoulder holster. It had occurred to him, on the first trip in fact, that there was no guarantee it would even work. They probably had ways of affecting things like that, like the stuff they could do with electric power. But he felt better having it around.

The water around the boat started to become glassy, losing motion until it felt like solid land. Everything went quiet.

Then bang—the light went on. Eddie flinched, cursed, and refused to look up into it. The light came down like a cylinder, a circular beam that was a couple of times wider than the boat was long. Though it looked just like someone had turned the world's biggest halogen flashlamp on him, Eddie knew it was more complicated than that. The boat was now rock steady, and the sea within the beam frozen in place. The light wasn't just a source of illumination. It grabbed hold of things, and could pull them up.

'It's Edward Kruger,' he said, loudly, shielding his eyes with his hands. 'Turn that fucking thing off.'

There was a long pause, during which the light stayed exactly as bright as it had been. Then it dimmed—very, very slightly.

'I want to go to the island,' he said. 'I've got business there. And I want to go the old fashioned way, because this isn't my boat. Okay?'

Another pause, and then the beam went out.

Eddie looked up, but as usual there was nothing to see. The boat lights slowly came back on, in the order they'd gone off. Eddie started the engines.

It took another twenty minutes before he could see the island. There was a single light at the dock, and he headed for it. The tying point was at the end of a long wooden walkway, as they often were on the Keys, because the water around the islands was so shallow.

In the old days there had used to be an island on the chain called No-Name Key, a few miles north of Key West: presumably so-called because the early settlers had run dry of the creative energy required to name the hundreds of local bumps in the sea, some little bigger than sandbars with a couple of trees. That island was called something else now, he couldn't remember what. Something dull, or quaint, or both.

The island he was about to land at wasn't even called something as unimaginative as No Name. It wasn't known as anything at all, and never had been, because as far as Eddie could tell, he and Connie were the only two humans who'd ever been aware of its existence—and Connie had never actually set foot on it. It wasn't on any of the maps, and Eddie had never been able to find a reference to it in any of the painfully exhaustive and quasi-literate local history books. He'd come to believe that for most of the time it simply wasn't there. Some kind of cloaking device, he guessed—in place for a very, very long time.

He got the boat tied up to the dock, and climbed out. Took a deep breath, looking back the way he'd come. You couldn't see the lights of Key West from here, or any of the other islands. It was very quiet, just the sound of his footsteps and a faint creak from the walkway swaying in gentle time with the water. You might just as well be on a different planet.

At the land end of the walkway was another light, which showed the path ahead through the forest. Apart from the dim lamps every couple of yards along it, the path was the only sign of artificiality on the island. As far was Eddie could tell, the rest of it was entirely covered in trees and brush. He lit another cigarette before he set off. He didn't really need it, but it was nice to have something man-made in your hand. It was grounding. Rah-rah for the humans, something like that.

After a few minutes on the path, he heard a sound over on the right, amongst the trees. He stopped, listened. Nothing. There weren't even any insects on the island, and it was deadly quiet. It was much warmer than it had been on the boat, and humid.

He started walking again, and this time heard the sound from the left side, maybe five yards into the trees. He kept on walking.

And then he suddenly turned around.

Behind him on the path, caught and frozen, were three small humanoid figures. About four feet high and thin, grey in colour, with bulbous heads and large black eyes that looked like those sunglasses people were wearing a couple of years back.

He laughed. 'What's the matter, someone leave the cat flap open? Going to be trouble when they hear you're out.'

The little guys looked at each other, then back at him. One of them cleared its throat.

'Hi Eddie,' it said. It voice was a poor approximation of human speech, more of a clicking rasp. 'You got anything for us?'

Eddie reached in his pocket, pulled out a spare pack of cigarettes. He tossed it to the nearest grey.

'Thanks, Eddie,' they said, in unison.

'Yeah,' he replied. 'Now scoot.'

They scuttled off into the undergrowth. Eddie shook his head. If they were his, he'd electrify the compound.

The path wound across the island for nearly a mile. Towards the end the ground rose slightly, and then gave out into a circular clearing. This was about fifty yards across, and was completely clear of trees and bushes. It was covered in short, manicured grass, soft like you got in Europe instead of the sharp and tough Florida scrub. In the middle were four armchairs—three of which were black leather recliners, the other the kind of worn affair you'd find in a cheap motel—and a standard lamp, which shed a warm glow for a couple of yards around. Eddie walked straight over and sat in the chair that didn't recline.

'I'm here,' he said.

They kept him waiting for a while, as usual.

George, meanwhile, was walking back to his room from the Marquesa's reception, after making a dinner reservation for the following evening. He was one of those people who really enjoy their food, and look forward to it, and take enjoyment in from planning where the next meal is going to come from. That evening—after careful consideration—they'd gone to Crabby Dick's on Duval, and had good steak and blackened dolphin while sitting on the upper deck and watching people wandering past below. The Marquesa's bistro was supposed to be pretty good, so that was where they were going to be eating tomorrow night. George didn't quite have his whole menu planned out, but he'd made some ballpark wine list plans and narrowed his appetizer options down to two. Though at the last minute he might go wild and switch to something else. You never knew.

Planning food events was also useful because it gave George something simple and practical to think about. Jen had accepted his story about getting sidetracked on the way to buy Danish, and been touched by the flowers. They'd had a nice day, just wandering around. Stood on the Southernmost point, looked at Hemingway's house and all the cats, drunk their own volume in iced fruit drinks. Then spent a late afternoon hour around the Marquesa's pools: there were two, both small, hidden in the leafy courtyards created when three wooden Victorian houses had been loosely combined to form the hotel. Jen floated around, gently paddling this way and that, while George sat in a chair wearing a T-shirt and holding a copy of the local newspaper. Though it was no longer an exactly recent development, he'd never quite got over the disappointment of finding that he'd somehow become housed in an older man's body, and preferred not to inflict the sight of it upon the world.

He watched his wife swim, glad that he'd gone to see Eddie that morning. He'd been nervous, and expecting many things: blank incomprehension, ridicule, or one of several different methods of extracting money. Instead he seemed to have been taken seriously, which for an hour or so had made him feel light-headed with relief. There was no way of telling whether the guy could actually do anything—could be that it was just a more complex scam than he'd been expecting. But he felt better for having done it, whatever happened. When your wife's touched because you bring her flowers and the only reason you did it is to cover up the fact you've been lying to her, that's a bad feeling. You realise that you should bring them more often, and that you'd like to, but somehow you don't. It mainly just doesn't occur to you. Unless you're hiding something, and the guilt that engenders makes you realise how much you love the person you're lying to. He didn't want to be covering up any more. He wondered briefly what percentage of flowers in the world were bought for the right reasons—then shitcanned that stream of thought and tried to read a story about a local group of poets. He couldn't. It wasn't interesting. If there was a local poet in the whole world who wasn't shit then George believed he must be in hiding somewhere, along with all the good local artists.

That, at least, was what anyone peeking would have found in George's mind that afternoon. He'd grown very used to covering up what was actually going on in his head, because he was finding it increasingly inexplicable and disturbing.

At night the pool area was deserted, with that strange, restful atmosphere public places get when the public isn't there to clutter them up. It was dark except for a couple of low yellow lamps, the vivid blue-green glow of the pool, and a few stars visible through the palm cover above. George was passing almost exactly the same spot where he'd been sitting in the afternoon, when he thought he heard something. At first he assumed it was another guest out for a stroll, and got a smile ready. No-one appeared. He stopped, looked around. Someone had put in a lot of effort growing plants in and above the courtyard, with big hibiscus and ground palms and all manner of other things Jen would know the names of. During the day you could see geckos, some of them pretty big, running all over the brickwork floor. Maybe that was what he'd heard. He started walking again, and started quietly to scale the low steps around the waterfall which was on the way to their suite.

He was still a way from home when he heard something that sounded like a door handle being turned, and then Jen's voice saying his name in the form of a question. As if someone had opened the door to her suite, and she'd looked up to see no-one there, and wondered if he was playing a game.

George started to run.

'Eddie, my man—how's it hanging? How are you, guy?'

Eddie looked down from the stars, to see that the three reclining chairs were now occupied. He'd given up hoping to see how they managed to do that—being not there one minute and then there the next—but it still irritated him.

'Hungry,' he said. 'And bored. You get a warning from when the assholes shine the big light in my eyes, you got video surveillance on the pier. You must know when I get to this chair. So how come it still takes you fifteen fucking minutes to get your asses out here?'

'Touchy,' said the first alien. Yag was his name. He, like the two others, had the recliner tipped back as far back as it would go, and was lounging with his arms and legs hanging off the sides. 'Think Eddie's a little out of sorts this evening, fellas.'

'It's just rude, is all,' Eddie said, and lit another cigarette.

'You know we don't like smoking,' another of the aliens said. He was about six foot eight, thin and spidery like the others. His skin was the usual pale golden colour, and glistened wetly. The way they looked, you'd expect them to smell pretty bad. Actually, they smelled of spearmint. His head was slightly elongated but otherwise not too different to ours. He was called Fud, and he was pretty drunk.

'You don't give a shit about smoking,' Eddie said, not putting it out. 'It doesn't even do anything to you guys. You're just being a pain in the ass, as usual.'

'We do too care,' Yag said, stifling a burp. 'Everybody cares. It's a zeitgeist thing.'

'You bring us anything?' the third alien slurred. Eddie didn't know his name. The spindly fucker had always been too wasted to pronounce it. Maybe that was how that Key got called No-Name too. Always too drunk to talk.

Eddie pulled the bottle of overproof Rum out of his pocket and lobbed it to the alien. It landed on his stomach and he went 'Ooof.' Then pulled off the cap and took a long pull, before handing it on to Yag.

'I had some cigarettes too,' Eddie said, 'But seeing as you guys don't like that kind of thing, I gave them to the greys instead.'

'What?' Fud demanded. 'Where were they?'

THE VACCINATOR

Eddie laughed. 'On the path. What's up with you guys? Masters of the universe and you can't even keep your pets under control?'

Suddenly Eddie found himself with the three aliens staring at him, and for the moment they didn't look so drunk.

'When we want a human's advice on how to run our affairs,' the unnamed one said, 'You'll be the first to know, Kruger. In the meantime, shut the fuck up.'

Eddie held the stare. 'Your call. But with those animals screwing around like assholes the whole time and flashing lights over people's houses, sooner or later it's all gonna go wide.'

'It's under control,' Fud said petulantly.

'Yeah right. Like that stupid autopsy video really made everybody think it was all just a hoax. You guys watch television ever? It's the greys who're the flavour of the decade, not you.'

'We don't give a shit what your stupid fucking species thinks,' Noname shouted, jumping to its feet and jabbing a long finger at him. 'I've wiped my *ass* on brighter life-forms than you, shit face.'

The sides of the alien's head were pulsing slightly, narrow slits opening in the temples. Eddie had seen this happen before, and suspected it was a prelude to something bad. Longing for a straightforward Colombian or two, he was glad of the gun in his jacket, even if it wouldn't work. At least he could hit one of them with it, if it came to it. He stood up.

'Gentlemen, gentlemen,' Yag said, mildly. 'Eddie, calm down. Come on. Have a drink.' He held the bottle out to him.

Eddie took it, made a couple of inches disappear, and then passed it on. Fud drank. His temples stopped bulging.

No-name glared at Eddie a final time, hiccupped, and took a drink. He sat down, then grinned. 'Give us a smoke, Eddie.'

Eddie passed him a cigarette, lit it for him, his heartbeat gradually returning to normal.

'That's better,' Yag said, and kicked the ground so his recliner spun in a gentle circle, making a quiet 'wheee' noise as it went. 'So, what you want to talk to us about, Eddie? Let's do business.'

'Man called George Becker,' Eddie said, sitting down. 'Lives in Illinois. I'm authorized to buy an abduction vaccine on his behalf.'

'Excellent,' Yag said, rubbing his thin, long hands together. 'What will the market stand?'

'Looking at him, I'd say forty thousand.'

'Then that's the price. Plus five thousand dollars.'

Eddie sighed. 'Why the extra five?'

'Because we feel like it,' Fud said, and the three of them cackled. 'You got a problem with that, ape-boy?'

'No problem at all,' Eddie said, reflecting that had these guys been a crew of humans out of Miami he could have just whacked the bunch of them six months ago. 'Forty-five thousand dollars,' he continued patiently, 'In return for which you leave him the fuck alone, stop freaking him out with phone calls and screwing with his car and faxing him and putting stuff in his dreams and memory and this shit about some forest with rocks in it.'

'Sure thing,' Yag smirked.

'And, of course,' Eddie said, having been caught out this way before, 'You don't abduct him either.'

'When do we see the money?'

'This weekend. And leave the guy alone in the meantime, yeah? He's on vacation. And get a mobile phone or something. I'm sick and tired of schlepping out here every time.'

'You want us to come find you instead?' Fud asked.

'No,' Eddie said.

'So we'll see you here in a couple of days.' The alien waved a hand. Eddie was dismissed. He got up, walked away.

As he disappeared down the path No-name said, with obvious satisfaction, 'Going to have to kill him sooner or later.'

Fud and Yag raised an eyebrow each.

'Eddie's okay,' Yag said. 'Does what he's told, doesn't talk to anyone, doesn't ask the right questions.'

'What do you mean?'

'Well,' Yag smiled, 'He didn't even think to ask if it was us who were buzzing this George Becker character.'

'Isn't it?'

'Hell no,' Fud laughed. 'Never heard of the fucking guy.'

'How were the weirdos?'

'Weird,' Eddie said, accepting the beer Connie handed him. 'Tell you the truth, they're really beginning to get on my nerves.'

'Why don't you just clip them, have done with it?'

'Yeah, right.' Eddie grimaced, and glanced around the bar. 'Jesus—what the hell's got into these people tonight?'

The room was crammed with tourists, apparently at one in a desire to demonstrate how much noise the human head was capable of producing. Sweating groups of guys and girls, quite a few couples, everyone happily talking and shouting and even singing—with the exception of a peaceable and remarkably sun-burnt couple sitting at the end of the bar, who appeared to be methodically establishing how many Golden Margaritas you could drink before your brain melted. Connie saw Eddie glance at them.

'From London, England,' he said. 'Just married.'

'And I would care...why?'

'Whatever,' Connie shrugged. 'Just filling you in.'

Eddie sat and quietly smoked a cigarette, working his way through a bowl of pistachios and piling the shells neatly where Connie could brush them in the trash with one negligent sweep of his hand. He'd told the weirdoes forty thousand on the assumption he'd put his standard ten on top. Fifty felt about right. The arbitrary and fuck-ass irritating extra five they'd stipulated left him with the dilemma of deciding whether George would go for fifty-five, or if Eddie had to take half rate this time out. Wouldn't be the end of the world, what with his overheads being not much more than zero, but no-one likes getting stiffed on a deal. Eddie in particular didn't like it, but he was exploring the notion on the grounds that not charging the extra might store him up some brownie points somewhere. He didn't really believe in karma, but every now and then he paid lip service to it or some other edited highlight of a belief system, on the grounds that you never knew—and that someone who'd put as many people under the ground as he had did well to hedge his cosmic bets.

Meanwhile he watched as Connie served the bar sitters, kept half an eye on the customers who looked likely to be first in line to cause trouble or be sick, and filled the orders that Fran brought in from the outlying regions. Fran was a cheerful and tough 23, had big hair even by Florida standards and tattoos on her wrist, shoulder and small of her back which Connie wasn't strictly in favour of. Wasn't his business, but he hated to see lilies gilded and he was of a mind that tattooing a woman's body was like air-brushing a pair of leaping dolphins into the background of the Mona Lisa, just to perk it up a bit. Fran, though attractive, had a voice which could bend trees when she was riled and Connie elected as usual to shelve the observation. Instead he reminded the English honeymooners that it was only just after nine and the bar was open until three and thus they could afford to take it easy with regard to volume of alcohol consumption per unit time. They thanked him for his insight and consideration, and ordered another couple of Margaritas. Connie moved them up to pole position in his internal list of People Most Likely To Pass Out Before Midnight, but mused that at least they were likely to do it politely.

Then he noticed Eddie turn his head sharply towards the door, and glanced that way himself. Two seconds later, George, the guy from the night before, came running into the bar. His hair was awry and his face red and he was panting like his heart was considering its options and leaning towards a CVA. Eddie was on his feet before the door had stopped swinging, and flashed two fingers on the way across. Connie quickly turned and sloshed out a couple of tequilas, yelled at Janine to get her butt out the kitchen and hold the fort a minute, and took the drinks out the side door.

On the sidewalk outside, Eddie was standing in front of George. He had a hand on each of the guy's shoulders, and was talking to him in a low, even tone. George's eyes were wide and he was still breathing badly, his hands down by his side and trembling. His weight was only vaguely distributed over his legs, and if Eddie hadn't been there George would have been flat on his face in a moment.

Eddie took one of the drinks and held it in front of George's mouth. 'Drink this,' he said. George shook his head as if trying to flick water off it, eyes staring at some point on Eddie's chest.

Eddie grabbed his hair, pulled the man's head back in one sudden snap and tipped the booze straight down his throat.

George spluttered like a man pulled up out of deep water and went into a coughing jag that sounded as if tissue were coming loose. Eddie meanwhile tossed the shot glass at Connie, who caught it in one hand and handed him the second with the other. But when George stopped blinking and rubbing his eyes, they were focused back on the things in front of him.

'Sorry for that,' Eddie said. 'But things really are going to be a lot simpler if you just do as I say. You need another drink?' George coughed once more, and hiccupped, then shook his head.

Eddie nodded, satisfied, and knocked the drink back himself. 'I take it something's fucked up,' he said.

George's finger had stolen up to his lips, and he was rubbing them like there was something ingrained there that he couldn't stand. 'They've. Oh. She's gone.'

When he'd managed these words he suddenly looked around, as if he couldn't understand what he was doing in this place talking to these people and was seized with a desire to go running away in some random direction.

Eddie reached out, grabbed his arm. 'Your wife?'

There were only two salient facts. Jennifer Becker had disappeared. George didn't know where she'd gone. In the time from him hearing her saying his name and him making it up the steps to their suite, someone had stolen her away.

'When was this?'

George looked at his watch. 'Forty, forty-five minutes ago.'

Eddie pursed his lips, looked away down the street. Two things immediately occurred to him. The second was that the woman had been taken round about the time he'd been sitting talking to the weirdos. In other words, the assholes had sat there and set a price, all the while knowing that some of their buddies were already on the way to abduct the target. As it was, they'd been too fucking incompetent—or drunk—to even get the right human, but that wasn't the issue. The issue was that they were jerking him around. No-one had ever successfully jerked Eddie around before, no matter what planet they were from. Not for long, anyhow, and never for long enough to tell the tale.

George started slightly when Eddie swung his gaze back at him. For a moment there was something in the younger man's eyes, something that made it very clear that Eddie wouldn't be your first choice of guy to have a fight with, unless you were a SWAT team on the top of your game. George didn't know it, which was probably just as well because it was the last kind of thing he needed at that time, but he was one of only two people who'd seen that look in Eddie's eyes and lived to see the next hour. The other person had been Eddie's father, a long time ago, and he'd since died of his own accord.

'Well George,' Eddie said, his voice eerily calm, 'Looks like we've got a situation. They sent some guys already, you weren't there, they got your wife.'

George pulled his hand away from his lip, visibly tried to pull himself together. 'Has this ever happened before?'

'No. The vaccine was negotiated. Even if it was just our bad luck that the fetchers were already on the way, they should have been recalled. Hopefully it's an error. If it's deliberate, then it's moving outside the usual rules of engagement.'

'So what do we do?'

'First thing, you go in the bar and call your room. Check she's not back there.'

'But why...'

'They could have realised the fuck-up, dumped her back and she's sitting there not knowing what the hell is going on. Go call.'

After George had shouldered his way into the mass of people in the bar and was out of sight, Connie looked at Eddie.

'What's going on?'

'I don't know. I don't think it's a screw-up. I think it's deliberate.'

'Could be the greys?'

'I guess, but I don't think so. They usually do their own thing and don't mess with stuff the big boys have set up. Plus they know better than to fuck with me. After that last time.'

'What you going to do? Head back out there?'

Eddie shook his head. 'Not tonight. If it's a screw-up, I want to give them time to put it right. If not, then I'm surely going to have to have a word with them.'

'Want a hand?'

'Could be. You ever whacked an extra-terrestrial before?'

'Not as far as I know. They really bleed green?'

'You got me. I never whacked one either.'

They mused on the subject for a minute, then Eddie started getting a sinking feeling. They went inside and checked the public phone where it stood a noisy yard from the gents toilets. Five minutes later the whole building had been checked, and it was for sure.

George had disappeared.

Sunrise found Connie standing out on the deck at Havana docks, on the off-chance. Eddie meanwhile was sitting on the little balcony outside the Beckers' suite at the Marquesa. He knew nobody was inside, because he'd checked. He'd also tossed the room and the luggage. Sometimes things got left behind. He didn't know whether it was because the aliens were careless, or out of a desire to leave behind some kind of annoyingly meaningless clue, but on occasion you found little globules of alloy, or scraps of stuff which looked like tinfoil but wasn't, or coins from some other century. Eddie had a collection of such things that would make a UFOlogist hyperventilate. He kept meaning to throw it out, but hadn't gotten around to it yet.

There was nothing in the suite, except what you'd expect two older people to take with them on a week's vacation.

At a quarter after seven on the dot he saw a guy in a white coat approaching, bearing a tray of breakfast and the morning paper. Eddie quickly dropped around the edge of the balcony, and waited until he'd heard a soft rap on the door and the footsteps walking away. Then he flipped back up and helped himself to coffee. Way things were shaping up, the Beckers weren't going to miss it and Eddie strongly believed it a shame to let good coffee go to waste. The toast, on the other hand, he let lie.

THE VACCINATOR

He'd had plenty of time in the small hours, and all his thinking was done. The odds were that George would be a very long way away by now, beyond reach of anything Eddie could do to help him. What had to be done had little to do with his client, though obviously he'd keep an eye out for the guy and his wife. Today's dealings mainly had to do with showing some skinny-shank weirdoes that you didn't fuck with the way things were done. A vaccine was a vaccine: if the Colombians could understand that, then assholes from the planet Zog could too.

When there was still no sign at a little after eight, Eddie left the hotel and went to meet Connie down at the docks and get some breakfast with meat in it.

Meanwhile, less than a mile away, George was sitting at the end of a long concrete promontory right at the opposite end of Duval Street. Either side of the first half was beach with a little restaurant down the way, but the last half poked right into the ocean and was in fact the southernmost point in the whole of the USA. That wasn't why George was sitting there, however. He'd already done the experience with Jen the day before, as a tourist thing, and actually neither of them had felt themselves come alive with excitement. It was a five-minute's-worth kind of attraction, though as pleasant a place to sit as any. Truth be told, he had no idea why he was there, or how it had come to happen. He was just sitting, his legs dangling over the end, watching the waves.

After a while a woman came up and stood behind him. 'Come,' she said. 'It's time.'

A few hours later Connie was sitting in back of the boat, running the engine and slowly working his way through the beers in the cooler. Eddie perched up front, smoking. The sun was bright out on the water, and the ocean ran flat out as far as the eye could see. It was hot, in the dry clear way you only get when you're moving fast over water. When they were still a way from the right area, Eddie swore. He grabbed the binoculars and glared through them at a dot on the horizon.

'What?' Connie asked, speaking loud against the noise of the engine.

'Spirit of Key fucking West.'

Connie looked at his watch. It was just before eleven. 'Kind of early for them, isn't it?'

A glass-bottom boat, capable of carrying fifty-odd tourists out to go stare at under-water things and be told stuff by earnest people in white shorts, the Spirit of Key West usually took its first cruise out of the Havana docks at around mid-day.

'It's coming season,' Eddie said. 'Guess Jack reckoned he could squeeze in a load of early birds.'

'It's going to fuck things up, isn't it?'

'There's no way the weirdoes will uncloak in front of a bunch of assholes with cameras.'

'So what do we do?'

'Any idea how long they stay out over the reef?'

'Never been. Got no real interest in denizens of the sea, unless there's cocktail sauce on the side. Plus, like, I live here. But shit, how long can you look at some fish? Fifteen, twenty minutes? And that's assuming you're stoned.'

Eddie swore again. 'I guess we just wait.'

Connie cut the engines and they drifted for a while. It was calm and very quiet, just the hollow slocking sound of water lapping up against the sides of the boat, and a few birds running the avian commuter routes up above. The seabed was maybe ten, twelve feet below, mainly bone-coloured sand but some white rocks and patches of weed. Eddie knew that, in a few places in the area, if you were to dig a few feet below the surface you'd find un-rusting metal caskets, places where the visitors stored things that included the buried remains of both their own kind and humans. But he had no real interest in finding them.

They gave the boat twenty-five minutes, and then Connie got on the radio to suggest to Jack that maybe his clients had seen enough fucking fish and would he like to get the hell back into harbor.

After about a couple minutes of trying Connie gave Eddie a look. Eddie nodded. 'Let's go see what's going on here.'

It took them ten minutes to get within shouting distance. Neither of them especially felt like shouting, so they went in a little closer. The boat, a sixty-foot Seabreezer IV, was stationery near the reef, though a hundred yards more to the West than you would have expected. The engine was off. The boat was drifting. Eddie tried again on the radio, and got no response. Then he tried shouting anyway, in case Jack had slipped out of the control room for a cigarette while his passengers were down on the lower deck inside. Nobody shouted back.

Meanwhile Connie brought the boat in closer. 'So now what?'

'Bring us up right to the back.' Eddie already had a gun in his hand, and one of the big knives slipped down into his boot.

Connie picked up the other gun. 'And if they suddenly kick in the engines?'

'There was anybody on the bridge, we'd have spoken to them by now.'

THE VACCINATOR

They got the boat up flat against the stern of the Spirit of Key West, and tied her on. Then they climbed aboard, Eddie first, Connie second: neither of them especially scared and both reconciled to the idea of shooting someone if the need arose.

The boat was a standard of its type. Open at the back so you could catch some rays on the way to and from the reef, a covered place at the front for sitting and the eating of potato chips. At the prow, an area where you could stand and pretend you were that baby-face asshole in *Titanic*. A bridge area, and, below decks, the lower section where you leaned on rails and look down through the bottom.

There were no people in any of these areas. There were also no bags, paperback books, jackets or other signs of things having been left behind.

After checking each of the levels, Eddie climbed back up to the top and stood and looked for a while at the desk where you bought soft drinks and cookies and stuff if you really couldn't go an hour without taking on some kind of sustenance.

Connie joined him after poking around in the bridge. 'This would be unusual, I feel?'

Eddie nodded thoughtfully. 'That about covers it.'

'So what's happened to all these people?' Connie capped a beer that he'd luckily thought to bring on board with him, took a long pull, and peered out through the windows at the tinted ocean.

'Obvious answer is there's been a mass abduction.'

'Right. That was kind of what I was assuming.'

'But,' Eddie said, 'I'm not sure that's working for me as an explanation.' He accepted the beer from Connie, took a drink, and then thought some more. Then he lifted the hatch on the food desk and went behind. Opened the cupboards and fridge.

Connie watched. 'I sense the Kruger intellect working overtime here.'

'Where's the stuff? Where the cans and the chips and those boring fucking cookies?'

'They are, I take it, absent.'

'This boat's not going to come out on a jaunt without them. You take a load of tourists out here in the sun and then tell them they can't buy a soda, you're going to have a mutiny. People are going to lose their minds with worry and just go berserk.'

Connie shrugged. 'Maybe Karen didn't make it in this morning, and Jack just took a chance on doing a trip without provisions.'

'Right. Or maybe the weirdoes had the munchies, and took all the stuff with them. I don't like either version.' Eddie got out his mobile phone, flipped it open. No signal. 'Go try the radio.'

Connie went forward into the bridge again. Eddie walked out back and stood on the sun deck, leaning back against the rail and watching the waves. He'd been holding a question mark in his head overnight. He was wondering if all this might provide an answer to it. Difficult to tell at this stage, but he was beginning to think it might. Trouble was, wasn't clear what the answer might be.

Connie came out, smiling. 'Just spent a few minutes talking to a guy who was ready to shit a brick.'

'Jack's back at the harbor?'

'You got it. With Karen, and those perky dudes in white shorts from the Marine Biology place. Not to mention a muttering hoard of sunburners who bought tickets yesterday afternoon and are really keen to come stare at some fish and been looking forward to it all last night, and are currently two short steps away from litigation. He's had to stand a round of free ice teas already.'

Eddie rolled his shoulders, flicked the safety back on and holstered his gun. 'There is something unusually weird going on here,' he said, 'And it's pissing me off.'

'So now what? Sorry to keep asking you questions and stuff, but this is, like, your area. Me, I'm just a spear carrier and happy that way.'

'What did you tell Jack?'

'Said we'd found his boat, it looks fine. Maybe we'd bring it back at some stage.'

'He's not barking for it now? We don't want to be dealing with some other guys come out here to fetch it.'

'Think he's sort of given up on the day. Sounded like he had started to face the situation with the aid of alcohol-based beverages.'

Eddie nodded. 'Okay. That's cool.'

'We have a plan?'

'We surely do.'

'Hurrah.' Connie neatly stowed the empty bottle in the trash and rubbed his hands together, his grey eyes sparkling with dangerous good humor. 'And what is it?'

'We leave the boat here, and get on with business. We go have a word with the weirdos, outline our displeasure at the situation in general, and if necessary kick some butt.'

'Eddie,' Connie said, 'That's a fine plan.'

Jennifer Becker sat as still as she could, covertly watching the two aliens. They hadn't spoken to her in a while. That was okay. She didn't want them to. In fact, she didn't think she could bear it if they did. She was only too aware that her life as it had been up until now, which she had by and large enjoyed, was over. A conversation with either of the beings who were standing a few yards from her could only rub this in further. She had also grown tired of trying to work out what they were saying. Occasional English words floated to the surface in their discussion, which otherwise sounded like the gurglings of a boisterous stream in early spring, trickle-fed out of melting snow and gathering volume and speed as it found its joyous way down a mountainside. At first she'd wondered whether this was because the aliens didn't have words in their language for what they were saying, like the French said they were going to have *un picnic* at *le weekend* while *camping*. Or whether it was more like Mrs Lal, the woman who worked at the Vietnamese grocery store in town and who'd been bilingual for so long that she seemed to forget which words belonged to which country—and who often turned to yell at her husband in a stream of gobbledygook which sounded remarkably similar to what the aliens were saying. But it was kind of an academic question and Jennifer hadn't found that she cared enough to pursue it very far.

Instead she was thinking about a friend of hers, Sally Dickens. Sally was the wife of one of the junior realtors in Becker & Marks. She was a little older than her husband Bruce, and Jen was a little younger than George, and the two had been close, up until a year ago. Then, little by little, Sally had started to act a little weird. At first Jenny had speculated her friend was having an affair, though she couldn't really get the idea to stick because while Sally was a really nice person—and great, acerbic company at a cocktail party—she wasn't what you'd think of as a hedonistic pleasure-seeker. Pretty serious, in fact, on the whole. Not the kind for sweated afternoons in darkness behind curtains in cheap hotels out by the Interstate, or hands held under the table in unpopular bars. Actually Jennifer thought that of the two of them *she* was more that kind of person, though of course she never had tested this theory, and had never even wanted to.

Then one afternoon the two of them had been having lunch at the quite good Italian that was part of the new mall and she'd pressed Sally a little, partly out of concern but also just a tiny bit because her friend's new twitchiness and silences had begun to get on her nerves. When your best friends start wigging out on you, it cuts at the heart of your life. Sally was already a few glasses of Chardonnay down at that point, and, after a couple more, and over the rest of the bottle, she tried to tell Jennifer a story. About something she claimed had happened one night when her husband was out of town, involving bright lights, strange noises, and a period of time out of time.

Jennifer hadn't believed her, and maybe hadn't hidden the fact too well. It all just sounded like something off a TV show, not very imaginatively adapted. The people she claimed had come to see her had been normal height or in fact a little taller, and not looked like those grey things you saw pictured everywhere. Apart from that it wasn't even a very interesting story, and Jen had smiled politely and sat there waiting for a gap long enough in which to ask for the check. Making it worse somehow was the fact that Sally had a bit of salad stuck between her teeth, which made her look vulnerable and sad. It wasn't the kind of thing you could point out, however, not while you were being told that kind of tale. Just something that could nag at your attention, and maybe make you pay an iota less mind than you should.

Over the next couple of months she saw Sally only once, at a party. She'd been drunk, and looked a little thin, but stood next to her husband listening to realtor stories and laughing at exactly the right moments. Her eyes had been flat, almost dry-looking, and when she saw Jen she smiled a small, tired smile that made Jen feel like a five-year-old, sensing for the first time that sometimes things happened to grown-ups which were too dismal and complex for children to understand. They barely spoke that evening, and when they did, Jen felt a little as if she was talking to someone who for reasons best known to themselves had decided to impersonate her friend, and had got the look more or less right but whose heart wasn't really in the rest of the job.

A few weeks after that Sally had tried to kill herself. Tried really quite hard, and only just failed. Since then she had been resident in a private place about twenty-five miles out of town. 'Depressed', was the official verdict: just sort of depressed about stuff, in general. From what Jen could gather no mention had ever been made of an otherworldly fantasy being a source for the situation. Bruce Dickens was bearing up reasonably well, probably partly because he and a female client who was trying to sell her gauche mansion over at the golf course had really quite a lot of meetings out of the office. There were no children, so that was that.

One afternoon Jennifer had driven out to the Hospital or Rest Home or Facility or Nut House or whatever it termed itself. She had got as far as parking in the lot, and sat in the car for half an hour. Then she'd driven home. She'd told herself that perhaps it wasn't a good idea for Sally to see her, that an unscheduled visit might interrupt whatever program the place had her on. Though actually Jen knew that the program would probably entirely consist of colour-coded pills and little measures of heavily-laced liquids, administered at regular intervals by brisk girls with dusty smiles. And really she just hadn't known what she was going to say, or how she should be, when the reality of the situation was that her friend had lost her mind.

Or so she'd thought. As she sat now in the grove of trees, very hot, extremely thirsty and being herself one step away from being driven insane by what was happening, Jennifer avoiding thinking about how she felt about her current situation by realising, finally, how guilty she felt about Sally. It wasn't even that she knew now that she might have been telling the truth. That shouldn't have mattered. Jen should have been a better friend to her anyway. And she wondered, pointlessly, whether she might have taken the whole thing just a little more seriously if there hadn't been that bit of salad caught between Sally's teeth, and how many of her judgment calls—and those of everyone else in the world—were made on such a trivial basis.

She wasn't surprised, only slightly relieved, when the aliens stopped talking and one of them turned and shot her in the head.

And the sad fact of the matter was that Sally Dickens hadn't been abducted. She really had just lost her mind.

'I'm hungry, is all I'm saying.'

Eddie shelved the idea of stripping his gun down. He'd already done it twice. No good could come of doing it again. No good had come of doing it the last time. He looked up at Connie. 'If you thought you were going to need to eat, you should have brought some food. That would have been the thinking man's approach.'

'Didn't think I was going to need it, mainly because I didn't think it was going to take this long. This is a protracted fucking afternoon we're having here, not to say one that's beginning to drag.'

'Really? Funny you feel like that, because I'm having a fucking ball.' He irritably started taking the gun apart again.

Connie shrugged. 'I feel like an ass sitting out here. Plus my head is getting sunburnt and that I can do without. Not to mention we're running out of beer.'

'You think things are bad now, wait until I run out of cigarettes. Then you're really going to see a downturn in the situation.'

Connie shook his head. 'This is no good, Eddie. You got to make a change in your working conditions. What kind of fucked-up deal is this, that you can't just go find the guys and whack them? Got to be the bottom line of any transaction of this nature. People fuck you around, they know they're going to get clipped. It's motivational management. Keeps them perky.'

'Connie, I run out of cigarettes, I'm going to whack *you*.'

'I'm just saying. That's all. This isn't dignified.'

It was just after five, Connie should have been at work hours before, and the sun was dipping low in the sky—but nothing was happening. Nothing had happened all afternoon, in fact. They'd sat in the right place for a while, then got so bored that they went back to the Spirit of Key West, tied the smaller boat on back, and taken the cruiser back to the harbor. Connie's intuition concerning Jack's coping mechanisms had proved to be correct. There was no danger he was taking the boat out again that day, unless he had some way of working it by remote control from the barstool he was already in danger of falling off. The tourists had lost interest and gone off to spend their refund money on T-shirts and driftwood sculptures. And food, probably, Connie mused, wishing he'd had the foresight to pick something up before they turned round and came back out again, instead of wasting the time ringing the bar to warn them he was going to be late. It wasn't that he was so damned hungry, more that the idea had gotten into his head and, in the absence of stimuli other than waves and sunlight and fucking seabirds, was proving pretty hard to dislodge.

Plus, actually, when he thought about it, he *was* kind of hungry. Eddie didn't seem to care either way, which Connie felt was weird. A guy had to eat, and breakfast was many hours ago and had anyway been compact and taken on the run. Eddie, on the other hand, seemed capable of existing solely on cigarettes and scowling.

'You never had to do this by day before?'

'No.'

'We can't just forget about the big light thing, go straight to the island?'

'It's just not there during the day. I've looked. It might be there at night. We have to wait and see.'

'Well, next time you'll know to bring a sandwich.'

'There isn't going to be a next time. Or if there is, it'll be a bazooka in the lunchbox, believe me. Look, eat a piece of rope or something, would you? I'm thinking here.'

Connie shrugged again, and opened one of the few remaining beers.

Meanwhile Eddie looked out over the ocean. He was indeed thinking, and what he was primarily thinking was that this would all be settled pretty soon. Once the light went, the weirdoes would be sure to pick them up. They didn't like people hanging around here after dark, as a few hundred years of disappearances testified. The only reason why Eddie wasn't on that list of anomalies is that the time when they'd picked him up and dumped him on the island he'd got the measure of the spindly ones pretty quickly, and had the balls to suggest a commercial arrangement to them. He'd known ever since then that the position was a perilous one. Of the three, he hated Yag the least, but he didn't trust him in the slightest. He especially didn't trust No-name. He'd met men like No-name many times, and they always ended up fucking you around. It was in their nature, even when it wasn't in their interests.

Eddie cleared his mind, set up what he knew, and what he suspected, and left it like that. It didn't do to be too locked in one mindset, when going into situations like this. The resolutions of violent events were generally short. You got killed, or you avoided getting killed—generally by killing someone else. That was what it came down to, and neither outcome took very long or could be meaningfully prepared for ahead of time. Like a tennis player facing a serve from someone you'd never played before, the best you could do was watch the other guy's feet, be limber, and skilled enough to whack back whatever came over the net.

So instead he thought for a while about finding a new line of work, but nothing came. After a time Connie opened the last beer and offered it to him. Eddie shook his head, but winked: and everything was relaxed in the boat once more.

That evening the restaurants and bars of Key West did good business. Nothing spectacular, because it wasn't yet full season, but everyone went home pretty happy—the proprietors to nice Victorian homes in the Old Town or Scholz-designed palaces on the North of the island, the waitresses and barmen to dwindling stashes of dope and rooms in ramshackle houses. Places like Crabby Dick's and Mangoes and Febe's Grill got in two solid covers of holiday spenders, and the Hard Rock Café doled out a hundred burgers or so, as an adjunct to its primary business of making people's ears bleed. The chi-chi bistros tucked away down sidestreets and in hotels raked in by far the best money—the human species having lost its bearings to such a degree that it thinks small portions on big plates are the Body of Christ, and that running when you don't need to is in some way life-affirming. Meanwhile Slappy Jack's and Sloppy Joe's and Jimmy Buffet's saw good Friday night crowds, and the usual pilgrimage was made by many down to the Havana Dock to watch the night come, despite the fact that before, during, and after sunset a uniquely talentless young woman armed with a battery of cheap synths rent the air with jerky covers of the songs of yesteryear, primarily the mid-1980s, and especially those with a maritime or vacation theme, however tangential; while another woman, who had once been beautiful but was now merely frightening, served long fruit cocktails in plastic cups and glared at the leavers of tips she considered insufficiently generous.

People walked up and down Duval Street in the warmth of the early evening, peering in stores, assaying menus, enjoying the company of their companions but with part of their minds distantly worrying about the children, pets, lovers and gas ovens they'd left behind. From above, the island was a patchwork of light and dark, groves of trees with house lights twinkling, a network of lit streets, the distant thud of music. You couldn't avoid the fact that life existed there, however far back you pulled: like a corner behind the fridge which never quite gets cleaned and is host to a variety of small microbular things going about their business with the happy, unmindful concentration of children.

This, or something like it but in heavier clothes and with no Internet access, had gone on there for hundreds of years—and would go on for hundreds more. What took place a couple miles out to sea that evening never made any difference to anybody and was, as Eddie expected, over fairly quickly.

The light came on eventually, but only for a moment and nowhere near as brightly as usual. The sea never froze. For Connie, who'd heard about the light from above but had never seen it, the experience was kind of interesting. For Eddie it merely confirmed what he'd already decided: something was notably fucked up.

They waited another few minutes to see whether something else would happen, but it didn't. Eddie cut the signal tone on the radio, and told Connie to start the engine.

'Which direction?'

'Straight ahead. That's where the island is.'

Connie peered eloquently out at the open sea. 'It's your call.'

'Yes, and I've called. Do it.'

They went fast and fifteen minutes later Eddie told Connie to slow it down a little. Connie took it back to pootling speed and watched as Eddie stood and looked ahead. There was still nothing to see. Eddie closed his eyes, got his bearings. He'd always been a good judge of space, even in the dark and in jungles and terrains he didn't know that well. It was just one of those things.

'I'd say we're a couple of hundred yards short at this stage,' he said.

'Keep taking her ahead, but slow.'

Connie drove. Eddie loaded his pockets with shells. Up above them the moon shed a cool, confident light that for several more minutes failed to reveal anything out of the ordinary.

But then, they saw something.

About twenty yards ahead. Something small and pale grey, about three feet above the ocean.

'Shit on me,' Connie said. 'What the blue fuck is that?'

Eddie didn't reply, but just waited until they were closer, by which time the question could be answered just through using your eyes. Connie slowed the boat right down, and then a quiet *thok* noise told them they'd found the walkway.

'Eddie, thank God,' the grey croaked. 'Boy am I glad to see you.'

Eddie tied the boat up, while Connie just stared up at the alien. Then he clambered onto the walkway. Not an easy task, while the pier remained invisible, but achievable.

He looked down at the creature. 'What's going on?'

'Weird shit, Eddie,' the grey said. 'That's all I know.'

'Do the tall guys know something's afoot?'

'I don't think so. They're kind of wasted. They even forgot to feed us this morning.'

'How many have you seen? What do they look like?'

The grey shook his head. 'Couple of the guys say there's four or five. Me, I only saw two. And those looked kind of like you do.'

Eddie turned back to the boat. Connie was still standing there. 'Are you coming up here, or what?'

Connie swallowed. 'Up where, man?'

'Up on the pier.'

'The invisible pier, I take it? The one where you're chewing the rag with something out of the fucking *X-Files*?'

'That'd be the one.'

'You know what? I'm wondering whether this is something I'm truly going to be up to on an empty stomach.'

Eddie leant down without a word and proffered a hand. Connie grabbed it, and scrabbled with relative grace up unto the walkway. He dusted off his hands and looked down at the alien, who looked back up at him.

'Hi, Roswell dude,' Connie said eventually. 'I come in peace.'

'That wasn't us,' the grey snapped, 'And I'm tired of taking flack for it.'

'Let's get on with this,' Eddie said, and started walking. The grey skittered round to trot in front. Connie took the rear. It felt like a good place to be for the time being. They walked the length, towards a yellow light. This, Connie observed, was also hanging a few feet above the sea. The situation didn't seem to be bugging Eddie, however, so he guessed it was okay. A couple of yards before they reached it, he got a flicker in his eyes. For a moment it looked like there was something behind the light, a body of land. Then the impression disappeared, to be replaced by a couple of oval heads around the light. There was some excitable chattering in a language that was neither English or Spanish, the only ones Connie had any real acquaintance with.

'Okay guys,' the grey said to them, as they got to the end. He nodded in the direction of the three other greys, who'd appeared from behind the light. All of them either waved or nodded at Eddie. 'What you have to do is get land-side of my buddies here.'

Eddie walked past the little aliens. Connie followed. The moment his back foot was past them, a whole island flicked into view. And this time, it stayed there. Connie shook his head.

'How the hell'd you do that?'

'Our science is many centuries ahead of yours,' intoned one of the greys. 'Do not adjust your television set.' The others giggled.

Eddie shushed them, and explained his plan.

Minutes later the greys quietly led Connie towards the path, and Eddie slipped alone into the trees. He waited until they were out of sight around the corner, and then cut a wide path around the island. Partly this was because it would probably turn out better if they didn't all approach the centre from the same direction. Partly it was to see if there was any evidence to bear out a hunch that had been slowly gaining hunchiness all afternoon.

In a grove close to the shore on the East side he found the body of someone he thought very likely to be Jennifer Becker, lying awkwardly on the ground. Eddie didn't bother to check for a pulse. She'd evidently been shot by a weapon of non-human provenance, which had punched a hole right through her head. A sad, crumpled end for someone who'd never really understood the situation she'd found herself in, but then Eddie could have said the same for many people he'd known, who'd fallen in the kind of fights that got covered on CNN and then been buried with full military honours. All around her in the sand were two sets of footprints of pretty normal shape and size. One of them bore the logo of a prominent earthling casualware manufacturer. The other showed all the signs of having been made by flip flops of equally terrestrial provenance.

Eddie decided he finally knew what was going on.

THE VACCINATOR

*

'So who the hell are you?' Fud demanded, glaring at Connie.

Connie looked right back at the alien. He'd already endured having his monkey-derived ancestry cited, and was rapidly discovering the truth of something Eddie had once told him: it didn't take very long in the company of these people before you started really, really wanting to kill them.

'Friend of Eddie's,' he said. 'He sent me here.'

'Eddie's an asshole,' slurred the No-name alien. 'I always said so. You're probably an asshole too.' He coughed, and then added in a wheedling voice: 'Did he send any smokes with you?'

Yag, who'd yet to say anything, shushed his colleague with a thoughtful wave of his hand, and carried on looking at Connie.

No-name hiccupped and stomped away to flop down into one of the reclining chairs. The greys meanwhile were standing together in a protective huddle a few feet away, under the standard lamp as if for warmth. Most of them were casting wary glances into the trees that stood all around the grassed clearing. The one who'd met them on the pier, who so far as Connie could tell was entirely indistinguishable from the others except that he was a little bit braver, coughed nervously.

'He told us to come warn you,' the little alien said to Yag. The others stopped peering around and gathered behind him, for moral support. 'Some bad stuff is happening. The guy he was arranging a vaccine for has disappeared. Plus his wife.'

'Wasn't us,' Fud said.

'He knows,' said the grey. 'Think he's going to want a word with you about that. And you know what he's like when he's pissed.'

'So who was it?' Yag asked.

'Us,' said a voice, and three species whirled at once.

Standing at the edge of the clearing was a man. Tall, dressed in grey shorts and nothing else. He'd lost the rest of his clothes during the day, no longer able to remember why he had to wear them. Only a shadowy vestige of an old propriety had kept the shorts in position. He stood in shadow, and at first Connie couldn't see his face. Then he took a couple of shambling paces forward, legs twisting as if he'd been knee-capped but was still somehow able to support his weight, a gun pointed in the general direction of the spindly aliens. Yag and Fud took small steps backwards.

No-name peered at the human and belched quietly. 'What the crap,' he rasped, 'is happening now?'

The man turned from the waist, as if he'd forgotten about his legs, and pointed the gun directly at him. 'Shut up,' he said.

'How did you get here, George?' Connie asked, his voice remarkably level. 'What happened to you last night?'

'By boat,' George said, his voice inflectionless. 'It had glass in the bottom. There were no sodas though. Jen was with us. But then she died. Well, we killed her, in fact. It was very sad.'

'Hold on,' said Yag, frowning. 'What do you mean, "Us"? There's only one of you.' The alien was hung over to hell and back, and something was telling him this might be a bad time to be in that condition. Also that it would have been a good idea to have thought to bring some weapons out with them, even some teeny little ones, when the greys and human had appeared in the clearing.

If in doubt, bring a weapon. It seemed so obvious now.

'And,' Connie added, spotting another flaw, 'you're one of the people who's been kidnapped, surely.'

'He's referring to me,' said another voice, female this time. A young woman stepped out of the shadows on the other side of the clearing. She had big hair, dainty tattoos, and a gun in her hand that looked like a bunch of big spiders fighting on a frog. 'You got a gun, Connie?' she said. 'Sure you do. Take it out, slowly, and throw it on the ground.'

'Fran?' Connie asked, his voice finally cracking, 'What in Christ's name are *you* doing here?'

'Could ask the same of you. But I'm not going to, because to be frank I don't really care. Just lose the piece.'

Connie reached into his pocket like a man in a daze, pulled out the gun, and dropped it on the ground.

'Great,' muttered Fud. 'Thanks for your help, banana-boy.'

'Yeah?' Connie said, still staring at Fran. 'Well, you're so tough, *you* do something.'

'We're not good at that kind of thing,' Fud muttered.

Fran motioned George forward with her gun. George picked Connie's weapon up and held it in his hand, as if unsure how to proceed. In the light that was always present in the clearing he appeared strange, shaky, as if holding himself together by will power alone. His face looked bulbous and pale, his skin damp.

Connie shook his head. 'Is Janine running the bar by herself?' he asked, evidently in need of clinging to something he could understand. 'It's Friday night. She's going to go ape.'

'No pun intended, presumably,' Fran smiled. 'I have no idea. I don't give a shit. I hate that bar. And those olive things you do? What are *they* about? Are they supposed to be food, or what? They're crap. Now, to business.' She pointed her gun at his head. 'You know too much. You have to die.' She laughed delightedly. 'Cool. I always wanted to say that.'

'I know shit,' Connie said hurriedly. 'Really.'

Fran did something to the gun that was clearly preparatory to using it to hurt people. 'Sorry, but that's the way it's got to be.'

'Seriously, it's overkill. There's fish in the bay got more idea of what's going on than me. Far as I know, you're just a waitress. A damned fine one, don't get me wrong. But a waitress, mainly.'

'Oh, I'm a lot more than that,' Fran laughed. 'In fact, I'm ...'

There was a sudden, short cry. Everyone turned, to see that George was now lying on his back on the ground with the air of someone who would be there for a while. Standing beside him, his gun pointed unswervingly at Fran's head, was Eddie.

Connie didn't think he'd ever been so pleased to see in anyone in his life, and in that moment, in a tiny, very male way, he loved the guy to bits. Eddie looked so casual. He looked so armed. He looked so much like if Fran even twitched then she'd be missing her head before she knew it—which, though a very specific way to appear, was easy to recognise and good to see.

No-name goggled. 'Are you seeing this too?' he hissed to Fud, in a low voice. 'People just keep *appearing*.'

'Yo, Fran,' Eddie said, carefully taking a couple of steps forward. His gun, while he did this, remained so steady that you could have rested a beer glass on it and not lost a drop. 'If that's your real name. Which frankly I doubt. Why don't you lower the gun.'

'Fuck you,' Fran said.

There was a quick, dry cracking sound, and Fran's right hand disappeared, taking the gun with it. She blinked, and a moment later a thick black gloop began to drip from the severed wrist. 'You *fucker*,' she said, with quiet amazement.

'Why don't you tell Connie what you are?' Eddie suggested.

'He doesn't want to know,' Fran snarled, shaking her wrist. 'Jeez, Eddie, have you any idea how long it's going to take to grow a hand back? Fingers are really hard to do.'

'Fran's from another planet,' Eddie said to Connie, slowly letting the gun drop. His tone suggested this was no more remarkable than her being a Pisces, or lifelong Blue Jays fan.

'I see,' Connie said, nodding sagely.

'So's George, though he didn't know it.'

Connie stopped nodding and stared at Eddie, like an owl that believed someone was trying to pull a fast one on it. 'Kind of hard thing to forget, wouldn't you say?'

'I'd have thought so, but that's what happened. For the whole of his life George believed he was just a regular guy who sold people houses and land. Jen believed that too, which must have made this afternoon rather difficult for her. But recently he's started to remember—because someone began dumping clues in his head. He thought it was a memory of abduction, and I assumed it was these assholes gearing up to make a play.' He indicated the spindly aliens, who were all wide-eyed and silent. 'And you guys didn't go out of your way to correct my mistake, which pisses me off somewhat. Given that I've now saved your gill-headed asses, I think there's going to be a change in pay and working conditions.'

'Saved our asses?' Yag said. 'How so?'

'This is some kind of significant staging post or trans-dimensional transportation thing you've got going on this island, right? And it's your job to guard it.'

'There's an element of that,' Yag admitted cagily. 'How do you know?'

'Worked it out. I figure that if there's a whole universe out there, chances are there's going to be more than one type of alien and their pets around.' He winked at the greys. 'No offence, fellas.'

'None taken,' the lead grey said. 'Hell, we like being pets. People give you food.'

'Sometimes,' one of the others added, pointedly.

Eddie turned back to Yag. 'Fran, she's not one of yours, so obviously she's one of a different type. Her attitude seems somewhat hostile. I didn't know from the beginning she was in on what's going on, but I figured someone other than George had to be—especially after George disappeared. My guess is that somehow, at some point in the past, she must have slipped through immigration and has been laying low. And last night I realised George wasn't what he seemed, or even what he thought he was himself. When I asked him how long ago it was since his wife had been abducted, he told me forty-five minutes.'

'And?' Connie asked. He took a couple of steps away from Fran, who was glaring unhappily at Eddie. 'So what?'

'Take about ten to get from the Marquesa to Slappy's,' Eddie said, 'Even if you were slow and got lost. Maybe he spent ten other minutes tearing his hair out in the hotel suite, or running around the grounds. Still leaves a block of time unaccounted for. I think he spent that time sitting staring into space in the room. I think that Fran abducted Jennifer as part of a process of getting George to remember what he really was.'

'What, like, gay or something?'

'No,' Eddie said patiently. 'George is a sleeper. An alien in disguise even to himself. She needed him to wake up, because she wanted him to help her take this base and open the floodgates.'

'So why'd George admit it was forty-five minutes?' Yag said. 'Why didn't he lie?'

'He'd stopped being wholly human,' Eddie shrugged. 'But hadn't yet reverted to his real type. He was confused. He no longer really understood what to say, or how to say it. When we saw him at the bar, the human part was temporarily back in control again. He didn't understand what the hell was going on, and he was afraid, and he told the truth because he thought it would help. He'd lost his wife. He wanted her back.'

'Hang on,' Connie said. 'Fran was in the bar at the time. How'd she do the Mrs Becker thing, when she was carrying drinks in front of my eyes?'

'I don't know,' Eddie admitted irritably. 'I also never understood the appeal of *Seinfield*, and the whole grassy knoll thing is a mystery to me too. I haven't got the complete thing worked out. But that's basically how it happened, right Fran?'

Fran had stopped shaking her hand.

She looked calmly back at Eddie.

'Four hundred and fifty years,' she said, eventually. She didn't look defeated, or worried, or frightened. 'I volunteered. I came ahead. I knew Florida when it was just a big swamp, just a few Indians wandering around. It seemed like a good place to wait for backup. It was quiet. It was hot. Then the white guys showed up. Decided this was Heaven on Earth. Whacked the first lot of Indians, and then let some more in and called them Seminoles. Let them stay. For a while, and then whacked them for the most part too. Meanwhile drained and farmed and did stuff, turning the mainland into a zoo. Then there was that stupid-ass fight about whether you were allowed to own other humans or not, so I came down the Keys to get out of the way. Watched the hotel guy, what was his name, Flagler?—lousy lay, whatever he was called—build the bridge right down through the Keys. Then the hurricane took it a couple years later. Then another got built.'

Eddie was keen on the idea of a cigarette by this point, but knew it would ruin Fran's sense of occasion and he figured that after a few centuries she had a right to that. Plus he was running very low. He just listened. The others did too. You sort of had to.

'All the time,' Fran said, shaking her head. 'You guys have no idea that you're all just barely-tolerated guests, and that these guys'—she indicated Yag and Fud with distaste—'have already laid claim. I wait, and I wait. They said they were going to send more after me. That there'd be enough for us to take this ridiculous island, which small though it is, is very fucking important in the general scheme of things. That was my job. But no-one appeared. No-one. For year after year after year. Until finally I learned what had happened. I got a message.'

'How?' Eddie asked, intrigued.

'They're beamed in, coded into *The Jerry Springer Show*,' Fran said. 'What else do you think is the point of that shit? Anyhow, the message told me that the controls had been tightened. They had managed to get someone over, but up in the North—and he'd only been able to stay for less than five hours. So he'd popped through, made a baby with a human, and then slipped back again. That baby was George, and he had no idea who he was. Until I finally found him, and started floating things into his head, waking him up to the way he should be. He got drawn down here, as all the sad abductee fucks do because they know something's going on around here and they think it's going to help them to be near. He still wasn't really getting with the program until last night, when I got a wino to go around to the Marquesa and grab the little woman out of her suite. And that about brings us up to date.'

Everyone looked at her for a moment. Then Eddie spoke again. 'All that waiting, just for *one more guy* to arrive?'

'One is all I need,' Fran said. 'Hell, one good man is all *anyone* needs.'

'And now it's all screwed,' Connie said, with satisfaction.

Fran laughed, with a kind of quiet contentment. 'Screwed? I don't think so.' She nodded at where George was lying prone. 'I really don't think that at all.'

Eddie was quick. He turned, stepped back and put three shells into George before anyone else had even moved. But it made no difference. By the time the erstwhile realtor was on his feet, his body was already halfway to changing. His knees had swollen to twice their usual size, and the skin was splitting like a dropped fig. The rest of his body was swelling too, unevenly but very quickly—some parts looking like their were about to explode, others dwindling to twig thickness.

'Oh shit,' Yag said, in a quiet, aghast voice. 'It's one of *them*.'

Eddie popped a measured three shells directly into what had been George's head, but was now a huge twisted thing that look like an old tree trunk covered in moss. It made no difference. Then he heard the greys gasp, and turned to see the same thing was happening to Fran. She was getting bigger. She was expanding and contracting in the same way George was, but as part of the process both of them were simply acquiring more mass. Somehow, drawn from somewhere, more stuff was going into them—and they were getting larger and larger. Both were making a low keening sound, though it wasn't clear whether this was coming from what was left of their mouths or if it was part of the process of change, flesh and bone screaming as it was pulled agonizingly into a configuration never meant to spend time on this planet or in our reality. It looked like something that *Hellraiser* dude might have come up with, the morning after far too much Mexican food.

As the creatures got bigger and bigger, and started to vibrate like gross, blood-spitting tuning forks, everyone suddenly drew breath and realised they wanted to be somewhere else. Yag and Fud ran to a point on the left-hand side of the clearing and started hammering their fists on something Eddie couldn't see, but assumed was the means of going back whence they'd come. Evidently it wasn't opening. The greys meanwhile ran in five random directions, got scared after a couple of yards, and then all hurtled back again to crash together in the middle. The two weirdoes gave up on the invisible door and tried to go sprinting off into the trees, only to find that something had happened to the air there and it had become an invisible wall. No-name, meanwhile, was evidently trying to crawl underneath one of the reclining chairs. Connie just stood, hands down by his side, watching events unfold with the air of a man who'd decided that if the world was going to drive him stark raving mad he might as well go along for the ride, and get the full value out of the experience.

Within two long minutes Fran and George stood ten feet high, looking like twisted figures painted by Francis Bacon around an idea by Miro, rendered in blood and bloat. They took a few shambling steps towards each other. Then stopped, at what looked like a prescribed distance, and stretched out to each other with what had once been hands.

Eddie knew what was about to happen, and emptied his gun into various parts of their anatomies, without much hope but knowing that he had to prevent the two of them becoming one. Fran had said that's all she needed, just one other of her species. Eddie didn't want to see, didn't want the world to see, what happened when two of these guys conjoined. He sensed it would be a bad thing.

He shouted at Connie and Connie slowly drew his eyes from the spectacle, realised what Eddie wanted, and pulled his gun.

They fired and reloaded, fired and reloaded, picking small divots out of the aliens' flesh but doing nothing to stop the inexorable progress of each's flesh towards the other's. The two bodies were now of slightly different shape, like halves of a biological jigsaw puzzle waiting to be fitted together like sperm and egg.

Michael Marshall Smith

The greys and the weirdoes stopped trying to run and just watched transfixed, as the two humans stood mere yards from the twisting nightmare and fired and fired and fired. In Eddie's mind everything in the world had disappeared. Everything within vision, everything he had seen and done and heard about, everyone he had known and killed and kissed and loved and found merely irritating. All he could see was two lumpen hands, straining towards each other, warm, glistening knobs of flesh yearning to become one thing and grow together. He hit the knobs time and again, but within seconds they were back again: while human fingers might be difficult to do, these creatures' real shape could evidently heal and regrow almost instantaneously. Eddie was coldly aware that such a species would be impossible to fight, once they came through, and that the fate of the whole planet might depend on him doing something now, that his mother's son held the future of the world in his hands.

He gave it his best shot. He tried. He couldn't do it.

And so it was just as well that, as the bridge was made and the two hands became one with a sound that was like a hundred happy people sighing at once, there was the sudden noise of a vicious, fizzing explosion. At that very same moment the whole collective top half of both what had once been George and what had never been Fran disappeared like dirt scraped off a windshield.

The remaining four-foot-high pieces shuddered, squirmed like sentient piles of shit, and then were blown to dust by two further explosions of the same kind.

The clearing was utterly silent for a moment. Everyone stood and stared at where the action had been, seeing only a large circle of scorched grass.

Then they turned.

Standing off to one side, each holding a complex-looking weapon and still looking sunburnt, were a pair of English honeymooners.

'Sorry we're late,' they said.

About half an hour later, Eddie and Connie stood at the end of the pier. The greys were gone. They'd been sent back to their compound and had complied with reasonably good grace, largely because of the promise of some extra food and being allowed to stay up late. The weirdoes were also absent. The two young English people had taken them off to one side in the clearing and had a long conversation with them, during which there had been much kicking of heels, sulky nodding and general averting of gaze by the spindly ones.

THE VACCINATOR

Eddie and Connie stood right where they'd been, guns still in hand, waiting for everything to start making sense. Eventually the weirdoes had come reluctantly over, obviously sent by the young couple. They'd mumbled short and insincere apologies for any inconvenience they'd caused, and then tramped in a line back over to the far side of the clearing, where this time the invisible door was evidently working again. Then the English couple had invited Eddie and Connie to accompany them back to the pier.

'So,' Connie said, after a while of standing looking down at the boat. 'Guess you're not from London, England after all.'

'Oh no,' said the male one. He was wearing a white Gap T-shirt and khaki shorts, and had engaging blue eyes. 'Well, not originally. Though we do have a small place in Islington at the moment. A *pied a terre*, really. Very convenient for the centre of town.'

'Where are you really from?' Eddie asked.

'Oh, quite some distance away. Miles and miles. I'm not sure your chaps have even found it yet.'

Connie swallowed. 'Do you look as gross in your dimension as Fran did?'

'Hardly,' the female one laughed. She had a neat blonde bob, and was slim and pretty. 'Actually we look exactly the same as we do here, but a couple of inches taller. No idea why.'

Eddie nodded. 'So what happens now?'

'Well basically,' the male one said, glancing at his watch, 'we're all free to get on with our evenings. The invasion threat's been averted and, well, the night is yet young. Sorry to have involved you in so much trouble. Wished we'd known that Fran was the spy. Could have sorted the whole thing out last night—though to be honest we were a little tipsy by the stage it all went off.'

'What are you?' Connie asked.

The woman shrugged. 'Police, angels, inspectors,' she said. 'Pick your metaphor. We sort things out. Though to be honest, at the moment what I mostly am is starving. It's probably about time for some dinner, isn't it darling?'

'Absolutely,' the male one said. 'Now: the gatekeepers have been told not to mess around with this whole abduction nonsense any more, but of course they won't listen. Incidentally, Eddie, you shouldn't really have been doing what you've been doing without a license.'

'Well, you know how it is, out in the sticks,' Eddie said. 'We don't always do things by the book. But we generally get by.'

'Quite. Well...' The man dug around in his pocket, and pulled out a

461

thin black piece of paper. 'Here's a license. With our thanks.'

Eddie took it, turned it over. It had no writing on either side. 'This is it?'

'I'm afraid so. I suppose you could get it laminated it you wanted. One final favour: we're thinking of zipping up the coast tonight, Gulf side, maybe Sarasota and its environs, checking out some new restaurants. Any recommendations?'

'You could try Tommy Bahama's,' Eddie said, eyeing them carefully. 'That's pretty good.'

'What kind of food is it?'

'They specialise in a Floridian/Caribbean cuisine. Kind of a 'Floribbean' thing, I guess you'd call it.'

The man frowned. 'Which is?'

'American. But with fruit in it.'

'Sounds perfect,' the woman beamed. 'Thanks awfully.'

The two aliens thanked Eddie and Connie once more, took each other's hand, and then vanished into thin air with a quiet pop.

Eddie and Connie stood in silence for quite a while.

Then Eddie coughed quietly. 'Sorry about Fran,' he said.

'She was a good waitress.'

'You didn't...?'

'Actually, yes, we did, a couple times. I'd rather not think about it right now.'

Eddie nodded for a while, and let quiet settle once more. Then: 'Can I buy you a beer?'

'Hell no. I'll buy the beer. What you're buying me is *food*.'

'Crabby Dick's?'

'You read my mind.'

They climbed down into the boat, took a look back at the island before it disappeared, and then set off across the calm, flat water towards Key West and food and drink and the things we do so well. They figured they might as well make a night of it. It was only just after eight o'clock.

Couple of weeks later, Eddie was standing on the upper deck of the Havana Dock early one evening, bathed in soft peachy light and waiting for the sun to go down. Even after seven months on the Key, he liked to watch it, and for the time being he liked living there too.

All around were couples and small groups, dressed smart casual for the evening, sitting in warm expectation and sipping at fruity drinks. Many were tourists, but there was a good sprinkling of locals, come to enjoy a thing of beauty because living with it hadn't staled them to its charm. There was a hum of loose chatter, but mainly it was quiet, largely because the female synth player was taking one of her all-too-infrequent breaks. Eddie hoped that by the time she came back, and discovered that someone had removed the fuses from each and every one of her keyboards, they would all have been able to watch the sunset in peace.

He was sipping his Margarita, which was punishingly strong because the woman who made them had a frightening crush on him and was also in his debt because he'd sorted out a problem she'd had involving the most psychotic of her many ex-husbands, when he saw a young woman walking up the way. She had long brown hair and was pretty, but her eyes were watchful and there was something in the set of her shoulders which said she wasn't here for the sunset but rather because she was worried and afraid and had heard in a bar there might be a man on the dock who could help do something about it.

Eddie lit a cigarette, and settled down to wait for her to find him.

Enough Pizza

I first saw him in the lobby, on the Friday afternoon. I was sitting sipping the last of my tepid Coke, leafing through the convention brochure and planning when to attack the book dealers' room. I'd decided that Saturday morning would probably be the best time, swaddled in what I assumed would be my first hangover of the convention. I like buying books when I'm hungover. It's very comforting.

I was running through an internal checklist of the items I'd be looking for when I happened to catch sight of a small group of people who had just entered the hotel through the unpredictable revolving door. An elderly guy in a good suit, a tall and fluttery young woman holding a sheaf of folders, and a porter carrying a single battered suitcase. The old guy came to a halt for a moment, looked around the foyer with a practiced eye, and then set off at a decent clip towards the registration desk on the other side of the room. The woman followed somewhat chaotically, eyes darting in all directions as if expecting an air attack at any moment. The porter waited impassively, waiting to be told where to go.

For a moment I wondered why I was noticing all this, and then with a rolling feeling in my stomach I realised I had just seen the man who was my reason for being here in the first place.

'Here' was *Smoking Gun IV*, a crime fiction convention being held at the Royal Britannia in Docklands, a hotel so appalling I imagine the only group of people who actually enjoy attending events there are sadomasochists. More likely just masochists, because the hotel's staff are drawn from species so far down the evolutionary ladder that I doubt it's possible to make them feel any real pain, as we understand it. If the barman in the lounge had greeted my earlier request for coffee with just an ounce more insolence, I might have tried to find out. Instead I'd rather meekly settled for the Coke.

Michael Marshall Smith

Crime fiction is my passion. I have an insanely dull job in computing, and there are times when the knowledge that I can go home in the evening and immerse myself in a fictional world is the only thing that prevents me from seeing how far I can push a hard disk up a client's arse. I'm not obsessive—I don't stand in my bedroom in an old mac and tilted hat, firing my finger into the mirror and quoting lines from old movies in which people get over-excited about stealing sums of money which wouldn't pay off my overdraft. I don't even go to conventions very often. They're all the same: you go to some anonymous hotel, listen to people talk and launch books, meanwhile drinking glasses of cheap white wine and eating small slices of free pizza while wondering who everyone else is. This convention was different. The very morning I received the flier and read the guest list (I'm on a couple of mailing lists, from specialist bookstores), I wrote a cheque and put it in the post, even though I'd been to the Royal Britannia before and knew what I was letting myself in for.

The man who was now standing at the registration desk, favouring the sullen woman behind it with a raised eyebrow that would have sent most people into a decline, was Nicholas Price. Chances are you won't know the name, but believe me—thirty years ago you would have done. Without Price's novels, most of the crime fiction that people read nowadays wouldn't even have been possible. Back in the 1990s he plunged a big stick into the genre and gave it a stir that changed the flavour forever, bringing crime into the mainstream in the way Stephen King had done with horror twenty years before. For two decades Price was one of the biggest wheels in crime, never quite achieving true pre-eminence or stellar book sales, but very much the man in form. And, judging by the small press biography I'd read, rather a handful as well. The author of the booklet had discretely referred to him as a 'bon viveur', but the real story was there between the lines: he and his group of cronies, between them making up most of the big names of the age, had drunk a good many bars dry before they'd even got into their stride for the evening. A representative anecdote tells how Price and his wife Margaret had once been discovered in the ornamental fountain outside a convention hotel in Houston at half past nine in the morning, having retired there only two hours before. The fountain was in full working order, and the pair was somewhat wet. Half an hour later, after a change of trousers and with a small Scotch in front of him, Price was on a panel concerning techniques for using flashbacks in crime narrative. History does not relate how telling or otherwise was his contribution to the debate.

466

ENOUGH PIZZA

That was half a century ago. Later his novels became less frequent, and began to feel like reworkings of earlier material. Younger guns came to the fore, unknowingly building on foundations Price had laid. It doesn't matter how good you are; sooner or later you're going to be yesterday's man.

There hadn't been a new Nicholas Price in twenty years—in other words, since I was ten and not reading any books, crime or otherwise. But now there was a new novel. *The Days* was to be launched at the convention, and I was going to be first in line to buy a copy and get it signed. I discovered Price six years ago, through an awed reference to him in an introduction to a book by a contemporary writer. I tried one of his early novels—not easy to get hold of, but then neither were the later ones—and I was hooked. I read everything I could find, and I'm here to tell you Price was the best. The absolute best.

The tall young woman with the folders was involved in a heated discussion with the girl behind the hotel's registration desk. I could guess the subject. Despite the fact that check-in time was three o'clock, and it was now past four, Mr Price's room wasn't ready. I'd been through the same thing myself, and my bag was currently stowed in the room the porter was now carrying Price's suitcase towards. Price himself had evidently lost interest in the dispute, and was gazing serenely into space. His minder fired one last salvo at the apathetic troll behind the counter, then turned to Price and gesticulated apologetically as she led him in my direction.

I held up the convention brochure again, feigning deep interest in its contents, and watched from behind it. Price walked slightly ahead, the woman consulting notes from her file. By now I'd worked out that she was from his publisher's PR department, and something told me this was her first experience of author-wrangling. She looked nervous and distracted, as if her head was so full of things she was reminding herself not to forget that she couldn't remember what any of them were. Price looked far from nervous. It wasn't so much that he exuded confidence, more that he could have been anywhere. Walking down a street, on a stroll in the park, crossing his own living room. He didn't look left or right as he walked, checking out the delegates standing and sitting all around, as most people would have done. He headed straight for the bar. His suit was charcoal grey, of modern cut, and fit well, and he was wearing a white shirt and a dark tie. For an old guy he looked pretty sharp.

But he also looked old. He had every right to. He was eighty-four, and if I'm still moving around under my own steam at that age, and doing so with a publishing person at my side rather than full medical backup, I'll feel I'm doing better than okay. Price's eyes were clear, his grey hair was neat and his tie was knotted immaculately.

But his skin was pale, and papery, and despite his best efforts to hide it, he was heavily favouring one leg. It was hard to believe that this was the man whose mind had mapped the brutal worlds of China Sofitel, Bill Stredwick and Nicole Speed—not to mention the countless minor characters who had moved through his fiction with damaged grace. Apart from what I'd gleaned from the thin biography, everything I knew about Price had been intuited from between the lines of his fiction—as if his narration placed him in a permanent present tense in the company of wild people in dangerous places. Now he stood at a characterless and danger-free bar in a Docklands hotel, a couple of fat and bearded members of the convention's organising committee converging on him from behind, and a blank-faced barman in front.

'I'd like a coffee,' Price said, reaching in his pocket for his cigarettes. The barman immediately embarked on the kind of dismissive dumb show he'd used on me earlier.

Price ignored him, and turned to his PR person. He asked if she'd like a coffee. She shook her head.

Price winked at the barman. 'Just one then.'

The barman, provoked to speech, said that coffee was impossible.

Price raised an eyebrow. 'Impossible? How so?'

The barman looked away. The exchange was obviously over, as far as he was concerned. The two convention organisers stood sheepishly behind Price, knowing they ought to do something but evidently realising they'd have no better luck. I empathetically shared their embarrassed fury at being pushed around by someone who's supposed to be serving you.

'Listen, Jean,' Price said mildly, evidently having read the man's name off his tag. The barman turned to him, ready to be affronted, but his face turned to caution as he caught Price's eyes. 'This is a bar. Behind it I see all the paraphernalia of coffee production, namely a coffee machine, milk and sugar. I notice that many of the bar mats bear the name of a prominent coffee manufacturer, and that a price for a 'cup of coffee' is displayed on the badly-punctuated sign behind your alarmingly bulbous head. Coffee is clearly not only *not* 'impossible', but a noted feature of this establishment. So serve me a cup.'

Jean, full of injured innocence, explained how it simply wasn't feasible that he do so, on account of the fact that he had no cups, that the cups were in the restaurant on the other side of the lobby—a journey of about ten yards—and he had no backup to prevent a riot in his absence.

ENOUGH PIZZA

He was sure the customer saw how it was.

'I do,' Price agreed. 'And this is the way it is. You're going to get out from behind that bar, and go fetch a coffee cup. Bring a couple, so the problem won't arise next time. Then you're going to pour my coffee into one of them, in return for which I will give you some money. The alternative is I stand here waiting until the queue gets so long it stretches out the front of the hotel. Eventually it's going to go across the road, and when it gets dark, someone's going to get run over, and their relatives will hunt you down and avenge their kin with fire and pointed sticks. I have all afternoon. It's your call.'

Jean stared at him. Price smiled gently, lit his cigarette and looked away.

Jean lifted the hatch and walked stiff-backed out from behind the bar. 'And don't you be a slowcoach,' Price advised, 'Or when you get back this bar won't be nothing more than a few broken bottles and an empty till.'

Shouldn't have worked from a man in his eighties. But it did. Jean scooted across the lobby.

I turned away from the bar, to hide the broad grin on my face.

The highlight of the afternoon's programme was Price in conversation with the convention's Chairman. I sat about four rows back. I had a slew of questions I wanted to ask, mainly about the China Sofitel series, but also about some of the short fiction.

I didn't get a chance, but I didn't mind. Most of my questions got answered anyway, in a fascinating, often hilarious conversation that overran by half an hour. Price lounged in his chair on the stage, whisky glass in one hand, a cigarette usually in the other, and turned the Chairman's carefully planned questions into a freewheeling discussion of crime-writing that, a few days after that weekend, led to me starting my first short story.

I wish I'd taken a tape recorder into that session, and preserved it for posterity and myself. It was Price's last convention panel. He died three months later.

Midnight found me back in the lobby bar. In the meantime I'd been to dinner with a gang of acquaintances, drunk an awful lot of red wine, and had a long and mildly flirtatious conversation with an American fan I'd never met before. She was called Sheryl and came from Kansas, and at eleven had abruptly announced that she needed to go to bed. I was still buoyed up by the way I'd dealt with the waiter in the pizza restaurant, and said I hoped it wasn't my company that was provoking her departure. She explained that it wasn't, but that she'd consumed too much wine and had to go throw up, and we arranged to meet for coffee the next morning.

I wandered into the part of the bar that overlooks the water, and sank heavily into a chair. I had most of a pint left, and intended to drink it. They weren't many people around, and none that I recognised, but I didn't mind. I'd had a good day, and it was nice to be out of the normal rut. I didn't need company to enjoy that feeling, and when I realised that someone was standing behind me I didn't turn and bid them a cheery hello. Everyone I knew had gone to bed, and you can get into some very dull and mood-destroying conversations with strangers at conventions.

I heard the sound of a cigarette being lit. Then:

'Mind if I sit here?'

I turned. Standing behind me was Nicholas Price.

'Christ yes,' I said, completely flustered. 'I mean no, go right ahead. You're very welcome.'

'You may change your mind. I've had a certain amount to drink.' Price sat gingerly in the chair opposite me, and placed his glass and cigarettes within easy reach.

I stuck around wildly for something to keep the conversation, such as it was, going. 'Impressed to see you're still smoking.'

Immediately I regretted it. It sounded like I thought he was old. All I meant was that it was good to see someone who'd resisted society's moral and emotional pressures to give up: and to give up for their own good, of course, though it's strange that people don't feel able to order complete strangers to give up fatty foods or alcohol or hang gliding—for their own good.

I dithered, wondering whether I should try to explain this or if it would just get me deeper into trouble.

'Always meant to stop,' Price mused, no offence taken. 'Never got round to it. Just as well. Last time I tried was when I was thirty-five. Do you have any idea how galling it would have been to suspect I could have spent the last fifty years smoking? Margaret used to say there were smokers and non-smokers, and everyone should work out which they were and be willing to pay the price.'

I knew who Margaret was, of course—and Price had just used her name as if I had a right to know. I was sober enough to realise it meant nothing, which he obviously just used her name instead of saying 'my wife', but I still felt dangerously excited.

Nonchalantly: 'She's not coming this weekend?'

'No. She left me nearly ten years ago.'

Aghast, I tried to apologise. 'I'm so sorry.'

Price smiled. 'It's okay. So was she. It was cancer she left me for. Came and swept her off her feet, charmed her away from me. Now she doesn't even write. Still, that's ex-wives for you.'

He was quiet for a moment, and then continued. 'We were together from the age of twenty. She smoked then, she smoked all her life. She made her choice. There are three types of decisions you can make in life. Good, bad and unavoidable. In the latter reason plays no part, no matter how much you think it does. Emotion or circumstance or pure that's-the-way-it's-got-to-be makes the choice, and it's those decisions that shape your life and build the house you live in. All the good or bad decisions ever do is change the colour of the walls.'

'I'm not sure I understand what you mean,' I said.

He laughed. 'Neither do I. Just thought I'd try it out. Came across that little observation in a notebook of mine from back when I was fifty. Obviously meant something to me then. Sounds like complete gibberish now.'

'I really enjoyed your panel this afternoon,' I blurted.

He looked at me levelly. 'You're not going to ask me about my work, are you?'

'Oh no,' I said, immediately shelving my first question, and the fifteen subsequent ones.

'Never used to talk about my work,' he said, looking out across the dark river. 'None of us did. Now it's all anyone ever wants to hear about. What did I mean in this story, what was I saying in that one. Who cares? Chances are what I was saying was just what it occurred to me to write, on that particular morning, with a hangover and a deadline. You want meaning, ask a tree. Work's just what you do to pay for your life.'

'It must mean more than that,' I ventured.

'Sure. I can go into the study, look at the books on the shelves, know I'm not going to leave this place entirely unmarked. We didn't have any kids. We had books instead. Plus I liked some of the characters in them. They were just imaginary, but then so is everybody else these days.'

We sat in silence for a few moments. I sipped my beer slowly. I didn't want finish it too quickly, because then I'd need to order another—which would involve going over to the bar and dealing with a barman—and Price might take that as a signal to leave.

'What time is your book signing tomorrow?' I asked, eventually.

Weak, but the best I could do.

'Eleven,' he said.

So much for that gambit. 'I don't know anything about the new one. Does it have any of the old characters in it?'

He shook his head. 'Couldn't find them,' he said. 'Went away, no forwarding address. Maybe even died.'

Then, for no reason I could see, he raised his right arm. Jean the barman appeared from nowhere. 'Yes, Mr Price?'

'I'm going to have one more Scotch,' Price said. 'And for my friend here…'

Jean accepted my order, inclined his head, and then turned on his heel and scooted off.

'How the hell did you do that?' I asked Price delightedly.

'It's a knack,' he said. 'Spend the rest of your life in hotel bars, chances are you'll pick it up. What is your name, anyhow?' I told him, and he nodded. 'Sorry to abandon you after this one,' he said, round the end of another cigarette, 'But I got to be in reasonable shape for tomorrow afternoon.'

'Why? What's happening then?'

'I'm getting an award.'

'Really? I didn't know that.'

He winked. 'I'm not supposed to know either. Actually, nobody's said that I am. But I'm getting it, sure as hell.'

'What for?'

'Lifetime achievement. What else?'

'Well, congratulations in advance,' I said. 'That's quite something.'

'Yes, I suppose it is,' he said, looking away. 'You ever hear of a guy called Jack Stratten?'

'He was your best friend, wasn't he?'

'Yes,' he said, and appeared pleased. 'That's exactly what he was. If I asked most people here what I just asked you, they'd most likely know the name. They'd've read a book of his, or heard of one, at least watched one of the dumb movies they made from them. Seen his name somewhere, or heard about that time he punched his editor out in Chicago.

'But that's not what Jack was. Nor Geoff McGann, though yes, he did write a lot of good books and made a sight more money than me or even Jack. Nor Nancy Grey, though she was my editor. They were my friends. I liked them and they liked me and we had some good times. *That* was my life achievement, not the fucking books.'

I waited, feeling a little cold.

ENOUGH PIZZA

'And so tomorrow morning I'll get up and put on a suit and go write my name in some more hardcovers. Jo from the publishers will be there, and she'll make sure I'm okay, and I'll sign books for a bunch of strangers who probably weren't even born the last time I did a line of coke. Then in the afternoon I'll sit in the banquet and people will be polite to me and I'll probably get this award. I'm pretty sure I will. They were awfully keen I came, and most people don't get too excited about me any more. So I'll get a statuette with my name on it, which is supposed to be a big thing, and it is, except it's too late. Who's going to hold my hand when I get back to the table? Who's going to see it on my shelf except me?'

He stared at me, his eyes bright. 'I don't want an award. What I want, for just one afternoon, is to have them all back. Margaret, my friends. The people who knew me when I had a life, instead of a bibliography. Who'd seen me walk fast, deal with hangovers, throw up...make people laugh because I'd been funny, rather than just out of respect. People who'd always be surprised to see me with grey hair or walking with a limp. Someone who'd tell me to stop fucking smoking.'

He stopped, and I swallowed, not knowing how to react.

Jean appeared, and politely placed our drinks in front of us. I noticed that Price's hand shook quite badly as he signed the room service slip, and racked my brains for something to say.

Price watched Jean walk away across the lobby. 'It's like breaking in a horse,' he said. 'Trick is to get their respect, and then tip big. Works every time.'

I laughed and realised I didn't have to say anything.

'So,' he sighed, sitting back in his chair. 'Ask me your questions about what I wrote.'

'I don't have any,' I said.

'Yeah, you do. Ask them. I'll do my best to come up with some answers.'

So I did, and he did. After he left I had one small nightcap, then slowly walked up the stairs to bed.

I met Sheryl for coffee at ten o'clock the next morning. This went well enough that we toured the book dealers' room together afterwards, and it was only when I found a very battered copy of Nicholas Price's first novel that I realised I'd missed his launch.

I checked my watch. I was definitely too late. 'Expected somewhere?' Sheryl asked, suddenly appearing at my shoulder.

'No,' I said, keeping the disappointment out of my voice. It was the truth anyway. Price wouldn't be looking out for me. I still wanted to get the new novel signed, but at the launch I'd have been just another stranger in a queue.

'Good,' she said, and linked her arm through mine.

I saw him twice more before the end of the convention. The first time was at the banquet. Sheryl and I were sitting at opposite ends of the room, the seating plan having been put in place before we'd met. I was on a table with the people I knew, and had fun, though I felt strangely anxious throughout the dinner.

When the speeches started I realised I was nervous for Price, though I had no right to be. He was sitting at the top table, and seemed to be having a reasonable time, nodding when the people either side asked him questions or told him things. He started smoking before the dinner was over, but nobody seemed to ask him to put it out.

After the speeches came the awards ceremony, which took half an hour. Best short, best novella, best novel; best this, best that, best the other. And at the end, Life Achievement. Best life, I guess.

The Chairman got up, and before he was two sentences into his speech I knew Price had been right. The applause that greeted the eventual revelation was tumultuous, and our table was one of the first to stand. Price got to his feet, wincing slightly, helped by those on each side. He made his way to the lectern where the presentation was to be made, watched carefully by the organisers. He was given the statuette, several people shook his hand, and then pointed him to the microphone. Everybody else sat down.

Price stood at the lectern, and looked slowly around the room. 'What a pleasant surprise,' he said, eventually, and someone at the back of the hall cheered.

'Thank you very much for this award,' he continued, 'and for treating me so well. Thank you also to my publishers, and to Jo, my publicist.' He smiled at her, and she blushed.

Then he turned and stared ahead, at the far wall or at nothing at all. 'Most of all I'd like to thank four people, without whom none of it would have been possible. Jack, Geoff, Nancy. And especially Margaret. Thank you all.'

I could see several people craning their heads, trying to see the people whom Price had been referring to. Nobody seemed to realise they were all imaginary now.

ENOUGH PIZZA

*

After the ceremony there was a drinks reception in one of the other rooms. I latched up with Sheryl and we stood by one of the walls, working our way, in a roundabout fashion, to suggesting to each other that we hang out together for the evening. At last it got said, and agreed, and we relaxed: sipping complimentary white wine and nibbling on small slices of free pizza.

After about an hour I saw Price on the other side of the room, and told Sheryl I'd be back. I gently pushed my way through the throng, getting gradually closer. The bookroom was shut, and I didn't expect Price to be carrying a few copies of *The Days* on his person just in case the need arose. I'd found a piece of blank paper, and was going to ask him to sign that instead. I was only a few yards away from him when I saw something.

Price was standing alone, Jo-from-the-publishers momentarily in conversation with one of the convention organisers. The head of Price's award statuette was sticking out of his jacket pocket, and he was slowly panning his eyes around the room, listening to the noise of two hundred voices, watching the groups of people.

He saw something that made him smile—a cute couple maybe, or someone on the way to being spectacularly drunk—and turned to one side to say something. But he turned the opposite way to where Jo stood, and tilted his head very slightly down—as if to speak to a woman a little less tall than him. He framed the first word, and then he remembered, and his mouth shut.

I froze in place.

Price raised his head and took a sip of his wine, as if nothing had happened, but his eyes looked flat. After a few moments his publicist extricated herself from her conversation, and turned back to face him.

'Hello,' she said warmly, as if greeting the grandfather she secretly preferred. 'You must be ready for another glass of wine by now.' This was said sweetly, a nod in the direction of the reputation she must have known he'd had. I realised that Jo was maybe better at her job than might at first appear.

'No thank you, my dear,' Price said quietly. His voice sounded very old, and unsure of itself. He put his glass on the table and looked up at her. 'I'm tired,' he said, 'I've had enough pizza, and I think I'd like to go home.'

*

475

When I checked out of the hotel the next morning, I was puzzled to find a parcel waiting for me at the registration desk. God knows how something left by one guest for another, with the name spelt correctly and everything, had actually made it to that guest—but it had. I would have though it getting lost was a mere formality. Someone in the hotel was obviously slipping up.

I paid my bill, haggling briefly over a small cache of entirely fictitious charges hidden on the second page, and went to sit and wait for Sheryl. She wasn't flying home for two days, and I was going to show her some parts of London. Including, I'd been given reason to suspect, the inside of my flat.

As I waited I opened the package. Two things were inside.

The first was a copy of *The Days*. It was signed to me, with best wishes. I read it soon afterwards and it's a good book, but it's not classic Price.

The second object stands on the shelf above my computer, where I can see it as I write.

A small statuette, a monument to an ex-life, given to me by a man I once had a drink with.

Afterword

On Not Writing

It is Saturday, the 26th of July, 2003. It is raining a little outside my window. I am sitting in my study in London, wondering what I'm going to do for this Afterword. A friend suggested last night that I write down what I know about the craft of writing. I replied that, if I was honest, I wasn't sure I *knew* anything about it.

'Well,' he said, 'There you go. That's your start.'

And so there it is, above this paragraph, that start. This is very often the way stories begin for me, in fact. A line, an idea, a character suddenly appears and does something, inviting me to discover or create the place he or she is going. Sometimes they arrive with that destination already in mind—a point or twist or final line. Equally often they just turn up at the door, full of themselves and convinced I should pay attention, but with nothing but shrugs to contribute when it comes to explaining what I'm actually supposed to *do* with them. So I just pull the keyboard closer and see where it takes me.

Like I'm doing now.

There's a famous story about Coleridge, which you may already know. Apparently he was just hanging out one day, not-writing (which is many writers' favourite form of relaxation, and certainly one of mine) and he fell asleep. Some say restricted substances were implicated, but I'm not one to cast aspersions on long-dead poets. Snoozing is a very popular activity amongst those who ply the scrivener's trade. You don't need drugs to bring it on. I find deadlines do it just as well. Anyway, Coleridge woke a couple of hours later having had this great dream about a fabulous pleasure palace. A huge poem about it popped right into his head, and so he got up and immediately started writing it down. He was barely underway with this great work, however, when a man from a town called Porlock arrived at the door. This jerk distracted Coleridge just long enough that, when he finally went away, the poet found the rest of the poem had gone, faded like the dream that inspired it. All we have of the intended masterwork is the part he got down before the interruption.

Now I don't know whether this story is true, or if this alleged 'man from Porlock' was actually Coleridge's dope dealer, and the poet thought he'd better be convivial and split a pipe with the guy, or what: but short story ideas are often rather like an inverted form of this interruption. Here I am, not-writing, and there's a knock on the mental door. I open it, warily. I'm enjoying not-writing. I don't necessarily want a creative visitor, not today—not least because I'm generally not-writing something in particular, and the last thing I need is something else to not-write. It can really stack up, the not-writing. You've got to be careful not to let it get on top of you. Then suddenly the visitor is standing right there. I realise that the idea has opened the door by itself, from the outside, and that I never had any control over whether it came into my life.

'Hey,' it says. 'Here I am. Now tell me: where do I go?'

A short story has arrived. That's the truthful answer to where ideas come from: the bastards come and interrupt you when you're busy trying to not-write.

Hmm. This is often how it happens too. You get that first chunk, the kick-off. And then your fingers stop moving, and the spell wavers, and you reach for your cup of cooling tea; you glance out of the window, or wonder whether you've got any new email or if that site with all the cool icons on it has updated or if your favourite online typographer has come up with some new face. That initial burst of speed fades, and you don't know how to proceed. You turn to your visitor, that intrusive idea, to check if it has any suggestions, but see it has settled down in a chair in the back of your study, flicking through an old magazine, and realise it's going to be no help at all.

'Hey,' you say. 'So what happens next?'

'Beats me,' he mutters. 'You're the writer.'

So you push sturdily forward into this second part, the section awkwardly called 'Okay, I've typed some words and saved them to disk with a name and everything, so this is officially a new story, but what's it actually *about*?' This is the place where it can all fall apart. This is when you can suddenly decide the idea isn't worth writing (rightly or wrongly), or when you can most easily be derailed by a phone call, some other commitment, or just plain laziness. That first chunk may go in a virtual drawer at this point, and never be seen again. Or you may come back to it weeks or months later, idly, and make it a little longer—before putting it away once more.

ON NOT WRITING

I'll come back to this scenario in a while. Idly.

This time can also be the best part, however. Some stories just bull straight through that first blank return. They've come with serious intent. They're good to go. They know where they're heading and are impatient to get there and are willing to do most of the work. These are my favourite sort. Some stories from right at the beginning of my time as a writer, like 'The Man Who Drew Cats'—my very first—'Always', 'Everybody Goes' and 'The Dark Land' came like this: delivered whole, and written in a day. More recent ones too, like 'Being Right', which I wrote specially for this collection. I came back to the house one morning, having walked up the road to buy lunch, and sat down to note an idea I'd had on the way back. I wound up never getting round to eating, but having two thirds a story by the end of the afternoon. Good deal.

There are others which take a little more time. Not because the idea comes with insufficient wind in its sails, but because the story it requires to keep it alive needs just a little more structural thought. 'A Place To Stay', for example, with its interlocking time zones and deliberately nebulous import; and 'The Book Of Irrational Numbers', which I wanted to progress as a series of only semi-related observations, and so was better left to come at its own pace.

And there are other stories which are started not just because of some random idea or opening paragraph, but because something about the world strikes you forcefully at a particular time—'Enough Pizza' was one of those; as was 'What You Make It'. Here it is not an idea that stirs the blood so much as a frame of mind.

There are still others where the basic idea occurred to me long, long before I wrote the story. The basic notions for 'The Handover' and 'Maybe Next Time', for example, were in my head for years before some internal switch was flicked and they were ready to come out onto the page. These tend to come out fast when they arrive.

At around this time, if not before, I'll go back to the beginning and edit right through; or go back a page, or a single paragraph. It warms me up for the next assault, and often you find you can cut the first sentence or two, and pare stuff down throughout. Cut, add, cut, cut, add, cut. Writing is not like picking apples for a farmer, where you get paid for the weight you bring home. It's more like knowing you're going to make a pie that evening, and walking out into your own orchard to pick ten really good apples to make it right. Eleven is too many. You don't need eleven.

But nine will be too few, of course.

Michael Marshall Smith

*

One of the intriguing things about short stories is that they seldom stand alone. When first published, they're in either an anthology or a magazine, and thus contextualised. The anthologist will have gone to some trouble to create a balance and structure to his book; a magazine's editor will likewise have placed a story in a particular position relative to other fiction, non-fiction and advertising. This is what makes the first publication of a story unique. Following a short, elegiac story from someone you've never heard of is different to preceding some mammoth piece of genius from Peter Straub; and you better have your very best foot forward if you're going to be put anywhere near a Ramsey Campbell or Stephen King. You may also be contextualised with regard to subject. If the story's in a book about vampires, then it's a fair bet that bloodsuckers are going to crop up somewhere along the line. On the other hand, if the author knows that's where the story's going to be published (as I did, with 'Dear Alison'), then—when blessed with an editor with eclectic tastes—this gives you the chance to write it from a very oblique angle. You don't need a vampire on the very first page. Actually, you may not need one at all. This was also the case with 'To Receive is Better' and 'Later', both of which were written for anthologies which wore their subjects on their sleeves, and thus afforded opportunities for this sideways glance approach. 'Charms' also came into being through an oblique version of this kind of genesis. I originally wrote it for an anthology celebrating the 45, those seven-inch singles which I guess are now the stuff of yard sales and collectors' fairs and not much else. I deliberately wrote against expectation here, and the editors justifiably sent it straight back. Luckily its slightly Bradburyesque tone made it appeal to another editor, a few years down the line. Stories will do that, sometimes; they will find their own home. Of all the tales in this collection, 'To See The Sea' is probably the one which most squarely met its invited brief, that of being part of a collection which spun further tales inspired by H. P. Lovecraft's 'The Shadow Over Innsmouth'.

And then there are the ones which you do for yourself, and are just pure fun to write, like 'The Vaccinator' and 'When God Live in Kentish Town.' Stories where you think you've got the easiest and best job in the world. To be honest, though, *all* of the stories in this collection were fun to one degree or another. None of the ones I had to struggle with have made the cut, which probably tells its own story.

For me, fast is good, and I believe there's a statute of limitations for getting an idea down on paper. Once you've let it sit on the stove too long, it curdles. It becomes a chore. The guest who turned up has stayed far too long, and become an unwelcome squatter in your head. I recently went through a folder on my hard disk which contained about twenty abortive starts; some only a few lines, others a couple of thousand labori-ously-hewn words. I threw all but three of them away. Straight off the disk. Erased and gone forever. In my experience, you have to do that with ideas. Show them who's boss. They have to earn their keep; they have to do their thing. Otherwise they just sit there, making you feel guilty and getting in the way of the door. I don't need that kind of crap from a notion. I can not-write effectively enough all by myself.

This collection's one exception to this rule is 'They Also Serve', which I started a long, long time ago. I knew where it was going, but never quite got it there. I just tinkered with it from time to time. Then a home appeared for it, and I revisited it with renewed intent. I'm glad I did. I'm not going to provide a note on each story in the collection, you'll be relieved to hear, as I've recently done that for a dizzyingly compre-hensive bibliography by Lavie Tidhar, currently in production with PS Publishing. If you want the blow-by-blow, that's the place to look. Not everyone wants to know the tale of how a story came about, of course. For some it's a little like having a favourite song—the tune they first danced to at their wedding, the melody they hear in their head when they're wistful, the song that makes them turn to their partner with a misty eye and dawning smile, suddenly sure all's well with the world—and being told the guy wrote it about his favourite pebble when stoned out of his head in a hotel suite in Idaho.

So I won't say how the story called 'My Favourite Pebble' came about. It's too personal. And I lost it in the end, anyway. In every story you gain something, and you lose something, as in life; you gain experience, and in the process lose a period of time you can never get back.

And then you're at the end. You've got where you were going, and the story is contained by a concluding sentence. At that point I immediately go back through the whole thing again. Several times, and before I stand up.

The balance of everything that has gone before is shifted slightly by the story's sudden finiteness, by the fact that this tale will now always be about five thousand words long, or fifteen hundred, or eight thousand. Now you know its extent, you understand better what the emphasis should be, whether the story will support that long rant about something that just happened to piss you off yesterday, and whether the ending you always planned for it is actually a step too far, and more powerful if never quite reached. I flit back and forth throughout the story, nipping and tucking, making those last little alterations before the concrete sets: because once I've stood up from the computer, walked away from a story with an end line, it's never quite the same again. The art is over, and the craft begins. Craft is fun too, and it's what pays the bills. But art is what builds the house in the first place.

Next day, another pass, but by then the story is getting bored of my meddling. It wants to go. You print it out. You give it to your/it's first reader, in my case my wife, Paula. She reads it and she tells me what she thinks, and I know most of it before she opens her mouth.

After that, chances are you will very rarely be present when someone reads this story, this nugget of your life which started out so intensely, or so trivially. The idea from Porlock finishes his tea, winks, and thanks you for your hospitality, for doing what you could with him. Then he puts his coat back on and leaves your house forever, going into the world, out of your hands now.

Great, you think. *Now* I can get down to some serious not-writing. And then just when you're getting into it, you hear another knock on the door.

So there you go. This all came out in a day, which is the way I like it. Turned out I didn't know anything much about writing after all, but I hope you enjoyed turning the pages. That's what fiction's for, in the end, and all it's ever about. Ultimately the writer's job is very simple.

Getting you to this sentence here.

Michael Marshall Smith
London, July 2003

Copyright & Additional Information

A Long Walk, For The Last Time © 2002 by Michael Marshall Smith. First appeared in Dark Voices 6 - United Kingdom: Gollancz 2002, edited by Stephen Jones and David Sutton.

A Place To Stay © 1994 by Michael Marshall Smith. First appeared in Dark Terrors 4: The Gollancz Book of Horror - United Kingdom: Gollancz 1998, edited by Stephen Jones and David Sutton.

Always © 1991 by Michael Marshall Smith. First appeared in Darklands 2 - United Kingdom: Egerton Press 1992, edited by Nicholas Royle.

Being Right © 2003 by Michael Marshall Smith. Original to this collection.

Charms © 2000 by Michael Marshall Smith. First appeared in *AbeSea* - United Kingdom: 1997 (a small press magazine, no other details available).

Dear Alison © 1997 by Michael Marshall Smith. First appeared in The Mammoth Book of Dracula: Vampire Tales for the New Millenium - United Kingdom: Robinson 1997, edited by Stephen Jones.

Dying ©1994 by Michael Marshall Smith. First appeared in *Omni* - United States: Omni Publications International 1994, edited by Ellen Datlow.

Enough Pizza © 1998 by Michael Marshall Smith. First appeared in The Ex Files: New Stories About Old Flames - United Kingdom: Quartet 1998, edited by Nicholas Royle.

Everybody Goes © 1992 by Michael Marshall Smith. First appeared in When God Lived In Kentish Town - United Kingdom: HarperCollins 1998 (promotional paperback).

Happy Holidays! © 2003 by Michael Marshall Smith. Original to this collection (appears in the lettered edition only).

Hell Hath Enlarged Herself © 1996 by Michael Marshall Smith. First appeared in Dark Terrors 2: The Gollancz Book of Horror - United Kingdom: Gollancz 1996, edited by Stephen Jones and David Sutton.

Last Glance Back © 2001 by Michael Marshall Smith. First appeared in Girls' Night Out/ Boys' Night In - United Kingdom: HarperCollins 2001, edited by Chris Manby, Fiona Walker, and Jessica Adams.

Later © 1992 by Michael Marshall Smith. First appeared in The Mammoth Book of Zombie Stories - United Kingdom: Robinson 1993, edited by Stephen Jones.

Maybe Next Time © 2003 by Michael Marshall Smith. Original to this collection.

More Bitter than Death © 1991 by Michael Marshall Smith. First appeared in Dark Voices 5 - United Kingdom: Pan 1993, edited by Stephen Jones and David Sutton.

More Tomorrow © 1995 by Michael Marshall Smith. First appeared in Dark Terrors: The Gollancz Book of Horror - United Kingdom: Gollancz 1995, edited by Stephen Jones and David Sutton.